Cynthia Harrod-Eagles won the Young Writers' Award with her first novel, *The Waiting Game*, and in 1992 won the Romantic Novel of the Year Award. She has written over fifty books, including twenty-five volumes of the Morland Dynasty – a series she will be taking up to the present day. She is also the creator of the acclaimed mystery series featuring Inspector Bill Slider.

She and her husband live in London and have three children. Apart from writing, her passions are music, wine, horses, architecture and the English countryside.

Visit the author's websites on:
http://www.morland-dynasty.co.uk
and
http://www.cynthiaharrodeagles.com

Also in the *Dynasty* series:

DYNASTY

24

The Homecoming

Cynthia Harrod-Eagles

timewarner
paperbacks

A *Time Warner* Paperback

First published in Great Britain in 2001
by Little, Brown and Company

This edition published by Time Warner Paperbacks in 2002

A CIP catalogue record for this book
is available from the British Library.

ISBN 0 7515 2531 6

Printed and bound in Great Britain by
Clays Ltd, St Ives plc

Time Warner Paperbacks
An imprint of
Time Warner Books UK
Brettenham House
Lancaster Place
London WC2E 7EN

www.TimeWarnerBooks.co.uk

THE MORLAND FAMILY

James — Lucy

James

BENEDICT
1812–1870
m. (1) Rosalind Fleetham   m. (2) Sibella Mayhew

Mary
1837–1869
m. 1854
Fenwick Morland

Preston
b. 1855
Ashley
b. 1856
Corton
b. 1858

Edward
b. 1850

George
1849–1885

EDWARD
b. 1885

HENRIETTA
b. 1853
m. 1871
Edgar Fortescue

ELIZABETH
b. 1872

REGINA
b. 1857
m. 1875
Sir Peregrine Parke

7 Children

Lucy

Thomas Weston
1803–1874
m. Emily Thorn

TOMMY
b. 1849
m. 1875
Emma Hobsbawn

FANNY
b. 1877
Thomas
b. 1878
Ada
b. 1880
Alfred
b. 1881
Octavia
b. 1883

Rosamund
1797–1867
m. (1) Earl of Chelmsford   m. (2) Earl of Batchworth

CHARLOTTE
b. 1822
m. Oliver Fleetwood
D. of Southport

VENETIA
b. 1850
m. 1885
John Winchmore
Vsct. Hazelmere
OLIVIA
b. 1851
m. 1876
Charles Du Cane
HENRY
b. 1853
Marcus
b. 1853
d. 1885
AUGUSTA
b. 1855
m. 1881
John Vibart

Cavendish
1831–1871
m. Alice Phipps

William
Earl of Batchworth

ANNE
FARRALINE
b. 1863

BOOK ONE

Proserpina

I must stop short of thee the whole day long,
But when sleep comes to close each difficult
   day,
When night gives pause to the long watch I
   keep,
And all my bonds I needs must loose apart,
Must doff my will as raiment laid away –
With the first dream that comes with the
   first sleep
I run, I run, I am gather'd to thy heart.

Alice Meynell: Renouncement

CHAPTER ONE

When Henrietta stepped joyfully into the arms of her one
true love in the churchyard of St Mary's, Bishop Winthorpe,
it was like the ending of a fairy story. It ought to have been
followed by nothing but those magical words, 'and they lived
happily ever after'. But life – and love – are rarely disposed
to be so tidy.

Her husband, Edgar Fortescue, rector of St Mary's, had
been dead twenty months on that September day in 1885
when Jerome Compton suddenly reappeared in her life.
Jerome was everything a story-book prince ought to be:
handsome, dashing and independently wealthy. Nominally
he shared a small house in the village with his sister Mary,
but he had always enjoyed a gypsy life, travelling widely
abroad, migrating between friends' houses while in England,
and returning to Mary when other forms of amusement
failed him.

For years Henrietta – trying hard to be a good wife to
an elderly, unaffectionate and increasingly reclusive husband
– had seen Jerome come and go in Bishop Winthorpe, un-
announced and mysteriously, a figure of romance. She ought
not to have fallen in love with him, but the spark was unde-
niably there between them. Perhaps if they had both made
an effort it might have been quenched; but from the beginning he had shown her preference, sought her out, and she
had allowed herself to enjoy his company. At all events, their
love had grown. At last he had tried to persuade her to leave
her husband and come away with him, and when she refused
he had left her in a fury and gone travelling to try and forget

her. The next thing she had heard was that he was married.

So she had given up all hope of seeing him again. But now her husband was dead and, by some magic, some alchemy, Jerome had suddenly appeared from nowhere and claimed her love; his own, he swore, unaltered by the years.

In the days afterwards they talked and talked, trying to make up for years of drought. They walked for miles along the lanes and through the fields, for she was living with her sister and brother-in-law, and there was no privacy for them indoors. It was fortunate that the September weather was exceptionally fine; but perhaps they were due some small piece of good luck.

'It was very wrong of you to pursue me when I was a married woman,' she chided him once.

'I didn't really mean anything by it at first,' Jerome confessed. 'I was simply amusing myself by paying you attention – though of course it is a monument to my good taste that it was you I singled out to flirt with! But I was served out in the end: I fell in love with you. And you remained virtuous, so there was no harm done.'

'I didn't give in to you, if that's what you mean,' she said. 'But harm *was* done, all the same. I loved you, and that was wrong. And I was unfaithful to my husband in my heart, if not in the flesh.'

'Well, it came out all right in the end,' he said, too happy to regret anything.

But had it? The years of being separated from each other had taken a toll; and their 'happy ending' had a complication. Henrietta was a widow, her period of mourning was well over, and only an unreasonable person would take offence at her marrying again. But Jerome's wife was still living.

'Julia and I are divorced,' Jerome said – more than once, whenever they reached this sticking-point. 'You know that. I can show you the papers if you like. And Julia wanted it as much as I did. She's perfectly happy with the situation. Don't you believe me?'

'Yes, I believe you,' Henrietta said. But it didn't make any difference, as he knew very well. Julia was still living, and in the eyes of the Church still his wife. Jerome was a divorcé, and that was just a fact. No amount of talking or good will on anyone's part could make it otherwise.

'But you've said you will marry me,' he urged.

'Yes, I will,' she said, and her clear level look defied him to deny the difficulties.

He did see them, of course. As a divorcé he could only marry in a register office, by a civil ceremony. For himself, he didn't care a bean: marriage, in his view, was a civil contract, and like any civil contract could be entered into and terminated according to the law.

As to the spiritual aspect, he felt he was quite capable of answering to God for his own actions; and God, he believed, would take a flexible view of things. After all, God knew his heart, which was more than could be said for any cleric.

But he knew that Henrietta, brought up differently, didn't feel that way; and nor did society at large. She would marry him, and bravely defy the Church; but a large part of the world they had to live in would regard them as living in sin, and therefore beyond the pale. He did not want his beloved to be the object of snubs, cold looks or reproaches. He would do all he could to protect her from them; he could not, of course, protect her from the reproaches of her own conscience.

During those long walks, in between lovers' talk, they discussed the practical aspects of their situation.

'I don't even know where the register office is,' Henrietta confessed.

'There isn't only one,' he said, amused at her innocence. 'They have them in all the large towns, and there are several in London.'

'London?' Something seemed to strike her.

'Yes, love?'

'Perhaps it would be better if we were to do it there, where no-one knows us.'

'Ah, you're ashamed of me!'

'No! You know I – oh, don't tease!'

'Well, if not ashamed, what, then?'

'It isn't only ourselves we have to consider. There's our families. If there's whispering about us, if we're cut, it will come back on Perry and Regina. We can't jeopardise their position, and their children's futures.'

He looked at her quizzically. 'In that case, no matter where we get married, we can't live in Bishop Winthorpe. Nor in York, since your brother lives there.'

'I don't see how we can.'

'Then what do you say to living in London?'

She eyed him askance. Something in his look made her suspect she had been manoeuvred to this point. 'I don't know. I've never thought about it.'

'Then think about it now. Think about the advantages: complete anonymity, a new start, a chance for you to make new friends – interesting friends. All the music and theatre and galleries and museums – there's so much I long to show you! And we can always rent a house in the country for a few weeks in summer if you begin to pine for the pleasures bucolic.'

His eyes were bright with enthusiasm, and she loved him so much just then she'd have agreed to anything. She did feel constrained, however, to point out that in the past his ultimate ambition had always been to buy an estate. His father had never had time to buy land, and Jerome had inherited his fortune in cash.

'Perhaps I shall, one day,' Jerome said. 'But at the moment I don't think I could settle down to a life of country idleness. I want to be doing, to be using my wits. I have a tremendous fancy to have a crack at stockbroking.'

She was completely nonplussed. 'You've never mentioned it before.'

'Well, the thing is,' Jerome said casually, as if he had not been leading up to this all the time, 'there's a good friend of mine who has a friend who's a stockbroker, who wants a partner. My friend's written to me suggesting I go in with him.'

'Isn't it awfully risky?' she asked. 'You hear of people losing all their money on the Exchange.'

'Oh, not these days – not if you know what you're doing.

6

On the contrary, I shall increase my fortune several-fold. And to be perfectly frank, my love, my fortune is not what it was. It's enough to keep a bachelor in reasonable idleness, but to keep a wife as well, and perhaps children—'

'Children,' she said, feeling hot and cold all over.

He looked amused. 'It has been known to happen. As a married man I shall need an establishment, and I'm afraid the Compton rhino won't sustain that. But stockbrokers can make princely sums in very short order. In a few years I shall be rich enough to buy a splendid pile where we can lounge in luxury for the rest of our days.'

'But will you like it?' she pursued. He had not been used to work.

'Living right at the heart of things, pitting my wits against the bears and bulls? What an adventure! Better than Africa – don't you see, love?'

His mind was made up, she could see that much. 'Will I like London? I've never even been to Leeds.'

'Oh, you'll love it,' he said. 'You're too intelligent to be shut away in the country with inferior minds. I have a fancy to see you do the hostess to artists and musicians and the great men of politics. You'd be so good at it.'

A little thrill of excitement ran through her. 'I expect the shops are wonderful,' she said. 'They say you can buy anything in London.'

'Anything at all! The riches of the whole world pour into it daily. You'll have a wonderful time.'

She smiled at his boyish boasting. 'Shall we get married in London too?'

'Yes, I think so, and then no-one will be upset. I'll have to find a suitable house and furnish it. I've very little to bring down from here – one or two pieces I'm fond of, and a few pictures.'

'And I, of course, have nothing,' Henrietta said dolefully.

'It will be fun to start afresh,' Jerome said quickly. 'Like a young bride, with everything new.'

'Yes,' she said. 'I suppose it will be rather an adventure. When shall we do it?'

'As soon as possible. I want to be done with this foolery

and have my wife to myself. And we've nothing to wait for.'

'Except that first we have to talk to people.'

'Ah, yes. A number of painful interviews lies ahead of us. But,' he added, 'perhaps they'll be more understanding than we expect.'

Henrietta's once large family of siblings was now reduced to two. There was Regina, the sister with whom she lived, who was married to the squire of Bishop Winthorpe, Sir Peregrine Parke; and there was her brother Edward, a bachelor who lived in York.

Their older brother, George, the head of the family, had died a few months ago. On his death it had been discovered that he had mired his estate so deep in debt that even the family seat, Morland Place, would have to be sold to satisfy the creditors. There was nothing for Edward – Teddy as he was known – to inherit; but he had his own independent fortune, partly in property, shops and commercial ventures in York, and partly in three cotton mills and some houses in Manchester. While the agricultural slump had brought landowners and farmers into dire straits, and business in general was suffering a downturn, manufacturing had been enjoying solid progress. Teddy was comfortably off – the more so since he had no wife and children to eat up his money.

'London, eh?' he said, when Henrietta had told him everything. He lapsed into silence. Knowing he was not particularly fleet of thought she waited patiently, looking round the room in which they sat. Teddy had inherited Makepeace House from their father, who in turn had inherited it, rather shamefacedly, from a wealthy widow who had been his mistress in his youth. At one time Teddy had been meaning to sell it and live permanently at his club, but he had somehow not got around to it, which was typical of him. He had also not got around to redecorating, and as Papa had never lived here, the drawing-room, like everything else in the house, was exactly as Mrs Makepeace had left it, the perfectly preserved fossil of the taste of the 1820s.

There was a light film of dust over everything, some faded and crumbling dried flowers in the grate, and no sound to be heard but the solemn, heavy ticking of a clock somewhere out of sight. The autumn sun oozed in through the window but penetrated no more than a few feet, so that they sat in a gloom which seemed to her to smell slightly of damp. Teddy had servants, but as he never entertained at home and there was no mistress of the house, they did little to make the place comfortable.

Henrietta felt there was something terribly lonely about Teddy's life, though he appeared to be content with it. She studied his face and could not imagine what he was thinking. He was impenetrable to her. He seemed much older than her, a portly, well-dressed clubman with an air of brandy and cigars about him. He might almost have been a genial but rarely visited uncle.

'Well,' he said at last, 'I don't know but what you're right. It's probably for the best, though it's a shame you should have to go so far away. But people *will* talk, and it would make things unpleasant for everyone. He means to do the right thing by you?' he added anxiously.

'Of course. I've told you, we'll be married, only—' She hesitated, and Teddy ended the sentence for her.

'In a register office. Hmm. Well, I can't say I like it, Hen, but you know your own mind. No-one can say you've had an easy row to hoe. And times change. These things are not so *outré* as they were even ten years ago. And I dare say people in London won't mind it as much as they do here. Still, if I were you, I'd keep mum about it anyway, when you get there. Just in case. No sense stirring up trouble.'

'Of course,' Henrietta said. She felt obscurely hurt. Perhaps she had hoped her new love would prompt more rejoicing than this. He hadn't even congratulated her, or wished her happy.

'I suppose Compton's pretty well-to-do?' Teddy said next.

'He lives like a gentleman. But I have no way of knowing what his fortune is.'

'No, of course not. You wouldn't. I see that. Wouldn't do

9

at all to ask. Not but what . . .' He paused again, thinking. 'Look here,' he said, coming to a decision, 'I'd better have a word with him. Here, or at the club, perhaps. A little talk. Man to man.'

She almost smiled. 'Interview him?'

'Make sure he's all right and so forth. Well, I'm sure he is,' Teddy said hastily, in case she was offended, 'but all the same, someone ought just to have a bit of a chat with him. You're a grown woman, of course, but after all I am your brother. Head of the family, too, so it's up to me to see he's got your best interests at heart.'

Now she did smile. 'Thank you, Teddy. You're very kind.'

He looked shy at her praise. 'Don't want him thinking no-one cares. Very fond of you, Hen.'

'I know. I love you, too.'

'Not many of us left now,' he said, and cleared his throat to hide his emotion. 'And, you know, I always liked him. I'm sure you'll be very happy together. Much more the sort of fellow I'd have liked to see you marry than old – well, well, water under the bridge now.' He coughed again, and stood up. 'Glass of sherry? Don't have to rush away, do you?'

The tray and decanter were in the room, so he didn't have to ring. Henrietta was sure there was dust on the glass he handed her.

'So tell me about your life,' she said. 'What have you been up to lately?'

'Oh, this and that, you know,' he said vaguely. 'Hither and yon. Keeping busy.'

It seemed to be the best she would get from him. She asked the question uppermost in her mind. 'What's happening at Morland Place?'

'Nothing at all.' He caught her eye and read her dissatisfaction with this answer. 'Really nothing. Between the bank and the lawyers, it'll be months before anything's decided. Two slowest moving things in the world, a bank and a lawyer.'

'You would be the first to know?'

'Oh, yes. And don't worry, I'll be sure and let you know

as soon as I hear anything. There's no money left, I can tell you that already. The question is, will Morland Place have to be sold as well?'

'I hate to think of strangers living there,' Henrietta said.

Teddy agreed. 'There've been Morlands at Morland Place for five hundred years. I'd almost sooner it burned down.'

Henrietta shivered suddenly as cold air seemed to brush across the back of her neck. 'How is it with Alice?' she asked.

'Oh, she's still there, taking care of things.' Alice Bone had been a housemaid at Morland Place. She had also, in the last days of his madness and misery, been George Morland's mistress.

'But she must be near her time,' Henrietta said anxiously, feeling Teddy wasn't taking the matter seriously enough.

'Near her time?'

'The baby is due in October, isn't it? And babies can come early, you know.'

Teddy felt out of his depth. These were not matters for a bachelor. 'She's got the old woman with her. And a message can be sent to the Waltons. Mrs Walton will come and help out, I dare say.'

'But, Ted, Alice must be taken care of. And she won't be able to housekeep after the baby's born.'

'Oh, we'll see about that when the time comes. I'll see she's all right.'

'But you haven't made any plans, have you? You hadn't thought about it until I raised the question.'

He frowned. 'I expect she'll go back to her father's house to have the child.'

'Her parents might be sticky about it,' Henrietta warned. 'Sometimes fathers won't have anything to do with a daughter who's a fallen woman.'

'I'll square it all right. I dare say he'll take her back if enough money's offered.'

'But what if—'

'Now, Hen, I've told you I'll take care of her, and I will. You have my word. I'll go out to Morland Place today and

11

talk things over with her. Or – wait. Can't go today. Fellow I have to see at the club. But I'll go tomorrow, you can bank on it.'

Henrietta had to be satisfied with that. 'You'll let me know what happens? To her and to Morland Place? You won't – forget me, when I'm in London?'

'Of course I won't. And, look, whatever anyone else feels about it, you'll always be welcome here, any time you want to visit.'

'Thank you, Teddy.'

He regarded her solemnly for a long moment. Little Hen, his shy little sister – a grown woman now, but still looking very young to him, with her soft brown hair and hazel eyes and little pointed face. About to embark on married life at last – almost as if for the first time, because somehow old Fortescue had never seemed like a husband, more like a crusty old grandpa she had been obliged to housekeep for.

And after all her years of servitude with the rector, it looked as though the old miser was going to leave her with nothing. Though the probate hadn't gone through yet, it was known that the agricultural slump had severely damaged his fortune; and of what was left, he had bequeathed so much in memorials to his old colleges that it didn't look as if there would be anything for Henrietta. Even her wedding china and linen had been sold off.

Teddy's conscience prickled him. He supposed Compton was pretty well to live; and a registrar marriage was legal all right, so Compton would have to take care of Hen. But still she was his sister, and a Morland, and she ought not to be a pauper bride.

'Look here,' he said, 'when the time comes – when you marry the fellow – I shall give you something.'

She was taken by surprise. 'What do you say?'

'A cash sum for you to invest,' he explained. 'When Papa died he didn't leave anything to you girls. Don't know whether you knew it at the time, but he left it up to Georgie to take care of that. Well, Georgie didn't. Maybe he wanted to but Alfreda wouldn't let him. I don't know. Don't want to speak ill of the dead.' He waved all that away with his hand. 'Well, it seems it's up to me now.'

Henrietta said slowly, 'I don't think anyone could expect it of you.'

'I expect it of myself,' Teddy said. 'Anyway, that's what I mean to do. A girl getting married ought to have a little something of her own. Mind, it'll be your money, for your own use. Put it in the Funds, and it'll provide you with pin-money, so you ain't dependent on him for every groat.'

'You're a kind, good person, Teddy. Thank you,' Henrietta said.

When she smiled, Teddy reflected, she wasn't at all bad-looking. Quite pretty, in fact. Compton was a lucky man.

When she rose to leave, Teddy didn't ring for the servant, but saw her out himself, all the way to the street door. When she looked back at the corner, he was still standing there on his own steps, dwarfed by the high, shadowed house, and she thought of the undusted drawing-room and the heavy silence within, and felt bad about leaving him there all alone. Absurdly, she wished she could take him with her.

Sir Peregrine Parke was an indolent, good-natured man, who had been an idle and expensive youth. He had come into his fortune and title early, and had indulged his new freedom by marrying the rector's wife's pretty little sister. Regina was an orphan with no dowry, and no education either, but she was as sweet-natured as Perry himself, and adored him. He had no older relatives to find fault with his choice, but if there had been any, he could have argued that she was of good stock: the Morlands of Morland Place were one of the oldest families in the Riding.

But having married, as it were, frivolously, the realities of his position suddenly came home to him. He was squire of Bishop Winthorpe, and a great many people's lives were dependent on him in one way or another. He was a husband and, very soon afterwards, a father: he now had six children, and another was on the way. He was, in addition, responsible for his younger unmarried sisters, Amy and

Patsy; and since Fortescue's death he had taken Henrietta and her thirteen-year-old daughter Elizabeth into his household. Good-natured and indolent he might be, but he was no stranger to responsibility, and his moral education had been sound. He thought as he should on most subjects.

So he looked grave when Henrietta told him she and Jerome Compton were in love, and graver still when she said they meant to marry. 'I was afraid something like this was brewing. I didn't want to think it, but when you went all those walks with him—'

'How did you know I was with him?' Henrietta asked in surprise.

He seemed to find the question fatuous. 'A village is a small place,' he said. He shook his head and sighed. 'I wish you hadn't done it. It's not the thing at all, you know, especially with you being the rector's wife.'

'The late rector's widow,' she corrected impatiently. 'Surely my husband has been dead long enough?'

'Hardly more than a year. There has been talk, you know.'

'Perry, that's absurd. How long must a woman wait before making another attachment?'

'I don't pretend to agree with it myself, but a lot of the older sort of folk think a woman should never marry again, especially when she's been married to a man of the cloth.' He raised a hand slightly, anticipating her protest. 'I said I don't agree with it, but you have a position in the village to keep up. You must see there's bound to be talk. Jerome arrives back in the country and the next minute you're thick as thieves with him. It looks hasty. It looks heartless. And with Mary still away . . .' He hesitated a moment before adding, 'Some people are saying that you visit him in the cottage.'

Henrietta grew angry. 'How dare they? It's a lie!'

'Oh, I'm sure it is. I'm just telling you what they say.'

'And even if it were true, why should I not visit him? I'm a grown woman.'

'You know perfectly well why. You can't do just as you please in this world,' Perry said. 'Especially when you live in a small village. And the more so, given that you're living in the squire's house. Come on, you must see that. Your conscience is your own affair, but you must think of us – or if not of me, of Regina and the children, and poor little Lizzie.'

Henrietta took a breath. 'You've been very kind to me, Perry, and I'm sorry if anything I've done has upset you. But I assure you Jerome and I have done nothing wrong.'

He looked awkward. 'Oh, Lord, I know you haven't. Anyway, you don't have to answer to *me*. It's just that—'

'It's just that as long as I live here there will be talk,' she supplied. 'So we must marry and move away.'

Perry stuffed his hands into his trouser pockets and walked a few steps up and down the room, trying to assemble the right words. 'Look here, Henrietta, you're my sister-in-law and I'm damned fond of you. I don't like to see you getting into a pickle. Jerome's a fine chap and I like him awfully. Damnit, he's my cousin. And I know you two've always had a soft spot for each other. But he's a married man! Can't you see the trouble you'll be making for yourselves?'

All the arguments, for and against, were lined up in Henrietta's head, but suddenly she couldn't bring herself to recite them again.

'Perry, I love you dearly, but I'm going to marry Jerome and you can't talk me out of it, so please don't try. Just tell me what you want us to do so as not to cause you trouble.'

He was silent, looking disturbed and unhappy. She went on, 'We thought we would marry in London, where we're not known; and Jerome wants us to live there afterwards. The question is, can I stay here until then, or will it embarrass you? May I leave Lizzie with you until we're settled? And may we visit you afterwards, or will we be banished for ever from your sight?'

Perry frowned. 'It's a serious matter, you know.'

'Do you really think I don't realise that?'

'You might sound as though you did, then,' he said crossly. 'I can't give you answers this minute. I shall have to think. And talk to Jerome. Thank heaven the girls are abroad with Mary! At least they'll be spared the worst of this. I'll give you my decision in a day or two, but in the mean time, please try to be discreet. And for heaven's sake, stop rambling the countryside with Jerome. If you want to talk to him, talk to him here. There's no reason he shouldn't visit this house, and it will give the gossipmongers less to chew on. You can see him alone in one of the downstairs rooms if you must. The servants will probably talk about that, but if it's under my roof at least everyone will know there's nothing worse going on.' His frown intensified. 'Unless, of course, they think I condone it. Oh, Lord, what a mess this is! A man in my position, giving countenance to adultery!'

She began to see it more clearly from his point of view, and was sorry for the trouble she was giving; but felt constrained, even so, to protest, 'It's not adultery. He is divorced.'

'The Church doesn't recognise divorce,' Perry snapped. 'I'm the squire; I have to take the Church position. And you're the rector's wife!'

For ever and ever, amen, she thought. No more myself, but his. She could say that about Jerome gladly, with a full heart; but the world said it of her about Mr Fortescue. He owned her still, even from beyond the grave.

Henrietta's conversation with her sister went much more easily.

'Dear Hen, I'm so glad for you. You love him, don't you?'

'Yes, I do. I have for a long time, but I thought it was hopeless.'

'Well, I suppose it was,' Regina said. They were in the morning-room, engaged in the inevitable sewing – 'parlour work', as it was called – and Regina had her feet up on a footstool. She was in the early stages of pregnancy, but there had been one or two worries and she had been ordered to be careful. 'I've always liked him, though he frightens me a bit. He looks so dark and – *pirate-ish*, and he smiles at the wrong things. I never know what he's thinking. I expect he thinks me an awful fool. But I'm sure you and he will be very happy together.'

'I think we will,' Henrietta said, cheered by this unequivocal endorsement. 'Of course, there is the problem that he's a divorcé.'

Regina looked up a moment. 'Yes, I suppose that is a problem. Not so much of one as if *you* were, of course, but I expect people will be horrid about it. But if you love him, it's worth it, isn't it? I know if Perry had been in the same position I'd still have married him, whatever the consequences.'

Well, that was the woman's view, Henrietta supposed: all for love and the world well lost. How many women had been ruined through that very feminine weakness?

'So you don't mind, then?'

'Mind? Why should I mind?'

'A lot of people will consider that I am living in sin.'

'I suppose so. But you're my sister and I want you to be happy. I don't think marrying a divorced man can be so *very* terrible, can it?'

Henrietta leaned forward and laid a hand over her sister's. 'I'm glad you feel like that. But Perry thinks differently, and he'll want you to agree with him; so when he talks to you about it, don't feel you have to argue my side. I don't want to be the cause of a falling-out between you. Perhaps it would be best if you didn't even tell him we'd had this conversation.'

'All right,' she said placidly. 'I expect he'd say we were talking behind his back. Men can be so touchy. But what do you think he'll do? You don't think he'll throw you out?'

'I really don't know,' said Henrietta. 'But don't worry. I can always go and stay with Teddy. And it won't be for long.'

The last interview turned out to be the easiest. Henrietta met her daughter Elizabeth outside the rectory, their former home. She went there three times a week for lessons with the new rector, Mr Chase. She shared her cousins' governess at the Red House, but her education was further along than theirs, and Mr Chase took her for Latin, Greek and mathematics, subjects that were beyond Miss Bell.

Mother and daughter walked home together along the dusty lane which took them through the village – the rectory and the Red House were at opposite ends – and Henrietta told her, in the straightforward terms one can use to a child, what was in train.

Lizzie's reaction was gratifying. 'Oh, *good*! I do like him awfully, though it will be a bit queer to think of him being my father. Will I call him Papa?'

'I hadn't thought about that,' Henrietta said, bemused. 'I dare say you can decide it between you. And there's another thing, Lizzie – we're going to live in London. What do you think of that?'

Her face lit up. 'Not really? Oh, how topping! I've always wanted to go to London!'

'I'm glad you feel that way. There'll be lots to do, and it will be very good for your education.'

The word *education* rang a bell with Lizzie. One of the children she and the cousins played with, the daughter of a widower, had been sent away to school when he had remarried. She asked cautiously, 'Shall I go to school?'

'We'll have to see,' Henrietta said. It would cost money, and she couldn't commit Jerome's without consulting him. 'Would you like to?'

'Not if it meant going away from you,' she said promptly.

'Then there's no reason why you should,' said Henrietta.

They were passing St Mary's now, up on its bank above the street. The mellow stones were framed by the high beeches behind, and the churchyard was littered with fallen leaves, small and bright yellow like a scattering of gold coins. The church clock struck the half-hour with a solemn note, and Lizzie glanced up automatically at the sound. As the rector's child, almost all her life so far had been governed by the hours and seasons of the Church. It was like a second mother to her – sterner and more demanding, but perhaps more tellingly present than her fleshly mother had been, for her father had kept them much apart.

Henrietta tried to read her daughter's face. 'You won't mind leaving here, then?' she asked cautiously.

But Lizzie said easily, 'Oh, no. I shall miss the cousins and everyone, of course, and I did rather think it would be nice for us to live by the sea, but it will be lovely to have a home of our own again, and – well, *London* makes up for everything.' She looked sidelong at her mother. 'Do you love him *awfully*?'

'Perfectly dreadfully,' Henrietta answered solemnly; and they both laughed.

CHAPTER TWO

At the end of October 1885 probate was finally granted on the estate of the late rector of Bishop Winthorpe. The trusts and memorials to honour the memory of Edgar Fortescue had been so complex to set up that the third largest beneficiary of his estate turned out to be the solicitors who had handled the business. It was unfortunate that Fortescue had named his widow and child only as residuary legatees, for when the debts were paid, the named pensions allowed for and the legal fees extracted, there was not much residue. Under the terms the larger part was put in trust for Lizzie's dowry, and Henrietta was at last made mistress of the sum of six hundred pounds.

She hadn't been expecting much, but it surprised even her. Six hundred pounds would generate an income of thirty pounds per annum, or eleven and sixpence a week, and she knew that would not support her and Lizzie. Even farm labourers in Yorkshire earned more. Had she not been about to remarry, she would have been destitute and dependent on her brother-in-law's charity. She was entitled to feel bitter at the rector's lack of provision for her, and Perry, with the privilege of family, expressed himself vigorously on the subject; but Henrietta was too happy in her new love to resent it now.

Teddy honoured his promise and gave her a thousand pounds as a wedding present. Henrietta felt rich indeed. She would have thirty shillings a week purely as pin-money: wealth almost beyond imagining for someone who had never owned anything in her life before. For the money was really hers, to do with as she pleased. As Teddy explained to her carefully, the Married Women's Property Act, which had been passed three years ago, meant that even after she married Jerome, what belonged to her would continue to belong to her. Moreover, if she were to acquire anything else in the future, by inheritance or her own efforts, she would be entitled to keep it for herself.

'It doesn't seem quite right,' she demurred. 'How could I hold anything back from him, when he has all the trouble of taking care of me and Lizzie?'

Teddy patted her hand. 'Dear old Hen! You don't *have* to keep it from him. The money is yours and you can give it to him or spend it on new hats or – or throw it to a passing beggar, just as you please. What matters is that the choice is yours.'

'I'm not used to having choice.' She smiled. 'Perhaps it's a good thing Mr Fortescue left me so little. How would I bear having a large fortune to manage?'

'I'll take the thousand back, if you like,' Teddy offered amiably.

'Oh, no! I wouldn't put you to the trouble. I'm sure the worry will be good for me,' Henrietta assured him.

Jerome was growing restless. Early in November he took command, whisked Henrietta away to London, and married her by special licence in a register office.

She had been afraid that the proceedings would be rushed and careless, would seem irreligious or in some way simply not legal; she was afraid she would be ashamed. But the registrar was an educated man of mature years, with a fine face, well-groomed silver hair, and a voice and presence a clergyman would have envied, and he conducted the ceremony with dignity. The words were simple but profound, the intent manifestly serious. She shivered with emotion when Jerome placed the ring on her finger, and at the conclusion turned a joyful face up to him, longing to babble of her relief that she really did feel married after all.

Still, it seemed a little flat as they walked out alone and got into a cab outside. No cheering crowds, no beaming friends and relations to wish them joy. Two members of staff had acted as witnesses, and they, of course, had remained on duty. A wedding ought to be shared with *somebody*, she felt.

'What do we do now?' she asked her new husband.

'You'll see,' he said, with a secret smile that raised her spirits again.

The cab took them to Brown's Hotel, to which he had dispatched their bags from the station. There, in a private room upstairs, a wedding-breakfast had been laid, complete with a wedding-cake, nicely decorated, and lots of flowers.

'You must have ordered it beforehand,' Henrietta discovered.

'Of course,' he said, enjoying her pleasure. 'And here are some friends to help celebrate our nuptials. My love, let me introduce my *other* new partner, Richard Sutton, and Mrs Sutton.'

The couple came forward, all smiles and congratulations. Jerome signalled to the staff and champagne was poured and handed, while Sutton slapped Jerome on the shoulder and Mrs Sutton shook Henrietta's hand and hoped she would be very happy.

'Don't mind my tears,' she said, dabbing her eyes with the back of her glove. 'I always cry at weddings. I wanted to bring some rice to throw over you, but Dickie said the hotel wouldn't like it.'

Mrs Sutton was a very thin woman, and quite plain in the face, with a bony nose and rather bolting eyes; but she was smartly dressed and carried herself with an air of confidence Henrietta envied. Richard Sutton was short and stocky, with a thick neck and a wide, ruddy face. His broad, rather lumpy nose, combined with the speed with which he emptied his champagne glass, made Henrietta wonder whether his appearance was due to over-indulgence. Neither of them was quite what she would have expected Jerome's friends to be like; but they were cheerful and not at all stand-offish, which in her new situation Henrietta appreciated.

'What a pretty dress!' Mrs Sutton exclaimed. 'That colour

22

is so becoming. Did you have it made specially?' It was a woollen dress and jacket in old-rose trimmed with grey braid, which Henrietta had had made when her official period of mourning had ended, but had never got up the courage to wear in Bishop Winthorpe. She was about to reply when Mrs Sutton went on, 'Oh, but of course, you didn't know, did you? Dickie said it was all a secret. So romantic, my dear! Jerome is such a love of a man! And you haven't long put off your blacks, poor thing! I imagine up in northern parts people are very old-fashioned about such things. Dickie always says you go back fifty years into the past when you travel north, and I remember my grandmother didn't put off blacks to the day she died, and she lived twenty years after Gran'pa. But you'll find it much less stuffy here in London – quite a change, if you've lived in a village all your life.'

'Indeed, Mrs Sutton,' Henrietta said, rather stiffly.

'Oh, please call me Marion! I'm sure we're going to be very great friends. We can hardly help it with our husbands being partners, can we?'

That was a consideration. Henrietta made an effort. 'Marion, then.'

Mrs Sutton smiled roguishly. 'It's Mary Ann, really – that was what I was christened. But Marion is so much more romantic, don't you think? I changed it when I was seventeen, and I've been Marion ever since. That's my deep, dark secret. I hope you'll keep it.'

They sat down to eat, and by the end of the meal Henrietta knew a great deal about Marion Sutton, and through her, about her husband. They lived in Bayswater and had five children aged from four to sixteen. Marion's mother, Mrs Pewsley, also lived with them. Marion's father had worked for a newspaper in Winchester so had just escaped the stigma of being in trade; Richard's father had been in orders and attached to the cathedral there, which was how they had met. Richard had a brother in the army and a mother and sister still living in Winchester whom he supported. He had inherited money from an uncle and used it to set himself up in the City, on the advice of a friend who had told him he would make his fortune. He had luckily got in early on the South American railways boom, and they had done very well out of it. Now Richard wanted a partner so that they could take advantage of other opportunities opening up. 'They're finding gold in South Africa, you know. They say Transvaal is riddled with it.'

Henrietta also learnt that Mrs Sutton knew a great deal about her. 'My dear, what are you going to do about a house? You ought to come and live near us. Bayswater's such a nice place, and so convenient for everything. And what about your little girl? Is she coming to live with you? How does she like Jerome? Do they get on? Not that I can imagine anyone quarrelling with him. He's so charming! Your late husband must have been a strange man to leave you so poorly off,' and so on. Henrietta felt as though her life had been rifled through as if it were a drawer.

When the meal was over and the Suttons had taken their leave, with long-drawn-out farewells and renewed congrat-ulations, Jerome escorted Henrietta to the room he had booked for them.

'In the name of Mr and Mrs Jerome Compton,' he mentioned, ushering her in. 'Does that excite you? I must admit it gave me something of a thrill, worldly-wise old cynic that I am.'

'You, a cynic? I've been hearing all afternoon from Mrs Sutton what a *love* you are, and how *romantic*.'

'That's for you to judge. Have I done well? Does madam approve her apartment?'

'It's lovely,' she said. It was large and luxuriously appointed, with a sofa, chairs and a table as well as the bed, from which she at present shyly kept her eyes. The curtains were drawn against the winter darkness and fog, a fire was burning welcomingly in the grate, and the gas lamps had been lit. Henrietta was charmed by them. 'I've never had gas lights before.'

'They aren't very romantic. Shall I call for candles?' he said, stepping nearer.

'Oh, no. Gas is very modern, and we are a modern couple, aren't we? How long have you taken the room for?'

'A week,' he said, nibbling her neck. 'I thought London was as good a place as any for a honeymoon.'

'Oh, yes. I'm sure there'll be lots to do. But will we be seeing a great deal of the Suttons?'

'Didn't you like them?' Jerome asked, fingering the buttons of her dress.

'She was a little – overwhelming,' Henrietta confessed.

'Not quite our sort?' He smiled. 'Don't worry, we shan't be living in their pockets. I doubt,' he said, approaching his lips to hers, 'that we'll be seeing much of anyone in the next week. Except each other, that is.'

Surrendering to the long-awaited moment, Henrietta thought that would suit her very well.

Love was a revelation to her. She felt she was drowning painlessly in delight, her senses ravished by what it could be when every part was engaged, heart, mind and body. He had only to look at her to make her skin tingle as though he were touching her; she wanted to be touching him all the time; and words were as much a caress as fingers and lips.

A week was hardly enough, even for a honeymoon, and it would be impossible now, they both agreed, to go back to Yorkshire and live apart. At the end of the week Jerome extended their stay so that they could look for a house. The agent he consulted recommended Kensington as a fine and fashionable suburb for the professional classes, which Jerome was amused to find he had now joined.

At the end of the seventeenth century the village of Kensington had been chosen by King William III as the site for Kensington Palace, his country retreat, for the sake of its clean air and leafy tranquillity. When Queen Victoria was born there it had still been a rural place, set amid orchards and market gardens, and notable only for the presence of the palace, and of Holland House half a mile further west along the Great Bath Road.

But during the next twenty years, as London's growing population gradually spilled westward, the stretch of road between the two great houses had developed into a thriving

High Street. Now it was joined through South Kensington to Knightsbridge ('So handy for Tattersall's,' Jerome said) and thus to the heart of London. Kensington was no longer a separate village, and the countryside was far away.

In 1868 a scheme of street widening and rebuilding had been put in hand to alleviate the narrowness of the roads and the notoriously awkward junction of High Street and Church Street. New, smart establishments replaced the poky, dark village shops, including a handsome 'department store' – John Barker's – which could rival William Whiteley's famous emporium in Bayswater. Terraces of smart houses went up on the fields – part of the Phillimore family's estate – which sloped down from the crown of Campden Hill to the High Street. Towards the end of 1868 the station for the Metropolitan Railway was opened, and in 1884 the Inner Circle had been completed, so that now, as the agent explained, fast and frequent trains linked Kensington with both the City and the West End.

'You could hardly want a more convenient place,' the agent assured them, his keen eyes still searching them for clues as to their status and situation. Evidently he could not quite pin them down. 'And it attracts a very nice class of person. You would not be embarrassed by your neighbours, I assure you, sir, madam.'

He showed them a house in Thornton Place. The previous occupant, a wealthy widow, had died suddenly, and it was still furnished with her things. As she had no close relatives it seemed likely that the furniture would not be wanted and the agent agreed that enough basic articles to set up house-keeping could probably be bought quite cheaply from the estate. Jerome said that speed was of the essence for them and the agent seemed to think that nothing would be put in the way as the legatee was anxious to secure his inheritance in cash.

'It would be rather a lark living here,' Jerome said to Henrietta aside, 'all among the solicitors and bankers and such. I'm rather looking forward to going to the City on the "metro" every day. And the great thing is that no-one here would know us. We'd be quite safe. What do you think, my love?'

It all seemed strange to Henrietta. She had never lived in a modern house before; never lived in a house that was attached to those on either side. Wouldn't they all be on top of each other? How did Londoners survive the crush and noise and lack of room? In Kensington High Street the press of people and traffic had seemed extraordinary to a country girl; but up here on Campden Hill it was quiet enough, and the tall, clean-looking houses, the trees and the shrubs in the gardens all made it look very pleasant, even on a chill, grey winter day. Besides, if it was what Jerome wanted, it was her business to fit in.

'I think it's very nice,' she said.

'You won't mind the old lady's furniture? We'll just take the minimum to begin with, and you can choose what else you want as we go along, as you find out what we need.'

'Buy new things, you mean?' Henrietta asked.

Jerome grinned. 'Would you rather I stole them?'

It was another strange thing for Henrietta. In her experience women did not get to choose where they lived, or to choose their furniture. They moved, after marriage, from their father's house to their husband's house. They settled in with their husband's existing household goods and routines, and the best they could hope for was to add to or change some part of it. Being consulted by Jerome was a heady experience for a wife who would have expected to have everything decided for her.

'I'd be happy living anywhere with you,' was what she eventually said.

Messrs Pickford's van had come and gone, delivering Jerome's bits and pieces, and he spent the afternoon unpacking his books and arranging his study and dressing-room while Henrietta made a start on unpacking the new china and linen, which had been delivered the day before by Whiteley's in boxes that were standing inconveniently in the hall.

Then they had a rather exotic picnic dinner out of the hamper he had had the foresight to order. It was very cold, and Henrietta had not taken off her coat all day; but Jerome discovered fuel left in the coal-hole downstairs, and managed to kindle a fire in the morning-room grate. So they sat on the rug before it and ate with their fingers. It was bliss to be completely alone and free to do anything they wanted.

'Make the most of it,' he said, smiling at her over a chicken leg. 'Once Lizzie's installed and the servants are here, we won't be able to behave like pagans any more.'

'Is this pagan?' she asked. 'It doesn't feel it to me.'

'How do you feel?'

'Married,' she said.

He put down the bone. 'No regrets?'

'No regrets.'

He reached out for her hand and brought her fingers to his lips. 'I hope I shall never give you cause to regret it, my darling. Do you like your new home?'

'It's not like anything I've ever known before,' she said, 'and that's good. A new start with you. A new life.' She looked round the room, at the shapes and emptinesses flickering in the firelight. Every outline was a stranger to her eye, and it was both refreshing and a little unnerving. In a few weeks everything familiar in her life had been stripped away. Now there was only Jerome – and he was perhaps the most exotic element of all. Even sitting here on the rug inches from him, she found it hard to believe it was reality. 'Perhaps we shouldn't buy any more furniture,' she said. 'I rather like it bare like this.'

He laughed. 'A thoroughly romantic notion! But I value my comfort. And after a couple of days of continually putting out your hand for something we haven't got, you'll be begging me to set up accounts for you with all the shops.'

'I expect you're right. But meanwhile—'

'Meanwhile, Mrs Compton, you shall play the lady who ran away with the raggle-taggle gypsies, if it pleases you. Do you insist on lying with me in a bare open field?'

In the brief silence that followed, the same idea occurred to both of them.

'Would you rather stay here tonight than go back to the hotel?' he asked, a little huskily.

'We do have a perfectly good bed upstairs,' she said. He

28

kissed her lengthily. 'Only I do hope it won't be damp,' she added, dropping abruptly into the practical.

'You can turn the sheets down bravely, can't you? Didn't I see you unpack the new linen?'

'Yes, but can one put them straight on the bed out of their wrapping? I suppose new sheets can't be damp? And the room will be cold.'

'If I lit a fire here, I can light one in the bedroom,' he said.

'Where did you learn all this kindling of fires?'

'Oh, as a boy, sleeping out of doors with an old poacher friend of mine. It was a skill that came in handy in Africa.'

'You know so much, and I know so little,' Henrietta said. 'I've never been anywhere or done anything.'

'The fox knows many things, but the hedgehog knows one thing. Would you like some more wine?' he asked.

'Let's go to bed,' she said.

It was their first night together in their own bed, and there was a great deal to keep Henrietta wakeful. But as she lay thinking, she discovered at least that London was quiet enough at night. It was quieter, in fact, than the country, where there were always owls and foxes, cattle and cockerels, the sound of wind in the trees, dogs barking, unexplained alarms among the chickens, occasional gunshots. Several times she woke with a jerk and a fluttering heart to realise that it was the absolute silence that had disturbed her.

The next day Jerome went off to the City to begin his new life in stockbroking. Henrietta had to go to meet her daughter from the train. The journey posed rather a problem. Jerome had given her instructions on how to do it by underground railway, and had insisted that she could not get lost. But Henrietta was perfectly sure she could, and besides she was afraid that down in those smoke-filled tunnels she would choke to death. She knew it was an irrational fear, since thousands of people must have done it every day and survived, but still she did not want to go down there alone.

There were plenty of omnibuses in the street, drawn by pairs of big, well-fed, well-groomed horses, but though they had their destinations written up in front or along the side, she did not see one that said King's Cross, and she had no idea where she would have to change. So she walked along to the cab stand and took a hansom. That in itself was an adventure: she had never done it before, and it made her feel rather 'fast' to be travelling in one alone, though Jerome had said that it was quite acceptable these days. Londoners, he said, had largely come to rely on public transport, and few people kept their carriage. Indeed modern houses, like their own, were built without mews or stables attached.

Travel above ground was very slow, however, because of the density of traffic, which got worse the longer the journey went on. She began to be afraid that she would be late for the train. Perry was sending a servant with Lizzie, but would the girl wait if Henrietta was late? She imagined Lizzie left stranded, tearful and frightened, alone in a strange place. The station seemed so dreadfully far and she didn't recognise any landmarks, so had no idea where they were. She wondered whether the cab driver was trading on her ignorance and taking her out of her way; then she worried that she would not have enough money to pay for such a marathon; and finally she feared that the horse, which seemed in very poor condition, might drop dead between the shafts. In contrast to the omnibus horses, most of the cab horses seemed sickly specimens.

When they finally pulled up in front of the station she was a quarter of an hour late, but she felt obliged to give the jarvey a good tip for having taken him so far from his home ground, and for the sake of the weary horse. She wanted to enjoin the cabbie to give the poor beast a good feed but was too worried about Lizzie to wait. She hurried into the terminus and spent futile moments trying to see some sign for the train, before seizing a passing porter and getting directions to the platform. 'It come in – ooh – twenty minute ago now, mum,' he told her with relish. She ran. The last of the passengers from the train were dispersing, and – praise be! – there was Lizzie, standing by the barrier with her bag at her feet, looking perfectly composed.

'I'm so sorry – the cab was so slow – were you dreadfully worried?' Henrietta cried breathlessly.

'Oh, no,' Lizzie said. 'I knew you'd come.'

Martha, one of Perry's housemaids, was standing behind Lizzie guarding her trunk and holding a large basket. She stepped forward now and proffered it.

'Master sent this for you, ma'am. He thought you'd like some fresh country vittles. He sends his compliments and says the pheasants wants to be hung another week.'

'Thank you, Martha,' Henrietta said, taking the basket, which the servant seemed eager to be rid of. 'You've got your ticket home?'

'Oh, yes, ma'am. And master gave me dinner money, too.' Her head was trying to turn after every new sight and sound, and she was having difficulty restraining it.

'What time is your train?'

'Half past three, ma'am.' Martha looked at her piteously. 'Did you want me to go with you and help with the baggage?'

Henrietta understood. Martha would probably never be in London again and she was yearning to spend her time here profitably. She took pity on her. 'No, that's all right. I shall manage. You can run along now, Martha. My thanks and respects to master and my love to mistress, if you please.'

'Yes'm.'

'Keep an eye on the time and don't miss your train, will you?'

'Oh, I won't, ma'am. I won't go far. And thank you very much, ma'am,' Martha beamed.

'Off you go, then.'

The servant gave a hasty bob and departed to taste the joys of the great metropolis, as far as she could in three hours. 'I hope she'll be all right,' Henrietta said, when she had disappeared into the crowds. 'I suppose she can look after herself.'

'I expect she'll be careful. She was very worried when you weren't here to meet us,' Lizzie said. 'She kept talking about white slavers and told me not to catch anyone's eye. What's a white slaver?'

'People who kidnap girls and turn them into slaves,'

31

Henrietta said vaguely. She was looking around for a porter.

'But there aren't slaves any more, are there?'

'Not in England. They take them to France usually, I think.'

'Is there slavery in France, then?' Lizzie asked, with interest.

'No – that is – not that sort of slave. Lizzie, don't ask so many questions.'

Lizzie eyed her a moment and said, 'I expect you mean odalisques.' Henrietta's head spun round. 'Don't look so surprised, Mama. They have odalisques in all the classics – only they call them different names, of course.'

Henrietta looked at her daughter's shiningly innocent face, and was quite sure she had no idea what an odalisque actually did. She melted into a smile. 'Was it a good journey?'

'It was topping!' Lizzie said enthusiastically. 'I've only been on a train to Scarborough and Whitby before, and this was much more exciting. So many different places we went through, and all the interesting people who got on and off! Martha didn't want me to talk to anyone, but I don't see how you could *not*, shut in together for such a long time. She said I'd talk to the Ferryman when he came for me. Where are we going now, Mama?'

'To the house. I'm sure you want to see it. But then I want your opinion, whether we should stay there or go to an hotel.'

'Go to an hotel? But I thought the house was ready.'

'We haven't got any servants yet. There's a girl coming tomorrow that Mrs Sutton recommended, but for today there's no-one to light fires or cook or anything.'

Lizzie gripped her arm urgently. 'We could manage all that, couldn't we? Oh, please, do let's stay at the house! I do so want us to have a proper home again. It's silly to go there and go away again. Please, Mama!'

Henrietta smiled at so much passion. 'I thought you'd say that. I feel the same way. Papa and I stayed there last night just for fun, and I said you'd be sure to say the same, so that's what we agreed. I just hope we can manage everything between us. Ah, there's a porter! We'll need a four-wheeler with all this luggage.'

Like her mother, Lizzie had never lived in a modern house. She had spent all her life in her father's large Queen Anne rectory and the vast spaces of the sternly Palladian Red House. As they paused before the tall, narrow façade of their new home, Henrietta wondered what Lizzie would think of it. 'It's rather Londony,' she said, breaking the silence, 'but it's bigger inside than it looks. Land is so expensive in London, they have to build upwards, you see.'

'I think it's lovely,' Lizzie said emphatically. 'It's so tall! It'll be like living in a tower, like the princess in the fairy tale!' She ran up the steps to the front door.

Henrietta let them in with a latch-key – another new experience: always before in her life there had been a butler or footman to open the door for her. The hall was narrow, with the stairs climbing away steeply to one side. 'The kitchen and so on are downstairs,' she said. 'You won't want to see those.'

'Oh, please! I want to see everything!' Lizzie said, so they descended to the semi-basement. The kitchen was large and well lit from the window onto the area. It was very modern: fitted with a coal-burning stove, a fine dresser and a range of cupboards. It had a refrigerator – 'The ice goes in here, you see,' Henrietta explained – as well as a meat-safe, and there was a patent knife-cleaner, which Lizzie found fascinating. There was a separate scullery containing the sink and the hot-water copper; a small boot-room; a coal-hole with a chute to the street; a bedroom; and, most wonderfully, a water-closet for the servants' use. 'Indoors!' Lizzie marvelled.

'There's piped water,' Henrietta said, allowing herself just a little tremor of excitement. 'Right up to the top floor. And gas lights.'

'Goodness! It's like a palace. It's warm, too.'

'Papa lit the range before he went to town this morning,' Henrietta said. He had needed hot water to shave in, of course, and she had boiled a kettle on the range. They had breakfasted out of the hamper – adequately, though rather missing a cup of coffee.

When Lizzie had examined every corner of the basement, they went upstairs. On the ground floor were the dining-room, morning-room and a small, square room that Jerome had claimed as his study. The first floor was taken up with two large rooms with patent sliding doors between, making an enormous L-shaped drawing-room with long windows onto the street and onto a narrow balcony over the garden. Lizzie was fascinated by the sliders, which instead of folding back to the walls in the usual fashion, rose up into a slit in the ceiling.

'It takes up much less space that way,' Henrietta commented.

'But where does it *go*?'

'I suppose it must go up into a space between the bedroom walls.'

'Isn't it clever the way it fits into the hole?' Lizzie said, craning upwards. 'You can hardly see the join.'

The previous occupant had evidently been inspired by the Aesthetic Movement, for the wallpapers everywhere were William Morris prints, divided by panels of plain colour, and with embossed and gilded friezes. The drawing-room windows had stained glass in the upper sections, and the marble fireplace was carved with fruit and flowers, swags and serpentines. Lizzie had no doubts about the taste. 'I think it's *lovely*,' she said. All the homes she knew were solid and plain and stuffed with heavy old furniture.

On the second floor was the master bedroom, with a dressing-room attached for Jerome's use, and two small bedrooms. 'That's the spare room, and this,' Henrietta said, stepping into the smaller of the two, 'is yours.'

'Mine? A bedroom of my own? No nursery?'

'I think you're getting too old for the nursery,' Henrietta said, enjoying her pleasure. 'Look, you've got a nice window over the garden, and a cupboard here to put your things in until we can buy you a wardrobe and dresser. One of the things I like about this house is that it has so many cupboards.'

Lizzie was still a sentence behind. 'Really, no more nursery? But who will look after me?'

'I thought I would,' Henrietta said. 'Later on, perhaps, you might have a governess, but – well, we've never really had any time together, have we? There's lots to do to get the house right – all the furniture and so on to choose, lots of shopping and unpacking and arranging. I thought you might like to help me.'

Lizzie hugged her wildly. 'I'd love it! It's the nicest thing I can think of!'

On the third floor were the day-nursery and night-nursery, which Lizzie viewed with a pleasant glow of detachment, and two servants' bedrooms. But the wonders of the house didn't end there: on the first and second half landings there were proper plumbed wash-down water-closets; and on the top landing was an indisputable bathroom, with a bath and wash-basin and piped water. Lizzie was entranced. She tried both the flushes and all the taps, watched the water swirling away with interest, and speculated on its destination so that Henrietta had to relay what she had learnt from Jerome about Mr Bazalgette's monumental achievement deep under London's streets.

The bathroom, of course, was solely for the use of the gentlemen of the house. 'I wish I were a boy,' Lizzie sighed at last, rubbing one of the big brass taps with an affectionate hand, as if it were a dog's head.

Henrietta smiled. 'No you don't. A cold bath every morning, whatever the weather, instead of a nice warm tub by the bedroom fire? I think not.'

'Why do gentlemen have to wash in cold water?' Lizzie asked.

'Would you want to marry one who didn't?' Henrietta countered unanswerably.

Lizzie was hungry, her breakfast a distant memory, so they had a cold luncheon out of the remains of the hamper, and inspected Perry's basket. There was a brace of pheasant, a cheese, a crock of honey, a mutton ham, butter and some apples.

'How kind of him,' Henrietta said. 'Still, with the

pheasants not ready we'll have to go to the shops to buy something for dinner tonight. We can't expect Papa to dine on cold ham on a day like this.'

'Who's going to cook it?'

'I shall have to.'

'*Can* you cook?' Lizzie asked doubtfully.

'I really don't know,' said Henrietta. 'I've seen it done many times as a child, but I've never tried it myself. But Papa won't expect more than a simple dinner. I don't see how it can be so difficult to fry a beefsteak and boil potatoes, do you? In fact, I don't see that any cooking can be hard to master, given what a fool Uncle Perry's cook is.'

Lizzie could think of no nicer adventure than to sally forth to those exciting shops they had passed on their way home and actually buy the food they were going to eat: choose it, hand over money for it, stow it in their basket. It was like a wonderful game.

'It's lucky Uncle Perry sent this basket,' Henrietta said, unpacking it, 'because I haven't another.'

It was a cold afternoon, and their breath clouded the air as they walked; the lights in the shops glowed deeply yellow in contrast with the grey dimness of the failing day outside, making them seem like magic caves of treasure. Happy in each other's company they wandered, staring, examining goods, listening to the strange accents around them, noting what everyone was wearing. The choice of emporia and of goods was almost bewildering, especially to Lizzie, fresh from a village which was considered exceptionally well endowed for having four shops.

At a greengrocer's (there was more than one!) they bought potatoes and carrots, and mushrooms for an *hors d'oeuvre*. At a butcher's shop they bought beefsteak, and then Lizzie said shouldn't there be fried onions, so they went back to the greengrocer.

At the fishmonger, Lizzie fell in love with the lobsters for their bright colour and exotic shape. But Henrietta said, 'I don't know how to cook lobster, love. And I don't know that we have the right tools for cracking them.'

'Oysters, then. You eat oysters raw, don't you?'

'I think so.' She bought the oysters. 'Now then, that's fish and meat; what for a sweet course? I really can't cook a pudding. It had better just be dessert, I suppose.' So it was back to the greengrocer. 'We've got Uncle Perry's apples, and the cheese.' They bought pears and watercress. 'Oh dear, I wish it weren't winter. There's so little choice. What else do we need?'

Lizzie thought deeply. 'Coffee?'

'Coffee – good Lord, we'll need things for breakfast, too, won't we? We'd better find a grocer's shop.'

They found a very handsome and comprehensive one, where Henrietta bought eggs, coffee and tea. The basket was heavy now, and she was exhausted by all the to-ing and fro-ing.

'Just bread to find, and then we can go home,' she said.

In the baker's shop, Lizzie persuaded her to buy a cake, too. 'For a sweet, in case he's really hungry after working all day in the City.' The bread and cake Lizzie had to carry, for it wouldn't go in the basket.

They set off home, and the hill seemed horribly steep and the house very far off. Henrietta, adding up all the purchases in her head, felt she had spent far too much. Were things dreadfully expensive here, or had she been cheated? Or simply chosen the wrong shops? When they finally reached their own front door, Henrietta realised that the door key was in the bottom of the basket, and they had to take everything out to get at it, and then put everything back to carry it in. It was almost dark, and there was a foggy smell in the air, which was somehow melancholy.

'I must have a cup of tea before I do anything else,' Henrietta said, as they walked down the narrow stairs to the basement. 'I suppose I'll have to light the gas lamps,' she added nervously. 'I do hope I don't blow us all up.'

She had never had to do it before: there was no gas in Bishop Winthorpe. When the hotel servants had done it, there had been a horrid hiss and pop at the moment of combustion that she was rather afraid of.

'Where are the matches?' Lizzie asked, pattering about with youthful confidence in the subterranean twilight.

'Let me see, Papa had them when he lit the range this morning. I expect he put them on the mantelpiece.'

'I can't reach,' Lizzie said, on tiptoe. 'Can you come and try?' She stepped aside to let her mother in, and shivered. 'It doesn't feel warm down here any more.'

'Oh, Lord!' said Henrietta. There was no warm glow from the range. There was no fire in its belly. It sat black, cold and accusing under the chimney. 'It's gone out!' She hadn't looked at it since that morning. She hadn't made up the fire. 'Of course I know that fires have to be kept up, but I just didn't associate the fact with myself,' she confessed miserably.

'Do you know how to light it?' Lizzie asked.

Henrietta braced herself. 'I watched Papa do it this morning. I ought to be able to remember.'

Flinchingly she lit the gas jets, giving a little shriek at the moment of the 'pop', and then fetched the wherewithal for the range from the coal-hole. Half an hour later it was quite dark outside and the range's firebox was full of nothing but burnt paper. 'The wretched thing *won't* hold!' Henrietta said almost tearfully. 'It just flares up and goes out again.'

Lizzie didn't like her mother to be upset. 'I expect Papa will do it when he comes home,' she offered.

'But I can't let him come home to a cold house! And it will make dinner so late.' They stared at each other for a moment.

'P'raps we can find someone to help us?' Lizzie said. 'What about the people next door?'

'That would be a fine introduction to the neighbours,' Henrietta said.

'No, I mean we could go to their kitchen and ask their servants. They'd be bound to know how to do it.'

'It would still get back to the master and mistress. But I suppose you're right, there's nothing else for it.' She got wearily up from her knees. 'I'd better wash my hands, at least,' she said, for she was black from her labours. 'Thank heaven for piped water.'

She went through to the scullery. Lizzie, meanwhile, opened the kitchen door and stepped out into the area, smelling the chill foggy air and marvelling at the street lights all nicely burning, extending London's useful day. She went half-way up the steps to be able to see into the street, and saw someone coming: a man trundling a barrow that carried the unmistakable glow of fire inside it, deeply orange in the gas-lit twilight. She ran the rest of the way up. A wonderful smell wafted from the barrow, and the old man pushing it paused at the sight of her. 'Hot chestnuts! Lovely hot chestnuts a penny!' he chanted hopefully.

When Henrietta emerged from the scullery, rolling down her sleeves over her damp arms (there was no towel down here yet), she saw Lizzie coming in from the area leading a small and indescribably dirty old man in shapeless black clothes and a greasy cap. His chin was a hedgehog of white whiskers and his hands were blacker than his clothes. Speech fled her.

'Mama, this nice man is going to light the range for us,' Lizzie cried. 'He's a hot-chestnut man, so he knows all about fires.'

Henrietta and the old man stared at each other, almost equally at a loss to find themselves in this situation. Then Henrietta asked, 'Can you really do it?'

'Nuffin' easier, mum, if yer got the matches,' he said, still poised for flight.

He seemed too small and old to do them harm. Henrietta tried to be more gracious. 'Then, if you please, I should be grateful.'

He turned to Lizzie. 'Please you to stand by the winder, my maid, and see no-one don't make orf wiv me barrer. Nah then, mum.'

In an amazingly short time he had cleaned out the cold ashes and relaid the fire, and as soon as he applied a match a fat orange flame obediently bloomed within. He did intricate things with the little doors and dampers, and then said, 'There she goes. She'll hold now, mum – only need to keep 'er stoked up.'

'I'm very grateful to you,' Henrietta said.

He eyed her thoughtfully. 'Got any other fires you want lightin' while I'm on the job?'

He was a man, even though he was old, and she was in

a strange city. She thought of letting him loose in the house, and of what he might steal while her back was turned. 'Oh, no. We'll do very well now, thank you,' she said quickly.

He must have read her face, for he looked hurt. 'Only tryin' to 'elp, mum. Your little maid arsted me so nice, else I wouldn't a persoomed.'

Henrietta felt ashamed. She mustn't let London make her suspicious and untrusting; and the house was horribly cold. 'Well, since you are so kind as to offer . . .'

The old man smiled, mobilising his bristles and exposing more gaps than teeth. 'Thass right, mum. Blandy's my name, mum. Glad to oblige. Lived in Kensi 'n all me life. Everyone round here knows me.'

'Thank you, Mr Blandy,' Henrietta said, giving him the 'Mr' to make up for having insulted him before.

Lizzie almost danced on the spot. She was having the most deliciously different day of her life.

The three of them sat down to dinner together – Jerome, Henrietta and Lizzie – for their first meal as a family. Lizzie had hardly ever 'eaten down' before, so it was another first occasion on this wonderful day. In the intervals between helping Henrietta to cook, she had found a piece of paper and a pencil and had written out a menu for Jerome. She had worked on the kitchen table so the final result was not pristine in appearance, but she had decorated it round the edges with curlicues and flowers, and Henrietta had collaborated on the wording, so it looked and sounded very grand.

MR COMPTON'S DINNER
Tuesday, 6th December 1885
at 12 Thornton Place, Kensington

Hors d'oeuvre
Mushrooms Henriette

Poissons
Oysters au nature

Entrées
Beefsteak fried aux oignons

Entremets
Pommes de terre boiled
Carrots boiled aussi
Gateau acheté de Kensington

Dessert

Apples	Pears
Cheese	Butter
Watercress	

Jerome laughed over it very much, admired the artwork, the French and the mischief equally, and said Lizzie's education obviously hadn't been wasted. He also enjoyed the story of Mr Blandy's heroic rescue, and hoped Henrietta had tipped him well.

'I gave him a shilling,' she said, a little anxiously. 'Was that right?'

'Nicely judged,' he said. 'Any more and you'd never have got rid of him. It was very brave of you to call on his services, my love. From what you say he must have looked villainous.'

'Oh, he was quite harmless really.'

'It was me that found him,' Lizzie said.

'I can see life with you is going to prove eventful,' Jerome murmured. 'I hope I can stand up to the excitement.'

It was as well that they had plenty to laugh about, for the dinner left much to be desired. The oysters weren't fresh: 'If the shells are open you shouldn't buy them,' Jerome told her. 'It means they're stale.' The beefsteak was so tough it was almost impossible to cut – 'The butcher swore it was tender!' Henrietta cried wrathfully – and the potatoes were hard – 'Who'd have thought they would take so long to cook?' The pears also were rock hard, but the apples, cheese and watercress were nice.

'It's a good job we bought my cake, isn't it?' said Lizzie.

'Plainly there's more to shopping and cooking dinner than I thought,' Henrietta said sadly.

But Jerome's good humour was unquenchable. 'Never mind, darling, cooks can be acquired, but only you could have made this dinner tolerable to me. I'm having a delightful evening.'

'You aren't,' Henrietta said, eyeing him suspiciously, but he laughed and assured her he was. And after Lizzie had retired to bed, Jerome had some brandy by the remains of the fire and Henrietta sat on his lap and the delight of the evening became manifest even to her.

CHAPTER THREE

The next day Henrietta had to meet the housemaid at the station – Liverpool Street this time – and Lizzie pleaded so hard for them to make the journey by underground train that Henrietta yielded. Liverpool Street was on the Inner Circle, Jerome said, so they wouldn't have to change trains. This was a consideration with Henrietta: she was much afraid of getting lost, imagining a subterranean maze of dark, dripping tunnels, and herself a kind of Ariadne without the Clue.

The maid was coming from East Dereham, in Norfolk, and was recommended by Mrs Sutton, who had once employed her sister. The servant problem was something that exercised Mrs Sutton greatly. Henrietta had discovered this on the occasion, during the 'honeymoon' week, that the four of them had gone to the Savoy Theatre for a performance of *The Mikado*, a new operetta by Gilbert and Sullivan, which was enjoying a very long run.

'It's the best thing they've done,' Mr Sutton had assured the Comptons as he led the way to the box. 'We go to all their productions.'

'This will be the third time we've seen *The Mikado*,' Mrs Sutton enthused.

Perhaps because she had seen it twice before, Mrs Sutton did not seem to mind talking most of the way through it, with the result that Henrietta never gained any real understanding of what was happening on stage. She did, however, learn that 'The servant problem in London goes from bad to worse. It's as much as one can do to get a maid to stay three weeks – and such maids! Dirty, lazy, and I don't know what else! In my mother's day nice girls all wanted to go into service, but now there are jobs in shops and factories there's no luring them away. I don't know what their mothers are thinking of. If I were a mother of that class I'd want to know my girls were in decent households where they'd be watched, not working in a shop by day and doing God-knows-what by night.'

Henrietta, trying to make sense of the play out of the corner of her eye, murmured an agreement. It was only the second time she had ever been in a theatre, and she wished she could have been here without the Suttons so that she could enjoy it in peace.

'Most of the new girls come from Norfolk these days,' Mrs Sutton went on. 'It's a poor county, and there's no work there for women. It's as well to get a nice fresh country girl if you can, before they've been spoilt by London. You have to train them, of course, and a tiresome business that is – and then just when you've got them to understand your ways they up and leave and you've to start all over again. But better that than some of the slatterns who answer advertisements.'

In the course of the evening's lecture – which included a tirade against drunken and foul-tempered cooks and 'indecent' girls who had 'followers in the kitchen' – Henrietta learnt that employing servants in London was a very different matter from in Yorkshire. She was glad therefore to be getting one girl by recommendation. Emma Holt was eighteen and had never left her village before, so there was some hope she would not have been 'spoilt' in Mrs Sutton's meaning.

Between Henrietta and her new maid, however, there lay the underground railway. She bought the tickets and she and Lizzie made their way down to the platform, where a number of people were waiting for the train and ignoring one another in a remarkable fashion, just as if they weren't standing barely feet apart. It was gloomy down there, the air smelt heavily of sulphur, and every surface was coated with soot. A small grimy boy was selling newspapers from a box by the entrance, and a very fat and dapper gentleman was sitting on the red velvet cushion of the penny-in-the-slot weighing machine – not from any desire to measure his avoirdupois, Henrietta decided, but simply to rest his feet, which were encased in tight shiny boots with pointed toes.

Lizzie loved it all. She was especially absorbed by the advertisements on enamelled metal plates fixed to the walls – so many of them that very little of the original surface was visible. 'Pears Soap,' she read to her mother. 'Nestlés Milk. Alsopp's Pale Ale In Bottle. Bryant and May's Matches. Vinolia, Vinolia – two this side and another one over there. What's Vinolia, Mama?'

Henrietta didn't answer. She was listening apprehensively to a distant deep rumbling, like summer thunder, which rapidly grew louder. The rails began to thrum, the thunder became a roar, and the long-funnelled black engine burst out of the tunnel in a cloud of smoke and steam. Henrietta jumped backwards in fright. The wooden platform vibrated beneath her feet as the engine tore past with a glimpse of orange fire, and the rattling chain of carriages followed like the jointed tail of a dragon. Smoke blatted down off the carriage roofs and enveloped the waiting passengers, and in the murk the brakes squealed and the train jolted to a halt. At once all was confusion. Doors opened and people descended, those waiting on the platform surged forward, and a porter who had appeared to shout the name of the station was besieged by people waving tickets and wanting to know the train's destination. Henrietta would have liked reassurance on that point herself, but Lizzie tugged her sleeve and pulled her confidently towards the nearest door, so she yielded and climbed in.

Inside the carriage there was a narrow wooden bench running down either side, and thanks to Lizzie's prompt-ness they managed to get the last two empty places on it. Others climbing up after them had to stand, and hold on by means of leather straps suspended from the ceiling. A very fat lady in a hat decorated with birds' wings ('How cruel!' Lizzie whispered) stationed herself beside the gentleman seated next to Henrietta and glared at him, breathing heavily; but he refused to see her, only lifting his *Daily Telegraph* closer to his face in defence.

There was a thunderous banging as the porter ran down the train slamming the doors, and then the train jerked into motion again and plunged into the tunnel. Henrietta did not enjoy the journey at all. The carriage was lit with gas jets, but they were far apart and the lighting was very dim, and they made the atmosphere close and stuffy. She did not like being confined at close quarters with so many strangers, which made her feel nervous and uncertain, though they all seemed to be ignoring each other quite comfortably, obviously used to it. The air smelt of coal, and there was nothing outside the windows but blackness.

When the train pulled at last into the next station, she found that the windows were so dirty, there was no seeing through them. It meant there was no way to spot the station's name except through an open door, which was not easy given that people were standing in her line of sight, and that the door was obscured by those getting on and off. The problem was compounded by the fact that the station nameplates were few and small and hidden amongst all the advertisements. Her various fears – of being confined, of being lost, of being suffocated – began to coalesce into a slow panic.

'How will we know when we get there?' she whispered to Lizzie. 'Can you see the name of the station?'

'The porter's shouting it out,' Lizzie whispered back. 'Like he did at our station.' Her younger ears had filtered the sound out. 'But we can't get lost anyway. It's the Inner Circle. Even if we go past the station it will come round again.'

Henrietta shuddered, imagining them going round and round the track for ever, always just missing the stop. Some of the other travellers, she noticed, seemed to know their destination by instinct, and never looked up at all until they rose to leave the train. She supposed they knew the number of stops until the one they wanted, and wished she had thought of counting them before getting on. But in the event Lizzie heard the porter coming along the platform shouting,

'Liverpool Street!' quite clearly; and then Henrietta was in a panic to get out before the train moved off again.

Climbing up the stairs to the main-line station was like being released from the Underworld rather than the Underground. There were trains, smoke, steam and hundreds of people up there, but in daylight under the high, arching glass roof everything seemed normal and the air almost mountain-top fresh by comparison. 'Never again,' she vowed to herself – but silently, so as not to disappoint Lizzie too soon.

Emma Holt turned out to be a fresh-faced girl, easy to pick out, in a brown coat and an old black hat with rather worn artificial cherries on it. She had a basket at her feet: her box she had been instructed to send. She picked out Henrietta at once by a sort of instinct, and smiled a ready greeting.

'Did you like the journey?' Henrietta asked.

'Yes, thank you, mum.'

'Have you ever been on a train before?'

'No, mum. I've never been out of Dareham.' That was how she pronounced Dereham. 'I liked it very much, only I was afraid when the train rushed through all they stations, how it wouldn't stop at Lunnon at all, and then what would I have done?'

Her accent was strong, but quite comprehensible. Henrietta could see that Lizzie was fascinated by it, and that she had taken an instant liking to Emma. Henrietta liked her too: she seemed good-humoured and patently honest.

Henrietta felt justified in taking a growler home, so that she could ask about Emma's previous experience – conversation was impossible on the 'metro', she decided. It would be a chance, too, for the girl to see some of the sights of London; but Emma did not seem greatly impressed by the scenes passing by the cab windows, though she was quite willing to talk.

Henrietta learnt with relief that though she had never 'had a place' before, she was quite accustomed to housework. 'Down hoom I been a-helping Mother ever since

Bessie went to Lunnon,' she said. Bessie was the sister who had worked for Mrs Sutton. 'Bessie's done ever so well for herself, married ever such a nice man. A butcher, mum,' she added, nodding impressively. 'Mother's back's bad, so I been a-doing all the washing and cleaning. But Sarah's fourteen now and she can help, so Father, he say to me, "Goo you up to Lunnon, girl, 'fore you gets too old to catch a husband," and hare I am,' she concluded cheerfully. She turned round blue eyes on Henrietta. 'I'm ever so grateful to you, mum, for taking me. Mother says to say she hoop I will give satisfaction.'

'I'm sure you will,' Henrietta said, glad she liked this friendly person who was to share her first real home. On the rest of the journey Lizzie questioned Emma with the directness that is a child's licence, and a picture emerged for Henrietta of the rural depression she had read so much about, and seen a little of in Yorkshire, of poverty, large families, farms failing, men out of work and young women forced to leave home and travel far away for a job. Service might not be an inviting prospect to girls with other choices, but Emma would be warm, dry and well fed, and able to send a large part of her wages back to Norfolk 'to help with the little ones'. And besides, with no work for the men at home, there was no-one there for her to marry. Bessie had caught herself a butcher, and Emma hoped to do as well for herself. Marriage was the ultimate goal of all maids.

Though she had little interest in the sights of London, Emma became keenly noticing when they arrived at Thornton Place. She was very impressed with the house, and even more so with the size and modernity of the kitchen. Her box had arrived by the time they got back, and she got it upstairs on her own, exhibiting both strength and initiative, which pleased Henrietta. Emma was thrilled with the bedroom. Lizzie, thinking she might be sad to be leaving home for the first time, had tried to make her welcome, arranging some evergreen leaves and ivy in a vase at the bedside and pinning a drawing of her own to the wall. This attention reduced Emma almost to tears, and she promised to treasure Lizzie's rather wobbly dog for ever.

48

'I'll get my coat and hat off, mum, and come right down and start,' she said earnestly.

She proved a treasure from the beginning. She knew how to light both the range and the copper and to 'keep them in'; and she was energetic and skilful about her cleaning. She sang over her work all day long, mixing hymns with popular songs, 'Lead Kindly Light' with 'Father's Donkey', 'Jesus Loves You' and 'Hoom Sweet Hoom'. The words mutated through her country accent, sometimes with surprising results. 'My hoops and my dreams are my noon,' she would warble jerkily, as she polished a doorknob; and 'Say olive oil, say not goodbye!' There was never any difficulty in knowing where she was in the house.

Most excellently of all, she knew how to cook, which proved an immediate blessing, as the five cooks who were sent that afternoon by the agency to be interviewed were all hopeless. Three were so old and decrepit it seemed a cruelty to have dragged them all the way up the hill, one was obviously a drinker, and the other was dirty and so stupid it was impossible to get answers to the simplest questions.

'I'll have to go to another agency,' Henrietta said, when she took the news down to the kitchen, 'but I'll never get anyone today, which means there's tonight's dinner and tomorrow's breakfast at least to be got over.'

'I can manage, mum, if that's not too fancy,' Emma said; so Henrietta blessed her again, put on her coat and went out to harangue the agency and to make the purchase of a 'bit o' plain fish' and some mutton chops. Lizzie preferred to stay at home with Emma: her accent, her songs and her stories were more alluring just then even than the High Street shops.

Jerome was putting most of his money into the business, and until it generated returns, he told Henrietta, they would have to live in a small way. Henrietta was content with that, having enough new situations to cope with, without a large new staff to control. So by the end of the second week she declared the household complete with a cook and two housemaids. All the washing was sent out, and charwomen could be hired on a casual basis for heavy cleaning, so the two girls would probably be able to manage everything else.

The cook was surprisingly young, only in her thirties – most of those Henrietta had interviewed had been elderly. Marion Sutton predicted she wouldn't keep her 'five minutes' and warned her to keep a sharp eye out for followers in the kitchen. The cook naturally had the courtesy title of 'Mrs' Bond, but she had never been married and because of her comparative youth it seemed more natural to call her Sarah. She seemed a good cook but was ferociously possessive of her kitchen and, like most cooks, flew into a temper if anything went wrong or she was crossed in any way.

'I dassn't pass her shadow when she's in a bate,' Emma said. 'Cross as crabs, she is, mum.'

The other housemaid, Edie, came from Fulham and had been in service before. She seemed lethargic and stupid compared with Emma, but she had a good character from a place where she had been for two years, which seemed a good omen, and Emma, who had to share a room with her, said she was 'all right'. The cook slept in the basement room next to the kitchen.

Tradesmen were not slow in calling to get the new household's business, and ordering the basic foodstuffs was now Sarah's concern. But most mornings Henrietta went to the shops, accompanied by Lizzie. There was always something needed – dusters, writing-ink, a new frying-pan, tin tacks, more towels – as well as the more out-of-the-usual food to order.

There were other things to be bought that required longer shopping trips. Henrietta could not get over her dislike of the underground railway, so she and Lizzie walked or took the omnibus, and in this way began to go further afield and piece together the map of London. They went to William Whiteley's famous store in Westbourne Grove and found it everything that had been promised, but expensive. They walked to Sloane Street for Harvey Nichols, found their way to the Baker Street Bazaar, to Marshall and Snelgrove in Oxford Street, Maples in Tottenham Court Road, Gamages in Holborn. Harrods she didn't like – it was very cheap but also very dirty, a warren of cramped little rooms.

The shopping trips were interspersed with visits to galleries, to museums – the Victoria and Albert was only a walk away at South Kensington – and to look at Buckingham Palace, the Houses of Parliament, Nelson's Column and the famous pelicans in St James's Park. And, of course, when the legs wearied and the spirit flagged with all this exertion, they had the perfect excuse to pop into Charbonnel's for a cup of chocolate, Gunter's for cake or Gatti's for ices. It was a delight to Henrietta to have the freedom to decide her own itinerary, to enter a place of refreshment and spend her own money on her own choice of purchase. Even Lizzie could hardly have found it more exciting.

Faithful to her promise, Henrietta wrote long letters to Regina, including all the detail she knew her sister liked.

I have been to the dressmaker Mrs Sutton recommended in Hans Square, and her work seems very good, though like all her tribe she is as haughty as an empress. I had an appointment at 11.30 but Madame Tessier kept me waiting almost half an hour and then was as cross as if *I* had kept *her* waiting! She is making me an evening dress of blue and fawn striped silk, which I think will look very well. Bustles are being worn again for evening, and it has a full skirt – much more attractive than the tie-backs we've suffered for the last few years. Madame T is very expensive, as I suppose one must expect in London, and though Jerome tells me not to mind it, I thought I would try something else as well. Some of the larger stores here sell ready-made clothes, which they alter on the premises. I bought a barathea dress and jacket at Harvey Nichols and had the sleeves refitted and different braiding put on the collar and cuffs, and I'm sure no-one would know it came from a shop. I shan't tell anyone, of course! I can just imagine what Alfreda would have said if she had known, but I wonder now as I look at other ladies' outfits if they are harbouring the same secret.

I am making Lizzie a frock in the loveliest brown velvet which I found in Barker's, and a little hat to go with it. But I've found that Whiteley's sell very nice cotton combinations and drawers more cheaply than I could make them, so I think I shall buy all our underwear from now on.

We went to dinner with the Suttons on Saturday. The only other guests were a rather stiff, elderly gentleman – another stockbroker – and his even stiffer wife, and a very vulgar, red-faced fellow who I think was an old friend of the family. He put his elbows on the table and talked very loudly and splashed his soup when he ate, and the stiff couple grew ever stiffer and the whole evening could have been a failure. But the Suttons have a very good cook, which soothed everybody, and Jerome put himself out to be charming, and made everybody laugh with funny stories about his travels. I suspect he regards the Suttons and their odd friends as so many more interesting African tribes to be studied, which I'm afraid is not at all proper but must make everything much easier to bear!

We have not made any other new acquaintances yet. The neighbours on one side have left cards; on the other side they are not back in Town. Quite a few houses are still shut up – Jerome says many families don't come back until after Christmas. We have not entertained at home. Some time we will have to have the Suttons back, but at the moment I am excused as being 'not settled in yet', though Mrs Sutton won't let that go on much past the festive season, if I understand her hints. This period is a sort of respite for me. I can't say so to Jerome, but I dread going into wider society and facing difficult questions and perhaps cold looks. Dear Reggie, you were so lucky to meet your love first time. I love Jerome so very dearly, but there is always that shadow, though I try not to think of it.

Regina did not write back, though Henrietta knew her sister too well to read anything into that: she had always hated any exercise involving the pen. But, somewhat to Henrietta's surprise, Teddy did send a letter. Written in his sprawling, impatient hand, it was hard to decipher, but Henrietta was warmed by the thought of the effort it had taken him. In all the years she had been married to Mr Fortescue, Teddy had never written to her. Now, knowing that she felt a little lost and forlorn so far from home, he had forced himself to the repellent task.

He had two things to tell her: 'I rode over to Crockey Hill the other day to see that everything was all right with Alice and the boy.' Alice Bone had gone back to her father's house in October and there had given birth to a son whom she had called Edward James – much to the surprise of Henrietta, who had expected her to name him George after his father.

Alice is over the birth now, but seems a bit blue and mopish – worried about her future, perhaps. Her pa is a dragon, and no doubt makes her know her sin. I was much frowned at for presuming to call and – you'd laugh, Hen – but though he takes my money, he does it reluctantly and with a grim face, as though he was supping with the devil and his spoon not nearly long enough! But the boy is a splendid little kid, much better-looking than babies usually are, and already showing a propensity to smile at Uncle Teddy.

This caused Henrietta wry amusement, for 'Uncle Teddy' had never shown the slightest interest in any other of his nephews and nieces, and in fact had always had a positive aversion to babies. It would do Alice's poor infant no harm to have the interest of a wealthy bachelor with nothing else to spend his money on. A servant-girl's bastard might otherwise have a very hard life, and perhaps a short one.

After Alice's departure Morland Place had stood empty, which had worried both Teddy and the bank, for an empty house soon deteriorates, and is vulnerable to damage by tramps and other undesirables.

In fact [Teddy now wrote], the bank is so worried about leaving it empty, that they are willing to consider selling it to me rather than wait and auction it in the hope of getting a higher price. Skelwith's are to give a valuation and if both sides agree, I shall stump up, and Morland Place will be mine. I can tell you, Hen, I feel a bit queer about the idea of owning the old house, and Lord knows what I shall do with it, but there's a prickly place in my head that tells me it's the right thing to do.

Henrietta knew exactly what he meant. She was overcome with relief herself that Morland Place would not be sold off to a stranger. The house itself had been built by a Morland ancestor in 1450, but it had replaced an even older house: there had been Morlands on that land since before memory. It had been a constant nagging grief in her mind that it was to pass out of Morland hands after all those centuries.

The letter came just before Christmas, and she hurried to tell Jerome about it. 'This is the best Christmas present I could have had. The old Place safe! Dear old Teddy!'

Jerome read the letter and said, 'The bank is probably wise: better to have the money in hand than risk fire or flood. And who knows if the price will hold up, the way agricultural land is falling? The bank has a charge on the place, I suppose? Well, provided the executors are satisfied that the valuation is fair, I can't see that any difficulties will arise. But does your brother mean to live there?'

'I don't know. I think he just means to *have* it, at the moment.'

On Christmas Eve there was another new experience for Henrietta: she received an invitation from the Suttons for Lizzie to attend a 'juvenile party', something she had never heard of before.

'What on earth is a juvenile party?' Henrietta asked Jerome, and before he could answer added, smiling, 'Lizzie thought I said "Juvenal party". She quite thought it would be dedicated to construing Latin.'

Jerome laughed. 'An erudite version of the spelling bee,

54

I suppose! No, a juvenile party is just a party given exclusively for children.'

'What a strange idea.'

'I believe they're becoming very fashionable in certain circles. Lizzie will be required to mingle with a dozen or so other children of various ages in their best frocks, partake of a meal featuring far more sweet stuff than is good for them, and play games. Meanwhile I believe the attendant mothers will sit in a separate chamber drinking tea and talking about servants.'

'It sounds dreadful,' Henrietta said.

'I'm glad you think so,' he said. 'There's a deplorable school of sentimentality growing up around children these days – calling them "little angels", talking about them trailing clouds of glory and such like. But I might have known my wife would see through the nonsense,' he added, stepping closer. 'A very superior woman, my wife.' They kissed for rather a long time, and then he added, 'She had better go, all the same. The Suttons may not be quite our sort, but they have wide connections. It won't do to snub them; and she might enjoy it.'

So Henrietta had quickly to finish the brown velvet for Lizzie, who was, indeed, excited at the prospect of the party. Unsure how much she herself would be on display, Henrietta wore her new barathea outfit from Harvey Nichols, with a lace jabot fixed with her pearl brooch, and her smartest hat, which was trimmed with fur. When she and Lizzie arrived at the Suttons' Bayswater house, she was glad she had 'dressed up'. They had come in a cab, but a stream of private carriages was depositing smartly dressed women who looked as if they had never put on their own stockings in their lives, together with obviously pampered offspring, some of whom were accompanied by nurses. One little girl was even carrying a pet dog dressed in a coat that matched her own.

Lizzie looked at Henrietta apprehensively. 'Do we have to go in, Mama?'

Henrietta pulled herself together. 'I'm sure you'll enjoy it. And your dress is as pretty as anything anyone else will be wearing.'

The Suttons' house was wide enough to have an entrance hall, which was dominated by a large Christmas tree in the German style. This was a fashion that was spreading downwards from the Royal Family, though old families mostly resisted it as an affectation. The Suttons evidently had no such doubts. The tree was a seven-foot-tall fir, hung all over with gilded nuts, apples and tiny ornaments that twisted on their cotton threads and caught the light. Already it had gathered a crowd of children, and Lizzie's eyes were drawn to it as though by magnetism.

A maid took their coats and then they were passed along a receiving-line consisting of Mrs Sutton, her mother Mrs Pewsley, and all five of her children, down to the four-year-old whose hand was being clutched by a nurse in a desperate attempt to keep her still. Marion Sutton greeted Henrietta effusively, kissed Lizzie – much to her embarrassment – and said, 'Now you must let me introduce my dear children. I *know* you are going to be such friends! This handsome rogue is my eldest, Roy.'

Roy was sixteen, a lethargic-looking youth in a light-coloured suit and a very high collar. He had his mother's protuberant eyes and his father's pudgy nose, but he was not so very plain as to make his mother's description ludicrous. What he mostly looked was bored and chagrined at being forced to attend a juvenile party when he was obviously, in his own estimation at least, a man. Apart from his rather startling suit, he wore his hair parted down the centre, and had a little, jaded, forced rosebud in his buttonhole. Lizzie, shaking his hand as he smirked self-consciously past her left ear, thought the rose looked as if it longed even more than its wearer to be elsewhere.

The second Sutton was a girl of twelve called Mignonette, who Mrs Sutton decreed would soon be Lizzie's best friend. Then came boys of ten and eight, Leonard and Fred, who were looking sulkily rebellious and had to be threatened with a cuffing before they would shake hands. The baby was called Alicia – Marion evidently had a taste for romantic names – and was a confection of white muslin, frills, a blue sash, and golden ringlets. She was evidently very much spoiled. Told to curtsey, she obeyed, but then dragged hard to release her hand from the nurse's grip, and when that failed, swivelled her head round with the speed of a trapped stoat and bit her wrist. The long-suffering nurse flinched but did not let go, evidently used to such assaults. Miss Alicia then stuck her tongue out at Lizzie as far as it would go, dropped to the floor like a stone and let out a wild scream of rage that made everyone except the Suttons duck.

As Henrietta led Lizzie away in the direction everyone else was going, Lizzie tugged at her arm and whispered, 'Can't we go home? Please, Mama!'

'Darling, we can't. It would be so rude. I'm sure you'll have a nice time. There are lots of other children here. There's bound to be someone you'll like.'

And in fact Lizzie did have a nice time. After an initial phase of standing around in an embarrassed fashion, the juvenile guests began talking to each other and tentatively making friends. A very authoritative lady (who turned out to be Mr Sutton's sister and had taught Sunday school all her life) came in and organised games – Blind Man's Buff, followed by Musical Chairs. Then everyone trooped into the dining-room where a sumptuous tea had been laid out: sandwiches, cold ham, bread and butter, savoury rolls, jam tarts, iced cakes, biscuits, blancmanger and three colours of jelly.

After tea a conjurer came and did magic tricks while the feast was digested, and then there were more games for the younger ones, while the older children were herded, somewhat against their will, into a separate room where they were obliged to dance with each other. Lizzie would have been happy to be classed with the little ones, but Mignonette (who was known to her family, unromantically, as Minnie) wanted to dance, and since she had seized on to Lizzie like a mussel to a rock, Lizzie was obliged to go too. Soon she found herself dancing with a more-bored-than-ever Roy, who tried to impress her with his conversation.

'Have you ever been to a ball, Miss Compton?' he asked. 'I don't mean one of these wretched juvenile balls, but the real thing?'

'No,' Lizzie said. 'At least, I haven't danced at one, but

at my uncle's we're always allowed to watch. He isn't at all strict.'

'Oh? And where is your uncle's?' Roy asked, in his strange drawl – an imitation of a masher, though Lizzie didn't know it. She just thought he had a cold.

'In Yorkshire. It's called the Red House.'

'Has he much of a place?' Roy asked, in the tone that expects the answer *no*.

'I don't know exactly. I think he owns most of the village,' Lizzie said innocently. 'They call him the squire.'

Roy's eyes opened fully. 'Do they? What is his name? Perhaps I know him.'

'He's Sir Peregrine Parke,' Lizzie said, 'but why on earth should you know him? You're only a boy, aren't you? I know you're older than me but you don't look more than fifteen.'

This devastating frankness hit Roy like cold water in the face. All he could manage to say was, 'Sixteen. I'm sixteen.'

'Oh, I'm sorry,' said Lizzie. 'But that's still not old enough to know a grown-up in that way, so stop pretending.'

Roy gulped a few times, like a fish. 'I might know him,' he defended his position. 'I go places with Papa. Last year I went with him to Mr Gambol's place in Norfolk, shooting. Papa showed me how to hold the gun and I nearly got a pheasant.'

'Did you? How interesting. Do tell me all about it – only,' she added hastily, 'can you talk in your ordinary voice? I can't understand you properly when you use that funny one.'

Roy stared at her, struggling to swallow the great lump of his pride in one go. But she was looking up at him with such innocent candour that he could not suspect her of deliberate cruelty; and though she was only a kid, she was very pretty. Also, it was not often that anyone told him he was interesting or actually asked him to talk, so under the outrage he was flattered.

'All right, then,' he said at last. 'What do you want to know?'

'Everything,' said Lizzie. 'Start at the beginning. Did you go by train?'

Mrs Sutton, coming to the door to check that everything was going as planned, saw her handsome rogue dancing with the little Compton child and talking so earnestly that the girl was evidently fascinated. She smiled a satisfied smile, avoided noticing that Minnie was dancing with the dreadful red-headed Worsley boy, and returned to the drawing-room where Henrietta, glazed with boredom, was trapped in a sea of mothers who were all, as Jerome had predicted, talking about servants.

The juvenile party ended with a distribution of presents to the guests by the young Suttons, a proceeding that one of the mothers described as 'sweetly pretty'. 'Marion Sutton always has such sweet ideas,' she went on. 'She's quite my favourite person in the whole world.' Henrietta agreed as best she could with this startling announcement and hurried away to look for a cab.

On the way home, Henrietta asked Lizzie if she had enjoyed herself. 'Yes, I did, thank you,' she said. 'I didn't think I would, but I did. The tea was very good and the games and things were jolly. If it hadn't been for Fred and Lennie Sutton running about punching each other and tormenting people, and the littlest Sutton screaming all the time, it would have been perfect. I didn't even mind dancing, though I'd sooner have played a game.'

'Mrs Sutton said you danced with her son Roy.'

'Yes, I did. He told me some interesting things about shooting and house parties. He was all right, really – when he stopped being peculiar,' she concluded judiciously.

Henrietta smiled to herself, remembering Marion Sutton's report that 'your little Elizabeth is absolutely moon-struck, gazing up at my Roy as if he were a god. It must be flattering for a little girl to have the attention of such a splendid boy – well, almost a *man*, really! I dare say,' she added, with a laugh, 'she's quite given her little heart away to him already!'

Lizzie's present, when she unwrapped it, proved to be a pen-wiper in the shape of a flower. An enclosed slip of paper explained proudly that it had been made unaided by Miss Alicia Sutton who was only <u>four years old</u>. Henrietta begged leave to doubt the 'unaided' part, but held her peace for the sake of diplomacy.

Christmas Day began cold and foggy. Henrietta woke early, disturbed from her sleep by the extra depth of the silence, compounded by the holiday and the muffling effect of the fog. She lay awake for a while, thinking of other Christmases, especially those in her childhood, before her mother had died: how they would go out and bring the Yule log home; how the servants and tenants would come up to the house and be given presents and hot punch and mincemeat pies; how they would go to mass in the chapel and sing all the favourite carols; how the dogs would make a shaggy, living carpet before the roaring fire in the great hall fireplace, where the boys roasted chestnuts on a special long-handled shovel. And one year one of the mares had given birth on Christmas evening, and they had all gone out across the snowy yard to look at the newcomer, damp and leggy and blinking in the yellow lamplight in the warm, straw-smelling stable.

Then Mother had got ill and died, and all the warmth had gone out of the world for twenty long years. But now she had a home again – for home, she thought, turning over and moving towards the sleeping bulk of her husband, was not just a house, but the people in it. Being home was being with the people you loved, who loved you. As she touched him, Jerome murmured in his sleep and opened his arms for her, and she snuggled against his blissful heat, and sank into a delicious drowse. The next thing that woke her was Edie coming in to make up the fire.

After breakfast, which featured some exceptionally fine sausages, presents were distributed. Henrietta had bought Lizzie a little musical box she had seen and admired in a shop in Sloane Square. It was German-made, and played six German songs – 'Ach du Liebe Augustine', and 'O Tannenbaum', and 'Kennst du Das Land', and three others she didn't know. Lizzie was enchanted with it. Henrietta had made Jerome a rather handsome silk dressing-gown, which he insisted on putting on straight away over his clothes, to Lizzie's amusement. Lizzie had bought her mother a box of chocolates and Jerome a pack of playing-cards with the kings and queens of England on the back. 'For when you play whist with the other gentlemen,' she told him, and added anxiously, 'They had them with flowers, too, but I thought kings and queens were more suitable for gentlemen.'

'Much more suitable,' Jerome said solemnly. 'And educational, too. I shall keep them for our first card evening here at home. How I shall amaze our guests when I produce them!'

His presents, which he carried in from his study, were inspired. For Henrietta he had bought a sewing-machine. 'I saw how you laboured over Lizzie's dress. If you will make clothes here at home, you shan't wear yourself out doing it.'

Henrietta examined the mechanical wonder with a touch of anxiety. It was enamelled shiny black, with curly decorations in gold paint, and set on a polished mahogany base. 'It's beautiful!' she said. 'But how shall I ever learn to use it?'

'Oh, it's simple, I believe, but the company will send round someone to teach you whenever you like,' he said.

His present to Lizzie was even more wonderful: a magic lantern, together with a box of a hundred and twenty slides he had selected personally. Lizzie was overwhelmed, and could only look her gratitude as she examined this marvel of the modern world. 'We'll have a show after dinner tonight,' he told her.

After breakfast they went down to the kitchen to take the servants their presents, and Lizzie took her musical box to show them. After that the servants were free for the rest of the day to go and visit their families. Emma, because her family was so far away, was going home with Edie, but coming back in the afternoon to help Henrietta cook dinner, and would have an extra day's holiday tacked on to her next day off instead, so that she could get up to Norfolk and back.

Jerome, Henrietta and Lizzie went off to church for the

Christmas service. The fog had lifted and it was a cold, sunny day, a little pink and misty round the edges, the air so perfectly still they could almost see the frost falling through it. The emptiness of the streets was delightful to Henrietta: no wheeled traffic at all passed them on their walk up the High Street, and the only people about were also on their way to church. It was almost like being back in the village.

The church was beautifully decorated with white flowers, candles and evergreen wreaths; and the service was lovely, with all the right carols, and a very good sermon. They walked home to a cold luncheon, and then Jerome took Lizzie to see St Paul's cathedral, while Henrietta began preparations for dinner. It pleased her very much to see her daughter and Jerome walk off together so companionably, arguing the relative merits of the underground and the omnibus. Truly, she thought, I have been blessed.

They came back, rosy with the cold, in time for tea. Lizzie was full of the things she had seen, the beautiful cathedral, filled with candles like stars; the fog rolling in up the Thames like a strange tide – 'The top of it was quite flat, Mama, like a table-top, and the ships' masts stuck up through it!'; and how they had ridden on the top of the bus, right next to the driver. 'He was so nice, he told me the names of his horses – Bessie and Ramsey – and who lived at all the different places we passed. You could see everything from up there! Right into the windows above the shops. We saw some people having dinner, and a little boy waved to us. And we played roadside cribbage as we went, and I won twice.'

'What's roadside cribbage?' Henrietta asked.

'Papa taught it me. You score points for the things you see, and try to get to thirty-one. It's five for a man carrying a baby, five for three in a hansom, one for a ladder or a perambulator, fifteen for a cat in a window—'

'Really, I'm not sure it's proper to play games on the way to church,' Henrietta said, though she was laughing.

'Oh, but we didn't!' Lizzie said quickly. 'We played it on the way back.'

Sarah had made a special cake, and Jerome had to take off his jacket and roll up his sleeves to get the knife through the white sugar icing. 'We ought to keep it for next year,' he said, panting. 'Just slip a new cake into it when the time comes – much easier than trying to eat it.'

Emma came in and was persuaded to sit down with them for a cup of tea and a piece of cake. 'Though really, mum, I don't know where I shall put it. Edie's ma didn't half pile up my plate.' Jerome further persuaded her (without much difficulty) to sing for them. She sang 'I Saw Three Ships' and 'Mr Polly's Parrot', and then heaved herself out of her chair with a sigh and began clearing the cups. 'I'd better get along, else I shall be all behind meself, like the cow's tail.' She was full of little sayings like that, which fascinated Lizzie.

Henrietta and Emma cooked dinner – or rather Emma cooked and Henrietta helped – while upstairs Jerome and Lizzie laid and decorated the table and set up the magic lantern, then played at backgammon until dinner was ready. The table looked lovely, with dried flowers, nuts and fruit, trails of ivy, little crackers in red and gold paper, and candles in white candlesticks with red shades. And after dinner they went up to the drawing-room where Jerome had hung up a sheet from the picture-rail for the show. Lizzie put out the lights, and with nothing but the firelight to distract them they gazed at mountain scenes and famous buildings, cathedrals, Greek and Roman ruins, and a whole menagerie of strange animals, many of which Jerome had seen in the flesh in Africa. There were some lovely kaleidoscope slides, and at the end some comic ones, too, of a man eating rats one after another, a woman whose nose grew and grew, a dog doing a somersault, a man who looked into a looking-glass and saw an ass's head, and many more.

After that, Lizzie was unwilling for the anticlimax of bed. 'If only we had a piano,' Henrietta said.

'But we have Lizzie's music box,' Jerome said.

He put it on, bowed low to Lizzie, and swept her, giggling, into a manic dance, which he said was in the German style. They bounded exhaustingly round the room, while Henrietta claimed that the only true German dance was the

63

waltz, and circled sedately with an imaginary partner. Jerome and Lizzie were still galloping when Henrietta came over faint and had to sit down. Fortunately they didn't notice, and it was not until an amazed Emma put her head round the door that they stopped and fell breathlessly into chairs.

'We won't be able to romp like that when we have more furniture,' Jerome panted. 'Perhaps we ought to leave the room as empty as it is.'

'I've had such a lovely day,' Lizzie said. 'I think it was the nicest Christmas ever. And thank you so much for my lovely presents.'

When she had seen Lizzie off to bed, Henrietta came down to the drawing-room and found Jerome in the big chair by the fire, a glass of brandy at his side. He opened his arms silently to her, and she went across to sit in his lap, her head on his shoulder and his arms wrapped round her: her favourite way to end any evening.

'Well,' he said, after a while, 'did you have a lovely day too?'

'The loveliest ever,' she said. 'And thank you, dearest, for both my wonderful presents.'

'Both?' he said. 'I only bought you one.'

'The other didn't cost any money, but it's more precious than gold,' she said. 'Haven't you guessed?'

His heart seemed to lurch. 'You don't mean—?'

'Yes. We're going to have a baby.' He didn't say anything, and her smile faltered. 'You are pleased?'

'Oh, my darling,' he said, and squeezed her very tightly. Absurdly, he found his eyes filling with tears, and rested his face against her hair to hide them. 'I love you,' he said at last.

'I love you too,' she said. 'So very much.'

After a little silence, he said, 'It wasn't my present to you, it was yours to me – and the best Christmas present I could ever have.'

CHAPTER FOUR

Perhaps inevitably, Henrietta saw a lot of Marion Sutton. Though her manner was sometimes overbearing, and she gave a great deal of unrequested advice, she meant it kindly, and Henrietta bore with it, aware that friendship was a thing to be cherished, in whatever guise it came.

The thing Henrietta found hardest to bear was Mrs Sutton's endless concern with social position. Marion knew to a nicety the relative status of everyone with whom they came in contact, and was a stickler for the exact rules of etiquette. 'Oh, my dear,' she would say, shocked, 'you ought not to leave cards at her house! It's for *her* to leave hers with *you* first.'

'Does it really matter?' Henrietta would ask tentatively.

'Of course it matters! If no-one attended properly to these matters, where would we all be? And,' she would add as the clinching argument, 'you must think of Lizzie's future.'

Henrietta had been brought up to be easy and affable with everyone, and rank and status had not entered her calculations at all. She had known an extreme form of Mrs Sutton in her late sister-in-law, Alfreda, her brother George's wife. Alfreda's life had revolved around minute calculations based on *Burke's*, *Crockford's*, the Army and Navy lists and the society pages of the newspapers, and it would have pained her as much to fail to be haughty to someone beneath her as to be snubbed by someone (there were not many, in her view) above her.

Henrietta supposed it had to do with confidence. Alfreda, though brought up a baronet's daughter, had lived for years after her father's ruin and death as a penniless dependant, and having married George had been determined never to suffer such humiliation again. Marion Sutton, she imagined, was trying to distance herself from the lowliness of her forebears, and secure a higher place on the ladder for her children.

Many of the people Henrietta met through the Suttons were similarly obsessed, and it did make her wonder from time to time why Jerome had chosen to plunge them into this world of the striving middle classes. She feared it appealed to his sense of humour; but of course he was not exposed to it in the same way that she was. In the world of work, men were much more equal; and men in general seemed less aware of the whole status question than women. It made it very difficult for her, harbouring as she did the dire secret of her marriage to a divorcé. She was forced to be on intimate terms with the very people who would most object if they found out.

Though Henrietta was, in Marion's terms, born far above her – being of the 'landed gentry', and old-established landed gentry at that, while Marion was a newspaper journalist's daughter – Marion obviously felt it was she who was patronising Henrietta and not vice versa. The reason for this, Henrietta concluded, was that she was a country woman, ignorant of the sophisticated ways of London, in which Marion regarded herself as an expert.

However little she felt inclined to compete with Mrs Sutton, she would hardly have been human if she had not wanted, when giving her first dinner-party, to show her in a quiet way how the thing should be done. The occasion was the return to England of Perry's twin sisters, Amy and Patsy, and Jerome's sister Mary, who had been travelling abroad together for almost a year. They were to arrive in London at the end of January and Jerome was to meet them at the docks and bring them home to stay for a few days before they went down to Yorkshire.

Henrietta was nervous about meeting Mary again, for they had parted on unfriendly terms. As a fond sister, Mary could never bear her brother to be deprived of anything he wanted. She had tried to persuade Henrietta to leave her husband for Jerome, since he loved her so much and Fortescue loved her not at all. Henrietta had been shocked at such lack of principle, Mary at Henrietta's cold-heartedness.

But though the first few moments were a little awkward, they were soon got over. Now that Jerome had his love, Mary was willing to forgive her. 'I'm glad I can call you sister now,' she said. 'It was always my secret hope.'

Henrietta embraced her, remembering the friendship and kindness that had preceded the rift. In her darkest days of loneliness as the rector's wife, Mary had been her refuge.

The twins were exactly as they had always been, plain and friendly, neat and quick as birds, full of talk and laughter, sharing their sentences as they shared their lives. They had a portfolio of sketches and paintings to show, and more experiences to relate than they could get through in two days.

As soon as he had word they were coming, Jerome had said to Henrietta, 'We must give a dinner for them. We shall have to ask the Suttons, of course. They've been kind, and it would be too cruel to deprive them of the chance to see Amy and Patsy.'

'Who else shall we invite?' Henrietta had said.

'Oh, leave that to me,' he had said airily.

Henrietta felt she would pretty well have to, since apart from the Suttons the only acquaintance she had made was that of the neighbours who had left their cards. They were a Dr and Mrs Charles Hensman. On her return call to leave her own cards she had been invited upstairs by the lady of the house, but she had managed to learn nothing more than that Dr Hensman lectured in archaeology at University College and that Mrs Hensman deplored modern manners. She couldn't imagine who Jerome would have to invite, unless it was other stockbrokers, for she had no idea what he did all day or whom he might know; but when he presented her with a guest-list, it seemed that stockbrokers were in a position to call on a wide circle of connections.

'You see, you won't be disgraced,' Jerome said teasingly.

'And, more importantly, you won't be dull.' He had invited Frank Burnand, the editor of *Punch*, and his wife; the Alma-Tademas, husband and wife both accomplished artists; Signor Ribero, the newest tenor to take the London musical scene by storm, and his lovely wife; 'Alec' Macdonald, the distinguished botanist, traveller and plant-finder; and Cyril Agnew, the critic and man of letters, and his wife.

'I think we should include the Hensmans, too – it's polite, and the girls will enjoy talking archaeology with him,' Jerome said. He scanned the list again, pleased with himself. 'A little bit of everything, and every soul a talker – with the possible exception of Madame Ribero, who I understand hasn't a word of English. There'll be no awkward silences round your table, I promise you.'

Henrietta counted. 'With us and the Suttons, that will make sixteen.' She looked up. 'Can I manage it? Sixteen to dinner! I've never done anything like that before.'

'You entertained at the rectory,' he pointed out.

'But it was the housekeeper who arranged our parties. I was never allowed to do anything.' Another thought occurred to her. 'We've only twelve chairs. And the dining-table isn't big enough. And what about the servants? I don't know whether Sarah's ever cooked a big dinner.'

Jerome captured her hands. 'We can buy more chairs – ought to, in fact, for I mean us to entertain often. There's another two leaves to the dining table up in the box-room. Servants can be hired, extra ones just for the night if you like, though with the three girls staying you might want to get another maid in. And if Sarah can't cook the dinner, we'll hire someone who can, and she can assist. As to whether you will manage, my darling wife, I can only say I have every faith in you. Intelligence will always find a way. And, mind, I expect Mrs Sutton's nose to be put thoroughly out of joint!'

It was ignoble, of course, but she couldn't help agreeing with the last part. Everything, she felt, was in the planning, and she made lists and decided exactly what had to be done in what order; but on the day itself it was not to be wondered at that she was preoccupied, and the returned travellers found that her mind was not fully on their wonderful stories.

Another dozen chairs had been purchased – fortunately the twelve they had were of a standard pattern. Sarah, delicately questioned, said indignantly that of course she could cook for sixteen, or sixty if required; and then, in the illogical way of cooks, she slammed saucepans about and muttered that people thought she was an octopus with eight arms and could do everything without help. So Henrietta went to the agency for a kitchenmaid, to be hired on a permanent basis. They sent a young Irish girl called Emily, who seemed a hard worker and had a healthy fear of Sarah's temper, and she settled in quickly.

As for serving at table, Henrietta decided to hire two waiters for the night of the party. Mrs Sutton had parlourmaids. Before she came to London, Henrietta had never come across the parlourmaid phenomenon, and was indebted to Jerome for the explanation that they were what the middle classes had when they couldn't or wouldn't afford menservants. Before she came to London, Henrietta had never been served at table by a female. Here at Thornton Place Emma served her and Jerome and Lizzie, but for various reasons there had been something of a temporary, picnic feeling to life so far, and she had accepted it. A formal dinner party was different, though. It must be men who served her guests.

She interviewed half a dozen waiters sent by the agency and after quizzing them in detail about their experience and inspecting their persons for cleanliness she chose the two best. On the day, she decided, she would create a small servery in the morning-room, whose door was right next to the dining-room door. Then when everyone was seated Emma and Edie could help carry things upstairs and place them ready so that the waiters could simply bring them through. In the same way they could clear into the servery and the girls could carry the dirty things down. The wine could all be set up there, too. Jerome would order the wines from a merchant in St James's: the house had no cellar.

After long consultation with Sarah, the menu was decided: artichoke soup; fillets of sole with white sauce; stewed sweetbreads; fillets of beef with brown gravy, thimble potatoes; goose pieces in tomato sauce with garlic and parsley; saddle of mutton with redcurrant sauce, chopped spinach; coffee savoy, chestnut meringues, frangipane tarts; anchovies, soft cheese, watercress.

'That ought to hold 'em,' Jerome pronounced cheerfully, when he read it.

'The soup and the sweets can be made the day before. That should ease things a little,' Henrietta said, and added, 'I asked Sarah if she wanted extra help in the kitchen on the day, but she said there would be enough trouble with her and Emily and the girls falling over each other without adding strangers to the chaos.'

'That sounds encouraging. Shall we call the whole thing off?' Jerome asked.

Henrietta squared her shoulders. 'Not at all. I mean to show you what I can do.'

She had hoped to keep the trouble of the dinner party from the twins and Mary, and present them only with the finished article – polished, effortless, delightful. But given her state of tension and the fact that one or other of the maids was coming to her with a question every quarter-hour, while occasional sounds of rage drifted up from the kitchen, it was not possible.

But when they found out, they were eager to throw themselves into it. 'You must let us help you,' the twins said. 'What is there left to do?'

Henrietta had almost everything in hand, but the twins got out their paintboxes and spent the day creating a beautifully decorated menu card for each guest, while Mary, who was longing for exercise, went out to scour the shops for flowers for a centrepiece, which she then made up with the addition of greenery snipped from the otherwise empty garden. And when Emma came upstairs to say that Emily had broken one of the meringues and Sarah had sworn that either Emily must leave or she would, it was Mary who went downstairs to soothe ruffled feathers.

By the time they all went up to dress, Henrietta had gone so far through her state of nerves she had emerged on the other side and told Jerome she felt 'numb, simply numb'. She put on Madame Tessier's blue and fawn striped silk with the wonderfully full, draped bustle and felt better. The gown had been expensive, but it was worth it. Only a fine dressmaker could achieve that look of the dress being moulded to the skin. Jerome came through from the dressing-room, and she said, 'What do you think?'

He studied her a moment, and then, to her pain, shook his head. 'It won't do. With that low *décolletage*, you need something around your neck. You look unfinished.'

'Oh, but I was going to put on my necklace,' she said hastily. She had very little jewellery: she had inherited none, and the rector had not been much in favour of women bedecking themselves.

'That thin little gold chain with the turquoises?' He shook his head again. 'Won't do at all. No, what you need is something more like this.' And from behind his back he brought out a box which he presented to her. She opened it, and caught her breath. It was a collar of three strands of pearls. In the front, like a boss, was a large sapphire surrounded by twisted gold wires. It was beautiful, and she couldn't begin to imagine what it had cost. Jerome watched her, amused. She wouldn't even put out her hand to touch it. 'Shall I put it on for you?' he said at last. 'Turn round, then.'

He fastened it round her throat, and then placed a kiss on the back of her neck, just below the soft little curl of hair that never grew long enough to be caught up. In the years he had been away from her, that curl had haunted him. He turned her to the looking-glass, and looked with her, over her shoulder. 'That's more the sort of thing I like to see my wife in.'

'It's too beautiful,' she managed to say at last, her eyes dangerously bright.

'Nothing is too beautiful for you,' he said.

She turned inside the circle of his arms, and they kissed. 'I don't understand,' she said, when he paused for breath, 'why you want me. You've lived such an exciting life, I'm so afraid you'll find out how ordinary I am, and go away again.'

'There's just no accounting for love,' he said lightly. 'It strikes where it will.' And seeing that that hadn't reassured her, he said, 'Darling one, don't you know I am contented at last? I only rushed about the world like that because I *didn't* have you. I'm home now. They couldn't drag me away with a team of six wild horses.' They kissed again, and then he said, 'Now put on your pearl earrings, and we'll go down. It's time.'

When they went out onto the landing they found Lizzie peeping round her bedroom door, waiting to see them dressed. They posed in front of her and she cried, 'Oh, you look *beautiful*!'

'Thank you,' said Jerome, 'but what about your mother?'

Lizzie laughed. 'You *both* look beautiful. I hope you have a beautiful dinner.'

'Emma shall bring you up something on a tray later,' Henrietta promised, and turned to the stairs.

'Allow me to help you with your train, my lady,' Jerome said. So Henrietta went down to her first dinner party feeling like a queen, a wife and a mistress all in one – a good combination for a hostess.

The dinner was a great success. Because of her planning, everything went smoothly. The waiters seemed to know their business, Sarah's cooking all came out well, Jerome was generous with the wine, and there was only one mishap, when Edie and Emma collided in the morning-room doorway and broke a sauce-boat on the doorknob.

But the best thing of all for Henrietta was the conversation. As Jerome had said, all the guests were people who would talk, and even poor Signora Ribero cheered up when she found that five people around the table spoke Italian fluently and two others had a smattering. The conversation flowed and eddied like a sparkling river, swirling this way, diverting that. It was wonderful to Henrietta to listen to intelligent people who had things of interest to say, opinions to offer, experiences to relate. She found herself joining in, amazing herself with things she had not known she thought. It was conversation that developed and grew like a living thing, and did not depend on personal anecdote or reiterated prejudice; and not once in the evening did anyone mention the servant problem. Even the Hensmans, the unknown quantity, brightened up when they discovered the quality of the food and company, and Dr Hensman joined a vigorous discussion with Mary on the Egyptian tombs, while Mrs Hensman fell under the spell of Signor Ribero's melting vowel sounds, and grew quite pink and animated.

As for Marion Sutton, Henrietta had never known her with so little to say for herself. She would have been afraid Marion was not enjoying herself, had she not caught her in a delightful argument with Mr Burnand and Mr Agnew as to whether the success of Gilbert and Sullivan depended more on the music or the words.

After dinner they went up to the drawing room and Ribero sang for them – unaccompanied, since they had no piano. Then at the request of the Alma-Tademas, who had admired the menu cards very much, the twins passed round their portfolio and talked a little of the places they had sketched and painted. Mr Macdonald admired Amy's flower paintings and praised their accuracy; and Mr Burnand said Patsy's comical sketch of their guide at Petra and his camel was worthy of a place in his magazine.

Finally carriages were called, the guests departed, the waiters were thanked and paid off, and Henrietta went downstairs to congratulate the staff and tell them to get to bed as soon as they could.

'Tired, Mrs Compton?' Jerome said, as he and Henrietta walked upstairs.

She turned a bright face on him. 'Yes, but, oh, so happy! I never knew dinner parties could be like that. I feel so – so *alive*!'

He smiled. 'It was what I always wanted for you. From the first time I saw you, pining in your cage, I knew this was where you would shine. I shall surround you with interesting people, my love. I can do that for you.'

'I thought I might not like living in London,' she confessed, 'but I could never have had a party like that in Bishop Winthorpe.'

He laughed at the idea. 'But this is just the beginning. What fun we're going to have!'

Despite the late night, everyone was down early the next day. Mary and the twins were to catch the train to York that morning so they were eager not to waste any of their remaining time.

'It was a *wonderful* party!' Amy said, the moment she saw Henrietta. 'I never had such delightful talk in all my life! Mr Macdonald was *so* interesting. He has travelled all over Africa collecting plants, and next year he means to go to South America. I must say, I wish I could go there. Imagine sailing up the Amazon!'

Patsy, for a wonder, did not agree. She dismissed South America as, 'nothing but mosquitoes, crocodiles and hostile Indians'. She seemed rather silent that morning. When prompted she said she had enjoyed the party very much, but she ate her breakfast with hardly an exclamation, and seemed to be watching Amy out of the corner of her eye.

Mary, by contrast, was more talkative than she had been with Henrietta since their quarrel a couple of years back.

'An excellent evening,' she said. 'Everything was done just as it should be. I can see you're going to turn into a very good hostess.' Henrietta made a deprecating noise, and Mary, looking at her keenly, said, 'Jerome always said that you would be. I suppose I must admit that he was right, though I wish it hadn't taken so long for you and him – oh, well, that's all done with now. This is a very snug house, and I envy you your acquaintance. I half wish I could stay here. I won't get such company in Yorkshire.'

'You know you are welcome to come and stay at any time,' Henrietta said warmly.

Oddly, Mary seemed disappointed with that answer, and after a moment's silence said only, 'Thank you. But you will have enough to do without family visits.'

Later, when all the bustle of seeing them off was over, Henrietta wondered whether Mary had wanted to be asked to stay permanently. Had she misunderstood her? But no,

Mary was too independent-minded, surely, to want to live under another woman's roof.

When she got back from the railway station she told the maids she was not at home that afternoon, so it was not until the next day that Mrs Sutton was able to call. She arrived very early. 'I'm sure everyone will be calling to congratulate you, so I wanted to be sure of having you to myself for a little while. It was a splendid affair. I am most impressed.' She stared a moment, seeming to sum Henrietta up and wonder at the score. 'You will outshine us all in Bayswater,' she went on. 'I confess the conversation was a little too bluestocking for me – I don't claim to be a great intellectual – but there is something very . . .' She searched for a word. 'Very *smart* about having that sort of company.' Smart didn't seem to be the word she wanted, and she searched some more. 'Very stylish. There is something *about* you and Jerome. I said so to Dickie yesterday.' And she shook her head as if it were too much of a mystery.

Henrietta was embarrassed, and to divert Marion from the subject asked her what news there was from the outside world. 'I haven't seen a newspaper for two days. Has anything interesting happened?'

'Oh, the politics is all dull as usual. Home Rule and Socialism. Such stuff! It's all one with this dreadful weather,' Marion said. 'But the society columns are full of the news of the Fleetwood–Hazelmere marriage. Now there *is* something to wonder at! Some years ago Lady Venetia Fleetwood created a terrible scandal by jilting her lover practically at the altar. She's the sister of the Duke of Southport, the Prince of Wales's friend, you know. Well, she jilted poor Lord Hazelmere good and hard. That was in the time of the old duke, I believe. Or, wait, didn't he die soon afterwards? Yes, that was it, because otherwise I suppose he would have done something about getting her another husband. But as it was, she was disgraced and sent down to the country and simply disappeared from the social columns.'

Henrietta opened her mouth to speak but Marion continued, 'No-one could understand at the time why she jilted him. He was rich and handsome and popular besides – all the young women were mad for him. Well, now, if you please, they are to get married after all! The wonder is that he's forgiven her. But it says in the paper that he never offered for anyone else, so perhaps it was a love-match in the beginning. You won't remember the story, of course, but it was all the talk at the time. It must have been ten years ago, if not more.'

Henrietta was slightly nettled by the assumption that she was an ignorant country mouse, and it made her indiscreet. 'I do remember it, very well. My brother was to have gone to the wedding. He and his wife were very disappointed when it was cancelled.'

Marion stared. 'Your brother?'

'The Fleetwoods are cousins of ours,' Henrietta said.

Marion's eyes almost stood out of her head. 'No! Really? Cousins? Why ever didn't you say so?'

Henrietta was sorry at once: it was pleasant to see Marion so thrown off-balance, but it was an ignoble thing to boast of important connections.

'Distant cousins,' she amended. 'My father and Lady Venetia's grandmother were first cousins. I'm not sure what degree of removal I stand in. But in any case, I've never met them.'

'Still, if your brother was invited to the wedding,' Marion said, 'the connection was an acknowledged one.'

'Papa and the old duchess were acquainted, so when Lady Venetia was to marry, she invited my brother as head of the family, out of respect. So you see it is a very remote connection. I'm sorry I mentioned it, really. It's nothing to speak of.'

Marion found her voice. 'Oh, but, my dear, don't say that, never say that! No connection of that sort is too slight to be important. This is not just a baronet or even an earl – it's a duke! If you don't care for your own sake, you must think of Lizzie. Think how much good it would do her, if she were to be invited to a party, or asked to stay – even if it were only once! It would establish her for ever. It would give her such advantages as you could never buy with money, not if Jerome were as rich as Croesus.'

'Oh, really,' Henrietta said, 'I hardly think—'

'You must let me persuade you on this,' Marion overrode her. 'On this one topic, you really must allow me to know better! You are so unworldly, my dear, and it does you credit, but we all have to live in the world, one way or another, and as a mother you must want to give your daughter every chance to do well for herself. What she makes of it is up to her, but to deny her such an advantage for want of a little – a very little – trouble is what I cannot believe you would do.'

Henrietta shook her head. 'I can't conceive what—'

'You must write to Lady Venetia, of course, offering your best wishes on her marriage. As a cousin, you have every right, and a delicate attention like that cannot offend. If nothing comes of it, you'll have nothing to reproach yourself with. But if she should be moved to extend the hand of friendship . . .' Marion paused to let the golden vision unfold in imagination. 'If anything a quarter as exciting came up for one of my children, I should die before I let it pass!'

Fortunately at that moment Emma came in to announce Mrs Agnew, and saved Henrietta from answering. She was rather afraid that Marion might introduce the subject in Mrs Agnew's presence, but she held her tongue, and since after discussing the dinner party Mrs Agnew wanted to talk about the play her husband had just reviewed, and Marion was a confirmed theatre-goer, the new topic held until both ladies departed.

When Jerome came home from the City, Henrietta told him what Mrs Sutton had said.

'What troubles me,' she went on, 'is that I *had* thought, before she said anything, that I might send Lady Venetia a note. I felt so sorry for her years ago when she jilted Lord Hazelmere, and everyone was so angry with her; and now that it seems she loved him all along I feel even more tender on her behalf.'

'It seems a good thought. What is your difficulty?' Jerome asked.

'Marion has made me doubt my own motives. I don't want it to seem as if I am trying to gain some advantage from the poor lady. I don't want her to think that's why I'm doing it; but then perhaps, deep down, it really is.'

'What do you hope will happen, if you do write? What is the very best outcome you hope for?'

'The best? Oh – that she should write and say she was obliged for my good wishes. That it would have given her some small pleasure.'

'Is that all? A very modest hope. I don't see that you need do all this soul-searching.'

Henrietta looked anxious. 'I really did think of it before Marion suggested it.'

'I believe you,' Jerome smiled. 'Why don't you believe yourself? What does it tell you in here?' He tapped his breast.

She thought. 'That I should write. That I would be sorry afterwards if I didn't. Not to write for such a mean reason would be worse than writing in the hope of gain.'

'Darling one! If such a little thing causes you such anguish, I am heartily glad not to have a conscience. Write your letter and be easy.' He turned away to the dressing-table. 'Marion Sutton is a good sort, but a talking fool. Your judgement is better than hers, so use it. You are strong enough to face the consequences of your own actions, aren't you?'

Henrietta hardly expected more than an acknowledgement to her letter, perhaps even penned by a secretary, given that such an eminent bride must have much to do on the eve of her wedding. But in a very short time a cordial note came in Lady Venetia's own hand, thanking her for her good wishes and asking her to call on Monday February the 8th.

In Marion Sutton's rules of etiquette, you could not call upon a person of higher rank than your own until they invited you to do so; to receive such an invitation was a great honour, particularly when they were so far above you as a duke's daughter is above a commoner. Henrietta tried to feel these things only to a reasonable extent, afraid of finding herself becoming too much like Mrs Sutton. But it *was* a compliment to be asked to call; and, unexpectedly, Lizzie was excited on her behalf, and sat watching her dress with round eyes.

'A duchess is higher than a countess, isn't it?'

'Yes, love. But she isn't a duchess, only a duke's daughter.'

'But is that higher than a princess?'

'It depends. Lizzie, you're sitting on my hairbrush.'

'Sorry.' She fished it out. 'Will she be wearing a crown?'

'No, of course not,' Henrietta said indistinctly, her head bowed as she pushed another pin into her chignon. 'Don't be silly.'

'It isn't silly. Dukes wear crowns. I've seen a picture. Does she live in a castle?'

'The address is Welbeck Street in London,' Henrietta said, 'so I doubt it.'

'I expect it's a very grand house, anyway. Grander than Mrs Sutton's. And I'll bet she's very beautiful.'

'I expect she is,' Henrietta granted generously, 'but don't say "I'll bet", darling.'

'I wish I could come too,' Lizzie said wistfully.

But when Henrietta's cab pulled up at the address she had been given, she thought Lizzie would have been terribly disappointed. It was a nice house in the centre of London, near Oxford Street, but it wasn't nearly grand enough to satisfy a romantic idea. In fact, even Henrietta thought she might have come to the wrong address.

'Is this right?' she asked the cabby.

'It's where you asked for right enough, mum,' he said.

Even more puzzlingly, when she trod up the steps to the front door, she found there was a doctor's brass plate beside it. *Dr Venetia Fleet, MD.* The similarity of the name confused her. Could there have been some awful mistake?

A very smart maid with sharp, noticing eyes opened the door. Henrietta presented her card and said hesitantly, 'Is Lady Venetia Fleetwood at home?'

She half expected a set-down, but the maid stepped back and said, 'Please to come in, ma'am. I will enquire.'

In the hall there were conflicting signs. There was a stack of parcels against the wall, which could be wedding presents, and a pile of cards on the table, which could be acceptances to wedding invitations. But the table itself was somewhat battered and scuffed about the legs, and the stair carpet was definitely wearing thin. She didn't know what to think. The maid returned to escort her upstairs, and in a moment she was stepping into a large drawing-room and a tall lady of about her own age was coming forward with her hand outstretched and a cordial smile.

'Mrs Compton. How kind of you to call.'

The voice, the manner, the beautifully cut suit of slub silk in a dusky shade of rose fawn were right. The face was vivid, without being conventionally handsome; the eyes looked into Henrietta's with an unusual directness that was almost mannish. There was a great assurance about this person, and Henrietta did not doubt she was a duke's daughter.

'It was kind of you to ask me to call, your ladyship,' she said.

Lady Venetia laughed. 'We could dispute all day over whose kindness was the greater! Let us call it quits, and sit down and have some tea.'

She was so welcoming that Henrietta suddenly misgave about her own situation. It was one thing to keep it a secret from the Suttons, but it would not be fair on Lady Venetia to put her in an embarrassing position, especially as she was a relative. Before she could lose her nerve, she plunged in.

'I should like nothing better, your ladyship, but I feel I ought to make you aware of something.' She felt herself begin to blush. She hated having to do this. 'My first husband died two years ago. I have recently remarried, but my second husband, Mr Compton, is – is – a divorcé.' She lowered her eyes from that bright gaze. 'In the circumstances, I will understand perfectly if you wish me to leave. I perhaps shouldn't have called, but I did so want to give you my good wishes in person.'

There was a pause, which seemed to extend itself agonisingly though in reality it could not have lasted more than a second. The warm, low voice said, 'Do you love him very much?'

She looked up, startled by the question. 'Yes, very much.'

'Do you find it hurts, right *here*? I love Hazelmere like

that. Please do sit down, Mrs Compton. It was good of you to warn me, but I have been far more of a disgrace in my time than you can have any idea of, or you wouldn't have come calling on me!'

Henrietta obeyed the gesture and sat, a little dazed. She said the first thing that came into her head – 'Then it was a love match all along?' – which was hardly tactful.

But Lady Venetia, who had gone to the chimneypiece to ring the bell, turned and smiled at the words. 'Oh, good, we are to have a frank conversation! I like that. I thought when I saw you you wouldn't be one of those dull people who talk commonplaces. There are too many of them in the world.'

Henrietta laughed. 'Yes, I know just what you mean! But still, it was impertinent of me to ask such a question, your ladyship. I'm sorry.'

'Oh, please, don't be.' With a rapid and impulsive movement she came to sit on the sofa beside Henrietta. 'And please don't "your ladyship" me! I hoped we would be friends. We are cousins, after all, are we not?'

'Of a sort,' Henrietta said. 'It's a distant enough connection for you to repudiate it if I become a nuisance.'

'You have a sense of humour too – that's nice! Well, my grandmother and your father were cousins, to be precise. But my mother knew your father well, and thought highly of him. And he and Uncle Tom were great friends. And now I've seen you I'm sure we'll be friends too. Do people always like you the moment they see you? You have such a nice face.'

'I could easily ask you the same thing,' Henrietta said. She liked this tall woman with the abrupt, frank way of speaking. She felt, absurdly, as if they had known each other a long time. 'But there's so much else I'd like to ask you.'

'Ask away, then. I don't mind, as long as I can ask you questions in return. Such as why, if you thought I might mind your being married to a divorcé, did you write in the first place?'

'Because I remembered all the fuss about your wedding being cancelled, and I felt so sorry for you then. I thought how unhappy you must have been to do it, and how much more unhappy you would be afterwards.'

'Because a girl who jilts is a social outcast?' Venetia said wryly.

'Everyone who spoke about it seemed angry with you, even though it was none of their business. I thought that so unfair. It must have taken great courage on your part.'

'You'll never know how much! My father was a terrifying person when he was crossed. And of course I did love Hazelmere quite dreadfully. Even in my fury, I hated hurting him.'

'Then why—?' Henrietta asked tentatively.

'Wait,' said Venetia, as the door opened. A maid carried in a tray, followed by a second carrying kettle and spirit lamp. When they had arranged everything and were withdrawing, she said, 'No disturbances, Patty, unless it's an emergency.' When the door closed behind them, she said to Henrietta, 'Now we shall be private. Patty's a good girl. She's been with me a long time. Let me pour you some tea, and then I'll tell you the whole story from the beginning. And afterwards you can tell me yours. It's so nice to have a female friend to talk to. However much you love a man, it's never quite the same.'

CHAPTER FIVE

Venetia didn't know what impulse had made her respond to Henrietta's letter in the way she did, or why, from the first moment of meeting, she felt so drawn to her. But in the course of that visit, shyly at first but with increasing confidence, they told each other almost everything.

Venetia explained how as a girl she had wanted to be a doctor. 'Everyone said my ambition was not only foolish, because women could not be doctors, but wrong, because women ought not to *want* to be doctors. Papa was outraged. He forbade me even to speak about it. I was *his* daughter, and I was to do as he wanted – which was to marry respectably.'

Henrietta nodded, understanding. That was the way things had always been for girls. 'So what did you do?'

'I have a lot of my father in me. I was equally determined I *would* be a doctor, but the only way I could even try was to leave home. That was the most frightening thing of all,' she added reflectively. 'For a girl from a protected back-ground, to go out in the world alone is almost unthinkable. If it hadn't been for my dear aunt Fanny I couldn't have done it. She wasn't really my aunt, but she and Mama were friends, so that's what I called her.'

'She looked after you?'

'She set up a house and let me come and live with her.'

'Didn't your father object?'

'Oh, of course. I was over twenty-one, so he couldn't legally stop me, but he disowned me, stopped my allowance and forbade me to see my mother or sisters until I came to my senses. That was a miserable business. But Hazelmere stood by me. He visited us and brought news of the outside world, and took me out for drives to make sure I got some fresh air and a change of scene.'

'That was kind.'

'Yes, he always was kind,' Venetia said. 'Kind and loving and handsome and amusing. I really don't deserve him.'

'I'm sure you do,' Henrietta said. 'Go on, what happened next?'

'Well, I managed to get myself taken on as a medical student, through the help of a friend of my mother. It was tremendously hard work, but I passed my first-year examinations with good marks – at which point the male students decided I was making them a laughing stock, and got up a petition to have me thrown out. No other medical school would accept a female, and Aunt Fanny's health was failing, so I had to go home with my tail between my legs. And at that point Hazelmere asked me again to marry him.'

'Like a knight riding to the rescue,' Henrietta said.

'Just like that! I've always thought he would look wonderful in full armour. He used to be in the Blues, you know: he was always the most dashing and popular officer in the cavalry. His nickname in those days was Beauty. Beauty Winchmore. That was before he inherited the title, of course. All the girls were mad for him, but he had eyes only for me – undeserving wretch that I am!'

'So you accepted him. Was your father pleased?'

'Oh, yes. Hazelmere wasn't a great match by his standards, but by then he was glad to have me marry anyone respectable. He planned an enormous wedding at the Abbey and a vast banquet afterwards. Every person of note from the Prime Minister downwards was invited. Then on the eve, practically, of the wedding, I found that Hazelmere had assumed once we were married I would give up my ambition and be a normal wife and mother. He said it was impossible for *his wife* to be a doctor.' Venetia spread her hands in a helpless gesture. 'What could I do? I couldn't marry him on those terms. I had to break it off.'

'Yes, I do see,' Henrietta said. 'I don't see how you could have done anything else. But they must all have been so angry with you.'

'It was as if the sky had fallen in! My father raged, my mother retired to her bed, my brothers nagged and my sisters wept. Even now when I think of the trouble and expense of first arranging and then cancelling that wedding it makes me shudder! Hazelmere went abroad and I was sent down to the country in disgrace. Then when my father died soon afterwards, my eldest brother, Harry, blamed me, and said it was the worry that had killed him. He's never really forgiven me.'

'Oh, that was cruel,' Henrietta said. 'I'm so sorry. But you don't believe it, do you?'

'I did for a long time. But Mama persuaded me eventually that I wasn't to blame. She came round to my side after Papa died. She's a wonderful person! You must meet her one day.'

'I'd be honoured. But go on, what happened next?'

'Oh, the next shock was when Papa's will was read, and I found he'd cut me off with a shilling. So now I was disgraced *and* penniless! Oddly enough, it did give me a strange sense of freedom – as though I had nothing more to lose.'

'But how did you manage to live?'

'Harry said he would pay me a small allowance, as long as I didn't live alone or do anything to shame him. So I found someone respectable to share lodgings with, and went on with my medical studies.'

'Didn't your brother disapprove of that?'

'I studied under a false name. Eventually I qualified, and set up in practice, and I've been self-sufficient ever since.'

'Ah, now I understand the name plate on your door!'

'Dr Venetia Fleet, MD. I was so proud when I first put that up! Those two letters after my name were so hard won, and mean so much to me, far more than any title, because I did it all on my own, and against opposition.'

'It's a tremendous achievement,' Henrietta said. 'Of course I did know that there were lady doctors, but I've never met one before. And to think of *you* doing it, a duke's daughter! Don't your patients find it strange?'

'To most of them I'm just Dr Fleet. As far as possible I've never admitted to anyone who I was. Of course, the game will be up now I'm marrying Hazelmere,' she added thoughtfully.

'How do you come to be marrying him after all?'

'We met again by chance. He said he had never loved anyone else, and that he'd changed his mind about my abominable profession and wouldn't mind in the least being the doctor's husband. So everything was all right.'

Henrietta sighed with satisfaction. 'It's a wonderful story. To be one of the very first women ever to become a doctor! I've never done anything but be a wife and mother, and I'm not sure I've been any use at those. When I was a girl, I used to wonder what women were for. Do you believe women can do anything men can do?'

'Yes, I do – if they want to. And if they want to, I think they should be let to. Of course, lots of women are happy to be wives and mothers, and that's just as well. But no man can understand the frustration, when you have a brain, and nerve, and abilities, of being told to run away and play. Things are beginning to change now, thank God, but there's a long way to go yet. Women like us must keep looking for ways to advance the cause.'

'Ah, now I know why you asked me here – to recruit me!' Henrietta laughed.

'Would you mind being recruited?'

'No, I think it would be good to have a purpose in life. My husband wants to make me a great hostess, and great hostesses can do a lot in bringing people together in a good cause.'

'I should like to meet your husband. Tell me your story now.'

So Henrietta told an abbreviated version. 'Not that there's much to tell. You've lived such an unusual life, and mine is very dull by comparison.'

She spoke of her happy childhood at Morland Place, scrambling about the country on her pony, helping at harvest and shearing, being taught how to shoot by the gamekeeper. 'I was such a little ragamuffin! After my mother died there was no-one except our nurse to care if I was clean and tidy, and no-one at all to care if I had any education. I was as ignorant as a cat, until Jerome and Mary started me on a course of serious reading.'

'I've always had a strong desire to see Morland Place,' Venetia confessed. 'My great-grandmother was born there. It must be the Morland blood in me, I suppose, for I feel a strange attachment I can't explain, since I've never been there.'

Henrietta told of her brother's marriage to Alfreda, and how soon afterwards she had been married to Mr Fortescue. 'And then my life seemed to end. Nothing happened to me after that but my daughter Lizzie; and even then I wasn't allowed to have much to do with her. Mr Fortescue educated her and kept her with him. It wasn't until he was dying that she and I were able to become close.'

'Were you very unhappy when he died?'

Henrietta found that hard to answer. Not even to this friend and cousin could she speak of the strange and horrible details of her marriage. 'He was a great deal older than me,' she said. 'I thought he loved me at first, but he soon seemed to forget all about me, and lived his own life quite separate from me. I hardly ever saw him. And yet he was Lizzie's father.' She was silent a moment. 'I think what I mostly felt when he died was anxiety. He left me no money, and I didn't know what I was to do, and how I was to support Lizzie. I'd never been on my own in the world. I went from my father's house straight to my husband's. What *do* women do, without a man to take care of them?'

'I understand how you must have felt.'

'Yes, I think *you* do. But then Jerome came back,' Henrietta concluded, 'and now everything's all right.'

'Is Lizzie very clever? It sounds as if she had a good grounding from her father. What do you mean to do with her, now you're settled in London? Will you send her to school?'

'I have thought about it,' Henrietta admitted. 'It seems a

waste not to continue her education, but we're very fond of each other, and we'd hate to be parted for week after week.'

'Oh, but there are day schools in London: she could come home every night. I should like to meet Miss Lizzie. Will you bring her to see me?'

'With great pleasure. She would be thrilled to meet you. She asked me this morning if you wore a crown and lived in a castle.'

At that moment a gentleman came in, who Henrietta knew at once must be Lord 'Beauty' Hazelmere. He was handsome and smiling, and Lady Venetia's eyes leapt to his the instant he appeared with a look of great tenderness. There was no doubt they were in love, Henrietta thought with satisfaction. Being in that state herself, she wanted the whole world to share it.

Introductions were made, and Hazelmere shook Henrietta's hand and said he was glad to see her. But then he added, 'I hate to seem inhospitable, but if you were thinking of going home, I would not wait any longer if I were you. When the meetings break up there's no knowing what may happen.'

'Meetings?' Henrietta asked.

'The rival meetings in Trafalgar Square. The socialists and the radicals.'

'Oh, yes,' said Henrietta. 'I'd forgotten all about it, though Mr Compton did mention it.'

Trade had been bad all winter, and the Social Democratic Federation had organised marches and meetings of the unemployed all over the country. The monster meeting in the capital was a culmination of these activities. But in addition, the London United Workmen's Committee, a rival radical group given to violent protest, had announced a meeting in the Square on the same day.

'The Home Secretary should never have allowed it,' Hazelmere said. 'But Childers has only been in the job a week, and Gladstone has him running round in circles over the Home Rule Bill.'

'But is there really any danger?' Venetia asked.

'The numbers are beyond what anyone expected,'

Hazelmere said, 'and there are some very rough types amongst them. There's a huge crowd in Trafalgar Square – they say five thousand or more. At the moment they're confined in one place, listening to speeches. But the speeches are intended to inflame, and once they leave the square and spread out . . .'

'Won't the police keep them in order?' Henrietta asked.

Hazelmere shrugged. 'They haven't made nearly enough provision, in my opinion – just a small force of constables in the square, and a couple of hundred reserves on standby. What use will that be against five thousand? Henderson is a fool. If anything happens, it will cost him his job.'

'Who is Henderson?' Henrietta queried.

'Sir Edmund Henderson,' Venetia said. 'Commissioner of the Metropolitan Police.'

'The trouble is that there've been no public-order difficulties since he was appointed,' Hazelmere continued, 'and he has no imagination. And the District Superintendent is Walker, who's over seventy and quite past it.'

'I shouldn't have asked you to come here today,' Venetia said to Henrietta. 'I'm sorry, it was thoughtless of me. I hate to end your delightful visit, but Hazelmere's quite right, you had better go at once.'

'If you really think there's danger,' Henrietta said, rising. 'Perhaps you'd call me a cab.'

'You'll never get a cab now,' Hazelmere said. 'In any case, I couldn't allow it. Venetia, you must send her home in your carriage.'

'Of course,' Venetia said, crossing to the bell. 'There's no knowing which way the demonstrators will go when they leave the square, but if my man drives straight out along the Bayswater road it should be safe enough, as long as you leave right away. I wish I had a footman to send with you but we don't keep any male servants.'

'Perhaps I'd better go with you,' Hazelmere said.

But Henrietta protested, 'Oh, no, I'm sure there's no need. Please, you mustn't think of it.'

So the visit ended rather abruptly. With warm farewells and promises to meet again soon, she was bundled downstairs and out to the waiting carriage. The air was bitterly cold and slightly foggy, and already a frost was forming on cold surfaces like railings. The horses stamped and their breath clouded the air. She hurried shivering into the carriage, and it set off at once at a brisk trot.

Henrietta had a great deal to think about, which kept the monster meeting out of her mind until they were on the Bayswater road driving alongside the park. Then it was drawn to her attention how many rough sorts there were about, ambling in groups through the park, gathering at the gates and lounging against the railings. All of a sudden she was nervous. They looked poor, badly clad for the cold day, and, with the encroaching dark, dangerous. At the Victoria Gate a large crowd was spilling out onto the pavement. Some of them seemed to be looking at her as she approached. She wished the driver would go faster. Then one of the men, a great burly brute, left the group and stepped out into the road. He seemed to be heading towards her; she saw him raise his hand as if to strike, and thought he meant to break the window to get at her. She jerked back away from it with a muted shriek of alarm – and then they were past, and she realised he had only been intending to cross the road behind her carriage, and had been waving to someone on the other side.

She felt foolish, and guilty for having misjudged the poor man, who was probably out of work and miserable. All the same she was glad when they were past the park, and turning down familiar Church Street, with only ordinary people about their ordinary business in sight.

Jerome was late home, late enough for her to begin to worry about him; and he brought the news that the meeting had broken up in disorder, and that there had been rioting in the streets afterwards. A garbled message had been sent to the reserve constables that the crowd was planning to march down The Mall, and they had hurried off to guard Marlborough House and Buckingham Palace. In fact, the mob was surging along Pall Mall, just a few yards to the north of them. They smashed the windows of the gentlemen's clubs in St James's, and crossed over into Hyde

Park where a further and more inflammatory meeting was to be held.

'I saw some of them,' Henrietta said, with a shudder. 'They did look like dreadful roughs.'

'Thank heaven you passed when you did, and not later,' said Jerome.

Venetia had had a great deal of contact with the Marylebone and Paddington District police in the course of her work, and in particular with Inspector Morgan of the CID, with whom she had worked during the Parliamentary Commission on child prostitution in 1882. So when he sent a message later that day asking her to come to the Marylebone Lane station as soon as possible, she did not hesitate, but picked up her bag, put on her coat and hat, and left.

'Wait for the carriage to come back,' Hazelmere begged her.

But she said, 'It's only a step. And Morgan did say "urgently". Don't worry, darling, I'll be quite safe.'

'You won't let me come with you, I suppose,' said Hazelmere, of old experience.

'Certainly not. But don't worry, I'll be back in time to change for the theatre. I wouldn't let a parcel of radicals come between me and Clara Schumann!'

Out in the street the pavements were slippery with frost and it was bitterly cold. Venetia drew her scarf up over her lower face and walked quickly, glad of her thick gloves. She saw nothing untoward, but there was a feeling of disturbance in the air, and the other people she passed had an air of tension about them. As she crossed Wigmore Street she saw three dangerous-looking toughs lounging on the other side, and they pushed themselves off the wall as they saw her. But she was only a few steps from Marylebone Lane, and the police station was just round the corner, so she hurried on, and they did not follow her.

At the station she found Inspector Morgan waiting for her.

'I beg pardon for the liberty of calling you out, Doctor,' he said, 'but we've quite a lot of casualties – broken heads and black eyes and the like, broken bones and some knife wounds. We've set up a makeshift dressing station, and I hoped you wouldn't mind, being as it's on your patch.'

'I suppose we must all do our duty in time of war,' she said, with a tight smile.

'Glad you see it that way, ma'am. But first up, and the reason I called you in particular, there's a female that got caught up in the crowd and went into labour. If you wouldn't mind coming this way . . .'

As he took her to the woman, he told her some of the details of events not available to Hazelmere. 'The Superintendent was charged with maintaining public order – Mr Walker, that is—'

'Oh, he's the one who's over seventy, isn't he?'

'That's right, ma'am. Seventy-five next birthday. Well, he went to the square in plain clothes to supervise the meeting and the constables on duty there, but not being a very robust gentleman he got swallowed up in the crowd and they lost touch with him. When he finally turned up,' Morgan suppressed a smile, 'he complained he'd had his pockets picked. By that time the mob was already streaming off west, out of control. I suppose you heard about the mistake over the Mall?' Venetia nodded. 'Five hundred uniformed reserves guarding it, while every window in St James's was being broken. There'll be the dickens to pay over this.'

Venetia was glad to find the pregnant woman not very far along in her labour, more frightened than hurt and playing up the attention for all she was worth. Discovering that she lived only half a mile away and had a family at home waiting for her, Venetia told her the baby wouldn't be coming for a couple of hours and sent her home in a cab.

She then concentrated on tending the real wounds, keeping one eye on the time. There were bones that needed to be splinted and cuts that needed stitching, but she was determined she would not be kept from her concert by mere bruises. When a fellow practitioner, Dr Folie, who she knew also treated the poor, turned up, she decided she had done enough and began packing up to leave. It was at that moment that Morgan came back in some agitation.

'Excuse me, Dr Fleet, but I think it's time you went home. We've just heard the meeting in Hyde Park's broken up and the mob is coming this way bent on mischief.'

'Coming this way?'

'Streaming along Oxford Street from the Marble Arch,' Morgan said grimly. 'One of our informants ran ahead to say they mean to break the shop windows and steal whatever they can get their hands on. It won't be pretty to be in their path, and you might want to get home and get your shutters put up.'

'I was preparing to leave anyway,' Venetia said. 'Thank you for warning me.'

She stuffed everything into her bag, struggled quickly into her coat and followed Morgan. 'You'd better go out the back way, to be on the safe side,' he said.

In the back room the duty officer, Inspector Cuthbert, was parading the relief of a sergeant and fifteen constables who were ready to go out on routine patrol. Morgan stopped at the sight of their calm preparations and said, 'Haven't you heard? I sent a message to you as soon as I got the news.'

Cuthbert shook his head. 'No message has reached me. Is it about the demonstrators?'

Morgan quickly repeated the news. Cuthbert didn't hesitate for an instant. He drew himself up and said, 'It's up to us to get between them and those windows, men. Draw your staffs and follow me!'

Venetia had to hold back to let them leave first, and when the mass of bodies in blue had surged out through the door, Morgan turned to her and said urgently, 'I'm going with them. Get straight home, Doctor, and, if you'll take my advice, stay there.'

'I will,' Venetia said. 'But take care of yourself!'

He bared his teeth in a savage sort of grin. 'I'm looking forward to taking a crack at them, the beggars! Wouldn't miss this for worlds!' And he was gone at a run.

Venetia hurried home, where Hazelmere was waiting for

her, beside himself with worry. She told him the latest news, but even before she had finished speaking they heard the sounds of riot – shouts, screams, glass breaking – coming from the south, from Oxford Street, presumably.

'We'd better get the shutters up,' Hazelmere said. 'Come, come inside. My love, why are you waiting?'

Venetia looked away towards the noise. 'There will be people hurt. Perhaps—'

'Absolutely not!' Hazelmere said at once. 'In fact, we shan't even be going to the concert. There's no knowing what they'll do or which way they'll run, and the streets won't be safe tonight. Come in, quickly!'

Venetia obeyed him, but eyed him askance. 'Is this how it's going to be when we're married? You are very masterful, my dear.'

'When I need to be. And I'm glad to see you meek and obedient, as a wife should be.'

Indoors, he supervised the servants as they closed the shutters and barred the door, and tried to calm their fears, though all of them could see that they were perilously close to the scene of action. When all was secure, Hazelmere and Venetia repaired to the drawing-room, and when they were alone she said, 'With the house locked up like a fortress, and the street in a state of riot, I can't see how you are going to be able to go home tonight.'

He smiled a little shamefacedly. 'To say the truth, I hadn't intended going. I feel I must stay here and protect you.'

'A fine excuse for ruining my reputation!' Venetia said.

He came closer. 'There's an old saying that comes to mind – something about being hung as well for a sheep as a lamb . . .'

In the morning, the news came that Inspector Cuthbert's prompt action, and the determination with which his men launched a baton charge, had been enough to scatter the mob and prevent any further rioting. But London remained nervous. Tuesday had dawned as dark as twilight. A thick, black fog had descended, and visibility was almost zero. The papers were full of rumours of serious public disturbance in the offing, with the threat of a full-scale attack being launched from the East End and talk of the troops having to be called out to meet it. In the blindness of the fog, one didn't know if the rioters had left the capital or were gathering on one's own street corner.

Jerome did not go to the City – no-one left the house, for it would have been impossible to find one's way even to the end of the road. The whole household stayed indoors all day, waiting for news. In Welbeck Street Hazelmere was still putting his foot down and Venetia stayed home too. No wealthy patients came to her door, but there was a stream of people to the dispensary, mostly with injuries sustained during the riots or as a result of the fog.

For three days the freezing fog held London immobile, silent, and waiting with bated breath for disaster. On the third day the rumour was that another mob was marching on Oxford Street, and the traders there hastily barricaded their windows and stood by with makeshift weapons to repel attack. But in the event the fog made it impossible for the socialists to organise anything; and when it finally lifted, it seemed to have cooled tempers. The rioters had dispersed also, and the threat seemed to be past.

Fog was very much a feature of the first months of 1886 – fog, bitter cold, heavy snowfalls, and socialism. William Morris, whose designs graced Henrietta's wallpaper, had founded the Socialist League at the end of 1884 and through his personal fame brought the movement to public attention. In that same year, the artisan's franchise had given the vote to most working men, and some were beginning to question whether the structure of society treated them fairly. In particular the miners, who were strong trade unionists, were threatening trouble, and considering how they might put up one of their own as a candidate for Parliament, instead of having to vote for a landowner.

The disturbances around the country went on. There was another monster meeting in London on February the 21st, when fifty thousand gathered in Hyde Park, and had to be dispersed by the police. Now she had been made aware of the situation, Henrietta noticed how many roughs were hanging around the streets. There were really three Londons, she concluded: the respectable, middling one she inhabited, the gilded sphere of the rich and titled, like Lady Venetia, and the low streets, taverns, courts and lodgings of the poor. All three existed side by side and hardly ever noticed one another, until the inhabitants spilled over into another's compartment for some reason.

Parliament, however, was concerned with other matters. Mr Gladstone had become Prime Minister again at the end of January, forming a government pledged to introduce Home Rule for Ireland, and throughout the spring both Houses were locked in battle over the Home Rule Bill.

One notable warrior for radical causes missed the fray: Sir Charles Dilke, MP, had been cited as co-respondent in a divorce case, and those pages of the newspapers that weren't full of Home Rule were full of the Crawford case and Dilke's appearances in the witness box. Henrietta found it painful to read, yet she felt herself drawn to peruse every detail, as one is drawn to probe a mouth ulcer with one's tongue. Though the judge in the case said there was no evidence worth the name against him, Dilke was held to be disgraced simply by association with the very word 'divorce'. His political career was over and he was widely shunned, though the Prince of Wales, who was a personal friend, remained loyal.

Venetia's most vital interest through those same months was, naturally, in Lord Hazelmere. They married in February. They had wanted it to be a quiet affair, with just one or two close friends present; but after the newspapers had caught wind of it there was no hope of privacy. It was a newsworthy story, by any standards, with the scandal of the previous jilting to be dredged up; but add to that the fact that the bride was one of the pioneer 'lady doctors', and had been treating people of all ranks these many years (*a duke's daughter! Touching people's bodies!*) and you had a sensation to rival any.

Besides all that, the newspapers were not slow to notice that Venetia's brother, the Duke of Southport, was one of the Prince of Wales's fast set. Along with Dilke, Lord 'Charlie' Beresford and Colonel 'Johnny' Vibart, he was a close friend of the Prince and took part in all those drinking, smoking, horse-racing and 'corridor-creeping' activities that so shocked and intrigued the reading public. All four were well known to the scandalmongers. Southport kept an actress as mistress, the beautiful Alicia Booth, known as the Kentish Songbird. Dilke, of course, was involved in the notorious divorce case; Beresford was having an open affair with Lady Brooke, the wife of the heir to the Earl of Warwick; and Vibart was married to Venetia's youngest sister, Lady Augusta, who was rumoured to be the Prince of Wales's latest mistress.

All in all, the Hazelmere marriage was a journalist's dream.

'It makes it hard to remember sometimes,' Venetia said to her betrothed, shortly after Henrietta's visit, 'that I'm the family black sheep.'

And in the face of all this bad behaviour, it was almost ironical that Henrietta felt burdened with guilt for having married a divorcé.

'She's obviously as innocent and virtuous as a newborn lamb, and yet there's Daisy Brooke, deceiving her husband—'

'Hardly deceiving,' Hazelmere protested.

'Well, cuckolding, then. If anything, it makes it worse that Lord Brooke knows all about it. He's such a nice, genial man.'

'If Brookie doesn't mind, why should you? It's well known he prefers a day's fishing to any of the hotter pursuits.'

'Whether he minds or not is hardly the point,' Venetia began, but Hazelmere hadn't finished.

'And it's hardly surprising if Charlie Beresford strays, given Lady Charles's age and peculiar appearance.'

Venetia's eyebrows shot up. 'Are you telling me that my only surety for your fidelity is my youth and beauty? Good God, Hazelmere, I can't marry you on that basis!'

Hazelmere hastened to take her in his arms. 'No, no, no! My love, I wasn't talking about us. Ours won't be that sort of marriage. Don't you know my heart – and my fidelity – are hopelessly yours?'

There was an interesting interval, at the end of which Venetia released herself with a satisfied sigh. 'I'm glad we have that settled. What was I talking about?'

'Daisy Brooke and Charlie Beresford, but I can't remember why.'

'Oh, yes! I was comparing their blatant adultery with Cousin Henrietta's extremely minor transgression,' she said, going to the chimney glass to straighten her hair.

'Unfortunately for Cousin Henrietta, divorce is the one thing that really is beyond the pale. If Daisy Brooke and Beresford ran away together, which I understand has been talked about, and there were divorces, that would be a very different matter.'

'Yes, I know that,' Venetia said, 'but I don't understand it. I think the whole business of marriage is very much a man's domain. Women think differently about love.'

'The world well lost, eh?' Hazelmere said, looking tenderly at his beloved's perplexed frown. 'Would you like to invite them to the wedding?' he asked suddenly.

Venetia was startled out of her thoughts. 'Daisy and Beresford?'

He laughed. 'No, idiot! Your cousin and her husband.'

Her expression softened. 'Oh, darling, you are so kind! But no, I don't think so. There will be so many journalists dangling round, looking for scandal, and I should hate them to get hold of Henrietta and ruin her life. Thank you for suggesting it, but no. Let's invite them to dinner when we're back from our honeymoon.'

'Just as you please,' said Hazelmere agreeably.

'And while we're on the subject,' Venetia said, coming close again, 'let me make it clear that if you ever so much as think of straying—'

'You'll poison me,' he finished for her, 'having the wherewithal so handy. Serve me right for marrying a doctor!'

In March Regina was brought to bed of a daughter. Everything went smoothly, and the news reached Henrietta that Regina and Perry had decided to call the newcomer Amy Patricia, after her aunts. It was the first of Regina's confinements from which Henrietta had been absent, and it made her sad that she had not been there to welcome the little girl into the world. It occurred to her, too, that had she been there in the usual way, the child might perhaps have been named after her. But she banished unworthy thoughts and sent a long letter of congratulation, together with some baby clothes she had been making.

Teddy received the news at home in York, and immediately dispatched a ham for the parents and a silver spoon for the baby. It was what he had sent for all the other little arrivals, and it saved thought to send the same again. He had other matters to occupy his mind. The deeds of conveyance on Morland Place were just completed, and on payment of the agreed sum (raised by selling some of his other interests) Mr Edward Morland at last took possession of his ancestral family home.

What he purchased was far less than his brother had inherited. The Morland estate had once consisted of nine farms, but these had been sold separately, some by his brother, some to satisfy creditors. Now only Low Farm, always known as the Home Farm, remained. With its fields and paddocks, together with the pleasure gardens and parkland, it was all that came with the house.

Teddy did not repine. He was no farmer, and since he had never expected to inherit the land, he had never wasted time cultivating any love for, or knowledge of, its ways. From a life of undergraduate idleness at Oxford he had come into a commercial inheritance that provided him with income without his having to do anything about it. He was a town bird, he freely acknowledged. He had been moved by a sort of atavistic family pride to buy Morland Place rather than see it in the hands of strangers, but having taken possession of it, he had no idea what to do with it.

The first thing, he supposed, was to find time to go and visit it. The weather continuing dreadful all through March, with bitter cold, dark days, heavy snowfalls, and freezing fogs, it proved impossible for him to go further from his own fireside than to that of his club. But in April, when the snow had melted, and the cold relented somewhat, he felt a wakening of curiosity; and on the day when the newspapers were full of Mr Gladstone's stirring and impassioned Home Rule speech to Parliament, he sent round for his horse, put on his warmest coat and hat, and rode out of the city.

The way to Morland Place was familiar beyond thought. It was the 'way home', which remains grooved deeply into the mind, and comes back to haunt in puzzled or wistful dreams to the very end of life. Teddy had not been out of the city in months, and looked around him with interest at the brave beginnings of spring. But the home farm was untenanted, and its fields were empty. It was the middle of lambing season, but there were no lambs, no symphony of ewes and their young calling to each other – what old Caleb, the Morland shepherd when Teddy was a boy, used to call 'ship music'. There were no mares in the paddocks, either, and no new foals stilting about madly on their fragile-looking legs, play-boxing and shaking their woolly tails.

The hedges were overgrown, the ditches choked with last year's leaves, the paths full of holes and the holes full of water. Dead branches, broken off by winter storms and the weight of snow, lay scattered under the trees. A gate had fallen off its hinges and was half sunk in the mud, proof of how long it had lain there untended. Teddy was no farmer, but he had been brought up on the land, and somewhere deep inside him he felt unease and something close to sorrow at the sight of such neglect. It was not right. It was a kind of sin, which he understood with his very bones, to let the land go uncared-for.

He rode in at last under the barbican into the courtyard of the old house, wondering who had left the gate unlocked and open. It had not changed so much since he last saw it. What struck him most was the silence. In his childhood it had been home to a host of people, his parents and siblings and a small army of servants, and there had always been people coming and going besides, visitors and tradesmen, tenants and villagers. It had been the beating heart of a great enterprise. Now the silence of emptiness was like death; it was melancholy, almost awful.

He dismounted and led his horse into one of the stalls to the left of the yard and tied it up. It snuffled hopefully around the empty manger for a moment, and then sighed and settled in resignation, cocking one hind foot. Teddy patted it remorsefully, for there wasn't so much as a scrap of hay anywhere in sight. 'I won't be long, old fellow,' he promised.

He had been given a great ring of keys when the house became his and, walking up to the front door, sorted through them, wondering which was which. The enormous thing eight inches long with the massive square ward was the key to the great door, as he knew well. He had seen it many a time in the hands of the butler, who had brandished it almost as a badge of office. He tried it, but though the lock turned and he heard the latch fall, the door would not yield, so he assumed that the bar was in place across it on the other side. Whoever left the house last must have come out from one of the subsidiary doors.

He didn't mind going in by the buttery door, but it left him with the trouble of finding the right key by the primitive method of trying them one after another. When he finally managed to get it open, it let him into the kitchen offices, cold, dark, and smelling mustily damp. This part of the house had been remodelled by his brother and he was not familiar with the various new rooms, but he was not much interested in them. He passed into the kitchen itself, stopping for a moment to wonder what struck him as odd, and realised that it was the lack of a fire. In his childhood the fire had never been let out, except to sweep the chimney – an event of surpassing excitement, involving a black man and an even blacker boy, who scrambled up into the wide flue like an enormous escaping spider; quantities of soot, falling in a soft, deadly thunder to the delight of him and his brother and the horror of the maids; picnic meals and that general sense of impending chaos always so delightful to a well-regulated boy's heart.

He went out by the kitchen passage and through into the

great hall. Yes, the great door was barred. The hall was empty of furniture. There were muddy footmarks all over the fine marble floor, and scraps of rubbish and dried leaves blown into corners, as if the door had been left open a lot some time last autumn. In a sudden, piercing access of memory, he saw his father and mother standing in the middle of the hall receiving the workers and tenants at Christmas, paying the former their wages, receiving the rent from the latter, and distributing presents to all. In his vision there was a huge log burning in the fireplace, and a tangle of dogs spread before it, hogging the heat; there was mulled ale and spiced wine and mincemeat pies, a babble of voices, and cheerful faces; the smell of pine resin from the branches hung about for decoration, and of sour wool and mothballs from the coats of the farmers and their wives.

The old Morland Place, the old ways, the old life! Traditions that had gone back hundreds of years. And himself, a chubby little boy, running around between the staid and gaitered legs, a mince pie in one hand and sugared almonds in his pocket, having his hair ruffled in passing – 'Now then, Master Ted!' – as he played a chasing game with the children from Whitehouse or Huntsham; not a care in the world because it was Christmas and there'd be no lessons for a week and lots of good things to eat.

He bowed his head a moment, as the bright vision faded and he saw himself as he now was, a stout and prosperous man in his thirties, utterly alone, standing in a cold and empty house. What a good thing it was, he thought, that we can never see the future. This present would have broken a great many hearts.

He shivered; and pulled himself together, and tramped off briskly to inspect the rest of the house. It was all empty and melancholy, too big without people in it. Most of the furniture was gone. One or two pieces, too inconveniently large for any other house, had been left – like the ancient four-poster called Eleanor's Bed, which stood in the blue bedroom – along with the paintings that were of no particular value, mostly family portraits by unknown or minor artists. The things that were left, achingly familiar as they were from childhood, only seemed to emphasise the strangeness.

He did not look into every room – it was too depressing. Halfway along the bedroom corridor he gave up and turned back. He ought to inspect the attics to see if the roof was leaking, but he hadn't the heart, nor the will to climb all those stairs. At the foot of the great staircase, though, on an impulse, he went to look at the chapel. The massive oak door was ajar just sufficiently to admit a body. The sound of his own footsteps was beginning to trouble him, and he eased himself through, as though afraid of disturbing something. The day outside was grey and the chapel was dim and full of shadows. Instinctively he raised himself onto tiptoe as he walked down the aisle. The sanctuary lamp was out – something that had never happened before in his memory, even during Alfreda's reign when there had been no chaplain – and the altar furniture was gone. He wondered if it had been sold like everything else to pay the debts, and felt that such a thing was vaguely sacrilegious. At least the pews were fixed, so they could not be removed; and of course the marble and brass ornaments on the walls remained.

And here, to one side, was the lady-altar, and the statue of the Lady was still there. He paused. She was so old, older than the house, a stumpy thing carved of wood, the face almost eroded by the years, though the slender hands, unexpectedly delicate, were still clear. There were legends aplenty in an old house like this, and one of the most persistent was that the Lady wept when disaster threatened the Morlands. Real tears would be seen running down her face. Teddy looked at her sidelong, half afraid of what he might see now. There was something frightening about her sheer age and endurance. She had survived everything, and even the bailiffs had not dared to touch her. Now she stood all alone in this empty place, keeping guard over the house and its memories. So she would stand, through the cold days and the dark nights, blind with age, her beautiful hands held out and open, offering or asking, he could not tell which, until a Morland came again.

The smell of damp here was penetrating, and it occurred

to him suddenly that just below his feet, separated from him only by the stone floor, was the crypt, where stood, row on row, the coffins of his ancestors. It was no wonder the house was haunted, built as it was on a foundation of bones. He imagined suddenly the floor giving way, tumbling him helplessly into the void; saw his fall broken by coffins, the coffins breaking open, the bones spilling out; himself trapped down there, unable to climb up again into the light.

You are master now. Don't betray us.

In his mind the skeletons assembled round him, their empty eye sockets turning to him reproachfully. He shivered violently and the image vanished; but he found himself staring at the worn, almost featureless face of the Lady, and that was almost as bad.

Don't betray us. Don't betray me.

Was that *her* whisper? Teddy was a man almost without imagination and it frightened him to be so besieged by images. He bowed to the Lady awkwardly, took a few steps backwards, then turned for the door, stopping himself from running only by an act of will. Outside the chapel he shut the door firmly, and only then, leaning against it, did he feel some measure of security.

He took out his handkerchief and, despite the chill of the day, mopped a sweat from his face. He could not live here. He ought to have known before he came, given that he was a town-bird by preference; but even if he had pined for the country, he could not live here among the ghosts.

He hurried outside, away from the voices and visions and sadness; and then found that, stupidly, he had not separated the buttery key from the rest, so now he had to go through the trial-and-error process all over again. As he was fiddling with the job, someone hailed him from behind.

'Hey-oop! Now then! What're you about there, feller?'

Teddy turned and found a man standing just this side of the barbican, a country fellow in working clothes, accompanied by two sheep-dogs, which were inching towards Teddy with their muzzles wrinkled and their teeth unpleasantly on display.

But as soon as he turned, the man's face cleared and he

pulled off his cap. 'Eh, it's Maister Morland. Coom, Shep, coom, Tab. Get by 'ere. Ah'm sorry, maister, Ah didn't recognise you.'

The dogs' hackles subsided and they sat, sweeping the ground tentatively with their tails. Teddy moved forward a pace or two, trying to see who the man was.

'It's Davy Walton, maister,' the man helped him out. 'Jeb Walton's son, from Huntsham Farm.'

'Yes, of course! Stupid of me. How d'ye do? I wasn't expecting to see anyone here,' Teddy apologised.

They shook hands.

'Likewise, sir,' said Davy, grinning. 'Ah were passin' by an' saw t' gate open, so Ah coom in to see if everything were all right. There's soom rough folk about, these days, an' it'd be a right shame if th' old house got brokken in to. Even if there's nowt to steal, these tramping men can do a lot of harm.'

'That was kind of you,' Teddy said. 'The gate was open when I got here. I don't know who has the key – unless it's on this bunch.' He held it out and rattled it forlornly. 'I'm just trying to remember which one I used to open the buttery door, so I can lock it again.'

'Let me, maister,' said Davy, taking the bunch obligingly and going to the door with the dogs surging round him eagerly. In a very short time he had chosen the right one (by instinct? Or was there a skill to recognising keys?) and locked the door. 'Ezra Banks from Woodside Farm has the key to the barbican gate, though Ah don't know if there's another,' he went on. 'The Bankses tend the kitchen garden.'

'Do they?' Teddy said vaguely, receiving his keys again.

'It were an arrangement wi' the old maister,' Davy explained. 'They tended it and took the produce, except for what maister needed. Now they tek it all, o' course. But it's better for the garden to be tended than left,' he added defensively.

'Oh, quite, quite,' said Teddy.

'And Ezra keeps the barbican key because he stores some o' the stuff here – potatoes an' apples an' the like. He keeps an eye on the 'ouse at the same time. Ah suppose he must have left gate open by mistake last time he were here. Ah'll have a word with him about it, if you like.'

'Yes, thank you. Good fellow,' said Teddy.

Davy eyed him curiously. 'Ah heerd y'd bought t'old Place, maister. Dad were right pleased it weren't goin' to strangers. Are you thinking of cooming back – beg pardon for askin'?'

Teddy stirred out of his reverie. 'Oh – no. No, I don't think so. I came up here thinking I might, but it's too – too big for a bachelor.'

Davy looked at him wide eyed. 'Aye, maister. It needs a fyow people about. Ah couldn't live 'ere maself, not wi' all them ghosts.'

Teddy laughed. 'You don't believe in ghosts, surely?'

'There's soom reet funny stories about Morland Place. Allus has been. Not that the ghosts were bad 'uns – but Ah reckon you need a bit o' company to face 'em. So what will you do, maister? A house needs livin' in.'

'I shall have to get a caretaker, I suppose, or a house-keeper.' He had bought it so that it might not fall into the hands of strangers, but if he could not live here a stranger must.

Davy nodded. 'It's a shame to see that good land not used, too. But things are bad all over. Still, I reckon Ezra Banks'll keep tending the kitchen garden, if it suits you, maister. And Dad and I'll keep an eye on the house when-ever we pass this way – until you get someone in, any road.'

'Thank you,' said Teddy. 'You're a good neighbour.'

Davy shuffled a little with embarrassment at being thanked, and wiped his nose on the back of his hand. The dogs, lying down, watched his face intently for the first hint that they might be leaving.

'Aye, well,' he said. 'Ah knaw that Dad and Mam – well, we're all glad to be stoppin' on at Huntsham, whoever we pay the rent to. But we'd sooner we were Morland tenants again, when all's said. There've been Morlands at Morland Place time out o' mind.'

'Yes,' said Teddy. The grey sky was darkening for more rain, and he felt the empty house at his back like a hole he might too easily fall into. All he wanted now was to get his horse and ride back to the city as quickly as he could. He would do something about finding a caretaker for Morland Place tomorrow. Or if not tomorrow, the day after. There was no hurry, really. It was important to get the right person.

CHAPTER SIX

The Hazelmeres had only a brief honeymoon, planning to take a longer trip later in the year. For the moment they had a lot to do, setting up house in Manchester Square. Though he was not a rich man, Hazelmere had a gentle-manly income of his own, and Venetia's practice was flourishing, so they could afford something in a more comfort-able style than the house in Welbeck Street. Besides, the old house had the dispensary in the basement, and Hazelmere was not keen to be living 'over the shop', as it were.

'I'd sooner you weren't so continually available, my darling. If we live over the dispensary, patients will be calling on you at all times of the day and night.'

When Hazelmere had proposed to her the year before, he had suggested – given how hard she worked and how little he would see of her otherwise – that she needed an assistant. Venetia agreed with him, and before the wedding she had interviewed a number of hopefuls and taken on a Dr Andrew Foreman. He had been qualified three years and was married and already had two small children, which meant he was both keen and not too expensive. The house in Welbeck Street seemed suitable for them – Mrs Foreman thought it a palace compared with their previous lodgings – and it would be convenient for Foreman to be on hand for the dispensary. The rent was a little higher than they had paid before, but their other outgoings were not great, and Miss Ulverston, who had shared the house with Venetia for propriety's sake, was happy to stay on as lodger, which helped.

So while the Hazelmeres were on honeymoon, the Foremans moved into Welbeck Street. The house in Manchester Square, though only two streets away, was much more suited to a viscount: not vast, but roomy and handsome. Hazelmere also said very firmly that they could not live without a manservant, so they soon had a household their peers would not be ashamed to visit.

The sensation in the papers about the pioneer lady doctor turning out to be a duke's daughter had barely died down when their return from honeymoon wound it up again, and unsolicited visits were a real nuisance at first. The manservant, Hobson, quickly proved his worth. He was a young man, a Scot from Aberdeenshire, who despite his youth had developed a freezing manner which went well with his very precise English. He had been trained by the butler of a great house, and was 'a whale', as Venetia said slangily, on forms and procedures. Though Hazelmere was a viscount, Venetia's rank, as a duke's daughter, was higher, so the correct address for her was Lady Venetia Hazelmere. Anyone foolish enough to enquire at the door for 'Lady Hazelmere' was told in the iciest tones that no such person lived there.

Besides Hobson, who doubled as valet to Hazelmere, they had a cook, a kitchenmaid, and two housemaids; a charwoman, a lamp boy and a secretary for Venetia all came in by day. The horse and carriage had been kept in Little Welbeck Street Mews, just behind the old house, where the coachman also had his room, and since he was comfortable there and it was hardly a quarter-mile away, they decided there was no point in moving them.

Hazelmere had hoped that having an assistant would mean that Venetia would have more time for him, and he had planned all sorts of things to do together. He had reckoned without her new fame. She still operated at the Duchess of Southport's Hospital (founded by her mother many years ago) and at the New Hospital for Women, and she liked to keep in touch with the free dispensary she had opened in Marylebone Lane. But the dispensary in Welbeck Street she gave over entirely to Foreman. She had hoped he would take over a large number of her regular patients too. What she had not expected was the rush of new patients.

'I have always hated the mere thought of doctors,' one lady said. 'You can't think what a relief it is to be seen by one of one's own.'

And 'Confessing one's frailty to a commoner has always pained me dreadfully,' said another.

But there were those who were simply agog at the thought, or longing for the thrill, of being examined by a duke's daughter. Venetia would have liked to turn them all away, but the rich paid large fees, which subsidised the work she did with the poor; and besides, she was a doctor, and if they were genuinely ill she wanted to help them. After a while the unnatural excitement died down, and since her secretary was very strict about pursuing bills, the idly curious soon dropped away.

She did end up with more surgical work. The rich were always operated on in their own homes, and they preferred to have someone who knew how to behave. Now the ladies had the extra comfort of a person of rank who was of their own sex as well. She had to choose her surgical cases carefully, however. Now she was married to the amiable Hazelmere, her social life was expanding, and it took a particularly well-balanced person to sit down to dinner with the lady who had recently had their blood on her hands.

The increase in the number of invitations they received was not only due to Hazelmere's amiability. In March Venetia received an attention she had by no means expected: an invitation to attend a Drawing Room at Buckingham Palace. She had been presented as a débutante, of course, back in 1867. It was usual for ladies of rank to be received again when they were first married, but Venetia had not expected it because of the notoriety attaching to her. But the Queen was mellowing with age, and her antipathy to females undertaking men's work – always a patchy thing – was weakening.

The focus of that particular Drawing Room was the presentation of Princess May of Teck. She was the daughter of Mary Adelaide, the Queen's cousin – the Mary Adelaide, affectionately known to the public as Fat Mary, whose brother George, Duke of Cambridge, had once been expected to marry Queen Victoria and was now her Commander-in-Chief. The Queen had always been close to the Cambridges, and was particularly fond of Mary Adelaide, who had married the Duke of Teck, a handsome and well-liked man, though penniless and of lower rank than her. Victoria Mary, known as May, was their eldest child. Though brought up in poverty and having a mere Serene Highness for a father, May had many advantages, not least having the Queen for her godmother.

After presentation, Princess May was invited to stand with her mother and the Princess of Wales in the semi-circle of princesses and royal duchesses beside the throne – a privilege that would not have been accorded her in any other European court, and a sign of the great affection of the Queen for the Tecks. Venetia examined her covertly as she approached the throne, and thought her attractive, with her mother's fair hair and complexion and her father's blue eyes, a pretty figure, and a rather determined little chin. She was more interested, though, in her own position, and hardly dared look at the Queen as she went down in her curtsey.

When she rose, however, she found the Queen was actually smiling. 'Welcome back, my dear,' she said affably. 'You have been too long away. Some time or other I shall be interested to hear about your work. You and Hazelmere must come to dinner. The Court needs new blood. We are sometimes *very* dull, you know, knowing each other's conversation as well as we do.'

A flood of things came into Venetia's mind but she restricted herself, wisely, to 'Thank you, Your Majesty,' and to contemplating the twinkle in the royal eye. The Queen was the byword for propriety, but being by nature stubborn and contrary she also liked to flout convention and surprise people. It was a trait that could work as easily against someone like Venetia as for them, and she could only be grateful that for the moment it seemed to be working to her advantage.

The Princess of Wales also had a kind word for her and said she must come to Sandringham some time, and the Duchess of Teck, who had been wildly unconventional in her youth, pressed her hand and said they must have a long talk about her work in the slums. 'The poor live in such terrible conditions, and there is much to do. People like us can help so much – but so few of us do. I'm pleased to meet someone who is really *doing*.'

Venetia felt a little dazed at all this attention, and looked forward to telling Hazelmere how far he had rescued her from oblivion by marrying her.

When the Drawing Room was over and the Queen had withdrawn, she had an opportunity to speak to her sister Olivia, whose husband was a permanent member of the Household.

'Come to my sitting-room,' Olivia said. 'I long for a good, cosy chat.'

Olivia had been invited to become a maid-of-honour at the tender age of eighteen, and had been at Court ever since. She had married Charles Du Cane, who was now Assistant Keeper of the Privy Purse, and was a favourite of the Queen, who enjoyed having about her pretty women with pleasant voices. Olivia played the piano and sang in four languages, and the Queen liked to have her read aloud too. She was skilled with brush and pencil, and was the Queen's favourite companion on sketching expeditions. She and Charlie also took part in palace amateur dramatics; and though she had no children of her own – a sorrow to her – she was devoted to them, and was often called on to play with or otherwise attend the youngest royals.

The Court was her whole life, and in the years since Venetia had fallen from grace they had met infrequently; but as soon as the door of the sitting-room closed behind them, Olivia fell on her neck and hugged her.

'Dear, dearest 'Netia! How I've missed you!'

'Dear Livy!' Venetia hugged her back. 'I've missed you too.'

'Let me look at you.' Olivia released her and stepped back, brushing a tear from her cheek. 'Just the same old 'Netia! You look very well.'

'You look better than well. You still look nineteen! Are you happy, darling?'

'Oh, *yes*! And you? I'm so glad you married Lord Hazelmere at last! I always thought he was the right person for you. So very kind and handsome.'

'The poor man's served a lot more than seven years for his Rachel. Do you remember when we used to have our "at home" days, and all the jolly officers came and paid us outrageous compliments?'

'Yes,' Olivia said, 'and you were always the favourite. You had witty things to say, while I could only look on.'

'But you were so beautiful, you didn't need to speak,' Venetia said. 'My God, that's a barbed compliment, isn't it? I didn't mean it quite like that.'

Now Olivia laughed too. 'Papa used to say I had more hair than wit, and it's true. I've never been clever, like you. But I've always been happy in what I did, and I've hoped and hoped so much that you would be too.'

'I am happy,' Venetia said. 'It was my whole ambition to be a doctor, and—'

'Yes, but I hated to think of you being so cut off from everything, as you were.' Olivia's 'everything' was different from Venetia's, but Venetia forbore to say so. It was a point on which she knew they would never meet. 'And now you've been received, we shall meet often,' Olivia went on happily. 'Charlie and I will be able to invite you to dinner.' She faltered. 'You understand why we couldn't before.'

'I understand. Don't think about it. But to what do I owe the change of heart? The Queen almost *beamed* at me.'

'Well, a married woman doctor is very different from an unmarried woman doctor,' Olivia said. 'And one can never be quite sure what the Queen will approve of.'

'I'm sure you must take a lot of the credit for my rehabilitation.'

'Oh, no! Well, I do try to speak to her about you when I have the chance. And she does so admire people who work with the poor. And, of course, she's interested in everything to do with medicine.'

'And in addition,' Venetia said with a smile, 'she likes to show now and then that *she* does not have to abide by the rules.'

'Of course not,' Olivia answered simply. 'She *makes* them.'

'I did wonder if there was anything other than coincidence in my being included in the list that contained Princess May. The Tecks would not be so prominent in a German court.'

'The Queen is very fond of them. And she's loyal to those she likes.'

'Still, you must have had to work very hard,' Venetia said, 'given the wickedness of our brother.'

'Oh, it doesn't matter so much with men,' Olivia said. 'And he's much more a Marlborough House person. We don't see him much at Court. But the Queen has said once or twice that he ought to get married. She believes dukes, even if they're not royal dukes, have a special responsibility to produce an heir.'

'There doesn't seem much chance of Harry doing that.'

Olivia did not pursue this line. She said, 'The Queen's much more concerned about Gussie's behaviour. I think, in an odd way, that was what persuaded her to receive you in the end. To show disapproval of Gussie.'

'I suppose I must be grateful for small favours,' Venetia said wryly. 'But now, tell me about you. I want to hear all about your life, everything that's happened to you since we last met.'

They sat and chatted for almost an hour, but what Venetia heard from her sister was a catalogue of Court news, the minutiae of royal routines. Olivia had no life of her own outside her service. Yet there was no doubt that she was happy. Venetia observed her sister, looking so neat and prosperous in a plain, well-cut dress of fawn silk trimmed with narrow maroon velvet ribbon, her golden hair done up as it had always been in a large, soft mass behind, like a plaited loaf. Her smooth, unlined face was serene, her voice gently animated. Serving the Queen and married to dear Charlie, she had everything she wanted.

They were disturbed by a tap on the door, and Arthur Bigge, assistant to the Queen's private secretary Sir Henry Ponsonby, put his head round the door.

'Ah, there you are. I thought I might find you here,' he

said, nodding to Venetia. 'Sir Henry sent me to enquire about a date for you and Hazelmere to dine here. Will Tuesday suit?'

'Yes, indeed. Thank you,' Venetia said.

'Good. I'll see the invitation goes out today. You know the form, of course?'

'I've never dined with the Queen before,' Venetia said.

'Well, I'm sure Lady Olivia can advise you,' Bigge said pleasantly.

A Buckingham Palace dinner might be dull, but at least it occupied only part of one day. The invitation to Sandringham, which arrived not long afterwards, was for Friday evening to Tuesday morning.

Hazelmere looked at it in dismay. 'What have you got us into, my love?'

'It's not my fault. It's your respectability that's to blame,' Venetia retorted. 'I was untouchable before I married you.'

'You must have impressed the Princess of Wales at the Drawing Room. She doesn't want to be left out, now the Queen likes us.'

'Well, we can't refuse,' Venetia said. 'Will it be so very bad?'

'That depends,' Hazelmere said, 'on how much you enjoy boredom. HRH is genial and the Princess is as kind as can be, but neither of them has any pretence to intellect, and they choose their guests likewise.'

'Then all we have to do not to be invited again is to be horribly clever.'

'You won't be able to,' Hazelmere said. 'You'll be sucked in. That's the power of royalty. However little you mean to, you'll find yourself being sucked in.'

'Why is it so boring?'

'Sandringham parties are run like military exercises. And HRH is such a stickler for punctuality he has all the clocks set half an hour ahead. Every moment is planned for. No sitting out allowed. No allowance made for individual preference. He'll even tell your servants what he expects you to wear, and woe betide you if you wear an order in the wrong position, or a waistcoat of the wrong colour for the liturgical season.'

'I'm sure you exaggerate. But anyway, it won't kill us for once. This invitation is by way of marking our marriage, and as we're not the Waleses' sort, it won't be repeated.'

Despite Hazelmere's warning, Venetia was excited – or perhaps, rather, intrigued – as the time approached. It would be, if nothing else, a novel experience. But there were preparations to be made. Hobson would be going with them to valet Hazelmere, but Venetia didn't have a personal maid, and having considered the housemaids she was convinced they would fall into hysterics at the very idea of such an exalted destination. What she needed was a trained lady's maid. After some thought she approached Lady Cordelia Cleveley, a distant cousin and a friend of her childhood, and asked to borrow her maid for the occasion.

Lady Cordelia agreed with great readiness to lend her Wilmot, but when she enquired further as to what clothes Venetia was taking, she threw up her hands in horror and said it would never do. 'You change five times a day at Sandringham. A certain amount can be done by varying hats and scarves and so on, but not everything. You really must make an effort, my love!'

'It's too late to get a lot of new clothes,' Venetia said rebelliously.

'Oh, it doesn't signify if they're new. None of that set has the *slightest* taste or discrimination, but you must have enough different things to be seen to be *trying*! And take *all* your jewels. Everyone's expected to gossip, and think how tiresome if what they're gossiping about is *you*.'

Now Venetia laughed. 'But I don't have any jewels! I was cut off with a shilling, if you remember.'

Cordelia frowned. 'Then you must borrow some,' she said firmly.

'I suppose I mustn't let Wilmot down,' Venetia agreed.

In the end, she borrowed from her cousin Lady Anne Farraline, who had a generous brother and had inherited all her mother's things as well. Between them, Anne and Cordelia took Venetia in hand, determined she should not look out of place, however rebellious she felt. Anne also lent some gowns, which Wilmot skilfully altered for Venetia. They were much of a height and build, so it was not too difficult, and Anne had good taste. It was impossible to keep all this activity from Hazelmere, and he was at first inclined to feel the pangs of hurt pride – for a man likes to feel he can provide for his wife – and to insist on Venetia's buying new things. But she pointed out that this was an unusual demand on her wardrobe, and persuaded him that it would be foolish to buy things she would probably never wear again. He was not too difficult to distract. He was in a flap over his guns, and the prospect of having to play baccarat every night with hardened gamblers, even though it was said the Prince did not play for high stakes.

The day came, and they travelled down by train from St Pancras to Wolferton, the nearest station, in a special carriage laid on for Sandringham guests. There were fourteen others, most of them unknown to Venetia, though Hazelmere murmured a name or two in her ear. She was amused to note how everyone was eyeing everyone else and trying to work out the social precedence; amused also to note that she and Hazelmere were obviously not in the first rank of Sandringham invitees, for apart from Lord de Grey, heir of the Marquess of Ripon, and the widowed Countess of Lonsdale, there was no-one very eminent there. The gentlemen began at once to talk politics and sport together, but the ladies – to Venetia's relief – were more wary, and passed only commonplace remarks while covertly examining each other's clothes.

At the station a veritable caravan of carriages was waiting to convey the guests, together with wagons for the maids, valets, loaders and luggage. If Venetia had thought her preparations excessive, she was disabused of this idea by the mountains that were disgorged from the luggage van for the other guests.

As the light faded the carriages pulled up in front of the 'Big House' – as it was called – at Sandringham. It did not look like a palace, nor even like a family pile. With its monotonous red brick front, imitation Tudor chimneys and gables, and large stone *porte-cochère* it looked, Hazelmere murmured wickedly to his bride, exactly like a Scottish golf hotel.

But the icy Norfolk wind was blowing off the Wash, whence it had arrived straight from the Arctic wastes, and in the gathering dusk the long windows were shining a welcome yellow, promising fires and hot water within, so Venetia was glad just to hurry inside.

The Prince and Princess were waiting in the entrance hall to greet everyone, and their affability was palpable. Venetia was surprised at how warmly the Prince spoke to her. He took her hand and held it, beaming down at her as if they had been meeting every week all their lives.

'I am *very* glad to see you here, m'dear,' he said. 'How well you are looking. Marriage suits you, hey, what? We shall have a long talk later. I shall be very interested to hear all about your work.'

What Hazelmere had not mentioned, though she remembered she had heard it spoken of, was the Prince's enormous charm, his ability to exude real, personal interest in whichever person he was talking to. Venetia looked up into that face, familiar from a hundred public portraits, and found herself smiling in response. His own smile widened perceptibly; the amazingly bright, pale blue eyes crinkled, and he patted her arm with his free hand and said, 'That's right, that's right. I hope you'll be comfortable, m'dear.'

As she moved away to allow someone else their turn, she reflected that of course if she didn't know him, he certainly knew her, being a bosom friend to her brother and, probably, lover to her sister. But the thought did not destroy the warm feeling that he really did like her and was interested in her. She was glad, though, that he had had the tact not to invite Gussie and her husband in the same party.

From the entrance vestibule they were swept into the saloon, a mock-Elizabethan hall with a minstrel's gallery and Tudor fireplace, cream-painted stone walls, and large, ugly but comfortable chairs and sofas, upholstered in the Prince's racing colours of red, blue and gold. It was brightly lit by gasoliers and there was a roaring fire. To break the rather awkward silence, the Prince began to discourse, with gathering enthusiasm, about the private gas-works he had had built to supply the house. With a little skilful prompting from Francis Knollys, his secretary, the Prince went on to the wonder of his private water supply, and the purification tower he had built to ensure he never got typhoid again.

Tea was served, a little desultory conversation got up, and then it was time to go and dress. A platoon of servants led the guests off to their rooms which, like the rest of the house, were comfortably furnished but without any pretension to style or elegance. It was really much more like an hotel, Venetia thought, than a private home. She saw not one old piece of furniture or painting of any merit on her trek through the corridors; but there was hot water in her chamber and a good fire.

At half past eight everyone assembled again in the drawing-room, a room decorated all in white elaborate plas-terwork, like a wedding-cake, with painted panels containing chubby rouged cherubs. Smoking was not permitted and no drinks were served, so they had nothing to do while they waited for the Prince and Princess but stand about and make awkward conversation. Francis Knollys drifted about the room murmuring a word or two to each guest. When he reached Venetia, she found he was telling them the order in which they would go in to dinner, and with whom.

'HRH will take you in himself, Lady Venetia,' Knollys said, 'so you'll be leading the way.'

She knew him from their youth, though they hadn't met in years. 'Oh, Lord, Francis, must I?'

'Of course. The Prince is a stickler for precedence, and as a duke's daughter you outrank the other ladies present. And, of course, you're newly married.'

'It's an honour I would happily pass up,' she said. 'I'm out of practice in small-talk.'

Knollys smiled. 'Some skills are never forgotten. I remember the night we danced at Grosvenor House in – 'sixty-eight, was it, or 'sixty-nine?'

'Longer ago than you have any business remembering,' she said, laughing. 'Who does my husband take?'

'Lady Lonsdale. De Grey takes the Princess.'

Hazelmere had had a lucky escape, Venetia thought: the Princess was as deaf as an adder, which made her hard work as a dinner partner.

The royal pair appeared, the couples formed, the doors were flung open, and Venetia found herself leading the way, her gloved hand resting on the stiff, expensive sleeve of the man who would one day be King of England. With his stout figure, his clean, pink skin, neatly trimmed beard and scanty hair, he looked like a genial uncle, though he was hardly ten years older than her. She felt the rumble of his voice as he spoke to her; her own seemed light and insubstantial as a dried leaf in reply. He was talking of her father: 'A great sportsman, fine rider, damned fine shot. My father said he was the finest shot he ever knew. Went stalking with him at Balmoral. Needs a good eye to shoot a deer in the open, y'know. Clever cove, too. Spoke Russian, of all things! Did you know that? Of course you did, what am I saying? He was your father, after all.'

'He spent a long time in St Petersburg, sir,' Venetia said. 'There was a story that he once shot a bear there.'

'No, did he? A bear! What did he use, d'ye know?'

'His army pistol, I believe it was,' Venetia said demurely, and at the Prince's stare of astonishment, she added, 'It was an accidental shooting, I'm afraid. The bear was a pet belonging to Prince Orlovsky and it wandered into the shooting gallery where Papa and the Prince were practising. Fortunately it was only a flesh wound, or the poor Prince would have been heartbroken. He doted on the creature.'

The Prince gave a delighted shout of laughter. They reached the dining table, and he waved the footman away to draw out her chair for her himself. Obviously she had made a hit. 'Glad you married Hazelmere,' he murmured to her, as they sat down. 'Good fellow, Hazelmere – one of the best. Just the right sort of fellow for you.'

She was surprised and touched, not having supposed before that he had ever given her a thought in his life.

The footmen glided in with the first course, and the long, sumptuous dinner began. The Prince, though not a heavy drinker, was a great eater, and delighted in fine food. The meal was excellent, though of a scope and length Venetia had become unused to. She could only nibble and taste the succession of dishes, but that was as well, for her function at this table was to entertain the Prince. The success of her first story had given her confidence, and she called up the resources that had not been used for so many years, and chatted to him lightly and vivaciously. In her youth she had been accounted witty and amusing, and if she could do it then, from a position of profound ignorance, she ought to be able to manage it now, with so much experience behind her. The Prince was an excellent listener, and kept her supplied with appropriate prompts, and she seemed to be pleasing him.

After dinner the gentlemen were taken away to play baccarat – Hazelmere rolled his eyes piteously at his wife as he followed them out – while card tables were set up in the drawing-room for whist for the ladies. The Princess of Wales presided. Though deaf and lame, she had kept her girlish figure and her face was amazingly unlined, beautiful and sweet of expression. When later two of her daughters, Louise and Victoria, came down, she might have been their elder sister, so young did she look. The girls did not join the play, but hung affectionately about their mother, watching over her shoulder, chattering to her; leaning on each other like girls half their age and playing idly with each other's hair. They were pretty enough, but from being always sickly they lacked animation, and as Lady Lonsdale, Venetia's partner, told her, they were 'as ignorant as foxes, having never had the slightest scrap of education in their lives'.

At midnight the Princess stood up and announced that everyone was to retire, but there was no sign of the men returning. Venetia took the opportunity to ask Lady Lonsdale when they would come to bed, and she said, 'Not until the Prince does, and he likes to play until three or four. He hardly seems to need any sleep.'

'Three or four?' Venetia said in dismay.

Lady Lonsdale made a grimace. 'It's hard on them, especially as they have to get up to shoot tomorrow. But generally those who don't like to gamble slip into the billiard room and sleep in the chairs, and a footman keeps watch and wakes them when the baccarat breaks up.'

Venetia tried to stay awake, but she was sleepy from the long day and the wine, and she did not hear Hazelmere tiptoe in, sore-eyed and smelling of cigar smoke, in the small hours. She woke, however, when he got out of bed in the morning to go to the window and check the weather.

'What's it like out there?' she asked sleepily.

'Dreadful,' he said. 'Wet and windy. We all have to shoot, even so. No crying off allowed. Half past ten on the dot. Shooting breakfast at nine.'

'Oh, Lord,' Venetia said, and then began to laugh. 'What poor things we are, not to mutiny! What time is it?'

'Just after eight. I didn't get to bed until three, and then I couldn't get to sleep at once,' he said fretfully.

'Poor love! Come back to bed for a while now.'

'I must get back to my room. Hobson will be coming in to call me at half past eight.'

'Then we have half an hour. Need I remind you of your duty, sir?' she said sternly. 'You have a wife – a new wife.'

He smiled and came back to bed. 'You're not a duty, you're a pleasure,' he said, kissing her. The kiss prolonged itself. 'What folly all this is,' he said, when he paused to take breath. 'Why aren't we at home pleasing ourselves?'

'I don't know. Because we are subjects of the realm, I suppose. Never mind, please me some more now.'

So he obliged.

Hobson's father had been a gamekeeper and he had handled guns all through his childhood, so he was to act as loader to Hazelmere as well as valet. The two of them tramped out just before half past ten to join the group waiting outside the house, the gentlemen in tweed shooting suits, flat caps and gaitered stockings, the loaders in tweed jackets with stiff collar and tie. Soft-mouthed gun dogs ran around, waving their tails and sniffing the new crop of unknown legs; one or two flasks were already being plied, for the east wind cut like a knife and brought tears to the eyes of the unwary who faced into it.

The ladies spent the morning lounging, reading, writing letters and gossiping. They were not expected to go out with the shooters, though occasionally a lady might venture, if she were having a particularly passionate affair with one of the gentlemen.

'Though they don't encourage it,' Mrs Penshurst said. 'Distracts them, you know.'

'Do you remember the time Bel Watson went out with Charlie Stanmore?' Lady Murray said. 'They were shooting at Six Mile Bottom and something fell down the back of her neck – a raindrop or something of the sort – and she let out a shriek. HRH turned sharply just as he was firing, and peppered a beater's leg!'

'Shooting is no pleasure for spectators,' Lady Lonsdale said firmly. 'An hour after luncheon is *quite* enough.'

'Luncheon in a tent is enough for me,' Mrs de Brisay said, with a shudder. 'The wind whistles quite through one. Last time I simply couldn't get warm afterwards.'

'There are some ladies who shoot, though,' said Lady Murray, 'and I dare say they find it interesting enough.'

'Yes, Lady Augusta Vibart always goes out with the guns,' Mrs Penshurst said. 'Handles a Purdey like a man, I hear.'

'But she does have *other* reasons for going out,' Lady Murray added. 'The Prince couldn't be separated from her last time I was here. One can only admire the Princess for putting up with it.'

'Oh, but I forgot,' Mrs Penshurst said, turning wide eyes on Venetia. 'She's your sister, isn't she, Lady Venetia? Goodness, how indiscreet of us!'

'Come away, Romola – not up to your usual standard of tact this morning!' Lady Murray said, and the two moved away to sit in a different corner and whisper.

'Don't mind them,' Lady Lonsdale said, noting Venetia's pink cheeks. 'Empty vessels, you know, make the most noise. You, I'm sure, have much better things to occupy your time with. Tell me about your practice.'

But it was impossible to get away from the gossip. Even trying not to, she heard from one source that Lady Lonsdale was having an affair with Lord de Grey, and from another that Mrs Penshurst was receiving Lord Murray in her bedchamber at night. She overheard whispered discussion of her own old scandal, of her brother Harry's habits and proclivities, and at another time intercepted great hilarity that her jewellery was borrowed (now how the dickens could that have got out?).

Moving seats, she came in for the edge of a complaint by Lady Boyle to Mrs de Brisay about her losses on the horses. 'I can't think why my bookmaker is so stingy with credit. He knows he'll get it in the end. But I can't ask Archie because I promised to give it up.'

'I could let you have something for a few weeks if it would help,' said Mrs de Brisay.

'Oh, darling, you are so sweet! I hate to dun my friends, but I had such a shocking time at Newmarket. I could let you have it back at the end of the month. Archie pays my quarter's dress allowance then.'

'Would two be enough?'

'Loads, darling. Thanks so much. I wouldn't have got in so deep if I hadn't been trying to outdo that ghastly Gussie Vibart. I can't bear the way she lords it over us all.'

'Well, dear, she has the Prince to pay *her* debts.'

'Vibart's a saint to put up with it.'

'Not at all. He was all to pieces before he married her, but HRH paid off all his debts on condition he gave her his name . . .'

Venetia was very glad when the moment came to change into tweeds, furs, stout boots and hats to be taken out in the brake to the chosen spot for luncheon. A marquee had been set up just behind the gun stands, and a lavish luncheon laid on, with full deployment of snowy linen, china and crystal. Cold dishes were supplemented with hot, kept warm in hay boxes, and for entertainment an equerry read out a list of how many head each gentleman had bagged. Venetia thought this rather vulgar, but Hazelmere said the Prince encouraged competition between his guests.

'It does foster some bad feeling, though,' he admitted. 'In fact, you ladies arrived just in time: tempers have been growing short in the last half-hour. Archie Boyle was complaining that de Grey has been taking his shots all morning, and Murray and Penshurst almost came to blows when they both picked up the same bird.'

'My, what a wonderful spirit sport breeds,' Venetia said. 'Have you had a nice morning?'

'Three hours of hearing my own and my family's characters being torn to shreds.'

'Oh dear, poor love!'

'At least no-one can think of anything bad to say about Olivia.'

After luncheon the ladies were obliged to stand behind the guns and watch a *battue* or two, murmuring admiration as the birds tumbled from the skies. Venetia could not feel it was very sporting for a gentleman to stand in an appointed spot while flocks of birds were driven past his nose for slaughter, but it seemed to satisfy something in the male character. The noise was head-splitting, and even though the rain had stopped the cold was intensifying as the invisible sun went down the grey sky, and the ladies were glad when they were summoned to go back to the house. Even Venetia thought the gossip and idleness would be a price worth paying for a fire before which to thaw her aching fingers and toes.

Back at the Big House, the ladies changed into tea-gowns for the men's return, and after tea there were cards and conversation, until it was time to change again for dinner. Wilmot proved her worth by advising that a high standard of dress would be required for this evening. '*With* tiara, my lady.'

It was an even more lavish dinner – twelve courses this time. Hot and cold soup, thick and clear, gave way to poached turbot and salmon mayonnaise, oysters and prawns; entrées of chicken davenport, turkey in aspic, cutlets, fillets of leveret were succeeded by roasts. Game came in elaborate form, pigeon pie, pheasants stuffed with truffles and oysters, boned snipe stuffed with *foie gras* under a Madeira sauce; and there were besides sorbets and numerous *entremets* – lobster salad, maraschino jelly, stuffed mushrooms, truffles in champagne. And after all that there was an elaborate sweet and then a hot savoury, before the board was cleared and pyramids of hothouse fruits and dishes of bonbons were placed amongst the banks of flowers that decorated the table.

After dinner the Prince led some of the gentlemen to his famous indoor bowling alley, while others repaired to the billiard room. This at least gave Venetia a chance to escape the gossip of the women: ladies were allowed to watch, even to play, billiards.

She and Hazelmere came together like survivors of a storm. 'How was your dinner?' she asked.

'Hard work,' he replied. 'I had Miss Whittaker this time.'

'So I saw. Pretty girl. American, isn't she?'

'Yes, a steel heiress from Pittsburgh, I believe. But I couldn't rouse the slightest gleam of interest from her. I talked myself hoarse on every subject I could think of – theatres, paintings, the weather, food, even gardening. Nothing! Not a glimmer.'

'She must be made of stone to resist you.'

'Not everyone has your good taste,' he smiled. 'But at any rate, I was just admitting defeat when a footman placed a tiny screw of paper beside my plate.'

'Not really?'

'Yes, I was as mystified as you. I unrolled it under cover of the tablecloth and on it, written in pencil, was "Try the zoo."'

'Just that? No signature?'

'No, but when I looked round the table, I saw Mrs Monkton Joins laughing at me in a sympathetic sort of way. You know she and her husband brought Miss Whittaker over from New York – friends of her parents? So I tried my partner with the zoo, and suddenly she burst into bloom, and chattered away, just like a little monkey herself.'

Venetia laughed. 'I doubt whether it's proper to call your dinner partner a monkey.'

'I think we are all monkeys to go along with this sort of nonsense,' said Hazelmere.

She squeezed his arm affectionately. 'I know you enjoy it, really. You're such a sociable soul. But it's penance for me. I so long to be back at my work. And there's two whole days more!'

'You wait until tomorrow! If you thought Saturday was dull, you'll simply adore Sunday!'

There was no shooting on Sunday, but a late breakfast followed by compulsory church attendance. Then came luncheon, after which everyone was taken on a tour of inspection of the grounds, including kennels, stables, model farm, kitchen gardens, gas-works and ornamental ponds. After tea the Princess took the ladies to see the special kitchen where her pack of pet dogs had their meals produced, and on the return to the saloon she was thrown into ecstasies to find her two sons had arrived.

Venetia was interested to meet the young princes, having never seen them before. Prince Albert Victor, the elder, always known as Eddy, was tall and thin, with a rather lugubrious cast of feature; but he was not ill-looking, had a sweet smile and a great deal of his parents' charm. His manners were engaging, and he chatted lightly and pleasantly to everyone. He came first to Venetia, as the new bride, and talked to her easily of London things, and of her sister Olivia, whom he met when visiting his grandmother. Venetia liked him. He was obviously no intellectual and his sentences had a way of trailing off as if he had forgotten halfway through what he was saying, but he seemed to have a genuinely warm heart.

She had little chance to speak to his brother. Prince George was shorter, and rather frog-like in appearance, with bulging eyes and a loose mouth; he seemed more solemn and reserved than his brother, though his rare smile was pleasing. The Princess of Wales cooed over both of them, and petted them as if they were five and six instead of twenty-one and twenty-two, but they seemed to like it, or at least not to find it embarrassing.

They remained to dinner, and afterwards the two elder daughters joined the party again. There was no gambling on Sunday night, but there were cards: Venetia, partnered with Prince Eddy, found he played a rather good game of whist, which was one of his passions. Later the Princess of

Wales, to Venetia's surprise, organised nursery games – Blind Man's Bluff, General Post, Hunt the Slipper and so on – which she made everyone join in. The young Waleses grew very boisterous and noisy under her urging, until the two young princes ended by having a soda-siphon battle, with the Princess, helpless with laughter, egging them on.

Everyone retired to bed at midnight, and when they were alone Venetia turned to her husband with a rueful look and said, 'Lord help us all!'

He embraced her. 'Never mind, darling. Only one more day.'

'Thank God I have my profession,' Venetia said. 'Even as a girl I couldn't bear to be idle, but now I think it would kill me to lead a life like this. How do these people bear it, going from one party to another, and all exactly like this? The same faces, the same gossip, no useful occupation, no goal to aim for.'

'They are not like you,' he said reasonably. 'And it is better for the men – at least we have sport, and politics to discuss. But I'm beginning to feel that I ought to have something useful to do, like you. Perhaps I ought to involve myself in some good cause. What would you recommend?'

'There's so much to be done, I hardly know what to pick,' Venetia said, sitting at the dressing-table and removing the diamond clips from her hair. 'The most pressing perhaps is housing for the poor.'

He looked faintly disappointed. 'There are so many people and organisations involved in that.'

'Yes, but the task is so huge they can only nibble at the edge of it. And bad housing is the root of so much evil – disease, violence, crime. I begin to think . . .' She paused, frowning.

'Yes, darling?'

'I wonder whether it *can* be remedied by individual action. With such a huge, intractable problem, perhaps we ought to have legislation, and government intervention.'

Hazelmere raised his eyebrows. 'It's not the government's business to provide people with housing.'

'I know that's what we've always believed.'

'What about freedom? This country has always been the champion of personal liberty.'

'Even the freedom to suffer, to be sick, to die?'

'Freedom is indivisible,' Hazelmere said. 'Yes, the freedom to make the wrong choices, the freedom to fail. Each man has his own path to work out. It's between him and God. How can the soul grow if we interfere in those choices?'

'Doesn't charity interfere?'

'That's a matter for each person's conscience. But if once you allow the government to interfere in a man's private life, there'll be no end to it. The State will take more and more power, and the individual will become helpless, dependent, a mere parasite. And a tool for the unscrupulous – look what happened in France.'

Venetia continued to remove her borrowed finery, looking troubled. 'But if help is needed, more than private charity can provide? Government already interferes – the factory laws, for instance. We prevent children from going up chimneys and women down mines. Is that wrong?'

'Some people believe so. Should we prevent a person from selling his labour on his own terms? Or from bringing up his children as he thinks fit? Compulsory education, for instance—'

'The 1880 Act is a dead letter anyway,' Venetia said with a shrug. 'Magistrates simply won't enforce it. The poor can't afford the fees, and farmers want their children working in the fields.'

'I'm talking of a principle, my love. Can it be right to force people to send their children to school?'

'But surely education is better than ignorance? That's just a matter of fact.'

'Is it? The man who spends his life in the fields may think differently, and what right have we to come between him and his family? To take decisions for other people is to interfere without responsibility: if we get it wrong, it's not we who will have to bear the consequences, but them.'

Venetia thought. 'Can't we say it's better for the country to have an educated population? Isn't that a reason for compulsion?'

'My dear,' Hazelmere said anxiously, 'you are beginning to sound like a socialist.'

She looked at him coolly. 'I don't know any socialists. I don't know what they think.'

'I'm afraid you will come to. They are getting more and more noisy. For the best possible reasons they will try to persuade us to give up our historical liberty, and there will be many who will listen to them for the best reasons. But the thing about liberty is that it's easy to surrender and very hard to win back.'

She relented. 'The one thing I do know, from my work with the poor, is that they *hate* being told what to do, even if it's for their own good. Even in the worst slums they relish their freedom. That's why I think Miss Hill's schemes are wrong-headed. But they do *need* help. I don't know what the answer can be.'

'For each of us to do our best, I suppose,' said Hazelmere, coming over to stand behind her and kiss the back of her neck. 'And from now on I shall make sure I do more. If we survive until Tuesday, that is.'

She smiled at his reflection. 'Shooting tomorrow. You'd better go to bed and to sleep so as to be fresh. You'll have the two young Waleses to compete with, as well as all the rest.'

'I'll be happy to go to bed,' he said, running a finger down her bare shoulders, 'but sleep? That's another matter.'

CHAPTER SEVEN

Returning from Sandringham was to Venetia like returning to sanity, and she threw herself with renewed vigour and gratitude into her work. It was so good to have a proper occupation, to have the skills to do something useful.

Somehow, in the mysterious way these things worked, it became known that she and Hazelmere had been invited to Sandringham and that she had been admired by the Prince of Wales. Invitations to all sorts of social gatherings began to arrive, some from people who before had looked down their noses at the duke's daughter who had let herself down so far as to become a doctor. She and her husband were very careful which they accepted. She had no wish to be lionised, or to be popular with and beloved of the idly fashionable; but they began to build a circle of friends from among the well-educated, amusing and philanthropical.

She did not forget her cousin Henrietta, and in May the Hazelmeres invited the Comptons to the promised dinner. It was a pleasant occasion. The two men took an instant liking to each other, and were soon deep in discussion about investments, horses, foreign travel, the Home Rule Bill and other masculine topics, while on the other sofa Henrietta and Venetia chatted like old friends, and Henrietta confided her expectations.

'It's due in September,' she said. 'I'm so very happy. It was what I've been hoping for ever since he asked me to marry him, but I hardly dared dream it would be so soon.'

At which point, Venetia revealed that, though it was early

to be sure, she rather hoped she might be in the same way herself.

Henrietta's face lit. 'Oh, I'm so happy for you! How wonderful that it should happen to both of us at the same time.'

'Our children will be born within months of each other,' Venetia said. 'Wouldn't it be nice if they were friends? They could call each other "Cousin".'

Henrietta was touched by such generosity, and agreed happily. 'Who will you have to look after you when the time comes?' she asked.

'I don't know. It's a puzzle, isn't it? I've delivered more babies than I care to remember, but it's a case of *quis custodiet ipsos custodes*, I suppose. And I am rather advanced in years to be having a first child.'

'I'm not much younger than you,' Henrietta said.

'Yes, but you've done it before. A first child is always a trickier matter. Though, now I come to think of it, Mrs Anderson was thirty-six or -seven when she had her first, and she had no trouble at all.'

'Mrs Anderson? Oh, you mean Mrs Garrett Anderson, the first lady doctor.'

'Yes. I seem to have been following in her footsteps all my life, so perhaps that's a good omen. Still, I should have someone. There are plenty of female colleagues in London – but perhaps I should ask Dr Foreman to attend me, and keep the fee in the practice!' Venetia laughed. 'Tell me, does your Lizzie know the good news yet?'

'I was afraid it might upset her at first, but she's very excited about it, as if it's a special birthday present planned just for her. Her birthday is in September too, you see.'

'I would dearly like to meet her. Will you bring her to see me? Not tomorrow – I'm operating at the Southport. What about Wednesday? I should be free in the afternoon. Come at three and stay for tea, and we can have a long chat.'

Lizzie was so excited about the visit that she could not speak, but held herself rigid as Emma helped her dress, her lips tightly shut and her eyes shining. The weather was still very cold, so she was to wear her brown velvet, which was a relief to her. There had been talk of a cotton frock, and she felt that such an inferior material could not possibly be good enough for the occasion.

'Lord bless us,' Emma said, 'you're as tight as a drum-skin. Are you scared?'

Lizzie's eyes opened wide. 'Scared? No!'

'There, don't you get yourself too worked up, or you'll only be disappointed,' Emma said kindly. 'Sing a song. That's what I do if I'm a little bit upsy-downsy.'

'You sing for me,' Lizzie said. 'Do, Em. You've such a nice voice. Sing "Mr Parry Wants to Marry".'

Emma laughed. 'What'd your ma say? I'll sing you a nice hymn instead.'

So it was with her head full of 'To Be a Pilgrim' that she went downstairs to the cab. She liked travelling in a hansom nearly as much as the omnibus, and there was always so much to look at, with building going on everywhere, and pedestrians and other traffic, and shop windows to stare into. Manchester Square, by contrast, was quiet, but the houses seemed wonderfully grand, which was as it should be.

When she and her mother were shown into the morning-room, there was not one tall, handsome lady to greet her, but two. Lady Venetia was thin-faced and commanding and had reddish hair and was dressed in a severe brown worsted suit. She would have been terrifying if she had not had such a lovely smile. She came and took hold of Lizzie's hand while she was still curtseying and shook it in a grown-up way and said how pleased she was to meet her. Lizzie felt at ease with her at once.

Lady Venetia greeted Mama with a kiss on the cheek, and then said, 'You must allow me to present Lady Anne Farraline,' and explained that Lady Anne was the daughter of her mother's half-brother, Lord Batchworth. 'So we are all cousins to each other, to some degree,' she concluded.

Lady Anne was young, jolly, and very beautiful. She had golden curly hair, done up on the top in a chignon, and blue eyes, and a lovely face, and she was dressed in a dusky pink grosgrain, quite plain but with just a hint of bustle, and hussar braid on the upstanding collar and the cuffs.

She, too, shook Lizzie's hand and said, 'I understand you have recently moved to London. How do you like it?'

'I like it *very* much,' Lizzie said. 'We lived in the country before and that was nice, but London is so much more exciting.'

Lady Anne laughed and said, 'A woman after my own heart! Here I am in London again for a few blissful weeks, but then William – my brother, you know, and a heartless tyrant – will want to be going down to the country and I shall have to go with him. I simply *ache* with boredom in the country.'

'William is nothing like a tyrant,' Venetia said, sitting down on a sofa and drawing Henrietta down beside her. Lady Anne and Lizzie took the sofa opposite. 'He's indulgent to a fault. It's only for your sake that he keeps taking the house in St James's Square every year, at Lord knows what expense!'

'Yes, in the hope that he can still marry me off!' She turned to Lizzie again. 'I am a complete disgrace, you know. Can you imagine, nearly twenty-six and not married! A shocking example to set to other young women. Your mama should have been warned before bringing you here. Take me as an awful object lesson, if you will, and promise her not to grow up like me.'

'I should *like* to be like you,' Lizzie said, 'only I don't see how I can. I'm not beautiful.'

'Beauty is a snare and a delusion. Don't they tell you so in church?'

'I think my papa thought so. He was the rector of our village before he died. But he thought all earthly things were snares. He only valued things of the spirit – and the mind, a bit.'

'In what way, a bit?'

'He valued the things of *his* mind, and some other gentlemen's, but not of ladies' minds. He taught me, and I *think* he thought I was clever, but he didn't want me to grow up, because then I'd only be a woman instead of his pupil. But, of course, I can't help growing up, can I? It just happens.'

'It does indeed,' Lady Anne said. 'But you mustn't be ashamed of being a woman, whatever your papa said. Women are just as wonderful as men, only in a different way.'

'I know,' Lizzie said. 'My new papa likes women – especially Mama.'

'Well, that's a fortunate thing!'

'Yes, isn't it? I like him, too. He talks to me like a proper person, and not in that silly way – you know.' She screwed up her face. 'Like some of the people we meet at the Suttons', who put on a silly voice and talk as if one were only three.'

'Yes, I know just what you mean. But I'm afraid that goes on all through life. Men are always telling us we can't do things, and not to bother our pretty heads about this and that. Even my own brother – who's a dear, really – can't think of anything but to get me a husband. I've told him a thousand times I don't want to be married, but he can't see what else you can do with a female.'

Lizzie saw that it was all right for her to laugh. On the other sofa her mother and Lady Venetia were deep in conversation, and did not glance across. 'What *do* you want to do?' she asked this goddess-like creature boldly.

'I want to be like Cousin Venetia, and do something worthwhile, and push back the frontiers for women. A long time ago she said to me that since she was going to be a doctor, I would have to be the one to get the vote for women, because she wouldn't have time. I think she was joking when she said it, but I took her seriously. There are lots of other areas too, where women need more freedom, especially in education and employment, but getting the vote is tied up with all of them.'

Venetia looked across. 'What's this? Are you proselytising that poor child, Fairy? And you've only known her five minutes!'

'We're having an interesting conversation about women's rights. Don't interrupt,' said Anne with dignity.

'Fairy?' Henrietta asked.

Anne made a face. 'It was my father's name for me when I was a tiny child. Nobody calls me that now but Venetia – and she only does it to annoy.'

'Someone has to take a pull on your reins now and then,' Venetia said, 'and William seems to be too much tied up with his wife and children to do it.'

Anne opened her eyes wide. 'But don't you know I *long* for you to take me in hand?'

'Only because you think I'd be too busy to keep a close watch on you, and would let you run wild.'

'Darling, you're so clever! You see through me. But look,' Anne became serious, 'you remember what it was like for you when you wanted to do something more than go to balls and parties. I'm a grown woman, only in William's mind I never get beyond ten. All I want is to live in London all year round. You can't think how deadly it is at Grasscroft. I love William, and I'm devoted to Maria and the children, but they never go anywhere or entertain anyone interesting, and there's *nothing* to do.'

'What are you leading up to, you wicked child?' Venetia asked, narrowing her eyes.

'Only for you to let me live here with you,' Anne said meekly. 'William won't let me live with another girl, but now you're married you count as a respectable chaperone. You've this lovely big house, so you can't say you've no room for me, and William will pay my allowance so I won't be a burden – I'll be a help, in fact. And you needn't really be bothered with chaperoning me. I can look after myself perfectly well. In fact, you need hardly know I'm here.'

Venetia looked at Henrietta and spread her hands ruefully. 'You see what I'm up against. She chooses the moment when you're here to attack me, thinking I won't be able to make a fuss in front of visitors.'

'No, no,' Anne laughed, 'you misjudge me. It just came up in conversation. But of course, had I not known that Cousin Henrietta was one of us, I wouldn't have mentioned it.'

'One of us?' Henrietta queried.

'A believer in equality for women,' Anne said.

'And how, pray, did you know that?' Venetia asked.

'Because I've been talking to Lizzie, of course. "By his works shall ye know him." Won't you throw your weight on my side, Cousin Henrietta?'

Henrietta smiled. 'I can't tell Cousin Venetia how to arrange her household. But I don't blame you for wanting to live in London. I wasn't sure I would like it before I came, but now I'm here, I don't want to leave.'

'There!' said Anne with satisfaction. 'If that's not an endorsement, I don't know what is. Please, Vee, do say yes.'

'I'll talk to William about it,' Venetia said. 'But the decision will be his. He is your guardian, after all.'

'No, darling, only my trustee!'

'Well, it comes to the same thing, doesn't it? He who pays the piper calls the tune. Ah, here's tea.'

Despite being a party to this very grown-up conversation, Lizzie was still girl enough to be deeply impressed by the tea. Even at the juvenile party she had not seen anything to rival the buttered muffins, the anchovy toast, the little French fancy cakes. There was cinnamon toast besides, with plenty of sugar, and dainty little sandwiches, and cream horns and a lovely lemon cake. She was rather afraid that the grown-ups would be too ladylike to eat much, and then she, of course, would have to feign indifference too. But Lady Anne looked as pleased at Lizzie felt and said, 'Oh, lovely! You do have the nicest teas, Vee. Aren't buttered muffins heaven? I could never be unhappy about anything as long as I was eating muffins.'

And Lady Venetia said, 'God bless your appetite! I'm famished myself. I had so many patients this morning I missed luncheon. I didn't even have time to change before you arrived, Henrietta. I hope you forgive me for entertaining you in my "business" suit.'

So it was perfectly all right for Lizzie to tuck in. The conversation was wide-ranging, but when she was eating what she knew, reluctantly, must be her last French fancy, the attention suddenly came round to her again, as Lady Venetia said, 'So, Miss Lizzie, I understand you would like to go to school?'

Lizzie flung a look at her mother, hardly knowing how to answer; Henrietta nodded, to encourage her to speak for herself.

'Well, ma'am,' she said slowly, 'I think I would. I've read *Tom Brown's School Days*, and I think it would be tremendous fun – not the bullying, of course, but the other parts.'

Venetia smiled. 'I don't think it would be quite like that in a girl's school. Is that what you want to go to school for – the fun?'

'Oh, not only that, of course. I really enjoyed my lessons with Mr Chase, before we came to London. He taught me Greek and mathematics, because my cousins' governess didn't know any. He made things so interesting. And although everything in London is exciting, I would like to be an educated woman when I grow up.'

'A woman after my own heart,' Anne said. 'Is there any possibility,' she enquired of Henrietta, 'that she can go to school?'

'Certainly there's a possibility. But I don't know anything about schools, and I don't think I should like her to be boarded away.'

'Oh, no, that would be dreadful,' Anne said. 'But there's no need to think of a boarding school when the biggest girls' school in England is right here in London. You must have heard of the North London Collegiate?' Henrietta and Lizzie both shook their heads. 'But you have heard of the headmistress, Miss Buss? She is a leading light in education for girls. Only Emily Davies is more famous.'

She seemed so certain they must have heard of the lady, that neither liked to say no, and they remained silent and rather shamefaced.

'At any rate,' Anne continued, 'the North London Collegiate is the best girls' school there is, with a proper academic syllabus that prepares girls for examinations. And it's a day school – no boarders. I don't think you could do better.'

Henrietta looked at Venetia, and saw agreement in her eye. 'Would you like to go, Lizzie, if Papa agrees?'

'Oh, yes, please!'

'Very well, I shall ask him, then.'

'Of course,' said Anne innocently, 'education is rather wasted on females. I expect Lizzie will get married straight out of school and that will be that.'

Lizzie turned to her passionately. 'Oh, no, I shan't! I want to earn my own living! I shall *never* get married!'

Anne laughed, but Henrietta said, 'You might spare a thought for me before you swear it, Lizzie. I might like to have grandchildren one day.'

Jerome thought that they could find the fees, and was all in favour of Lizzie having a proper education. 'The sort of man who insists on having an ignorant wife is not worth marrying. It's a paltry attitude. Mary is a much better example of what a woman should be, to my mind. I shall write and ask her if she knows anything about your Miss Buss.'

Mary wrote back that she had indeed heard of Miss Buss.

She and Dorothea Beale and Emily Davies have been the pioneers of women's education these fifteen or twenty years. They are all friends of Mrs Garrett Anderson, so I dare say that's how your Manchester Square ladies know her. I don't know anything of the school in question, but it must be better than the usual 'academies' where girls are taught nothing but how to languish and pout. Plainly Lizzie must do *something*. Better she's equipped to earn her own living – unless *you* mean to find a dowry for her, or keep her at home for ever, which I can't imagine you'll want to do, especially with one of your own on the way. I'm fond of you, brother dear, so if the fees are a problem let me know and I shall be a dutiful aunt and find them out of my income. I don't spend much here in the depths of the country, especially now you don't come any more.

This was not a letter Jerome felt he could show to Henrietta, but he gave her the gist of the first part, and on that recommendation she wrote to the school, describing

Lizzie's previous education and asking for information. A letter came back very promptly describing the fees and hours of study, and saying that Lizzie might enter the school in the autumn, provided she passed the entrance examination.

'Oh, I'm so glad it won't be until the autumn,' Henrietta said.

And Lizzie said, 'Entrance examination? Oh dear, I shall really be up against it!'

'You will if you talk such slang,' Henrietta reproved her. 'But never mind, dear, you can only do your best. Don't worry about it.'

'May I go and tell Emma?' Lizzie asked, and dashed away downstairs.

She found Emma in the kitchen cleaning silver and singing a song which, though lugubrious, had the right rhythm for rubbing. 'Satan is glad, when I am bad, and hopes that I, with him shall lie, in fire and chains, and dreadful pains.'

She left off and listened to Lizzie's bubbling news, and then said, 'Well, I am glad for you! Going to school, eh? And what'll they learn you there?'

'Oh, everything, I dare say,' Lizzie said, with a wide gesture. 'Only I have to pass an examination first. I shall have to cram and cram.'

'Why, won't they give you anything to eat?' Emma asked.

Lizzie laughed. 'Cram books, I mean. Study.'

'Think of reading books one after another!' Emma said. 'There! If you get any cleverer, we s'll have to pay to talk to you.' And she sang again, to the same tune, '"I'm such a fool, there is no school, that could teach me, for any fee." 'F I was like you, I'd read books too.'

Lizzie hugged her. 'I think you're perfect as you are. And no-one sings better than you.'

On the appointed afternoon, Henrietta and Lizzie took a series of omnibuses to Camden Town. 'It's a long way,' Henrietta said doubtfully as the omnibus crawled along through the usual London traffic.

'It would be much quicker on the underground train,'

Lizzie said. 'I could take the Inner Circle to Euston and then walk. It's only a mile from there.'

'How do you know that?'

'I asked Papa,' Lizzie said simply. 'I'd much sooner go on the train. I think it's lovely!'

'Lovely?' Henrietta said, amused at the adjective. 'Well, I think perhaps you'll have to go that way. You'll be late every single day if you go by omnibus.'

The school was a large, grim-looking building, of which every door seemed to be shut tight. But Lizzie spotted some steps leading down into the basement, which had 'Pupils' Entrance' over them, and holding hands tightly they ventured down. The corridor in which they found themselves had a stone floor and glazed tiles halfway up the walls, which made their footsteps echo in an accusatory way. They were very relieved when an ample-figured and motherly looking woman appeared round a corner, walking briskly.

Henrietta cleared her throat nervously and explained their mission.

'Yes, of course, we were expecting you. I am Miss Biggar. We are rather late, I fear,' she added sternly.

Henrietta, feeling as if she were a new girl too, humbly explained the matter.

'Yes, I see,' said Miss Biggar. She looked down at Lizzie. 'Well, dear, you must allow ample time for your journey if you are accepted into the school. We do not allow lateness.'

'Oh, yes, ma'am, I shall come on the train,' Lizzie said eagerly. 'You see—'

'Yes, dear, very well,' Miss Biggar interrupted. 'Now just sit down in here while I take your mother to the waiting-room, and then I shall bring you the papers.'

She ushered Lizzie into a room furnished with two or three desks and chairs and nothing else, except for a row of coat hooks along one wall, and a sink in the corner with a tap that dripped. Lizzie chose a desk and sat, then changed her mind and moved to another. She felt very nervous. Some tremendous feat of intellect was going to be demanded of her, and she feared to fail. This was the best school in England, and the strictest. She tried to remember the content of the last lesson she had had with Mr Chase and found her mind distressingly blank. She could not even remember how to decline a fourth-declension noun in Latin.

Hollow footsteps sounded outside in the corridor and the door opened abruptly to admit Miss Biggar, who placed sheets of paper, ink and pens in front of Lizzie, and then handed her several sheets of questions. 'Answer them in any order you like, dear,' she said, 'and write your name at the top of each page. I shall leave you now and come back in a little while.'

Nervously Lizzie drew the first sheet towards her. It was a series of arithmetical problems, and as she read through them, her heart started to pound and her hands grew damp – not with fear, but with excitement. Why, these were easy! Ridiculously easy! The answers were popping into her head even as she read, and she was frantic to start writing them down.

She lost all sense of time as she wrote and wrote, ink spreading up her fingers and transferring itself to her face as she absently scratched her nose. *List the Kings and Queens of England, in order, with dates, from Edward the Confessor to the present day.* She could have chanted them in her sleep. *In your own words, explain what causes the tides.* Papa – her first papa – had been very interested in astronomy, and had taught her all about the planets. She drew diagrams of the earth and the moon, and then, carried away with enthusiasm, drew another of the rest of the solar system, joined by a series of beautiful concentric rings.

And here was a blank map of Africa with the instruction to fill in all she knew. Africa! Ever since Mama had married her new papa, she had been interested in Africa. He had told her lots of tales of his journeys there, and on many an evening they had pored over the atlas together. She was still filling in mountains and rivers when Miss Biggar came back and said, 'You must stop now, dear.'

Lizzie put down the pen, feeling a wave of reaction sweep over her like weariness.

Miss Biggar collected together the papers and looked

surprised. 'Why, what a lot you've written.' She glanced down a page, and then another, and her eyebrows went up. She didn't say 'very good', but it was implicit in her expression, and in her tone of voice. Then, having set the papers aside, she brought forward a small sewing-box, and said, 'Now just make me a buttonhole, dear, and then we'll be done.'

Cold air seemed to trickle down Lizzie's back. 'I'm afraid I don't know how.'

'You don't know how?' Miss Biggar seemed astonished.

'I didn't know they were made. I thought they – were just *in* things,' Lizzie said.

Miss Biggar threw up her hands in shock. 'A great girl of your age, not know how to make a buttonhole! I've never heard of such a thing.'

Lizzie looked at the ground, miserably. 'Does that mean I can't come to the school?'

'Well, we shall see. I can't say at once. But you must go home and learn how to make a buttonhole, and then come back this day week and let me see you make it. It's a rule of the school that no girl may enter who cannot make a buttonhole. Now come along, and I'll take you back to your mother.'

Henrietta's heart sank when she saw Lizzie's drooping head and miserable face, but on the way out, when she heard the reason for the despondency, she brightened up. 'Is that all it is? I can teach you that. Our old nurse taught all of us girls that sort of thing while we were still in the nursery, but of course you've never had a nurse or a governess in the usual way. It isn't difficult. With a week to practise, you'll have it off perfectly. But what an odd thing to ask.'

'She said it was a rule of the school.'

'But what about the examination? Were the questions hard?'

They were outside now in the mild grey afternoon, and Lizzie felt her spirits surge upwards with release. 'No, they were easy. Quite piffling, really! No Latin or Greek; no mathematics, only arithmetic. Oh, and they asked about

Africa – wasn't that lucky? I'm so glad you married Papa! Suppose you'd married someone who'd been to India instead.'

Henrietta laughed too. 'We've both had a lucky escape.'

Lizzie returned to the school alone a week later. 'Of course I shan't get lost! And I shall have to go on my own if I get in, shan't I?'

It thrilled her to travel alone on the underground railway, and the walk up the long straight road from the station seemed full of interest. One day soon, she thought, I shall know every shop and house along here, perhaps every crack in the pavement. Her elation was a little subdued as she approached the grim-looking building and went down the stairs again to the echoing basement; but everything was as easy as could be. She was conducted into the same room, given a piece of calico and needle and thread, made a buttonhole and was dismissed.

A few days later a letter came from the school, signed by Miss Buss herself, saying that Lizzie might enter the school after the summer recess. She must agree to obey all regulations while on school premises, must attend on time every day ('lateness is *not* permitted'), and must dress plainly, with no unnecessary ornament. Enclosed was a list of equipment and books that would be required, and a bill for the fees, 'which must be paid in advance before the beginning of term'.

'It sounds more like a convent than a school,' Jerome said when he read it. 'Are you sure you still want to go there, Lizzie? We could find you a nunnery instead, if you liked.'

'Oh, no, I really, *really* want to go! Please! May I?'

'Well, if you insist,' he said gravely. 'I expect your mother will be able to manage without you.'

What with one thing and another, the problem of Morland Place and finding a suitable caretaker for it went out of Teddy's head. When he did remember it was always at some unsuitable time – like in bed just as he was falling asleep, or at dinner just as the waiter was carving the rare side of the sirloin – a moment when he couldn't do anything about it; and by the time he was in a position to act, he had forgotten again.

It was brought forcibly to his mind one day in June when his manservant came to him as he was dressing for dinner and said, with a look of deepest disapproval, that there was a person at the door asking to see him.

'What sort of person?' Teddy asked.

'A female person, sir,' said Waller.

'I can't see anybody now,' Teddy said indignantly, struggling with his studs. 'I'm going to the club. Meeting Travis and Dr Havergill. You know that.'

'I tried to send her away, sir, but she was most insistent, and rather than have a disturbance on the doorstep . . .'

Teddy looked perplexed. 'But what does she *want*? I don't know her, do I, Waller?'

'She would not tell me what she wanted, sir,' Waller said, and the reason for his disapproval followed, 'but she is carrying a baby in her arms.'

Teddy's conscience in that regard was so clear that for a moment he did not realise what Waller was thinking. Then his eyebrows shot up, and he said, 'Not want a disturbance on the doorstep? Damn your impudence! If you weren't such a good servant, Waller, I'd give you your warning!'

'I beg pardon, sir.'

'Where have you put this female?'

'In the business-room.'

'Very well, I'll go down and see what she wants. Some charitable case, I suppose.'

The business-room was the room from which Serena Makepeace – the benefactress who had first given the house to the Morlands – had conducted business, and since Teddy had no business but enjoying himself, it was never used now, and had been left pretty much the way it had been at her death. It had a massive desk, some cupboards and a few hard chairs, and a large and gloomy painting over the fireplace of Salome being presented with the head of John the Baptist on a platter. The head had its eyes rolled up and its mouth open and was plentifully bedaubed with gouts of blood of the apparent consistency of raspberry jam. It was impossible to sit anywhere without facing it, so as a waiting-room this dour chamber was an excellent exactor of penance.

Teddy reached the open door and found his visitor staring at St John in awful fascination, but she turned as he approached and got to her feet. It was Alice Bone. She was pale and looked thin, and had obviously been crying. She was holding her little boy in her arms and had a bag on the floor beside her, and Teddy's heart sank. It was not hard even for him to deduce the situation from these observations. But, deuce take it, what was it to him? And to come at *this* time of night, when he was about to go to dinner with two of his most agreeable friends!

'Oh, sir! Oh, Mr Morland!'

'Yes, yes, Alice. There there. Calm yourself. What's the matter?'

'Oh, sir, my father – he's cast me out! He never did approve – well, you know – and there were terrible rows, nearly every day, and Mam worn out with it. But now it's all come to a head and he vows he won't have me in the house, or my little Edward, and says he never wants to see us again, and, oh, sir, if you are not kind to us I don't know what I shall do!'

She began to cry again. In the hall the long-case clock struck the three-quarters. Just time for him to walk down to the club. If he didn't go now, he would be late.

'Well, well, that's most unfortunate. Can't you go and ask him to take you back? I'm sure he would if you said you were sorry and promised not to do it again, whatever it was.'

'I can't, sir! I can't go back there. Father's been angry since the first day I went home. He only took me because you asked, and he never liked it. It's been terrible there, sir, with Father on at me day and night, and Mam in tears half the time. Now he says he was wrong to take me and it's encouraging sin to be kind to girls like me. He says I should be whipped at the cart's tail rather than housed and fed by decent folk. He won't have me back no matter what, and it was so bad I'd nearly rather lie down in a ditch than go even if he'd have me, if it wasn't for little Edward.' All this was splurged out through tears as thick and copious as St John's blood, and the baby, who had been placidly surveying his surroundings from his mother's arms, began to grow upset and seemed to be preparing to add his wails to hers.

Teddy felt helpless in the face of female tears. He had had the usual youthful adventures, but women's emotions worried and puzzled him, and since he had left university he had avoided them as much as possible. He had an arrangement with a nice, obliging little person in York, who treated the whole thing as a business transaction, and was pleased to see him when he came but never made the slightest fuss when he left, and would have been as perplexed as him had any question of feelings arisen. As a matter of fact, he didn't go and see her all that often now. Food, he had found, was a much more reliable pleasure.

So to have this distraught and weeping woman inside his own house, invading his citadel, was very upsetting. And now Alice added, as her final plea, the killing stroke, 'Oh, please help me, sir. It's not for myself, but for the child. What's to become of him, sir? He is your brother's son.'

Aware of Waller hovering somewhere behind him in the hall, Teddy said hastily, 'Well, well, don't cry, there's a good girl. Something will be done, I promise you. Look here, really, don't cry – you're upsetting Edward. He's grown since I saw him last. Quite a little man now, isn't he? How old is he?'

Alice made a great effort to control herself and managed to say, 'Eight months, sir.' She fumbled with her free hand in a pocket and produced a handkerchief and blew her nose.

'Well, look here, Alice,' Teddy said, aware of the clock's inexorable ticking, 'this is not the time to talk about it. I have to go out. You can stay here for the night and we'll think what to do in the morning. Yes, yes, very well. Don't thank me. Just go with Waller, here. Waller!'

The manservant came forward from where he had been fiddling with things on the hall table, his ears out on stalks.

'Take Alice to Mrs Cox and tell her to see she's made comfortable. Something to eat, I dare say, and milk or something for the baby. She'll know what's what. And they're to be found somewhere to sleep for the night.'

'Yes, sir,' Waller said, his face stationary and his mind busy. 'Which room, sir?'

'Oh, I leave that to you and Mrs Cox,' Teddy said hastily. 'Off you go now. I must get along myself.' He turned away, and then called the departing Waller back so as to address him out of Alice's earshot. 'Put 'em as far away from me as possible. Aren't there spare rooms in the attics?'

'Yes sir. There is a spare servant's bedroom.'

'That'll do, then. It will only be for one night, I hope. Tell Mrs Cox I'm sorry for the extra work.'

And with that he made his escape, just as the overtaxed nerves of his nephew and namesake gave way, and a penetrating juvenile wail broke the peace of the house.

By the next morning, opinion among the servants had divided itself sharply over Alice and her child. Mrs Cox, the cook-housekeeper, was a sentimental soul and had been won over by Edward's shy smile. She was outraged that Waller should so have misjudged his master as to think Alice was an entanglement of *his*, and was therefore all the more determined to see noble generosity in Teddy's action. Waller was relieved that Teddy was not the culprit, but in that case saw no need for him to risk any misunderstanding on the subject. Besides, he tended to take Mr Bone's attitude that fallen women should be punished and outlawed *pour décourager les autres*. Alice was a loose woman and should be made to feel the full weight of society's disapprobation. Sarah, the housemaid, agreed, with a frisson of interested horror, that Alice was beyond redemption, but thought the little baby was sweet and that it wasn't *his* fault, the duck. Master should throw out the woman but keep the little boy. After all, master was his uncle, when all was said and done. Waller told her to keep her ignorant opinions to herself as befitted her inferior position, and Sarah subsided resentfully, feeling it was not playing fair for him to pull rank in an intellectual argument. She confined herself to observing *sotto voce* from time to time that blood *was* blood when all was said and done.

Teddy woke from a well-deserved and peaceful slumber at nine o'clock and rang for his breakfast tray. It was a long time in coming, and when it arrived showed all the evidence of having been assembled hastily. When he turned pained eyes up to his manservant, Waller set his lips in their most uncompromising line and said, 'There is somewhat of a rumpus in the kitchen this morning, sir. Routines have been disrupted. Mrs Cox has been put behind trying to feed an egg to the child.'

Teddy stared a moment uncomprehendingly, and then memory flooded back. 'Good God, yes, the child! Well, not to worry. I have come up with the perfect solution to that problem. Tell Alice that I will speak to her in the morning-room directly I come downstairs.'

Breakfasting, reading the papers, bathing and dressing followed their normal course, and just after eleven Teddy went downstairs and into the morning-room, where he found Alice, very nervous and erect, supervising the baby as he sat on the floor playing with his toes and the fringe of the carpet.

'Good morning, Alice. Did you sleep well?' he asked cheerfully.

'Oh, sir, yes, sir, thank you,' Alice began breathlessly, 'but I'm afraid I've upset your servants, sir. At least Mr Waller says – that is, I don't think they like me to be here.'

'Never mind 'em,' Teddy said. 'I'm master in my own house and I shall do as I think fit. And in any case, I've come up with a plan for you. How would you like to go back to Morland Place?'

'Oh, sir!'

It was hard to tell from Alice's expression what she thought of the idea, but Teddy chose to take it as approval. 'I need someone to live there and take care of it. The work will be light enough. Just do a little cleaning, and light fires in each of the rooms in rotation to keep the damp at bay. And look out for any repairs that need doing, and report them to me. Gatson, who used to be the estate carpenter, lives nearby and he can turn his hand to most things. I've a mind to see if he would like the work of patching up whatever needs patching. These little repairs are nothing if they're kept on top of, but let them run away and before you know it the house is a ruin. So what do you say? You'll have a roof over your head and I'll pay you – let's see – twenty pounds a year besides. You'll have to provide your own food out of that, but you can have whatever you want out of the kitchen garden, and you can always keep a few hens in the orchard.'

'It's a big house, sir,' Alice said at last.

'What of it? A sensible girl like you won't mind that.' He thought briefly of the ghosts, but then dismissed the idea. They wouldn't bother Alice – she wasn't a Morland. 'Lots of room for your little boy to run about. And it's not far to Woodhouse Farm in an emergency, or even Huntsham.'

Alice thought of living alone in the huge house so far from anywhere, of the emptiness and the dark at night, the echoing chapel, the bare yard with its melancholy tang of horses past; of the long walk from the kitchen to any living room across the great hall with its rearing spaces into which candle- or even lamp-light could only penetrate a few feet. Houses made noises, especially at night when you couldn't sleep and had nothing to do but listen to them. And she thought – though she didn't want to – of all the stories she had heard while she was a housemaid there, of tragedies and ghosts and strange goings-on.

But what choice did she have? On the one hand here was a home for her and her son and twenty pounds a year besides, and on the other the workhouse, shame, separation from the child and probably early death.

'You're very kind, sir,' she said. 'I'm very grateful to you, and I'll try to keep everything nice.'

'Good! Excellent! Well, I think if you go over there today and see if there's anything you need to set yourself up – I don't know what's left in the way of bedsheets and cooking-pots and so on – you can get them this afternoon and then move in tomorrow. Mrs Cox or Sarah can look after the child while you do that. Oh, and you'll need to check on the state of the coal-cellar. I don't imagine the creditors took the coal but you never can tell. I ought to go over myself some time and take an inventory, but I have a rather pressing engagement today so it will have to be another time.'

'Sir, what must I do for money – if I do need sheets or anything?'

'Oh, Lord, yes, I was forgetting. Well, look here, make a list and bring it back to Waller, and he can go with you and buy everything – I have accounts at most of the shops in York. And you'll need some food items as well. What say I give you an advance on the first quarter's wages? Will two pounds do?'

Such generosity brought tears to Alice's eyes, and she began to thank him stumblingly and ever more moistly until he managed to make his escape.

BOOK TWO

Oenone

The days have slain the days
And the seasons have gone by,
And brought me Summer again;
And here on the grass I lie
As erst I lay and was glad
Ere I meddled with right and with wrong.

William Morris: *The Half of Life Gone*

CHAPTER EIGHT

Life was very pleasant to Henrietta. She had settled in now, and the house was comfortable. She enjoyed the daily domestic routines of shopping, supervising the servants, 'parlour work' and the cleaning of special items, which she undertook herself. There always seemed to be plenty to do, even without the extras of entertaining, visiting, and receiving callers. An increased social life meant more clothes, too, which meant visits to Madame Tessier and Harvey Nichols, and making things on the sewing-machine for Lizzie.

The servants were working out well for her. Emma continued to be a tower of strength, and very funny besides. There was the occasional violent outburst from Sarah, usually followed by floods of tears from Emily, and Edie was lethargic and needed to be chivvied; but on the whole Henrietta had little to complain about with her staff. The small crises that occurred from time to time – the laundry mislaying a shirt, a stray cat getting into the kitchen and licking the butter, a broken plate that no-one would admit to (with bitter recriminations all round), the kitchen sink blocking up – did not upset her. She actually enjoyed coping with them. In her previous marriage these things had never come to her attention. She had not been allowed to run her own house, everything being done by the housekeeper, who guarded her domain jealously. Life then had been very dull: it never was now.

Jerome was amused to see how much she enjoyed the domestic life. 'Playing house' was what he called it.

'Whenever it ceases to amuse you and you want more servants, let me know,' he said to her affectionately. 'I don't want you turning into a drudge.' But that was far from the case. They had regular dinner parties, saw many of the new plays, and, under guidance from the Hazelmeres, went to concerts, too. The Albert Hall was only just down the road, and there and at the Italian Opera House and various recital venues, Henrietta heard Clara Schumann and Franz Liszt; Albeniz and Patti; Joachim, Hofmann, Henschel, Rossi and Ribero.

Inevitably, much of Henrietta's time was taken up with visiting and being visited – 'calling', as it was known. Partly through Marion Sutton and partly through Jerome's acquaintances, she now had quite a long calling list, and methodically made a note of each lady's 'at home' day. Marion's was Thursday, for instance, Mrs Alma-Tadema's Monday, Mrs Burnand's Friday, Mrs Rider Haggard's Wednesday. Henrietta made Tuesday her day, and rarely had fewer than half a dozen visitors.

Alec Macdonald, the botanist, was a frequent caller, and she concluded that, having spent so much of his life travelling, he was short of friends in Town. He seemed rather a lonely man. When the Hensmans invited her and Jerome to dinner, Henrietta was glad to find Mr Macdonald also a guest, he having met Mrs Hensman again at Henrietta's house. She felt she had done him some good by extending his acquaintance; and Mrs Hensman confided that *she* was extremely glad to have met *him*. 'Presentable bachelors are such a prize, my dear. And any new person Dr Hensman doesn't think a fool is doubly so.'

Lizzie was now of an age to go with Henrietta when she went to pay her calls, and was happy to do so when they went to see 'interesting' people. Lizzie liked to go where the conversation was 'clever'. She did not so much enjoy visiting the Sutton set, who she thought were dull compared with the artists, writers and politicians. But visits to and by the Suttons were inevitably frequent, and Minnie Sutton was generally agreed to be Lizzie's 'particular friend'. Marion Sutton's closest friend, a Mrs Roughley, was regularly encountered at the Sutton house, and was on Henrietta's list. She had two daughters, Thelma and Julia, of fourteen and fifteen, whom Lizzie liked, and who were much closer to being her best friends in her own estimation than Minnie.

Relations between Henrietta and Marion remained cordial, and Henrietta was at pains to keep them that way, given that their husbands were so dependent on each other, and even seemed to enjoy each other's company, going riding in Hyde Park together, and to cricket matches – Dickie's passion. The only awkwardness that ever arose was caused by Marion's jealousy of Henrietta's friendship with Venetia. Marion so desperately wanted to rise, and it irked her that Henrietta, her *protégée*, should so effortlessly have 'got herself into' a titled circle when Marion herself had no titled friends. Whenever Henrietta mentioned that she had been to see Venetia, or that she and Jerome had gone to a concert or to dinner with the Hazelmeres, the struggle to remain civil was visible in Marion's face. Out of tact, Henrietta did her best not to bring up the subject, but Marion could not leave it alone, and would ask the question direct, to which Henrietta could not lie. And if she missed calling on Marion for several days, or was obliged to refuse an invitation, or was out when Marion called, Marion would inevitably attribute it to the Hazelmere connection. When they next met she would say, 'I suppose you were busy with your illustrious cousin,' or some other remark to that effect. Henrietta felt sometimes that Marion thought she should have introduced her to Venetia, but of course it was not for her to do so, as Marion must know quite well. But it was a small awkwardness in the grand scheme of her happy life, and Henrietta felt that it was as well to have at least one cause for complaint, so as not to tempt fate.

At the house in Manchester Square she met a different kind of person. Being a working woman, Venetia did not have 'at home' days, but when she was expecting anyone interesting to call, she would send a note round to Henrietta. She (and Lizzie) met Mrs Garrett Anderson and her sister Mrs Fawcett, Miss Emily Davies, Lady Frances Balfour and Miss Lydia Becker, Mr Stansfeld and Tommy Weston –

people whose lives were given in one way or another to improving the lot of women.

Lady Anne Farraline was often there, and called at Thornton Place, too; and she and Lizzie struck up a friendship, despite the difference in their ages. Lizzie rather worshipped her, but Anne was too down to earth for it to do Lizzie much harm. As the weather improved and Henrietta's condition led to a reduction in her mobility, Anne frequently called to take Lizzie out to exhibitions, lectures and so on, while Henrietta rested at home.

Lizzie had also struck up a friendship with Blandy, the hot-chestnut man. It began with her looking out for him and running out to talk to him whenever he passed. Henrietta was grateful to him for his help that first day, and did not discourage her; and when she discovered that he had handyman skills in other fields, she sometimes called him in to do small jobs for her. It transpired that he lived quite close by, just across the other side of the High Street where the poorer, meaner houses from a previous age had not yet been demolished to make way for better. One day Lizzie met Blandy in the High Street when she was on her way alone to the shops, and he invited her home to meet his wife, who was bedridden. After that she often called in when she was nearby; Henrietta saw it as charitable work and allowed it. Mrs Blandy was very cheerful in her disability, but she had been a proud housewife. Lying all day looking at a crooked table-runner or forgotten dead flowers in a vase was a subtle torture, and she 'didn't like to nag poor Blandy', who had enough to do to make them a living. So she was glad to let Lizzie dust and tidy for her. During their conversations it transpired that Mrs Blandy had also been a first-rate needlewoman, and after that Lizzie was able to take her sewing jobs from Henrietta, which helped the family budget and allowed her to feel less dependent.

Summer came, and with it at last some warm weather – though warm weather in London, Henrietta discovered, was not a thing that brought unalloyed pleasure. Chimneys, both domestic and factory, still belched out smoke night and day, and as the air warmed up it gave rise to summer fogs, thick, yellow and enveloping, making some mornings as dark as winter. The mixed smell of sulphur and horse manure – the natural perfume of London – was even more unpleasant in warm weather than in cold, and Henrietta could understand now why Londoners fled the capital as soon as the Season was over, if they possibly could.

The movement was not all one way, however. At the end of June Amy and Patsy telegraphed their intention to visit. Henrietta was surprised that they should want to come, especially at that time of year, but not displeased. She had hoped to be asked to the Red House at some time in the summer to see the new baby, but no invitation had been forthcoming. At least a visit from the girls would bring some news.

When the girls arrived, there was a further surprise: Mary was with them.

'How lovely! But I wasn't expecting to see you,' Henrietta said, as she kissed her.

'Weren't you?' Mary said. 'I thought it was understood. I hope I shan't be in the way?'

'Good heavens, no,' Henrietta said hastily. In her head she quickly revised plans. Lizzie could sleep in the nursery and Mary could have Lizzie's room. The turkey would easily go round, and perhaps Sarah would have time to make some little tarts – strawberries were plentiful and Emily could run out and buy some for a filling, with whipped cream . . . 'It's lovely to see you. We have some excellent company for you tonight. The Burnands are coming to dinner. And the Westons – he's an MP, and they're both interested in better housing for the poor. And perhaps I can ask Mr Macdonald, to make the numbers even.'

'My, what a giddy life you lead nowadays,' Mary said. 'What a good thing I packed my best frock.' The twins were giggling together, and there was something in Mary's expression that gave Henrietta the feeling they all knew something she didn't, but she had too much on her mind to worry about it.

But all was soon revealed to her. When they reached home,

Henrietta had refreshments served while she hastily despatched Edie to prepare Lizzie's room for Mary. Then the travellers went up to their rooms to rest a little; but Patsy was soon down again and sought out Henrietta in the dining-room where she was counting out silver and inspecting napkins.

'I have to tell you – I can't keep it a secret any longer!' she burst out. 'Jerome wanted to surprise you but I don't think it's fair you should be the only one who doesn't know.'

'Know what? Is it something nice?'

'Nice? It's *splendid*! I've been corresponding with Mr Burnand ever since January, and sending him my work, and now he has written to say he thinks he might be able to employ me on his magazine.'

'Employ you?' Henrietta was dumbfounded.

'Yes – isn't it a lark? He liked my drawing when I showed it to him here, and I wrote when we got back home and asked if he could use anything of mine, and that I liked to do humorous sketches. He wrote back and said a cartoonist had to be able to draw on any subject, to order. Then I wrote and said I could do that, and he sent me a test – four things I had to draw for him, on subjects he'd chosen. I did those, and sent him two more that I'd thought of for myself on things I'd read in the papers, and he said they were very good and just what he needed, and that he'd like to see me and talk about it. So I wrote and told Jerome and he arranged it.'

She came breathlessly to the end, and Henrietta said rather blankly, 'I didn't know about any of this.'

'No, well, I asked Jerome not to tell you, because there's a small difficulty. I shall have to live in London, and I haven't told Perry yet. I know he's going to make a fuss about it, and say it's impossible.'

'But why shouldn't I know?'

'Because I thought you might feel bad about keeping a secret from Reggie, you being so very *good*, you see, and one couldn't tell Reggie and hope to keep it from Perry. She'd just blurt it out.'

Henrietta felt obscurely hurt to have been left out – though it ought to be a compliment to be thought too good to practise even so benign a dishonesty. She also felt that Regina had been misjudged: she was quite capable of keeping a secret. However, she put those feelings aside and said, 'I'm very pleased for you, but if Perry's against it, how will you manage?'

'I don't know yet,' Patsy said carelessly. 'We'll have to see. I think if we present him with a *fait accompli*, he's bound to see sense.'

'Amy would come to London too?'

'Of course,' said Patsy, as if the question weren't worth asking. 'And, after all, we're not green girls, and we've travelled in far wilder places than London. It's nonsense to put that sort of dull propriety before actual physical danger, don't you think?'

'Well, yes and no. I can see his point,' Henrietta said cautiously. 'You and Amy wouldn't think of living alone, surely?'

'That's a contradiction in terms, isn't it?'

'You know what I mean. Two unmarried girls living together without a chaperone . . .'

Patsy sighed. 'We're over thirty, you know!'

'Yes, it's just that you seem much younger,' Henrietta said. 'And somehow, unmarried ladies living alone—'

'Well, never mind now,' Patsy said hastily. 'Just be glad for me about *Punch* wanting to take my work. It's so exciting! I don't think a female Parke has ever earned a shilling in all of history. Won't it make Perry's eyes pop?'

'Modern times,' said Jerome when they were dressing for dinner. His voice was strained because his neck was stretched as he tried to fasten his collar stud. 'Things are changing. I should have thought you of all people would welcome the change.'

'I do, of course I do,' Henrietta said. 'Why shouldn't women earn money by using the skills God gave them? It just seems—'

'Yes?'

She searched her feelings. 'Rather hard on Perry,' she concluded, 'to be doing it behind his back.'

Jerome abandoned his recalcitrant stud and came to put his arms round her. 'Bless you! Always so tender for other people's feelings. But with people like Perry it's always wise to play from strength. And Patsy's quite right – two females who've travelled through Italy and Egypt, not to mention South Africa, can surely be trusted in the most civilised capital in the world?'

'Of course. It was never a question of not trusting them. Here, let me,' Henrietta said, and tackled his stud. When it was in, she reached up and kissed him, and said, 'I hope our baby grows up as handsome as you.'

'What if he's a she?'

'Phooey! Do you think I'd give you anything but a son? First time, anyway. Will you fasten my pearls for me?'

Dinner was a great success. Frank Burnand was an intelligent, amusing man, and his wife Rosie, who had been an actress before her marriage (how Perry would stare if he knew that, Henrietta thought guiltily) was the merriest creature, full of fun and energy and invention. Mr Macdonald seemed a different person in this company from the shy, rather melancholy man who so often sat in silence, sucking the head of his stick, in Henrietta's drawing-room. He not only grew animated, but exhibited a vein of frivolity she would not have suspected in him. And the Westons (he was a sort of cousin of Venetia's and therefore, Henrietta supposed, of hers) were nice, plain people, very straightforward and pleasant. After dinner Henrietta had a long conversation with Mrs Weston about children (she had a large family) while Mr Weston talked politics to Mary with some animation.

Later she found herself beside Mrs Burnand, and the conversation turned to the summer vacation of London. 'Have you something in plan?' Mrs Burnand asked, and when Henrietta said she hadn't, she went on, 'You have not yet experienced an August in London, I believe?'

'No, I've always lived in the country until now,' Henrietta said. 'The idea of going away in the summer is new to me.'

'Then I really must urge you to consider it – especially

in your delicate state of health. You can't imagine how nasty London is – how airless.'

'Our friends the Suttons have invited Lizzie to stay with them. They and the Roughleys always go to Margate for three months, until the end of September. They have children Lizzie's age, so it will be nice for her to have the company.'

'Then you have only yourself to worry about,' said Mrs Burnand. 'Let me persuade you to take a house in Ramsgate. Frank and I always go there. It's quieter than Margate, and very pleasant, with lovely gardens and squares, a theatre, and excellent company. The nicest people seem to take their holidays there.'

Henrietta was struck by the idea. With Lizzie away, the house would be too quiet, and the thought of fresh sea air was very appealing. 'How does one manage it?' she asked.

'One shuts up one's London house and takes one's own servants, so it's very comfortable. And the great advantage of Ramsgate for the gentlemen is that the train to London takes less than two hours, so it's perfectly possible for them to go up every day. I would never be able to get Frank away on any other terms, and I must admit I shouldn't care to have to go away without him.'

Henrietta agreed. It had been her one last doubt on the subject.

'There are lots of excellent houses for rent,' Mrs Burnand concluded. 'I can give you the names of some people to write to.' Henrietta promised to speak to Jerome about it, and Mrs Burnand said, 'I expect Frank will have mentioned it already. He likes to secure good company when he can.'

When the coffee cups had been cleared away the conversation became general, and when the subject arose of the twins' coming to live in London, there was no dissenting voice.

'Things are much easier in that respect nowadays,' Mrs Burnand said. 'And it's not as if they would be without friends near at hand.'

'No indeed,' said Mr Macdonald eagerly.

'A neat house in a quiet street in a respectable area,' said Mr Burnand, 'would cause no outrage, I'm sure.'

Jerome looked across and caught his sister's eye. 'And to make assurance doubly sure,' he said, 'why doesn't Mary come and live with them?'

She laughed at him. 'You're casting me in the role of chaperone, are you? Am I such an old maid that I must be respectable?'

'I'm sure he couldn't have meant that,' Mr Weston jumped in gallantly.

'Certainly not,' Jerome said, but with a grin. 'I merely meant that there's safety in numbers. Could you bear to give up your rural retreat for life in the Metropolis, sister dear?'

She laid a dramatic hand to her breast. 'For the sake of my dear cousins, I could even undertake that privation!'

Mrs Burnand laughed. 'I can see I'm not the only actress in the present company. How long has this been decided amongst you?'

'If you could tell it was already decided, my acting skills have failed,' Mary said.

'I think it's a splendid idea,' Mr Macdonald said. 'And with three such elegant ladies in residence, I predict this neat house, wherever it may be, will be the most popular in Town.'

'Hear, hear,' said Tommy Weston. 'I hope we shall all be invited to call, having been the first to offer our moral support.'

Mary and the twins stayed a week, looking at houses, and finally agreed on one to rent from mid-September. It was on Eaton Gate, near Sloane Square, so not too far from Jerome and Henrietta, but closer to the centre of London and therefore more elegant. The house came on a recommendation from Tommy Weston, who with his wife and family had recently moved to Belgrave Square. The Eaton Gate house belonged to the same landlord. The Westons were pleased that they would be living 'just round the corner'.

'Mrs W hoped I would drop in often,' Mary confided to Jerome, 'but I can't see myself doing so. She is a good creature but dull. Too many children, you know. He is amusing, though.'

'Well, I'm glad you aren't too far from us,' Jerome said, 'and though I couldn't call it "just round the corner", I hope you'll drop in often on *us*.'

'I'm glad you chose this side of the Park,' Henrietta said cheerfully. 'The Suttons are always praising Bayswater and urging us to move.'

Mary raised an eyebrow. 'My dear Henrietta, I may not be a Londoner, but I do know that nobody who is anybody would choose Bayswater over Kensington.'

Henrietta laughed. 'Oh dear, you sounded just like her. I'm so glad Jerome and I got it right, though it was the sheerest luck!'

'Luck she calls it!' Jerome said, in offended tones. 'You have no faith in me.'

When the guests had departed for Yorkshire, armed with their campaign for persuading Perry, it was time for Henrietta to start preparations for going away. Lizzie was excited about her trip to Margate, and in particular with the promise that she should be allowed to sea-bathe. Henrietta made her a bathing-costume, and a new seaside outfit of a blue serge skirt and pink blouse together with a little sailor-hat, in which, Jerome said generously, she looked 'at least sixteen', much to Lizzie's delight.

For her own departure, Henrietta had to let Emma and Edie do most of the packing, for she was very large now and found bending tiresome. She wanted no new seaside clothes for herself – where was the point, when they would not fit her for long? – and ached only to be out of the city's heat. It would have been nice, she thought, to have gone back to Yorkshire, to spend the last month of her pregnancy on a sofa in a shaded room with Regina, holding the new baby and chatting comfortably; but that was not to be.

On the day itself, the servants went off by an early train so as to be able to settle in and have everything ready for her, and Henrietta went down by the two-thirty. Jerome took the afternoon off to escort her, and as they headed out through the grimy suburbs and at last into open country, Henrietta felt herself revive. It was lovely to see lushness again, rolling hills, the darkness of trees and hedges against the yellow-buff of harvest fields. At Ramsgate the railway station was right on the sea front, and as soon as she stepped down from the train she could smell the sea, and noted that the birds perched on the station roof were not pigeons but seagulls.

The house they had rented, on Rosie Burnand's recommendation, was not large, but had a good-sized drawing-room, and a morning-room on the cool side of the house. It was pretty and bright, recently decorated, and though you could not see the sea from any of its windows, you could hear it at night, when the town was quiet. Henrietta slept with the window open, and fell asleep to the soft rush and pull of the waves.

Jerome seemed happy to be there, especially on Sunday morning when he did not have to get up early to catch his train to London.

'It's like a second honeymoon,' Henrietta sighed blissfully, lying in his arms.

He raised an eyebrow. 'I didn't know the first one had ended.'

While he was away during the days, Henrietta didn't want to do much. A stroll to the sea front in the morning, a seat where she could watch the world go by, a chair and a book in the small garden for the afternoon – these encompassed her pleasure. In courtesy she had to call on the Burnands, and was happy to do so, for Rosie understood she had no inclination to talk herself, and supplied all the conversation, while the five Burnand children provided the activity. Rosie Burnand called on her in return, and one day Mrs Sutton and Mrs Roughley drove over from Margate for the day with Lizzie, Minnie, Julia and Thelma. Henrietta was glad to see Lizzie and to hear she was having a wonderful time; but she was quite glad when they all departed again. Pregnancy held her in a sort of waking sleep, a luminous, impervious bubble of happiness in which she had nothing to do but wait.

On a morning at the very end of August, Henrietta lay in bed gazing out of the window. Jerome had gone to London, and when he had crept out of bed she had told him she was wide awake and asked him to pull the curtains back. Propped up comfortably against her pillow, she could see the large chestnut tree in a garden a few houses along. The early morning was milky with a sea-fog, through which she could see the colour of the tree – green just beginning to be touched with gold against the white of the sky – as if it were an old watercolour that had faded over the years. The baby, which had been active lately, was quiet, and she lay with her hands cupped over it, gazing at the tree, which seemed to her just then the most beautiful thing she had ever seen.

The sun strengthened as it rose, and the fog seemed to be rubbed away from the tree like the bloom from a plum, until it stood clear in its full colours, lovely, but an everyday thing. The magic was gone; and as the early quiet began to be invaded by daytime noise, Henrietta felt it was time to be stirring. She pushed back the covers and swung her legs out of bed. As she stood up she felt something give inside her, and a moment later a low, grinding pain seized her.

She sat down again on the bed until it was over, and then rang the bell. Emma was a long time coming, and arrived with a tray of tea, which was evidently what she had thought was being rung for. When Henrietta explained things her eyes widened so alarmingly it made her hairline shoot backwards. 'But it's early! We haven't got our things with us! What'll we do, mum?'

'We shall manage,' Henrietta said. Naturally they had had to give consideration to the possibility of the baby's coming while they were still in Ramsgate, and had made arrangements with a doctor recommended by the Burnands that he should be called at need. And Henrietta had taken the precaution of packing a set of sheets and baby-linen just in case. 'The first thing we must do is send for Dr Gresham to confirm that the baby is coming. It may be a false alarm.'

'Yes, mum,' Emma said doubtfully.

'Even if it is the baby,' Henrietta said to reassure her, 'I don't expect anything will happen for a long while yet. It was hours and hours when I had Miss Lizzie.'

'But first babies always take longer,' Emma said. 'I remember when Mother had our Billie, he came like lightning.'

This was not reassuring, but Henrietta tried to concentrate on what needed to be done.

'I want you to send Emily round for Dr Gresham, and in the mean time you and Edie can strip off the bed in the small spare room and put on the sheets that you'll find in the bottom of the wardrobe over there.'

'Yes, mum. Hadn't I better light the fire, too? That might be damp in there.'

'Yes, perhaps it would be wise. And warn Sarah that she might be asked for hot water later on.' It was a pity they were not at home, she thought. No copper here – all water had to be heated in kettles on the kitchen range.

Dr Gresham lived only two streets away, and was soon on hand. He examined her, smiled, and said someone must be sent for the nurse. Emily dashed off on this errand, while Emma helped Henrietta to transfer herself to the spare room.

'What a shame it didn't start before master set off,' Emma said.

'He ought to be let know,' Henrietta said, through the gritted teeth of another pain.

'Shall I send Edie to the post office?'

Henrietta doubted Edie could be trusted with so complex a task. 'No, you'd better go. Bring my purse and I'll give you the money.' As Emma was leaving the room with the coins in her hand and the message and address in her head, Henrietta felt a moment of panic at being without her. If anything happened before the nurse came, Edie would be no help. 'Hurry back,' she said.

She hurried, and was back with the receipt before the nurse arrived, and sat chatting eagerly, seeming even more excited about the impending addition than Henrietta was. When the nurse finally came, she proved a small, bustling, cheerful person, who spread waves of activity about her like a stone dropped in a pond. She seemed to feel that something ought to be being done at every minute, and Henrietta was hardly left alone for an instant, but at least it distracted her from the pains. As they grew harder and longer, she wondered that she could ever have forgotten them from the first time.

But Emma was a great comfort: having seen so many brothers and sisters born she took everything for granted. Dr Gresham came back at half past ten, said she was coming along splendidly, and by removing his jacket and rolling up his sleeves demonstrated that he didn't think it would be long now. And not long after noon Henrietta's second child made its appearance with a little rush and a penetrating wail.

Emma shed happy tears. 'It's a boy, mum,' she proclaimed, while Henrietta was still in no position to know. 'A lovely little boy! Oh, master will be so pleased!'

Yes, he would, she thought. A son for Jerome. She was glad too, not only for him, but for Lizzie. Another daughter might have proved a rival, but now she would still hold the girl's place in Jerome's heart.

Jerome must have left the City early, for he arrived soon after five o'clock, when Henrietta had just awoken from her first sleep, and was sitting up with a tray of tea and bread-and-butter which Emma had brought her up.

'My darling, are you all right?' he asked frantically, as he came through the door – an absurd question, given the tea tray and the happy face that confronted him. 'Is it all over?' he asked next.

'Yes,' she said. 'It was very quick, and your son was born at ten minutes past midday.'

'My son?' he said. Emma, beaming, hurried to beat the nurse to it and bring him the child, to place it in his arms.

All the way home, Jerome had rehearsed in his head what he might feel and what he might say at this moment, but his imaginings had fallen very short of the mark. In fact, what he said was nothing at all; and what he felt as he looked down at that tiny, tightly closed face was an astonished wonder. His child? His son? Slowly an extraordinary joy spread through him, and a love that was so piercing it was almost like terror.

'He's so small,' he said at last. 'Is he all right?' If this little life should be snatched from him now, he didn't know if he could survive the injury.

'He's perfect,' Henrietta said. 'He'll soon grow, you know.'

He came to the bedside and bent to kiss her almost reverently, and then sat beside her, cradling the baby in one arm and holding her hand. He asked her how it had been and how she was, and listened to her account attentively, but he could not look at her. However much he loved her, he was simply unable to drag his gaze away from his child.

Much later that evening he sat again by her side, in the firelight, and alone at last. This time Henrietta held the baby, and it was her turn to gaze.

'He's so perfect,' she said. 'Lizzie was red and crumpled when she was born, but he's as smooth and pink as a shell.' She looked at her husband with enormous gratitude, remembering how when Lizzie had been born Mr Fortescue had not come home for two weeks. She had been so alone then. 'I love you so much,' she said.

He smiled at her, his particularly ravishing smile, and lifted her free hand to kiss it. 'I love you, too, my dearest. More than ever. I wouldn't have thought it was possible to love you more, but I see I was wrong.' He kept hold of her hand, playing with her fingers as he gazed at his sleeping son.

'He will have to have a name,' Henrietta said after a while.

'We've never discussed names,' he observed. 'I have no idea what your views are on the subject.'

This was another new thing to her. In her life up till now it was the father who chose the name. For that reason she had given the matter no thought. 'Have you a preference?' she asked.

'There's such a vogue for fancy names nowadays,' he said.

'All your Cuthberts and Wilfreds and Percivals. Perhaps I am merely being perverse, but I feel a desire for something absolutely plain for him. I imagine him in a few years' time when he's a sturdy boy running about, and I call after him to keep him from some minor peril. I can't imagine myself calling out "Clarence!" or "Algernon!" or "Phineas!"'

'What do you imagine, then?'

He was silent a moment, projecting it in his mind. And at last he said, 'Jack. That's a nice, plain, manly name.'

'The plainest,' she agreed. 'You want to name him John, then?'

He gave her an apologetic smile. 'No, just Jack. Do you mind, my love? It must be your choice too.'

She was not yet used to choice. She looked down at the baby. 'He looks like a Jack to me already,' she said.

Lizzie never forgot the trip from Margate to Ramsgate to see her new brother. As soon as the news of the birth had arrived by telegraph, Minnie had become very grave and, taking her aside, had warned her solemnly that here was the end of all her fun. 'They won't want you now, depend on it,' she said. 'Not now they have a boy.'

Thelma Roughley agreed with her. 'I know a girl at home, who's the eldest of four, all girls, and her mother and father couldn't have been nicer, until her mother had another baby and it turned out to be a boy. After that it was "Willie this" and "Willie that" and they hardly ever spoke to her again except to scold her.'

'You'll never have any new things any more – it will all be for the baby,' Minnie affirmed. 'And as for your papa – well, he'll probably turn quite savage, this being his real baby and you only a step.'

Thelma nodded. 'Step-fathers are always cruel, like Mr Murdstone.'

Lizzie thought of Jerome and knew he could never be cruel. But the jolliness they had shared – yes, she could quite believe that would be a thing of the past. Everything she heard the grown-ups say confirmed this. A son was evidently what all men wanted, and their daughters were nothing to them. Only Julia Roughley dissented. 'Why should he be different? *You* are the same person. So is he.'

Lizzie tried to keep hold of this common-sense idea, but the prognostications of the others gave her an uncomfortable journey. Emma was waiting for her at the station to escort her home, and the sight of her red, smiling face did Lizzie good.

'Oh, Miss Lizzie, what a day that's been!' she exclaimed. 'You never saw such a pretty baby. Master's fit to float off like a kite, he's so pleased.'

On the short walk she regaled Lizzie with as many of the circumstantial details as were fit hearing for a young girl, and Lizzie grew more and more silent with doubt. But when they entered the house the first person they saw was Jerome, who swept down on her and enveloped her in a hug, crying, 'Here's my Lizzie! Now we can be jolly! Come and see your little brother. I think there was never such a perfect child in all of history, but I may be mistaken. You must set me straight. I depend on your opinion, you know!'

He was just as he had always been, and all her fear was washed away. She was now only ashamed to have listened to Minnie and Thelma rather than trusting her own judgement. In the spare room she found her mother in bed, but sitting up and looking perfectly well, and when she had hugged and kissed her, Jerome scooped the baby out of his makeshift crib (the top drawer of the tallboy) and put him into Lizzie's arms as if making a gift of him. Lizzie took him, looked down into his face, and was lost.

'He's so *perfect*!' she cried. 'His little fingers! The tiny fingernails! And doesn't he smell lovely?'

In a minute Jerome took him back. 'I must have a turn. I haven't held him for ten minutes!' He laid the baby in the crook of his arm in a very professional manner and walked up and down with him, talking about the things they would all do together in the future, both immediate and distant. 'You'll find it a great convenience to have a brother, Lizzie, when it comes to courting. He'll be able to interview your suitors and see off the undesirables. I know he's quite a bit younger than you, but if we feed him up he'll soon grow;

and if they're tall, he can always stand on a soap-box.'

'You are nonsensical!' Henrietta laughed at him, and he only beamed at them both. 'Lunatic with happiness,' he affirmed.

Lizzie went back to Margate to finish her holiday in good spirits, only a little worried about what would happen when it was time for her to go to school. Minnie had got it from one of the Sutton servants that ladies who had just had babies could not stir from their beds or be moved for a month without risking death, so it was to be assumed that her mother must stay in Ramsgate until October.

'You can stay with us,' Minnie said, 'and go to school from our house.'

Lizzie acknowledged the kindness, but she didn't want to embark on the adventure, challenge and strangeness of school from a strange house, and with no Mama to come home to.

But in the event, both Henrietta and Jerome were quite aware of her situation, and equally determined nothing should spoil it for her. At the end of a fortnight Henrietta was declared well enough to travel, and the household moved back to Kensington with four days to spare before the beginning of term. Jerome had put an announcement of the birth in *The Times*, and all sorts of free gifts arrived in every post from commercial firms hoping for future trade: soap, baby powder, patent foods, ointments – even a photograph of the notice from a photographic studio. There were also letters of congratulation from friends and acquaintances and even from Jerome's business acquaintances whom Henrietta had never met.

And people visited – how they visited! It seemed everyone wanted to see the baby and exclaim over him. And everyone brought or sent presents. Even Mrs Blandy sent a dear little baby chemise she had made and embroidered herself; Mr Macdonald brought an exquisite carved lapis-lazuli bead on a leather thong, which he said was a good-luck charm from ancient Egypt; Lady Anne Farraline brought a beautiful embroidered shawl; Mary sent a silver cup, and the twins an order for flowers for a month from the nearest florist.

And Venetia, who could not call, for she was large with child herself, sent a long letter, and a very practical dozen of champagne,

> not only for wetting the baby's head, but for recruiting the strength of the mother. It is the very best restorative after childbirth, so make sure you get your share, dear Henrietta. As soon as I am delivered and out and about again, I shall come and see you both (or you shall come to me if it suits better) for I long to see your dear baby, whom I know I shall be very fond of.

Henrietta wrote back thanking her, and asking, a little diffidently, if she would agree to be Jack's godmother. Venetia wrote that she would be honoured, but asked if the christening could be delayed until she could be present. 'If things go along as anticipated, my baby should be born early in October, so perhaps the ceremony could be postponed until November.'

Henrietta had had no plans for any particular date and was perfectly agreeable to this. It was a very human impulse that had her counting backwards and considering that either the baby was going to be very premature, or Venetia and her beloved had been cohabiting before the wedding. She did not judge her cousin for this, only reflected how differently it was possible to act in different sections of society. Money and position had a great impact on moral questions; and so, too, did London. In Bishop Winthorpe, whispers about Henrietta's meeting Jerome at Mary's empty cottage had given her and Perry great pain; but Venetia did not even consider pretending that her baby was not due until the respectable month.

CHAPTER NINE

Lizzie was intensely excited on her first school day, nervous of what her new life might hold, but wildly happy to be embarking on it. It seemed to promise vistas of unimaginable freedom. Through her childhood in Yorkshire she had been obliged to be quiet, docile and obedient. Though her father had taught her to a high intellectual standard, he had not granted her the slightest licence, and she would never have dared even to speak without permission in his presence. All that had changed in the brief time she had been under the rule of her 'new papa'. Jerome was as different as he could be from the rector. He encouraged her to talk, to think, to question, to be independent of mind and spirit. Little Miss Fortescue would never have dreamt of travelling alone across London; young Miss Compton relished the idea.

Jerome had bought her a season ticket from Kensington High Street to Gower Street, a stout square of card on which was printed 'with the privilege of alighting at intermediate stations'. The grandiose words enchanted Lizzie as much as the promise of new places to explore. She thoroughly enjoyed, on the first morning, walking past the barrier with it in her hand and saying, 'Season,' in as grand a manner as possible, as if she had been doing it all her life. She enjoyed the underground journey: nothing about it troubled her as it did her mother. She liked being in a carriage with a lot of strangers and shooting through a dark, mysterious tunnel. She liked the noise and the rattle, the flickering lights, the smell of sulphur; she liked all the bustle, and the odd people she saw.

The walk at the other end, which she had so blithely dismissed as a trifle, did seem very long and she began to worry about being late. Lateness, it had been emphasised in the letter that had been awaiting her on their return from Ramsgate, was a cardinal sin. On this first morning the new entrants were to arrive an hour later than the normal time, so the streets were unsettlingly empty of schoolgirls. But when the building hove into sight at last, she was glad to see some other young ladies converging on it, reassuring her that if she was late, she was not alone in her delinquency.

They were conducted first to the cloakrooms and then into the assembly hall: very fine and dignified, with a high platform at one end and a gallery at the other. On the platform a tall-backed, heavy chair stood like a throne, and behind it rose the pipes of a great organ. There were rows of folding desks and benches, and the sun shone in cheerfully through a stained-glass window, which a plaque said was a memorial to someone – Lizzie could not read the name.

The rest of the school was already at work and it was impressively silent. Lizzie thought eagerly how good it would be to study again. What magnificent intellects would teach them at this, the best school in the country! What clever and dedicated girls she would have around her, and how their minds would be stretched! She glanced around her at her fellow newcomers to see if they had the marks of greatness on them, but they seemed very ordinary. Only one stood out at first glance, a young woman who looked a little older than her, who had smooth hair the colour of honey and dark eyes in a vivid face. She seemed to feel Lizzie's gaze on her and turned, met her eyes and smiled.

But at that moment the proceedings began. A lady in a dull purple dress climbed up onto the platform and after a stern preamble began to read aloud the school rules. A copy of these had already been sent to each girl, close-printed in double columns, a daunting number of them. Read aloud in a dreary monotone they dulled some of Lizzie's elation. The purpose of this assembly seemed to be to impress on the new girls that discipline was all and that no nonsense would be allowed *here*. There were so many 'thou shalt nots' that Lizzie's mind began to drift, but it was brought back sharply when a moment later a girl sitting in front of her turned and murmured something to her neighbour. At once the lady on the platform stopped, glared, and, pointing at the offending girl, snapped, 'You must not speak in Hall, dear.' The girl turned bright red with vexation, and Lizzie felt for her. The pointing finger seemed unnecessarily brutal, and the addition of the 'dear' did nothing to soften the rebuke. (In fact, she was to discover that the teachers always called the girls 'dear', no matter what they were saying to them.)

At last the recital ended and they were dismissed, with instructions to repair to the form that had been assigned to them in the preliminary letter. 'You will find the name of the form on the door.'

They streamed out and dispersed along the corridors. The doors to the classrooms had glass panels in the top half, through which could be seen rows of girls busily – and silently – learning. As the crowd thinned, Lizzie found herself beside the fair girl she had noticed earlier. 'What form are you in?' she asked pleasantly.

'Lower Fourth,' Lizzie said.

'Oh, so am I,' the girl exclaimed, with obvious pleasure. They looked at each other with interest.

'My name's Elizabeth Compton,' said Lizzie.

'Mine's Mary Paget. How old are you?'

'Fourteen – just. How old are you?'

'Fifteen and a bit. You must be very clever to be sent to the Lower Fourth.'

'I don't think I am.' All the other girls had disappeared and they were alone. 'We'd better find it, though, or we'll be in trouble.'

'No speaking in the corridors,' came the voice from behind them of Miss Hucksby, who had read them the rules. They turned guiltily to find her glaring at them. 'If you speak again you will have to sign for it,' she said. 'Now hurry along to your form.'

'We don't know where it is,' Lizzie said.

The woman frowned. 'You must say "please" when you speak to me, dear.'

'Please, we don't know where the Lower Fourth is.'

'That way, down the stairs and turn right. Hurry along now. Remember, no speaking, and no running on the stairs.'

They found the room with no more difficulty, and entering, found thirty or so girls seated at the desks with a teacher out in front of them, her desk on a low dais and a blackboard beside it. They gave their names, and the teacher said, 'I am Miss Webster. There's an empty desk over there. Sit down quickly.'

In the middle of the morning there was a break, and they all filed in silence down to the basement, where they were allowed to buy a biscuit or a bun to eat. They then had fifteen minutes to eat it, and during this time talk was allowed; but they had to stand in straight lines, so it was only possible to talk to the person next on either side.

Lizzie and Mary Paget – she asked Lizzie to call her Polly – stood together. 'What do you think of it so far?' Polly asked.

'I'm not sure. It isn't what I expected.'

'What did you expect?'

Lizzie hesitated. 'I thought the teaching would be more inspiring. Miss Webster just read out of Haldane and then asked questions – and I did Haldane years ago. And French was even worse – just translating out of *Picciola*, no conversation or stories.'

Polly nodded. 'I thought it was dull, too. Where did you go to school before?'

'Nowhere. My father taught me at home, and after he died I shared my cousins' governess, and did extra lessons with the rector. Did you go to school?'

'Yes, to Miss Barrow's, in Hertfordshire, where we lived. It was fun there – not strict like this. There are so many rules, aren't there?'

'I'll never remember them all,' Lizzie sighed.

'What do you suppose the lady in the hall this morning

meant,' Polly asked, 'when she said if we talked again we would sign for it?'

The girl beyond Lizzie on the other side heard the question and obligingly answered. 'When you break a rule you have to write down what you did in the Appearing Book and sign your name. You know, you write "I ran in the corridor" or "I spoke in Hall" or whatever it was.'

'And then what happens?' Lizzie asked.

'Oh, nothing,' the girl said.

'Aren't you punished?' asked Polly.

'No, but they send home at the end of term, "Reported thirty-three times for breach of regulations", and then your parents are disappointed in you.'

'Oh,' said Lizzie. Yes, she could imagine the scene.

'And you can hardly help signing for *something*, there are so many rules,' said the girl, with the relish one reserves for telling bad news. 'There are new ones practically every day – rules, I mean – so they catch you one way or another.'

'Why do they do that?' Lizzie asked.

The girl shrugged. 'Just to annoy, I suppose. But signing's nothing, really. If you do something really bad – or something *they* think is really bad – you get sent for to Miss Buss's room and she jaws you. That's dreadful. There isn't a girl in the school who could stand up to it. She *always* makes you cry. Bessie Forrester in the Upper Fourth is the boldest thing you ever knew, but when she was sent for, Miss Buss made her sob so hard she almost fainted.'

Break was over so there was no time for more revelations. Lizzie filed back to class with the others in sober mood, wondering at this daunting regime. She didn't even survive her first day without 'signing', for during the next lesson when she put up her hand to answer a question she unluckily swept her pencil-box off the desk, and was called up to the front to write in the book 'I dropped my pencil-box' and sign her name. She felt dreadfully upset by this, for it seemed that there was no way, as the helpful girl had said, that one would be able to avoid blame, if even accidents were punishable.

The day's lessons ended at half past one. There was no

afternoon school, for most of the girls came from a fair distance away, and it would have taken too long for them to get home and back. But the afternoon was not to be spent in idleness: there was homework to be done. A printed time-table was issued to each girl, on which she had to enter the time she began work, the time she finished it, and the total time taken. It had to be filled in in ink and signed by a parent as a guarantee of honesty (no ink was allowed in school).

As Lizzie joined the other girls streaming out of school at twenty-five to two, her mind was a ferment of new impressions, a bedwilderment of rules (*Girls must not walk more than three abreast. No girl may be out of doors hatless*); but what she felt most of all was *hungry*. She had breakfasted before eight o'clock and the mid-morning bun had done little to fill the gap. The walk to Gower Street and the underground journey home stretched before her like a desert to be crossed, and she felt just then that she would willingly have 'signed' a dozen times for things she had not done in return for a sustaining bit of bread.

'Goodbye! See you tomorrow!'

She turned and saw Mary Paget smiling as she turned the other way. 'Yes, see you tomorrow!'

I've made a friend already, Lizzie thought, brightening. And then she felt a little surge of excitement at the thought of getting home and telling Mama all about it, and seeing little Jack, and the journey ahead of her did not seem so daunting. She walked down the road with a swing to her step and wondered what Sarah would have cooked for luncheon.

Gradually over the next few weeks Lizzie settled down to a routine. School was not what she had expected. The lessons were generally too easy for her, and therefore boring, and they were taught without any great originality, generally straight from the textbook. Read a passage, answer questions, perform a test: this seemed to be the approved method. Tests were frequent, and the desks were provided with a board that could be fitted into iron brackets to prevent the next girl from seeing what was written. Papers were then exchanged for marking, and the marks recorded in various ledgers.

'Marks' seemed to be a huge preoccupation of the school, and were given and subtracted for almost everything, so that the collection and calculation of them took up much time and effort. Lizzie had imagined the great intellects of the teachers inspiring the eager young minds of the pupils to ever higher feats of originality. In fact, she seemed to be a small cog in a machine whose purpose was purely to produce order. What seemed to matter was that everyone did the same thing at the same time and did it tidily. Marks were given for tidiness and accuracy in work, never for originality, and subtracted for any sound or movement that spoiled the clockwork appearance of thirty girls simultaneously performing the same task.

But though she would have preferred the school to be other than it was, she would not have given it up for anything. It was good to have set tasks to perform, even if they didn't always stretch her mind; and she was learning things, even if not in a very interesting way. She enjoyed the discipline of regular hours, and she enjoyed being with other girls, after a lonely upbringing.

There were other pleasures, too. She began to learn German, which her father had never ventured on. She enjoyed morning assembly, and the mid-morning break when, with a little contrivance, it was possible for a few friends to chat together. She and Polly always stood together, and soon had made friends with another girl, Agnes Grey, who had red hair and a droll sense of humour. She enjoyed exercise periods in the gymnasium when they would perform Swedish exercises, drills, and bounce balls and swing poles about. And though the regular teachers were limited in their teaching, from time to time guest lecturers would be brought in to address the whole school on some subject of art or science, giving a taste of the wider world outside, and a contact with real expertise and enthusiasm of mind.

And once a month the school held a 'Dorcas meeting'. For this the girls stayed on at school for the afternoon. Each would bring a package of food from home, which was eaten picnic-style, and then they would sew cotton chemises for the poor while being read aloud to by a mistress from a book of her own choice. As it was a charitable activity, the usual strictness was relaxed, and talking and even laughter were allowed; and since there was no requirement for their minds to be improved, the mistress would choose an amusing book that she enjoyed herself.

When Lizzie had been at school for a couple of weeks, Mary Paget brought in a note from her mother, inviting Lizzie to come home with her for the afternoon on the following day. Lizzie came back the next day with permission and a return invitation for Polly for the following week. At the end of school, the two girls walked together to the Pagets' house, which was on Primrose Hill. It was delightful on the walk home to be able to talk without restraint, and to discover what they had suspected from the first, that they liked each other very much, and thought alike on many subjects.

The Pagets' house was a large one, detached and standing in handsome grounds, overlooking the park and with a gravel 'in and out' carriage sweep. Mr Paget, Lizzie understood, was a merchant banker. Mrs Paget greeted her kindly, and, understanding the most urgent need, sent them straight in to luncheon. The meal was plain and plentiful, the sort of 'nursery food' Lizzie had been accustomed to at the Red House – Scotch broth, mutton hash, and rice pudding with jam – and just what two starving schoolgirls needed. However, Mrs Paget did Lizzie the honour of sitting down at the table with them while they ate, and made conversation, which meant that Lizzie had to put down knife and fork to answer while her stomach cried out for uninterrupted attention. While too well-bred to be openly curious, Mrs Paget evidently wanted information as to whom her daughter might be consorting with, and Lizzie was wise enough in the ways of the world by this time to mention the most creditable things: her father's being both a rector and a noted academic, her uncle's being squire of Bishop Winthorpe, her mother's coming from an old landed family, her new papa's being a gentleman.

After luncheon Polly took her round the garden, and then upstairs to show her her room. Lizzie examined her books, her old toys, her collections of seashells and butterflies, and then the two of them knelt on the window-seat with their elbows on the sill and gazed out at the passing world while they talked and talked and talked.

After that they went for a walk in the park, and came back to tea, laid cosily in the old nursery, which was Polly's sitting-room: Mrs Paget was entertaining some ladies to five o'clock tea in the drawing-room. While the girls were engaged with hot buttered toast and greengage jam, Polly's brothers came in. Lizzie had only just got a brother for the first time, and deeply envied Mary hers. Dryden was seventeen, Cambourne sixteen, and both were at school at Merchant Taylors'. They seemed to Lizzie splendid young men, well-formed, handsome, with the same fair hair and brown eyes as Polly, but above all so friendly, frank and open-mannered. Unlike Roy Sutton they did not seem to feel the need to be superior and put on airs; nor did they treat their sister and her friend with lofty contempt. They greeted Lizzie with apparent pleasure, begged for toast, and sat down to be agreeable.

'You'd get a better tea in the drawing-room,' Polly pointed out.

'It's quantity we're after, not quality,' Dryden said.

'Besides,' said Cambourne, 'the company's better here. I distinctly saw Mrs Montague's hat as I passed the door.' He gave a theatrical shudder.

'Ma has all her *bêtes-noires* assembled down there,' Dryden agreed. 'She likes to get them all over in one go. We crept past on tiptoe so we shouldn't be seen.'

'You're a disgrace to polite society,' Polly said, 'but I'm glad you chose us. I wanted to show you off to Lizzie. Aren't they adorable?' she enquired innocently of her friend. 'And perfectly tame. I have them eating out of my hand.'

'It's true,' Dryden said, open-eyed. 'She makes us beg and lie down and "die for the Queen".'

'And all for a sugar lump,' Cambourne added, and going down on all fours made believe to lick Polly's hand.

'Well, now you're down there,' Polly said, 'make yourself useful. Here's the toasting-fork and there's the bread.'

In a short time all of them were sitting on the floor in front of the fire, taking turns to make toast, and the talk was so easy and jolly Lizzie felt as if she had known them all for years. The party was only broken up by Mrs Paget's coming in. They all scrambled to their feet, and though she didn't say anything, she looked with raised eyebrows, standing just inside the doorway with her hands folded magisterially before her. But if she was disapproving, it was evident she could not resist her sons' charm, and they soon diffused the atmosphere. It was time for Lizzie to go, and all three young Pagets put their coats on and walked with her to the omnibus, to see her safe on her way.

'How was it?' Henrietta asked, when she got home.

'Lovely,' Lizzie said. 'Mrs Paget is rather stiff and proper, but not in a horrid way. And Polly and her brothers are awfully nice. And Mrs Paget says Polly may come back with me next Tuesday. Here's the note. We had greengage jam at tea; but the cake was dull. Polly doesn't eat down at all, though she's a year older than me.' She smiled sunnily. 'Home's best, isn't it? Can I go and see Jackie?'

Henrietta was happy with this endorsement. 'Yes, but don't wake him if he's asleep. He's been crying all afternoon. A touch of colic, Emma says.'

Apart from the brothers, Lizzie did not learn to envy Polly. She enjoyed going to the Paget house, and grew fonder and fonder of Polly, but she continued to think home was best. Jerome, when he came home from the City, was always interested in what she had done at school. He laughed at its absurdities, but helped her with her homework, and remembered, in the most flattering way, which girls she liked and disliked, and the peculiarities of all her teachers – whom he would sometimes imitate to ludicrous effect. Mr Paget, when he came home from the City, brought an awed hush to the house, as at the descent from Olympus of a minor deity. Everything was arranged so that he should not be annoyed by anything, and his dinner and his undisturbed pleasure were all that mattered to the household.

When Lizzie got home from school, there was her darling mama, still at first resting on the couch, but ready to be interested in what Lizzie had to say. She would discuss school, happily play at cards or tables, struggle through French or arithmetic with her, hear her learning by heart, or demonstrate sewing techniques that Lizzie had need of. Now she had leisure from housekeeping she liked to chat, and had a thousand stories about her own childhood at Morland Place, which had the fascination of a foreign country for Lizzie. In addition there was little Jack to hold and pet and help to feed and bathe; and the servants, especially Emma, were like friends. Lizzie knew all about their families, complaints, pleasures and trials, and little went on in the kitchen she didn't know about. Sometimes Sarah would even let her 'make messes', and try her hand at pancakes, omelettes, jam tarts or lemon squares.

Polly's mama, though perfectly amiable, never relented from her formality, and such conversation as was exchanged was very much *de haut en bas*. The Paget house ran like clockwork and the servants were servants and not friends: the cook would have been horrified if Polly even showed her face in the kitchen, leave alone ask to try cooking anything. Polly's home was very fine but, to Lizzie, cold; and if it weren't for the glorious brothers, Lizzie would have felt very sorry for her. But Polly was obviously quite happy. Lizzie wondered how Dodie and Cam, as she was soon calling them, had managed to grow up as they did; little Jack, she concluded, with twice the benefits would turn out the perfect man.

Polly's was not the only house she visited, of course: she was still frequently invited to the Suttons' and the Roughleys' – more to the former as Julia and Thelma were generally there anyway. When Lizzie had first started school, she had naturally wanted to tell all about it, but she soon learned to curb her enthusiasm. Minnie was scornful of the North London Collegiate, and asked questions only to ridicule. '*I* would not stand for being spoken to so. Mama says teachers are a low, ignorant sort. Fancy being told what to do by a pack of dowdies! What a stupid rule! Why on earth should you want to do that? Lord, it sounds horribly dull. What a lot of nonsense! *I* should have told her what I thought of her,' and so on.

She was also contemptuous of the girls who went to the school. 'They're nothing but a pack of scarecrows. I've seen them going in and out. Dreadful old dresses and horrible boots! Some of them look as if they've been wearing the same frock for years. I don't know why your mama lets you be with pauper girls like that.'

Lizzie had been unwary enough to deny that they were all paupers and to introduce Polly as an example of wealth, which only gave Minnie more ammunition. She had inherited her mother's jealous streak, and deeply resented Lizzie's having another friend, particularly one she didn't know. 'Going to see your precious Polly?' she would enquire nastily if Lizzie said she could not come on any particular day. 'I'm sure we mustn't let anything upset *her*, even if I was your friend first.'

So Lizzie learnt not to speak about school or Polly. She could only congratulate herself on never having mentioned Dodie and Cam, for it was still an accepted idea in the Sutton household that Lizzie was heartstruck for Roy.

Julia and Thelma had no particular animus against the school, though they thought all schools boring, and agreed with Minnie that the Collegiate girls were dowdies. It was true, Lizzie acknowledged, that many of the girls came from moderately poor backgrounds, and all of them were obliged by school rule to dress plainly, but one of the things she liked about it was that the girls there never made fun of or even noticed each other's clothes. In the Sutton world, it was disgraceful to be poor, and every effort had to be made to conceal poverty where it existed, and to display to the world the newest and most expensive aspect possible.

But as long as she avoided mention of school, she got on well enough with the Suttons and Roughleys. She was glad of their company, and enjoyed the games and conversations they had, though she did notice anew how ignorant they were. And even more than their ignorance, she noticed their restlessness. Never having been obliged to follow a regular and disciplined course in anything, they seemed incapable of concentrating, flitted from one thing to another, and frequently complained of being bored. Lizzie was always too busy to be bored and sometimes longed for the luxury of having nothing to do; but to Minnie, Thelma and Julia – particularly the first two – boredom was a common agony, for they had no means of alleviating it except by the physical activity of going to each other's houses or – their favourite occupation – of going shopping.

She talked to Jerome about this, and he said that the longer he lived, the more he wondered that females could bear the do-nothing of their lives. 'It's all right for people like my sister Mary, who read widely and have plenty to think about – and have country pursuits and good works into the bargain; and of course the poor have to labour so hard to keep themselves they never have time to be bored. But I would not be your friend Minnie for all the gold in Africa. Nor marry her, either, come to that.'

Lizzie thought of him married to Minnie and burst out laughing; and following her thought he grinned too, and said, 'Yes, but just mind who *you* marry, when the time comes!'

Mary Compton and Amy and Patsy came to London to take up their new lives in September, not long after Lizzie started school. It made for another agreeable variation in routine, visiting and being visited by them. Mary showed a detached interest in Jack, called him 'my nevvy' and brought him presents, and handled him with all the skill she had learnt at the Red House; but confessed that little babies had no appeal for her. 'When he can talk rationally to me, I shall be the best aunt in the world,' she said.

Amy and Patsy exclaimed over him a great deal, but never offered to pick him up, and obviously had much more interesting things on their minds. Patsy was intensely occupied with her new work, and with the new friends it was bringing her. Everything about *Punch* thrilled and fascinated her, to the extent that she could not hold any other subject for more than a sentence or two without bringing it in. Amy said it made her want to scream, but in fact she seemed too happy really to object to anything. It soon became apparent that she was being courted by Alec Macdonald, and had succumbed, at this relatively late age, to the pangs of love. How Mary spent her time was never revealed, but as the whole of London, with its arts and society, was at her command, it was not a question that worried anyone. Though she was over forty, she was more handsome than she had ever been, besides being witty, intelligent and independently wealthy, and the wonder was, Henrietta thought, that she was not being courted too. But perhaps she was, and drove her suitors away. It was not easy to imagine her submitting herself to a man's authority.

Venetia's baby was born on the 10th of October. Her colleague Elizabeth Garrett Anderson attended her during the birth, generously finding time despite the pressure of work: with Venetia out of commission she was the only person undertaking major surgery at the New Hospital for Women. The unshakeable rule there was to have no masculine member of staff, 'not even a tom-cat', as Mrs Anderson said – not out of spite, but because if there were male staff, any success would automatically be assigned to them. Nine years on from Venetia's qualifying, lady doctors were now more numerous, but none would perform anything but minor operations.

Venetia's labour was uncomplicated, and at half past six in the morning she gave birth to a small but perfect baby boy.

'You are obviously doing so well, I shall have no qualms about going into the hospital this morning,' Mrs Anderson said. 'I have a tumour patient I want to keep an eye on – a very interesting case.'

'But you've been up all night,' Venetia demurred.

'It's not the first time and it won't be the last,' Mrs Anderson said. 'You of all people know how it is.'

'Yes, I know how it is.' Venetia smiled up at her over the tiny white bundle she was holding. 'Just tell me before you go if he isn't the most perfect baby you've ever seen?'

'Without a doubt!' Mrs Anderson laughed. 'No matter how many babies I deliver, the wonder of it never decreases. Well, I shall leave you to get some rest. No doubt your visitors will start arriving in a few hours, so you had better sleep while you can. I wish you might have helped me with the tumour operation, but I shall probably do it tomorrow. I'm not inclined to leave her any longer.'

'I wish I might have too. Good luck with it – and thank you for all you've done.'

Mrs Anderson raised her eyebrows. 'It was nothing at all.' She rolled down her sleeves, preparing to go. 'As soon as you feel well enough to work, let me know. I always have more cases than I can handle myself.'

The nurse finished tidying her, and word was sent to Lord Hazelmere that he might approach and view his first-born. Venetia heard his tread along the passage outside, uncharacteristically hesitant. He appeared in the doorway, afraid to speak too loudly or move too quickly, his eyes shadowed from his sleepless night, but full of hope.

'Come and see him, then,' Venetia said, and he crossed to her, and stood staring. She made a little offering gesture with the bundle, and his hands whipped behind his back. 'Take him,' she said.

'Lord, no – I should drop him, or break him, or something.'

'Don't be an idiot, Beauty! Babies don't break.'

He grinned slowly. 'You haven't called me that for a while. Very well, then, give him here. I'll show you I can make a fist of it.'

He was very awkward about it, but once he had hold of the baby he seemed to gain confidence, and soon shifted him into one arm so that he could use the other hand to pull the shawl away from his face so he could study him. The smile that came to her husband's lips was all Venetia could have wanted. It was a thing of such perilous and tender joy she understood at last why women went on having baby after baby, despite the tremendous labour – in all senses – involved.

'We shall have to think of a name,' she said, after a bit.

Hazelmere did not seem able to take his eyes off his son and answered without looking up, 'Should you care for Oliver, after your father?'

'Mm,' she said equivocally. 'How about John, after my husband?'

'You never call me John,' he pointed out.

'That only means the name is fresh and unused.'

'Foolish! No, I tell you what, I have a fancy for Thomas. That's a good old English name. What do you think?'

'It's a nice, manly name. Thomas it shall be, then, if you please.'

Hazelmere slipped a finger into the baby's grip and joggled his hand. 'The Honourable Thomas Winchmore. He seems determined to ignore me – won't even open his eyes. Hey there, young rascal, this is your papa speaking!'

'He's had a hard night of it, poor little man,' Venetia said. 'Don't wake him.'

Hazelmere looked up at last. 'But I've got a lot of things to teach him! How to ride and shoot and fish and play cricket.'

Venetia held out her arms for the baby, hungry for him even after so short a time. 'Perhaps tomorrow.'

Hazelmere handed him back reluctantly. 'Very well, but no spoiling him, mind, or making him soft.'

'He shall begin boxing lessons first thing in the morning,' Venetia promised, and took her baby back. He fitted into the curve of her arms as naturally as if they had known him all her life, and she gazed down at the small sleeping face, feeling she could never have enough of looking at him.

Hazelmere came and sat beside her and gazed too. 'He is wonderful, isn't he?' he asked, stroking her free hand with both of his.

'Oh, yes.' She looked up a moment. 'And so are you. I love you, dearest, in case I hadn't mentioned it.'

'I love you too. So very much,' he said, and lifting her hand to his lips, kissed it with something close to reverence.

As Mrs Anderson had guessed, the visitors were not long arriving. Hazelmere held off the first-comers, while Venetia and young Thomas were enjoying a well-earned sleep. The first to be admitted was the Dowager Duchess of Southport, Venetia's mother, who arrived at lunchtime, having travelled up on the train from Ravendene with her maid Norton.

Charlotte was sixty-four. The illness that had plagued much of her life since her experiences in the Crimea seemed to have gone into remission at last, and she was enjoying an untroubled old age. Her pinkish gold hair was quite white now, and she wore it wound in a crown on the top of her head, as her mother had used to, which gave her a regal look. She had kept her figure, and moved briskly, as if she wanted to make up for all the years she had been forced to lie immobile on a sofa.

When she arrived, Venetia had just woken again, so she was admitted at once.

'So this is my grandson. He's perfect, isn't he?'

'I think so,' Venetia said. 'Do you want to hold him?'

'What a question! Of course I do. How are you, darling? Was it very bad?'

'Not bad at all, only tremendously hard work. Don't I look well?'

'Disgustingly so. Ah, here's your luncheon tray. No, it's all right, I'll hold him. You needn't be afraid, Nurse, I shan't drop him. I've had five of my own. What do you mean to call him?' Charlotte asked when the nurse had retreated.

'We've decided on Thomas.'

'Oh, that's nice! I've always liked the name. My uncle Thomas was the dearest person.' Venetia began on the omelette and peas that had been prepared for her. 'My first grandson,' Charlotte went on, gazing as Venetia had gazed. 'I remember when you were first put into my arms, darling. It's the most wonderful feeling, isn't it? Your father was transfixed.'

'Beauty was too. It's a strange feeling, isn't it – to have that power?'

Charlotte nodded. 'I hope he won't be my last grandchild. It seems I shall have to rely on you. With Marcus gone, poor Olivia seeming not to be able to, and Harry and

Gussie leading such irregular lives – well, thank God for you, that's all I can say!'

Venetia looked up and laughed. 'Darling Mama, doesn't that strike you as funny? After being the black sheep all my life, suddenly I'm the favourite!'

'To let you into a secret, you always were. Mothers aren't supposed to have favourites, but there it is – human weakness. Your father too. He always liked you best, in spite of everything. I wish he were here to see you, and his grandson.'

'Perhaps he is,' Venetia said, touched.

Henrietta came to visit a few days later, taking the opportunity to bring Jack to see his potential godmother. The two women exchanged hugs, and then babies.

'Thomas is handsomer, I think,' Henrietta said.

'You are just being polite. I can't believe you don't think your baby is the most beautiful creature in the world.'

Henrietta laughed. 'Well, perhaps you're right.'

'And, in fact, I can't choose between my son and my godson for beauty. Your Jack is quite delicious. I'm sure they're going to be great friends.'

After a little they put both the babies into Thomas's crib, which was quite big enough for two. There they lay contentedly, Jack staring up and clenching and unclenching his hands, Thomas sleeping hard, as if content Jack was on watch.

They chatted for a while, and then Henrietta raised the question of the christening. 'Not that I mean to rush you, but I would like to start making plans. You said perhaps in November? Does that still seem all right to you?'

'Plan for the end of November,' Venetia said. 'The twenty-eighth or twenty-ninth. And what do you say to a joint celebration?'

Henrietta was almost taken aback. 'Oh, but surely . . .'

'What is it? Don't you like the idea?'

'No – I mean, yes, it would be wonderful, but surely you'll be having something very splendid? Your position in society—'

Venetia stopped her with a hand on her wrist. 'Thomas is only an honourable, not a royal duke. I wasn't planning on the Abbey! The local church, a few close friends, a small reception back here. It would be very pleasant to share it with you. As I am to be Jack's godmother, I was hoping you would consent to be Thomas's.'

Henrietta was pleased, but she met Venetia's eyes and said painfully, 'Forgive me, but are you sure it's what Lord Hazelmere would want? You aren't forgetting that I am married to – that Jerome is a divorcé?'

For the moment Venetia *had* forgotten it, and in the moment of remembering she was angry with herself, and even angrier with society, whose rules mitigated against someone so obviously good as Henrietta. But her mind moved quickly and she said without a pause, 'I've told you before, I am too much of a scapegrace myself for that to matter to either of us. We *both* want you to be godmother. I hope you won't disappoint us.'

For all Venetia's efforts, Henrietta *had* seen her expression waver, and it hurt. But to refuse now, since Venetia wanted to champion her, would hurt both of them, damage their pride and their affection, so she smiled and said she would be honoured, and went on to discuss plans as if there were no shadow on either of them. While they talked, Venetia was telling Hazelmere in imagination and trying to gauge his reaction, and half wishing Henrietta had not been so honest as to tell her in the first place; and Henrietta was busily blaming herself for her weakness in marrying Jerome, while knowing that given the choice again she would do the same thing, and puzzling over why doing what the Church said was wrong should feel so right and make her and Jerome *and* Lizzie so very happy.

Venetia did not expect a visit from her brother Harry, the duke, and she did not get one, though she informed him of the birth of his nephew, as she felt was right given that he was the head of the family. Her brother Marcus, Harry's twin, had died at Khartoum, but before he left for Egypt he had visited Harry and found him in a bad way, not only drinking too much, frittering a fortune on gambling and actresses, but also smoking opium and taking cocaine. He had passed on the substance of this to Venetia, and from that time she had expected nothing of her brother, and only hoped their mother did not know the worst.

But to her surprise she received a visit from her youngest sister, Lady Augusta Vibart. Gussie as much as Harry moved in the Prince of Wales's circle. 'Johnny' Vibart was one of his closest friends, along with Charles Carrington and 'Charlie' Beresford, at the noisier end of his acquaintance, and Gussie moved among people as far removed from Venetia's friends as it was possible to be. Not only that, but Gussie had disliked her for a long time, blaming her for spoiling her come-out year so long ago, and believing her bad behaviour had led to the death of their father.

So when the maid came to Venetia to say that she was below, Venetia thought at first the girl must have made a mistake. But in a moment Gussie came in in her old energetic way, staring around her with open curiosity. She looked very prosperous in a dress of grey lace over satin, with a cuirasse bodice and a ruched, draped and pleated skirt. Over it she wore a velvet jacket trimmed with fur, and a hussar hat of grey fur was tilted forward on her much-curled head, decorated with a stiff little cockade fixed with a diamond brooch. She had four strands of pearls round her throat, pearls at her ears, and pearl and diamond bracelets over her grey suede gloves.

'Well, goodness, here you are,' she said. 'I was afraid of what I might find when I came here, but I must admit you're living in better style than I expected. This isn't a bad house. On the small side, but at least you have a decent manservant to answer the door.'

'Thank you. I'm glad you're satisfied,' Venetia said drily. 'How are you, Gussie? Please sit down.'

Gussie sat, beginning to pull off her gloves, though her restless eyes still combed the room and would not yet rest on her sister. 'But it does look awfully bare. There seems hardly any furniture and no pictures worth mentioning. I know you haven't been married long, but surely Hazelmere must have had family things? When we were girls I thought he had quite good style. You've no big glasses in here – how do you dress?' She didn't wait for an answer. Her roving eye had alighted on a pair of figures on the mantelpiece. 'Aren't those Mama's Meissen goddesses, from her sitting room at Southport House?'

'Yes. She gave them to me as a wedding present.'

'I thought I recognised them. Oh, and the black Davenport vases, I see. Goodness! Did she give you those as well?'

'Of course. Did you think I stole them?'

Now at last Gussie looked at her. 'Of course not. Don't be silly.' She inspected her sister at length. 'I must say, you don't look half bad, considering. So you had a boy?'

'Yes. How did you know?'

'Oh, these things get about. Vibart says Hazelmere is thrilled. He met Tommy Weston at Brooks's and Tommy said he couldn't talk of anything else. How tiresome *that* must be! What do you call it?'

'Call what?'

'The baby,' Gussie said impatiently.

'Thomas,' Venetia said. From her sister's demeanour she guessed there was some reason for her visit, and she was waiting for it to surface. She saw no reason to put herself out in the mean time.

'Oh,' said Gussie blankly. She had one glove off now, and was fiddling with a diamond band on one of her fingers. 'Well, I suppose at least it keeps you from doctoring. Does Hazelmere really not mind? I can't believe he likes you to do that. It is quite disgusting, now do admit.'

'I can't admit anything of the sort, but I don't expect you to agree. Our ways parted long ago, Gussie. I hope you haven't come here just to take up an old grievance?'

'I came to see how you were. Is there something wrong with that?' Gussie retorted, though not with quite her old sharpness. 'I can't *like* you being a doctor – what normal person could? – but after all, you've been to Sandringham now, and Buckingham Palace, so I suppose we all have to accept it.'

She lapsed into silence, her eyes far away, and after a moment Venetia asked politely, 'How is your husband?'

Gussie's eyes came back sharply into focus. 'How on earth should I know?' she said. 'He's shooting grouse up at Dromore with Sutherland and Granby. I dare say we'll meet up at Newmarket, but I can't pretend I care.'

Venetia felt a pang of unwilling pity. 'Oh, Gussie, why did you marry him?'

'I thought you knew,' Gussie said, with elaborate carelessness. 'Vibart was all to pieces. He owed twenty thousand pounds – think of it! So when a Certain Person asked him to oblige . . .'

'What do you mean?'

Gussie met her eyes nakedly. 'It was all arranged between them by Harry and the Prince. I dare say they both put something up. I never cared to ask. But the thing is . . .' She swallowed. 'The thing is, you see, that now I'm pregnant.'

Venetia stared, trying to understand. 'But that's wonderful – isn't it? A baby! Why, Colonel Vibart must be delighted, and even if things haven't been quite right between you, it will make all the difference.'

'Oh don't be a fool,' Gussie said roughly. 'It isn't *his* baby.'

Venetia remembered the whispers she had half overheard. 'My God, you don't mean – is it the Prince's baby?' Gussie nodded. 'You're sure?'

'There's no-one else. What do you take me for?' Gussie said, turning her head away. 'I told you, mine is a marriage of convenience. Vibart knows the set-out. He always did.'

There was a silence, at the end of which Venetia said valiantly, 'Well, it's still good, isn't it? The Prince cares for you, doesn't he? And he's a very fond father, from everything I've heard. He'll make sure you're looked after.'

Gussie sighed, a long, deep sigh dragged up from the bottom of her shoes. 'I never wanted a baby. It will spoil everything!'

'You may think that now, but you'll love it when it's here,' Venetia said.

'I shan't! I hate babies! And it will ruin my figure. I'll look hideous for months, and there'll be no going anywhere or having any fun. And then – and then—' She swallowed.

'It will mean the end of everything. *He* won't want me any more, not once I've had a baby.'

'You can't think he'll abandon you?'

'Oh, he'll give me money, if that's what you mean. But he won't want me to be with him any more. My life will be over!'

'Do you love him so very much?' Venetia asked, a little surprised.

Gussie looked at her wildly. 'You don't understand! As it is I'm the most important person in society. I go everywhere. Everyone wants me on their guest list. Wherever he's invited, I'm asked too. I'm first in every company. People copy my clothes, and repeat my sayings, and find out what my favourite foods are before they plan their menus. But if he drops me that's all over. I'll be nobody – and soon there'll be a new one, and I'll have to watch everyone fawn over her instead. I can't do it! I can't give it all up, not now. I'm only thirty-one,' she finished pathetically. 'Not old at all.'

'Oh, Gussie,' Venetia said, with terrible pity.

Gussie leaned forward abruptly and grabbed Venetia's hand. 'You can help me. Please, Venetia, please! I know you can.'

'Help you?' Venetia said, though she guessed what was coming.

'Help me get rid of it. You know how to do things. You must have helped other people, and I'm your sister, damnit! You must help me. I can't have this baby.'

'I can't do that,' Venetia said, trying to withdraw her hand.

But Gussie held tighter. 'No-one will ever know. I haven't told anyone about the baby yet, and I know how to keep my mouth shut. And I'll pay – you needn't worry about that! Anything you ask for. I know you and Hazelmere aren't well off. I'll make you rich if you just do this one thing for me.'

'Gussie, I can't. It's against the law and against my Hippocratic oath – and besides all that it's just plain wrong.'

Gussie dropped her hand. 'Oh, don't give me that cant! Women do it all the time! All those prostitutes you work with, they can't afford to have babies. Don't pretend you've never helped them out of a spot.'

'Not that particular spot. Yes, they ask me sometimes, but I say the same to them as I do to you.' Venetia rubbed her crushed hand, staring at her sister sadly. 'Poor Gussie, how have you come to this pass? Is there no love in you at all?'

'Love?' Gussie's lip curled bitterly. 'For what? For this baby? Why should I love it?'

'Because it's part of you, and part of the man you love. You must have felt something for him to become his mistress.'

Gussie stood up impatiently, shaking this line of reasoning away as a dog shakes water from its coat. 'Let's get this straight. Are you refusing to help me?'

Venetia held her gaze steadily. 'I can't do it.'

'You won't do one small thing for your own sister, to help her out of trouble?'

'It's not a small thing to take a life. And don't you realise how dangerous it is? It could kill you, or leave you paralysed. Even if it weren't illegal and wrong, I wouldn't do it. I wouldn't take that risk with your life and health.'

'Then there's nothing more to be said.' Gussie turned away, tugging angrily at her glove.

'Have the baby, Gussie. You'll love it and so will the Prince. What do you think he would say if he knew you'd tried to get rid of it?'

'I don't have to listen to your pi-jaw,' Gussie said, with her back turned. Her voice sounded uneven. When she reached the door she paused and said, still not turning round, 'Does it hurt?'

'Having a baby? No – not in the way you mean. It's just – very hard work.'

Gussie made a strange small sound in her throat, like a snort of laughter gone the wrong way. 'Yes, I might have expected you to say that. What was that fable Mama used to tell us – about the fox that lost its tail?'

'I haven't lost anything. I'm happier than I can possibly tell you to have had Thomas.'

Gussie threw her a searing glance over her shoulder. 'It's all right for you!'

Venetia thought of Gussie's life, married to Johnny Vibart

as a cover of respectability for her precarious relationship
with the Heir to the Throne, and pity rose up in her, strong
as a flood. 'Have the baby, Gussie,' she said gently. 'Promise
me you won't try to harm it. You'll reproach yourself for
the rest of your life if you do.'

But Gussie only shook her head, and was gone, leaving
Venetia feeling shaken to the core.

CHAPTER TEN

On March the 10th, 1888, the Emperor of Germany, Kaiser Wilhelm, died, and his son Frederick succeeded. 'Fritz' was Queen Victoria's most loved son-in-law: married to her daughter Princess Victoria, he was the most ardent adherent to all the late Prince Consort's teaching and wisdom. The love was mutual: the new Emperor's first official act was to send a telegram to Queen Victoria, the content of which Olivia repeated to Venetia when she went to visit her at the end of the month.

He had written, 'My feelings of deep affection to you prompt me, on succeeding to the throne, to repeat to you my sincere and earnest desire for a close and lasting friendship between our two nations.'

'But it's so terribly sad,' Olivia said, sitting in Venetia's drawing-room with her hands folded in her lap, neat and precise as always. 'The poor Emperor is so sick – Princess Victoria wrote to the Queen about it at the same time. He has a cancer of the throat and it seems there's nothing to be done about it. He's dying, 'Netia! It's such a blow. They've waited so long to come to the throne, and now it's too late.'

'The Queen must be very upset,' Venetia said. It was well known in Court circles how things stood in Berlin. The late Emperor had not seen eye to eye with his son, and there had effectively been two courts in Germany – the reactionary, militaristic court of Wilhelm and his first minister, Prince Bismarck; and the scholarly, liberal and artistic circle of the Crown Prince and his English wife. The worst thing of all was that Fritz's son and heir, William, had been flattered and seduced by his grandparents' circle into a contempt for and neglect of his parents. For thirty years Fritz and Vicky had clung on to their dignity in their backwater, waiting for the time when they would rule and be able to bring about the liberal reforms Germany so needed; now it looked as though that backwater was to become a mere oxbow, while the river of history ran another course.

'Dreadfully upset,' Olivia replied. 'The Queen loves the Emperor like a son; and it incenses her that the German Court prefers to cluster round William as though he were already dead. Sir Edward Malet, our ambassador in Berlin, wrote to Sir Henry Ponsonby that Prince Bismarck's son called the Emperor "an encumbrance", and the Queen found out – she always does, of course. So she means to go and visit them, to show Bismarck and his circle what she thinks.'

'The Queen is going to Germany?'

'Yes, at the end of April.'

'To Darmstadt?'

'No, to Charlottenburg. The Emperor and Empress moved there straight away. However short a time they have, they mean to use it.'

'That must have taken some courage,' Venetia commented. 'So, and will you be going too?'

'Yes,' Olivia said. 'Charlie and I will both be going. Just think, 'Netia, I shall tread in your footsteps, and see all the things you saw.'

'Not quite all, I hope,' Venetia said. She had been in Berlin during the war with France, helping out in the military hospital. It was there that her ambition to be a doctor had crystallised, hardened by the dreadful sights she saw, and the callous incompetence of so many of the doctors.

The conversation was interrupted at that moment by the entry of the nursemaids bringing young Thomas to see his aunt, along with Venetia's new baby, Oliver, who had been born in January. Olivia loved babies, and these little ones put the sad thoughts out of her mind entirely.

The Queen set out for Germany on April the 22nd. The

visit to Berlin was short, but the Queen found time to give Prince Bismarck an audience.

I was surprised to see him so nervous and ill-at-ease. He was mopping his neck with a handkerchief as he went out [Olivia wrote afterwards to Venetia]. But I suppose the Queen of England is so high above him, he might well feel daunted. The Queen spoke about the might of Germany and how they must all desire peace, which he agreed with; and she mentioned the Emperor's illness and urged Bismarck to stand by the Empress, which he promised he would do. He seemed to be very impressed with the Queen. Sir Arthur said that as he went out he muttered to his aide, 'That is a woman! One could do business with her!'

I did not see the Queen's leave-taking of the Emperor, which was in private. It must have been affecting, for she knows she will never see him again, and she loves him so dearly. At the station the Empress climbed up into the carriage to say goodbye to the Queen, and they clung together and kissed and cried so dreadfully. It was heartbreaking to see the poor Empress stand there on the platform weeping as the train pulled out.

Venetia had been kindly treated by the Empress (then Princess Victoria) and her husband when she had been in Berlin – had it not been for the Empress's early patronage she would probably not have been a doctor today – and she felt desperately sorry for them. If they were isolated now, how much worse would it be for the Empress after her beloved husband had died?

That April Henrietta and Jerome moved to a larger house a few streets away. They both wanted to stay in Kensington, which Henrietta liked and Jerome found convenient. Mary might laugh at him for 'wallowing among the middle classes' and urge him to move further into Town, but he smiled and shrugged it off. The air was better up on Campden Hill, he said, and he preferred the speed and convenience of the 'metro' to wasting his life sitting in a stationary hansom in a jam of traffic. Mary's strictures were only a tease: she never refused an invitation to their house. She enjoyed meeting the eclectic variety of friends Jerome brought home, and was a favourite with them for her lively mind and wit.

A larger house was possible because Jerome's business was flourishing; necessary both because of the constant entertaining and the increase of their family. Henrietta had had a second son in September 1887, whom they had called Robert. They needed room to set up a proper nursery, and to employ extra servants.

Emma was still with them, part of the family now. She had taken so strongly to Jack that she had become, first unofficially and then by agreement, his nurse. On Robert's arrival she was given, to her delight, the title of Nanny, and a girl under her. She still sang all day long, and now she had a permanent, and very appreciative, audience: Jack loved her songs, his favourite being 'Father's Donkey', which he pronounced, Emma-fashion, as 'Faather's doonkey' when he begged for it one more time.

Emily the kitchenmaid had long left to improve herself; another Irish girl, Bina, had her place. Edie, too lethargic for ambition, was still with them, along with two other house-maids, Doris and Sarah; and there was a male element now, a footman, Frank, who also took care of Jerome's clothes and the wine cellar he was beginning to lay down, and a boot-boy, Jim, who went home at night.

Sarah the cook had left to get married, and a series of unsatisfactory replacements had come and gone in short order: Mrs Trumper who drank; Mrs Eddows who was impertinent and dirty; Mrs Beech who stole; and Mrs King who was possessed by religious melancholia (Jerome said the reason her gravy was always so thin and salty was that she wept into it while singing gloomy hymns). It was all very depressing, and Henrietta realised that her fortunate experience with servants, as Marion had warned her, had not been typical.

But soon after the move her latest advertisement in the

Daily Telegraph produced Mrs Dark, a very nice and seemingly normal woman who, for a wonder, actually was married – unique in Henrietta's experience of cooks. Perhaps her married status accounted for her normality. At all events, Fanny – as she soon became known – gave satisfaction, and proved a very good, and even sometimes imaginative, cook. Her only drawback was that she 'slept out' – went home at the end of every day.

Marion Sutton was scandalised when she learnt of it, and said it was unheard of and would never work. 'And if you don't have trouble with her, you'll have trouble with the husband,' she insisted, to Henrietta's mild defence of Fanny's nature. 'I had a married cook once and it was disastrous. He kept turning up drunk and making a scene. In the middle of the night, once – broke the basement window trying to get at her. The language! We never knew a moment's peace. Of course, she was separated from him, but the principle's the same. Don't take her on, my dear. You're asking for trouble.'

But Fanny Dark's husband seemed to be as nice and normal as she was. He worked at a brush and broom factory in Shepherd's Bush, and was as steady and sober as anyone could wish. He had been in service himself, and understood the demands of his wife's position, and when the Comptons had dinner parties that kept her late, he often came along to help wait at table. The only difficulty Henrietta encountered from the situation was that occasionally when the fog was down and the public transport was consequently delayed, Fanny might be late arriving in the morning. However, the housemaids were perfectly capable of getting breakfast, especially with Emma (who seemed to feel, as the one who had been there longest, that she had some kind of responsibility for the smooth running of the household) chivvying them along.

Fanny and Emma got along well, both being Catholic and from large families, which made things comfortable: many households were riven by animosity between cook and nanny who, ruling their separate kingdoms as autocrats, each felt they should have authority over the other. Though Emma and Fanny came from different parts of the country they had many of the same sayings. Lizzie found it irresistibly comic to hear them finish each other's sentences.

'Needs must when the—'

'Devil drives.'

'Boughten bread makes the—'

'Mistress fine.'

'Rooks fly high—'

'Clouds go by.'

They would nod to each other encouragingly when this happened, like two cage birds. Lizzie called them the Bookends.

Lizzie was still attending the North London Collegiate where, having progressed now to the upper school, she was finding the lessons more interesting and the discipline less irksome. Her closest friends were still Polly Paget and Agnes Grey. Agnes lived in Chipping Barnet. Her father owned a very large chandlery business, buying up fodder from the great hay belt that encircled London to the north and west and selling it to the large commercial stables in the capital – the omnibus companies, breweries, hackney companies and railway yards.

Mr Grey had made such a fortune in this essential business that he had been able to move from the crowded and dirty surroundings of Long Acre where Agnes had been born to the clean air and green fields of Hertfordshire. The Greys now lived in a large new house with extensive grounds, and kept their own carriage, which delivered Agnes to the railway station every schoolday morning and was waiting for her when she alighted in the afternoon. Agnes was her father's pet, a sharp-witted girl and a droll, who had pleaded for education not because she would ever need to earn her own living but because she was bored at home, and her father would not deny her anything. Despite the wealth of her background, Minnie Sutton referred to her witheringly as 'the ostler's daughter', and whenever Lizzie went to stay with her would make jokes about her having to sleep in a haystack and eat oats out of a nosebag. Lizzie didn't pay any heed: by now she was used to Minnie's jealousy, and understood why she was so unkind about anyone who rivalled her for Lizzie's attention.

Lizzie liked visiting the Greys. Agnes's mother and father were simple, hospitable people, and the style in which they lived had done nothing to change their basic nature, which was friendly, unassuming and charitable. When they had lived in Long Acre they had known all their neighbours, as happens when people live on top of one other; and though they now had four acres of pleasure grounds round their house, they still knew everyone in the village, kept their doors unlocked, and were ready to lay an extra place without notice at any meal. Covered bowls, baskets and packages of food made their way from the kitchen door to the homes of the poor and old, and many a weeping boy had his cut knee or bloodied nose tended by Mrs Grey's own hands as she passed through the village.

It was a very different household from the Pagets', and Lizzie felt at home there. There was always lots of fun at the Greys'. Agnes had three older sisters, all married but living nearby, who were in and out of Grey Lodge as often as their own homes; and a younger brother, Rodney, who was everyone's pet. Polly was often invited at the same time as Lizzie, and sometimes another girl from school, Lilian Bowling, was asked too. Agnes had her own horse, and the girls would go riding together, borrowing Mrs Grey's mare and a neighbour's road horse for Lizzie and Polly – Lilian did not ride. Back at the house there was always something going on – the Greys were very inventive about games – and company coming and going.

Part of the grounds at Grey Lodge had been given over to a tennis lawn, and it was here that Lizzie was first introduced to the game, which had been invented sixteen years before by a retired army officer, Major Wingfield, and patented under the unpromising name of 'Sphairistike' – probably the only game in history to have been subject to a patent. Lawn tennis (as it was now called to distinguish it from 'royal' tennis) was beginning to overtake croquet in popularity, especially amongst the prosperous middle orders, whose new suburban houses had big enough gardens to accommodate it. The first time one of the Suttons' friends had a tennis party to which they and the Comptons were invited, it galled Minnie to discover that Lizzie already knew how to play, and handled the 'racquet' with great insouciance. In fact, Lizzie was not yet very good at it, and at Grey Lodge could only ever win when paired against Rodney Grey, who was only ten, or Lilian, who was very short-sighted. But she made a good show at the Hendersons', where everyone was even more of a novice than she, and Minnie's pique only amused her: she had learned to take a rather reprehensible pleasure in provoking her. Her performance won her deep admiration from Roy Sutton, who said she looked as graceful as a fairy when she stretched for a ball; and though she did not seek or enjoy his compliments, it made her realise that being good at tennis might well prove a social asset in the future.

In May Mrs Paget went to stay with a sister who was ill and needed nursing. She expected to be away for some time, and as Polly did not want to miss school, a letter was sent to Henrietta asking if she could come and stay with the Comptons for a few weeks. Henrietta sent a very cordial reply saying that Polly was welcome to come for as long as she liked. Lizzie was so wildly excited at the prospect of having a friend to stay that Henrietta wondered why she had not thought of suggesting it before.

Dodie and Cam arranged to stay with friends, and Mr Paget was to move in to his club, an arrangement that suited him perhaps better than being at home, since it was much closer to his place of work, and there was never anything there to disturb his reading of the newspaper. The Paget house was shut up and Polly came with her trunk to Kensington and moved with her belongings into Lizzie's room.

After the first week, when Jerome asked Lizzie privately if she was enjoying the new regime, she replied that it was perfect bliss. 'To have your favourite person with you all the time, day and night, so you can talk to them any time you want! Now I understand why people want to get married. It must be just like this – isn't it?'

Jerome laughed at this reply, and for some time afterwards referred to Lizzie and Polly as 'the Mr and Mrs'. To Polly the Compton household was a revelation, and if at first she found herself a little bewildered by the noise and movement and lack of formality, she soon found her feet and joined in with everything. On two occasions her brothers were invited to spend Sunday there, so that she shouldn't feel too homesick; and on the second occasion Marion and Dick Sutton, together with Minnie and Roy, were invited too. Thus Minnie at last fulfilled her ambition of meeting her rival. Her fury at discovering that Miss Mary Paget was not only pretty and elegant, but well dressed too, was mitigated by the handsomeness and charm of her brothers. Dodie and Cam, assessing the situation at a glance, dedicated themselves to the entertainment of Miss Sutton and gave a passable imitation of being smitten by her. In fact, Polly thought it overdone, and made faces at them when no-one else was watching; but they had the bit between their teeth and would not see her, only redoubled their efforts and made their speech even more absurdly flowery. Fortunately Minnie was not accustomed to young men whose wit enabled them to dissemble, and she saw nothing wrong with the performance. Nor did Roy, who not only found it natural that *his* sister should command wherever she went but was glad that the handsome, debonair young men were not devoting themselves to Lizzie, whom he regarded as his own property.

By the time school ended for the summer vacation, Mrs Paget was back from her sister's, and issued a return invitation to Lizzie. She and Polly were to go down and stay with Mr Paget's brother and his wife in Sutton for a month. The Sutton Pagets had a large family, including four of a suitable age for Polly and Lizzie; and Dodie and Cam were also to be there just at first, before going off with some other young men on a trip to France. Henrietta did not hesitate to accept the invitation on Lizzie's behalf. She was glad that her daughter was having the opportunity of company of her own age, knowing that a wide circle of acquaintance would serve her well in later life. She would miss her, but she was feeling rather tired and would not be sorry to have a little peace and quiet, for she had just discovered that she was pregnant again.

Emperor Frederick of Germany died on June the 15th, quietly at the end, with his wife at his side. His reign had lasted only ninety-nine days. Queen Victoria at once telegraphed their son William: 'I am broken hearted. Help and do all you can for your poor dear mother and try to follow in your best, noblest and kindest father's footsteps.'

How little this advice was heeded was soon apparent. The Prince and Princess of Wales travelled to Berlin to represent the Queen at the funeral on June the 18th, and Francis Knollys told Hazelmere about the trip afterwards. The new Emperor's behaviour had been 'trying, to say the least.' He had fidgeted about during the service as if he had wished to be anywhere else, showing not the slightest piety or even respect. Bismarck had claimed he had too much work to be able to attend, and William had not insisted that he did. And the Court Chaplain had laughed and joked throughout the ceremony, but far from rebuking him, William had seemed to enjoy his performance, and looked across, grinning encouragement.

'Shocking though that is, it's not the worst,' Hazelmere said, when he relayed Knollys's words to Venetia. 'His first act as Emperor was to surround the palace where his mother is living with a regiment of Hussars. It's now virtually sealed off from the outside world, as if she and Fritz had been criminals. He's had his father's private writing desk ransacked twice, looking for what he calls "secret documents". The second time, he arrived himself in full dress uniform halfway through the proceedings and shouted at his mother, accusing her of concealing State papers.'

'My God,' Venetia said, horrified. 'He must be mad!'

'Knollys says there's quite an element at Court who think he must be,' Hazelmere said. 'I suppose there is a sense in which all rulers are mad, or have the potential to be. But William has been subverted all his life by an element who loathed Frederick for his peace-loving nature and hated him for marrying an English princess.'

'Yes, I remember the anti-English feeling in Berlin when I was there,' Venetia said.

'It's astonishing when you think of the happy relations between England and the German states in the Prince Consort's time,' Hazelmere said. 'But I suppose the united Germany is a different creature.'

'It's Bismarck's creature,' Venetia said. 'And so now is the Emperor.'

As the weeks passed, more details coming out of Germany provided no comfort or reassurance. William had always had a passionate love of all things military, especially of uniforms, of theatrical display and the demonstration of power. Now that he was Emperor, he was able to give his passion full rein. He declared that he was the reincarnation of Frederick the Great and required his ministers to call him the All Highest. He held huge military parades, with brass bands clashing and cannon firing salutes, and made sure they passed the windows of the palace where his grieving mother sat in mourning. In the Reichstag he promised to be guided by the example of his grandfather, making no mention of his father. Elsewhere he announced that his father's reign had been happily terminated by Providence, and the sooner it was forgotten the better. And against his mother's most urgent wishes, he insisted on a post-mortem of his father's body, which produced a report, authorised by him, that ignorant, clumsy and untrustworthy English doctors had given Frederick the wrong treatment. His grandfather had always encouraged him to blame his deformed arm on the English medical men who had attended his mother at his birth. Now, it seemed, he had a new grievance. He announced publicly: 'An English doctor killed my father, and an English doctor crippled my arm – and this we owe to my mother, who would not have Germans about her.'

When Olivia visited Venetia, she told her of the Queen's fury over the way the Emperor was treating his mother, and her grief for the dowager Empress. For her own part Olivia wondered that anyone could behave so badly, and supposed that the Queen must be correct that he was 'not quite right in the head'. But she did not seem to draw any conclusions beyond the immediate. Venetia, however, brooded that the future of Germany was now in the hands of a – to put it no more strongly – hothead with a passion for the force of arms and an obsession with his own power; that the most militarily powerful nation on earth was governed by a party with a taste for war and a hatred of all things English. And where would that end?

One day in June Venetia was visited by Mrs Anderson, who came to talk about the New Hospital.

'The lease on our two houses runs out soon, and though I've asked Lord Portman to renew it, he refuses absolutely.'

'Really? Why is that? I didn't know he was hostile to us,' Venetia said.

'I think when we began he had not thought about what it would mean,' Mrs Anderson said. 'It's not the hospital itself, but the crowd of poor women and babies waiting outside on the pavement every afternoon for the outpatients' clinic to open. He thinks they give the area a bad name.'

'I suppose they don't look very tidy,' Venetia said. 'And the numbers have grown so rapidly, haven't they?'

'We treated more than five thousand last year, and already this year it's double that. As it happens, I don't mind too much having to move, because we badly need larger premises. The quality of our work is as high as anywhere in the land – I insist on that – but we are not helped by poky rooms and overcrowding.'

'So will you look for somewhere else?'

Mrs Anderson sighed. 'I already have been looking, and really, I might have saved myself the time. If we were free to choose a house as private people would, I could have found excellent quarters over and over again. There are lots of large houses suitable for conversion in Bloomsbury and Marylebone. But everywhere I enquired, the landlord objected to a hospital on his premises, and the local house-holders objected to having a hospital next door. The only houses we could have bought were wretched tumbledown places in the most squalid districts.'

'So what will you do?'

'We've decided – the Committee has decided – that the only answer is to buy a vacant site and build a new hospital.'

'That sounds like good sense. Have you anywhere in mind?'

'Yes, there's a suitable plot in Euston Road, further east than we are now, but nearer to the London School, which is convenient. We can get a seventy-year lease on it.'

'Oh, excellent! Long enough to settle in,' Venetia said, with a smile.

'Quite. And we have decided on a hospital of forty beds.'

'So all you need now,' Venetia said, well aware of how these conversations went, 'is the money. I take it that's why you've come to me?'

'Of course, I was hoping for a donation. I shall be launching the fund next month. There'll be an opening meeting – the Lord Mayor has offered the Mansion House, which will look well – but I'd like not only to raise money but to educate the public about the work of women in medicine. So I was hoping that I could persuade you to address one of the meetings, and perhaps to write a piece for one of the newspapers. You are very well known now, and you have the ear of people in the higher ranks of society.'

'I believe I could manage to do that,' Venetia said, 'if you think that my fame is of a positive sort now. I remember you once thought me too notorious.'

Mrs Anderson shook her head. 'Don't let's bring up the past. You and I have come through difficult times, but I believe the tide is with us now, and this is the moment when we can take public opinion with us. Women doctors now pursue the same education as men, pay the same fees, pass the same examinations. All we lack is the practical experience after registration, because general hospitals will not offer us house jobs. But you operate at the New and at the Southport, and you can tell people how important this practice is.'

'So can you.'

'It's better coming from two of us. And they've heard me before – yours will be a new voice.'

'Well, I'll do all I can to help you,' Venetia said. 'And Hazelmere shall give you a cheque. I'll write to my cousin Batchworth – he should be good for a thousand, if I press him. My mother will give something, too, I know. By the way, have you approached Miss Nightingale?'

Mrs Anderson nodded. 'She's my trump card, as far as the general public goes. She has sent fifty pounds, and a very warm letter, which I mean to read out at the opening meeting. And she has agreed to look at the building plans when we have them finished, and give them her seal of approval. That should open purses in the provinces.'

'You're right. Hers is a magical name. If you have her on board, you might even get the Queen to endorse you.'

Venetia approached Anne Farraline for a donation to the fund, and found that she had already been drawn in via another source. It was not the first time Venetia had remarked how closely all the women's groups were inter-connected.

Anne's main interest that year was the Local Government Act. In the past, the counties had been administered in the ancient way by the justices of the peace through the quarter sessions. Under the new Act, councils were to be elected to do the work: the first institution of the democratic principle, which was intended eventually to extend to all local government. The aspect of the Act that had caused intense excitement to the women's suffrage groups was that women were to be allowed to vote in the council elections – the first time women had been included in an electorate.

They were particularly interested in the elections to the London County Council. For the first time the capital was to acquire a popularly elected authority, which would have the power to affect issues like paving, lighting, cleansing and public health. Before, these had been in the hands of an anti-quated jumble of historic authorities such as vestries and district boards, too small to do much good, and usually too lazy and corrupt to want to. The influence of the London

County Council would be enormous, and its prestige – as for the first time the fragmented parts of London would take on a unified identity – would be beyond imagination. And the most exciting thing of all was that the wording of the Act did not preclude the election of women to the Council.

After an intense campaign, two ladies were elected, and with good majorities; but in the end they were not allowed to take their places. That same ambivalence in the Act was used against them, and it was claimed that, as it had not been made clear that women *were* allowed to serve, it must mean they were not. The position was strengthened by the refusal of the men who had been elected to serve with women, and so the women's cause suffered another disappointment.

It was a blow, but Anne refused to be completely downcast. 'We soldier on,' she said. 'Another opportunity will present itself. Look how many years it took for women to become doctors.'

'And we still aren't accepted,' Venetia reminded her.

'But making the first foothold is always the hardest thing. We benefit by your pioneering work.'

Venetia laughed. 'God bless your optimism!'

In the January of 1889, Venetia and Hazelmere were invited to a hunting party at Easton Lodge in Essex, the home of Daisy Brooke. She had been born Frances Maynard, and had inherited estates worth £20,000 a year from her grandfather, the last Viscount Maynard. Besides being fabulously rich, she was also extremely beautiful, vivacious and intelligent – so eminently eligible that it was said she had once been considered as a match for Queen Victoria's favourite son, Prince Leopold. Whatever the truth of that, Miss Maynard had all the confidence and determination of an only child who had inherited a fortune at the age of three and was used to command all those around her. She would make her own choice of husband. She chose Lord Brooke, the heir to the Earl of Warwick, whom she married in 1881 in Westminster Abbey, at a service whose guests of honour were the Prince and Princess of Wales.

The Brookes' London home was in Carlton Gardens, but for their country home they continued to use Easton, which Lady Brooke loved with a passion. She adored giving house parties, hunting, playing billiards, and driving a four-in-hand, but these things, and the indolent affection of 'good old Brookie', did not add up to quite enough excitement. So, having provided her husband with an heir or two, she took a lover.

Her choice fell on Lord Charles Beresford, something Venetia could never understand. Lord Charles was a sea-officer – he had commanded a gunboat during the Egyptian campaign, and in 1886 had been appointed to the Admiralty by Lord Salisbury, at the Prince of Wales's request. He was part of the Prince's most intimate inner circle: in 1875 he had been one of those friends, along with Charles Carrington and Venetia's brother Harry, who had accompanied the Prince on his official trip to India; and his brother, Lord Marcus, was the manager of the Prince's stud.

As well as being a successful sailor, Lord Charles was extremely handsome and dashing; but he had a violent temper, was impetuous and careless of consequences, and was a notorious adulterer. From what Venetia had heard, he had little love for his conquests, and his was not a kindly nature: Francis Knollys told her he had once said he liked to make women cry because it was such fun to hear their stays creak.

But he and Daisy Brooke fell passionately in love, and had conducted an affair so torrid that at one time they had talked of elopement, and even complaisant Lord Brooke had been roused to murmur about divorce. But perhaps they had met their match in each other, for if he was unfaithful to her, she was equally not averse from bestowing her favours elsewhere. At all events, the affair seemed to be cooling when the invitation arrived at Manchester Square, and Venetia supposed with a sigh that they ought to accept it.

'I should think so indeed!' Hazelmere laughed at her. 'Refuse an invitation to Easton?'

'Oh, but you know I don't enjoy house parties,' Venetia said.

'I understand why you don't like shooting parties, but hunting parties are different. Lady Brooke offers to mount you, so you'll have something to do to keep you out of the house. A something, moreover, at which you can excel.'

She smiled. 'You are remarkably confident in me. I haven't hunted for years.'

'It's not something you forget,' he said easily.

'I may fall off in the mud and make a fool of myself.'

'You won't. I shall put money on you to be up in the first flight. I rely on you to put Daisy Brooke's perfect nose out of joint, my love.'

'Oh, really, Beauty, I don't think I can be bothered!'

'Shame on you! That's pure idleness. But in any case, you can't refuse. The Prince of Wales will be there, and I hear he has asked particularly for you.'

'Who told you that?'

'Brookie himself. I met him at the club and he passed on the message.'

'Poor Brookie. What a life he leads, sent hither and yon like a telegraph boy!'

'Oh, he doesn't mind. He won't be there anyway. He'll be shooting at Blenheim.'

So to Easton they went. The weather was dry, cold and hard – not good hunting weather, but pretty to look at as the train rushed through the frozen countryside, while the sky drained pink down to the trees and the winter dark came up from the east.

They were met at the door of Easton Lodge by the Groom of the Chambers and a platoon of footmen in livery, all six feet tall and broad at the shoulder. Daisy Brooke had matching footmen, a conceit Venetia did not know whether to laugh at or cry over. To match servants as one matched carriage horses seemed both ludicrous and wrong-headed; but then she supposed if you had vast sums of money and nothing but your home and your pleasure to think about, you might well be tempted to such excesses.

'At all events, we can be sure we'll be comfortable here,' said Hazelmere.

Country-house visits were often an agony: draughty,

ill-lit passages; Spartan bedrooms with smoking fires, dreadful old beds that felt as though they were stuffed with rocks, and where any light was positioned so that it was impossible to read in comfort; nothing but cold water to wash in; and appalling food, which had to be carried so far from the kitchens it was always cold and congealed. And even the public rooms were sometimes so poorly heated that the ladies in their low-cut and sleeveless evening gowns would find the smooth arms they prided themselves on puckering up like dead chickens.

'Yes. Remember Eaton Hall?' Venetia said. 'The drawing-room was so cold we all turned blue.'

'But if rumour is true, Easton can be relied upon for creature comforts.'

'What a difference a single consonant can make!'

Rumour proved to be true. The whole house was warm – not just the rooms but the passages too – and well-lit. The bedchamber to which Venetia was shown had a large bed with a good mattress, and was elegantly furnished with big comfortable chairs and a sofa; lamps were placed so that reading would be a pleasure, and there were more looking-glasses than Venetia knew what to do with. Everything a guest might conceivably need was to hand. On a side table was a bowl of fruit and a pretty tin box full of biscuits to guard against starvation in the night; the latest travel books, biographies and talked-about novels were placed where they could be reached from the sofa without getting up; the writing desk was provided with pens, paper, reference books, gazetteer and even a box full of stamps.

'The person who could find fault with this room must be unreasonable indeed,' she remarked to her maid, as she changed for tea. Since her first experience at Sandringham their social life had expanded so much that she had given in and employed a housemaid capable of doubling as lady's maid when they went away. Greevy was a very good girl and a positive demon with a flat-iron, and her only complaint about her present position was that when at home her lady refused to be properly maided and would put on her stockings and boots herself. Greevy adored country-house visiting, and was never so happy as when travelling away. Easton represented her highest peak yet, and she was thrilled to the marrow to be here.

'The Prince of Wales himself is here, my lady! Imagine! Of course, His Royal Highness's servants keep separate from us downstairs, but it's such an honour even being in the same house with the man who brushes the clothes of the future King of England!'

Downstairs in the saloon the company gathered for tea, laid out on a vast round table for people to help themselves from an array of every kind of sandwich and cake, besides muffins, crumpets, scones, jam, honey and Devonshire cream. It was not the custom here for people to be introduced to each other: it was assumed everyone knew everyone else; or perhaps it was thought to be an insult to assume anyone did *not*. Venetia was glad to see that Charles Beresford was not present. Perhaps the rumours of the cooling-off were accurate.

The Prince of Wales was present without the Princess, and Venetia recognised Sir George Chetwynd, a particular friend of Johnny Vibart's, and Charles Carrington, Harry Chaplin, Fred Somerset, Bentley Greville and 'Buck' Middleton. Amongst the ladies she recognised Meriel Denbigh and Lady Edward Marchant. Apart from herself and Hazelmere, the only married couple present was Lord and Lady de Grey. So, she thought with a little sinking of heart, it was going to one of *those* parties. She was not *au fait* with who was flirting with whom, and looked forward to a confusing and possibly embarrassing few hours.

But her inclusion in the company seemed to be explained by the presence of her brother, the Duke of Southport. She started when she saw him, and wondered for a moment if Daisy Brooke could have made a mistake. But as he caught sight of her he smiled – a little awkwardly, but it was a smile nevertheless – and as soon as it was possible he came over to her side.

'Well, well,' he said, and then, as if it helped, repeated it. 'Well, well.'

'Hello, Harry,' Venetia said cautiously. She hadn't seen

him for years. He had refused the invitation to her wedding, and the only time since then that she had even written to him was to tell him of the birth of her first child. She surveyed him covertly, remembering what their brother Marcus had said about Harry's state of health; but he seemed to be sober and of a normal state of mind, was properly dressed and groomed, and though rather thin and looking older than his age, he did not seem to be unwell. 'How are you?'

He had been surveying her with equal interest. 'Oh, tol-lol, you know. Good to see you here. Seem always just to have missed you wherever I go, I don't know how it is. Turn up the week before or the week after. You're looking well. Damned well. Hazelmere here?'

'Yes, he's talking to Lady Denbigh,' Venetia said. Harry looked vaguely in the direction, but he evidently had other things on his mind, and feeling impatient, Venetia cut through to the question: 'Harry, did you ask for me to be invited?'

He seemed a little offended at such directness, and stared a moment before saying, 'I suppose I did, in a way. Mentioned to HRH that I'd be glad to see you, at any rate. He must have done the rest. Not that he'd need persuading. Uncommon fond of you, is Tum.' This was the nickname that a few of the closest to him – Carrington and Chetwynd, for instance – had bestowed on the Prince.

'Is he?' she said stonily.

'Oh, yes. Thinks the world of you. Often says—' He stopped in mid-sentence, and seemed to be working out whether the rest of it was repeatable or not.

'I shan't rely on that, however,' Venetia said. 'He used to think the world of Gussie.'

'Oh, hush!' Harry murmured, stepping nearer. 'Gussie's all right. It's her own fault she was dropped – made a fuss, you see. Don't *you* do it.'

'I don't mind whether I'm dropped or not,' Venetia said impatiently.

'Yes, you do,' Harry said. 'Got to live in the world, 'Netia. Got to think of your family – children and so on. Olivia and

Charlie. Even poor Gussie. Don't make a fuss, that's the important thing. People will forgive anything except people making a fuss.'

Venetia knew it was true. The Prince of Wales was a kindly man and had taken good care of Gussie, and after the baby was born – in the May of '87 – she could have come back into society. But it was plain that the Prince was out of love with her, and instead of accepting it gracefully she had tried to get him back, accused him of neglect, and put it about that the baby was his and not Vibart's. Probably everyone in the inner circle had guessed that anyway, but it should never have been *said*. The Princess of Wales frosted her, the Prince requested her to be cut from a guest list on which his name appeared, and in a matter of weeks she and Vibart were untouchables. They had had to go to France, where they were living, the last thing Venetia had heard, in a small *hôtel* on the Ile St Louis – which, she reflected, would be torture to poor Gussie, who had never learnt French and hated the very idea of 'abroad'.

'Have you heard from her?' Venetia asked now.

'She wants to come back,' Harry said, unsurprisingly. 'Thing is, it may be possible. Fuss has died down, people have forgotten. I'm working on HRH, so don't make any waves, will you?'

'Of course not,' Venetia said. 'But why did you want me here, Harry?'

'I wanted to see you,' he said, after a moment's hesitation. 'To bury the hatchet. Make peace. It's not good for a family to be at outs. We ought to be friends. Don't you think? I am your brother, after all – your only brother now.'

Venetia stared, trying to make sense of it. It was he who had cast her out and maintained the ban ever since. Why the sudden change? Because the Prince 'thought the world of her'? Surely not. He had had the Prince's ear for years on his own account. 'Does my being a doctor not trouble you any more?' she asked acidly.

'Very brave women,' he said. 'Everybody says so.'

'So I'm respectable now?'

'Hazelmere's a good fellow,' Harry said, with rather more

sincerity. 'And—' He seemed to have come to the point of confession. 'You see the dark-haired female over there? In the blue? Talking to Gladys de Grey?'

'Oh – yes,' Venetia said. A slim young woman with a mass of dark hair and a pale face, and something indefinably foreign about her dress – the cut or the trim, she couldn't decide what immediately. 'Who is she?'

'Miss Culpepper. Nancy Culpepper. She's American. Her father's one of these millionaires. Or perhaps not quite that, but frightfully rich, at any rate. A wheat magnate, they call him. Very keen on horses, too. Has a stud in Maryland or Virginia or one of those places, that would make your eyes stand out on stalks. So Marcus Beresford says, anyway.'

'You seem to know a lot about her,' Venetia said, a suspicion forming in her mind.

'I'm nearly thirty-six,' Henry said starkly. 'Marcus is dead. Mama's been lecturing me.'

'You mean to marry her?'

'That's the idea,' Harry said, though without great enthusiasm. 'Could do with the money, too, but it's the heir business that's most pressing. So I've given Alicia her *congé*.' This was Alicia Booth, the actress, his mistress of many years. 'And I'm courting Nancy for all I'm worth. Her pa is all for the title, of course – "his little girl an English duchess", and so forth – but he wants to be sure it's all above board. *Entrée* into society all present and correct. The right connections. So I've got to square Mama, get Gussie back, show I'm in Tum's good books, and—'

'And you thought I'd be an asset?' Venetia said drily.

He had the grace to fidget. 'They look at lady doctors differently over there. Admire 'em. Females who get on and do things are – well, respectable. And Hazelmere's a good fellow. Knows everyone. And now you're on the Sandringham list . . .' He let the sentence fall.

She looked at him with suppressed exasperation, and wondered whether any right-thinking female ought to encourage the American heiress to marry a reprobate like her brother. But then the whole thing began to strike her as funny. And Miss Culpepper ought to be able to look after herself, if half what she had heard about American girls was true.

'All right, Harry, I'll do my best for you. But I rather doubt my contribution will be the deciding factor.'

'Thanks, Sissy,' Harry said, reverting in his relief to an affectionate name of their childhood, which more recent events had made painfully inappropriate.

Hazelmere had been right: a hunting party was much more bearable than a shooting party. Daisy Brooke in the most generous fashion provided Venetia with a superb mount, a sixteen-hand dark chestnut called Munstead whom she had hunted at the beginning of the season and said was 'going superbly'.

'I know you are a fine rider by reputation,' she said to Venetia, 'and I only ask you to be kind to my dear boy's mouth. He's big and he's strong, but he never pulls. He has a mouth like a kitten, so be careful with the curb, won't you?'

Hazelmere was given one of 'Brookie's' hunters, a fine old fellow of twenty-one called Grenadier. When they walked out together in the morning to claim their mounts, Hazelmere compared Grenadier, standing peacefully chewing his bit, with the curvetting youngster wearing the sidesaddle, and said ruefully, 'I can see which of us Daisy Brooke thinks is the rider. It seems I wasted my youth in the cavalry.'

Venetia eyed Munstead doubtfully. 'Perhaps she sees me as a rival and wants to do away with me. Does that look to you like a "dear boy" with a "mouth like a kitten"?'

'*Do* kittens have good mouths? I should have thought they were dangerous – not soft, at any rate. I think you've been hoaxed, my love. Want to call it off?'

'Laugh at me all you like,' Venetia said coldly. 'I'll show you. I'll show you all!'

The morning was promising for a good day's hunting. The wind had gone round in the night and the hard cold setting in from the east had been replaced with a damp mildness from the south-west. The bone was out of the ground, the scent was good, and they found at once. Venetia had had 'Buck' Middleton appointed to her as a pilot. It was usual for a lady who hunted to be piloted by a man, especially if she did not know the country. It was harder to ride sidesaddle than across, and if one came off, almost impossible to get back on without help. The pilot would find a line for his lady, pick out the jumpable places, generally take care of her, and ensure she had a good day.

But as soon as they started to run, Middleton, riding up alongside her, shouted, 'You don't need me to guide you. You're on a real topper there. Daisy's a trump to give you him! You can take him where you like, and find your own line.'

Munstead had gone straight into a hard gallop, and feeling the power of him under her, Venetia called back, 'I don't think I can stop him.'

Middleton grinned. 'Why should you want to stop him? Hounds are running!'

'But I doubt if I can turn him.'

'You don't need to – they're running straight.'

Venetia could only laugh. The thrill of the hunt was taking hold of her, the old, remembered exhilaration of speed and power, the thunder of hoofs, the surge of muscle beneath her, the sting of the air on her cheeks and the tight, pricked ears before her. Her busy life in London left no room for riding, and she discovered now how much she had missed it. Suddenly she felt absolutely confident. Munstead was putting his feet down beautifully, and she didn't believe he would stumble; and Daisy Brooke had been right after all – though he was going full out, he wasn't pulling. She believed she could stop him if she wanted, but she didn't want. She wanted to be up with the first flight, with Daisy herself and the Prince. Perhaps that was why she had been given Mr Middleton as pilot: it was a compliment to her reputation, just as Munstead was.

A vast double oxer was looming up, and Fred Somerset was between her and it, lumbering along on a heavyweight and already slowing for a cautious approach. She couldn't stop now. Venetia leaned forward a little and shouted, 'Get out of the way! Get out of the way!' Somerset turned his head, checking his horse automatically. Venetia shot past, catching a glimpse of bulging eyes and a mouth open in surprise. Middleton was close at her shoulder, and they both took the oxer soaringly.

She had a wonderful day, and rode back towards the house in the gloaming with the rest of the company, aching pleasantly in every muscle and with a mind perfectly at peace. Hazelmere came alongside her to say, 'I hope you've had a good day. I have! I take back any unkind thoughts I had about my old fellow here. He went like a train. You'd never know he was twenty-one.' He patted the damp neck enthusiastically.

'I had a wonderful day,' Venetia said. 'My only regret is that it was so good, the rest of the weekend must be an anticlimax.'

'Especially as you haven't a lover to intrigue with,' Hazelmere said. 'I must say it's dull to be here with one's own wife. Would you like me to pursue one of the other ladies so as to leave you free for Mr Middleton?'

'Not for your life,' she said, with a laugh. 'Oh, I'm glad this is Easton! There'll be good fires and hot water when we get in. And a decent bed. Even as it is I shall be as stiff as a board tomorrow. I haven't ridden for so long, and this was hardly a gentle easing back into the saddle!'

'The thing is to keep moving,' Hazelmere said wisely. 'Perhaps there'll be dancing tonight. Or if not, you had better go to the billiard room and knock the balls about. There'll be a good dinner, at any rate – that much we can be sure of. And an evening not entirely without interest, I fancy.'

'Guessing who will be corridor-creeping to whom?' Venetia said, with a faint grimace.

Hazelmere lowered his voice and said, 'I can give you some information on that subject. It throws light on many unanswered questions.'

'Gossip, Lord Hazelmere? Well, what is it?'

'The Prince is in love with Daisy Brooke. Yes, it's true! He can't take his eyes from her. Carrington says he's never

224

seen him so smitten. I fancy we are seeing the beginning of the next grand royal romance.'

Venetia thought of Gussie, and of Gussie's little baby Edward. Well, at least her sister could console herself that her replacement was the most striking, intelligent and desirable woman in society.

CHAPTER ELEVEN

Mrs Anderson's fund for the new hospital building grew so rapidly that only a few months after its inauguration, it had been possible to purchase the lease of the site in the Euston Road for three thousand pounds. There were advantages to the new position over the old: it was close to King's Cross and St Pancras stations, the Metropolitan railway had a stop nearby, and there were omnibuses that passed it, which would be helpful to women living at a distance who had need of the specialist treatment available, and those patients too sick to walk far. And the site was flanked by areas of crowded streets, back alleys and mean tenements – Somerstown and Agar Town – full of the poor and needy people the hospital was intended to help.

At the beginning of 1889 work began to clear the site, and on the 7th of May the foundation stone was laid in a grand ceremony, which was planned by Mrs Anderson and the Committee to gain the maximum amount of publicity for the hospital and for the cause.

Venetia attended, and offered a place in her carriage to Henrietta. Henrietta accepted gladly. She had hardly been out of the house since the birth of her third child – another boy, Francis – at the end of February.

'The time goes by so quickly when you have a new baby,' she said. 'Here we are with spring in full flood, and I've hardly noticed it arrive.'

'I've noticed it,' Venetia said. 'Not by the leaves on the trees and the birds in the nests, however. It's the upsurge of infections and diseases that tells me winter's over.'

'I expect you're glad of a change of scene,' Henrietta said. 'It's kind of you to ask me. I wish Lizzie might have come – I think she'd have found it interesting – but she wouldn't miss school for anything.'

'It's her last year, isn't it?'

'No, she has one more to go. She's only sixteen – seventeen in September.'

'What does she want to do after that?'

'We've talked about it a little, but she doesn't really know. Jerome tells her there's no hurry to decide. I think in the back of his mind he thinks she will get married, so it doesn't matter.'

Venetia laughed. 'I know, however modern men are in their thinking, the backs of their minds never change! Hazelmere is just the same, really. Every time I'm called out, he has to make a conscious effort not to tell me I'm a lady and ought not to expose myself to such disagreeable things.'

The day, though warm, was grey and overcast. Venetia, craning to look out of the window, hoped it would not rain. 'It always *does* on these occasions, just to annoy.'

'It won't rain,' Henrietta said. 'The clouds are too high for rain, and the wind – what there is of it – is from the south-east, which is a dry direction.'

Venetia looked amused. 'How do you know that?'

'The first thing I do every morning is look out to see what the weather will be,' Henrietta said, faintly surprised. 'I suppose it must be because I'm a country person at heart.'

'I used to think of myself as a country person,' Venetia said, with a sigh, 'but I've spent so long in London I've forgotten all the country lore. The back alleys and the Agar Towns are my natural habitat now.'

'But you move in the best circles too,' Henrietta said. 'Don't you find it difficult to be going from your poor patients to your rich friends?'

'I do sometimes feel like a species of Jekyll and Hyde, living my two separate lives. But in fairness, I don't spend *very* much time lolling on silken divans! I'm sure I know more prostitutes than peeresses.'

'Better be careful who you say that to!' Henrietta said; and then as Venetia's words triggered a memory, her smiled faded. 'That dreadful business last year – those poor women murdered in Whitechapel – is it all over now, do you think?'

'It seems so,' Venetia said cautiously. 'There've been no more since November. The police think the murderer must have either gone hopelessly mad or killed himself, after the last one. That murder was particularly horrible.' She stopped, recollecting to whom she was talking. From the end of August to November 1888 a series of murders of prostitutes carried out in a small area of Whitechapel had become front-page news, and brought about such public concern and even panic that the resignation of the commissioner, Sir Charles Warren, had been demanded, petitions had been sent to the Queen, and private citizens had offered cash rewards for the capture of the murderer.

As Inspector Morgan, Venetia's particular police friend, had said to her, 'It's not the murders, particularly, but the method of them – the mutilations. There've been five other murders of prostitutes in the Metropolitan area this year, but they're just common murders: the women were killed by their menfolk, usually in a drunken fight. It happens all the time, as you know.'

'Yes,' said Venetia. The strains of the kind of life lived by the poorest – always in debt and in want, living on top of each other in the vilest conditions – led to drunkenness. 'Lush' was the only escape from an unbearable reality, and drink all too often led to violence.

But the Whitechapel murders were different. An unknown man stalking and murdering women with whom he had no connection, and killing them moreover in such a calculatedly vile way, was something to send chills down any spine.

'The tails expect to get knocked about by their men on a Saturday night,' Morgan had continued. 'That's something they understand. But this!'

Venetia heard something of their fears from prostitutes in her own area whom she treated. Translating their inarticulate plaints, it seemed to her it was the randomness they most feared – how do you defend yourself against the incalculable? – plus the violent hatred the actions seemed to suggest.

'We ain't never done nothin' to 'urt no-one. We're juss tryin' ter make a livin',' one said, appealing to Venetia as if she had some means of stopping it. 'What'd they do if they was us? If men didn't want it, we wouldn't be doin' it, would we?'

Despite the horrible nature of the killings, Venetia was a little surprised at the way they became national news. The East End, after all, was to most people the place where such things happened, and the victims were 'only' prostitutes. Hazelmere pointed out that the part of Whitechapel involved was very small, and that the rest of the area was quite respectable, home to decent, hard-working people who saw their livelihoods threatened by an unchecked wave of crime. It was the honest traders of Whitechapel who had got up the first petition.

Venetia thought there might be something in that, but in her view what both fascinated and horrified the reading public was the same thing that terrified the prostitutes – the idea of a stranger killing at random for no apparent reason. If such a thing could happen, who was safe?

But there had been no more killings since November, and though the killer had never been brought to justice, things were beginning to settle down again.

'What do you suppose it was all about?' Henrietta asked. 'Was it someone trying to rid the streets of vice? I read that somewhere.'

'Oh, there are a dozen theories,' Venetia said. 'I don't suppose we'll ever know, now. Much better not dwell on it – there was altogether too much unhealthy interest last year, in my view.'

The carriage was passing the Southport Hospital, and Venetia pointed it out, glad of a change of subject.

'It's very imposing,' Henrietta said. She hadn't seen it before: a massive building, plainly Georgian in concept, with a multitude of tall sash windows and heavy stone copings.

Mama's hospital, Venetia thought. *What an achievement*

that was! Nothing I can do can ever equal it. Now here was the elaborate Gothic of St Pancras and the starkly neo-classical King's Cross, and they had hardly passed the usual tangle of station traffic when they came upon the tail of a carriage jam. 'If these are all bound for the same place we are,' Venetia said, 'the occasion will be a great success.'

The crush was so great they had to abandon the carriage and walk. Venetia sent it home, telling her coachman they would take a cab back. A huge crowd had gathered, filling the pavement and spilling over into the road, further impeding the traffic. They were mostly women, but with a fair sprinkling of children and idlers. They were very good-natured and, when Venetia told them who she was, made way for her and Henrietta and almost bundled them through.

The site itself looked very gay, with a huge marquee flying strings of bunting – rather limp on this windless day – and masses of potted palms, ferns and flowers banked all around it to disguise the otherwise bare nature of an empty plot. There was a red carpet laid from the marquee to the pavement, and a detachment of volunteer rifles in gaudy uniforms for an honour guard. A military band was formed up to one side, playing a selection of popular tunes, and a crowd of press reporters and two photographers were gathered at the entrance, hungrily noting down the names of the invited guests who were chatting together while they waited for the arrival of the royal party.

At the centre of attention was Mrs Anderson herself, standing with the Archbishop of Canterbury, who had come to bless the endeavour, and the leading lights of the New Hospital and the London School. Venetia exchanged a few words of greeting with them, introduced Henrietta, then moved on to mingle with the other guests.

'Everyone's here. How gratifying! Look, there's Miss Octavia Hill and her friend Miss Jekyll. Mrs Fawcett – she's Mrs Anderson's sister. And the Balfours, over there. Mr Stansfeld – what a good friend he's been to us! Henry Cust and John Burns: lots of radicals here – that's a good sign. Oh, and there's dear old Miss Ulverston. I must speak to her.'

There was a number of lady doctors present, who greeted Venetia as an old friend, and most of the female medical students from the London School, who pointed her out to each other with awe. She and Henrietta made their way slowly through the throng, smiling and greeting. The band played, and the level of conversation rose, to form a blanket of sound as unbroken as the grey sky. As more and more people arrived, it became harder to move, and it was only over people's heads that they saw Patsy, who had come with Mary, holding a sketch pad and drawing rapidly. Mary they could not see because of the crowd. Venetia waved, but Patsy did not see her. And at a distance she saw her cousin Tommy Weston, talking to a fellow MP and the eminent physician Frederick Treves. She couldn't see Tommy's wife, her old friend Emma.

The band, which had been playing a selection from *The Mikado*, now came to a stop with a crashing chord, and the din of conversation trickled away into a murmur as it was plain something was happening. The sound of cheering rose from out in the road, and there was a general stirring as people tried to see the arrival of the guest of honour.

And then there she was: the Princess of Wales, a slender, youthful figure in a green velvet dress with diamonds flashing on her bonnet, with two ladies-in-waiting behind her. She smiled and exchanged a word with the Archbishop; Mrs Anderson curtseyed and shook the gloved hand; a little girl in a white dress came forward, after a covert shove from behind, to curtsey and present a nosegay, which the Princess took with a sweet smile.

Conducted by Mrs Anderson she came walking up the red carpet, smiling and nodding to the people on either side. Venetia said quietly to Henrietta, 'It's wonderful that she's here – the first royal endorsement the hospital has ever had. Mrs Anderson did well to secure her. It ought to make a big difference to the funding.'

The crowd of guests folded in behind the royal party and passed into the tent; the press reporters were admitted from the other end and gathered respectfully to one side, pencils at the ready. Mrs Anderson made a speech; the builders,

Mr Higgs and Mr Hill, and the architect, Mr Brydon, were presented to Her Royal Highness, and the Archbishop prayed for the success of the venture, the relief of suffering, and for God's blessing on all concerned. Then the Princess was handed a new silver trowel with which to perform the ceremony.

In the general shuffling for position, Venetia caught sight of Tommy again, standing with a woman now, seemingly engaged in a very absorbing conversation. It was not Emma, however – this woman was too tall. Venetia could not see her face, only her hat – a smart black hussar with a stiff black hackle at the front.

The business was completed, everyone applauded, the band struck up again, and the royal party retreated, with more handshaking and words of good will, smiles to either side, and a final wave of the hand as they climbed into the carriages; and then the carriages pulled away to huge cheering from the crowds outside, who loved any sort of royalty, but the Princess of Wales most of all.

The press and some of the guests departed, and as the pressure eased it became possible to move again. Conversations were struck up with more purpose, now the official ceremony was over. Tommy Weston suddenly appeared at Venetia's side.

'There you are! Splendid affair, isn't it? I think every single newspaper has sent someone: very good publicity for the hospital.'

'It's needed,' Venetia said. 'We're nowhere near the total wanted yet.'

'But doing well, I understand?'

'Oh, yes. But where's Emma? Isn't she here with you?'

'No, she didn't feel up to coming.'

'Is she unwell?' Venetia asked. Emma had recently been confined with her seventh child – but not so very recently. It must be five weeks now, she calculated.

'Oh, no, but she won't be venturing out for a week or two yet. You know how it is,' Tommy said vaguely.

Venetia would have asked more, but at that moment Mary and Patsy joined them.

'Hello!' Patsy said brightly. 'I've got some topping sketches. Frank Burnand wants me to do something on today's little ceremony. Do you suppose I'd be clapped in the Tower if I dared to draw the Princess? I've thought of the most wonderful caption. The Archbishop hands her the trowel, you see, and she says—'

'You can't,' Mary said. 'You really can't. Yes, you would be clapped in the Tower, and beheaded as well! Hello, Henrietta. Lady Venetia. Tommy, how are you? I didn't know you'd be here.'

'Couldn't miss an important occasion like this. A landmark in the progress of the Cause,' he said.

'As a Member of Parliament, tell this cousin of mine she can't lampoon the Princess of Wales,' Mary went on.

'I wasn't going to lampoon her,' Patsy objected. 'But I expect it would be safer to leave her out. I have a good sketch of Mrs Anderson, which I suppose is more to the point. But now I have to go to the British Museum and draw some Egyptian mummies.'

'Why on earth?' Henrietta asked. 'What have they to do with it?'

'You'll see,' Patsy said.

'Well, I'm not going with you,' Mary said. 'It's very dull work watching someone draw. I shall take a cab home.'

'Perhaps I can give you a lift,' Tommy said quickly. 'I have my carriage with me.'

'Oh, thank you. That would be kind,' said Mary.

Venetia looked from her to Tommy and back again, a little puzzled. There was something about the exchange that did not seem quite spontaneous. And Mary was wearing a smart black hussar hat with a stiff black hackle at the front.

She shook away the thought. *I've been spending too much time with the Sandringham set,* she thought. *Seeing intrigue where there is none.* If Mary had been speaking to Tommy earlier, she would not have said she didn't know he would be there, would she? And hussar hats were all the fashion at the moment – lots of people were wearing them.

Tommy turned to Venetia and said, 'Can I offer you ladies a lift too? Or have you your carriage with you?'

'Thank you, but we go in the other direction,' Venetia said. 'Give Emma my love, tell her that I'll come and see her soon.'

The party split up, and walking back to the road with Henrietta, Venetia asked if she would like to come home with her for luncheon.

'I would like to very much,' Henrietta said, 'but I have to get home to the baby.' She lowered her voice discreetly. 'I'm feeding him, you see, so I can't be away too long.'

'Yes, of course,' Venetia said, and then felt better about Emma's absence. 'Yes, of course, I understand.'

'But perhaps you'd like to come home with me?' Henrietta suggested. 'Luncheon would be pot-luck, but we'd love to have you, and your little godson would be so pleased to see you.'

There were a thousand things to do at home, and she had rounds this afternoon, but suddenly she wanted a little of Henrietta's normality, her ordinary domestic life.

'I'd love to,' she said. 'I shan't be able to stay long – I have rounds at three – but I can manage it as long as we can get a cab fairly quickly.'

'If we walk up to the station, we're bound to get one there,' Henrietta said sensibly.

In the autumn of 1889 the Duke of Southport married Miss Nancy Culpepper, with all the splendour that money could buy, in Westminster Abbey with the Archbishop of Canterbury conducting the ceremony. Everybody who was anybody was invited, including the Prince and Princess of Wales and the Prime Minister, Lord Salisbury, and there was to be a massive wedding breakfast afterwards at Southport House, where the champagne, to employ an expression beloved of newspaper reporters, would flow like water.

'It reminds me horribly of our first wedding,' Venetia said to Hazelmere, when she first heard about it. 'The one we didn't have.'

'This will be grander,' Hazelmere assured her. 'Culpepper *père* means to have his moment. Think in terms of *le roi soleil* and Versailles.'

'In that case, I shall have to have a new dress,' Venetia said. It was not entirely a joking matter. Money was a little tight just then: Hazelmere's investments had not been performing as well as they ought, and Venetia's income always fluctuated, depending on the proportion of paid to unpaid work she undertook. To add to the complications, she suspected she might be pregnant again.

'Perhaps we won't be invited,' Hazelmere said.

But they were. Harry intended to assemble all his family about him, for the reassurance of the Culpeppers, and not only were Venetia and Olivia to be there with their spouses, and the dowager duchess, but even Colonel and Lady Augusta Vibart were to travel back from Paris for the occasion.

'How will the Waleses feel about coming face to face with her?' Venetia wondered.

'Southport seems to think it will be all right,' said Hazelmere, who had more contact, through the gentlemen's clubs, with the ducal set than had Venetia. 'Gussie has sworn to behave herself.'

'That's not much reassurance. When did Gussie keep her promises?'

'Apparently she's been chastened by her exile. Carrington met them over there at Easter, and thinks she'll hold to it. And Knollys has discreetly sounded out the Prince, and believes he doesn't care a bit, now he's in love with Daisy Brooke.'

'I hope you're right,' Venetia said.

'In any case, if she looks like reneging, Du Cane and I will jump to it and hustle her out.'

'Are you so devoted to Harry's peace of mind?'

'Don't care a bean about Harry,' Hazelmere said, coming closer, 'but we can't have her sisters being embarrassed in public.'

'Darling Beauty,' said Venetia, lifting her face for his kiss. 'I'm so glad you persevered and married me.'

On the day before the wedding, London filled up with all the distant Cavendish and Manvers cousins Venetia hadn't seen since her father's funeral. There was a family party in the evening for the viewing of the presents, and Venetia and Hazelmere met the bride's parents for the first time. Mr Culpepper was a big, broad man with a shiningly bald head and very large whiskers, perhaps in compensation. He had got himself up in full Court evening dress – breeches, stockings and rosetted slippers – and such was his self-confidence that he managed to make everyone else look wrong rather than himself. He was at the party *en garçon*, explaining loudly when Venetia politely enquired that, 'Mrs Culpepper could not leave Nancy on this evening of all evenings. That girl is as nervous as a turkey at Thanksgiving.'

'Quite understandable,' Venetia murmured, repressing a smile.

Culpepper examined her frankly. 'So you're the lady doctor? Well, ma'am, if I was wearing a hat I'd take it off to you! That must have taken some pluck, not to say snap and just plain gumption! Tough enough for any lady to get on, 'specially in this country, but for a duke's daughter to take on the whole of society – well!'

'You don't disapprove, then?' Venetia asked demurely.

'Why, no, ma'am, not a bit. I reckon whatever the good Lord puts into a person, that's what has to come out, and it's not a bit of use to fight against it – just makes for friction and turns a person sour. If my little Nancy had wanted to be a doctor, Mother and I would have helped her along. Mind you, I can't pretend I'm not glad she *didn't* want it. Would have seemed a waste, Nancy being such a pretty, perky little thing. Made for a good marriage, that's what Mrs Culpepper always said – and she's proved right, you see! It'll be the proudest day of our lives when our little girl becomes a duchess.'

Venetia could only hope he would find the bargain worth all the money he was laying out, but it would not have been polite to say so. Instead she asked if he would be staying long in England, or whether business would call him back to the United States.

'To tell you the truth, ma'am, we're thinking of settling here permanently. Mother likes the country and I like the horses, and we'd be glad to stay near Nancy, she being our only chick. Besides, my business is mostly between the States and England, and I'm thinking of expanding into France and Germany, so it would make sense to be here.'

'You are a – a wheat magnate, I believe?' Venetia asked, searching her memory for what Harry had told her.

Culpepper smiled. 'So some folks call me. I'm a shipper and exporter. I've used an agent in this country up to now, but darned if I'm not thinking of setting up my own office in London, now Nancy's marrying into the country. After all, why pay a middle man when you can take the profit yourself?'

'Why indeed?' Venetia said. So Harry was going to have his in-laws on his doorstep, she thought. How would he like that? She rather suspected his good behaviour was a strain on him, and if his bride's parents were watching he would have to keep it up permanently.

It was not until the wedding itself that she saw Gussie. She and Vibart did not arrive in Dover until late the night before so they weren't at the party. Venetia and Hazelmere were sitting in their seats in the Abbey, with Olivia and her husband to one side and two empty seats on the other, when the Vibarts arrived, very late, only just managing to get in before the royal party. Venetia thought her sister much changed, looking older – thinner too – and with a discontented frown that seemed to have become permanent. Vibart seemed much the same and, idling in behind her, merely nodded a vaguely smiling hello to everyone; but Gussie had hardly sat before she leant forward and addressed her sisters in a penetrating whisper.

'*What* a journey we've had! God, how I hate boats! And here you all are, sitting comfortably – you've no idea how some people have suffered to be here!' Her eyes raked her sisters' dress and coiffure. 'New frocks, too. Very nice. I told Vibart I *had* to have new, no matter what! People who think it's cheap to live abroad ought to try it, that's all. Foreigners are so nasty, always cheating one, and pretending they don't understand. It's impossible to get anything done right!'

'You look very nice,' Venetia murmured, hoping to shut her up, but it had the opposite effect.

'Do you think so? Well, I believe when you have taste, you always have it. You don't lose it just because you have to live in some God-forsaken place abroad. I *hate* abroad! And who is this girl Harry's marrying? Some uncouth, simpering miss, I suppose. Why on earth marry a Yankee? He could have had anyone he liked, and he has to choose a foreigner. I suppose he did it for the money. These Yankees are buying up all our old families. It's too bad! But how on earth could Harry have gone through Papa's fortune already?'

'This isn't the time and place,' Venetia whispered, trying to hush her. 'And I'm sure he loves her.'

Gussie's rather popping eyes opened wider. '*You* needn't take up for him. You got nothing out of him, and what Livy and me have had is just the bare bequest, when it was plain to everyone Papa meant Harry to add to it once he inherited. But he won't part with a penny, and now he's marrying this millionaire's daughter, just watch if he doesn't hide it all away and swear he can't afford to give us anything!'

Venetia abandoned tact. 'Gussie, for God's sake, shut up!' she whispered. Olivia, beyond her, also leant forward and placed her finger urgently on her lips. Gussie subsided, but it was more likely because the royal party had just entered than from any respect for her sisters' wishes.

Once the Waleses were seated the ceremony began. The groom and his groomsman, Lord Arthur Somerset, took their places and as the great organ struck up with a processional march, the bride entered on the arm of her father and started down the long aisle. There was no doubt Mr Culpepper was bent on getting the full value out of the situation. Miss Culpepper was attired in silver lace over white satin, an elaborately draped, ruched and ruffled gown drawing back into an eight-foot train decorated with silver and gold thread embroidery and encrusted with silver-gilt appliquéd roses. Her veil, also of silver lace, was fixed with a diamond tiara, she wore a diamond necklace – her father's wedding gift – and carried a sheaf of white roses and lilies in a silver holder. Eight bridesmaids walked behind her, all in white tulle over pink satin, with coronets of pale pink roses in their hair. It was a magnificent sight, but Venetia couldn't help thinking the gown too heavy and over-elaborate for a young bride. Flowers in the hair and a simple veil of gauze would have been more becoming than diamonds and silver lace, and pearls rather than diamonds round the neck. But she supposed it was Mr Culpepper's idea of how a duchess should look, and there was no doubt from his rapturous expression that he was happy with the arrangements.

Soon enough the young lady was coming back down the aisle, Miss Culpepper no more, but Her Grace the Duchess of Southport, with all the precedence that entailed. It was an odd thought to Venetia that now not only she and her sisters but also her mother would have to fall back and give place to the wheat magnate's daughter. Only royal duchesses, the princesses and the Queen ranked above her. Her veil was back now, and she was smiling – was there a touch of relief in it? Harry was smiling too, though in a rather fixed way. When the royals had left their seats, Mr Culpepper offered his arm to the dowager, and Hazelmere hurried forward to take Mrs Culpepper on his, and the rest of the guests filed out afterwards. Gussie and Vibart disappeared on the way out of the Abbey, separated by the press of the congregation, and Venetia, Olivia and Charlie Du Cane got into a carriage together and were swept off in the procession to Pall Mall.

The grand saloon in Southport House was banked with flowers, and everything was spotless and shining from a cleaning so recent Venetia could still smell the polish. It was strange to be here again in her childhood home – even to see one or two of the same footmen, grown older in service: ducal servants, like the royal household, tended to stay for life.

She congratulated Harry, who was looking bemused, and kissed the bride's cheek. The new duchess was pink, shiny-eyed and elated with happiness.

'Oh, thank you, Lady Hazelmere! I'm so glad you could come.' The new duchess would need guidance to negotiate the complexities of English titles, Venetia thought.

The Prince of Wales was genial. 'Good to see you, good to see you! Haven't seen so much of you these last months. Been busy, I dare say?'

'Yes, sir, always busy.'

'Splendid affair, this. Damned glad Southport's tying the knot at last. Do him good. Settles a man down, getting married.'

This, Venetia thought, from a man who conspicuously had *not* settled down. 'We're all pleased, sir. Especially my mother. The dukedom wants an heir.'

'Ah, yes. Family's a wonderful thing, even if it does give you grey hairs. How are your little ones?'

'Very well, sir, thank you.'

'Good, good. Well, come and see us soon. Come to Sandringham for the shooting. Liven us up with your witty conversation.'

It was a hearteningly warm reception for a former social outcast and black sheep, but Venetia thought, as she moved away, that she could have done without the invitation to another shooting party.

She finally caught up with Gussie just before they all moved in to take their places at the table.

'What happened to you at the Abbey?' Venetia asked. 'You and Vibart were supposed to be in our carriage.'

'Oh, I was talking to some friends,' Gussie said. 'You can't think how nice it is to talk to English women after all these dreary Parisians.'

'Did you speak to the Prince and Princess?'

She made a face. 'The Princess frosted me, but at least *he* spoke to me, though he was very grave. When I think—'

'Don't think,' Venetia said quickly. 'When a thing is over, you have to let it go and move on.'

'Fine talk from *you*,' Gussie said discontentedly. 'You don't know what it's like to be dropped like that.'

Venetia thought painfully of the scandal she had endured over her affair years ago with Ivo Jennings. 'Don't be so sure of that,' she said.

Gussie looked incredulous. 'You? You've always been the one to do the jilting.'

'I'm not going to go into details, but I do know what it's like to be rejected. It's painful and humiliating, but, Gussie, it's much worse to go on throwing yourself at him when he doesn't want you. Have a little dignity; don't let people see that you mind.'

At that moment the luncheon was announced and everyone was on the move to find their partners, so there was no time for Gussie to reply. Venetia had no hope that her words would have any effect; but the meal went off without a hitch and Gussie seemed to be behaving herself, from what little she could see. It was a magnificent feast, with ten courses from the pheasant consommé through to the cauliflower in Bombay sauce, with sorbet served just before the roast pigeons, and then a sweet and a savoury before the dessert was put on. The table was a mass of floral decorations, the crystal and silver glinted, the women's diamonds and the men's orders flashed, the talk swelled and the laughter tinkled. Two glasses of champagne before she sat down gave Venetia a feeling of complete unreality. She seemed to stand outside herself looking on, and the scene before her was utterly fantastic. She thought of her other milieu, the courts and alleys of the poor parts of Marylebone and Westminster, and of the operating theatres of the New Hospital and the Southport, and they seemed as bizarre and unreal as this. The only reality, she thought, was her own cosy home, the few rooms she shared with her dear, familiar husband and her sweet babies. Honour that it was to be included in this ducal wedding feast, she would much sooner have been at home dining on cod, neck-of-mutton and rice pudding!

After the meal was over, the royals did not stay long, and when they had departed, many of the other important personages also left. Harry and his bride went up to change, and when they had been seen off in the carriage to the railway station on their way to Biarritz, the rest departed, leaving only the immediate family. Olivia, Charlie Du Cane and Charlotte were talking to Mrs Culpepper; Vibart and Hazelmere to Mr Culpepper. That left Gussie for Venetia to entertain. They sat together in a quiet corner, near one of the tall windows that looked out on Pall Mall.

The noises of the street came up muted to a murmur by distance and glazing; it had begun to rain, and the drops pattering on the glass made the greater sound. Gussie talked for a while about the wedding and the Culpeppers, and then of her life in France. Eventually she wound down like a clockwork toy and sat picking absently at the braid on the chair back, her eyes distant.

Eventually, Venetia said, 'So, what are your plans now? Will you go back to France, or do you think you might stay in England?'

Gussie pushed her lips out in a little puff. 'Harry's made it plain he doesn't want us to stay. Afraid we'll dun him for money, I suppose.'

'And would you?'

'I suppose that is your notion of humour,' Gussie said crossly. 'What is one supposed to live on? Vibart hasn't a penny, and my allowance wouldn't be enough for us to stay in England. You don't know what it's like, having to live on a pittance, and scrimp and scrape for every little thing.'

'Don't I?'

Gussie shrugged. 'Oh, I suppose you went through a bad patch after Papa died, when Harry cut you off – but that was your own fault. And you're living like a coach horse now you're married to Beauty Hazelmere. It's not *fair*.'

Venetia did not bother to enlighten Gussie about her financial state of affairs – what use? Her sister had always thought she was unfairly treated. She was about to ask another question when Gussie went on in a different tone.

'You've always had your ambition to be a doctor to keep you going, and nothing else really mattered, not even what people thought of you. And now you've succeeded, so everything's all right. You know where you belong and what you're going to do tomorrow and the next day and all the rest of your life. But for *me*—' She looked up suddenly, her eyes bright. 'You remember, Sissy, how I always wanted to be popular – to be the best dressed, and go to the best parties, and have all the men running after me. I know you thought it was a paltry ambition, but what else did I have? I hadn't your brains, and even if I had I could never have defied

Papa the way you did. I was a duke's daughter and I knew what my place was, and what I ought to have, and it was all I ever wanted.'

'Well, and didn't you get it?' Venetia asked, but gently. There was something new in Gussie's eyes, a vulnerability she had never seen before.

'Yes, of course I did,' she said. 'I became the Prince of Wales's mistress. I was the leader of society, the highest, the first lady of the land. Only the Queen and the Princess of Wales were higher, and they didn't count in my circle. I was at his side always, I was invited with him automatically, everyone wanted to know me, everyone was interested in what I said and did and thought, what I liked and disliked. It was everything I dreamed of, Ven. I had it all. And now,' she made a flat, downward gesture of her hand, 'now it's all been taken away from me, and what do I have left?'

Venetia saw, and felt desperately sorry for her. 'Is it really what you wanted? You never planned to make a good marriage?'

'What use would that have been? Marry some paltry duke's son, or marquess's son, give him a quiverful of brats and see him run after someone else's wife while I stayed home and got fat? No, I was the mistress of the heir to the throne. I thought I could keep him, and then in the end I'd be the King's mistress. How could a marriage compete with that?'

'But you married Colonel Vibart.'

'That was what *he* wanted – the Prince. To keep it respectable. Kings can't have unmarried mistresses. And now,' her expression twisted into despair, 'now I've lost him and I'm stuck with Vibart. And we can't even afford to live in England. Not that I'd want to. I hate abroad, but at least I don't have to see people laughing at me and talking about me.'

'I'm sure they don't.'

'Yes, they do,' Gussie said fiercely. '*I* would, if I was them.'

Venetia didn't know what to say. At last she asked, 'What about your little boy? How is he?'

'Oh, he's been a dreadful nuisance,' Gussie said crossly.

'Sick all the way across the Channel, never stopped crying, and my maid was an absolute *pig* about it. Well, I couldn't afford the fare for more than one servant, so she was supposed to look after him as well as me, but as soon as he started to be seasick she refused to go near him.'

Venetia was bewildered. 'Do you mean you've brought him with you? Here, to the wedding?'

'Well, of course.' Gussie stared. 'I couldn't leave him back there, could I? Who would look after him?'

'Poor little boy,' Venetia said.

Gussie's expression had altered again. Now there was something of her old calculation in her eyes. 'He's awfully sweet, really. I don't mean to say I'm not fond of him, and after all he is You Know Who's child. But I'm not really the motherly sort. I've never been any use with children. Not like you.'

Venetia began to suspect a trap. 'What makes you think . . . ?'

'Oh, you're good with sick people, it's the same thing. And you've two of your own.' *Three soon*, Venetia thought. *God willing*. 'The thing of it is,' Gussie went on, 'that our life in France is no good for him. He ought to have a proper English nanny – French ones are worse than useless – and other children to play with, nice children. And eventually he ought to go to a proper school.'

'Gussie, I don't think—'

'*You* could take him,' Gussie burst out, throwing guile to the winds. 'Three would be just the same to you as two, since you've got your nursery set up already. Please, Venetia, don't say no. Think of the poor little brute, stuck with me for a mother – and Johnny not even his real father. Think of him living in horrid lodgings in horrid France, with horrid French food and nasty French drains, no-one to play with, not being brought up properly. I know you don't think much of me, but I do love my little boy, and I want the best for him. I don't want him to have to live the way we do. I want him to be English, and have everything he should have had if – if he'd been brought up by his own father. Please take him – oh, *please*!'

Venetia stared, in mingled pity and exasperation. And yet . . . and yet she saw her sister meant at least some of what she said. It was not just a ploy to be rid of an encumbrance. Before she could say anything, Gussie went on in a low voice, 'He's a dear little boy. He deserves better than me. Let me do what little I can for him. Let me give him to you.'

'I can't just make a decision like that,' Venetia said. 'There are all sorts of things to think about. Your husband would have to give his consent – he is the legal guardian. And what would the Prince say? In any case, I should have to ask Hazelmere, and I doubt if he'd be very happy about it.'

But even as she spoke, she already knew the outcome. She knew she would take little Edward – and she saw in Gussie's eyes that *she* knew it too.

It was not long after the Duke of Southport's wedding that a dreadful scandal broke out concerning a house of ill-repute in Cleveland Street. The matter came to light because the police were investigating the theft of money from the Central Telegraph Office, which was thought to have been taken by employees. During the enquiries it came to light that some of the messenger boys were earning money outside their employment by providing sexual services at number 18, Cleveland Street.

Venetia was quite well aware that there were homosexual brothels in London as well as the ordinary sort, but it was Inspector Morgan who provided her with another nugget of information: that messenger boys were a particular target of homosexuals, who sent each other meaningless telegrams for no other purpose than to ensure a visit from a telegraph boy.

'Sooner or later,' Morgan said, 'there's going to be trouble from that new legislation. Would to God Mr Labouchère had kept his nose out.'

The new legislation he referred to was the Act of 1885 whose main purpose had been to protect young girls from being forced or lured into prostitution. Venetia had given evidence to the Select Committee in advance of the Act, which was how she had first come to meet the inspector; and they had since worked together on many occasions where the police and medical worlds intersected.

But at the last minute, at the instigation of Henry Labouchère MP, a further clause had been added to the Act, making gross indecency between two males an offence punishable by up to two years' hard labour. Until that point, although sodomy had been illegal and punishable by anything between ten years and life imprisonment, lesser homosexual acts had not been proscribed by the law.

'But surely,' Venetia said, 'you don't condone that sort of thing?'

'What a couple of gentlemen do privately to each other is none of my business,' Morgan said, 'and I'd like to keep it that way. I don't want to have to go and ask them what they get up to, and I don't want them to tell me.'

'I agree with you, up to a point,' Venetia said cautiously.

'Sodomy's one thing, and that's always been against the law, and so it should be. But the other games they get up to – why, Doctor, you must know yourself that half the chaps in Parliament have been to Eton, and the other half to some other public school, and they've all tinkered about at that sort of thing. Boys will be boys – and not only at public school, either. Go down any back-street, look in any crowded bedroom after dark, and you'll find them experimenting. It's curiosity, that's all. Mostly they grow out of it.'

'And if they don't?'

Morgan shrugged. 'As I said, I'd sooner not know. And do you think any of us will be better off for having that sort of thing shouted in court and spread about in the news-papers?'

'I don't know,' Venetia said. 'I'm thinking about those messenger boys. I hate to think of children being corrupted.' She was thoughtful for a moment, and then looked up. '*All* boys, do you say?'

He caught the gleam in her eye and said, 'Excepting myself, of course. And his lordship.' He sighed. 'Well, the law is the law, and we'll have to enforce it. But this Cleveland Street business is bad. A lot of high-ups are involved.'

It was Hazelmere who brought home the news that one of the 'high-ups' known to frequent the Cleveland Street house was none other than Lord Arthur Somerset, who had been Harry's groomsman, and was equerry to the Prince of Wales. All that was as nothing beside the fact that shocked Hazelmere most – that Lord Arthur was a major in the Blues. 'The old regiment,' he moaned. 'There must be some way of keeping it out of the papers! And Euston as well!' The Earl of Euston was another eminent military figure.

'Euston? I thought he was a ladies' man,' Venetia said.

'So did we all. I suppose these things are not exclusive – though God knows how any man—' He broke off, becoming aware, as often happened to him, of how odd it was for him to be speaking about these things to his wife. But of course Venetia probably knew more about them than he did – a consideration that did nothing to soothe him.

'Inspector Morgan says the police have enough evidence to prosecute – and, after all, they are obliged to uphold the law, now it has been changed.'

'Yes, of course. It's the devil of a business. If only—'

'If only Mr Labouchère had minded his own business,' Venetia finished for him.

But a few days later Hazelmere came home with more serious news. 'I hate to mention something like this to you,' he said to his wife, pulling at his moustache. 'It's something no lady ought to—'

'Dearest,' she interrupted him, 'whenever you begin with "what no lady ought to know", it turns out to be something I have known all about for years. Out with it.'

He pulled himself together. 'Yes, of course, you're right. Well, then, to brass tacks. I was buttonholed in the club today by Lord Arthur Somerset's colonel. He felt he could talk to me, as a former Blues man myself, and, I think, more particularly because of my connection, through you and Harry, with the Prince of Wales.' He paused, looking troubled.

'It's something about Cleveland Street?' Venetia tried to help him along.

'Yes. Something Lord Arthur confided in him,' Hazelmere

went on. 'It seems he was not always alone on his trips to – to *that place*. And the person who went with him was someone very eminent indeed.'

Venetia paled. 'Not the Prince of Wales? Surely – *surely* you don't mean . . .'

'In a way, it's worse,' said Hazelmere. 'The Prince at least is capable of dealing with matters himself. No, this was his son – Albert Victor.'

'Prince Eddy,' said Venetia. 'The heir presumptive to the throne. Oh dear!' She saw it all in a flash, how disastrous it would be. 'But I am surprised. A vapid boy, and yet I thought attractive to – and attracted by – women.'

'You're probably right,' Hazelmere said. 'Except that he's no boy any more. And often those vapid types will swing either way, as the wind blows them. Of course, it could have been a mistake, and Eddy didn't know what he was being let in for.'

'Yes, I'm afraid he's slow-witted enough for that to ring true.'

'The problem is, what do I do about it?'

'Do? You're not his father!'

'Thank God! But, darling, think – it's bound to come out. And once the police get hold of it—'

'Never mind the police, what if the newspapers get hold of it?'

'It would not be good for the country,' Hazelmere said.

'An understatement if ever I heard one. Well, it seems to me that the prosecution must be stopped.'

'I agree. Had I better go to the Prime Minister?'

Venetia thought. 'The difficulty may be that Salisbury is so very honest. I think it would be better perhaps to approach the Prince first.'

Hazelmere blanched at the thought. 'Tell the Prince of Wales that his son and heir frequents a homosexual brothel?'

Venetia smiled faintly. 'Not a task anyone would relish. It needs a man of very great courage to face up to it.'

'Thank you! I am not comforted.'

'No, my love, but you know I'm right. I would do it for you if I could, but that's impossible.'

'I know. Well, then, if it falls to me, the sooner the better, before the police move – or I lose what little nerve I have.'

So it was that Lord Hazelmere sought and was granted an audience at Marlborough House and went through what he afterwards said was the worst half-hour of his life. As a result of the interview, and with Hazelmere acting as go-between and buffer state, wheels were put in motion. Lord Salisbury intervened and was able to halt the prosecution. Favours were called in, the newspapers were squared, and little of the scandal emerged into public knowledge. The owner of the house, Charles Hammond, and Lord Arthur Somerset went into exile abroad, and Prince Albert Victor was sent off on an official trip to India in the hope that it would invigorate him and, at the very least, keep him out of trouble.

There was one further consequence: in the new year Hazelmere was given a sinecure in the Prince of Wales's household, which provided a modest but welcome addition to his income, and Francis Knollys murmured that when the Prince succeeded he might look for further honours, perhaps an earldom. Venetia was pleased for him, though it meant his absence from home for several weeks a year; but she was never entirely sure whether the favour had come as thanks for Beauty's part in hushing up the Cleveland Street scandal, or because the Prince of Wales's unofficial son was now resident in Venetia's nursery, along with his cousins Thomas and Oliver.

CHAPTER TWELVE

Lizzie enjoyed her last year at school. In the Sixth, lessons were challenging, and the teachers were friendly and approachable, which gave an agreeable sense of common purpose and trust. Lizzie was made a prefect, a position of honour marked out by a special badge on blue ribbon. She was particularly pleased because the prefects were chosen by election, with all the girls in the form voting in secret. They were lectured beforehand on the importance of not choosing their best friend, but voting for the person who would be best for the school as a whole. Jerome laughed when he heard that, and said it would be a noble sort of person indeed who followed the injunction; but Lizzie was pleased either way, whether it meant she was a general favourite or thought to be a force for moral good.

The prefects were meant to help keep discipline throughout the school, and to this end had the authority to make any girl 'sign'; but Miss Buss, at their inaugural meeting, insisted that it was by their influence she expected the prefects to improve the school rather than by the power of office, and in practice the 'signing' power was never used. Prefects enjoyed certain privileges, the most valued being the right to enter school by the front door, and to be excluded from the no-talking rule. Meetings were held at which the prefects were consulted by Miss Buss and senior staff on matters of policy or discipline, and they gave their opinions gravely, pleased to be thought mature enough to consider such matters.

Miss Buss was warmer and more open with the prefects

– almost affectionate, Lizzie found. 'I think she likes us better than some of the teachers,' she said one evening, to her mother and Jerome.

'Perfectly understandable,' said Jerome. 'Shouldn't a mother love her children more than their governess?'

Lizzie made a face. 'We aren't her *children*!'

'Of course you are – her intellectual children and her spiritual heirs.' The idea made Lizzie giggle, and she made a mental note to tell Polly next day.

Polly Paget was still her closest friend, along with Agnes Grey and Lilian Bowling, but during term-time Polly's was the only house she visited, and Polly the only girl who came home with her. They liked to do their homework together, and each had tea in the other's house at least once a week.

The school work that last year was aimed towards taking the university matriculation, which involved a series of stiff examinations and, in the school, carried a prestige second only to the achievement of getting into Girton. The question of what one was to do afterwards was never far away, and it was something that exercised Miss Buss considerably. Any sixth-former meeting her in the corridor was likely to be taken to one side and quizzed, or solemnly warned about the consequences of having no ambition.

'You have too much about you to resign yourself to the dreadful career of stopping at home and helping Mother,' she would say. 'Dusting the drawing-room and arranging flowers – what a horror!' And another favourite saying of hers was, 'Why did the good Lord create Messrs Huntley and Palmer to make cakes for us, if not to give our clever girls a chance to do something better?'

Some girls had already decided on their futures. There were those who were going to be married – had either become engaged already, or who expected to find a husband in the usual way as soon as they were old enough or 'came out'. Many of the poorer girls, who needed to earn their living, were destined to be teachers, there being little else open to educated females. The unthinkable thing was to be a governess: that was considered too shameful to mention.

But school-teaching was respectable, and most of those intended for it thought it might even be agreeable.

Miss Buss took a particular interest in them. She and some other like-minded females were determined to raise teaching to the status of a profession, like medicine or the law, and had formed a society called the Teachers' Guild to pursue that end. The poor quality of some of her own staff was a trial to Miss Buss, and it was obviously in her own interests to encourage her best girls to take up teaching in a serious way.

It was an uphill struggle, since most teachers were female, and therefore an object of amusement to lofty mankind; and public-school ushers, who were all men, scorned the idea that they needed to learn how to teach. But the Guild had managed to get together subscriptions sufficient to start a new teachers' training college which, to give it prestige, was sited in Cambridge. Cambridge was already home to the famous women's colleges of Girton and Newnham, so the atmosphere there was helpful and supportive; and Miss E. P. Hughes, one of the most brilliant of Newnham graduates, became the principal. The college was only a collection of tiny rooms in a row of cottages with the party walls knocked out; but one day, it was dreamed, it would have its own great building and be as famous as King's.

Lilian Bowling was destined for this college, if she matriculated high enough to win a scholarship. Polly Paget was hoping for Girton; Agnes Grey had surprised everyone by revealing a desire to become a dentist, to which end she would be studying over the summer for the Edinburgh matriculation, the school there being the only one that would admit women.

Lizzie felt left behind by these friends, for she still had no idea what she wanted to do.

'Try for Girton with me,' Polly said, as they sat on opposite sides of Lizzie's 'studying desk' in her bedroom. 'Do, it would be so nice to have you there!'

'I don't know,' Lizzie said, chewing the end of her pen. 'I like the idea of Cambridge, and it's fun working with you, but – but what's it *for*?'

'For?'

'Yes – all the study. Where does it lead? I don't want to study just for study's sake.'

'Don't you?' Polly looked surprised. 'It seems to me better than the alternative, at any rate.'

Lizzie shook her head doubtfully. 'It reminds me of my father – my real father, I mean. He studied and studied until he'd taken all the juice out of everything. The last weeks before he died he worked night and day on a paper he was writing – you never saw so much effort go into anything! – and after he was dead when we came to read it, it didn't mean anything. It was just words. It all seemed such a waste.'

Polly stared at her a moment, and then said, 'I think you think too much. Some things are worth doing and some aren't, and since we don't know what the future holds, we might as well do the worthwhile things and see how it comes out. Otherwise you're back to helping Mother and—'

'Dusting the drawing-room!' Lizzie joined in and they chanted it together, and laughed.

The door opened and little Jack came in, holding something carefully in his hands. 'Are you laughing?' he said, eyeing them consideringly.

'What if we are?' Lizzie said.

'I like laughing too. I can laugh also, if you like,' he offered.

'Where's Emma?' Lizzie asked. 'Does she know you're here?'

'Emma's soopising Bobbin on the pot,' he informed her importantly. 'Soopising' was 'supervising' – Jack had a liking for words and seized on new ones eagerly. And Bobbin was what he called Robert – a cross between Bobby and Robin, both of which abbreviations had been used in his short life. 'Bobbin's a baby, being soopised. I went on my own when I was three.'

'You're a very wonderful fellow,' Polly said. 'Come and kiss me, darling.'

'Boys don't kiss girls,' he said sternly.

'Well, come and see me, anyway. What's that you've got in your hands?'

He came over and showed her, opening his hands over

her lap. 'It's a great big spider. I call it Daddy Smith Brown.'

Unfortunately Daddy Smith Brown, suddenly exposed to the light, decided to make a break for freedom, flowed over the edge of Jack's hands and dropped into Polly's lap. She was not particularly squeamish about insects but the surprise of it and the eight-legged speed of movement made her jump up with an exclamation, brushing instinctively at her skirts.

Jack was upset. 'Don't, don't, you'll hurt him! Oh, be careful!' He dropped to hands and knees, searching the carpet. 'Now you've lost him!' he cried reproachfully.

'I'm sorry, darling. Never mind,' Polly said tenderly. 'You can find another one.'

'I don't want another one, I want Daddy Smith Brown. I was going to teach him tricks.' He stood up, pouting a little, lowering his long lashes over his beautiful blue eyes. 'He's been my friend for ever and ever. I caught him this morning on the window-sill in the nursery.'

'I expect he came out of the ivy,' Lizzie said. 'You'll easily get another. There's lots of them living in the ivy.'

The blue eyes filled rapidly with tears. 'I told you, I don't want—'

Polly interrupted, 'I've got a piece of toffee in my pocket that you could have, if you liked.'

The flood checked cautiously. 'Let me see.'

Polly pulled out the battered paper bag, to which adhered the last two pieces of a quarter bought four days ago to sustain the girls on their walk home. Jack inspected them minutely and then selected the larger piece. The tears miraculously sank to their source, and he placed it, with the snag of paper it was stuck to, in his mouth. 'Fank you,' he said politely. 'I like paper on it also.'

In the open doorway Robert appeared, in his dress and boots but carrying his knickers in his hand. He was two and a half, fat and fair and impassive, always following in Jack's wake. He saw Jack's cheek bulging and said, 'Me sweetie too.'

An anguished pattering of feet heralded the nursemaid, who arrived with baby Francis. 'There you are! Oh, and

Jackie, you naughty boy, disturbing the young ladies! I'm ever so sorry, Miss Lizzie. Emma went out of the room for just a moment, and I had my back turned with Frankie. I'll take them away now.'

Baby Francis, tucked under her arm and dangling, suddenly saw Lizzie and Polly and his face broke into a delighted beam. He put his arms out to be taken, making a little snatching movement with his hands to hurry them up about it.

'Oh, he's so adorable!' Polly exclaimed. 'Let me hold him a moment.'

'We'll never get this work finished,' Lizzie objected. 'You can go and coo over them afterwards. Take them all away, Katy. Go on, Jackie, there's a dear. We'll come and see you later.'

'I aren't a deer,' Jack said with dignity, 'I'm a caterpillar,' but he went away, and Katy grabbed Robert's hand and followed.

'You're so lucky having babies in the house,' Polly sighed. 'They are such heaven!'

Lizzie, getting up to close the door, said, 'I suppose they are, though one gets used to them a bit.' She reflected that it was odd how clever, academic Polly, who was destined for the intellectual rigours of Girton, was so 'soppy' over her baby brothers. It showed, she supposed, that women were complex creatures.

In March 1890 the building for the New Hospital for Women was finished. It was very impressive to look at, built of red brick and terracotta tiles; four storeys high, with tall, narrow windows, much decoration, steep gables, turrets and high chimneys.

Florence Nightingale had been shown the plans for approval back at the time of the foundation-laying, but Venetia had learnt from Tommy Weston, who had it from Sir Douglas Galton, that Miss Nightingale had *not* approved them, sending a detailed criticism of the layout with a stern stricture that the first thing for a hospital was that it should *do the patient no harm*. Whether anybody on the committee read the criticism or not, it was certain that the plans had not been modified in any way, and when Venetia finally got to see inside the building, she found much that was wrong: narrow corridors, sharp turns round which it would be hard to manoeuvre a trolley or stretcher, badly placed stairs, dark corners, windows that opened too much or not at all. But for all that the wards seemed pleasant and homely, with parquet flooring, bookcases, cheerful red counterpanes and in each one an open fire – just for the look of it, since hot-water pipes provided heating throughout.

A three-day bazaar was held before the hospital was opened to raise money for the moving expenses. Venetia and Anne organised a stall between them, and enlisted Henrietta's willing help. Theirs was the fancy-goods stall, always a popular one, and there was no shortage of contributions. Henrietta provided a great deal of her own sewing and embroidery – handkerchiefs, pillow-slips, nightgown cases, antimacassars and the like – and begged from Patsy some pretty sketches and watercolours. Amy, who had married Alec Macdonald after a short but surprisingly passionate courtship, was home for a spell with her husband, and gave some of her African mementoes, wood carvings and pokerwork animals. Mary volunteered some exquisite arrangements of pressed flowers mounted on white card, which could be used for 'greeting cards' – delicate work which quite surprised Henrietta, who would not have thought Mary had the patience. Anne Farraline contributed decorations made of dried flowers, some tied in bunches, others set into little baskets or fixed into mounts like pin-cushions. Olivia sent some beautifully knitted baby-clothes, and even the dowager duchess made a dozen peg-dolls, dressed like princesses in scraps of silk, satin and velvet decorated with sequins for diamonds and tiny pearl beads.

'Everybody's made something but me,' Venetia said, as she and Henrietta were arranging the last of the fancy goods on the stall.

'No-one would expect you to. You don't have time on your hands the way we do,' Henrietta said soothingly, trying to get a small looking-glass with seashells stuck round its frame to stand up.

Venetia gave her a sidelong smile. 'A fair effort, but I still feel guilty.'

'You'll do your part by selling the things,' Henrietta said. 'A good salesman can double the takings, and I believe you'll prove a master at it.' She propped the looking-glass against a quill box, and added, 'Besides, being famous you'll be a tremendous draw.'

The bazaar was a great success, and all three days attracted such crowds it was sometimes difficult to move about. The public found plenty to intrigue them. Dr Garrett Anderson presided in person over a hat stall, and the famous Dr Venetia Fleet was on the fancy-goods stall performing like a fairground barker to 'talk up' the prices. The MP Tommy Weston did a turn in the fortune-teller's tent, with large earrings, a silk robe and a turban round his head, making great play with an upside-down goldfish bowl, and reading palms for sixpence. In another part of the hall was a pretend Indian temple where Hindu ladies in saris sold brass Benares ware, lacquer trays and embroidered linen; and in yet another corner Linley Sambourne, one of the cartoonists for *Punch*, drew people's portraits on the spot, taking turns with his colleague P. Parke who, many people were amazed to discover, was a woman.

The fancy goods went so quickly that there was a continuous hunt for replenishments, and by the third day they were ransacking their attics and begging patrons to thin out the content of their whatnots and china cabinets. Henrietta even baked some batches of biscuits, which Anne tied up prettily in coloured paper and ribbon, and contributed pots of home-made jam, for which Lizzie made tie-on covers out of offcuts of pretty material.

Lizzie was thrilled to be able to attend one day of the bazaar and help behind the counter. Polly came with her mother and looked envious at the fun Lizzie was having. All Jerome's friends came at some point, urged at least to show their faces. William Gilbert had his caricature sketched by Patsy and presented it with a bow and a laugh to Mrs

Gilbert; Mrs Alma-Tadema came and bought a fringed evening scarf of a peacock-eye pattern (which had been Anne Farraline's and she had always hated and never worn); the Burnands seemed to be everywhere, and creating laughter wherever they paused. The Suttons came and spent lavishly in a good cause, Mrs Roughley arrived with Julia and Thelma and bought a Benares brass tray for the front hall for visiting cards. Most wonderfully to Venetia, on the third afternoon there was a sudden hush and a falling back from her stall, and into the gap stepped the new Duchess of Southport, sumptuously swathed in furs and multiple strands of pearls, diamonds twinkling in her fur hat, and followed by what was obviously a very highly paid lady's maid who looked as if this was not what she expected when she entered Her Grace's service.

'Hello there,' the duchess said shyly to Venetia. 'I heard what you were doing and thought I just had to come and see. I do think this is all splendid. I wish I could help some way.'

Venetia smiled at her sister-in-law. 'You've helped just by coming,' she said, noting the heads together whispering in the background as people told each other who the newcomer was. 'But you could buy something, if you liked. I'm afraid the best stuff is all gone, but—'

'Oh, I'd like fine to buy something,' the duchess said eagerly. 'Let me see. Hmm. I think I'll have *that.*'

That was the ugliest thing on the stall, a vase of hideous shape and even worse colour, which had been donated by a distant cousin of Hazelmere's, Lady Paisley. It had been on the stall since the first day, effortlessly avoided by even the most eager shoppers. Venetia felt guilty, opened her mouth to suggest she might choose something else, and then realised that the duchess was deliberately buying what she thought would not otherwise sell. It was a charitable gesture that deserved reciprocation. Venetia would have sold the vase for fourpence if she had felt she could get it, but to the duchess she said, 'A fine choice, ma'am. That will be fifteen shillings, please.'

Henrietta beside her choked back a gasp, but the duchess

smiled on and waved her maid forward. 'Pay for it, will you, Dawson?' The maid produced a reticule and handed over a sovereign, and as Venetia began picking out change, the duchess waved it away and said, 'Never mind, I hate to carry all those heavy coins about.' The maid received the vase into her arms with a stony expression that suggested it might well meet with a fatal accident on the way home, but the duchess seemed delighted with the whole process, and leaning forward a little said confidentially, 'Do you know, the thing I'd like most in the world is to come behind the stall with you and sell something? Do you think I could? I'm real good at it. We had a bazaar at my school the last year and it was the greatest fun!'

Venetia had only to seize the opportunity, and in a moment the duchess had stripped off her furs and was cajoling the crowd with greater gusto even than Venetia. The crowd was so delighted at the novelty of buying something from a real live duchess that in no time all the unsaleable items had gone at record prices. When the duchess left half an hour later, she looked wistful as her maid helped her on with her furs and said, 'This has been such fun.' Venetia could not help deducing that life otherwise was not providing Harry's wife with much of that commodity, and felt sorry for her.

The bazaar served its purpose. March the 25th was moving day, and a week later Venetia was performing her first surgery in the new hospital theatre. In six weeks every bed was filled, and the out-patients' department was fully operational. The cause of women doctors had taken a leap forward, for in the medical hierarchy there was immense prestige attaching to a teaching hospital, and now the women doctors had a proper one of their own, in a building designed for the purpose.

The matriculation examinations took place in Burlington House in June. They were held over a number of days, and making the excursion there, sitting in the tense silence of the examination hall, scribbling away against the clock in the company of dozens of strange girls from other schools as well as the North London contingent, gave Lizzie such a feeling of unreality that it quite killed any nervousness she might have had. Afterwards Polly looked upset and said she was afraid she hadn't done well, but Lizzie could get no sense of her own performance. She had written a lot, but couldn't tell if she had written the right things or expressed herself clearly. 'Well, there's nothing we can do about it now,' she said philosophically.

On the day the results came out, the girls concerned stayed on at school after luncheon while a senior teacher went up to Burlington House to collect them. It was a nerve-racking time, but it seemed some kind of perceptive self-assessment permeated through the group, for those who grew really quiet and depressed turned out to be the ones who were called tactfully away to be told of their failure in private. To the rest the teacher announced, smiling, 'Every girl here has matriculated.' Polly, Agnes and Lilian had all won scholarships. Lizzie had passed well, but with a mark just below the scholarship level. She was surprised, and felt almost hurt, as if she had been slighted by the examiners. Self-knowledge had not worked in her case. She discovered now, belatedly, that she had always assumed she was at the top of the class, and it hurt to find that she wasn't.

'But you passed,' Polly said, as they walked home together, anxious to comfort her. 'And I'm sure you're as good as me. Sometimes people just aren't good at exams.'

'But I thought I *was* good at exams.'

'Well, you studied every bit as hard as me.'

'And I wrote pages and pages.'

'Perhaps you wrote too much,' Polly said tentatively. Lizzie only frowned, trying to remember. Polly put her hand on her friend's arm. 'You passed, Lizzie. You matriculated. That's the important thing.'

Lizzie shook away her thoughts, smiled, and said, 'Yes, you're right.' They had agreed beforehand to go home together to Lizzie's house, either to celebrate or drown their sorrows, as appropriate, and she determined now to be cheerful. Henrietta had a special tea waiting for them, with bread and butter and the best strawberry jam, a lemon cake, and Yorkshire curd tarts, a delicacy from her child-hood she had persuaded Fanny Dark to learn how to cook. Lizzie talked and laughed and smiled as much as anyone, joined in the conversation about the examination and school and everyone's futures, and chatted to and played with the babies when they were allowed in to join them. But in the background of her mind she was working and working on the problem. Tutored by her father from an early age, always set apart from other children by the lessons, always far ahead of her peers, she had assumed, without conceit, that she was exceptional. Now it seemed she was not – among the cleverest girls in the country, yes, but not the cleverest of the cleverest. So what, then, was to become of her? If she had not known before, it was now even more of a puzzle.

One of the drawbacks to being a leading citizen of York, in Mr Edward Morland's view, was having to sit on all these improving committees. He didn't mind that he was always one of the first to have to make a donation to every fund and collection; he didn't really mind sitting through all the speeches, even though he'd have been happy to put his hand up in agreement to anything they wanted without hearing the arguments; but they *would* insist on having their meet-ings at two thirty in the afternoon, just at a time when the digestion of his luncheon was demanding a far more hori-zontal posture, and his mind was at its least alert.

Today he was drifting gently in and out of consciousness as his fellow civic leaders discussed the insanitary conditions around Peaseholme Green. Many of the foul areas of York, which had been such scourges in his childhood, had been tackled and cleaned up, but in other places the poor still crowded into tenements made out of the old decayed town-houses of the rich, to which rackety wooden additions had been tacked over the years to form a warren of intercon-necting tiny courts.

'Still far too many midden privvies,' Mr Micklethwaite was saying. 'We calculate there are some eight thousand inside the city, and a good many of them, gentlemen, are in the Peaseholme area. Some of them serve anything up to twelve families.'

'Come, sir, come,' Mr Peckitt objected, 'you exaggerate. Since we built the new waterworks, everyone's been putting in water-closets. Half the houses in York have them now.'

'Not nearly half,' said thin little Mr Sidlow, who always had facts and figures at his fingertips. 'Not more than a quarter, if that.'

'And in any case, the poorest people who live in places like Peaseholme are not the ones with water-closets,' Mr Micklethwaite added. 'That must be obvious even to you, Mr Peckitt.'

Mr Peckitt bridled. 'I don't know what you mean by "even" to me, sir. All I know is we are forever paying down good brass to put in pipes and sewers and I don't know what else all over the place, and still you ask for more. There's no satisfying this town's appetite for water, it seems to me.'

'There's a sight too much water in Pug's Court at the moment,' said Mr Obadiah.

'Pug's Court is one place that does have a sewer, I know that for a fact,' Mr Peckitt said triumphantly.

'Much good it does 'em,' said Obadiah. 'It's not laid right, as anyone knows, and every time it rains hard the sewer runs backwards and floods the cellars with—'

'Yes, thank you,' Mr Micklethwaite interrupted. 'Pug's Court is not the subject of our meeting today. Taking into consideration Mr Peckitt's objections, I still feel we ought to have a resolution to set up a working committee to look at the drainage and sewerage in the Peaseholme area. Can I have your views, gentlemen?'

'If it's to come out of the rates, I'd sooner the money went into providing a public library,' said Mr Havergill.

There was a general groan. The public library had been a subject of contention for the last thirty years, and no-one wanted to go over the arguments again.

'A public library won't stop cholera and plague, which new drains for Peaseholme will,' Micklethwaite said. 'What do you say, Mr Morland?'

Teddy shot back into consciousness at the sound of his

name. 'Oh, absolutely,' he said on general principles, having lost the thread long ago.

'You agree with me? You're for the resolution?'

'Indeed, indeed. Excellent idea. Just what I've been thinking myself,' Teddy said. A glance at the clock on the mantelpiece told him the meeting was almost over, and his sleepy time was past, too. He felt better, quite alert now, in fact.

'Can we have a show of hands, then?' Micklethwaite looked round. Only Havergill's and Peckitt's were down. 'Excellent. Then that's agreed.' An imp of mischief whispered in his ear, and he went on, 'May I suggest that Mr Morland undertakes chairmanship of the committee? I feel his enthusiasm – and his late father's great contribution over the years – make him the best fitted for the task.'

There was a chorus of 'ayes': no-one, it seemed, begrudged Teddy Morland responsibility for investigating middens. Teddy looked round, a little bewildered, and seeing the enthusiastic smiles, nodded amiably.

That was how it was that he found himself in the company of his fellow councillor Mr Sidlow and a civil engineer, Mr Thomson, picking his way through the narrow, evil-smelling alleys that criss-crossed the area between Aldwark and the city wall. The walls of rotting buildings stood sometimes so close to each other that Teddy had difficulty in getting through without his coat touching them, which he was anxious to avoid. If there had ever been pavement or even cobbles underfoot, they had long gone, and there was only a species of slimy mud, liberally strewn with rubbish of various kinds. Where the alleys opened – if that were the appropriate word – into a court, it only seemed to make more room for rubbish, including in many cases a dungheap on which chickens scratched, or pigs rooted, and sometimes children played. Women in sacking aprons came to doors or windows to look suspiciously at the gentlemen so out of their element. Such men as were around were either old, crippled, or so conspicuously of the 'idler' class that Sidlow began to fear for his life and his wallet, and crept closer to Teddy's bulk for protection.

But Teddy was conscientious, and they quartered the area thoroughly before deciding they had seen enough. They were glad to pass at last into a wider lane, one with cracked paving underfoot, which actually had a name plate up on the wall, and a gas lamp at the far end where it joined St Cuthbert's Yard. Collet's Pass, it was called.

Mr Sidlow and Thompson were walking ahead, there not being room for three abreast. Teddy, who had been smoking a cigar against the smells, came to the end of it and paused to stub it out, so he was lagging a little behind. Moving on, he passed an archway on his left, giving onto a lightless passage that ran under the building to the yard beyond.

A girl stepped out from the darkness into his path. 'Please, sir,' she said – or, rather, whispered. 'Please.' She was small and thin, in ragged clothes with a cloth pulled over her head like a shawl, and eyes that seemed to take up most of her face.

She looked up at him, and seemed unable to go on. Teddy was not a man of imagination, but he suddenly felt the large, well-fed bulk of his body around him, the safety of it, his clean clothes against his skin, the bulwark of knowing he had money in the bank, a home and servants of his own, and food whenever he wanted it. She seemed so exposed to the elements, so unprotected; and she looked at him as though she half expected a cuff on the side of the head. What must it be like to be her?

'What do you want?' he asked, trying to make it sound kind.

She licked her lips once or twice, as though she were having difficulty in getting it out. Her face was intense with some desperate emotion, her little hands were down by her side, bunched into tight fists. Did she mean to attack him? But that was absurd. She was so small and thin he could have broken her in half between his two hands.

She spoke at last. 'Mother's sick,' she said. 'We've no fire and nothing to eat.'

That seemed to be all – and, indeed, what else was there to say? In a strange way, she did not seem to him to be begging. She had not asked for money, nor had she held out her hand, as practised beggars did. She just looked at him, as though she had simply wanted to tell someone, as though telling was the limit of her strength.

Teddy put his hand in his pocket and drew out all the change that was there. 'Here,' he said, and held it out to her. She made no move to take it, still staring at him as if not understanding what was wanted of her. 'It's money,' he said, feeling foolish. 'All I have about me. Take it. Get food, or whatever you need.' Still she did not move. 'Take it,' he said.

She put out her hands at last, cupped under his, and he spilled the coins into them carefully. There was silver as well as copper – even, he fancied, a half-sovereign. She looked at it, and her lips moved. 'It's all right,' he said.

She looked up again, and folded her full hands against her breast in a gesture that seemed to express something almost unbearable – perhaps merely the change from despair to hope. He hurried on, not wanting to see more, not wanting her to impinge on him more than she already had.

It was a small and unimportant episode, and he had forgotten it entirely by the next day.

One morning two weeks later his manservant Waller came to him when he had just finished breakfasting and was idling over the newspaper, and said, with his most long-suffering look, 'There is a person asking to see you, sir.'

Teddy looked up, remembering the last time they had had this conversation. 'If you mean Alice Bone, then say so.'

'No, sir, it is not Alice Bone. This is altogether a lower kind of female.'

'What the deuce do I want with her, then?'

'I could not say, sir. She asked with some urgency to speak with you, and I did not care to assume that you would not wish to have her admitted.'

'Oh, very well,' Teddy said, in the hope that it would annoy Waller more for him to see the girl than to send her away. He was glad to see Waller's expression of suffering intensify.

'Shall I show her in, sir?'

'In here? Of course not. You put her in the business-room, did you? Very well, I'll see her there.'

When he entered the room a few moments later, under the boiled-cod gaze of John the Baptist, he saw a complete stranger, a young female in a threadbare plush dress and an old, cheap hat with a dirty feather. For a moment his speech failed him as he considered what had been going through Waller's mind when he admitted her; but before he could explode, the girl turned a face of desperate appeal up to him, and he recognised the waif to whom he had given money in Collet's Pass. She had evidently attempted to clean herself up for this interview, for he could see quite clearly the ring round her white face to which the dirt had been washed back. Her hair was pinned up and frizzed under the horrible hat. The dress, which hung on her thin body, had once been somebody's idea of finery, and in style seemed far too old for her; and there were scuffed boots on her feet, though they looked far too big for her skinny ankles. Despite her efforts she was still dirty, and she smelt.

'It's you,' he said, going no nearer. 'What do you want?' More money, he supposed. How had she found him?

'Sir,' she said, 'I wanted to thank you. What you did, sir – it saved us. Mother would've died. She's getting better now, I think.'

'I'm glad to hear it,' he said warily.

'I bought food, and coal,' she said. 'There's only me now. Dad's gone, and my brothers are dead. I have to look after her.'

'I see. Well – er – what's your name?'

'Charley, sir. Charlotte. Charlotte Byng.'

'Well, Charlotte, I'm pleased your mother is better. Er, how did you know who I was?'

'I asked at the shop – Magby's the baker's. At the end of the lane. You passed it, sir, after. They knew who you were by sight, sir.'

'And how did you know where I lived?'

She looked faintly surprised. 'Everyone knows you, sir. You're famous.'

It was rather flattering, he thought, even from the mouth of such a waif. He smiled without realising it, and found her smiling in response. It lit her face so that for an instant she looked almost pretty, despite her pinched and dirty face. Her eyes, which were dark, seemed as large as a deer's.

'Well, well,' he said. 'So, what did you come here for?'

'Like I said, sir, to thank you.'

'Quite all right,' he said. 'Off you go, then.'

But she came closer. He saw her swallow, and some desperate resolve came into her eyes. Faint alarm bells rang. He tried not to step back.

'I want to thank you properly, sir. We're not beggars, me and Mother, not really. But we've got nothing. Mother says . . . she says to offer you – something in return.' She swallowed again, and he could actually see the pulse fluttering in her throat. She was afraid, yet driving herself on. 'I would – I would do anything for you, sir,' she said, 'anything you wanted.' Her voice faded through the sentence, so that the next bit came out in a whisper. 'Mother says you are a gentleman and would be kind to me.'

Understanding, horror and pity came all at once. He understood now the dress, the hat, the pinned-up hair. How old was she? Twelve, thirteen? It was monstrous. 'Good God!' he exclaimed.

She flinched away from his anger. 'I'm sorry, sir,' she whispered.

He caught himself up. 'It's all right, I'm not angry with *you*. Did your mother really say that? Did she tell you to come here and – and offer yourself?'

She nodded, her eyes filling with tears. 'I didn't mean to offend, sir. I only wanted – Mother said – the way things are, we've got nothing else. And I thought—' This last was something different: her expression said it was a new idea.

'Well? What did you think?'

'That – that you might be lonely.' It was only a husk of a voice now.

Teddy looked at her and something moved inside him, like a great rolling over of a sleeping beast. Lonely? When had anyone last wondered if he was lonely? This little pale waif had just the faintest look of his sister Henrietta about her – the big dark eyes and the little pointed chin.

'How old are you?' he asked abruptly.

'Fifteen, sir.'

'No, I mean really. Tell the truth.'

'Fifteen, sir,' she said, and her slight surprise told him she was not lying. He supposed her emaciation made her look younger.

'I'd like to help you, Charlotte,' he said suddenly, 'but you don't need to – to do anything for me.'

The eyes brightened with tears again. 'But, sir, I must. It wouldn't be right. I've never begged before.'

'Never mind. It's all right. What do you need most? Can you work?'

'I could, sir, if it wasn't for looking after Mother. She's bedridden, you see – a cripple. I was a housemaid before, when my little brother was home to take care of her. I kept us all. But when he died, I had to give up my place. I did my best, but what we had ran out, and with no fire Mother got cold and then she got ill, and I didn't know what to do. Then – then I saw you and—'

She stopped, making a little gesture of her hand. He didn't know what it meant, but it caught at his breath, that little, white, graceful, downward movement.

'Well, I'll find some way to help you. Some work you can do and still take care of your mother. Look, here's some money now, to tide you over. Come back the same time tomorrow, and I'll tell you what I've decided.'

She put her hands behind her back. 'Thank you, sir, but I've a bit left from what you gave me before.'

The dickens, he thought, with an inward smile. Won't take more charity! Where does a poor child like that come by her pride?

So began the strangest friendship of Teddy's life. In helping Charlotte Byng and her mother, he felt he had achieved more good than with all his donations and sittings on committees put together. Here he could make a real difference. He visited – very briefly – the filthy, leaking room the Byngs were living in, and quickly found them another place, not large, but clean and with a ceiling and windows that kept out the elements, and access to water and a privy that were shared only between two other families. With shelter and decent food, Mrs Byng grew strong enough to sit up and do some things for herself. A decent neighbour promised to watch her for a penny a day, so that Charlotte – Charley, as Teddy came to know her – could work again. But at the last moment Teddy could not bear to think of her working for strangers who might not treat her right, so he took her on as a housemaid in his own house.

That was the first arrangement, but it didn't work. Cleaned up and neatly dressed, Charley was an attractive girl, and the other servants disapproved of her, bullied her and made her miserable. Teddy grew tired of having them come to him with complaints about her work, and of seeing her creep about with her eyes down and her lips trembling. Something must be done, he decided.

He discovered that she could read and write, so every day she came up to the house and he installed her in the business-room as his secretary. He had never felt the need of one before, his correspondence not being so heavy he could not do it himself, but it was certainly agreeable to walk about the room dictating replies to letters, and to discuss with her what needed to be done about this or that. The servants hated her all the more, but she was under his eye and they could not get at her.

She wanted to be properly employed, so when work was lacking he made it up for her, to salve her pride, and when he could not think of anything else for her to do, he had her read aloud to him. Bit by bit, she crept into his life, taking on all sorts of little jobs that a daughter-at-home might do for a father. The business-room no longer confined her. She ran errands for him, found things he had mislaid, dusted the more precious items in the drawing-room, reminded him of appointments, even conveyed his wishes to the other servants for him.

Home seemed more comfortable and welcoming now that Charley was there, and Teddy found he was staying in more often. They talked together, and she made him laugh. Properly fed, and with fear abated, she was a lively girl with an original mind. He stayed home just so that he could enjoy her company.

As she crept into his life, she crept into his heart, and seeing his affection for her, the servants scowled and assumed the worst – though how they thought the deed was managed was beyond Teddy to imagine. But he didn't care what they thought, and they valued their jobs too well to do more than think the worst, and gossip among themselves. He was happy: happy with the situation, and happy to think that this strange little creature liked him. Charley was his little pet lamb, and he would take care of her.

After the visit of the Duchess of Southport to the bazaar, Venetia made an effort to be kind to her. She left her visiting card, was invited to call and did so, and found the former Miss Nancy Culpepper, though puzzled and at sea in her new station in life, a livelier girl than she had suspected, and full of good sense. She enjoyed talking to her, and after that made a point of calling from time to time, sensing that the girl was lonely. She never saw Harry on those visits, and Nancy did not talk about him; she and Hazelmere were not invited to dinner or any other social gathering by the Southports, and until that happened it was not possible for Venetia to invite them. So the friendship remained limited; but she felt she had done something positive to improve her sister-in-law's life.

Hazelmere saw Harry sometimes when he was at Marlborough House, or otherwise attending the Prince of Wales, and said he seemed well, but that marriage did not seem to have changed him. He and his duchess appeared together in public and at private parties, went to the opera, the theatre, the races, to Eaton Hall, to Easton, to Sandringham, to Goodwood, to Glenalvie. Once or twice Venetia and Hazelmere would turn up at the same gathering, but they went less into society than the Southports, and Venetia found her work so much more absorbing that she often refused invitations where she would otherwise have met them. When she did find herself in a room with them, she thought they conducted themselves quite normally, but could not help feeling that the duchess was somehow a little out of things. There was a resentment of American money in some company, and a general rejection of outsiders, whoever they were. If you were not born into their ranks – and related to half of them – you might never be accepted by the *ton*; and Nancy did not seem to have the force of character to batter her way in.

One day when Venetia was at home alone, she received a visit from Mr Culpepper. She had been just about to go out, but surprised and intrigued, she said she was at home, and had him shown up.

He strode across the room and shook her hand heartily and said, 'Good of you to see me Lady Hazelmere – Dr Hazelmere – dash it all,' he shook his head, perplexed, 'what do I call you, ma'am? I haven't got a handle on these titles yet. I'm afraid I'm always offending!'

'I'm Lady Venetia in company, and Dr Fleet profession-ally. It does make for confusion – not your fault at all.'

'Good of you to say so, Lady Venetia – I'll call you that, if I may, since I haven't come to consult.'

'Won't you please sit down? May I offer you some refresh-ment?'

'No, no, thank you, nothing of that sort. I won't stay but a minute – I'm sure you're too busy to waste time with drop-ins. My official reason for calling was just to let you know, by way of courtesy, that Mrs Culpepper and I are leaving Town for a while. Going to France for a month, just for a visit. Mother has always had a fancy to see Paris.'

'I'm sure she'll find it fascinating. How kind of you to call and let me know.'

'I believe your sister is still living in Paris. If there was a message or a letter I could carry for you, I'd be more than happy.'

'I am much obliged, but I wrote to her only last week. If you should happen to find yourself in company with her, my love to her, if you please, and say that all is well; but please don't go out of your way.'

He bowed, and fidgeted his hat around on his lap. Venetia thought she had better help him along.

'You said that was your official reason for visiting me: is there another?'

He smiled. 'Can't put anything past you, can I? Sharp as a pack of needles! Yes, Lady Venetia, there is another reason. I wanted to thank you for being kind to my girl.' Venetia was taken aback, and tried to find the polite words for the situation, but he held up his hand a little to stop her. 'She's finding it hard to settle in. It's all strange to her – English society is as different as can be from ours at home – and she's a shy girl, sensitive, you know. And not everyone in the duke's circle is quite as welcoming as we might have expected them to be. Well, *you* know all that. You saw she was a little lonely and left out, and you took the trouble to be kind to her, and I do appreciate it, ma'am. I wanted you to know that.'

'It is not difficult to be kind to her. Your daughter is a charming young woman,' Venetia said awkwardly.

'Heck, she's just a kid! If you could give her a pointer or two, help her out a little – but I mustn't impose on you, busy as you are.'

'I'd be happy to help in any way I can, but you perhaps don't appreciate that the difference in our rank means all approaches must come from her. I cannot presume—'

'Presoom?' He spread his hands. 'You can't think she cares about that – or that I do either! Ma'am, couldn't you just be her friend, without worrying about rank?'

Venetia smiled. 'I've done enough unconventional things in my life; perhaps one more won't hurt.'

'That's the dandy!' he beamed. 'Thank you, ma'am, from my heart. My Nancy needs a friend, and I don't know a better person than you for it. A person knows where he is with you – not like some of these grand-society dames! And now, I won't trespass any longer on your valuable time.' He stood up to go, and Venetia stood too, rather enjoying this abrupt American way of doing business. Then something seemed to strike him. 'By the way, I believe you have a cousin – Nancy says she was at the bazaar with you – who comes from Yorkshire?'

'Mrs Compton – my cousin Henrietta,' Venetia agreed, wondering at this new approach.

'That's the one! Nancy says you've talked about her quite

a bit. And I think she said her name before she married was Morland?'

'Yes, that's right,' said Venetia. A conventional woman of her rank would have frosted this blunt man for impertinence by now, but she was intrigued.

'Now, here's a queer thing,' he said beguilingly. 'You know I've been setting up my office over here for the shipping business? Well, a fellow approached me for a job, an American fellow, said he'd been working in shipping back in the States, but wanted a change and came over here. I liked the cut of his jib and took him on. You're wondering why I'm telling you all this,' he said apologetically, 'but the man's name is Morland, and he said his forebears came from Yorkshire, so I wondered if he was any relation of your cousin's.'

'I suppose it might be possible, but I think it's unlikely,' Venetia said. 'Mrs Compton did have an older sister who went to America and married over there, but as I understand it the whole family was wiped out during the Civil War. At all events, nothing more was ever heard of them, and it was known that the plantation was completely destroyed and the house burnt down.'

Culpepper's face fell a little. 'Oh, they were Southerners, were they? Then there can't be any connection. This man is from Boston, as Yankee as can be. Ah, well, I thought I would just enquire. I'll bid you good day now, Lady Venetia, and thank you. I hope we shall meet again often.'

Venetia saw him off with good will, but not quite the same fervent hope. She liked him, but thought a little of him would go a long way.

CHAPTER THIRTEEN

For the summer of 1890, Jerome took a house in Ramsgate again – a larger one this time, necessary to accommodate his growing family. Though Ramsgate was neither very smart nor very fashionable, he found the journey to and from London easy enough, and Henrietta liked it there. She was pregnant, expecting to be confined in December, and would be glad of the peace and quiet, and the fresh air away from Town.

'As to you,' he said to Lizzie, 'you will soon be an extremely grown-up young lady, so I recommend you to spend one last summer as a child, and romp about as if you were twelve. You'll never be able to do it again.'

Lizzie laughed and said she would do her best. She was assured of a little time with Polly, for she had been invited to stay with the Pagets when they visited Mr Paget's brother in Sutton in September. Agnes she would not see again before she went to Edinburgh, but she asked if Lilian could come and stay with them in Ramsgate, and Jerome said yes. The Bowlings were not sufficiently well off to have a holiday, so it was a kindness as well as a pleasure.

But a week before they left for Ramsgate, a letter came from Mrs Paget to say that she had to go and nurse her sick sister again, and asking if Polly could come and stay with the Comptons. Lizzie was thrilled. 'Oh, please, please say yes! I'm sure we can all squeeze in. We can all sleep in the same bed – or I can sleep on the floor if I have to. Oh, please, Papa!'

'If it means so much to you,' Jerome said. 'But you three

will have to go fishing every day to ease the strain on the kitchen.'

'I don't think I know how,' Lizzie said doubtfully, and added, 'but I'm sure I can find out. It can't be *that* difficult – I've seen little children doing it.'

'He's teasing you,' Henrietta said. 'Of course Polly can come. She's a dear girl.'

'And you don't really need to go fishing,' Jerome added. 'I don't suppose a slim little thing like her eats much, and Lilian's as thin as a rake. One portion of everything will do between the three of you.'

The Suttons and Roughleys were going to Margate as usual, but they promised to come over and visit, and were promised visits in return, so everything seemed set for a happy summer. Lizzie was determined it should be. She still had no idea what she wanted to do with her life, but Jerome had told her very firmly there was no need for any decision yet, and she leant on that as a comfortable prop.

'I want you to have at least one season of fun and parties,' he had said. 'It's every girl's right.' There would be no formal coming-out, but it was his and Henrietta's intention to introduce her to adult company through parties and dances and the like, and Jerome in particular wanted to take her to the theatre, the opera and so on. He had done what he could to cultivate her tastes, and now that she was old enough to go to public performances he did not mean to miss the pleasure of witnessing her enjoyment.

Lizzie found she liked Ramsgate better than Margate. It was less crowded and there were lovely walks along West Cliff and round Pegwell Bay. On Saturdays and Sundays the beach might be crowded with day-trippers, but during the week it was always possible to get away from them; and the house Jerome had taken was big enough to have a large garden, in which the three girls were happy to lie on a rug in the shade and read or talk. Jerome had advised Lizzie to romp while she could, and there was a good deal of that, particularly when Jack bestowed his company on them, which was as often as he could. Polly loved children and Lilian came from a large family so they didn't mind a bit.

The three girls took him to the beach and paddled, shrimped and investigated rock-pools with him, and played all sorts of games in the garden.

But the other great privilege of youth is idleness, the golden ability to do nothing at all for hours on end, and the romps took place as a variation to those long, peaceful hours under the trees when the gentle voices would rise and fall like calm sea waves, and looking out from a window of the house Henrietta would hardly see them move from one hour to the next.

Happy as they were, it was a welcome diversion when Polly's brothers arrived quite unexpectedly one day in August. They received a rapturous welcome from the girls; and Jack, having surveyed them carefully for a moment, asked the important question.

'Can you play cricket?'

'We most certainly can,' Cam answered for both.

'I can play cricket also,' Jack said. 'I've got a ball. Lizzie broke a milk bottle with it.'

'A dangerous woman!' Dodie laughed, catching her eye.

'Girls can't play cricket,' Jack observed witheringly.

'But they can do lots of other things that are much more important,' Dodie informed him.

Henrietta greeted them with pleasure, but was worrying about accommodation when Cam said, 'We are staying at a boarding house down the road. Our landlady informs us we were lucky to get the room, but from the smell of the lunch that was cooking, I think she was lucky to get us! We told her we'd eaten already.'

'You must eat here, of course,' Henrietta said. 'I'd ask you to stay but I can't think where we'd put another bed.'

'We wouldn't dream of putting upon you,' Dodie said, 'but we'd be delighted if you'd allow us to spend all our days here.'

So they did, for what Lizzie afterwards remembered as the best fortnight of her childhood. Dodie and Cam and the three girls spent every day together, walking along the beach, paddling at the sea edge, strolling about the town. The boys hired a rowing boat and took them out on Pegwell

Bay. They had borrowed a fishing-rod from somewhere, and Dodie tried to teach Lizzie how to fish while Cam took the oars, and later they swapped and Cam tried showing Lilian, in neither case with any success. One day they all – including Henrietta – caught the train to Canterbury, looked at the sights of the old city, took a conducted tour around the cathedral and had tea in the Beckett Tea-rooms; on another day the boys hired an open carriage and took everyone for a drive along the coast road.

There was never any dull moment: even when it rained and they had to stay in the house, the boys could always think of some new way to pass the time. One evening they introduced the whole family to 'Consequences', and played amid great hilarity until it was time for them to go back to their lodgings. Even Jerome joined in, and proved very inventive.

And when nothing else was going on, there were those long, lazy conversations, more interesting than ever to Lizzie now that there was a male point of view to absorb and consider. Cam was a delightful clown, but it was Dodie's opinion she wanted to hear. Though he was playful too, he had a more serious cast of mind, and the sound of his voice, even in the midst of a clamour when everyone was speaking at once, always made her turn her head towards him. Sometimes when she did that, she found he was already looking at her, and it pleased her to think he wanted her, more than the others, to listen to him.

One hot afternoon she and Dodie were lounging on the blanket spread under the trees at the bottom of the garden. At a little distance Cam, Polly and Lilian were playing rounders with Jack, using his treasured ball and a rolling pin borrowed from Fanny in the kitchen. They had all been playing to begin with, but since Jack was unwilling to relinquish his turn, the game had degenerated into Jack taking strike and the other three taking turns to throw him the ball and field it afterwards. Lizzie had given up in disgust, saying the others spoiled him, and went to flop onto the blanket, and after a little while Dodie came to join her. 'It doesn't need four of us to serve one small tyrant.'

The afternoon was drowsy with heat, the leaves hardly moving in the lightest of airs. The voices of the others seemed to echo as if held in a hollow a long way off, and Lizzie felt as if she and Dodie were alone in the world. They talked of nothing in particular. Dodie rolled over onto his back, his knees up, chewing a blade of grass, and Lizzie leant on one elbow and watched the sun-dapples moving over his face. His front hair, she discovered, had been burnt almost white by the summer sun, and his brown eyes were not densely brown like Polly's, but had sparks of gold in them.

'Have you decided what to do now you've finished school?' he asked after a while.

'No, I haven't an idea. It's rather shameful, not to know what I want to do, isn't it?'

'I shouldn't think many people think so. Females aren't supposed to want to do anything. I think it's rather splendid that girls like you and Polly are different.'

'Polly's so clever – much cleverer than me.'

'Do you think so? She thinks you are streets ahead of her. You don't want to go to Girton, then?'

Lizzie made an equivocal face. 'Of course, I'd like to be with Polly but—'

'I'm glad you're not going,' Dodie said. 'Cambridge is such a journey!'

She didn't quite know what he meant by that. The consideration that he minded where she went made something flutter in her stomach, like pre-examination nerves, only pleasanter. But she said only, 'You'll be in your last year when you go back in October, won't you?' He was reading law at King's College, London. 'I suppose your future is all decided.'

'Yes, pretty well,' he said, removing the grass blade from his mouth and studying it as he spoke, turning it back and forth in his hands. Lizzie noticed how long and thick his eyelashes were – like gold-brown fur. 'I'll go into the family business.'

'I thought you would want to be a barrister.'

'Oh, no. The law's interesting enough, but I've no wish

278

to be called to the bar. And someone has to follow in Pa's footsteps. I'm the dull and steady one, you see.' The eyelashes fanned upwards as he looked at her, smiling. 'Cam's the adventurous one. I think university's wasted on him – he wants to go to sea.'

'Does he? I've never heard him mention it.'

'You're lucky. He talks about nothing else to me! I dare say he'll get his way in the end. He can usually talk Pa into anything.'

'Doesn't your father want him to go to sea?'

'He wants him to go into Parliament. But that would never suit Cam. He wants to do something really exciting and worthwhile – discover a new country, perhaps, or some wonderful plant that cures diseases.'

'Don't you want to do something worthwhile?'

'Of course. Don't you?'

'I'd like to think,' she said carefully, 'that my life had made a difference.'

He rolled over onto his side, facing her. 'I agree. But I happen to think one can make a difference without doing anything extraordinary. To lead a good life, do one's job well, to have children and bring them up to be good people – think how many lives one can influence.'

'Yes,' she said. 'It doesn't sound exciting, but—'

'But as long as one is married to the right person, it would be very satisfying, I think. And never dull.'

'No, not dull. As long as it was the right person. Someone you could talk to and share things with. Like Mama and Papa. They talk all the time, you know, and laugh, and seem so happy.'

Dodie smiled at her, his long, closed-lipped, mysterious smile, and then he rolled over on his back again. 'Ah, domestic bliss!' he exclaimed. 'When you consider it, it's a wonder they can find anyone to man their ships or go exploring or hunt tigers and whatnot. Really, wild adventure simply can't compare!'

She laughed, and then the ball came flying at her as Jack's rolling pin connected for once in a chance hit, and Lilian, running after it, said plaintively, 'It's so hot! Can we go down and walk by the sea, do you think? I'm getting awfully bored with this.'

'You're a heroine to keep it up so long,' Dodie said.

'A fool, I was going to say, for indulging Jackie,' Lizzie contradicted. 'Tell the others to stop and we'll go for a nice cooling walk.'

When Dodie and Cam had left, things seemed rather flat; but it was not long before the Suttons and Roughleys made their visit, and then invited the three girls back to Margate with them, to stay for a few days. They had rented a larger house than usual on the outskirts of the town, a modern villa with its own tennis lawn, so they were never without young people dropping in. Minnie had grown up no more than passably pretty, but she had an air and a stylishness that made her seem much more attractive than she was, so her mother's assertion that she was 'a beauty' was not too far from the mark. She was certainly very popular, and already had a string of young men dangling after her. The addition of three more girls of the right age did the villa no harm at all: there was something like a party there every day.

On the day after their arrival Roy and some of his friends hired a *char-à-banc*, and a party of twenty young people went off in it for a drive to the fine old port town of Sandwich, and a picnic on the shore. Polly was doubtful about the propriety of going, knowing that her mother would not have allowed it without an adult chaperone; but Lizzie said surely there could be no harm in it when there were so many of them together.

'It's not as if it were just two, four or even six of us. There can't be any idea of "couples", which I could see would be objectionable,' she said. 'I don't think Mama would mind. She always says girls go about much more now than when she was young.'

Polly was still uncertain, but since it would have seemed odd and even impolite for her to remain behind alone, she gave in and went. It was certainly a jolly outing, and Lizzie saw nothing to make her uneasy: even Minnie for once abandoned her arch and flirting ways in favour of simply having fun. The picnic was excellent, the weather clement, and they sang all the way home. It was not, though, as pleasant as the days she had spent with Dodie and Cam. The company's conversation lacked their wit and originality; and Roy would attach himself to her and explain things which she perfectly understood, as though she were an idiot or a five-year-old.

On the 9th of September she had her eighteenth birthday, and Henrietta and Jerome gave a special grown-up dinner party for her. Henrietta's present to her was a proper long dinner gown, of amber silk with a draped bustle and a small train; Jerome gave her a necklace of lapis lazuli which, he said, kissing her, brought out the colour of her eyes. She had her very first champagne that evening, and liked it, which made Jerome laugh and say she was a born sybarite. Henrietta said, 'I had my first champagne when I was just about your age, at my brother's wedding. It took me much longer to learn to like it.' And Jerome said, 'Ah, girls mature much younger these days.'

And then a week later it was off to Sutton to stay with the Pagets. Henrietta remained in Ramsgate with the babies. She was not going back to town until Lizzie left Sutton, at the beginning of October, when they would meet again at home, in Kensington, and the 'Little Season' would start.

Marion Sutton was bringing out Minnie next year, and expected to use the Little Season to break her in gently to adult company, and Lizzie was sure of receiving lots of invitations. Polly and Lilian would be off to Cambridge together so she would not see them for many weeks. She was sad about that, but could not help remembering that Dodie – and Cam, of course – would still be in London, and it was not out of the question that she might bump into them at some or other public event.

Henrietta's baby was born on the 12th of December 1890, and Venetia's on the 17th of May 1891. Both were girls and, by coincidence, both were given names of flowers. A week after the birth Venetia invited Henrietta to come and visit her, asking her to bring her newest baby, and sending the carriage for her for the purpose. So it was that Miss

Jessamine Compton first met the Honourable Miss Violet Winchmore, though both were fast asleep at the time.

Henrietta sat in a large armchair beside Venetia's daybed, and each held the other's infant. 'She's beautiful,' Henrietta said, stroking the tiny cheek with the back of one finger. 'How smooth and pearly she is! Jessamine was crumpled and red when she was born, and her nose was flattened, poor little mite – very unprepossessing.'

'She's lovely now,' Venetia said. 'But she's so big compared with Violet! Every time, I forget how quickly they grow.'

'Yes, Violet is like a tiny doll.' She looked up. 'We are lucky, aren't we? Five for me and three for you and all – so far – healthy.'

'Yes, thank God! But, you know, it does occur to me that it might be time to stop.'

'Stop?'

'Having babies. We've done well so far and ought not to tempt fate. We aren't so very young any more, either of us. I'm forty-one, and you're not far behind me. Childbirth becomes more dangerous the older you get.'

Henrietta sighed. 'I know. And I did feel very tired after last time. But when I hold a little one in my arms like this, it all seems worth it, whatever the risk. And besides . . .' She met Venetia's eyes with a conscious look.

'And besides, you don't know what you can do about it?' Venetia guessed. Henrietta nodded. 'Do you think Jerome would be willing to – limit your family by artificial means?'

'It sounds so horrid when you put it like that,' Henrietta said. 'So cold and calculating.'

'Well, it is calculating. But on the other hand, if it means you can go on expressing your love for each other in the fullest way, it's the opposite of cold.'

'I suppose you have a point,' Henrietta said. This was an embarrassing conversation, but Venetia was the one person she could have had it with. 'I suppose *you* know ways in which it can be done?'

'None of them is absolutely sure, but they're better than nothing if you do want to avoid pregnancy. If that is what you want, speak to Jerome about it, and if he agrees, I can advise you. If you want to go on having babies, there's nothing more to be said – except that there is a risk involved, and I should be sorry to lose my friend.'

Henrietta wasn't sure what to say to that. Naturally one always knew that things *could* go wrong, but it was impossible to live life on that basis, and she had never thought about having babies as dangerous. It seemed as mechanical and wrong a view of marriage as did the idea of contraception; but at that moment Violet woke up, yawned, and tried to suck at the front of Henrietta's dress. Finding it yielded nothing, she began to cry. Though it was not her baby, the sound made Henrietta's milk spurt.

'Here, give her to me,' Venetia said. 'I expect she's hungry.'

The noise had woken Jessamine, who began to wail too. 'Better swap,' Henrietta said.

'We can feed them together, if you like,' Venetia said. 'No need to go into another room.'

It was another strange idea to Henrietta, but she pushed down her self-consciousness, and once she was over the first shyness, it seemed a natural as well as a warm and friendly thing to do. Quiet fell as they suckled their babies side by side, and Henrietta thought that, though Jessamine and Violet would not remember this moment, perhaps it might form a spiritual bond between them, and make them friends all their lives.

In May, while Venetia was preoccupied with childbirth, the Tranby Croft scandal was coming to a head.

The previous September, the Prince of Wales had gone up to Doncaster races as usual for the St Leger, but was unable to stay with Christopher Sykes, as in other years, because of Sykes's financial problems. Daisy Brooke had arranged for him to stay at Tranby Croft, the home of Arthur Wilson, a wealthy ship-owner, though she herself could not be there because her step-father had just died. Other guests, though, included the Earl of Coventry, General Owen Williams, Reuben Sassoon – one of the Prince's new Jewish friends – and Mr Thomas Jefferson Culpepper, a friend of Mr Wilson, being in the same line of business. It was through

Culpepper that the Hazelmeres had learnt afterwards what had happened.

On the first evening, the Prince had suggested by way of after-dinner entertainment a game of baccarat – which, of course, was illegal in England. During the play, another of the guests, Sir William Gordon Cumming, was suspected of cheating. Gordon Cumming, who was a colonel in the Scots Guards, was an immensely rich baronet, but was unpopular in many quarters because he had cuckolded so many husbands and spoken slightingly of so many fools. He had also been suspected before, though never accused, of cheating in other houses.

On the second evening the game was played again, and under close scrutiny of several of the company, the suspicion was confirmed. In a stark scene around the green baize, with the cigar smoke drifting in strata above the lamps, Gordon Cumming was confronted with the accusation. Public knowledge of his behaviour would have ruined his career and made him an outcast from society, and all present vowed to keep silence on condition he signed a document promising never to play cards again as long as he lived.

Gordon Cumming objected that to sign such a note was tantamount to confession, but the General and Lord Coventry insisted, and eventually he signed, after which all those present, including the Prince, added their names as witnesses.

Within a short time, however, the secret was out. No-one knew who had broken the silence, but Hazelmere, gloomily, guessed it was Lady Brooke. 'HRH can't keep anything from her, and he went from Tranby Croft straight to York the day afterwards and met the Brookes on the train. And she can't keep anything from anyone – she's not known as "Babbling Brooke" for nothing!'

However it happened, by January of 1891 it was clear that the story had wide circulation, and Gordon Cumming had no choice but to issue writs against his accusers. Not to do so was to admit the truth of the rumours. But a trial would mean that the Prince of Wales would have to give evidence, and this raised such consternation and horror that desperate attempts were made to divert it. As Gordon Cumming was a Scots Guards officer, it was suggested the matter should be dealt with by a military court; then that it should be handled privately by the Guards Club.

At one point the efforts seemed to have worked. Charles Carrington told Hazelmere that Gordon Cumming had agreed that if he was allowed to retire from the army rather than being cashiered, he would remove his name from all his clubs and go abroad. Carrington and Hazelmere took this information to Francis Knollys at their club, and everyone rejoiced that a suitable compromise had been found. But at the last moment the 'society lawyer' George Lewis, who was acting for Gordon Cumming, could not resist the excitement of calling the Prince of Wales into court.

'Lewis said in my presence, "The public must not be disappointed,"' Hazelmere said in disgust to Venetia. 'He thinks it will be wonderful advertisement for him. He doesn't think of the damage it will do the country.'

'It's appalling that anyone should take delight in such a wretched, sordid business,' Venetia said.

So the Heir to the Throne of England was condemned to the ignominy of being 'dragged through the courts', and on the 1st of June 1891 the Tranby Croft trial came on before the Lord Chief Justice, Lord Coleridge, to an enormous sensation in the press and amongst the public at large.

Gordon Cumming, represented by Sir Edward Clarke, made a very good showing in court, giving his answers in a firm, clear voice, and the attorney managed to suggest he had been made the victim of a conspiracy. The Prince, when his turn came, did not do himself justice, having been made so ill with worry about the scandal that he looked tense and uneasy and spoke barely above a whisper. The gallery was on the colonel's side, and when at last judgement was given against him there was prolonged and angry hissing.

The Prince did not do well in the press, either. All the papers disapproved of his gambling, and *The Times*, in a long article, said that the dismaying aspect of the case was the discovery that the Prince should have been at a baccarat table, that the game had been apparently played to please him, and that he liked it so well he had his own set of counters, embellished with the Prince of Wales feathers. It was shocking, said *The Times*, to learn that the Prince's was a gambling, baccarat-playing set; and just as Sir William had been forced to sign a promise never to play cards again, it could be wished, for England's sake, that the Prince had signed a similar declaration.

'And that's mild, compared with some,' said Venetia, folding the paper. One journal said the kind of life the Prince led filled the editor with horror; another condemned him as a 'wastrel and whoremonger'.

'The news has spread across the Atlantic,' Mr Culpepper told her. 'The *New York Times* says this business proves that royalty is a burden on the British taxpayer for which he receives no return.'

'The *New York Times* ought to mind its own business,' Venetia said crossly.

Culpepper looked apologetic. 'I hope you believe, Lady Venetia, that I had no alternative but to sign that paper. And it was not me that spilled the beans.'

'Of course, of course. It's all Sir William's fault for being a disgusting cheat. It's so unfair – he seems to be getting off lightly in all this!'

'Even to the extent of getting married the day after the trial finished,' Hazelmere said. Gordon Cumming, like Southport before him, had married an American heiress, a Miss Garner.

'While the Prince was booed at Ascot,' Venetia concluded.

'Do you think it will blow over?' Culpepper asked anxiously. 'With the Duke being one of his set, I don't like to think of the consequences to my daughter if—'

'You mustn't worry about that,' Venetia said. 'No-one could ever believe that Her Grace was anything but sweet and good. These things soon blow over. It's only because he's the heir to the throne that the fuss is being made. I'm sure none of the scandal will rub off on his friends.'

When Mr Culpepper had gone, Venetia said, 'Do you think he was comforted?'

'Not in the least,' Hazelmere said. 'But you did your best, and you'll be proved right – it will blow over.'

'Olivia writes that the Queen has been beside herself, for fear that the Prince's behaviour will damage the monarchy, and if that article in the *New York Times* is anything to go by—'

'Oh, you mustn't mind that. The Americans are always foreseeing the end of our monarchy. They're jealous because they haven't got one, that's all.'

Venetia laughed. 'You cheer me up.'

'Here's something else to make you laugh – Francis Knollys told me the Queen wanted Tum to write an open letter to the Archbishop of Canterbury condemning all forms of gambling.'

'Bless her, she's so unworldly!'

'And given that ninety per cent of her subjects, at a conservative estimate, like nothing better than a flutter on the horses, or cards, or dogs, or rats, or anything else it's at all possible to bet on, the declaration wouldn't have had much effect.'

In July Madame de Souberville gave a ball at Queen's Gate Hall, to which both the Comptons and the Suttons were invited, de Souberville being a client of their firm. For Lizzie it was the largest private dance she had yet attended, and Henrietta decreed she must have a new gown. 'Especially as we dine there first,' she said. 'What do you say to something in blue taffeta?'

'Oh, Mama, that would be lovely. We could use the lace from my fawn silk, couldn't we? That would save a bit of expense. I know I've cost you an awful lot this year, what with all my clothes, and hiring carriages and everything.'

'Never mind, darling, it's worth it to see you enjoy yourself. You look so lovely when you're dressed for a party. And Papa will tell us when he can't afford it any more.'

Henrietta went to Madame Bocquet for Lizzie's gown – an expensive dressmaker recommended by Mrs Roughley, who had her make for Julia for special occasions. Madame Bocquet charged excessively, in Henrietta's view, but she certainly produced the most elegant toilettes; and, she thought, she could always economise on her own gown. The blue taffeta was a stunning success, of a delicate harebell shade that suited Lizzie's colouring. It had a closely fitted bodice with an almost square neckline, and little puffed sleeves which Madame said were so new a fashion that no-one else had them yet. The skirt had a long, sweeping hemline with the great fullness at the back that had replaced bustles, and a deep frill, single at the front falling to triple at the back, oversewn with the lace she had consented to re-use, since it was such very good lace. The dress was very simple, fitted to perfection, and depended for its effect on the superb material and workmanship. When Lizzie tried it on, she held her breath for a moment as she first looked in the glass. She had thought it might be too plain, but saw now how it would shine down all the bows and trimmings and furbelows that surrounded it by its sheer elegance.

There were almost a hundred people invited to dine first, and Jerome, Henrietta and Lizzie did not see anyone they knew at their part of the table. However, when they got up at the end to go and prepare for the ball, they soon met Marion and Richard Sutton, who had Minnie and Roy with them. Minnie was in pink satin, very *décolleté*, the bodice swathed in ruched net, the skirt decorated with vertical lines of large velvet bows.

She seized Lizzie's arm at once. 'There you are, you dear thing! I've been craning my neck looking for you. Is that your new gown? Let me see.' She pushed her back enough to study her. 'Yes, it suits you very well. It's rather plain, but I'm sure that doesn't matter, when you're as pretty as you are. Are you engaged for the first dance yet?'

'No, of course not,' Lizzie said.

'There's no "of course" about it! I'm booked right through to the fifth. I can't bear coming to a ball unengaged and having to start from nothing. Think if one was left standing! And, you know, the men always prefer to ask women they see dancing already. No-one likes to think he's dancing with someone no-one else wanted.'

Lizzie paid no heed to any of this. She was used to Minnie

by now and listened only to one sentence in four of hers when she was excited. But Minnie dropped her arm and hurried ahead to grab hold of Roy, who was in the process of sloping off to find somewhere to have a smoke. Lizzie saw an urgent conversation take place, after which Minnie came back and linked arms with her again, saying, 'That's all arranged! Roy will dance the first dance with you, so you needn't worry about being left out.'

'I *wasn't* worried,' Lizzie said, bemused.

'Oh, don't thank me,' Minnie said. 'If I can't do that much for a friend – and Roy quite dotes on you, you know.'

But when they began to filter into the ballroom, Lizzie thought that perhaps it was as well to have a partner secured, at least for the first, for the crowds were huge, and she didn't see anyone she knew. Minnie saw someone through a gap and squeezed her arm, saying, 'Oh, look, there's—' The end of the sentence was lost as she dashed away, and as the backs closed together after her, Lizzie found herself cut off from both Suttons and her parents. She was quite stuck, and could only shuffle forward at the pace of the crowd, without being able to see where she was going, and concerned for her skirt and her hair.

Then suddenly she burst into an open space and, pausing gratefully to shake out her skirt, found herself face to face with Dryden Paget.

'There you are!' he said, with a smile of great satisfaction. 'I knew you were to be here, and I've been looking for you.'

She smiled too. She hadn't seen him for months, and the sight of him now made her heart quicken so that she felt rather breathless. He had such a look of Polly about him, but wonderfully translated into maleness. 'How did you know I'd be here?'

'Polly told me, of course,' he said. Lizzie wrote to Polly every week, and must have mentioned it. 'I say, you do look perfectly lovely.'

'Do you think so?'

'Absolutely. So very – elegant.' The enthusiasm in his eyes confirmed for her everything Madame Bocquet had said about the evils of over-decoration. 'Would you do me the honour of dancing with me when the music starts?'

'I'd love to,' she said, her feelings rushing upwards like a Roman candle. And then she remembered. 'Oh dear, except that I'm already engaged for the first.'

'Oh, I see. Well, perhaps you'd spare me a dance later?'

'Of course. Any one. I mean, I'm only engaged for the first,' she said, tripping over her tongue in her eagerness. Bother Roy, she thought. And bother Minnie for interfering! She had been blissfully free when she arrived here.

The music started up, and people began to take to the floor. Dodie looked at her uncertainly. 'Is your partner nearby? Shall I take you to him?'

'I don't know where he is,' Lizzie said, feeling a fool. 'It's Roy Sutton, Minnie's brother.'

'Oh, yes, of course,' Dodie said. Was it her imagination, or was there a slight cooling of his manner? She stood stupidly silent, unable to think of anything to say. He said politely, 'Shall I wait with you until he arrives, then?'

Lizzie could not bear to have him see her claimed by Roy, who would treat her, as always, as his personal property. She said hastily, 'Oh, no, really, there's no need. You won't get a partner yourself if you delay. I shall be quite all right. He'll be here in a moment.'

Dodie hesitated, and then took himself off, leaving her feeling wretched. He hadn't secured a dance with her before he left, as he might have, and perhaps he would not ask her again. Suppose he found a partner he really liked? She might not see him again all evening. Suppose he thought she had snubbed him? She should have found a way to let him know she really wanted to dance with him, but her stupid brain had let her down.

A damp hand fastened over her wrist. It was Roy, in a bad temper. 'What are you doing here? I thought you were with Minnie. Come on, the dance is half over.'

'It isn't. It's only just begun.'

'Well, I'm wretchedly hot, searching all over the place for you. Do come on.'

'Please put your gloves on first,' Lizzie said firmly. She

didn't want him making sweat marks on her new taffeta.

'Sorry.' He fumbled them on, and then seized her again and dragged her onto the floor. 'I thought there was no-one here that we know, but I've seen several friends of ours, so it will be a jollier evening than I expected. There's the Cussons, the Hollands, the Watneys – do you know them? And a friend of my aunt in Winchester is here with a girl she's bringing out, Ada Winsham. The Winshams are frightfully rich. Ada's a very pretty girl.' He seemed to recollect his duty. 'Not as pretty as you, of course,' he said, giving her a smirk. As if, she thought, she cared whether he thought someone else prettier than her! 'New gown, is it? Yes, you always look your best in a new gown.'

The dance seemed endless to her. She disliked being patronised by Roy, who seemed to feel somehow that she could not get on without him. His conversation was dull, consisting of a recital of the people here whom he knew and how rich and important they were, interspersed with stories of his prowess at drinking and gambling, and how much he had spent at these hobbies that his father didn't know about. He didn't dance well, and she was afraid for her skirt, and afraid of being made to look a fool.

When the first dance ended she was extremely glad. Roy looked about for a moment and then said, 'I'll give you the next dance as well, if you like, but then I must go and dance with Ada. The Winshams are big people in Hampshire, so I must make sure she has a nice time.'

'No, really, it's quite all right. Go and dance with her now. Better make sure of her before someone else gets in front of you. I'm quite happy, really, Roy.'

He took a little persuading, but not much, and being assured she did not need escorting to the side of the floor either, he hurried away. Lizzie turned with a mixture of relief at his departure and disappointment that she had missed dancing with Dodie; but she had only gone a few steps when he broke through the crowds at her side.

'Has he really gone? I thought he was going to hang around you for ever.'

'Were you watching?'

'Of course. I had to make sure I knew where you were so that I could catch you before anyone else asked you. Will you dance with me now, dear Lizzie?'

'Oh, yes,' she said, her eyes shining with happiness. She was his dear Lizzie, was she? Well, from the brother of her best friend it might not mean anything; but at any rate, she was to dance with him, and nothing could take that away.

The music began, and though they were among two hundred people on the floor, Lizzie felt as though she were quite alone with him. He was so easy to dance with that she did not need to think about that: their bodies moved as one, and she was able to give her whole mind to his conversation. He talked of the exhibition at Burlington House, which she had seen, and of a concert at the Albert Hall; he talked of Polly's progress at Girton, and asked her about the babies, 'Especially my friend Jack.' They discussed the cricket match Jerome had taken her to at Lord's, and the latest Sherlock Holmes story. She told him about the musical party they had attended at W. S. Gilbert's new house at Grim's Dyke, near Harrow – a fantastic mock-mediaeval mansion designed by Norman Shaw – and of Mrs Gilbert's wonderful plans for the garden. And they discussed the strange novel, *The Picture of Dorian Grey*, by an Irishman called Oscar Wilde, which they had both recently read, and what it could possibly mean, or if it meant anything at all.

'Mama says it's unwholesome,' Lizzie said. 'I do see why she says that, but I can't think it's enough to say by way of a criticism.'

'I think Wilde is probably a little mad,' Dodie said, 'but sometimes people on the edge of madness do have interesting ideas. There's a fine dividing line between genius and madness.'

'Do you think this book a work of genius?'

'Perhaps not quite that, but interesting none the less. My mother read some of it and condemned it utterly. She was very angry that I insisted on finishing it. But I do think, don't you, that one ought to try new things before one makes up one's mind, and not just accept other people's opinions?'

'Oh, yes! If everyone refused to try things just because they were new and different, nothing would ever change. Change is so important! Without it society would wither and die.'

He laughed, not in ridicule but in happiness. 'Nothing withering about you! I like it when you are enthusiastic about something – your eyes sparkle like champagne!'

She looked into his eyes, and something changed. She couldn't define it, but she knew that it had happened, and to both of them. It was like something inside her unlocking – she could almost hear the click – and then a hot, excited feeling right in the middle of her.

Dodie seemed suddenly short of breath. He said, in a husk of a voice, 'You are lovely, Lizzie.'

And then they didn't talk any more. The dance ended and another began, and they stayed on the floor and danced together, still not talking, but looking and looking at each other as though they were newborn.

In another part of the ballroom Henrietta was being introduced by Marion Sutton to her sister-in-law's friend, Mrs Langley. Mrs Langley's *protégée* Ada was dancing with Roy, a circumstance Marion seemed to think would upset Henrietta to the extent that she needed to be distracted. So she explained in voluble detail that Peggy Sutton and Mrs Langley had gone to school together in Winchester when Mrs Langley was a Miss Dubbon, but that was before she married Mr Langley, of course, and moved to London; and the Dubbons had been next neighbours to the Winshams in Harestock, a village on the edge of Winchester, and Mrs Langley still kept in touch with them and visited them whenever she went back to Winchester to see her mother, which was often, so of course when the Winshams had asked if she would have Ada to stay and give her a taste of London society she had been only too pleased, especially as Ada was such a pretty girl and would have a very large dowry too, so obviously a London Season would be of more benefit to her than many girls, and it would be a wonder if she did not get engaged to be married before the end of the summer because all the young men would be mad for her, only they would have to compete for her with Roy because he was mad for her already having only just met her. All this having brought Marion back to the point she was trying to avoid, she stopped, drew breath, and asked Mrs Langley for news of a family in Winchester wholly unknown to Henrietta, so she had nothing to add to the conversation.

What was troubling her was the mention of the name Winsham. It was familiar to her – had some very strong significance – but she could not bring to the front of her mind what it was. Winsham. Winsham from Winchester. No, perhaps it was just the assonance that made it seem familiar. Winsham from Winchester. She couldn't—

It came to her with a cold smack like being hit by a wave while in a rowing-boat. Not Winsham of Winchester. That was not how it had sat in her memory. It was Winsham from Hampshire. Miss Julia Winsham from Hampshire. That was how Henrietta had first heard, via Mary, of the woman Jerome had married, all those years ago when he was in despair of ever being allowed to love her. Henrietta had not wanted to know the name, but Mary had told her, and those few syllables had burned down into her mind like hot metal searing a table-top.

It must be a coincidence. Mustn't it? Probably it was a common name in that part of Hampshire. Probably the Ada Winsham at present enduring a dance with Roy Sutton was no relation to Jerome's divorced wife. And even if she was a relation – a distant relation – probably Mrs Langley knew nothing of the circumstances.

But it was here, in front of her, the thing she had feared and held at bay ever since she had married him. If there were a connection – if it were known about – she was standing on the brink of disaster. At any moment any casual comment, the merest polite question, could precipitate discovery. She was standing on a thin crust of earth over a pit of fire, and if the crust should break—

'Henrietta my dear, are you all right?' Marion said. 'You look rather strange.'

'It's nothing,' she said feebly. 'Very hot in here.' There

was a ringing in her ears and she felt the horrid black swooping and nausea that told her she was going to faint.

Marion's face was very close, she was asking something – she was trying to be discreet, and only a few of the words reached Henrietta: '– not pregnant again?' But Henrietta could not hold on any more. The blood left her head and she sank to the floor, hearing little shrieks and squeals around her through the thumping of her own heart.

While the Tranby Croft reverberations were still rumbling on, in July the Prince of Wales faced further trouble, this time from Lord Charles Beresford. Beresford had been Daisy Brooke's lover before the Prince. When Daisy had discovered that Lady Charles was pregnant, she had written a heated and very silly letter to Beresford, accusing him of being unfaithful to her with his wife, and adding salacious and incriminating details about their affair. It had arrived while Beresford was at sea, and as he had given his wife orders to open all his correspondence Lady Charles read it and, incensed, sent it to her solicitor. Her solicitor was George Lewis, who had acted for Gordon Cumming, and the implication was clearly that publication would be the next step.

From there matters had grown complicated. Lady Brooke had begged the Prince to intervene. The Prince, infatuated, had taken her side and tried to persuade Lady Charles to have the letter handed over to him. She refused, and he, frustrated and irritated, hinted that she could either give up the letter or her place in society. After that, he made sure the Brookes were invited everywhere he went, and made a point of striking out Lady Charles's name from any guest list he was on. In retaliation, Lady Charles's sister wrote a pamphlet about the affair, containing passages quoted from Lady Brooke's letter, and threatened to circulate it.

Lady Charles, furious at being shouldered out of society, wrote bitter letters of complaint to her husband at sea, where he was captaining the *Undaunted*. The last straw was when she discovered that not only did no-one invite her anywhere but that the Princess of Wales had received Lady Brooke at a public function at Marlborough House. She wrote to her husband that she was going to leave London and live abroad, and at that point, on the 12th of July, Lord Charles wrote to the Prince. He accused him of high-handed interference, of insulting his wife, and of being a blackguard and a coward; he said that since the days of duelling were over, his only recourse was to publicity, which he would use at the first opportunity, to make his opinion of the Prince known.

Had he sent the letter to the Prince it would never have seen the light of day, but he sent it instead to his wife with instructions to show it to the Prime Minister and demand that he force the Prince to make a public apology.

At this point Lord Salisbury called on the services of Lord Hazelmere as an intermediary.

'Why me?' Hazelmere said, in answer to Venetia's question. 'Because I am a byword for tact, I suppose – and HRH trusts me after that Cleveland Street business. I'd as lief have nothing to do with it, though. It's a sordid business. And when you come between two fighting tigers – or I suppose you could say four in this case – you are bound to get mauled by one or another.'

'My poor darling!' Venetia said. 'Which tiger do you fear most?'

'Lady Charles, without a doubt. I have to go and see her, and try to persuade her to have George Lewis destroy the letter. Salisbury meanwhile is to write to Lord Charles. We discussed the best way to word it, to persuade him to be quiet, poor fellow.'

'Poor fellow? Beresford?'

'I don't like him, but he's doing the right thing in trying to defend his wife. It's a wretched business!'

He was quiet when he came back from the interview with Lady Charles, and Venetia did not press him. It was several days later that he told her about it.

'She seemed infinitely pathetic to me. Ten years her husband's senior, her face obviously painted – with her wig, and her false eyebrows she looked like a clown. And all to keep the favour of a man who has constantly betrayed her with other women.' He paced about the bedroom, his hands clasping and unclasping behind him. 'And yet – and yet – he defends her, even against the woman he so recently betrayed her with. He risks his career and reputation for her sake; and she forgives him all his trespasses and appeals to his protection. It's a strange business.'

'What did Salisbury's letter to Beresford say?' Venetia now dared to ask.

'Oh, that his complaints against HRH were unfair—'

'*Unfair?*'

'Because cessation of acquaintance cannot be construed as an insult, and that if there is any other insult in question it should have been expressed clearly to the Prince so that he had the chance to explain or refute it. And that publicity would harm Beresford more than the Prince, and do no possible good to Lady Charles. *She* seemed receptive to my pleas. Let's hope she and the letter between them change Beresford's mind.'

Venetia watched him walk back and forth across the room. 'So – you take the Prince's part in this?'

He stopped. 'My love, I was appointed to do a job. It's not my business to judge.'

'Isn't it?'

'The Princess is the only one with the right to blame him, and she supports him wholeheartedly. In our stratum of society the only sin is to be indiscreet, and the Prince has not been. The two women have made all the fuss between them. They are the ones who have broken the rules.'

'Is that all?'

He came to stand before her. 'I would not behave as any of them have – but then they do not have the inestimable privilege of loving you.' She gave him her hands, and he kissed them. 'I'm glad to be done with this whole wretched affair. If Salisbury should send for me again I shall feign sickness. Kiss me, love, and take away the taste of this folly.'

Lord Charles agreed to withdraw the original letter, and the Prince invited Lady Charles to a garden party at

Marlborough House; but nothing could stop Lady Charles's sister privately circulating copies of her pamphlet, and when London filled up again after the summer it was the hottest topic of conversation, and hostesses who promised a reading of it found their drawing-rooms filled to bursting.

With the gossip rumbling on, the Princess of Wales, who had gone for her usual visit to her family in Denmark, could not bear to come back to London, and went instead to stay with her sister, the Tsaritsa of Russia, in the Crimea. She was still away for the Prince's fiftieth birthday, which upset him; and his autumn was further marred by a serious fire at Sandringham, which did considerable damage. It had been a horrible year for him, and he missed his wife's support; and the worst was not yet over. The Princess's return from Russia was finally brought about by bad news: she hurried home on receiving a telegraph that her younger son, Prince George, was seriously ill with typhoid.

Venetia's sympathy towards the Prince of Wales was re-kindled by his continued ill-fortune, and she told herself that he was, above all, a kind-hearted man who never meant anyone harm, which was more than could be said for many of his detractors. And after all, he was the future King of England. She frosted anyone who abused him in her presence, and persuaded her sister-in-law Southport to do the same.

Prince George recovered and became convalescent, Lady Brooke agreed to leave Town for a while until things settled down, and the engagement was announced of Prince Albert Victor, Heir Presumptive to the throne, who had recently been created Duke of Clarence and Avondale. His bride had been chosen by Queen Victoria as a girl who was 'quiet and yet cheerful, so very carefully brought up and so sensible'. The girl in question was the daughter of the Queen's favourite cousin Mary Adelaide – little Princess May of Teck.

Venetia had a particular interest in her as they had been received on the same day, at the same Drawing-room, though their circumstances were very different. She seemed, for all Venetia knew, a nice girl, and though impoverished and only a morganatic, she had the right background to know what was involved in marrying the throne. Venetia thought of Prince Eddy, dull-witted but pleasant and kind-hearted, and supposed that Princess May could have been given to a much worse husband. No-one would have mentioned Cleveland Street, of course.

CHAPTER FOURTEEN

Henrietta's fainting fit prevented any further conversation that might have led to revelation. Jerome was sent for, Lizzie sought and discovered walking – or perhaps the word was wandering – round the perimeter of the ballroom arm in arm with Dryden Paget, deep in a dream. Henrietta recovered, and said that it was only the heat, but she looked nervous and pale, and the concern that she might indeed be pregnant again made Jerome decide to take her straight home. Marion offered to take charge of Lizzie so that she might stay on at the ball, but Lizzie thanked her and said she preferred to go. She could not enjoy herself while worrying about her mother; but her eyes parted so lingeringly and regretfully from Dodie's face they almost seemed to belie her words. Dodie bowed to everyone and took himself out of their way, only murmuring to Lizzie at the last moment that he would call the next day, if he might, to see how her mother was.

In the carriage Jerome tried to quiz Henrietta, but she silenced him with a look, and said again that it was nothing but the heat.

'More probably the tightness of your stays,' he said lightly, searching her face for information. 'When will you women learn to value your health more than fashion?'

'When you men learn to value our minds more than our figures,' Lizzie answered for her, with some spirit, which made him laugh, easing the tension.

Only when they were alone together at last in the bedchamber was Henrietta able to tell him what had happened. 'I expect it's nothing, really,' she began; and finished with, 'Winsham is a common name, I dare say.'

But Jerome had listened gravely all through, and when she stopped, said, 'No, not so very common. Harestock, you say? Julia's younger brother William lived at Harestock. It's about five miles from the family house – not two miles from the cathedral. He was married, so Ada could be one of his children.'

There was a silence. Henrietta said, 'So it's all up, then?'

He tried to hearten her. 'Not necessarily. I don't think I met William above twice, and if Ada is his daughter she must be one of the younger ones, so there's no reason for her to recognise me. Young people are never interested in grown-ups' affairs anyway. Why should she say anything to anyone? Wait and see before you fret yourself. I expect nothing will come of this. She may not even be William's daughter, but a wholly unconnected Winsham.'

'You said it wasn't a common name.'

'You shouldn't depend on my opinion. I don't know Winchester very well at all.'

Despite his assurances, Henrietta didn't sleep well, and woke the next morning to a feeling of heaviness and dread. Lizzie, knowing nothing about it and believing her mother's assurances that she was well, wrote a long account of the evening in her diary and then slept the sleep of deep happiness, and woke with the delightful sense of anticipation of Christmas morning, that something wonderful was going to happen.

She was in such a dream of bliss she hardly noticed that Jerome did not leave for the office until both the first and the second posts had come, or that both her parents were unusually quiet at the breakfast table. How early would he call? Proper visiting time was after luncheon, but he had said 'tomorrow morning', hadn't he? Or was that just a slip of the tongue? She had put on her prettiest day dress, and pinned up her hair with extra care, wetting the little curls on her forehead and by her ears and pinching them up for extra curl.

At five past eleven there was a rap on the door, and

Henrietta, who was making believe to sew, flinched. Lizzie listened, breath suspended. A male voice below – wasn't it? And now feet coming upstairs, and, the door being open, Doris appeared in the doorway.

'It's Mr Paget, ma'am.'

Henrietta stared, her face paling. Had it come to that already? Spread so far? What did he mean by coming in person – to berate her for contaminating his daughter by her hospitality?

'For Miss Lizzie,' Doris added, wondering at the mistress's frozen look. 'Mr Dryden Paget.'

Lizzie jumped up. 'Is he downstairs still, Doris? I'll come down, then. I'll go out and walk with him in the garden, Mama, so as not to disturb you. He said he'd call to see how you were.'

Henrietta moistened her lips. 'How kind. Tell him thank you, and I'm quite well. Just a little headachy.'

Dodie was in the hall, holding his hat in his hands and looking at one of the pictures. He turned as Lizzie ran down the last of the stairs and his face lit up. Lizzie's stomach turned a somersault, and then suddenly she felt calmly, divinely happy.

'Hello,' he said. 'I gather from your expression your mother is not ill.'

'She says to say thank you for your enquiry, and she's quite well. It was just the heat last night, that's all.'

'I'm glad,' he said. They looked at each other for a moment or two, until Doris had gone back downstairs and closed the door. Then he said, 'I was looking at this drawing. It's a Blake, isn't it?'

'Yes, Papa bought it a few weeks ago at the Grosvenor Gallery. It's quite mad, isn't it?'

'Interesting,' Dodie said. 'Your papa doesn't mind trying new things, then?'

'No, not at all. He's the least stuffy person I ever met – except for you.'

Dodie grinned. 'I hope I can do as well when I'm his age.'

'Do you have to go anywhere now?'

'No – nowhere in particular.'

'Come and walk in the garden, then. Mama says she's still a little headachy, so I don't want to disturb her.'

He put down his hat on the hall table and followed her gladly. 'Did you sleep well last night?' he asked, as they passed out into the garden.

'Like a top,' she said.

'No dreams?'

'I dare say I had some, but I can't remember them. Did you – sleep well?'

'Not for ages. I sat up at the window and watched the moon rise. I had a lot to think about.'

Now she felt shy, and could not look at him. 'Did you?'

'I was thinking about you,' he said, and her heart thumped so hard she felt it. They walked on until they came to the garden bench which, being past the curve of the laurels, was out of sight of the windows. There she stopped and sat, and he sat beside her. 'Don't you want to know what I was thinking?'

'If it's nice,' she said, still not looking at him. She was concentrating so hard it was making her feel faint, but what she was looking at was a patch of clover in the lawn that was attracting the attention of a number of bumble bees.

'Oh, it is nice,' he said. 'It's very nice.' His hand touched hers tentatively, and at once her fingers folded eagerly through his. 'They fit together, don't they?' he said. She looked at their linked hands – hers so pale and female, his so lean and brown and masculine – and then up at him at last. 'I think we fit together, too.'

'Yes,' she said.

'We always have so much to talk about, and we think alike about things,' he pursued. 'And we're always happy together, aren't we?'

'Yes,' she said. 'Very happy.'

He took courage from this. 'I love you, Lizzie, so very much.'

'I love you, too,' she said. They stared into each other's eyes for a long, breathing moment, and then he leant forward and kissed her. It was the first time she had ever been kissed,

303

and it was wonderful. Love filled her up so full she felt it must overflow, leak out of her eyes like tears, pour out of her mouth like the burst river out of a flooded house.

When he drew back at last and they both began to breathe properly, he said, 'I'm waiting for my finals results now, as you know, but I'm pretty sure to pass – m'tutor says everyone in our year will, and I'm not bottom by any means – and then I'll be to going into the family firm. I'll have to learn the ropes, of course, so I shall be a sort of apprentice for a year or two. But after that – well, not meaning to sing my own praises or anything of the sort, but the profession does pretty well as a whole, and once I'm established I ought to make a tolerably decent income.'

Lizzie listened to him as to a bird singing, hardly distinguishing the words. She didn't mind what he said, she just wanted to hear his voice. He looked quizzical, as if he realised she was not following him.

'What I'm trying to say is that it will be a while before I can support a wife, so it wouldn't really be fair of me to ask you now, when you'd be committing yourself to a long wait—'

'Oh, please,' she interrupted him, understanding now, 'do ask me!'

'Really?' he grinned.

'Really!'

'On one knee?'

Now she laughed. 'Yes! You might as well do it properly while you're about it.'

He slipped off the bench and onto one knee, still holding her hand, and though the pose was comic, his expression was not. 'Dearest Lizzie, I love you so very much. Will you marry me?'

'Oh, yes!' she said. 'Yes, please!'

He kissed her hand in solemn pledge, and then sat beside her again. 'I've asked and I won't go back on it. I know I shall always love you. But I just want you to know that if the wait gets too much for you, or you meet someone else—'

'I shan't!'

'Ssh! If you change your mind some time between now and when I'm in a position to marry, I shan't reproach you. You mustn't think of yourself as bound. That wouldn't be fair.'

She took hold of both his hands and drew them to her breast. 'I shan't change my mind. I shan't meet someone else. And I shall think of myself as bound. I love you with all my heart, Dodie.'

They sat in blissful silence for a while. Then he said, 'I shall have to ask your father, of course.'

'And yours.'

'Oh, mine won't be any trouble,' Dodie said airily. 'He'll think me the luckiest dog in London. The only question is whether you're too good for me.'

No note came from Marion that day, which might have been either good or bad. She usually did write on the day after a party, or call; and given Henrietta's indisposition, she might have been expected to enquire. Several times Henrietta began a note to her to say that she was not ill, but could not finish it. If the secret *had* been discovered, the note would seem deceitful, and Marion would hate her for it.

She wrote a thank-you to Madame de Souberville, and began her regular letter to Regina, but her attention was not on it. Emma brought Jack and Robbie to see her on their way out for their walk, and the sight of their happy, innocent faces almost made her cry. She hugged them, but they felt her emotion and wriggled away, not liking it.

'Where are you taking them?'

'Just along the street, ma'am. We might get as far as the shops and look in the windows.'

It seemed a dull walk. She wanted her little boys to have some pleasure, while they could. 'Take them to the Park, to the Round Pond,' she said. 'Here's the fare for the omnibus – it will be too far for them to walk all the way.' The boys beamed with delight and Emma smiled too, but looked curiously at Henrietta, knowing her too well by now to miss the signs of distress in her face.

Later, when Henrietta was sitting and staring out of the

window, Doris came in and asked if Mr Dryden was staying for luncheon.

'Oh – is he still here? Yes, of course he shall stay, if he wants to.'

She was too preoccupied over lunch to notice the young people's joyful faces. They talked lightly through the meal, of books and plays and art; Henrietta hardly contributed, but they were too bound up in each other to notice that. When it was over, Lizzie asked tentatively if she might go with Dodie to the Victoria and Albert Museum, as there was an exhibition he had mentioned that she would like to see. Probably if Henrietta had been herself she would have said no, the request being on the borderline of what was permissible; but as it was she said yes, as long as they went straight there and came straight back.

The long afternoon dragged by, heavy and silent. The skies clouded over and it came on to rain. Lizzie and Dodie came in laughing and damp, saying they had run all the way from the 'bus stop. 'It started just as we got off. May Dodie stay for dinner, Mama? He wants to talk to Papa.'

Still nothing connected in Henrietta's troubled mind.

'Yes, of course. Tell Fanny, will you? It will only be our everyday family dinner, Dodie, I'm afraid.'

'Whatever it is, it will be delightful to me. The proverbial dinner of herbs, ma'am. Thank you,' he said, and Henrietta smiled vaguely, having no idea what he was talking about.

Lizzie and Dodie spent the remainder of the afternoon at the far end of the drawing-room doing a jigsaw puzzle together on the small table in the window, while Henrietta, at the other end, sewed and rocked and brooded. The babies were brought down at six, and a few minutes later Jerome walked in, a good hour earlier than his usual time. He bypassed the clamouring boys and went straight to Henrietta, bent over to kiss her and whispered, 'Anything?'

'Nothing,' she replied.

He looked into her eyes a moment, and said, 'That's good, isn't it? Everything will be all right, I'm sure.' He kissed her again and straightened up, received an over-excited Jack full in the chest and, swinging him round onto one hip, went over to shake hands with Dodie. 'This is a nice surprise. Have you come to dinner?'

'Yes, he is staying, Papa,' Lizzie jumped in. 'He's been here all day,' she added, with stars in her eyes.

Jerome examined her flushed face, and then looked at Dodie with one eyebrow raised. 'Is there something I ought to know?'

Dodie straightened and put his hands behind his back, colouring a little. 'I did want to speak to you, sir, if you don't mind. About something rather important.'

Jerome wanted to laugh at his solemn earnestness, at the self-absorption of youth, at the unfortunate timing that brought him here a-lovering when Henrietta was waiting like the accused in court for the jury to come back with their verdict. But he controlled himself, looked from Dodie to Lizzie and back, and said, 'Now?'

'If you don't mind, sir.'

'Then you'd better come to my study.'

Dodie followed him out, casting a last, reassuring look back at Lizzie.

What to say to the boy? If the secret of his divorce was about to be broken, how would that affect young Paget? There was no knowing how people would react. It might be that no-one would care. Or it might be that the Pagets would care very much, and refuse to allow a match between their eldest son and a disgraced family's daughter. Was it right to let the lad commit himself without knowing all the facts? But how could he blight Lizzie's happiness, when perhaps it might not prove necessary to say anything at all?

He fell back on Dodie's own doubts, which he had expressed in an honourable way.

'I like you very much,' Jerome said, 'but I think she is too young. I'd like her to see a little more of the world before she settles for the first young man who asks her – however personable he is. And I agree that you are too far from being independent for any thought of a formal engagement between you.'

Dodie looked disappointed, but said, 'I half expected you

307

to say that, sir. I said the same thing to Lizzie – that it wasn't fair to bind her with so long to wait.'

'And what did she say?'

He grinned. 'That she wanted to be bound.'

'Ah, the impetuosity of women! That's why they need us to take care of them. Well, my lad, that's my decision: wait a year anyway, and then if you're both still of the same mind, an engagement can be entered into, with a view to marrying when you've established yourself. For the moment, however, you have my unofficial blessing. I should be delighted to have you as a son-in-law.'

Dodie stood up and shook his hand vigorously. 'Thank you, sir! Thank you! I won't let you down, sir, nor Lizzie.'

Jerome released himself, patting Dodie's shoulder as one might pat an excited dog. 'Just one thing – not a word to Mrs Compton tonight, if you please. She's been a little under the weather, and I'd like her to have a quiet evening. I'll tell her myself tomorrow what's been agreed.'

'As you wish, sir.'

'And tell Lizzie not to say anything to her mother either.'

Jerome told Henrietta in bed that night. As he had anticipated, she cried: he had not wanted her to cry in front of Lizzie like that.

He held her, loving her, sad for her, knowing she was suffering in a way that was strange to him. Her love for him had never faltered, and she had done what she did in full awareness of her actions; but in her deepest mind she did not believe they were married, and every year and every child she bore him compounded the sin, or error, or whatever it was to her. And there was nothing he could do about it. If the present blow did not fall, she would regain her equanimity, and they would carry on, but it would never be right for her, and it saddened him to know it.

And if the blow did fall – but he did not want to think about that. He held her close until she fell asleep, loving her so much and so tenderly; but it was as if there were an invisible barrier between them, a sheet of glass between her soul and his, so that they could not touch.

The letter came the next morning. Marion had evidently laboured long and carefully over it.

'In the circumstances, I do not think we should meet or communicate again. You will oblige me by not replying to this letter, or by calling, as I should very much regret the necessity of refusing you.'

All this must have been written and rewritten, but at the end was a sentence that came from the heart, that had burned its way out incoherent and uncorrected.

'How could you let me go on all this time living a lie, knowing what you knew and never mention, to think how much I liked you, it was so hurtful and wrong I don't know what to think.'

'Well,' said Jerome, tearing the letter into tiny pieces, 'you managed without Marion Sutton before you met her, and you can manage without her again.'

Henrietta was not comforted. 'It won't stop there,' she said. 'You see how she thinks about it. She'll feel it's her duty to tell others, and the others will tell their friends, and so on. It will be all over Town in a day or two.'

'It was the damnedest bad luck it came out at all,' Jerome said fretfully.

It *was* bad luck. Had Marion Sutton not gone to Miss Duckworthy's school for two years with Miss Dubbon, it would not have happened, for the Winshams were far above the Pewsleys or even the Suttons in social status, and though Marion had heard of the family she had never met any of them, nor would have been likely to, and she knew nothing of their circumstances. But Miss Dubbon was a notch or two further up the social scale, and had been acquainted with the Winshams; and through being pretty and lively had married well, which made a Mrs Langley a suitable chaperone for a young Miss Winsham wanting a season in Town.

Ada Winsham had not recognised Jerome – that was not how it had happened. It was purely the name that had done it. After Henrietta's departure from the ball, Mrs Langley had asked Marion thoughtfully whether she had heard rightly, that the gentleman who had just left was a Mr

Jerome Compton. Yes, said Marion. Jerome Compton from Yorkshire? Yes, that was where he had come from before he moved to London. Mrs Langley had said nothing further, but the following day Marion had called on her to discuss the ball and, in a ferment of unsatisfied curiosity, had pressed her as to how she knew Jerome. Having spent a night wrestling with her conscience Mrs Langley had decided it was her unhappy duty to tell.

The story lost nothing with telling. Julia Winsham became a sweet, innocent creature without the slightest understanding of the world, who had been lured into marriage with a designing rogue, an older man so sophisticated he bordered on being a reprobate. After the Divorce (the word made Marion gasp every time it was spoken) Julia had had the decency to live in quiet retirement with her older brother, Henry, acknowledging that, though it was not her fault, a divorced person was irreparably tarnished in the eyes of the world. But the Reprobate had shamelessly married again – if you could call it marriage, which obviously you couldn't. Everyone in Hampshire had heard that much. No-one knew what sort of a woman he had found who was abandoned enough to go through such a sham of a marriage, but they had all suspected she must be pretty low: her actions alone proved her degenerate. Mrs Langley was sorry to have to say it about a friend of Marion's, but Marion had evidently been imposed upon and Mrs Langley felt it was her duty to tell her what her 'friend' evidently would not.

So in the course of that heated and heating conversation, Jerome and Henrietta had become a reprobate and a degenerate who had deceived Marion and Richard in order to secure themselves a place in decent society which they otherwise could not have enjoyed. In fury, bitter hurt, and fear for how the association might have contaminated her family and spoiled her children's chances in life, Marion rejected Henrietta as hard as she could, and wasted no time in telling everyone of their acquaintance the horrid truth.

Former friends dropped away. Mrs Roughley wrote – kindly, on the whole – saying that she did not feel she could continue the acquaintance. Others wrote less kindly, repudiating the Comptons, and one enclosed a religious tract recommending repentance and penance for sins of the flesh. The Burnands stayed true, perhaps because of the connection with Patsy, or perhaps because, being 'artistic' they were more easy-going about such things. In the days after receiving the letter, Henrietta did not dare 'go calling' for fear of being refused admittance, a humiliation she could not have borne; but her own 'at home' day showed her who had cut her. On the first Tuesday she received only two visits; on the second Tuesday no-one called at all. Two letters came informing her that the writers were going out of Town and would not be visitable for the foreseeable future. Three couples who had already accepted withdrew from a proposed dinner party, and Henrietta cancelled it rather than face further withdrawals. Worst of all, a party to which Lizzie had been invited was cancelled 'owing to illness', and there was no way of knowing if that were the truth or if Lizzie alone had been cancelled.

Lizzie had her own letter from Minnie, rambling, ill-spelled and bereft of punctuation, ending with the injunction that 'she need not think of Roy, either, for he knew all about it and was rejoicing in his lucky escape'. Julia and Thelma did not write at all, and Lizzie did not know whether to be glad or sad about that.

Jerome and Richard rubbed along together at first, apologetically friendly towards each other. The business was what mattered, and Richard did not care about Jerome's marital arrangements, which made no difference to him. But Richard had to live with Marion, who nagged him day after day until he was worn down with it. At length, sadly, he told Jerome that he thought it would be best if their partnership were dissolved. 'It's so awkward as things are – you do see, old man? No offence meant, I'm sure, but I don't see how we can carry on indefinitely like this.'

To Henrietta Jerome said, 'I'm sorry about it, but I can see how difficult it is for him. I expect it's for the best.'

'But what will you do?' Henrietta asked.

'Set up on my own. I know enough about the business

now not to need Sutton, and I have my name and my reputation. And I have my own clients, too.'

'Will they stay with you?'

'Most of them,' he said. 'But others will come. There are always new investors, and a limited number of brokers to satisfy them.' He seemed suddenly invigorated, and she saw he was looking forward to it. 'It's an opportunity,' he said. 'I was just beginning to feel the need for something new to get my teeth into.' Had he been growing bored? Before he married her, his life had been one of constant movement and change. 'This will be something I can build up entirely alone, owing nothing to anyone. By God, I can hardly wait!'

She looked at him steadily, thoughtfully, and he came down from the clouds and patted her hand. 'We'll be all right, you know,' he said. 'I have great plans. And new markets are opening up all the time, for the man who knows how to take advantage of them. Don't you trust me?'

'With my life,' she said.

'This is a little more important,' he teased. 'This is your money!'

'*Your* money,' Henrietta corrected. 'And I shall try to be more careful with it. We ought to be able to economise on entertaining, at any rate. No more big dinners for a while.'

He put his arms round her. 'It will come right in the end. We'll make new friends. There are lots of people in London who don't regard divorce as a disgrace.'

'But how will we find them?' Henrietta said. 'How will we know unless we tell them? How can we make friends if the first thing we have to do is tell them our dark secret?'

'Yes, confession isn't the best lubricant to social ease,' he said. 'We must find another way of testing the water. Darling one, try not to be unhappy. What really matters is that we are together, isn't it?'

She nodded, pressed against him as though he might keep out the world.

Mary came to visit, and her opinion was robust. 'You don't need people like them anyway. Dreadful, small-minded *petit bourgeois*. How dare they criticise you?' To Jerome, privately, she said, 'Well, brother, have you had enough of your little adventure? You see where it leads – censured by such people as the Suttons! I never understood what you were about.'

'It was fun in its way,' he said. 'Seeing how other people live.'

'Why don't you get out of it now and buy a place?' she asked. 'You're a gentleman. You shouldn't be grubbing for a living among the middle classes.'

'Oh, but we're all middle class now,' he said airily. 'And, besides, I like "grubbing". You've no idea of the heady excitement generated by the Market! It's addictive, like gambling; and trying to outwit the bears and bulls has all the thrill of big-game hunting, without the physical discomforts. I even enjoy travelling up on the "metro" every day! I'm sorry if it shocks you, but I positively love being a stockbroker.'

She stared at him suspiciously for a moment. 'I don't believe you. But if you intend to carry on, at least move to a better area, and live among your own sort. Come and live somewhere near us. There are some nice houses in Belgravia.'

That part of her advice he mulled over, and finally put it to Henrietta. 'I think we ought to move away from here,' he said.

'Shake the dust of the neighbourhood from our feet?' she joked, to hide the slight sinking of her heart. She liked this house, and had grown comfortable in it.

'I think it would be for the best. You don't want to have to keep avoiding the neighbours and being afraid to meet people in the street. I was thinking we should move somewhere further in, so you could be nearer to your cousin Venetia.'

'But wouldn't rents be awfully dear? I suppose we'd have to have a smaller house.'

'With our large family? I don't think that would be practical. No, my love, I'm going to make our fortune, so we ought to begin as we mean to go on. We'll lease a place.'

The agent found a house for them in Trevor Square.

'Knightsbridge is a very desirable area these days,' he assured them.

It didn't have a very large garden, but as Jerome pointed out it was just across the road from the Park, which would make a big difference. 'Emma will be able to take the boys there every day. All that room for them to run about, and plenty to interest them: the Round Pond, the Serpentine, the bandstand, the horses. It's almost opposite the barracks, too, so they'll be able to watch the cavalry coming and going.'

This reasoning appealed to Henrietta, who had begun to worry about the lack of good places for the boys to walk. She went to see the house, and liked it, but worried that it seemed much more expensive. 'Are you sure we can afford it?'

Jerome said they could; and so the thing was decided.

The move was a thing of great disruption and inconvenience, and Jack and Robbie took full advantage of it. They 'helped' the removal men almost to distraction, broke a small table and a pair of vases, and ran wild about both houses when they were at their emptiest and most delightful. Emma apologised afterwards but said that it was very hard for her and Katy to keep control of the boys when they had the babies to care for as well. 'Truth to tell, ma'am, they're getting out of hand. They need a bit of learning to slow 'em down.'

'Jack certainly ought to be doing lessons,' Jerome agreed. 'And it wouldn't hurt Robbie, either.'

'Papa, I can do that,' Lizzie jumped in eagerly. 'I'd like to – please.'

'Tired of a life of idle pleasure?' he asked, smiling.

'Not entirely – but I've done nothing but cost you money since I left school.'

'I'll tell you when I can't afford it any more,' he said, touching her cheek affectionately. 'But if you'd like to help your mother teach the boys their letters, it will save having to hire another nursemaid.'

'I should like to be useful,' Lizzie said. She met his eyes, and understanding passed between them. Henrietta needed something to do to take her mind off things, and housework did not provide it: it was impossible not to think while washing delicate porcelain or arranging flowers, because those tasks occupied only the body, not the mind. But teaching the children would use up all one's resources.

And, Lizzie thought later, a little glumly, it would be good practice for her, too, in case she never married, and the time came when she had to earn her own living after all.

Lizzie had told Dodie what had happened. She felt she had to, for he was at the house so often he would not have been able to avoid knowing that something was wrong; and besides, she would not have anything less than honesty between her and her beloved.

He had listened in puzzled silence to her exposition, and after a pause said, 'I am very sorry. It must be upsetting for you. But after all, *you* can't be blamed for anything. Your mother and father were married, properly married by anyone's standards. No-one can point the finger at you.'

She looked at him doubtfully. 'Do you think they were wrong – Mama and Papa? Do you blame them?'

He was uncomfortable with the question. 'I can see that a lot of people would think so. I mean, divorce is bad enough, but to remarry afterwards – and yet, a lot of people have done it, people from some of the best families. It isn't against the law, so I don't see how it can be really wrong.'

'But what do *you* think?' she pressed him.

He assembled his words carefully. 'If your papa loves your mama half as much as I love you, I can't blame him at all. I don't know what I'd do if I couldn't marry you. And things are changing. People are getting more open-minded, and I wouldn't mind betting that in ten years' time divorce will be spoken about quite openly.'

'In ten years' time?'

'Well, it needn't concern us, anyway,' Dodie said hastily. 'As I said before, *you* aren't affected by it. Jerome's only your step-papa.'

But her mother, her mother, her *mother* was now an outcast, didn't he see that? And what people thought of her mother did affect her! She wanted to shout at him for not

315

understanding, but stopped herself. For the first time she felt a distance between them; but the feeling passed quickly. She ached all the time to be with him, and the days when she did not see him were endless.

There was no doubting his love and support. He did not stop coming to see her, and never changed in his manner towards Jerome and Henrietta. He still wanted to marry her. He hadn't mentioned anything about the divorce to his parents, that was all. His father, like Jerome, had been happy for him and Lizzie to be unofficially engaged, and he was leaving it at that, and hoping this other business would never come to light. He wasn't sure how his parents would take it if they ever found out, but he had a feeling his mother would not like it, and if she objected, his father would too. So it was best, he thought, to leave sleeping dogs lie. Once he and Lizzie were properly engaged there'd be nothing they could do about it.

Dodie passed his examinations, and began his 'apprentice-ship' at his father's merchant bank. Though his visits were less frequent, since he had to be at work during the day, they remained regular, and Lizzie leant on his unswerving affection as on a prop. Polly had been away all summer, staying in France and then in Germany with friends from Girton and their families, and Lizzie had not seen her before she went back to Cambridge. Acting on Dodie's advice, Lizzie had not written to her about what had happened. 'Tell her when you see her, if you must, but it wouldn't be fair to worry her when she's away from home, and with so much hard work to do.'

Lizzie had found it easier than she expected to keep it out of her letters. When she wrote to Polly, the whole business seemed so unreal, and so petty, that it was something that did not relate to her and Polly at all. In December Polly came home for Christmas, and came to see Lizzie at once. Lizzie was so happy to see her friend again, she did not mention their troubles at first, not wanting anything to spoil their reunion. Time enough, she thought, at the end of the holidays.

Venetia and Hazelmere had invited the Comptons to a performance of *Cavalleria Rusticana* at the Shaftesbury Theatre, and as it fell on Polly's first day home, they generously included Polly and Dodie in the invitation, saying the box was plenty big enough for all. It was a lovely evening, the performance was excellent and the music thrilling, and for several hours all the Comptons managed to forget everything and feel completely happy.

Unfortunately, unknown to them, Marion and Richard were also at the performance. From their dress-circle seats they were perfectly able to see into the Hazelmere box, to see who was there, and how happy everyone seemed.

Before that evening Marion would have said, if asked, that she wished Henrietta well, though she could never see her again; but seeing her laugh in the company of the friend-and-cousin who had always been the object of Marion's jealousy was too much for her. Henrietta ought to have been chastened, miserable, in retirement and pining for the friendship she had lost because she did not deserve it. Instead she was shamelessly enjoying herself as if she hadn't a care in the world, and as if such a person as Marion Sutton had never existed.

Pique, hurt and jealous rage demanded revenge. She had seen Mary and Dryden Paget in the box too, and would like to bet that the deceitful, underhanded Henrietta had not told them about her shame. After all, she had not told Marion, and if a kindly friend hadn't warned her . . . ! Well, a kindly friend should warn the Pagets, too. As soon as she got home from the theatre, she wrote to Mrs Paget, explaining what she had found out about the Comptons, and asserting that her only concern was to save the young Pagets from the contaminating influence.

Only Polly and Dodie witnessed the explosion (Cam was at sea), and neither of them ever told anyone what was said. Mrs Paget was shocked and incensed that a couple living in such irregular circumstances – tantamount to living in sin – should have thrust their daughter upon her family, and endangered her precious girl's reputation. Mr Paget, taking his cue from his wife, was extremely annoyed to have been imposed upon. 'And we don't know that there was ever any money. There can be no question of you marrying the girl now,' Mr Paget said to Dodie.

'Thank God there was never any real engagement,' Mrs Paget added, 'or I wouldn't put it past them to bring an action for breach. Probably that was what was in their minds all along. The underhandedness of people is not be be believed!'

Polly and Dodie leapt to the Comptons' defence. Both were forbidden ever to see the Comptons again and refused to be forbidden. There was a furious row. Polly was under her parents' control, and it was impossible for her to defy them; in any case, she would be back at Girton in a few days' time. But if she could not see Lizzie, she could write to her. She wrote even before she left London, saying that she would continue to correspond with Lizzie, but warning her not to send Polly letters at home, where they would be confiscated. She could write to her at Girton, and during the vacations care of Lilian Bowling, who would send them on under cover.

Dodie came to tell Lizzie in person. 'They can't stop me seeing you,' he said. 'Not without locking me up.'

'I don't want to get you into trouble,' Lizzie said miserably.

'I don't care,' he said. 'Pa said if I went on seeing you he'd stop my allowance and throw me out of the firm, but he wouldn't do that. It would cause such a stink – and, anyway, he wants me to carry on after him: Cam obviously won't. Don't worry, he'll never know. They can't control where I go when I'm not at home. But the thing is, I'm dependent on him for money for a while yet, so there'll be no question of our getting engaged until I'm earning a proper salary.'

'It's all right,' Lizzie said. 'It doesn't matter, getting engaged.'

'No, of course it doesn't. Getting married's the only thing that matters. And we will be married, I promise you.'

Just before Christmas an influenza epidemic struck Britain. It was a particularly virulent strain, and the death toll was high. Venetia was kept very busy, and she and Hazelmere turned down the invitation to go to Ravendene for Christmas, though Venetia would have liked to see her mother. There was little enough anyone could do about influenza, but to have turned her back on the pleas for help would have been beyond Venetia, and she toiled on, supported by Hazelmere's love and understanding. The weather was bitterly cold, and freezing yellow fog enshrouded London, both factors contributing to the mortality rate among the very poor. Getting about in a carriage was virtually impossible, and Venetia walked to her calls, heavily muffled up, though the clammy cold still penetrated in spite of many layers, and her fingers and toes never seemed to warm up until she was in bed at night and could thaw them on her husband's willing body.

It was not only the poor who died. The obituary columns in the newspapers were long. Every day there was the name of someone one knew, and the highest were not spared. One of the victims was Prince Victor of Hohenlohe-Langenburg, son of Queen Victoria's sister Feodora. The Prince of Wales and Prince 'Eddy' attended the funeral, and the Court went into mourning, causing a cancellation of a number of festivities. Among them was a grand ball at Sandringham planned for the 8th of January to celebrate Prince Eddy's twenty-eighth birthday.

'Thank God for that,' Hazelmere said, when he brought the news back to Venetia, having heard it from Francis Knollys. 'Have you any idea how cold it is in Norfolk at the moment? There's freezing fog all the way up the coast, and Francis says the lake at Sandringham is frozen hard enough for skating.'

'Won't you have to go at all?' Venetia asked. They had both been invited for the ball.

'No, it's to be a family-only affair now. Prince Eddy's wedding's fixed for the twenty-seventh of February and I shan't be wanted until then, or just before. If only the influenza would go away we could have a little belated Christmas all to ourselves.'

There was no hope of that, however. The disease

319

continued to rage. Venetia was exhausted from overwork, and could not even take comfort from her children, for to avoid the risk of infecting them, she would not enter the nursery nor have the little ones brought to her for the time being. She worried about infecting her husband, too, but nothing would keep Hazelmere from her.

'You know we never catch each other's colds,' he said. 'And someone must comfort and care for you.'

'I don't want to be separated from you,' Venetia said. 'Lying in your arms at night is the only thing that keeps me going.'

'You can be glad we were spared Sandringham, at any rate. Everybody there has a cold. Eddy caught one at the funeral, and poor little May of Teck's taken one down with her. The Princess of Wales is sniffing and dripping, Princess Victoria's in bed with influenza, Prince George is weak from his typhoid, and half the servants are out of commission. But Tum still insists on dragging everyone out shooting in the bitter cold.'

'You men must have your pleasure,' Venetia said. '*I* wouldn't be shooting.'

'No, but you'd have to join us for luncheon, in a delightful marquee open at the sides, and a carpet of frozen grass under your feet, the only entertainment to watch the men's breath form icicles on their moustaches.'

'You exaggerate!' she laughed.

'Not a bit. I tell you it's so cold I hear they'll be taking the champagne out in a hay box!'

But soon the news from Sandringham grew more grave. Prince Eddy's cold turned to influenza, and he was too ill on his birthday to attend his own birthday dinner and entertainment. The Wales children were brought up on Spartan principles, and in his chilly bedroom influenza turned to pneumonia. By the 12th of January he was delirious. On the morning of the 14th of January, 1892, he died.

The appalling tragedy for the Royal Family provoked a wave of sympathy in the press and the public at large, and the Tranby Croft and Brooke scandals of the previous year were forgotten by a nation where so many were mourning sons or brothers. Venetia spared a thought for poor little Princess May, so nearly a bride and queen-to-be, and now a penniless Court hanger-on again; but she had other troubles nearer at hand to occupy her mind. For a telegraph had come from Paris to say that Gussie was gravely ill with the influenza; and even before a reply could be sent, a second telegraph arrived to say that she had died.

Fog still locked the country in freezing obscurity as the black-bordered newspapers reported the progress of the obsequies of the Heir Presumptive. Those close to the Court were privy to the undercurrent of quarrels that marred the unity of mourning. The Princess of Wales wanted her dearest son buried at Sandringham, but the Queen insisted on a State funeral at Windsor. The Princess was then urgent that no women should be present, which annoyed the wider Royal Family who wanted to witness such an important ceremony at first hand. The Queen, advised not to risk catching influenza, agreed not to attend, and left Windsor Castle. The Sandringham household moved in, but found themselves at outs with the Windsor servants, who had their own odd ways of doing things, and queer rules that had been laid down by the thrifty Prince Consort. A sybaritic prince and his household might well raise their eyebrows at the ban on smoking, at one lump of sugar only in tea, and squares of newspaper in the lavatories.

The funeral was held on the 20th of January in St George's Chapel, which was tightly packed with the royalty of Europe and the dignitaries of England. Hazelmere was there, as was the Duke of Southport, and they found time afterwards for a brief talk before departing their various ways. Hazelmere told Venetia about it afterwards, and said that Harry seemed deeply shocked and affected by Gussie's death.

'They were always close,' Venetia said.

'He seemed quite ill with it,' Hazelmere said. 'There was a very affecting moment at the funeral when the Duke of Teck handed a wreath to the Prince of Wales to put on the coffin, a replica of Princess May's orange-blossom bridal wreath. Everyone felt it, but your brother broke down into sobs. I suppose he was thinking of Gussie's wedding.'

'It was Harry who promoted that match: perhaps he felt guilty as well.'

'He's arranging with Vibart to bring the body back. Harry wants the funeral to take place at Ravendene.'

Venetia nodded. 'I wonder what Vibart will do now. And what he will do with the child.'

Hazelmere looked at her sidelong. 'Shall you mind if he takes the boy away from here?'

'Yes, a little. I'm fond of him. Do you think he will? After all, he's not really his son. Gussie never pretended otherwise.'

'I can't see Vibart making a home for the child,' Hazelmere said. 'For one thing, how could he afford it? Perhaps he'll ask us to keep him. It would be a pity to separate him from his cousins now.'

CHAPTER FIFTEEN

The Vale of York was also locked in fog – slightly less yellow than London's, perhaps, but more freezing. Those who could stayed indoors, banking up their fires against the cold and thus adding to the fog. Animals had to be fed and cows milked, but no other farm work was possible. In the city, people crept from gas lamp to gas lamp, scarves over their mouths and noses. Policemen stood at main intersections with flaming torches. There were accidents, with people slipping on icy patches, falling down steps, being hit by vehicles as they tried to cross roads. And still the influenza raged, claiming victims who could not immediately be buried because the ground was too hard to dig.

Teddy Morland was glad that he had no need to leave his house. Makepeace House was comfortable now. None of the furnishings or decorations had changed, but it was cleaner and warmer; good fires were always lit, the linen was changed regularly, and something like a household routine had been established.

Since Teddy ate at home rather than at the club, meals had had to become fit for his exacting palate, and Mrs Cox had left at September quarter-day for an easier place. Teddy had acquired a new cook, Mrs Hopkins, a comfortable, pleasant woman who liked food and enjoyed preparing it – something that could be said of surprisingly few cooks. She liked the fact that Teddy appreciated when dishes were well prepared, and enjoyed discussing new ideas and recipes with him; and since it was a matter of indifference to her what the master's relationship with Charlotte Byng was or wasn't, she was happy to accept her as unofficial housekeeper.

Waller had teetered on the brink of leaving at the same time as Mrs Cox, but had decided in the end that the place was worth holding his tongue for. The work was not hard, and the master was an important man in York; and besides, now he was eating at home he had had to build up his wine cellar, to which, of course, Waller had the key. Waller was fond of good claret and good port, and saw the virtue in a master too indolent to count the bottles.

There was a new kitchenmaid and two new housemaids, and a boy who came in to do the boots and knives, and all of them accepted Charley's presence without question, knowing no other arrangement. Teddy's only regret was that Charley went home in the evening, to be with her mother. Occasionally she would stay on and have dinner with him, if someone could be found to sit with Mrs Byng, but she would always leave directly afterwards.

One morning in January, during the worst of the fog, Charley did not arrive at her usual time, and a little while later an urchin brought a note from her, begging Teddy's pardon and saying that her mother was too ill to be left. Teddy retained the child's services for the delivery of two notes, one to Charley to say that he perfectly understood, and that he would send the doctor to see her; and the other to Dr Needham to ask him to visit and charge the bill to him.

'It is the influenza,' Needham reported to Teddy later. 'Not much one can do about it. There's no cure, unfortunately. The strong recover by their own strength, and the weak . . .' He let the sentence hang.

'What's your prognosis?' Teddy asked.

'I can't hold out much hope. The patient's chronic condition tells against her. Frankly, it might be in the way of a blessed release if the worst happened.'

'Not to Charley,' Teddy said. Needham only shook his head slightly. 'What can I do?'

'Nothing, I'm afraid. The daughter seems a sensible nurse. Warmth, and good nourishment, if the patient can be persuaded to take it, are all that can help. Now, as to you, my dear sir, I hope you are not sickening for it yourself? You seem to have a little cold.'

'Just a snuffle. It's nothing,' said Teddy, his mind on Charley's predicament.

'No cold is nothing in these dangerous days,' said Needham sternly. 'I had better examine you while I am here, and make sure.' At the end of a quarter-hour he declared Teddy to be in no immediate danger. 'But I must emphasise, no-one can afford to be complacent, and a cold can easily turn to influenza. I urge you most strenuously to stay out of infection's way. Remain at home, if you can, and at all events do not go into any house of sickness.'

So any thought Teddy had of visiting the Byngs had to be abandoned. He wrote every day, however, and sent anything he could think of that might help Mrs Byng – baskets of delicacies, basins of nourishing broth, bottles of wine – and requested a daily report from Charley. He paid the same urchin a penny a time to bring messages, so the boy hung around Charley's door all day, ready to be used.

Charley sent word, day by day, sometimes hopeful, sometimes despondent; but the trend was downwards. Mrs Byng's immobility did not help matters. The influenza settled on her chest, and she grew weaker. Pneumonia would be the next thing, Teddy supposed, and then that would be that.

Late one evening, while he was sitting reading by the fire and thinking about going to bed, there was a thunderous knocking at the front door. At this time of night, he thought, it could only be bad news: it must be a message from Charley about her mother. He listened, straining to catch the sounds from the hall. A man's voice, but not an educated one. Not the boy, nor the doctor, then. What man had Charley found to deliver the message?

Waller came in. 'There's Dick Walton asking to see you, sir, from Huntsham Farm. He seems to think it's urgent.'

Dick was one of the younger Walton boys. 'Send him in,' Teddy said, puzzled. The Waltons were no longer his tenants, though he would always keep an interest in their well-being. Dick Walton came in, red-cheeked from the cold, his jacket, muffler and cap dewed with fog beads, his eyes and nose running from the bitter air outside. 'Well, Dick? What brings you out on a night like this?'

'Eh, Maister Morland, Ah'm sorry to disturb you so late,' Dick said, fumbling out a handkerchief to wipe his face. 'Fact is, it's tekken me that long to get 'ere. Fog's so thick, y' can't see a foot ahead o' y'.'

'You've walked here from Huntsham?'

'Ah thowt Ah might get a lift part o't way, but there's not a thing moving on't road – not a sowl abroad, man nor beast.'

'It must be something serious to bring you out, then?'

'Aye, Maister,' he said apologetically. 'It's yon Alice Bone from up the big 'ouse. She got sick with the influenza, Ah don't know how long since. Any road, she coom up to our 'ouse last night – Lord knows how. Ravin' she were, wi' the fever, sick as a cat, poor creature. Me mam put her to bed and took care of her, for there was no-one else. Alone up at the big 'ouse, she was, as you know, maister.'

Teddy nodded. 'And how is she now?'

Dick turned his cap in his hands. 'She's dead, maister. Died this afternoon. Wasn't nothing to be done about it. Dad, he said mebbe we should 'a' sent for th' doctor, seein' she were your caretaker, but Mam said it wouldn't make no difference, even suppose doctor could 'a' got out to us. So Dad told me to coom and tell you. Ah'm sorry, maister.'

'Yes, so am I,' Teddy said. 'Thank you for letting me know, Dick.' He was silent a moment. 'What about the child – her little boy? Was he with her? Is he all right?'

'Aye, maister,' said Dick, 'he's right as rain, as far as his 'ealth goes. Alice brought him with her. Ah'm not so sure it wasn't him brought her the last part, she were that sick. He were breakin' his little heart for his mother when Ah left home, but he's not got the influenza – not even a sniffle.'

'Thank God for that,' Teddy said. 'But what's to be done now?'

'That's what Ah came to ask, maister,' Dick said.

'Can your mother take care of the boy for a little while? I shall have to think what's to be done with him.'

'Aye, maister, Mam says she'll be glad to – anticipatin'

you'd be askin'. He's no trouble. But there'll need to be a buryin'. We've got her laid out decent-like in the back scullery, and this cold weather she'll hold a day or two, but for the sake o' the little lad, as well as me mam, we'd like to have her put away respectful as soon as possible.'

'Of course, of course. I'll deal with it. I'll have the undertaker sent out first thing in the morning – even if he has to lead the horse all the way. You must thank your mother and father for their great kindness – especially your mother.'

'That's all right, maister. Glad to be of help.'

'What will you do now? You won't try to go back home tonight? I'll have a bed made up for you here.'

'Thank you, maister, but Ah reckon Ah'll get started back, if it's all the same to you. Dad'll be needing me fust thing for the milking, and I'd sooner walk it now than have to start at three in t' morning.'

'Well, as you please, of course – but you'll take something to eat and drink before you set off?'

When Dick had departed for the kitchen with Waller, who had orders to tell Mrs Hopkins to provide something hot, Teddy settled back down by the fire, looking into the flames and thinking. He had a picture in his unwilling mind of Alice, in the grip of a fever, struggling through the freezing fog to take her child to a place of safety. And suppose she hadn't? She'd have died all alone at Morland Place, and the boy would be there alone now, frightened and helpless. He might have died too, not knowing how to get help. Teddy's conscience, that slumbering organ, stirred. He had employed Alice, but had rarely gone near the old place to see if everything was all right, supposing that she would send a message if she needed anything. He had not thought about illness or accident.

He had not done right by Alice. As his brother's former mistress she had a claim on the family, and nowadays he *was* the family. He ought to have made sure she was all right. He felt very bad. Well, he would do the best he could now. First thing in the morning he would see the undertaker. And – the happy thought occurred to him – he would have her buried at Morland Place in the crypt. That would solve the problem of the frozen ground, too. She could lie next to George – on the other side from Alfreda. No-one but him need ever know, so there'd be no-one to offend.

And one more thing he needed to think about – he braced himself for the effort, though the fire was sinking now and his bed was calling to him like a siren. The boy. What to do about the boy? He was, after all, George's son – Teddy's own nephew. He must be taken care of. Teddy's brow furrowed. Well, after all, he had a large house, and enough money to hire as many servants as necessary. Why not bring little Edward here? It might be rather nice to have a child about the house – liven things up a little.

He could see no flaws in the scheme, and went to bed satisfied.

In the morning Teddy entered into a period of unprecedented activity. First there were letters to write – and all without the help of his little secretary. He had grown unused to wielding the pen himself, and it took him some time to settle down to the task. First he wrote to the Waltons, thanking them for their help and kindness, explaining what he meant to do both about the burial and the child's future, and asking them to continue to keep the boy until he had been able to make the necessary arrangements to receive him.

A nursery would have to be set up, furniture and equipment purchased, suitable staff hired, he thought. That would take time. He must ask someone's advice over what would be needed. Perhaps he should write to Regina? Or, no, to Henrietta – she was more down-to-earth and practical than her sister.

He put that letter onto the end of the list of things to do, and now addressed his efforts towards his instructions to the undertaker, which included the request to deliver his letter to the Waltons. He was quite proud of himself for thinking of that. And next, a note to Charley.

He was engaged on that when he was interrupted by the arrival of a note from her to him. It was short, and the writing was uneven. Her mother was sinking. She did not think it could be very long now. She was very sorry not to be able to attend to her work and hoped Mr Morland would understand.

His hands trembling, Teddy drew a fresh piece of paper towards him to reply to this, but before he had written the first word he thought better of it. He had let one person down already, and that was a person he didn't care twopence about by comparison. He would go to Charley himself. She should not be all alone at such a time. He got up and rang the bell.

Having given instructions to Waller to take the two letters to the undertaker, he went in person to the kitchen – the first time he had ever set foot in it – to ask Mrs Hopkins what a person might take with him on such a mission.

Mrs Hopkins was quite upset. 'Oh dear me, the poor young lady! What a sad thing! Her poor dear mother's the only kin she's got. Well, sir, I don't rightly know what you might take. If she really is sinking, nothing will help now. They do say champagne's good for pneumonia, but happen that wouldn't strike quite the right note. Perhaps you might take a bit of brandy, in case of need – a nip for the dying or the bereaved can't be taken amiss, and there's no knowing but what she might swoon.'

So it was with a flask of his best Cognac in his pocket that Teddy finally ventured out, so swathed against the weather that his own kin would not have recognised him. It was still bitterly cold, but the fog seemed a little lighter, and there was more traffic around, horses looming out of the whiteness suddenly like pond creatures emerging from water. Sounds echoed strangely – footsteps, wheels creaking, a horse coughing, the loud bang of something heavy dropped – evidence of invisible presences: everyone in York was a ghost.

It was not far. He was afraid at one point that he had missed his way, but at the last moment recognised a shop on the corner when he had almost passed it, and turned back and into her street and in a few moments was knocking on the door. She opened it at once, and he saw in her pinched face all the signs of her suffering, and at the same time her gladness that he had come.

'How is she?' he asked at once.

Charley only shook her head. 'It won't be long. Oh, but thank you for coming, sir.'

'I didn't want you to be all alone,' he said.

The room was warm, the fire being well banked up: he had made sure she was properly provided with coal. The bed was by the window, and there was a screen between the two, presumably to keep any draught off. Mrs Byng was propped up on several pillows, a shawl over her bed-jacket, a handkerchief clutched in her fingers. She seemed to be sleeping, but when Teddy, invited by Charley's look, crept near, her eyelids fluttered, and she murmured something.

'I'm here, Mother,' Charley said. She took up her mother's hand. 'Mr Morland's come to see you.'

The eyes opened with an effort. They were shiny with fever, and she was struggling for breath, but she saw Teddy and seemed to recognise him. Her lips twitched in the ghost of a smile. 'So kind,' she whispered.

Teddy didn't know what to say. 'Not kind at all. Anything I can do—' He stopped, because it seemed so foolish to be asking that at such a time.

Mrs Byng's eyes closed again, as though great weights were rolling the eyelids over. After a moment her lips moved again, soundlessly. Charley bent her ear close to them. 'What is it, Mother?' she asked. 'What do you say?' After a moment she straightened up and looked at Teddy. 'It's you. She wants to speak to you.'

Embarrassed, Teddy took her place; hesitated, looking at the crabbed hand on the counterpane, and awkwardly picked it up. It was hot and dry, felt almost shiny to his touch. He bent over the closed face, towards the laboured breathing. 'Mrs Byng,' he said, feeling foolish – surely she was beyond conversation now? 'This is Edward Morland here. Do you want to say anything?'

There was a slight tug on his hand, and Charley touched his shoulder, pushing him very gently. Obeying the tacit instruction, he bent over and approached his face to the dying woman's. 'It's Edward Morland,' he said again.

The lips moved. There was no sound, only little movements of air, too faint even to be called whispers. 'I'm sorry,' he said, horribly embarrassed (*letting her down! Another one!*). 'I can't hear what you're saying.'

And then at last he did hear, just three words, widely spaced as if they were not joined in any meaning, but all the same plain to him, plain in intention, and, thank God, something he actually could do something about.

'*Take. Care. Charley.*'

Tears rushed to his eyes – of relief as well as sadness. 'I will,' he said. 'I promise.'

He relinquished his place then to Charley, and moved back, taking a seat on the other side of the room and waiting. The woman did not speak again, or try to, and Charley sat in silence, holding her hand; but it was a long time before the breathing finally hitched and stopped, and a dreadful silence filled the room instead. Teddy surreptitiously looked at his watch. More than two hours he had been sitting here.

Charley did not move at once. Then she laid her fingers against her mother's neck and cheek, slowly released the hand she was holding and, with a long, weary sigh, laid her head down on her folded arms and closed her eyes.

Teddy got up and went to her; hesitated, then laid his hand on her thin little shoulder. He had no idea what to say or do: such scenes were beyond him. But his affection for the girl moved his tongue at last to speech.

'I think she's gone, Charley dear. Gone to God. She'll be happy and comfortable now.'

Charley nodded, without lifting her face from her arms.

'I'll look after you,' he said. 'Always. I promise.' A pause – no movement. 'We'll have a lovely funeral for her – everything of the best. And then you can come and live at my house.'

She raised her head at last, looked at him, and then stood up, dragging herself upright as if tired to death. Probably she was, he thought – she must not have slept much for days.

'You're very kind,' she said, 'but—'

'No, no,' he said, sympathy making him unusually

perceptive. 'I don't mean to – nothing like that. I would never do you harm. Everything above board. You shall be—' A flash of inspiration came to him. 'I didn't tell you yet that I am having little Edward to live with me. His mother – another victim of this wretched influenza. He has no-one else to take care of him, so I'm bringing him to live at Makepeace House. You shall be his nurse, if you please, or governess, or what you will. You shall take care of him. Would you like that? At a salary of – of thirty pounds a year. That's respectable enough, isn't it?'

'Sir,' she said, 'I can't think – can't talk about it now.'

'No, no, I understand. We must do what's right here, first. Don't worry, I'll take care of everything. And then we'll go back to Makepeace House.' He looked round the room at the few things it held, the meagre appurtenances of Charley's life. He wanted to give her so much. 'We'll go home,' he said.

In the summer of 1892 there was a general election. The Liberals were returned by a narrow majority, and Mr Gladstone was recalled for a fourth term of office. The Queen was down at Osborne, and it was there he was summoned to kiss her hand.

Olivia wrote to Venetia:

I never saw a man so altered. The Queen thought so too. She said to me afterwards that she thought him dreadfully aged and weakened, even in his voice, and a weird look in his eyes. I think this last is due to his failing eyesight. I sat next to him at dinner and he asked me to read the menu to him. He is also dreadfully deaf now. However, it didn't matter very much because he talked constantly himself and didn't oblige me to answer – which was just as well, as I shouldn't have known what to say. When we ladies had withdrawn the Queen beckoned to me at once and wanted to know what Mr Gladstone had been talking about all through dinner. I said, 'Home Rule, ma'am,' and she gave a rueful laugh and said, 'I know! He always will!'

'Home Rule again,' Hazelmere complained to his wife when Parliament resumed. 'I wish he could think of something else! There are so many more important issues.'

'Such as?' Venetia invited. She was studying case notes for tomorrow's rounds and only half listening.

'Our obligations to Egypt. French and Russian belligerence. The fact that the Kaiser is building up the German fleet at a breathtaking rate, while our navy is starved of funds. The increase in trade-union membership.'

'Is that something to worry about?'

'Of course. What is a trade union for, if not to persuade its members to strike? I read in *The Times* yesterday that thirty million man-days have been lost in the last year through stoppages.'

'Yes, there does always seem to be a strike going on somewhere or other.'

'The docks, engineering firms, gas-works, the mines – it's one thing after another. And the next thing will be that they all get together and bring the whole nation to a standstill. Stopping people going about their legitimate business through brute force is blackmail, pure and simple. That's what these socialists won't admit.'

Venetia looked up at that. 'You know, wherever I go I seem to stumble across people who want to preach to me about socialism. The oddest people, too – not just Fabians and radical editors and that dreadful Bernard Shaw with his vegetarian nonsense, but society people like Lady Tonbridge. I think it's becoming fashionable, God knows why.'

'Because they've nothing else to think about, of course,' Hazelmere said. 'After years of nothing but pleasure and gossip, they're longing for a new thrill. Taking up for the poor oppressed working man has all the excitement of the forbidden to them. They'll drop it as soon as the next toy comes along.'

Venetia laughed. 'Oh, Beauty, you are so harsh! The poor things mean no harm.'

'The times are changing,' Hazelmere warned. 'Enjoy the world you know while you can, because it won't last long as it is.'

'Not all changes are bad,' she said, going back to her work. At the annual summer meeting of the British Medical Association in July, Dr Galton had proposed to the delegates that they should reverse the twenty-year-old ruling against having women members. Dr Garrett Anderson had been called upon to second the motion, and had given an amusing, and tactfully brief, speech about Darwinianism and the theory of evolution. If the BMA believed in Darwin's theory, she said, it should support the evolution of women out of one stage and into another. There had been appreciative laughter at that; and when the vote was taken, the proposal had been accepted almost without dissent. At last, after fifteen years of practice, Venetia had been able to enrol in the association of her profession. It was a wonderful moment, for her and all her colleagues. That one decision had changed the status of women substantially for the better.

The suffragists had experienced a flush of excitement in the return of the Liberals to office. At their headquarters at 2, Gower Street – just along the road from where Venetia had lodged as a medical student – Mrs Fawcett's fellow-workers allowed themselves a little cautious hope. One of their biggest obstacles was the animosity of Mr Labouchère. Only the previous year the Women's Suffrage Bill had been robbed of its Parliamentary day by his promise to let the Land Bill through if the Government would drop it. He not only did everything he could to prevent women's suffrage being discussed in Parliament, he also used his own paper, *Truth*, to pour ridicule on the whole movement.

He satirised Mrs Fawcett as 'one of those few ladies who want to go into Parliament as they prefer this to looking after their homes', and went on to say that they made so much noise no-one ever realised how few there were of them. This incensed Anne Farraline – who, now that she was twenty-nine, was allowed to come up to London alone, provided she stayed with someone her brother approved of. Very often this was Venetia.

'That unspeakable man,' she had proclaimed during her last visit, 'has had the impertinence to say that it would be as useful to extend the vote to rabbits as to women! Well,

I'll show him! I'm addressing a meeting in Kingsway tomorrow, and I'll use his own words to bring ridicule down on him. There will be several sympathetic newspaper men there. We shall see how he likes being on the receiving end!'

'Darling, I don't believe there's any such thing as a sympathetic newspaper man,' Venetia said.

She was proved right. The newspapers were all more or less hostile to women's suffrage. To most of them the very notion of women's rights was nonsense, and both boring and irritating. Reporting Anne's speech, one paper said that Mr Labouchère was quite wrong to say it would be as sensible to give the vote to rabbits as to women. 'Rabbits, if possessed of the suffrage, might be trusted to do no great harm to the constitutional machine, but if we had a million women armed with the same weapon the result might be different.'

And *The Times* merely said that the female sex was not always placed in a position of inferiority: the epicure preferred the female herring.

Venetia had to laugh. 'Oh, come, Fairy, you must admit the absurdity,' she said, to her enraged cousin.

'It's all right for you,' Anne replied crossly. 'You've got everything you ever wanted.'

'Never mind, come and see the babies,' Venetia tempted her. 'Unless you've become anti-baby since I saw you last.'

'Not at all – not where yours are concerned,' Anne said, forgetting her annoyance. 'You know I adore them.'

They went upstairs together to the nursery to visit Thomas, Oliver and baby Violet. Little Edward Vibart was still with them, too; between Thomas and Oliver in age, he fitted in perfectly, like a third son. His nominal father was still abroad: 'Johnny' Vibart could not afford to live in England any more and, as Venetia had predicted, had no interest in the boy now that Gussie was dead. The income from her dowry, diminished by extravagance over the years, was only just enough to keep her widower in France. It was unlikely he would ever return, and as far as anyone could predict, Edward would be staying where he was for good.

Anne chatted to the boys, and played with the baby. Violet was just beginning to get up on her feet, and with encouragement tried to walk, clutching a supporting adult finger in each fist, while her chubby legs bowed under her weight and her feet made wild inaccurate stabs at the floor. Reaching the far side of the room she would chortle with delight at her achievement, and then descend to the more familiar all-fours, in which position she could whiz about the room at astonishing speed.

Watching Anne 'walk' and then chase her with evident enjoyment, Venetia said, 'Don't you ever mean to get married? You would make such a good mother.'

Anne made a comical face. 'Me? I'd never be at home – always off at some meeting or other. What is motherhood for women like us? We hire other people to take care of our children.'

Venetia was taken aback. 'That sounds like a criticism of me.'

'It wasn't meant to be. Throughout history, whenever women have been given the choice of looking after their own children or having someone do it for them, they've always chosen the latter. Our vaunted "mother's instinct", you see, is nothing but economics.'

'I love my children,' Venetia protested.

'I know you do. But you love your work, too. Why should you have to choose between them, any more than a man does? You have a dressmaker make your clothes and a cook to cook your food, and no-one suggests that makes you any less a woman; so why baulk at having a nanny to look after your children? It's all cant and nonsense, you know, this stuff about a woman's nature. Now, I shouldn't mind having children if someone else would *have* them for me as well as caring for them. We ought to be able to buy them in shops,' she concluded. 'Or, no, wait – to hire them! That would be even better. Hire them by the hour, then you could send them back when you were tired of them.'

Venetia was laughing, not taking her seriously. 'That's precisely what you do with mine.'

'Yes, and I don't even have to pay you for them. Excellent arrangement!'

* * *

Anne Farraline had not forgotten her friend Lizzie. Venetia had told her about Henrietta's troubles, and though she did not care herself for the idea of love and marriage, she entered fully into Lizzie's feelings. If courtship needed a helping hand, she was not averse from providing it. That summer of 1892 Dodie had been away during the recess, staying with his parents with friends in Switzerland, and Lizzie had hardly seen him. Finding her drooping at home, Anne had decided to take her under her wing, and had recruited her to help at 2, Gower Street, doing unpaid secretarial work. It gave her something else to think about, varied the routine of her days, and got her out of the house for a little. Henrietta was only too pleased to agree. Since they had moved to Trevor Square they had not made any new friends, nor entertained at home, and though Lizzie threw herself into the teaching of the little boys, her mother was afraid it was a dull life for her.

So when Dodie came back and resumed his 'apprentice-ship' at the bank, he found Lizzie much revived, with new ideas to talk about and, as she was at Gower Street at least once a week, and often on other days to be found at Manchester Square, much more accessible to him. Anne tacitly encouraged him, and Venetia had no objection to the lovers meeting in her house. When she could, Venetia invited Henrietta to come too, for much the same reasons. She would send the carriage and Henrietta would bring Jack and Robbie to play in the nursery with her own boys, while the mothers enjoyed a cosy chat downstairs.

Venetia felt very sorry for Henrietta. Her 'sin', and Jerome's, seemed very minor compared with, say, the behaviour of Charlie Beresford or Daisy Brooke. And what of poor Gussie, having a baby of which her husband was not the father – something Daisy Brooke had also boasted about? To marry, quietly, a man with whom she was in love, and live with him faithfully and bear him children seemed virtuous compared with the peccadilloes of other people, and the fact that Jerome was a divorcé seemed almost irrelevant.

Of course, in Venetia's stratum of society, in a world where marriages were often arranged or undertaken for dynastic reasons, affairs, once the nursery had been stocked, were accepted, as long as the protagonists were discreet. And the same was true of divorce: it was not encouraged nor precisely accepted, but a quiet, discreet divorce between two consenting adults, who then, after a short absence from the scene, returned with a new spouse, would not nowadays lead to any outrage, except from the strictest of hostesses, and in Court circles. Indiscretion, fuss, scandal, making a public show of oneself – those were the real sins. But even those guilty of indiscretion were accepted again once the fuss blew over. Beresford and Lady Brooke were already back at the heart of things.

It was not so, she knew, among the middle classes. Before her marriage to Hazelmere, Venetia herself had slipped from the path of righteousness. She had had an affair with a man to whom she was not married; and when the thing had become known, her middle-class clients had abandoned her in outrage and disgust. It was very odd, she thought, how much more 'moral' they were. Poor Henrietta had received harsh treatment at the hands of her husband's partner's set, and was evidently smarting from it still. Jerome had a new partner now, a man called Harwood who seemed to be a gentleman, and having moved to a smarter area, it was to be hoped that the Comptons would find a new circle of friends. Venetia felt it her duty to help as much as possible, by inviting them when she entertained.

For Lizzie's twentieth birthday, she arranged a box at the theatre to see Mr Wilde's new play, *A Woman of No Importance*. His play of the previous year, *Lady Windermere's Fan*, had been the *succès fou* of the season, and the new work looked like repeating that success. Already it had received rapturous acclaim, and when the Prince of Wales went to see it on the second night and Wilde told him he was thinking of cutting it a little, the Prince begged him not to lose a single line – a story that was soon known all over London. Everyone wanted to see the play, and there could have been no more exciting outing for a birthday treat for Lizzie. They were all to go on to supper in a private room at the Café Royal after the performance, where some friends were to join them, and Mr Wilde himself had accepted an invitation to their table. This was rather a coup for Venetia: with two great theatrical successes in consecutive years he had become the most sought-after dinner guest in London.

Venetia invited Dodie for Lizzie; and as she had not seen them for some time, she also asked the Westons to share the box with them, but Tommy replied that Emma was rather under the weather, and that he was unfortunately already engaged. So it was just the six of them who met at Manchester Square to go to the theatre together.

Lizzie was wearing one of her gowns from the previous year, cleverly made over by Henrietta – a pink corded silk, the bodice newly trimmed with the fawn lace. Round her throat she wore a pink ribbon, and her hair was done up behind in a large chignon, with a mass of little curls in front. Now she had grown into her features, she was really a very pretty young woman, and the lively, intelligent expression of her face and eyes made her the more attractive. Dodie, looking extremely handsome in black-and-white evening dress, couldn't take his eyes from her.

They had the present-giving at Venetia's house before the theatre, and Hazelmere poured champagne to toast the birthday. Henrietta's present was a beaded evening bag to replace Lizzie's velvet reticule, which was growing shabby. Venetia and Hazelmere gave her a beautiful little painting of a woman in a flower garden. 'It's by Burne-Jones,' Venetia said. 'A small thing, but rather lovely, I thought. He's a friend of my mother, and she had him paint something a little like this for me for my eighteenth birthday. I have it still, and love it very much.'

'Oh, it's perfect! Like a jewel – the colours, the clarity!' Lizzie cried. 'I shall treasure it always.' Dodie leant over her shoulder, and made a breathy sound of appreciation. 'Exquisite!' Lizzie gazed and gazed. 'It's such a happy picture. I shall have it on the wall beside my bed so I can look at it first thing in the morning and last thing at night.'

Jerome's present came next. 'Take off that ribbon,' he said. 'I've something a little better for my girl.' It was a string of pearls, which he fastened round her throat from behind, kissing her neck affectionately when he had finished.

Lizzie danced over to the chimney glass and stared. 'Oh, Papa, they're beautiful! But so extravagant – I thought we were supposed to be retrenching!'

'I'll let you know when I can't afford to buy you a birthday present,' he promised. 'I shan't go bankrupt tomorrow, I promise you!'

'I never expected anything like this!'

'Well, I was going to give you pearls next year for your twenty-first, but I suddenly thought, Why make the poor girl wait twelve more months with a bare neck?'

'Oh, you are so good to me,' she said, turning to survey her benefactors, bright-eyed. 'You are all so good to me!'

When everyone was on the move, putting on coats and cloaks preparing to leave, Dodie sidled up to her and said covertly, 'I'm afraid my present will be an anticlimax after all that, but here it is anyway. With my love.' He gave her a small box. 'I didn't want to give it to you while your family were giving theirs. It seemed presumptuous.'

She opened the box and found inside a funny little charm, in the shape of a curved fish with a smiling face.

'It's a dolphin,' he said. 'For good luck. You know Cam's in the Baltic? I had him get it for me and send it home. It's amber. The best amber comes from the Baltic.' There was a tiny gold hoop on the highest curve of the dolphin's back. 'That's for the chain to go through. I'm sorry I couldn't get you a chain as well, but I'm a bit short of rhino at the moment. I'll give you the chain for Christmas, if you can wait.' Her head was still bent over it, and she had not spoken. He added, 'But of course you couldn't wear it right away, anyway, not with your pearls.'

At that she turned a shining face up to him. 'I *love* it. The pearls are for special occasions, but I shall keep this by me all the time, and wear it every single day, when I have a chain for it.'

'You really like it?' he said, hope reviving.

'If we were alone, I would *kiss* you!' she whispered. And

by way of proxy she kissed the dolphin, before stowing it safely in her new bag.

The play was most enjoyable, and was rapturously received by the audience. Jerome, who was sitting next to Venetia, asked her during the applause, 'You saw *Lady Windermere's Fan* last year? Did you find this somewhat similar?'

Venetia nodded. 'I suppose it was inevitable. *Lady W* was so successful that Wilde must have been urged to repeat it. Theatre owners have to make a living. But still, an entertaining piece.'

The others were less critical, or perhaps more easily swayed by the atmosphere and the verbal sleight-of-hand of the playwright. They admired the sparkling dialogue and witty epigrams, and enjoyed the plot with its wicked lord, fallen woman with her child of shame, and the dramatic secret excitingly revealed. They chatted brightly about it as they walked down the carpeted stairs into the foyer. From the vantage-point of halfway down they could see, over the heads of the crowd, Mr Wilde himself, surrounded and holding forth in his usual manner to a press of admirers and some theatre critics and journalists. His eye, always on the lookout for who was nearby, caught Venetia's as he talked, and he gave her a friendly wave. The crowds parted to let her through with her party, and she shook his hand, said she had enjoyed it, and that she would see him shortly at the Café Royal.

'*Dear* Lady Venetia, it will give me the greatest pleasure! I do so love the company of people who have the good taste to admire my work.'

Those near enough to hear (and he spoke penetratingly) laughed, and a murmur went round identifying Venetia – even without wanting to she heard 'Southport' and 'Prince of Wales' amongst the whispers.

'Won't you introduce me to your charming friends?' he asked. Venetia did so, uncomfortably aware that they were blocking the exit and being made conspicuous, but also having regard to the rapturous excitement on Lizzie's face. Wilde seemed particularly struck with her and Dodie, shook their hands lingeringly and inspected their faces with great attention. 'Ah, youth, youth!' he cried. 'There is nothing like it! You, my dear young people, have the most precious gift in the world, a golden inheritance! The middle-aged are mortgaged to life, you know. There is nothing I wouldn't do to win back my youth – except, of course, take exercise or become a vegetarian!'

Everyone laughed, the knowing all the more heartily at this oblique reference to Bernard Shaw, who had criticised Wilde's work unfavourably.

Lizzie had been gazing, fascinated, at the famous man. His florid face, drooping eyelids and thick lips were not in themselves attractive, but he had such an air about him, with his rather long hair, dandyish clothes and elegant gestures that there could be no doubt about his celebrity. She said now, 'I did *so* enjoy your play, Mr Wilde, especially the witty language.'

He seemed pleased, and flashed a smile at her. 'Words are the greatest inebriant known to man. I am perpetually drunk with them. I would throw truth out of the window in a moment for the sake of a phrase or the chance of an epigram.'

Seeing that Lizzie was becoming dazzled, like a rabbit by a poacher's lamp, Venetia detached her party at this point and they took their leave. At the Café Royal, so brilliantly lit with its vast chandeliers that it glittered in the comparative dark of the street like a crystal palace, they found their other guests just arriving, the Balfours and Lord and Lady Sherbourne. Introductions were made, and it transpired that Lord Sherbourne knew Jerome's partner Harwood, so the conversation quickly split, the gentlemen talking about the stock market and the South American situation, and the ladies and the young people talking about theatre and art.

'Mr Wilde is coming, isn't he?' Lady Sherbourne asked Venetia eagerly. 'I thought he would be arriving with you.'

'He was still holding court at the theatre when we left,' Venetia said. 'He'll be a little delayed.'

Lady Sherbourne was indulgent. 'Bless the man, he must depend on the press for his living, of course. Providence rarely arranges it that great artists are possessed of a convenient fortune.'

'Perhaps they wouldn't become great artists without the stimulus of poverty,' Venetia said. 'Not that Mr Wilde is penurious, of course. He lives in comfortable style, I believe.'

'You haven't been to his delightful house in Tite Street?' Lady Sherbourne asked. 'His way of decorating is quite unusual. Everything very pale. So modern, so amusing!'

'Yes, I have seen it,' Lady Frances Balfour said. 'It's a copy of Ruskin's idea, however. Ruskin did it better, in my view.'

'Oh, but of course Wilde would adapt it to his own inimitable style,' said Lady Sherbourne. She turned to Lizzie and Dodie. '*Did* you enjoy the play?'

'Very much,' said Lizzie. 'It was the most entertaining thing I ever saw.'

'Then you will be looking forward to supping with the great man himself! It is so wonderful to listen to him speak – not just the marvellous things he says, but his beautiful voice! It's quite wonderful – like brown velvet.'

'And he plays it like a cello,' Venetia said. 'I think we had better find our table and wait for him there. We are rather blocking the door here.'

They entered the dining room. As they were looking around for the *maître* to show them to their supper room, first Jerome's, and then Henrietta's eyes were drawn to a couple sitting at a table a little way off – one of those *tables à deux* discreetly placed by a screen of potted palms. They were absorbed in each other, so much so that they did not notice the group just entering until the very pressure of the eyes on them made them look up. The man saw them first, and he seemed to pale slightly as he recognised Venetia. It was Tommy Weston; the woman with him was Jerome's sister Mary.

CHAPTER SIXTEEN

Mary faced her brother in the drawing-room of her house in Eaton Gate, white-faced with fury.

'How dare you lecture me?'

'Because I'm your brother,' he flared back. 'Who has the better right?'

'You are not responsible for me! You have no authority over me! I am an independent woman!'

'Far too independent! What the devil do you think you're doing?'

She gave a short, hard laugh. 'Oh, that is really affecting, coming from you! The pot calling the kettle black, if you like!'

He stared, reddening. 'What? What do you say?'

'Have you forgotten, brother mine? What a convenient lapse! Let me remind you how for years you pursued a married woman and tried to lure her from the path of righteousness into your bed. But of course, when the saintly Jerome Compton does it, it doesn't constitute a sin. Mere contact with the greatness of your soul washes out any little blemish!'

'That was quite different,' he said.

'Was it? Pray explain to me how.'

'I loved her. I always loved her. I wanted to marry her.'

'And that makes it all right? Not adultery at all?'

'We never committed adultery.'

'Only for want of opportunity, And because *she* wouldn't. If she had been willing you would not have hesitated a second.'

He knew that was true, and it made him angry again. 'I never wanted to deceive anyone. I begged her to leave her husband and come away with me.'

'Ha! And I suppose you think it's different for me? That Tommy and I aren't in love, and don't want to marry?'

Now he was surprised. 'But – you surely can't believe he will leave his wife for you?'

'Why not?' Mary said defiantly. 'He loves me.'

'Because it would ruin him, that's why. It would be the finish of him. He would lose his seat. He'd be an outcast. Good God, Mary, you've seen what happened to us for far less cause. If Tommy Weston abandoned his wife and seven children—' He stopped, seeing that she knew it was true, that whatever she might have told herself she had never at the bottom of her heart believed it.

She turned her face away from him. 'We must all take love where we find it,' she said, in a hard voice. 'You did, and so must I. You've been lucky, that's all. I can't see how that gives you the right to censure me.'

'No,' he said unsteadily. 'Perhaps not. It's the calculation that upsets me, I suppose. You took the house here so that you would be near Weston's house, didn't you? So that he could slip in and visit you when Patsy was out of the way. Did you never think of that poor woman and her children when you were trying to take her husband, their father away?'

'Did *you* think of it in your own case?'

'But I wasn't trying to take anything from Henrietta and Lizzie. I was trying to give them something.'

'And Fortescue could fend for himself, I suppose?'

'Well, of course. He was a man.'

'You are hopelessly inconsistent,' Mary said. 'Your double standards are quite sickening. And it's none of your business. Tommy and I will do what we like without your permission.'

'Then for God's sake be discreet!' he cried. 'Dining with him in public! Decent women do not eat *à deux* in restaurants. And the Café Royal of all places! You could hardly have chosen a better advertisement if you wanted to bring the affair to public notice.'

'Oh, leave me alone,' Mary said, and he saw she was near to tears.

He softened. 'Mary, please. I don't mean to play the Puritan, but if it got out it would be a horrible scandal. If you don't care for Mrs Weston – and God knows why you should – think of Patsy. She'd be bound to be dragged into it, living in the same house.'

'Patsy knows all about it,' Mary said dully. 'She doesn't mind a bit. So you see I haven't been as underhand as you seem to think. Go away now, Jerome. I'm tired of this conversation.'

Tommy Weston had called at Manchester Square at Venetia's request, not because he wanted to in the least but because he could not see any way of avoiding the interview in the long run, and thought he might as well get it over with. He felt at a distinct disadvantage with her, as well he might.

'You had better say your piece,' he said, when they were alone, and added peevishly, 'It was damned bad luck your seeing us like that. Otherwise you would never have known a thing.'

Venetia raised an eyebrow. 'Bad luck, when you choose a public place like that to entertain your mistress?'

'It wasn't our usual table,' he muttered.

'And in any case, you are wrong. I would have found out sooner or later. I've already had the hint from Lady Frances that you two have been seen together in several places. Good God, Tommy, you aren't invisible, you know!'

'Well, I don't see that it's your business,' he said, as Mary had said to her brother.

'Emma's my oldest friend. We were brought up together – she's practically a sister to me,' Venetia said. 'Does she know?'

'Of course not!' Tommy said. 'Look here, you know, these things happen all the time. It's no great thing. I love Emma dearly, but we've been married seventeen years, and she's tired, and often unwell, and – oh, you know what that means. Damnit, you of all people know what I'm talking about.'

'You mean you don't have sexual relations with her,' Venetia said coldly.

Tommy blushed. 'There you are, you see, that's the very thing that's always made people upset with you. You not only know about things you shouldn't, you talk about them too. How you have got the infernal gall to lecture me about morality—'

'That's precisely what I was thinking about you,' Venetia said. 'I remember how you mounted a moral crusade and cut me off for years, simply for offering contraceptive advice to Emma. You wouldn't even let me see her in case I corrupted her, and now you – you—' She controlled herself, took a breath, and remembered that she did not, in fact, have any right to tell him what to do, except the right of caring about him and his family. 'Tommy, please,' she began again in a gentler voice, 'I can't bear to think what could happen if this gets out. It would ruin you.'

'Oh, nonsense – ruin me? It happens all the time. You're making too much fuss. These things are understood.'

'For Emma's sake, then, please give it up. If she found out about it, it would break her heart. You know how she loves you.'

'She won't find out. And if she did – she's a sensible woman. She knows I love her. The Princess of Wales is a fine example to her. She wouldn't make a fuss.'

She saw it was no use and gave it up. Afterwards when she was talking to Hazelmere about it, he shrugged and said, 'I don't know why you've let it upset you so. You know how these things are played. You've been to enough house parties to see it in action.'

'Yes, but this is different,' she said stubbornly.

He didn't laugh at her, only asked her, seriously, 'Why is it?'

'It's always different when it's someone you know, I suppose,' she said, and then, thinking again, added, 'Because I know Emma and she isn't like that. At those house parties no-one is hurt because everyone is playing by the same rules. But Emma will be hurt. And Mary Compton too, I suspect.'

'Mary Compton is old enough and sophisticated enough to know what she's about,' Hazelmere said.

'Hmm,' said Venetia, unconvinced. 'And besides all that, *I* am hurt by it. Look what a position he has put me in!'

'Yes,' Hazelmere said. 'You know a secret which you are obliged to keep from Emma for her own sake. A part of you believes you ought to tell her, because it is unfair that she alone does not know; and another part of you feels guilty, as if you are helping to deceive her, which in a sense you are. But to tell her would hurt her far worse.'

Venetia looked at him gratefully. 'You really do understand. Bless you, Beauty.'

'I do understand. And you won't tell her. But I should dearly like to knock Tommy down for putting you in that position; and I'd do it the next time I see him if it weren't that it would cause a scandal that would not do poor Emma any good.'

'I'm so jealous that you've been to Oscar Wilde's house and I haven't,' Lizzie said.

She was doing her stint at 2, Gower Street one afternoon in April 1893, addressing envelopes; and Dodie, having sought her out there, had been recruited to the task as well. 'No idle hands allowed here!' Miss Ulverston had said sternly.

'That's five times you've been now, isn't it?'

'No, only four,' said Dodie.

'Only!'

'Well, he can hardly ask you, can he? An unmarried girl – young woman, rather,' he amended hastily. 'Anyway, there never are any women there – or very few, and only married ones who come with their husbands.'

'So when we're married you can take me with you,' Lizzie said.

'Mm,' said Dodie doubtfully. 'I suppose.'

'What's it like? The house?'

'Red-brick, tall and thin, and very elaborate. Pretend mediaeval on the outside. Haven't you seen those Tite Street houses?'

'I've never been to Chelsea.'

'There are quite a few in South Kensington too.'

'I think I know what you mean. And what's it like inside?'

'Weird. All pale colours, and pictures everywhere, and strange *objects d'art*. But there's always so much going on one never really notices the decoration – after the first time anyway.'

'What does go on?' Lizzie asked, between licking and pressing. 'You never do say.'

'Oh, I don't know. It's talk, mostly. Mr Wilde talks a lot. Sometimes there's singing, or someone reads aloud, but mostly it's the conversation one goes for. There are always interesting people dropping in.'

'What sort of people?'

'Writers, painters, poets, that sort of person. Musicians. Actors.'

'It doesn't sound very respectable,' Lizzie said, not meaning it, but cross because Dodie was having so much fun that she wasn't.

'Of course it is. I met Conan Doyle there – that's respectable enough, isn't it? Your papa loves his stories. And Ernest Dowson, the poet. And Reggie Bacchus – he writes moralising pieces for religious newspapers, you can't get more respectable than that. He's married to an actress, Isa Bowman – she's one of the married women I mentioned, and Mrs Patrick Campbell's another. Oh – and of course I've met the Burnands there, did I mention that?'

'Unaccountably not.'

'Oh, yes, the time before last I think it was. They're very friendly with Mr Wilde.'

Lizzie sighed. 'Well if they go, I don't see why they couldn't take me.'

'I expect they will, one day.'

'Is the conversation *very* brilliant?'

'Very. To tell the truth, I don't always understand everything that's said, but that makes it more exciting, somehow. And there are some very queer sorts who turn up sometimes.' He paused, remembering, a frown between his brows.

'What sort of queer sort?' Lizzie prompted.

'Oh – I don't know.' He came back from his reverie. 'Just oddities. Mr Wilde is friendly with everyone. He's so kind and open and affable.'

'I suppose it is kind of him to ask you. Is Mrs Wilde nice?'

'Very nice – good and clever, and she plays the piano beautifully. But she doesn't often join us. As I said, it's mostly men. The only one I really don't like is Lord Alfred Douglas. He's always there.'

'What's wrong with him? Who is he?'

'He's the son of the Marquess of Queensberry, so he's very high up; and he's very handsome and he writes poetry – Mr Wilde thinks he's brilliant. I suppose it's natural that he always wants to be the centre of attention; but when he isn't, he gets silly, or sulks and makes a fuss. He's a dreadful sulker. And he's always interrupting – can't just sit and listen, if Mr Wilde is talking to someone other than him. Like a spoilt brat,' Dodie concluded, with some venom.

'That doesn't sound very brilliant, I must say. More like school,' Lizzie said, slapping down the last envelope. 'There, I'm done! What's the time? Oh, good. I'm going back to Manchester Square for tea with Cousin Venetia – shall you come too?'

'I can't, I have to get back to the office. I was only able to call in on you because I was in the area, delivering some papers to Gordon Square.'

'Oh. When will I see you, then? You haven't been to dinner for a long time.'

'No, that's true. I've just been so busy, and I have to go home sometimes, you know.'

Lizzie looked at him oddly. 'I wasn't criticising you. You don't need to defend yourself.'

He glanced round to see they were not observed, and leant over to kiss her, briefly. 'Foolish! I know you weren't. And I miss you dreadfully. Seeing you here even for such a short time is like an oasis in a desert.'

'I miss you too. What about tomorrow?' she asked, encouraged. 'Come to dinner tomorrow.'

'I can't,' he said, hesitated, and seeing she was going to ask, added, 'I'm going to the theatre.'

'Oh, how nice – to see what?'

'Pinero's new play.'

'But you've seen it. You saw it with us,' Lizzie said, and then, 'Oh, I suppose you're going with your parents. I understand. Well, another night, then. Do come as soon as you can – and you know you don't need to ask.'

'No, I know. I will,' said Dodie. 'I must go now. Goodbye, Lizzie.'

He was gone so quickly she didn't even have time to ask him which way he was going. He might have walked her to Manchester Square, or part of the way at least. She sighed, and went to get her hat and jacket.

The up-and-down fortunes of Princess May of Teck rose again when on the 3rd of May 1893 she was proposed to by Prince George, brother of her late fiancé, and now Heir Presumptive. Prince George, who had been created Duke of York on the Queen's birthday the year before, had been instructed to court her, but seemed not to object to the order too strenuously. As to Princess May, Venetia thought, if she had been prepared to accept poor Eddy as a husband for the sake of the throne, Prince George would be no harder to love. The only person not pleased with the arrangement was the Princess of Wales, who having lost one son into death had not been prepared to part with the other into marriage. But the Queen and the Prince of Wales persuaded her that it had to be, so she put a brave face on it.

The wedding was to be on the 6th of July in the Chapel Royal, St James's. On the afternoon of the 5th, the Waleses gave a garden party at Marlborough House, to which Venetia and Hazelmere were invited. They had lunch first with Olivia at Buckingham Palace, where she had arrived that morning with the Queen.

'I think it's a very happy arrangement,' she said. 'They are very well suited.'

Venetia laughed. 'Both utterly cold and indifferent, but determined to do their duty.'

Olivia looked pained. 'They're shy, that's all. I'm sure they have a great affection for each other.'

'Well, God knows there's enough trouble in our world caused by unregulated passion,' Venetia said. 'Perhaps this might be the better arrangement for the country.'

She did not repeat, of course, what Hazelmere had said about the jokes circulating in the clubs, concerning the forthcoming wedding night. Would the royal couple know what to do? Would they be able to bring themselves to do it? Would England get an heir out of them? She had said to Hazelmere that, personally, she agreed with Queen Victoria, that if you put two young people together in a bedroom, nature would take its course.

When they left Olivia to go to Marlborough House, the weather was appallingly hot and airless, the London smoke making the air grey and hazy, obscuring the sun so that it appeared as a moving reddish-yellow spot travelling across the sky. The leaves of the plane trees in the park hung limp and moveless and the grass was parched and failing. The heat, trapped between the buildings, seemed to propagate damply, taking up all the oxygen, and the air smelt of soot spiced with the sting of horse manure.

London was already filling up for the wedding, and the Hazelmeres' carriage could only crawl slowly in a great press of traffic. Sightseers were already thronging the procession route, some on foot, many more in vehicles of all sorts and sizes. Commercially minded enterprisers were making good money out of the visitors to London, taking them around the streets in wagonettes at sixpence a head to see the decorations, which were splendid, a gaily coloured mass of bunting, flags, ropes of greenery and flowers. The Mall was lined with the barrows of vendors of all kinds of food from oranges to hot pies, and 'souvenirs' of the occasion from lithographs to china mugs. Every detail of the wedding was of passionate interest to the eager populace, who devoured information about the bride's trousseau (*fifteen ball dresses! Forty outdoor suits!*) and the wedding gifts – worth three hundred thousand pounds and on view to the public for a shilling, all proceeds going to charity.

Five thousand guests had been invited to Marlborough House for the garden party, and the closer one got to it the more the traffic stalled. It was abominably hot, and stuffy in the carriage. Venetia, in a rose-beige dress and jacket of fine silk crêpe and a cream-coloured hat trimmed with marabou, felt sorry for Hazelmere, stifling in broadcloth. As there would be a great many royal personages present, the command for the day was for uniforms and orders.

Venetia had expected that among so many guests she and Hazelmere would go unnoticed and be able to seek out their particular friends to chat to, but they had hardly arrived when Francis Knollys appeared at Hazelmere's elbow and said, 'There you are, old fellow. Servant, Lady Venetia! Look here, HRH wants you to take care of the Tsarevich again. It seems he took quite a fancy to you the other evening. Just see he doesn't get buttonholed, or wander off, will you?'

A few evenings before, Hazelmere had been bidden to make one of a small party, gentlemen only, to take the Tsar of Russia's young heir to the theatre. The Comédie Française had been at the Drury Lane Theatre playing *Les Effrontés*, a tactful choice. The Tsarevich Nicholas and the Prince of Wales had both seemed to enjoy it; and after the performance they had all gone on to the Marlborough Club for brandy and cigars.

It had been a very relaxed evening, with the Tsarevich calling the Prince of Wales 'Uncle Bertie', and being addressed himself as 'my dear Nicky'. Nicholas's mother, the Tsaritsa, was the former Princess Dagmar of Denmark, the Princess of Wales's beloved sister. It was a compliment to Hazelmere that he had been chosen to make up one of such an intimate party – sign, he supposed, that his tactful services on previous occasions had not been forgotten.

During the course of several brandies young Nicholas had warmed and softened into confidential mode, and finding himself knee to knee in a corner in deep club chairs with Hazelmere, he had come around to talking of affairs of the heart. He had been in love for several years with his cousin, Princess Alicky of Hesse – daughter of Queen Victoria's second daughter Alice. They had met in 1889 when Alicky, aged seventeen, had spent six weeks in St Petersburg as the guest of her sister Elizabeth, who had married Nicholas's uncle Sergei.

Alicky had fallen in love with Nicholas, then aged twenty, but at that time there had been a plan afoot to marry her to Prince Eddy – Queen Victoria's dearest wish, though Alicky herself was far from willing. But by the following year that plan had been dropped, and Nicholas had talked of marrying her one day. The difficulty was that, as future Tsaritsa, any woman he married would have to adopt the Russian Orthodox faith, and Alicky was deeply religious and felt she could not abandon her own church.

Having murmured so many confidences into Hazelmere's kind ear, the Tsarevich greeted him at the garden party with the affection almost of a relative, with a hearty handshake and a beaming smile.

'Sir, may I present my wife, Lady Venetia Hazelmere?'

'But of course,' said Nicholas, bowing. 'How do you do, Lady Venetia? This would be a delightful party, don't you think, if only there were half as many people here, or the garden were twice as large?'

Venetia curtseyed, smiled dutifully, and said, 'Your Highness speaks perfect English.'

'We speak it a lot at home. We speak a lot of everything at home,' he added, 'English, Russian, French and German. We Russians love to talk! It's a good thing we are linguists.'

For the sake of conversation, Hazelmere mentioned that Venetia's father had been frequently at Court in St Petersburg in his young days, and Nicholas seemed interested, and spoke of having heard good things of her grandfather, who had been ambassador there; though whether it was merely politeness there was no knowing. He had very charming manners and a musical voice, so he made a pleasant companion.

Amusingly, several guests came up to offer him their congratulations on his forthcoming marriage, mistaking him for Prince George. Nicholas looked ruefully at Venetia and said, 'It happens all the time. People say there is a startling resemblance between me and Georgie. I am getting quite tired of hearing the same thing all the time.'

Venetia took her cue from his tone of voice. 'I beg your pardon, sir, but I don't see it. It is surely only the beard, and your general height and build that make people think so. Your features and the Duke of York's are not alike to my eye.'

She meant it. The Duke had one eye larger than the other, and a quite different nose – Nicholas's was much thinner and sharper; and the Tsarevich's hair grew differently, and his cheekbones were higher.

Nicholas seemed pleased with her reply. 'Thank you, thank you, I'm glad to hear you say that. I don't think we are a bit alike, but you know only yesterday one of *my* equerries went up to Georgie in a corridor and asked him if he wanted to wear the Preobrajensky or the Life Guard uniform to the reception. Taking him for me, you know!' he added, in case she should not have understood the joke.

They strolled and chatted pleasantly, being stopped very frequently by other guests who wanted the distinction of being presented to the future emperor of half the world; and Hazelmere intervened tactfully to extract his charge if anyone looked like sticking to him for too long. And then at last the Prince of Wales caught Hazelmere's eye and nodded, and they led the Tsarevich up to him, and handed him over.

'You must come and speak to Rosebery, Nicky,' the Prince said. 'He has the most promising horse I've laid eyes on for a decade. His stud is the envy of us all.'

Nicholas bowed to the Hazelmeres and said, 'I shall see you at dinner, I hope?'

'No, sir,' Hazelmere said.

'It's all family, Nicky,' the Prince said. 'Royalty only tonight.'

'What a pity,' Nicholas said, bowing over Venetia's hand. 'I had hoped I might have the pleasure of sitting by you.'

The Prince bade them farewell, then turned back to pat Venetia's hand and murmur, 'Not a chance of it! I'd have taken that place m'self.'

And then they were gone, and Venetia and Hazelmere let out identical sighs, which made them laugh. 'Parade's over. Off caps,' Hazelmere said.

'He seems a very nice, inoffensive young man,' Venetia said.

'Odd description of the person who will one day wield absolute power over the largest kingdom the world has ever known. But I agree with you.'

'I think he has quite a look of the Princess of Wales about him. No doubt that's why the Prince is so fond of him.'

'I think he has quite a look of Kaiser Willy about him,' Hazelmere said, 'which is odd because they're not related – except by marriage.'

'What a good thing for Europe that all these kings and dukes and emperors *are* related,' Venetia said. 'At least they won't go to war with each other. Do you think we can be very selfish and naughty now, and go home? I don't think I can bear the heat much longer, and the band's giving me a headache.'

'You prefer home to the most important garden party of the year?' Hazelmere said incredulously.

'I prefer peace and quiet,' Venetia said, smiling. 'Isn't that unnatural of me?'

Peace and quiet was not to be had. They were changing for dinner when there was a tremendous banging at the front door, followed by upraised voices. Venetia quickly put on a dressing-gown over her chemise and went to the door to open it a crack and listen. A woman's voice, hysterical and clotted with tears, and the measured tones of Hobson. Oh, Lord, Venetia thought, it must be an emergency. Why had the woman come here and not to Foreman? If it was something really serious she would have to go, but if it was only a childbirth, she decided firmly, she would send the woman elsewhere. She must have some time to herself.

Footsteps were coming up the stairs now. Venetia checked that she was decent and went out into the passage to meet them. Hobson was looking unusually perplexed. 'What is it, Hobson? I heard the noise.'

'It's Mrs Weston, my lady. She is – very upset, and demanding to see your ladyship.'

Venetia's heart sank. Could it be that she had found out? 'I'll see her, of course. Tell her I'm dressing, and that I'll be down in ten minutes.'

'I beg your pardon, my lady, but I'm afraid she won't wait that long. I've put her in the morning-room, but I fear she won't stay there if you do not go at once.'

Venetia stared, trying to read the warning in his eyes, and then shrugged and said, 'You had better show her up here.'

There was barely time for Hobson to have got back down to the morning-room before footsteps came running up, and Emma burst into Venetia's room. She looked quite wild. Her face was swollen with weeping, she had no hat, and her coat was misbuttoned. She flung the door shut behind her, placed herself against it, and said, 'Tell me you didn't know.'

Venetia, taken aback, hesitated an instant too long. 'Know what?'

A strange kind of cry was wrenched from Emma. She screwed her eyes shut and reeled away from the door, putting her fists up against her temples. 'Oh, oh, God, you knew! You *did* know! I told myself it wasn't *possible*!'

'Emma—'

'Don't you touch me! Don't touch me. I don't want your sympathy. Just stand there and look me in the eye and tell me how you could let it go on and not tell me.'

'I don't know what you're talking about.'

'*Don't lie to me!*' Emma was backed up against the wardrobe now, her hands behind her as if seeking support. She was not crying, but stiff with rage. 'For God's sake, don't I even deserve that – the truth from you? What am I? A child, an idiot? Tell me the truth!'

Venetia could not bring herself to frame the words. She faced Emma, feeling herself trembling with distress. 'How did you find out?' was what she did say.

'I didn't need to. The lady herself was kind enough to come and tell me.'

'*What?*'

'Oh, yes. Mary Compton. She came to tell me all about it. About her and my husband being lovers. She came to my house!' Her voice rose to an hysterical shriek. 'To my house – my house! To tell me that!' She began beating on the wardrobe behind her with her fists. 'She came – to – my – house!'

Venetia tried again to touch her, hoping to comfort or at least calm her, but Emma evaded her, pushing herself away from the wardrobe and across the room to the wall beside the door. She seemed to need a flat surface behind her. Now she said, in a voice of normal pitch, though it shook with emotion, 'I told you not to touch me.'

'All right, I won't. All right, Emma.'

'It's not all right.'

'No, I see that. When did this happen?'

'Just now. I came straight here. It was all I could think of – that you had known all along and not told me.'

'I couldn't – how could I? It would have broken your heart.'

'Ha!'

'I hoped it would end, and then there'd be no need for you to know. I told him – begged him—'

'How long?'

'What?'

'How long has it been going on?'

'Oh, Emma—'

'Tell me!'

'I don't know. Truly I don't. I found out last year, last autumn. I don't know, Emma.'

She closed her eyes, and drew a great, shuddering sigh. 'Oh, God,' she said quietly. 'Oh, God. You should have told me. You should have done that for me, if you were my friend.'

All Venetia's guilt rose up again, guilt and sorrow. And she found her own anger at last. How could Mary have done such a thing? So cruel, so pointlessly wicked? Pointlessly – yes, yes, what *was* her purpose? To precipitate something? What could she gain from such an action? To try to make Tommy leave Emma for her? Surely she couldn't be so foolish as to think he would?

'Emma, what did she say? Exactly.'

'For God's sake,' Emma said. Her eyes still closed, she seemed to be swaying with weariness.

'Please. I think it's important.'

'She said she and Tommy are in love. They want to marry. There'll be a d-divorce. I will be taken care of.'

'She's lying,' Venetia said, her chest tight with anger and distress, which made her voice shake. 'Don't you see? If it were true he would never have let her tell you. He'd have told you himself. I know what it is: he must have finished with her, or she's afraid he's going to, and she's trying to force the issue. She's desperate. It's the act of a desperate woman, not a loved one.'

Emma's eyes opened, and as she stared at her cousin they slowly filled with tears. 'Oh, Venetia! What does it matter?'

'Of course it matters. Darling, Tommy would never leave you. He loves you.'

'He doesn't. I've known for a long time that he doesn't.' The tears overspilled and she sobbed, just once, before taking a deep breath to control it, pressing her fingers against her lips. 'He's never home,' she went on, 'and when he is, he never looks at me. He doesn't want me with him when he goes to things. I don't exist for him any more. He loves that woman. I could see it in her eyes. She was – all springy and shiny with it, like a young dog.'

'But it's not the same sort of love,' Venetia said. 'You're his wife, Emma, and that's everything. His wife and the mother of his children. This other thing doesn't matter at all.'

'It matters to me.'

'I know, I know – but, look, Tommy won't leave you. He doesn't want a divorce. If you just ignore this—'

'*Ignore* it?'

Venetia spread her fingers placatingly. 'Stand on your dignity. Don't make a fuss. Be serene – above it. Like the Princess of Wales. If you show him how noble you can be, he'll love you more than ever, he'll be grateful. Everything will be all right.'

Emma looked at her oddly. 'And that's your advice, is it?'

'It's the best I've got,' Venetia said helplessly. 'I know you're hurt. He'll know that too. But what's done is done. The past has happened and there's no way to change it. What matters now is the future.'

'There is no future,' Emma said dully.

'But don't you see—'

'No,' Emma said, holding up a hand to stop her. 'Don't say anything else. I can't bear any more words.'

She pushed herself off the wall, swaying a little until she found her balance. Venetia thought she had never seen anyone look so dead tired.

'He's stopped loving me. I know in your circle these things don't matter. But we were never like that, Tommy and me. We belonged together. We were – one thing. Now it's broken.'

'Emma—' Venetia pleaded.

Emma shook her head. 'I'm going home now.' Her eyelids drooped, and almost drowsily she turned and took hold of the doorknob to let herself out. She paused and looked back, and said, 'I thought you were my friend.' And then she was gone.

Afterwards, Venetia thought that if that had been the end of it, she would have remembered those words as the worst moment of her life. But it was only the beginning of the horror.

Hazelmere came creeping in with his tie still undone and said, 'Is she gone?'

'You kept safely out of the way,' Venetia observed.

'I didn't think either of you would want me there.'

'You're right,' she relented. 'Oh, Beauty, here's a mess!'

'She's found out about Mary?'

'Worse than that. Mary went round there and told her.'

'What?'

Venetia explained.

'She must be mad,' Hazelmere concluded. 'What could she hope to gain by it?'

'I don't know. I suppose we shall find out. The question is, what do we do now?'

'There's nothing we can do.'

'Warn Tommy?'

'We don't know where he is. Besides, what good will it do? He'll have to face this one alone. Dear God, what could Mary be thinking of?'

'Herself, I imagine,' Venetia said.

Fortunately they were dining alone that evening. All of London was *en fête*, celebrating the eve of the royal wedding, and the Hazelmeres had had invitations to a dozen dinners, but had decided that the garden party would leave them wanting solitude. So rather quietly and thoughtfully they sat down opposite each other to dinner; and after dinner retired to the drawing-room where each took up a book. Conversation seemed too full of pitfalls; but the silence, broken only by the rustling of a page being turned, made Venetia nervous. She hardly knew what she was waiting for, but when the front door shook to another thunderous salute, she started to her feet, knowing this was it.

Tommy Weston came running up the stairs, leaving Hobson standing, and flung into the drawing-room, white and wild-eyed. 'You've got to come. Now. For God's sake. Oh, please—'

'What is it?' Hazelmere asked.

'It's Emma. Please – come now.'

Hazelmere would have asked more, but Venetia, seized with a nameless dread, silenced him with a look and said, 'Yes, we're ready. Is she ill? Do I need my bag?'

He stared at her so wildly he seemed uncomprehending, as though she had spoken in a foreign tongue. Behind him she saw Hobson hovering, his face one huge question.

'Hobson, we'll need a cab.'

'There is one waiting at the kerb, my lady.'

'Good. Go and make sure he waits.' When Hobson had retreated Venetia took hold of Tommy's arms and shook him a little. 'Do I need to bring my bag?' she asked again, quietly.

Tears of pain and panic squirted into his eyes. 'I think she's dead,' he said.

There was so much to do. Hazelmere was reminded grimly of the time Lord Marwood had tumbled to his death down the stairs of the house where Venetia was living, and it had fallen to him to keep scandal at bay. Venetia's business now was in Emma's bedroom. Tommy, returning home from a dinner, had learnt from the butler of Mary's visit and gone straight upstairs to Emma's room, where he had found her hanging by a long silk scarf tied round her neck from the chandelier hook, an overturned chair beneath her.

Somehow he had got her down, tried to revive her, and then in terror and panic had run for Venetia, not knowing where else to turn. If she were dead it must be covered up, it must not be allowed to be known as suicide, for the children's sake if no-one else's. But Venetia was a wonderful doctor. Perhaps it wasn't too late. Perhaps she could revive her.

In terrible sorrow, Venetia examined the body. 'Oh, Emma,' she whispered. 'Not this. Not this.' It was too late by many hours. She rolled the eyelids down over the unflinching eyes and held them until they stayed. Tommy had removed the scarf before he went for help. Being silk, it hadn't left too much of a mark. She stroked the dead cheek, puffy still with all the tears she had cried. By luck or judgement Emma had managed to hang herself properly, breaking her neck as she fell, like a judicial hanging. It was a very, very small comfort to know she had not strangled slowly.

By the time the Hazelmeres got back to the house with Tommy, the servants had guessed that something serious had happened, though as Tommy had somehow had the presence of mind to lock the bedroom door before he ran for help, they did not know precisely what. But the locking of the door was in itself a thing to arouse suspicion. How long before rumour began?

The nursery staff were fighting a rearguard action to keep it from the children. When Venetia emerged from the bedroom onto the landing where her husband and Tommy waited, a light voice called down the stairs from the next floor. It was the Westons' eldest daughter, Fanny, who was fifteen.

'Is Mama ill?'

Tommy looked up like a goaded bear. 'Go to bed, Fanny!' he said harshly.

'Please,' Fanny said, her voice trembling, feeling desolation in the air as a horse smells lightning. 'What is it? Is she ill?'

'Go to bed, damnit!' Tommy roared, and with a sob, his daughter retreated.

Hazelmere put an arm round him and turned him away. 'We have to decide what to do,' he said. In Tommy's business-room, with the door shut, he asked Venetia, 'Can you give the certificate?'

'She died of a broken neck,' Venetia said. 'But there'll have to be an inquest, you know that.'

'It mustn't be suicide,' Hazelmere said softly. Tommy lifted red eyes for a moment, before putting his face back in his hands. 'You know what that would mean.'

'Ruin,' Tommy answered. 'Disgrace. Unconsecrated ground.'

'It's up to us,' Hazelmere said, holding his wife's eyes urgently.

'What are you talking about?' Venetia asked. 'You know I have to tell the truth.'

'Only as far as you know it. Look, Tommy came home and found his wife dead on the floor. She had climbed up onto a chair for some reason – we'll work something out – and fallen. Tommy lifted her up onto the bed and tried to revive her, then came and fetched you. You found her lying on the bed with a broken neck.'

'Beauty—'

'She died of a broken neck. She could have got that by a fall, couldn't she?'

'She did get it by falling,' Venetia said.

'Then you can swear to it with a clear conscience. Only Tommy needs to lie. Think, Venetia, think of the children. Emma's dead now, we can't bring her back. We have a duty to the living. Think of Fanny.'

She drew a sharp breath, and let it out slowly. 'What about the servants?'

'Tommy?' Hazelmere said. 'What about them? Did you say anything to any of them? Could they have known?'

He looked up with an effort. 'No. No, I don't think so.' He screwed his brow down in the effort to think. 'I shut the door. I think I shut the door. Then I cut the – the scarf with her scissors. I took it off her before I left.'

'Where is it now?'

He looked blank, then said, 'In my pocket.'

'The rest of it will still be tied to the chandelier,' Venetia pointed out.

'I'll go and get it,' Hazelmere said.

'They're bound to talk,' Venetia said. 'They will wonder why he locked the door, why he didn't call any of them, why he came for me himself.'

'Well, if they wonder, they can't prove anything. Will they be loyal to you, Tommy? Tommy?' He only groaned. 'We'll have to hope so. When I come back down we'll get them all together in the hall and I'll address them. I'll give them a story they can believe.'

'Oh, God, what a mess,' Tommy moaned.

Venetia suddenly had a clear image in her mind of Emma as she had been earlier, pushing herself upright, bone weary, before leaving to go home. 'There is no future.' Oh, Emma, Emma. Not this! It wasn't worth this. But she mustn't let herself think, not yet. It would make her helpless, and there was so much to do.

The undertaker. The inquest. The reporters. The funeral. So much to do. Choosing a coffin. Blacks for the children, armbands for the servants. Blinds down, pictures and glasses turned to the wall, crêpe round the doorknocker. Flowers, letters, callers. Black-edged stationery. Choosing the hymns, ordering the carriages, enduring the sympathy and curiosity.

The inquest gave 'death by misadventure'. Mrs Weston had apparently climbed on to a chair to adjust the chandelier, had overbalanced and fallen, breaking her neck. It was not unusual for her to do things herself rather than call for a servant: she was an independently minded person.

There was a huge crowd at the funeral, for Tommy was a very popular man and a well-loved public figure. The children, from fifteen-year-old Fanny to four-year-old Percy, all dressed in black, made a very pathetic sight. There were seas of white flowers, twelve carriages with black-plumed horses, and 'O God Our Help In Ages Past'.

The royal wedding, which all the rest of London was celebrating on that terrible day when the concealment was set in motion, helped their cause, keeping the interest of the public and the press otherwise engaged. Everything went smoothly, there was no speculation, only sympathy for Weston, who had been known to be devoted to his wife; and if the servants had doubts, either they never voiced them, or at least they never came to the ears of a wider audience.

Only when it was all over, and things had settled down again into something like normality, did Hazelmere tell Venetia that Tommy had, in fact, thought of marrying Mary. He had told him, Hazelmere, that she had been pressing him, threatening to end the relationship if it was not going to lead to marriage, and he had been – or thought himself – so much in love that he had told her he would do it, tell Emma, and put matters in train for a divorce. But of course he never would have. It would have been the ruin of him, the end of his career, and though he was independently wealthy he could not have borne to give up his public life. As he delayed and delayed, Mary got more agitated, until, it was supposed, she had decided to precipitate matters in a way Weston could not reverse. The terrible results could not have been in her mind any more than his.

'Well, it's all over between them now,' Hazelmere concluded. 'He doesn't want to see her again. Unsurprisingly.'

'What a waste,' Venetia said.

'You don't think he ought to marry her after all, surely? I can't see her being a mother to Emma's children.'

'No, of course she wouldn't be that. I don't suppose she wants him any more, either. I didn't mean that – only, what a waste of everyone's lives.'

'I suppose Weston will marry again one day,' Hazelmere said. He looked at his wife curiously. 'He wanted to marry you, once.'

She evaded that memory. 'I thought he loved Emma. Really loved her, I mean. He's not the man I thought he was.'

Weston's eldest daughter, Fanny, grew up overnight, and quietly stepped into her mother's shoes, taking up the reins of the household and supervising the care of the other children. Venetia helped her all she could, hoping that this would not be another life blighted, that pretty little Fanny would not dwindle away into daughter-at-home before she had ever had a chance to taste life on her own behalf.

The secret of Emma's suicide was kept between Tommy, Venetia and Hazelmere. But in the course of a last, angry meeting between Tommy and Mary, when he asked what she had thought she was doing visiting Emma like that, she countered with a furious question as to when he had intended telling her himself. He said he had never intended leaving Emma, they quarrelled violently, and Tommy lost control of himself and the true facts slipped out. Ashamed of himself on a number of counts, he blamed her for Emma's self-destruction, and they parted with the greatest bitterness.

Mary's anger at finding herself the sole villain of the piece overcame any guilt or remorse she might have felt about Emma's death. She had been in the right: Tommy had promised her marriage, and all she had done was to try to move matters along. If Emma was such a weak-minded fool she couldn't stand a breath of reality, how was that Mary's fault? And if it was Mary's, it must be equally Tommy's, so why was everyone blaming her and feeling sorry for him? Furious with Tommy, out of love, humiliated by having been abandoned by him, she wanted nothing more than to escape to some place where she need never see or hear of any of the Westons again.

But where was there that she *could* go, a woman on her own? Bishop Winthorpe was the only answer. She needed capital, however, for the removal and to set herself up, and applied to her brother for it. Jerome knew only that Emma had died by accident, and supposed that Mary and Tommy had parted out of a sense of guilt for having deceived her. But he was glad Mary wanted to leave London. The whole affair had been unpleasant and the ending such a tragedy, it was for the best that she went as far away as possible. He gave her money. Through an agent he found her a small house in the main street of the village, not far from their old one, arranged the packing and transport of her belongings, and when the time came, travelled down with her on the train. They spoke little on the journey, except that at one point he said, 'I think you should say nothing of any of this. Let it be known that you tired of London and craved the peace of the countryside again.'

'Who did you suppose I would tell my story to?' she asked scornfully.

'I didn't suppose anything. It's just my advice. Remember, Henrietta has relations in Yorkshire, and what you do and say will reflect on her.'

Mary was too offended to reply.

'You've changed, you know,' she said, when she parted from her brother at the door of the new house. '*She*'s changed you. I knew she would. We used to be so close, you and I,' she mourned.

'Oh, Mary,' he said – and left it at that. What else was there to say?

With Mary gone, Patsy could not live alone at the house in Eaton Gate, nor did she want to. She gave it up, packed up her easel and brushes, and moved into the spare room at Jerome's house. Henrietta was glad of her company, as was Lizzie; and her contribution to the housekeeping was useful, for expenses seemed to go up almost week by week, and Jerome hadn't increased the housekeeping money for a long time. She thought of asking him, but he seemed so anxious and fraught these days that she didn't like to.

BOOK THREE

Ulysses

Come Worthy Greek, Ulysses come
Possess these shores with me;
The winds and seas are troublesome,
And here we may be free.
Here we may sit, and view their toil
That travail on the deep,
And joy the day in mirth the while,
And spend the night in sleep.

Samuel Daniel: *Ulysses and the Siren*

CHAPTER SEVENTEEN

In August 1893 a group of coal miners protested against the pit owner's demand for a reduction in wages of ten per cent, and were 'locked out'. Thus a strike began, which soon fulfilled Hazelmere's predictions of national turmoil. In previous strikes the aim had been to bring pressure against a particular owner, and the unions had been anxious that all those not directly involved continued working. But in this case the Miners' Federation – the union concerned – had a new tactic: to inflict shortage on the public in general in order to compel the government to intervene. Under the Federation's urging, smaller unions joined in and pit after pit went on strike, until every miner south of Durham was 'out'. The exception was in South Wales, where miners' wages were regulated by sliding scales. Here the Federation attempted to make the action universal by fomenting a hauliers' strike. Hauliers formed 'marching gangs', which went from pit to pit, stopping work and using violence if the miners objected. At last at Ebbw Vale the miners, who had been warned of the approach of an entire army of marching gangs, armed themselves and fought a pitched battle on the mountainside, defeating the hauliers and ending their strike.

But the miners' strike in the rest of the country continued. First coal prices soared, and then coal, especially house coal, became so short of supply that had the weather not been mild thousands would have died of cold.

'It's blackmail, plain and simple,' Hazelmere said. 'Just as I predicted. It's despicable to hold the public to ransom for something they have no control over.'

Tempers on both sides of the dispute grew short. In September there was a nasty incident at Featherstone, near Pontefract. There the pit owners had imported strike-breakers to work the mines, and a huge crowd of strikers and their supporters had gathered, their mood growing ugly. The police presence had been reduced because large numbers had had to be sent to Doncaster for the race meeting, and the strikers took the opportunity to attack. The remaining police were overpowered, and the mob rioted, wrecking buildings and machinery. A small body of troops was called in to stop the riot, and in the mêlée two miners were killed. Herbert Asquith, the Home Secretary, was blamed, as the minister responsible.

'It does seem unfair,' Venetia said. 'Riots have to be stopped. It was very unfortunate, but there's no need to call the poor young man a murderer.'

'He's much affected by it,' Hazelmere said. 'I saw him in Whitehall yesterday. He's always been on the liberal side of the party, which makes it the more ironic.'

'Perhaps it's time for Gladstone to do something,' Venetia suggested.

'There've been delegations begging him to intervene, but that would be to give in to blackmail. I can see why he's unwilling to get involved.'

But as winter approached and coal all but disappeared, it was plain that something had to be done, and in November Gladstone finally called a meeting between the two sides of the dispute, and charged Lord Rosebery to chair it. After four days, on the 17th of November, an agreement was reached and the strike of three and a half months was called off.

The lesson was well taken by the unions, who had seen the action of small men, when properly orchestrated, bring the government of the country in on their side. Formerly unions had been specific to skills or callings, but now seeing the importance of numbers they began recruiting more widely. The Miners' Federation would not only represent coal-getters in future, but hauliers, surface workers, horse-handlers, engineers – anyone who might be employed at a colliery, skilled or unskilled. Mass representation and mass action: it was a vision for the future, and one that Hazelmere said made him shudder.

The loss of his sister had affected Jerome deeply. He had always been very close to her, and for a long time, before he married, each had been the only intimate friend the other had. The two Comptons *contra mundi*: effortlessly superior to the rest, looking on in faint amusement at the follies and ignorance of ordinary mortals. Perhaps if Mary had not been his ideal of womanhood, he would not have been so hurt by her fall. He went on, to the uninformed eye, much as before, but a sparkle had gone out of him. He smiled a little less readily, talked less, and when he was silent his mouth sometimes set into a grim line.

Henrietta knew he was unhappy, and did what she could to reach him, but he would not talk about it. When she asked what was the matter, he would unbuckle his brow, smile at her and say, 'Nothing's the matter. Why should anything be?' And then he would tell her a funny story, or plan an outing, and the next day there would be tickets for the opera, or an extravagant present for her – which was agreeable in its way, but not what she wanted. What she *wanted* was not to feel him tense and restless across the dinner table from her, not to know he lay awake at nights. Sometimes he would say, 'I'll be up soon,' when she suggested it was bed-time, and then he would not come. She would fall asleep without him, wake and wonder, and go downstairs to find him in his study, working away at something, or even asleep at his desk with his head pillowed on his arms.

Lizzie's twenty-first birthday came in the middle of the miners' strike, and the national trouble together with Jerome's darker mood rather took the shine off the occasion. Lizzie told her mother she did not want a celebration. 'Just another year older,' she said. 'Not much to celebrate.'

'A family dinner, then,' Henrietta suggested. 'Us and Aunt Patsy and a few friends. It's your majority, we must celebrate that. You'll be an adult, able to do what you like.'

'Oh, Mama, as if that were true,' she said ruefully. 'I don't see that we can *ever* do what we want.'

'Your friend Polly is doing what she wants,' Henrietta tried. Polly Paget had passed her examinations in June with excellent marks, and had now started as a teacher in a girls' school in Sussex.

'But though she did all the work and passed all the examinations, they won't give her a degree,' Lizzie said.

The tired eyes and the sad droop of the shoulders told their tale to Henrietta. This was more personal than the position of women in society. 'Dodie hasn't called for a while. Has he written to you?'

'He's very busy,' Lizzie said lightly. And then, to her mother's insistent silence, 'There never was a formal engagement, you know.'

'Oh, Lizzie! Do you think he doesn't want to marry you any more?'

'I don't know. Sometimes I wonder. He's been working for his father's firm for two years now, and he never seems to get any nearer to being independent. He says he loves me, but – but if we can't ever marry, then what's the use?'

Henrietta wished she could ease her daughter's troubles, but was as helpless to do that as to ease Jerome's. 'Darling, if he should have changed his mind, isn't it better to know sooner rather than later? I'm not saying that he has, but . . .' She hesitated. 'He hasn't been to see you for two weeks, has he?'

'Only ten days. And we met at Gower Street last week, so you could count that.'

You shouldn't have to count that way, Henrietta thought, but she didn't say so aloud. They had been very young when they fell in love, and people grow out of each other at that age. That was one reason why Jerome had not wanted them to get engaged – and perhaps if the scandal had not altered their lives, Lizzie would have met some other young men and Dodie's spell would have faded quite naturally. The trouble was that she didn't go out enough to places where she might meet other young people. Henrietta thought she must try to find a way to introduce Lizzie to more company. Perhaps Venetia could help. It was important that it was the right company – the sort that would not probe for and object to the Secret.

Dodie called the next evening, and seemed just as he had always been; and Lizzie bloomed and smiled. Watching them together Henrietta could not flatter herself that Lizzie's feelings for him had changed; but equally, he seemed to treat her with the same easy warmth that had been such a noticeable feature of their relationship. He apologised for his absence, pleaded pressure of work, and then plunged into conversation with Lizzie which lasted, on and off, the whole evening. It was full of jokes, of esoteric references, of nicknames and code words, and was carried on at a level of intimacy unusual between young people of opposite sexes. It struck her, at one point, that it was like the conversation of brother and sister who have grown up together in the same nursery.

It happened at one point that she was alone with him, when Jerome and Lizzie had gone off together to find a book they had been talking about, and Henrietta took the opportunity to invite Dodie to dinner for Lizzie's birthday. 'Just a cosy, family dinner, but I felt we ought to mark it in some way.'

Dodie looked wretched. 'Oh – the ninth – I'm – I'm honoured to be asked, ma'am, and I wish with all my heart I could, but the ninth – you see, I'm afraid I'm already engaged.'

'Dodie, you can't *not* come to Lizzie's birthday,' Henrietta said firmly. 'How could you accept an invitation for that day of all days?'

'But you see, ma'am, it was my parents. They're giving a dinner party and I have to be there, and I couldn't tell them – I'm not supposed to see her.'

Henrietta lost patience. 'It's about time you resolved the situation. You're over twenty-one, and you can marry whom you like.'

'Yes, I know, but I'm still dependent financially on my father, and I know he won't have it. You see . . .' He hesitated, looking more wretched than ever, and then confided in a lowered voice, 'You see, they want me to marry someone else. The daughter of Pa's partner, Mr Venner. It's her and her parents who are coming to the dinner party.' Henrietta looked her shock, and he added hastily, 'But I'm not going to marry her! I've told them that. And they can't make me. As you said, I'm over twenty-one. I'm going to marry Lizzie. I *love* Lizzie. I don't even like Edith. I've told Pa I won't marry her, but he just thinks if we see enough of each other I'll come round to it, and he insists I attend this dinner. So I have to go, you see. But it won't make any difference to my feelings, truly it won't. If I can't marry Lizzie I don't want to marry anyone.'

Henrietta felt dismayed. It all seemed more hopeless and complicated than ever; but he seemed in earnest and quite sure about his feelings. 'Well,' she said at last, 'we'll have our dinner on another day. What day can you come?'

She had half feared he would make some other excuse, but he said at once, 'Oh, any other day. Whenever you like,' which seemed positive enough.

The others came back and she said no more then, but later when she was playing the piano and Dodie was turning for her, she asked him under cover of the music, 'Have you told Lizzie about this young woman – Edith?'

'Oh, no,' he said, looking shocked. 'It would only upset her, and for no reason. Mother and Pa will come round in the end, and see that I mean what I say.'

Seeing how happy Lizzie was when he was there, Henrietta decided to say nothing, only to keep an eye on the situation. They had Lizzie's small dinner party, and it was a great success. Venetia and Hazelmere were there, and Polly managed to get special permission to come. The reunion between the old friends was rapturous, and since Polly travelled up from Sussex and stayed overnight, she and Lizzie were able to talk into the small hours.

Through the autumn Dodie seemed more attentive, called more often, and Lizzie was happy, so Henrietta decided there was nothing immediately to worry about. But when, if ever, would Dodie be independent of his father? And if working in his father's firm meant he never would be, oughtn't he to leave it and go elsewhere? Perhaps merchant banking wasn't like that – she didn't know. Perhaps he couldn't work anywhere else. But in that case, how could he and Lizzie ever marry? She wished she could talk to Jerome about it, but he seemed so preoccupied just now she didn't like to bother him unless for an emergency, which Lizzie's love affair did not seem to be, at least not yet.

One evening in April 1894 when it was time for little Edward Bone to be brought down to see his uncle Teddy, it was the housemaid Sarah who came in holding his hand.

'There's my boy!' Teddy said, holding out his arms. 'There's my Edward.' And the boy smiled and ran to him, exchanged a hug and an unselfconscious kiss, and then climbed onto his favourite knee in the world as a young king onto a throne. He demanded too much attention for Teddy to pursue an enquiry into the whereabouts of Charley, especially as the maid curtseyed and hurried away as soon as the child let go of her hand, but it nagged at his mind all the time he was playing with his *protégé* and namesake.

Edward was eight years old, a handsome, sturdy little boy with fair hair and blue eyes, and something of the look, Teddy thought, of his own mother, Sibella, about him. Edward had been rather timid and silent when he had first been brought to Makepeace House, not only because of his recent bereavement and the shock of change but because he had been brought up until that point in a large, empty house with no company but his mother, who had not been either chatty or high-spirited. It had taken Teddy long hours of dedicated effort first to win the boy's trust, and then to break down the barriers of silence and teach him how to play and romp and laugh. Now at last he was beginning to see results; and the rehabilitation of Edward had helped Charley to get over the death of her mother. It had been good to see her grow cheerful again, to see colour return to her cheeks and smiles to her lips. She and the boy were very fond of each other, and together they made movement and sound and cheerfulness in Teddy's house. They made it a home.

Some weeks after Edward had come to Makepeace

House, Charley had spoken about school. The boy had never been taught anything, was lamentably ignorant, though obviously not stupid. He ought to go to school perhaps, said Charley – but she said it wistfully; and Teddy had no wish to part with Edward so soon. It would be unfair, he pronounced, when the boy was so far behind, to send him to a school to be laughed at and bullied. Better they teach him at home. Between them, surely Teddy and Charley could teach one small boy what he needed to know. Charley had agreed, all smiles. So Edward did not go to school. Charley taught him to read and write, and Teddy taught him his numbers, and since then he had had lessons every day with one or other of them. It had given Teddy a new purpose in life, and in the cause he had taken up and dusted off books he had not opened since his own boyhood. Now he was beginning to think it might be as well to employ a tutor, at least part-time, for there were things Teddy did not feel competent to teach, and Edward must not be left at a disadvantage. What Charley could teach he had left behind, but she had her role for him, as a substitute for his mother. Teddy still had things to impart; and besides that, there were the things a father taught – riding and houndcraft and how to shoot straight and hold a cricket bat, stand up for right and tell the truth, take punishment like a man and defend the weak against bullies. Having no father, Edward would need to learn all that from Uncle Teddy.

He came back to the present, to find that Edward had tired of not being answered, and had slid from his knee to the carpet where he was playing a game of soldiers with some walnuts out of the bowl on the side table, using the fender as a fort. He pushed them about, making little muted noises of gunfire and military commands under his breath. Teddy smiled. All those years of playing alone had made him remarkably self-sufficient.

'Tomorrow,' he said, and the war was broken off, the bright face turned instantly up to him. All those years of playing alone had also made him remarkably hungry for company and conversation. 'Tomorrow I think we ought to do something about teaching you to ride.'

'To ride a horse?' Edward said eagerly.

'To be sure. What else would one ride? In the old days, I could have taken you out to Twelvetrees and there'd have been all the horses we needed. But that's all gone now. I think what I shall do is make use of my old friends the Waltons just at first. They're bound to have a pony of some sort that I can put you on, just for the first lesson. Then as soon as you can stay on and know how to go and stop, we shall see about buying a suitable animal – and one for me, too, of course, so that I can ride with you. We can keep them out there – Walton will look after them for a fee – and go out in a cab whenever we want to ride. What do you say? Do you like that plan?'

'Me, to have a pony?' Edward breathed.

'Yes, indeed.'

'I say *yes*!' He scrambled up onto his haunches and leant against Teddy's knees. 'What about Charley? Shall she have a pony too?'

'I don't know whether she can ride,' Teddy said, as if it were remarkable that he didn't. And then, 'Where is she tonight?'

'Gone out,' Edward said. He inspected his uncle's face carefully. 'You do like Charley, don't you?'

'Of course I do.'

'Only you looked cross when you said where is she.'

'Just because I miss her when she's not here.'

'I do too,' Edward said comfortingly. 'But she's coming back.'

When Sarah returned to collect Edward and take him to the nursery, she entered at the same moment as Waller, come to enquire about what time dinner should be put on. When Sarah and the child had gone, Teddy asked Waller where Charley was.

'Gone out, sir,' said Waller, and then, defensively, 'It is her afternoon off, sir.'

'Is it?' In all the time she had been with him, living in Makepeace House, she had never taken her afternoons off, though they had been mentioned at the very beginning, along with her salary. They had not seemed relevant, for she was not, to him, a servant. When she wanted to go some-where – to a shop, or to visit her mother's grave, for instance – she went, just as she would if she were a relative living there, whether it was her day off or not; and, for the other part, she had never gone anywhere in the evenings, always dining with Teddy after the child was in bed. But just these last few weeks she had been taking her afternoon off as if it were a right she had to exercise. He missed her at dinner, and afterwards in the drawing-room, reading or playing cards or just talking. But she had not told him where she had gone, and he had not felt it right to ask. Just a trifle hurt, he felt it was treating him like an employer instead of a friend not to tell him; and as an employer he did not want to ask.

But now, to Waller, he said, 'Did she mention where she was going?'

'No, sir.' Waller was impassive.

'Or when she would be back?'

'No, sir.'

Teddy was silent, looking at the fire. A little green-blue flame ran along the top of a block of coal like a wave breaking. 'What time did she go?'

'At half past two, sir,' said Waller, as if it was something he should have known. 'Her afternoon off is from half past two. The young man called at the back door and she put on her hat and left.'

Teddy looked up sharply. 'Young man? What young man?' Waller looked suffering. 'I do not,' Teddy said sternly, 'allow followers. I hope that is understood.'

'Indeed, sir,' Waller agreed. 'But what the staff do on their afternoons off is, I believe, a matter for their own conscience.'

'Conscience? Who *is* this fellow? Come, you must know!'

'His name, I believe, is Archer. He is a man of the cloth, sir,' Waller added, condescending to reassure. 'The curate at Holy Trinity Church. Quite a respectable young gentleman.'

'Young gentleman,' Teddy growled. He was in a difficult spot now. He was quite entitled to disapprove of his maids walking out without his permission, but if he objected to this, it was making Charley his servant and not his friend. But if she *was* walking out, where did that leave him? And why hadn't she told him?

But he must not expose himself to Waller. It had been hard enough weathering the gossip and sly looks when he first brought her into the house, and they had only just died down. He pulled himself together. 'I'll have dinner as soon as it is ready. And when Miss Byng comes in, ask her to come and see me straight away.'

'Very good, sir.'

He had only just finished dinner, with the clocks striking eight all over the house (five of them in earshot, all slightly out of time with each other, forty strokes in all – wound and put right on a Sunday, and by Wednesday, Charley's half-day, they were spreading out like horses round a race-course) when Charley came in. She had taken off her coat and hat, but her cheeks were bright from the cold air and she smelt of the rain drying on her front hair. She looked young and vigorous and full of life, and he, sitting in his chair by the fire, felt suddenly old.

'Where have you been?' he asked. He hadn't meant to ask it like that, but he couldn't help it. She didn't reply, only frowned, and waited, as though he would find his own answer as to why he should not ask. He took a deep breath and summoned up all his self-control to speak reasonably. 'Any young woman living in my house is in my care. I stand *in loco parentis* – that is, I must worry about her when she is not at home. Many things can happen to a young girl, especially out alone and at night—'

'I wasn't alone,' she said.

'Ha! So I understand. You went off without saying where you were going, with a man, unchaperoned.'

She laughed, such a happy, innocent laugh. 'Unchaperoned? But he is Mr Archer, the curate. I walked along with him to his house—'

'His *house*?'

'Where he lives with his mother and father, and took supper with them. And then he walked back with me. I was quite safe.'

He considered this for some time, and considered her face, too, her dear, familiar face, and what it was telling him. Best to have it out, he thought, once for all. He stepped down off his high horse. 'Charley, why didn't you tell me?' he asked gently.

She flung herself down on the hearthrug, much where Edward had been kneeling, except that she rested her hands on the chair arm rather than his knees. 'I was afraid you'd be angry. But he's a very respectable young man, truly he is.'

Teddy screwed up his face in hurt. 'But what do you want with him?' She didn't answer. 'Are you – are you walking out with him?'

'I don't know. No, I don't think so. Not yet.'

'Not yet?'

'Do you mind? Would you mind if I did?'

Her pink cheeks and wide eyes were close to him, her sweet breath on his cheek. He wanted to snatch her up and press her close, keep her safe, keep her for himself. 'He's only a curate,' he heard himself saying. Oh, foolish, unready tongue!

She grasped the chair arm harder. 'A curate is something,' she said. 'Isn't it? Quite something for a girl in service.'

'You're not in service.'

'Am I not? What am I, then? What is to become of me? You don't think of that, perhaps, but I must. I'm all alone in the world and I must think about the future.'

'How can you say that – all alone? Don't I take care of you?'

'But—' Her hands were white-knuckled with the urgency of her thoughts. 'But what *am* I? What am I to *you*?'

He could not answer. At last he said, 'I thought you knew.'

She shook her head, getting to her feet; brushed down her skirts with that little, automatic movement that tweaked his heart, as almost everything she did had the power to. She was going. 'Charley,' he said, and she paused. 'You are like a mother to that child.'

'I am not his mother, however.'

'Don't you care for him?'

'I love him. But one day you'll send him away to school and then what will I be?'

He thought he was enlightened at last. 'Did you think I'd send you away because he didn't need you any more? Silly girl. *I*'ll still need you.'

'What for?' She looked at him, and asked it as a simple, direct question. 'What for?'

She stood with her hands at her sides, without an attitude, the firelight fluttering in her face and the gas light steady on the shine of her hair, a thing of simplicity and beauty, and he thought of a young horse he had helped to break, years ago, which, having frolicked and bucked all round the paddock, had finally stopped, turned at the end of the lunge rope to face him, and looked at him, much like that, as if to say, *Well, you have me – what now?*

Had he been stupid? Well, yes, undoubtedly, but had he also been blind? At all events, it was for him to give and hazard all he had, and take his knocks if necessary. It was not for her to say the words or ask the question.

'Charley—' He lifted his hands in a helpless gesture. He had never done anything like this before, and it was hard. 'I need you just for *you*. I love you.'

He saw her swallow. 'Do you?'

'Not like a daughter. I thought that was it, at first, but it wasn't. I love you, everything about you. You fill the house with light. You fill me with life. I don't want you to go away.'

She nodded, and her eyes glinted in the firelight, too bright – there were tears there. But she stood still and did not move.

One more fence to jump. One more hazard. 'I want you to stay here always, Charley. Will you – will you marry me, and stay?'

Her stillness broke and she ran to him; down on her knees before him again, this time burying her face in his coat sleeve. He curled his hand round the back of her slender neck, and felt a tingling rush through him at this first touch of her flesh.

'What? What did you say?' he asked tenderly, her voice being muffled by his fine broadcloth.

She lifted her face. 'I said, some people think we are already. Oh, if you had *heard* what they say sometimes!'

'Will you marry me, then? Marry me. Say yes, Charley, before I go mad.'

'Yes,' she said. And then it seemed perfectly natural for her to slip onto his lap and for him to put his arms round her. I'm not so old, he thought. I'm only forty-four. And I was a devil with the ladies when I was young. Why shouldn't I marry? And who cares what people will say? I'm an eccentric bachelor, that's what they think already. But I'm a rich one. I can do as I like.

'You won't mind if people think it odd?' he said.

'We're odd already,' she said, echoing his thought. 'Who cares what they think? Once we're properly wed, they can't say anything.'

I'm head of my family, he thought. I can do as I like. Charley, Charley, sweet Charley. 'I promised your mother I'd look after you.'

She laughed. 'I don't expect she meant you to marry me.'

'Didn't she? I'm not so sure,' he said. And then their eyes met, and he saw it was all right for him to kiss her.

It was not like he remembered, nothing like the kisses of his youth. They had been merely enjoyable; this made him feel weak with longing to possess and protect her. After a while, drawing breath, he said, 'We must get married *very* soon. I can't have the servants shocked again. Will you marry me next week?' He had a sudden thought. 'What about the curate?'

'I was never promised to him.' She laughed again. 'Perhaps he'll conduct the service. Now there's a thought!'

The marriage caused a sensation. He took the precaution of telling people afterwards rather than before, and the wedding itself was very quiet, just the two of them, with Edward in his best sailor suit in the charge of Mrs Hopkins who had always been kind to Charley, and the Havergills, Mr and Mrs – old friends of Teddy's – as rather bewildered supporters. Charley looked radiant in a wedding-gown bought ready-made in York's best store and quickly fitted, and a bonnet from one of Teddy's own shops. When the words were pronounced and the ring was firmly on the new Mrs Edward Morland's finger, Havergill took the usual privilege to kiss the bride, while Mrs Havergill embraced Teddy, and murmured tearfully, 'Bless you! You look younger already. It may answer very well after all.'

Teddy beamed, feeling younger, feeling the elderly habits of his bachelorhood falling from him like discarded clothing. He had been handsome and dashing as an undergraduate and he would be again, with Charley to love. They were going to the South of France for their honeymoon, while the Havergills took care of Edward, and it was on the way to the railway station that Teddy posted the letters to his family announcing his marriage. They might think and say what they liked now, nothing could change it. Henrietta, at least, he thought, would be happy for him.

It was while they were away that the tragedy happened. When Alice Bone had died Morland Place stood empty for a few weeks, before Teddy found a new caretaker – an elderly man called Craikes, who said he had been a butler to a large house in his younger days. He and his wife answered the advertisement placed by the agency Teddy employed, and since they seemed decent enough people and the other candidates were all single, he took them on. Like Alice before them, they lived in the bachelor's wing, which was turned into a sort of apartment for them, and their duties were only to look round the house regularly to check for broken windows, slipped tiles and the like, and to discourage tramps, fieldmice, bats, beetles and other destructive influences that plagued empty houses. More cautious since Alice's death, he required regular reports from them, visited about once a fortnight, and had a charwoman go in once a week to clean the downstairs rooms, and a workman in April and October to take down and put up the shutters on the upper floors, scoop the weed from the moat, clean the gutters, sweep the chimneys and generally do any little jobs that needed doing.

What he did not know, and the Craikeses managed to conceal from him on his visits, was that Craikes drank. It was a common fault in butlers, and the reason he had lost his good place and descended in the world to a man who would caretake an empty house in the middle of nowhere. One night during Teddy's honeymoon, Craikes was drinking by the fire in what had been the billiard-room, and which he used as his sitting-room. Mrs Craikes had gone to bed. Getting up at last from his chair, he picked up the oil lamp with the intention of lighting his way in the search for another bottle; but his balance was affected by the drink, and he staggered, caught his foot in the carpet, and fell awkwardly, banging his head on the heavy arm of the chair. It was enough, in his drunken state, to stupefy him. The lamp hit the floor, spilling oil which immediately caught fire, flames like running liquid flowing in three directions.

Mrs Craikes, deaf and a heavy sleeper, was only woken at last by the noise as a window exploded into shards, and was lucky to escape with her life. The fire was spotted from Woodside Farm, where Ezra Banks sent one of his men to raise the alarm. By the time the engine was able to gallop there from the city, a crowd of people from various farms and houses round about had gathered and were doing what they could with buckets, but the fire had a good hold. It was lucky that the moat was deep and had a good flow of water, for with the aid of the favourable wind direction and with pumps and ladders the firemen were able to stop it spreading to the main house, but they could not put it out until a sharp shower in the early morning proved the forerunner of steady April rain.

The whole of the new wing was destroyed, and the sitting-room and bedroom above it were much damaged, but the rest of the house, miraculously, was unharmed. Craikes was found dead under the ruins; and when the swans came picking their way cautiously back they found their moat reduced to a stream and partly blocked by charred beams and rubble.

The Havergills consulted with Mr Anstey, Teddy Morland's man of business, and decided, compassionately, not to send the news to Teddy in the South of France. There was nothing he could have done, after all. He had only a few days left, and it would be a shame to spoil his honeymoon. He would find out soon enough what had happened to poor old Morland Place, they thought.

In March 1894 another Local Government Act was passed, setting up a system of elected urban and rural district councils, bringing together various powers previously held by sanitary boards, boards of guardians and improvement commissioners, and adding some new ones. Since the rural franchise had been brought in, there had been an increased demand for local democracy in rural areas, which had not been completely satisfied by the creation of county councils in 1888. The difficulty was that in an area as large as a county, poor men could not generally afford the time away from their work to sit, so the new councils tended to consist of the same people as the old quarter sessions they replaced.

Henry Fowler, the Act's prime mover, brought it through by the exercise of prodigious energy and tact, and even managed to include an extremely liberal measure, which excited the women's movement both to hope and gratitude. For the Act that created the county councils had allowed single women to vote but not to serve; Fowler's Act allowed both single and married women to vote, and ruled that if they were qualified to vote, they were qualified to stand for election as well.

'A liberal, just and common-sensical conclusion,' Anne Farraline said. 'It's wonderful how long it takes our lords and masters to understand something which is so plain to the unclouded mind.'

Venetia laughed. 'You are harsh on them. Do you think if we women had had all the power and the privilege from the beginning of history, we should have been any more eager to give it up?'

'*You* say that? After the struggle you had to become a doctor?'

'I don't say that I approve of their attitude,' Venetia said, 'only that I understand it.'

'Well, they had better understand that this Act is a signpost and a weathervane – and a warning, too, that we shan't give up until we have the full franchise on the same terms as men. We do not ask for privilege, only simple justice: nothing else will satisfy.'

'Darling, you don't need to proselytise *me*!'

Anne grinned. 'Just practising my next speech, dear cousin.'

Though the Local Government Act had gone through, the Home Rule Bill had failed again, having been finally rejected in the Lords by a massive majority in September 1893. Gladstone, believing his own reputation to be involved in the Bill, had wanted to dissolve and put the matter to a general election again; but the Cabinet had objected, and both Parliamentary and public opinion was evidently more relieved than indignant at the failure of a measure that had taken up eighty-five sittings in the present Parliament alone.

Venetia, like most people who had no connection with the country, had no interest in Ireland, but she listened with interest to Henry Campbell-Bannerman on the subject, when she sat next to him at a dinner party. He had been a coming young man at the War Office when her father was there, trying to get the army reforms through, and the duke had always spoken highly of him. Campbell-Bannerman had been one of the drafters of the Home Rule Bill, and although he was disappointed by its defeat, he was not despairing.

'In 'eighty-six the Commons rejected Home Rule as a matter of principle,' he said. 'The House never even came to hear the details. This time we went through all the stages, passed the third reading, and it was a complete and adjusted measure that went up to the Lords. I think the principle has been accepted and the time will come when the public believes the Lords used its veto unfairly. Then we shall have our Act. In my view, it has become inevitable.'

'Like the women's franchise?'

He laughed. 'I'm not sure I'd go that far. You know, it isn't just the Parliamentary sort of man who objects to the vote for women. Working-class men – and especially the trade unionists – hate the idea too.'

'Not the very poor,' Venetia objected. 'Amongst them,

there has always been a curious kind of equality: everyone works and suffers alike.'

'Quite so. But I mean the new sort of working-class man, the decent, respectable, aspiring fellow – he wants nothing to do with it. He wants his wife meekly at home, cooking and cleaning and agreeing with him quietly when he comes home from work, not stridently challenging him for his job, his opinion and his mastery of his own little kingdom.'

'Dear me, is that what emancipated women would do?' Venetia murmured. 'How *horrid*.'

Campbell-Bannerman smiled. 'Dear Lady Venetia, you are an example to us all, male and female alike! But I tell you another thing, the working-class man believes that if women had the vote they would use it to abolish alcohol and tobacco – and probably gambling and football as well. And without those comforts, his life would not be worth living.'

Two days after this conversation, Gladstone announced his resignation. The official reason given was his failing sight and hearing; the immediate cause was a disagreement in Cabinet over finances for the navy, in which he found himself in a minority; but the real reason, as everybody told everybody else, was the defeat of the Home Rule Bill and the Cabinet's subsequent refusal to dissolve, which ended any hope of his settling Ireland himself – his great ambition.

He was eighty-four years old; it was sixty-one years since he had delivered his maiden speech in the Commons, and fifty-two since he had first been sworn in as a privy councillor. It was less of an exaggeration than such titles usually are when he was called the Grand Old Man of Parliament.

The Queen did not ask his advice on the choice of a successor, since such advice, if asked for, is deemed to be binding; instead she sent for Lord Rosebery. There could hardly have been a greater contrast with his predecessor. Rosebery was forty-six, handsome, charming, rich, eloquent, liked wherever he went. He had succeeded to the earldom just before his majority so he had the grace of long accustomedness in his great wealth; and he owned a string of racehorses the envy even of the Prince of Wales. He could make a public speech that would melt the roughest heart, and it was a tribute to his universal likeability that it was he who had been called on to settle the miners' strike the year before – and that he had succeeded.

'I like Rosebery very much,' Venetia said to her husband.

'So do I,' Hazelmere agreed, 'but unfortunately a large section of his party in Parliament consists of dour northern Nonconformists, probably teetotallers, who heartily disapprove of a racehorse-owning Whig aristocrat who is such an obvious favourite of fortune. I suspect he will have many difficulties with his own benches.'

'Well, his first act as Prime Minister was certainly shocking,' Venetia said, and Hazelmere laughed. On entering number 10, Downing Street, Lord Rosebery had announced that he intended to have electric lighting put in. 'What on earth next?' Venetia said. 'A telephone machine?'

Rosebery's Chancellor of the Exchequer was Sir William Harcourt, a grim and overbearing old man, who outside Parliament was regarded as the natural successor to Gladstone. In May he presented the first budget of Rosebery's premiership. The expansion of the navy, which was desperately needed in the face of the massive German expansion, had to be paid for somehow. Harcourt introduced a new tax, to be levied on the whole wealth, in whatever form, left by deceased persons. The beauty of death duty was that it was a direct tax, independent of income tax, capable of being augmented automatically and indefinitely by a simple turn of the screw.

'It's an appalling precedent,' Hazelmere said. 'He would never have got away with it under Gladstone. The Old Man hated income tax for that very reason, that it was a standing temptation to every government to increase public expenditure. If they *can*, his thinking went, sooner or later they *will*.'

'The Conservatives won't like it,' Venetia said. 'It's clearly intended to victimise the landowning sort.'

'Yes, and for the same reason the Liberals will like it, as a means to take money from the rich to pay for social reform.'

'Isn't that a good thing, on the whole?'

'To tax the income of the rich is one thing. But the reason I said it was an appalling precedent is that for the first time the State will be confiscating capital to spend it as if it were income. That's shockingly bad business. If any company regularly released capital to pay for day-to-day running costs it would soon be in trouble. Where will it end? And why is the State to be the arbiter of how the accumulated wealth of the country should be dispersed?'

'I don't know,' Venetia said helplessly.

Hazelmere suddenly grinned. 'You ought to know! These are the sorts of question you ladies will have to deal with if you have the vote.'

'Oh, when you men start to talk of "you ladies", I know it's time to stop listening!'

Rosebery opposed the introduction of death duties in Cabinet, but the measure was passed in spite of him. The following month, however, the Prime Minister enjoyed a success unique in history when his horse Ladas won the Derby. It was an immensely popular win with the racegoing fraternity and the public in general, but there could hardly have been anything more calculated to annoy his Nonconformist colleagues, who regarded gambling of any sort, and horse-racing by association, as works of the Devil.

One day in April 1894 Olivia was sent for to the Queen's private drawing-room. As Princess Beatrice was away, she was wanted to play duets with the newly arrived Princess Alicky of Hesse.

The pretty but rather wan-faced Princess was unusually glowing. She had just come from Coburg, where she had attended the wedding of her brother Ernie to her cousin Victoria Melita of Edinburgh, always known as Ducky. Ducky's father was the Duke of Edinburgh and Coburg, Queen Victoria's son Alfred; her mother was Princess Marie of Russia, the sister of the Tsar. So it was natural that the Tsarevich Nicholas should have attended the wedding as well; and under the influence of family intimacy and the romantic atmosphere, Alicky had finally accepted his proposal of marriage.

The young Princess was evidently overflowing with happiness, and when the music had sent the Queen to sleep in her chair, she took the opportunity to confide in Olivia.

'I'm so happy for you, Your Highness,' Olivia said. 'May I offer my very best wishes and felicitations?'

'I'm so happy for myself!' the Princess cried – softly, and under cover of the playing, knowing the Queen would wake if the music stopped. 'Everybody's pleased about it. Granny is *quite* reconciled now, and Nicky had the *sweetest* letter from his mama, the Empress. She said she already regarded me as her daughter and she wished I would call her Mama or Motherdear, because that's what I am to her now. Isn't that kind? And the Emperor wrote too, and *thanked* me with all his heart for consenting! Imagine! As if I had done his country such a great favour.'

'As you have, Your Highness,' Olivia said. 'You will be the next Empress, and mother of the heir to the throne.'

'Oh, I know, but you see I love him so very much, I can't think of it like that. It has been so *hard*, refusing him all these years, when I've loved him so much for so long! And now I'm so happy, I keep having to pinch myself to know it's real. But I had such a dreadful dream last night, and you know, I hardly ever dream. It was idiotical. I dreamt I wasn't engaged to Nicky at all, but to his uncle, but I still loved him – Nicky, I mean – and I was in despair, not knowing how to get out of it. What do you think that could mean?'

'I don't think dreams have meaning, Highness. As you say, they are nonsensical.'

The lovely eyes opened wider. 'Oh, I'm sure dreams *do* have meaning, if only we can find it out. But of course they can't mean what they seem to mean.'

'Thank God for that, Highness,' Olivia said, privately amused.

'But I do think—' the Princess began, but at that point the Queen woke up and the conversation was broken off.

It was resumed, however, at various moments during the stay. Seeing that her granddaughter had taken to Olivia so strongly, the Queen asked Olivia to attend her during her stay. From time to time, when they were alone together or the Queen was asleep – she frequently dropped off for ten minutes or so during the day, and for longer periods in the evenings – Alicky spoke of how much she missed her Nicky, how she kissed his dear photograph last thing at night and first thing in the morning in lieu of his dear face, how absurdly shy she was when in his company. 'In my letters to him I can pour out all my foolish thoughts and feelings, but when I am with him there is so much I want to say and ask, and yet I can't manage it. It's as if there's a strange lock on my tongue, and it won't form the words, even though they're in my mind longing to come tumbling out.'

'But that will pass, Highness,' Olivia said calmly. 'It is quite natural to be shy at first with a member of the opposite sex, however much one loves him.'

'Did you feel that way too with Mr Du Cane?' the Princess asked eagerly.

'Oh, yes, Highness. I could hardly lift my eyes to his face, though I longed and longed to look at him. I think, indeed, that one is more shy with the person one loves so very much than with any other man.'

'Yes, yes, you're right! If I didn't love him so, I could speak to him as easily as to Cousin Georgie.'

'But it passes, I promise you.'

'Oh, I do hope so! I'm afraid I must seem dreadfully cold to him sometimes. When we said goodbye at the station at Coburg . . .'

'I'm sure he understands very well, Your Highness.'

She spoke also of the struggle she had to come to terms with renouncing her religion. 'But I'm sure I am a better person for these five years. It has made me think more about God than ever before. Suffering always draws one nearer to God, don't you think?'

'Yes, Your Highness,' Olivia said placidly; her surface serenity never changed, but she and Charlie had longed for a child ever since they were married, and she knew a little of suffering.

'One thinks of what Jesus Christ suffered so patiently, and all our troubles seem so small by comparison, yet we grumble and fret.' She paused. 'God will understand, don't you think? That I am doing it for the best of reasons.'

'God sees into our hearts,' Olivia said. 'And I don't believe that a good thought or prayer can be made bad by the form in which it is spoken.'

The Princess seemed struck with that. 'Yes, I'm sure you're right! Oh, but there will be so much to learn! The religion, the language, the customs! If it weren't for Nicky, I could never do it, I know. We are to have a long engagement, so that I can learn everything. I'm going to ask him to send me lots and lots of books so that I can begin straight away. Your father was in Petersburg when he was young, wasn't he? What did he tell you about it?'

So Olivia dredged up what memories she had of her father's stories, and the Princess listened avidly, until it was time to talk of her beloved's beautiful eyes again; and his goodness, and her love for him.

The Queen spoke privately once or twice to Olivia about her misgivings. 'She is not strong, poor child, and she has had no-one at all to turn to since her parents' death.'

'Except Your Majesty.'

'Yes, I have been a second mother to her since her dear mother's death, but I do not see her often enough. She needs constant guidance, and I wonder if Nicky is quite steady enough to give it. He's a good boy, but when all's said and done he is a *Russian*. Alicky's feelings are very strong and good, but I fear sometimes her emotions are unregulated. The responsibilities and trials of her position will be very great. I'm afraid she doesn't properly appreciate how difficult it will be.'

'But she will always have Your Majesty to give her advice. And I'm sure she and the Tsarevich will often be visiting you.'

'Hmph,' said the Queen. 'Once she is in Russia I do not depend on her ever being let out again, for all their soft speeches. Russia is a foreign country, and that's all there is to it.'

Venetia had the opportunity to see the lovers for herself in June when the Tsarevich was invited to England for a month.

He had a few private days at first with his fiancée, staying with her sister Princess Victoria, who lived in Walton-on-Thames with her husband Louis of Battenburg; and then the young couple went to Windsor Castle. Venetia and Hazelmere were invited to dinner there one evening when the Prince and Princess of Wales were also present. Nicholas and Alicky seemed very happy, obviously in love, and the Princess unexpectedly serene. The Tsarevich remembered Venetia and spoke in a warm and friendly manner to her, joking, *sotto voce*, that he did not feel he was looking his best, since the Queen insisted that he wore the Windsor tailcoat, blue with red collar and cuffs, with stockings and shoes, like all the other men. 'How horrid!' he said. 'I must look a sketch! But it is traditional.'

'Yes, sir – and it was designed by the Prince Consort,' Venetia said, and saw by the twinkle in his eye that he appreciated the gravity of the warning.

The Prince of Wales spoke at some length to the Hazelmeres of how glad he and the Princess were about the match. Venetia congratulated him on the birth of his grandson, the first child of the Duke and Duchess of York, born at White Lodge at Windsor on the 23rd of June.

'Yes, clever May!' the Prince said. 'A boy first time. And a splendid little fellow he is, too, strong and healthy. We're both delighted – though we would have preferred him to have been born at Sandringham. Between you and me,' he said, leaning forward a little, confidentially, 'White Lodge was an unhappy choice for May, for she's been bothered to death by her mother. But she would have it so, and there's no arguing with ladies in a delicate condition.'

Venetia thought that if May had stayed at Sandringham, she would have been bothered to death by her mother-in-law, so there wasn't much in it; but she didn't say so, of course. 'Have you chosen names for the little Prince, sir?' she asked.

'Oh, yes: he's to be christened Edward Albert Christian George Andrew Patrick David,' he said, with a faint air of defiance.

'That sounds very fine, sir,' Venetia said. She knew Queen

Victoria would have wanted the baby's first name to be Albert.

'Yes, doesn't it? Names fit for a king. But at home we shall call him David. His grandmother has a fancy for it.'

A shocking thing happened in the House of Commons. Sir William Harcourt rose to move, on behalf of the government, that official condolences be sent to France over the assassination of their president, M. Carnot. Up rose Mr J. Keir Hardie, the Independent Labour Party member, to ask whether the same should not be done for the two hundred and sixty mine workers killed in a pit accident in Wales on the same day. There was a collective sigh of impatience, for Keir Hardie was well known for raising such issues and for not understanding the nature of protocol. Harcourt replied, curtly, that there was no question of it. 'I can deal with that now by saying that this House does sympathise with those poor people in Cilfynydd.'

Keir Hardie went red with fury as if he had been slapped in the face. A little later in the same session he took his revenge by standing up and opposing the vote of congratulation to the Queen on the birth of a son to the Duchess of York. The House erupted with scandalised gasps, angry comments, and cries of 'Shame!'

'He's a fool,' Hazelmere said, 'if he thinks that will win him sympathy. The ordinary working man is an ardent royalist, and insulting the Royal Family will only turn them against him. That's what these socialists never understand.'

'They are a troublesome set, aren't they?' Venetia said. 'Not long ago you never heard the word "socialism" and now you can't seem to open a newspaper without seeing it. Nancy Southport told me that Daisy Brooke – Daisy Warwick, I should say now – is a tremendous convert. She can't talk about anything else.'

Hazelmere gave a short laugh. 'That should please HRH. What jolly conversations they'll have together!'

In September 1894 the Tsar of Russia was taken ill, and was moved to Livadia, in the Crimea, in the hope of recovery.

There his condition deteriorated so rapidly that the Prince and Princess of Wales left London to hurry to his side. But he died while they were *en route*, on the 1st of November, and they arrived only in time to comfort the Tsaritsa, the Princess's loved sister.

The Duke of York was sent for, and the Waleses travelled with the imperial suite to St Petersburg for the funeral, to give their support and comfort. Just a week later, on the 26th, the marriage took place between the new Tsar, Nicholas II, and Princess Alicky of Hesse, who was proclaimed under the name Empress Alexandra Feodorovna.

'Awfully ill-omened,' Venetia said, thinking of the weeping and the black drapes, solemn music, incense and all the appurtenances of court mourning. 'Blacks put off for one day only, everyone in floods of tears. Poor things. They could have waited a few weeks, surely?'

'I expect he wanted her support,' Hazelmere said. 'It must be an alarming thing suddenly to find oneself Tsar of all the Russias.'

'How much more so for her? The poor girl hasn't had any time at all to get used to things, and now she's pitch-forked into the hottest part of the fire.'

'At least they have each other,' Hazelmere said.

CHAPTER EIGHTEEN

In September 1894 a novel called *The Green Carnation* had been published, which had provoked a great deal of gossip and speculation. It portrayed the relationship between a highly sophisticated middle-aged man and a young nobleman, and it was not difficult to deduce that it referred to Oscar Wilde and Lord Alfred Douglas. The green carnation itself, whose colour was artificially produced, was said to be the insignia of the homosexual, and Mr Wilde famously sported one in his lapel almost every day.

Though the circulation of the book was naturally limited, Mr Wilde's huge popularity with the public and in the drawing-rooms spread its fame far beyond its readership. Unspoken suspicions about him became spoken, and even those who knew nothing about homosexuality, and could not therefore recognise the symptoms of it, remembered *The Picture of Dorian Grey* and wondered if there were not something perhaps *unwholesome* about such a *particular* relationship as that between Mr Wilde and Lord Alfred.

Venetia's friend Inspector Morgan came to talk to her about it one day in January 1895. He was no longer attached to Marylebone but had been drafted into a special department working from Scotland Yard, so they no longer met about their normal business, but they retained an interest in each other and each other's work.

After exchanging news about their families and the neighbourhood, Morgan broached the subject of Wilde. 'I suppose you've deduced, my lady, that there's something not quite right about him?'

Venetia had seen enough of the dark side of London to know what he meant. 'Despite his wife and two children?'

'Of whom I believe he's very fond. He wasn't always what he is now, if my informants are to be believed. But at this very moment, according to those same sources, he and Lord Alfred are off on a jaunt to Algiers.'

He nodded significantly, but Venetia had to ask, 'Is that a bad thing to do?'

'Algiers is the favourite place his sort goes to. Full of little boys, Algiers is; and the locals will sell 'em for the price of a meal.'

'How dreadful!'

'Well, ma'am, Algiers is outside our jurisdiction, but there's a certain address we've got our eye on – thirteen, Little College Street – which isn't.'

'Just across the road from the Houses of Parliament?'

'Just so, ma'am. It's run by one Alfred Taylor, who's a friend – or at least an associate, to put it no higher – of Wilde's.'

'You say "run by"?'

'Indeed, ma'am. We have our suspicions, seeing the kind of people who go in and out and the curtains being drawn shut all day. Shaded candles and scented smoke and red velvet divans in every room and suchlike. More telegraph boys and messenger boys calling every day than can well be accounted for. Oh, we'll have Mr Alfred Taylor one of these fine days, believe me for it! You'd hardly credit a gentleman could fall so low – he went to public school, you know.'

'Did he?'

'Yes, ma'am. He went to Marlborough.'

'Oh, that hardly counts,' Venetia said, remembering Hazelmere's humorous comments on the subject. 'But have you a particular reason for telling me this?'

Morgan looked a little uncomfortable. 'I didn't like to presume, my lady, and there may be nothing in it, but having had the honour of working with you, and just in a friendly way, I thought I ought to mention—'

'Spit it out, man,' Venetia said kindly. 'You can't think I shall faint, or bite your head off, whatever it is.'

Morgan smiled. 'Well, no, I suppose not. You and I have seen things – and talked about 'em – stuff I couldn't mention to the ordinary person, male or female. The long and short is that we've reason to believe Wilde is one of Taylor's customers at his establishment, and that Taylor may have supplied services to Wilde at his home as well. And since a certain young fellow who's been a frequent visitor to Wilde's home, and is seen in public in his company, happens also to be a frequent visitor here, I thought it wouldn't be out of the way to drop a hint – a warning, you might say.'

Venetia stared. 'What young fellow?'

'A Mr Dryden Paget, son and heir of Paget and Venner's merchant bank. I'm not sure what his relationship with you is, my lady, but if he's a *protégé* of yours—'

'Dodie Paget? Good Lord! But it can't be,' Venetia said, her eyes fixed on the far wall as she searched her memory for clues. 'He's engaged to my young cousin – or not engaged officially, but pledged to her. That's why he comes here – it's a place for them to meet. Are you *sure* about this?'

Morgan spread his hands. 'It may be perfectly innocent on his part – probably is, in fact. Wilde attracts a lot of artistic young men – women too – who think the world of him, without there being anything insalubrious going on between them. And Wilde is welcomed in many a drawing-room—'

'He has dined here more than once.'

'Exactly, my lady – so young Mr Paget may not see anything wrong with him. But he has been seen going into Wilde's house at times when I wouldn't be happy about it if it was my lad, and there's no knowing what he may get led into. In a funny kind of way, the more innocent the young gentleman is, the more likely he is to get into trouble.'

'I understand you.'

'And with this Taylor business in the offing, if he was to be there when things came to a head and arrests were made – well, his name would have to be taken and questions asked and so on. He'd likely end up a witness, if it was nothing worse, and his father wouldn't be happy to see him dragged through the courts in a case of that sort. It would be very bad for him and his career – and his dad's business.'

'Yes, I see. Well, thank you very much for the warning, Inspector. I take it very kindly in you. I'm sure the young man has just been dazzled – he's passionate about art and theatre and so on but—'

'But when the moth gets dazzled by the flame, it's the moth that ends up in trouble,' Morgan finished for her, unexpectedly poetical.

When he had gone, Venetia wondered for a long time what to do. *Was* there anything in it, other than Dodie's worship of the arts? Was it possible that Wilde was corrupting him? Was that why Lizzie seemed discontented? Why the engagement had not got any further forward? She liked Dodie very much, had always thought him and Lizzie well suited, if only the difficulty with his father could be got over. But had he even mentioned it to his father? Was that merely a blind to prevent him being expected to fulfil his engagement?

Dodie was extremely handsome – just the sort of pretty boy men like Wilde favoured. That was hardly Dodie's fault . . . but was there something in him she had seen a glimpse of – a weakness, or softness? Or was she just imagining it now, in the light of Morgan's warning?

Well, she thought at last, it did not affect her course of action. One way or the other, she must warn Dodie that visiting Wilde's house could involve unacceptable risks. And perhaps in the course of warning him she might gather some clue that would tell her what to do about Lizzie.

When Dodie Paget appeared in Venetia's drawing room one afternoon in response to her request, he seemed a little ill at ease. There was no reason on the surface of it why he should have been. It was unusual for her to ask him to call, especially in the daytime, but these days it was not unheard of for ladies to want to arrange a loan on their own behalf, and naturally they would prefer to transact such business in the privacy of their home. But something seemed to have told Dodie this was not a business call. He entered with a wary smile and did not enquire why she had sent for him, but took the proffered seat and waited in silence for her to begin.

How handsome he was, she thought: clean-shaven, with his thick, fair hair swept back to show his fine forehead, his classical profile, his sensitive lips. His frock-coat and trousers were well cut, his hands nicely kept, his boots gleaming. He was not, she was relieved to note, wearing a green carnation. The only decorative thing about him, besides his looks, was a gold ring on his left little finger, which she had not noted before and which, under her silent scrutiny, he began to twist about with the other hand.

She did not know how to begin and, since he would not enquire, with an inward shrug she plunged in bluntly. 'What are your relations with Mr Oscar Wilde?'

He looked surprised, but he did not tell her, as he was entitled to, that it was none of her business. 'He's a friend. I'm proud to be able to say that, given what a great man he is, but he's very kind to me, and he calls me *his* friend, so why shouldn't I do the same?'

It was a complete answer, smooth as a carapace, giving her no toe or foothold. 'You seem to spend a great deal of time with him.'

'That's what one does with friends, isn't it?'

'More time with him than with your fiancée,' she pursued.

That provoked a gleam of something – resentment, perhaps? 'There are difficulties about that, you know there are. I wish I could spend more time with Lizzie, but as things are . . . Excuse me, ma'am, but why are you asking me these questions?'

She sighed. 'I wish you would not be disingenuous. You must surely know about Mr Wilde. If you're there so often, you must know better than me what he is.'

Now he blushed. 'You've been listening to gossip. It's not true, none of it's true.'

'What does he want from you, Dodie? You are a hand-some young man, and he likes handsome young men around him.'

'You don't understand,' he cried passionately. 'None of you understands. He's a great man and a great artist! He

402

has a brilliant mind, and he loves beauty. No-one loves it more or understands it better. And everything he does is beautiful. He is incapable of ugliness or wickedness.'

'Do you love him?' she asked quietly.

'Of course I do,' he said defiantly, but not quite meeting her eye. 'Everyone loves what is beautiful and brilliant and skilfully wrought. If you love art, you must love the artist. It is the purest love, that which exists between master and acolyte. It is a spiritual and perfect love. Plato made it the basis of his whole philosophy.'

These words, Venetia deduced, were not Dodie's own, but had been learnt at the feet of his new 'master'. She felt very sad. It was too late for Lizzie, she thought. If a marriage were to take place between them, it could never be a happy one. And indeed, if Dodie loved Wilde in more than a spiritual way, it must be prevented at all costs.

She summoned up her courage to face the unpleasant task. 'All that you say may be so, but the fact remains that Mr Wilde is a homosexual, and homosexual activity is prohibited by law. Already his habits are under scrutiny by the police. His behaviour in public – and that of Lord Alfred Douglas – is so little governed by discretion that sooner or later he is going to get into trouble, and it will be very bad trouble. My concern is that you do not find yourself caught up in it, because if you do, you will be ruined.'

Dodie had blushed violently at the word 'homosexual'. Now he seemed rather to have grown pale. 'You don't understand,' he said again.

'I understand very well,' she said. 'Much of my work is done in the back-streets amongst prostitutes and—'

The word made him jump, and he cut her short. 'You're against him, just like the rest! You want to destroy him! It's the jealousy of the common mind for anyone who is touched with greatness!'

She kept her temper. 'Please believe me that I do not care enough about Mr Wilde either way to want to destroy him. My interest is solely in you, and what your intentions are towards Lizzie. If you love her and mean to marry her, I think you must give up your connection with Mr Wilde, because any scandal that attaches to you because of him will attach to her, too.' He stared at her, pale and wild, unable to speak. She went on, ever more gently, 'If, on the other hand, Mr Wilde has taught you something about yourself that you were not aware of when you first attached yourself to Lizzie, I think you must in justice break off your arrangement with her and let her find happiness elsewhere. You could never bring anything but misery to her if your feelings run another way. Do they run another way, Dodie?'

He swallowed several times and licked his lips before he was able to make a sound. 'I never meant to hurt her,' was what he said, and it was the death knell of any hope Venetia might have had.

'I believe you,' she said. 'But now you must do what is best for her. A clean break. It will hurt her at first, but be better for her in the long run. Have you the courage to go and see her and explain?'

He lowered his eyes, shook his head miserably. 'I don't want her to know about – to know that.'

'Then you must tell her something else.'

'My father wants me to get married,' he said, still looking down. 'He wants me to marry his partner's daughter, for the sake of the firm. I could tell her—'

'That you've decided to give in to your father's will?'

He looked up. 'It's true that I don't see how I can ever marry Lizzie. Pa would never agree to it – more especially now – and if I defied him he would throw me out of the firm. How could I support a wife then?'

'There are other banks, other positions.'

'Pa would make sure nobody else employed me. And – you see, the whole business will come to me one day, when Pa dies. That would be all washed out if I married Lizzie against his wishes.'

He seemed to feel this did not show him in a flattering light; but Venetia could sympathise. To give up livelihood *and* inheritance, to abandon such a prospect of comfort, wealth and security, would need a love of no common order; and would such a love be wise, or lead to the happiness of either party? A little of the head was surely needed to temper

404

the heart. Even lovers had to eat, pay rent and get their laundry done.

'You could tell her that, I suppose. It is something she will understand, poor girl. But whatever you tell her, I want you to promise me to do it at once. Don't keep her waiting any longer on a false hope.'

He nodded. 'I will. I do see it isn't fair on her. I'll write to her tonight.'

'Not see her?'

He looked wretched. 'I couldn't. Please, I really couldn't.'

Venetia shrugged inwardly. Perhaps it would be better for Lizzie in the end to be able to despise him for his cowardice: it might kill her affection the sooner.

When he stood up to go, she said, 'Dodie, what has been said here today will never go any further, I promise you that.'

'Thank you.'

'But I must say one thing to you: give up Wilde. This is a serious warning. Stay away from him. Something is going to happen and it will be very bad. You will not want to be involved.'

Something else looked out for a moment from his eyes. 'I'm already involved,' he said. 'I can't give him up.'

Venetia sat for a long time after he left before she was able to compose herself enough to get up and go on with her day. Poor Lizzie, poor Lizzie! She felt very bad now about having given haven to the lovers and made it possible for them to meet. Not that she could have known how it would end, but perhaps any subterfuge was a bad thing that should never be encouraged.

It was Jerome who went up to Lizzie's room in the end. She had not cried at once when she read the letter. She read it through twice and then, looking up and seeing their eyes on her, had tried to say something, found she couldn't speak, and handed the letter over to her mother.

Jerome had gone to stand behind Henrietta's chair and read it over her shoulder.

'Oh, Lizzie,' Henrietta said, when she finished it. 'I'm so

sorry. But it's best to know now rather than later how things stand.'

Lizzie nodded.

'I think you were beginning to suspect it was going this way, weren't you?' Henrietta asked.

She nodded again, and then finding it imperative to speak, blurted, 'He didn't even have the courage to come and tell me face to face. Just – a letter!' Then she burst into tears and ran out of the room, and they heard her feet running up the stairs and the slam of her bedroom door.

Jerome laid his hand on Henrietta's shoulder. 'I thought something was wrong,' he said. 'Well, she's better off out of it, if the lad hasn't the gumption either to make his father agree or find some other way to make a living.'

'Yes, I know,' Henrietta said. 'But she does love him so. And she's waited for him so long.'

'I'd like to wring the little wretch's neck.'

'Lizzie's?' Henrietta said, startled.

'Paget's. He must have known before now it was hopeless, but he kept her dangling.'

'But he loved her, too. He hoped it would come out all right. I'd better go to her,' she said, rising.

'No,' said Jerome, 'leave her cry a bit. She needs to. Then I'll go up.'

When he did, he found her standing by the window, staring out sightlessly at the grey January garden, a damp handkerchief crumpled in her hand. She turned as he came in, and the sight of her tear-swollen, forlorn face tugged desperately at his heart.

'Oh, Lizzie,' he said gently. 'He wasn't good enough for you. He's not worth all this.'

At his words the tears started trickling again. He crossed the room and took her in his arms, and she sobbed on his shoulder. Then, when the storm had abated, he sat down on the chair by the window and took her onto his lap, as he had used to when she was a little girl.

They sat like that for a long time. The cold wind moved the bare branches of the ash tree in the garden and made a little hooning noise against the window-pane; a robin flew down onto the window-sill outside, trilled a few notes, flipped its tail and flew off again.

At last Lizzie drew a long, quivering sigh and said, 'What am I to do, Papa? What am I good for? I'm twenty-two years old, and I've done nothing. I've put all my thoughts and plans and efforts into marrying him, and now I feel – cut adrift. What can I do now? I must have some purpose in life.'

'It will come to you. Sometimes it takes a long time. But what you're for will find you out sooner or later. Look at me – I had to travel half round the world and reach middle age before I could marry your mother.'

'Is that what you were for?'

'It seems so to me. Dear Lizzie, you are lovely and clever and good, and it won't go to waste, I promise you. Only be patient.'

'I thought I had been patient already.'

'Yes, I know. Poor love.' He drew her head against his shoulder and stroked her hair. 'But you were both very young when you met, and Dodie's a boy still. One day you will meet a man, a real man, and fall in love; and then you'll wonder how you could ever have mistaken what you felt for Dodie for the real thing.'

'You think so?'

'I think only a very big man will be good enough to love someone as special as you.'

'I'm not sure,' Lizzie said, with a watery smile, 'that that's very encouraging.'

Oscar Wilde's new play, *The Importance of Being Earnest*, opened in February, and on the first night there was a disturbance which, to the initiate, was a sign of things to come.

Lord Alfred Douglas's father, the Marquess of Queensberry, was a strange man, choleric, intolerant, with violent opinions and no fear of confrontation. He had been sent to sea as a young lad, endured seven years of the Spartan life on board, and thereafter delighted in nothing but hard, masculine sports and the company of rough men. He was a superb rider and not only hunted but had ridden in the Grand

National. He was a superb boxer, too, and used his abilities along with his rank to bring some order to the sport, framing the 'Queensberry Rules' and forcing their acceptance. In the company of jockeys, gamekeepers and prize-fighters he shone. But he had no drawing-room manners, and a number of violent antipathies – for instance, to any sort of religion – made him an outcast from polite society. He had refused to take the oath of loyalty, calling it Christian tomfoolery, and was therefore barred from the House of Lords, which had caused a scandal and added to his sense of resentment. He had been divorced twice, and was said to have treated his wives and children with violent cruelty; and it was well known all over Town that his relationship with Lord Alfred was abysmal.

One of the things Queensberry loathed was homosexuality. Some years before, his eldest son, Viscount Drumlanrig, was private secretary to Lord Rosebery when Rosebery was Foreign Secretary. Queensberry suspected there was too great a degree of intimacy between them, followed Rosebery to Germany (where he was on a diplomatic mission) and confronted him in public, threatening to beat him with a horsewhip. When Drumlanrig died soon afterwards in a shooting accident, many thought he had in fact killed himself for fear of a scandal coming out.

So Lord Alfred's consorting with Oscar Wilde drove Queensberry to a frenzy. Not only did they disport themselves in public and, it seemed, delight in drawing attention to themselves, but fashionable society – the very people who rejected Queensberry – accepted and lionised them. He had had violent quarrels with Lord Alfred over it, but his son would not give Wilde up.

Now Queensberry's hatred of Wilde had become ungovernable. On the opening night of the new play he arrived with a 'bouquet' of carrots and turnips which he intended to throw at Wilde when he appeared on stage at the curtain, following it up with a public denouncement of his proclivities. News of the plan got out, however, and on the night he was refused entry to the theatre. There was a noisy scene, but in the end he could only leave the bouquet at the stage door, with a number of threats, to be passed on.

The play was a brilliant success. Venetia and Hazelmere went with Lord and Lady de Grey and Nancy Southport, who was a grass widow again – Harry had gone to Scotland before Christmas to stay with Lord Dromore and had not yet returned.

'I think it's the best thing he's done,' Lady de Grey said afterwards. 'So brilliant, so amusing.'

'Oh, yes, I like it tremendously!' Nancy said, looking much brighter than before the curtain rose.

'It's certainly the best thing he's done,' Hazelmere said, 'but I have to confess I don't think that says very much. It's an accomplished piece, but very lightweight.'

Venetia supported her husband. 'There's just one trick to Oscar. He does it very well, but once you've seen through it, what more is there to say?'

There was a chorus of protest.

'Oh, no, no, too harsh!'

'How can you say so?'

'His writing is delightful!'

'There is room in the theatre for the light and entertaining,' Hazelmere said. 'I don't say there is not. But he is no Shakespeare – nor even, not to stretch him too far, Bernard Shaw.'

As they came down the stairs into the foyer, they could see the man himself, in opera cloak and top hat, holding court as usual in the corner by the box office, and heard his liquid flowing voice between the admiring laughs of his audience. This was very much to be expected, as was the sight of Lord Alfred Douglas draped over his shoulder. What disturbed Venetia was that Dodie Paget was at Wilde's other side, very much part of the entourage and, at one point, having Wilde's meaty arm put round him as apparently something was said that concerned him.

Venetia was angry and upset. It was still possible for Lizzie to be hurt, though not compromised. But there was nothing she could do about it. She had delivered her warning, and if the boy was such a fool—

Hazelmere touched her arm. 'Do you see what I see – or who, I should say?'

'Yes. That stupid boy,' Venetia murmured.

'I hope your Inspector Morgan's net has wide mesh, and lets the little 'uns slip through.'

'He doesn't want to cast it at all. But these wretched people keep pushing and pushing! Why can't they do what they want to in private and leave it at that?'

'Love of the limelight, I suppose,' Hazelmere said, and they went on to supper.

A few days later Hazelmere said to Venetia, 'There's the queerest tale going around the club about Queensberry and Wilde.'

'Queensberry? What has the old wretch been up to now?'

'It seems that on the day after the opening night of the new play – you remember he had a plan to cause a rumpus and it was thwarted?'

'Yes. That must have annoyed him.'

'It did. The next day he went round to Wilde's club—'

'The Albemarle, isn't it?'

'That's right. Freddie Talbot troughs there sometimes, and he told me about it. Queensberry went round there, scrawled "To Oscar Wilde, posing as a sodomite" on his visiting card and gave it to the porter to give to Wilde.'

'Good Lord! What on earth did the porter do?'

'Well, Wilde wasn't there, as it happens, so he put it into an envelope and gave it to him next time he came in. Now Lord Alfred Douglas is urging Wilde to sue the old man for criminal libel.'

Venetia shook her head. 'He'd be mad to do so. Everything would come out.'

'But he can't just let the accusation stand.'

'Queensberry will have to plead justification and Wilde must know that there's enough evidence against him. His visits to Little College Street – I wouldn't trust any of that fraternity to keep the secret if Queensberry offers them money. Who is Wilde's solicitor – George Lewis, isn't it? He's canny enough. I wonder he hasn't warned Wilde against it.'

'Ah, no, Lewis has acted for him in the past but he's already been engaged by Queensberry in this case, so he can't. Wilde went to Humphreys, and from what I hear, Humphreys is quite willing to go ahead with it. But I don't suppose Wilde has told him everything.'

'Oh dear, this is going to cause terrible trouble,' Venetia said. 'And who knows what might come out? Can't you warn him, Beauty?'

'Me?'

'Tell him not to be such a fool. Tell him to tear up the card and say nothing.'

'Darling one, I don't know him well enough to be giving advice, especially on that subject. He's a grown man, he must take his chances. Apparently it's Lord Alfred who's pressing him. That boy hates his father so much he'd love to see him getting a bloody nose in court.'

'But what about young Paget?'

'Well, if it comes to that, he's a grown man too. And he has a father of his own to guide him.'

'But he can hardly ask *his* advice about this.'

Wilde took out the prosecution against Queensberry on the 1st of March 1895, and on the 9th Queensberry appeared before the magistrates, pleaded justification, and was committed to trial at the Old Bailey. The trial was to come on on the 3rd of April. George Lewis withdrew on the grounds that he knew Wilde socially, and Queensberry engaged another solicitor, Russell, who at once employed a private detective to gather everything he could about Wilde's private life.

One March day Venetia was coming out of a dispensary in Tothill Street to which she was occasionally called. The weather was bitter. The wind seemed to be coming straight off the river, damp and penetrating, and the air was foul with the smoke pouring down from the Gas Light and Coke Company's massive works in Holland Street. She huddled down into her collar and hurried towards Victoria Street where she hoped to pick up a cab, and at the corner bumped into Inspector Morgan.

'No surprise seeing you here,' she greeted him. 'This is your ground, now, isn't it?'

They chatted for a few moments, and the subject came round, unsurprisingly, to the Wilde case.

'Mr Russell's man's found out about Little College Street,' Morgan told her. 'A group of female prostitutes put him on to it – they don't like the boys taking their trade. Anyway, Russell's interviewed some of the male prostitutes there and got the information he needed. The question is whether they'll be willing to stand up in court. It would be incriminating themselves, d'ye see? Otherwise the only evidence Russell's got is that Wilde wined and dined various men and gave them presents.'

'That's bad enough, but it doesn't amount to anything criminal.'

'That's right,' Morgan said. 'But if Wilde has any sense he'll take his chance now and go abroad before the trial starts. It can't do him any good to stir all this up. I can't understand the man. He's seen the Plea of Justification – he knows they're not just talking about writing poetry any more.'

A bitter gust swept down on them, sending icy fingers down Venetia's neck. She shivered, and Morgan said, 'I mustn't keep you standing here, ma'am. Catch your death.'

'It was nice to see you again,' Venetia said. 'Come to tea one day next week, and see my children. Come on Tuesday.'

'Thank you, ma'am, I'd like to.'

Many people tried to persuade Wilde to leave the country, and many of his associates took their opportunity and fled to France; including, as Venetia heard in a roundabout way, Dryden Paget, persuaded to it by his frantic father, who had at last realised the significance of his son's friendship and the dangers of allowing him to mix with 'artistic' people.

But Wilde himself would not budge and events continued in their doomed course. The trial opened, Wilde was called into the witness box, and there disported himself like a character in one of his own plays, throwing off frivolous remarks, clever paradoxes and witty put-downs, and causing

412

so much laughter from the public gallery that the judge had sometimes to call sternly for order.

But on the second day counsel for Queensberry began to press Wilde about Taylor's house in Little College Street and the young men he had met there, and finally produced his trump card: that one of them, Charles Parker, an unemployed valet, would be taking the stand to give evidence.

It was the thing that had seemed impossible, and it would be the end of Wilde's case. On the following day, on the advice of his counsel, Wilde withdrew his prosecution against Queensberry, sending a letter to the *Evening News* to say that his reason was that he did not want to call Lord Alfred Douglas to the witness box to give evidence against his own father.

But at the same time Queensberry, grimly triumphant, was sending all the evidence he had gathered to the Director of Public Prosecutions, who consulted with Herbert Asquith, the Home Secretary. A warrant was made out, and at six thirty on that same day two detectives arrived at Wilde's door to take him into custody. They conducted him to Scotland Yard where he was charged with committing acts of gross indecency with various male persons.

'It has come into my purview now,' Morgan told Venetia when they met again. 'And now that it's a Crown prosecution, we can offer immunity to witnesses if they'll give evidence in court, so we can use the people at Little College Street – and a good few others besides that we've had our eye on. It's all up for Mr Oscar Wilde. He should have run when he had the chance.'

'When will the case come on?' Venetia asked sadly. It was all so horrible and tawdry. That all Wilde's verbal brilliance and wit should have come to this! It was like seeing a bird-of-paradise shot down, its bright feathers draggled in the mud. But she had to remember what he had done, the horror of places like Little College Street, and all the telegraph and messenger boys who had been lured into the trap.

'Twenty-sixth,' Morgan said. 'Nothing to delay for – we've got all our evidence lined up. We're putting Alfred Taylor up with him – that'll get another nasty piece of work out

413

of the way at the same time. Funny thing,' he mused, 'Taylor's the one man who wouldn't peach on Wilde, not even to save his own skin. Said it wouldn't be honourable. There must have been something in that public school of his after all, eh, ma'am, despite what you said?'

'Indeed there must,' said Venetia.

The trial was the sensation of the year. For three days the prosecution brought forth a train of witnesses, people of the lowest character, who described how they had been introduced to Wilde, entertained by him in fashionable restaurants, taken by him to expensive hotels, how he had given them gifts and had sexual congress with them. Then Wilde was brought again into the witness box and cross-examined endlessly about his writings, his friendships with men and his other activities. He looked pale and worn, answered now without frivolity but sometimes with a kind of desperate poetry in his choice of words, denying wrong-doing, speaking of beauty and love. It was plainly an agony to him to be dragged down from the clouds and into the mud, and to hear his actions described as sordid and tawdry.

And after all that, the jury decided after four hours' deliberation that they could not agree on a verdict, and the judge had no choice but to order a retrial in three weeks' time. He would have to go through it all again.

The newspapers were in an ecstasy of moral indignation; public opinion was in a frenzy of condemnation, disgust and contempt for the man it had once idolised. The theatre that was showing *The Importance of Being Earnest* blanked out Wilde's name on the billboards in the hope that people would then feel they could still go to see it; but they need not have worried – prurient curiosity ensured that it was sold out night after night.

Many people in the more civilised part of society felt that Wilde had probably suffered enough and that a further trial was unnecessary; but the names of people in high places had been mentioned during the trial, including that of Lord Rosebery, and the government felt it was important that there should be no hint of concealment. So the trial was to go ahead; and that it could ever be a fair one, in the face of what was in the newspapers, was doubtful. Again friends – and even his arch-critic, George Bernard Shaw, in an access of kindliness – urged Wilde to take his chance and go abroad, but he would not go. He seemed to have sunk into a fatalistic stupor. He was being hounded everywhere he went by a gang of thugs hired for the purpose by Lord Queensberry, and probably could not think clearly.

At the new trial the charges against him were whittled down from almost thirty to a mere seven. The same weary ground was trotted over, Wilde spoke again in his own defence, and his counsel complained that the trial was nothing but an act of indemnity for all the blackmailers in London, who were being given freedom from arrest for all their past crimes in return for accusing the prisoner. But after two hours the jury came back with a unanimous verdict of guilty.

The judge, in passing sentence, gave vent to his previously subdued inner feelings.

'People who do these things must be dead to all sense of shame, and one cannot hope to produce any effect on them,' he said. 'This is the worst case I have ever tried. That you, Wilde, have been the centre of extensive corruption of the most hideous kind among young men is impossible to doubt. I shall, under such circumstances, be expected to pass the severest sentence the law allows. In my judgement it is totally inadequate for such a case as this.'

He sentenced Oscar Wilde to two years' hard labour.

'Good God,' Venetia said when she heard about it. 'It will kill him.'

The newspapers published every word of the judge's comments; and Lizzie, reading them, came at last to understand what she had begun to have some faint suspicion of long before – suspected without understanding what it was she was suspecting. Even now, of course, she had no clear understanding of what 'gross indecency' might comprise, and she could not believe Dodie capable of doing anything gross. But she accepted now that he had loved Mr Wilde more than her, and that the one love precluded the other. She cried, alone in her room, almost every night, and surprised even herself by the vast reservoir of tears there seemed to be in her. By day she did her best to be cheerful so as not to upset her mother, who was not in the best of health, or to have Jerome feel she was weak and foolish. She took comfort in the children, particularly dear little Jessie, who was a running, bubbling, chattering four now, and attached herself to her older sister with sticky, adoring hands and an upturned face of blooming love.

'Don't fall in love, that's my advice to *you*,' she would say sometimes, hugging Jessie hard; and Jessie would laugh delightedly and patter kisses all over her face, or pull her hair hard, with an expression of devilish delight in her own tiny power.

It was a hard summer for Lizzie to bear, for everybody seemed to be getting married. In May, she attended the wedding of Lilian Bowling, who married a young man with a good position in the civil service. The following month news came that Agnes Grey was married, to a gentleman farmer with land around Enfield, so not too far from her happy family home. Also in June Patsy was married to the wealthy society portrait painter, Vivian Laine, whom she had been quietly seeing for months, since they met at an exhibition at the Grosvenor Gallery. He admired her work and was happy to allow her to continue to do it, which made things comfortable. He had a large house in Pont Street which, since it was three storeys high, not counting attics and basement, had two north-facing rooms, so they could each have their own studio.

'I couldn't have married him otherwise,' Patsy said, though the almost palpable glow she carried round with her showed she was very much in love.

Her brother Perry wanted her to be married up in Yorkshire, from the family home, but she could not hear of it. 'My life is in London now, and all my friends.' She chose to be married from Jerome's house and since Perry, sternly and regretfully, therefore refused to be present, Jerome agreed to give her away. Henrietta had hoped to see her sister again, and was disappointed; but she was pregnant and feeling very tired, with too little energy to feel very badly about anything. To save her the strain of organising it, the wedding breakfast afterwards was held in an hotel, and the couple afterwards went off on honeymoon on a tour of France, Austria and Switzerland.

The wedding, at which Lizzie was bridesmaid, was a little oasis of cheer in the middle of what was otherwise a subdued summer. Henrietta's continuing unwellness meant that Lizzie had to take over almost sole responsibility for her little brothers and sisters; Jerome was spending long hours at his office, and when home was too distracted to smile at her or play with them. He seemed worried and preoccupied, and was in his study more often than the drawing-room.

Towards the end of June Lizzie received a letter from Polly Paget, announcing her engagement to Leonard Cussons, the son of a man who owned a large chemical manufacturing firm, which he would one day inherit.

Lennie and I expect to be married in November, and at first we shall be living in the family house at Crawley, in Sussex, from which it will be quite easy for him to travel up to Town. The Cussons' have another house in Camberwell, nearer to the factory, where his mother and father will live with the younger ones, so we shall have Rylands to ourselves until summer, when they all come down. Eventually Lennie and I will take a place of our own; and then, dearest Lizzie, I shall exercise the greatest prerogative of the married women, that of choosing my own friends! I long to see you again, and shall invite you as soon as ever I can.

Polly did not mention teaching, and Lizzie supposed that she would give it up now that she was marrying a man wealthy enough to keep her. All that intellect and education, and the dreams of doing good, all come to nothing in the service of matrimony. Was that what it meant to be a woman? Perhaps, with rare exceptions like Lady Venetia, it was.

Towards the end of the letter, Polly said,

I have heard from Dodie – privately, that is, in a letter not meant to be seen by Mama and Papa. He is in Italy, where the living is very cheap, and seems to be enjoying himself studying art. He goes as a private scholar to the lectures at the University of Siena, but I suspect spends more time sitting in the sun drinking wine and discussing life with the other students than reading about the history of art! Papa talks of bringing him home in the autumn, and I hope he may be back in time for my wedding. Cam will have leave for it, and it would be good to be all together one last time.

Lizzie, I am so very sorry about you and Dodie. I know it will give you pain but I think you should know that he will be brought back on condition that he marries Edith Venner, and from what he says in his letter I think he is resigned to it. My only hope in telling you this is that it will end any longings you still have after him and make it easier for you to forget him. He behaved very badly by you, and I am ashamed of him, but he is my brother and we were very close in our childhood. He has always been very kind to me, and I can't help loving him. I don't think he loves Edith at all and I am sorry that the marriage should even be contemplated, but it seems to be a matter of business and I can only hope that Edith understands that and is happy with the arrangement.

The news caused Lizzie a little pain, but not a great deal, since she had long supposed the wedding would happen, and had accepted it. What she could not tell from Polly's letter was whether Polly knew anything about Dodie's relationship with Wilde, or whether Dodie was cured of that. If he was not, his marriage to Edith Venner would be an unhappy thing for them both – certainly nothing for her to envy. It was the smallest possible seed of comfort in an otherwise dreary situation.

In June 1895, the Prime Minister, Lord Rosebery, won the Derby a second time with his horse Sir Visto; and his War Secretary, Campbell-Bannerman, won an equally notable victory by forcing the retirement of the seventy-six-year-old Duke of Cambridge as Commander-in-Chief. He was still vigorous, and as the Queen's cousin he had Her Majesty's support and confidence; but his reactionary stance was impeding very necessary reforms of the armed forces. How Campbell-Bannerman persuaded the Queen to accept the duke's resignation was a mystery; yet another was his managing to baffle her wish to give the post to her son, the Duke of Connaught; and that he did both without upsetting her or earning her disapproval was a miracle.

'It just shows,' Venetia said, 'that behind his genial front he hides a will of iron. He ought to go far.'

But his advancement would have to wait a while: the government lost a vote of confidence in the House over the supply of cordite to the army, and resigned. A general election was held in July, the Conservatives were returned with a large majority, and Lord Salisbury became Prime Minister. Mr Gladstone did not stand. The unpopular Sir William Harcourt lost his seat – and so, too, did Mr Keir Hardie, leaving no Labour member of the House at all – to the relief of many.

Salisbury was to double the office of Prime Minister with Foreign Secretary; Arthur Balfour was Leader of the House of Commons. Joseph Chamberlain, thought of by many as the 'coming man', could have had pretty well any position he liked – Salisbury gave him the choice – but to everyone's astonishment chose the previously little-favoured Colonial Office.

'But everybody says that's a dead end,' Venetia exclaimed, when she heard.

'He's got a bee in his bonnet about the colonies,' Hazelmere told her. 'Feels he's "discovered" them; wants to be the man to make them the government's central concern.'

'But nobody cares much about the colonies – no politician, that is.'

'Yes, well, Chamberlain sees them as undeveloped estates. Compared with other Powers, I suppose we have spent very little on them over the past hundred years or so. Anyway, he thinks it's time to invest public money in them and develop them properly for the benefit of their inhabitants – which, of course, will create wealth for everybody, so he may not have too hard a task in persuading Cabinet to see it his way.'

'Invest in what way?' Venetia asked.

'Oh, railways, ports, roads, schools. Subsidies to steamship lines to open new routes. Promote the study of tropical agriculture and tropical medicine – that's essential: so little is known about either. And generally keep order, protect the natives from their own home-grown dictators, and give them access to a system of justice.'

'All the benefits of civilisation,' said Venetia.

'Everything but alcohol and death duties,' Hazelmere smiled. 'Well, let's hope he can sort out the business in South Africa to begin with. Kruger's getting a great deal too big for his boots.'

'If he can do that, the Queen may even come to forgive him his republicanism.'

The 'summer of weddings' brought dissatisfaction to Venetia, too, for she discovered that her cousin Tommy Weston was courting a young woman, Beatrice Abradale. She was the daughter of Abradale Engineering, a company that specialised in building railways and bridges. Tommy had always had a deep interest in railways, and Abradale *père* was bound to 'come down handsomely' over his only daughter's marriage, in return for the access to Parliament Tommy might provide; and though Tommy had a private income from the estate left him by his father, no man with seven children to get on in the world was likely to scorn such an addition to his wealth.

There was nothing at all to wonder at in the situation; but Venetia could not help resenting it all the same. It was only two years since Emma's death, a shocking and tragic death for which Tommy's behaviour had been, in her mind, wholly to blame. It would have been more seemly for him to see out his time as a widower; or, if he must have companionship, to have waited a few more years and then married a woman of his own age, a mature woman, preferably past childbearing, who would be a mother to Emma's children and raise no eyebrows. But Miss Abradale was only eighteen and extremely pretty. It seemed to Venetia a calculated insult to the memory of poor Emma.

'And what's Fanny going to think about having a step-mama who's actually two months *younger* than her?' she asked indignantly of her spouse.

Hazelmere sympathised, but said, 'There's nothing to be done about it, darling. And we know nothing against the girl. She might make a very good friend for Fanny – God knows, she needs one, poor child.'

Venetia was unconvinced, and couldn't help brooding on the situation. To cheer her spirits, Hazelmere proposed taking a holiday in August and accepted an invitation from Viscount Sandown, an old friend, to join a small party on his yacht for Cowes Week. It was just the thing to enliven Venetia. Getting out of London in August was imperative, and she loved the sea. The Isle of Wight offered plenty of inexpensive cottages where the children could be lodged with the nursery staff for their own holiday, and be within easy visiting distance from the yacht; and as a final inducement Olivia would, of course, be at Osborne with the Queen, so she might get to see her.

Sandown's yacht, the *Tutamen*, was a very comfortable affair, designed purely for gracious living, for, unlike the Prince of Wales, Sandown did not compete. The Prince was there, of course, with *Britannia*, which he loved to race, and with which he had won all the cups in the regatta at one time or another. He was Commodore of the Royal Yacht Squadron at Cowes as well as President of the Yacht Racing Association, and Hazelmere said the Princess of Wales, though not fond of the sea herself, was glad to encourage what she thought of as the most wholesome of his sporting interests.

It really was very pleasant at Cowes, and very restful, too. The weather was fine, and Venetia slept like a log in the gently rocking arms of the Solent. Breakfasting in the open air on the afterdeck, surrounded by the sparkling water and the many fine yachts, all gleaming with new paint and polished brass and gay with flags, was a delight. Sandown had managed to get a very good mooring quite close to *Britannia*, so they could see all the comings and goings; and as the Waleses knew Hazelmere was aboard, the whole *Tutamen* party was invited on board for drinks the first night and for dinner the second.

After breakfast there were races to watch, or sightseeing or shopping trips to make on shore. Tea was always taken in the Royal Yacht Squadron gardens: a thing of cucumber sandwiches and buttered scones on the lawn, selections from *HMS Pinafore* played by the military band, flags fluttering gently in the light breeze and the elegant and fashionable promenading past, immaculate and light-stepping as so many prize Borzois. Dinner was taken on board one or other of the larger yachts, in whose vast, wonderful staterooms one could easily forget one was not ashore, were it not for the very slight lapping of the wine in the glasses and the refulgence of the swaying chandeliers.

Venetia was not much interested in the racing, but she showed willing and watched the Prince win an early one so that she could congratulate him at dinner on the *Britannia*. He seemed pleased with her praise, was charming and expressed himself glad to see her. 'Hazelmere should bring you more often. It's too bad of him to keep you to himself. You must both come to Sandringham this autumn. Don't you think so, my dear?'

And the Princess, who was extremely deaf, replied, 'Yes, very fine, and they say it is set fair for the week.'

Olivia and Charlie drove over from Osborne to have lunch with Venetia and Hazelmere on their second day, and in the afternoon they all went to the cottage Hazelmere had rented to see the children. When they left to go back to Osborne, they delivered the Queen's invitation to dine later in the week, when Lord Salisbury would be there.

But all was not sweetness and light at Cowes that year. The Kaiser had been coming every year since 1889, when he had been made an honorary Admiral of the Fleet, and when the Prince of Wales had proposed him for the Royal Yacht Squadron. It was then that he had developed a passion for ships and the sea, which had initiated his obsessive expansion of his navy – something which had been worrying Her Majesty's Government for years.

It was not just battleships that interested him, though: in 1893 he had arrived with a spanking-new racing yacht of his own, the *Meteor*, with which he had managed to beat the Prince of Wales for the Queen's Cup, much to the Prince's annoyance. Since then, in the Prince's own words, the Kaiser had set about making himself the 'boss of Cowes' and, being bombastic and tactless, had put a great many noses out of joint in the process. But it was not only that he dominated the racing and inserted himself noisily into every social gathering: he also used Cowes week as a showcase for the stream of new German warships, which he flaunted like a bully daring a smaller boy to a fight, evidently believing that if it came to a test of strength he could not but win. More seriously, he used the occasion to gather information about the British navy which the government would rather he did not have. The Queen was one of the few people on earth he really did love, albeit erratically. Aware of this genuine affection, she could be persuaded by his wooing words and winning smiles to show him almost anything.

This year he arrived in the imperial yacht *Hohenzollern* escorted by Germany's two newest and largest battleships, *Worth* and *Weissenburg*, sleek ironclads bristling with guns and both named after German victories of the Franco-Prussian war. Venetia, who remembered the horrors of that war, thought it was in poor taste; but their simple arrival was as nothing to what happened the next day, when, as it was the twenty-fifth anniversary of the battle of Worth, the Kaiser assembled all his sailors and addressed them with a boastful and aggressive speech about Germany's military glory, saying that the victory at Worth had proved his army was invincible.

'This is not what regatta week should be about,' Sandown said when he heard about it – for the content of the speech soon spread everywhere, as the Kaiser, no doubt, had intended. The press was not slow to get hold of it, and there were angry leaders in most of the papers condemning the Kaiser for making such offensive remarks while a guest in Great Britain, which provoked equally angry ripostes from the German press.

The Kaiser meanwhile, seeming to care nothing that he had worsened relations noticeably between the two countries, went on to annoy the regatta committee by withdrawing *Meteor* from the Queen's Cup on the grounds – noisily broadcast – that the handicapping system was unfair to him. He referred to the Prince of Wales publicly as 'the old peacock', and made sure everyone knew that he had approached the designer of *Britannia* with a commission to build him a new yacht even bigger and faster than *Meteor* that would ensure nothing could beat him for the foreseeable future.

'This used to be a pleasant holiday for me,' the Prince complained to Hazelmere, 'but now my nephew's taken over the show it's nothing but a damned nuisance, perpetual firing of salutes and cheering and so on, and no pleasure to be had at all to compensate for the disturbance.'

Hazelmere murmured something consoling, and the Prince went on, 'It's a pity Salisbury encourages it. He thinks the Queen has a civilising influence over the Kaiser, but the fact of it is he was spoiled as a child by his grandpa and there's no doing anything with him now. Damned if I shan't give up racing altogether. The pleasure's gone out of it for me.'

On the day after their dinner at Osborne, Venetia was taking tea with Lady Sandown in the Royal Yacht Squadron gardens when she saw a very unexpected group approaching: Mr and Mrs Culpepper, accompanied by their daughter the Duchess of Southport. Nancy embraced Venetia with great affection, which bubbled over from her excitement.

'I'm so glad you're here! Francis Knollys said you both were, so I couldn't wait to come and see you. We're staying on the *Graceful* – Papa borrowed it from the Rutlands. Because, guess what? Harry's coming down! Isn't it splendid? He was staying at Goodwood with the duke and Angus Dromore, and he's coming to Cowes for a week before they go to Scotland for the grouse.'

'I'm very pleased for you,' Venetia said, thinking what a pity it was that she should have to be so excited at the prospect of seeing her own husband – and rather too aware that Lady Sandown must be wondering about the same thing and drawing her own conclusions.

'He's coming tomorrow morning,' Nancy went on, 'so we're going to have a grand dinner tomorrow night on the boat. Papa's inviting everyone, and you and your husband must come. Now *do* say you will!'

There was something so ingenuous about her, enhanced by her using the expression 'on the boat' in such a place and company as this, that Venetia had to smile. But she said, 'I'm honoured to be asked, but we're guests of Lady Sandown, and she already has tomorrow night's dinner planned.'

Nancy looked stricken. 'Oh dear! Oh, but you must come! Your sister and her husband will be there – the Queen's given permission. I can't bear it if you don't come! Oh, dear Lady Sandown, couldn't you possibly let them off just this once, please, as it is to see her very own brother?'

Alice Sandown laughed. 'My dear Duchess, "let them off"? You make it sound like a punishment.'

Nancy coloured. 'Oh dear! I didn't mean—! I'm awfully sorry.'

'Not at all, not at all. Don't upset yourself, my dear. Venetia and Hazelmere shall dine just where they please. I can't be less gracious than the Queen when it's a family occasion, can I? Mine was only an informal dinner, and we have seen them every day. Venetia, my dear, don't give it another thought. Of course you must want to see your brother.'

'That's very nice of you, Lady Sandown,' Culpepper put in. 'My wife and I take it most handsome of you, and if you could think of coming as well, with your husband, of course, we'd be more than pleased to see you. It'll be a fine dinner, I promise you, and the best band in Portsmouth to play on deck afterwards.'

Lady Sandown kept her lips under control and said seriously, 'Thank you so much, Mr Culpepper, but I will have to be present at my own dinner to take care of my other guests. But Venetia and Hazelmere shall come to you.'

Venetia felt it was likely to be an embarrassing occasion, and that she would sooner have dined on board the *Tutamen*; but on the other hand she never had enough chances to be with Olivia, and she admitted a curiosity to see Harry, and discover how he was with his wife.

So the next evening the *Tutamen*'s launch put off for the *Graceful*, with Venetia and Hazelmere in the stern, well wrapped against the evening damp, and full of curiosity. *Graceful*, as a late-comer, was on one of the furthest moorings, so they hadn't seen Harry come on board that morning, but the ducal flag flying at the masthead told them he had arrived safe and sound.

Safe, Venetia thought afterwards when reflecting on that evening, but not so sound; for it was plain from her first sight of him, even before she took his fevered hand in hers and kissed his waxy cheek in greeting, that he was very far from well.

CHAPTER NINETEEN

In October 1895 Vivian Laine was commissioned to paint a portrait of the Marchioness of Salisbury, his most important commission so far: not only was Salisbury the Prime Minister, but the Cecils were the next thing to royalty, having served the throne since the days of Elizabeth. The following month there was an exhibition at the Academy to which Laine took Jerome, thinking it would amuse him, as a very distinguished crowd was anticipated. It was indeed a huge crush, and almost impossible to see anything of the paintings; but Lord Salisbury dropped in, and finding himself face to face with Laine smiled pleasantly, said how fine he thought his wife's portrait was going to be, and allowed Laine to introduce his companion Jerome Compton.

From such little acorns great oaks may grow. Later that month a large party was held at Hatfield House, the beautiful beamed Elizabethan manor that was the Cecil family seat. As well as society people and political friends, the notables of the art world, such as Millais, Alma-Tadema and Burne-Jones, were invited, and both the Laines and the Comptons were sent a card.

Henrietta was at once thrown into an agony of doubt, and took the problem to Venetia. Venetia was robust. 'Accept, of course! Don't tease yourself about it. I'm sure Salisbury knows nothing about your situation, but I can assure you if he did know he would care nothing.'

Henrietta looked doubtful. 'Are you sure?'

'My dear Henrietta, every great family has a divorce somewhere in its past, or something far worse. And believe me, a Cecil – almost any Cecil – is too far above ordinary mortals for such things to signify in the least. You must go. It would be like refusing an invitation to dine with God because you had a broken fingernail.'

Henrietta laughed, and looked at once less strained. 'The other difficulty I have is the perennial one.'

'Nothing to wear? Haven't you anything tucked away?'

Henrietta spread her hands. 'I can't fit into anything I have tucked away. Besides, would it even be proper to go to such an important party in my condition?'

'Of course it would,' Venetia said promptly. 'You aren't very big yet. In fact, if you hadn't told me, I don't think I would know.'

'Thank you. That's a great relief. Well, I think I will go, then, if you say it's all right. Jerome wants to, and I ought to do anything I can to help his career. He thinks it may lead to new business, and I don't think things are going terribly well at the moment. He doesn't say anything to me, but I can tell. He looks worried all the time, and he doesn't sleep well – tossing and turning and muttering all night. If he can get the business of some great, rich men, it may make all the difference.'

'In that case, you had better take the plunge and have something new made up. Skilful dressmaking can conceal anything,' Venetia said. 'And a stockbroker must look successful if he's to attract new clients, which means his wife must look successful too. You had better go to my Madame Petruce.'

'Oh, but I don't think I could justify it, for one party,' Henrietta said anxiously. 'The expense . . .'

'Don't worry about that. Petruce will make for you for a reasonable price if I ask her. These fashionable dressmakers only fleece the sheep who won't stand up to them. She and I have an understanding. She'll make for you at the same price she makes for me – and I assure you *I* don't pay any fancy prices.'

When Hazelmere came home later that day, Venetia asked him, 'Have you heard anything about Jerome Compton being in difficulties?'

'In a business way, you mean? No, why?' Hazelmere asked.

'Henrietta was here, and she said he seems worried.'

'That needn't mean anything. There are plenty of things to worry about besides money. But I'll make enquiries if you like. I hope you warned her not go about telling people that? The one thing that can ruin a stockbroker is lack of confidence.'

'Yes, I did give her a hint. She's expecting, of course, and that can make a woman nervous for no reason. She wanted to consult me about a dress. Salisbury's invited them to a reception.'

'That doesn't look too much like a man in trouble,' Hazelmere said.

Lizzie was very excited about her parents going to Hatfield. It was her urging that got Henrietta through the business of having a dress made at short notice, for otherwise she could not have borne the thought of standing for fittings in a stuffy little room every day, feeling as she did. The gown made for her by Madame Petruce (who was actually an Italian of the name of Petrucelli: 'But everyone wants dressmaker to be French, so, *ecco*, one-two-three, I am French!' 'How do you get everyone to confide in you, Mama?' Lizzie marvelled) was beautiful, and so cleverly cut that even without a tight corset, which Henrietta couldn't bear at the moment, it would take an impolitely close scrutiny to tell that she was *enceinte*. It was of black chiffon over pink silk taffeta, a daring choice of colour, but one that suited Henrietta admirably, said Madame. Bustles were completely gone out now, and the fullness and slight train at the back of the skirt was achieved solely by the clever use of gores, which kept the waistline smooth and flat. Waists were very small this year, but bodices were softly draped and gathered and sleeves were ruched and very wide at the top, which helped disguise those ladies who for one reason or another could not achieve nineteen inches. The bottom of the skirt was shaped to points and edged with a triple frill of chiffon to give a swirling, flowing effect when she moved, which Lizzie admired extremely. 'It must make you feel deliciously wicked!' As a counterpoint to the wickedness, the guimpe and undersleeves were of chaste silk-embroidered cream net, with the close-fitting cuff and high collar of fashion trimmed with tiny pearls.

Even with Venetia's intervention, it was the most expensive gown Henrietta had ever had, and she broke the news of the bill to Jerome with trepidation. But he had seemed much more cheerful since the invitation came, and kissed her and laughed and said it was worth it to see his wife's beauty properly set off.

'You know, I think we ought to ask Laine to paint a portrait of you. We shall be able to afford even his ridiculous fees when I have my new clients from among the richest in the land. When I think of the Cecil wealth alone, it makes me feel weak at the knees.'

Henrietta was glad to see him happier, and encouraged it. 'Why just a portrait of me? Why not all of us? It would make a fine family group.'

'Yes, why not?' Jerome agreed airily. 'We ought to have it done soon, before Jackie goes off to school. He'll be ten next year, old enough for Eton.'

'Eton?' This was a new start to Henrietta. The most expensive public school in the land had not been mentioned before.

Jerome struck an attitude, with his thumbs tucked into his waistcoat. 'Don't you know that nothing but the best is good enough for my boys?'

The day of the party came, and Henrietta dressed with Lizzie's help, with Jessie and Frank running in and out in wild excitement and getting thoroughly in the way. Jack and Robbie were quieter, observing their father in his dressing room with minute and embarrassing interest, and asking a thousand questions, as if storing up information for their own future launch into high society.

The Comptons were called for by the Laines' carriage, and waved goodbye to Lizzie, the children and the servants, all crowded together on the doorstep, as they drove off to the station. A special train was laid on for the guests to Hatfield, which gave Henrietta some idea of the number expected. She and Jerome would be the least minnows in this exalted pool, which she thought on the whole a relief. It made it less likely that anyone would notice her.

The beautiful, stately old house was crowded with the nobility, the political fraternity, the *corps diplomatique*, minor foreign royalty, junior British royalty, the leaders of society, a few businessmen, and representatives of the worlds of art, music and the stage. The Laines quickly attached themselves to the painting fraternity, and Jerome felt that Henrietta was well enough protected under their umbrella to leave her side and make himself agreeable where it would do most good.

There was fine wine, delicate food and excellent music, and, most of all, talk. The conversation of the many guests became a solid wall of sound which soon left Henrietta behind, or rather *out*, for she felt as though there were a glass bubble encircling her that prevented her from touching or being part of the company. She ceased to hear what anyone said, only smiled and nodded and laughed when it seemed appropriate without being able to distinguish more than a syllable here and there. Jerome swam in and out of sight, returning to her side every now and then to see that she was all right before diving back into the silk-and-scented, broadcloth-and-ordered, glittering, chattering waters that seemed marvellously to have become his element. But they *were* his element, she remembered, by birth, much more than the world they now inhabited. He belonged here, and it must seem strange to him sometimes how far he had moved away.

But she did not feel she belonged, and though conscious of the honour, she began to long for it to be over. When at last they were on their way back to London it seemed to her to have been an enormous expense of time and trouble – and money, too – for a very small return. But the other three were elated, talked about whom they had met and what they had said, and were evidently in no doubt that it had been worth it. More even than having been there, it was the having been invited that meant so much, for them personally and for their careers. It's only me, Henrietta thought. I'm just too tired to care about parties. But she did her best to conceal it, and look bright and interested as the froth of excitement poured over her and only gradually subsided into a happy, remembering silence.

But she could not fool Jerome. The Laines' carriage delivered them to their door, and as soon as they were alone he said, 'What's the matter?'

'Nothing,' she said automatically. 'Nothing at all.'

'Don't say that. I know you've been unhappy ever since we got there. What is it? You haven't been worrying foolishly about that old business, have you? I've told you, and your cousin's told you, that it doesn't matter to people like the Salisburys and their guests.'

'No,' she said, 'I wasn't worried about that.'

'What then?' he asked impatiently.

'I'm tired, that's all.'

'Tired? You seem to be tired all the time. I hoped you might have made a little effort today, considering what it could mean to me.'

'I did try,' Henrietta said, dismayed at his rising irritation.

'Not very much,' he said. 'I work damned hard to keep you and the children, and when just once in a way I need your help I should have thought loyalty alone would ensure you gave it.'

Tears rose helplessly to her eyes. It was the first time in her life he had ever spoken sharply to her, and it hurt her dreadfully – quite apart from the injustice, when she had done her best not to let anyone see how weary she was and how she yearned to be lying down, ached just to close her eyes and be quiet.

'I'm sorry,' was all she managed to say, and that ended in a sob, quickly choked back. She turned away, not to let him see her cry; but he caught her wrist and turned her back, and took her into his arms.

'No, I'm sorry,' he said, holding her against him, cradling her head and kissing her hair. 'Darling, darling, don't cry. I'm so sorry! What a brute I am. I didn't mean it. Oh, please, forgive me.'

The comfort of his warmth and strength, his arms around

her, broke the barriers of her self-restraint, and she wept against his shoulder. 'I'm so tired,' she said, between sobs. 'So tired. Sometimes I can hardly get myself along.'

'You should have told me! Darling, you mustn't keep things like that from me. You should have had the doctor to see you if you weren't feeling well.'

She was crying so much she was hard to understand, but he thought he caught the words 'expense' and 'worry you'.

'Damn the expense,' he said, but gently. 'Nothing matters more than your health. Come, come to bed now, let me make you comfortable, and tomorrow we'll get the quack to come and look at you, just to make sure everything's all right. And if you feel tired, you stay in bed, that's all there is to it. There's nothing in the world you have to get up for if you don't want to.'

He coaxed and petted her upstairs, helped her – with surprising dexterity – to undress, put her into bed, and persuaded her to drink half a glass of wine. Then he sat on the edge of the bed stroking her hand and looking down at her.

'Better?'

She nodded, drowsy now. 'So comfortable. Thank you.'

'For being a brute and making you cry?'

'For loving me. Not worth it.'

He lifted her hand and pressed his lips to it, and then his cheek. 'Oh, darling, I love you so much. You are everything in the world to me, and if I sometimes forget it for a few hours, don't think it's gone away. Nothing really matters to me but you. They can take my money and my reputation and this house and everything in it, but unless they can take you from me, they still leave me the richest man on earth.'

Lying back in the pillows, she was comfortable at last, warm and eased and cared-for. She looked up at the man she loved, his face golden in the candle-light and firelight; saw the lines around his eyes and the tiredness of the muscles beside his mouth; saw that his forehead was higher than it had once been, and the hair at his temples was grey. It touched her unbearably that he should be mortal, that

433

time could mark him in this way; and that he should need, as she needed. Her private god was human. He existed in her mind on a plane that nothing could touch, and there he was as he had always been, the young and darkly fascinating stranger who had danced with her at the Red House long ago and stolen the heart right out of her. But here with her now, holding her hand, was the man she lived with, whose warm flesh she rested against in the night, whose lips and hands made delight for her, whose day-weary head rested against her shoulder in the darkness when she cradled him after loving. It was richness almost beyond counting.

'I love you too,' she said, and they seemed poor little words to express all she felt. But it was enough. He looked into her eyes, shining like dark jewels in the flowing light, and it was enough.

In the morning she obeyed his strictures and remained in bed, but begged him not to send for the doctor. She was tired, that was all, and a lazy day or two was all she needed. Lizzie brought the children in to see her on their way out for their walk and asked if she wanted anything.

'No, I think I shall sleep a little now,' she said. 'But when you come back, bring your lunch up and have it with me.'

Lizzie brightened and said she would, and took the little ones away. Jack and Robbie tiptoed ludicrously, evidently having been told that they must not disturb Mama, and Robbie overbalanced and lurched into the little table by the door, toppling the candlestick on it and only catching it with much clatter; and Jessie, following them, burst into uncontrollable giggles, poking her bright, funny face back round the door after they had gone out for one last look, making Henrietta smile.

She drifted off to sleep feeling happy and very blessed; but woke some time later to a biting pain deep inside her. Her clock said five past twelve. The house was absolutely quiet: it was the time of the servants' dinner. She didn't like to disturb them, and lay still, hoping it would go away. But the pain sharpened and deepened, and she suddenly felt very alone and frightened. She struggled upright and rang the bell; then rang it again, long and urgently.

A message was sent to Jerome at his office right away, but before he could arrive home, Henrietta had miscarried the child. The doctor met him at the door with the news, and told him she was very ill.

Princess May, now the Duchess of York, had a second child in December 1895. It was a boy but, to the horror of the close family and the Household, he was born on December the 14th, the anniversary of the day the Prince Consort died. It was always a day of deep solemnity and mourning, and known as 'Mausoleum Day' because the Queen liked to mark it with a visit to the Consort's remains in the mausoleum where her own would one day be laid; the rest of the day was usually shrouded in an impenetrable gloom. The Queen was deeply superstitious about the 14th of any month, but the 14th of December she awaited every year with dread of some disaster.

The Duke of York approached the Queen with the news with some trepidation, but to his surprise and relief she was extremely cheerful about it, and decided that the child was a gift from God and that the date of his birth would probably 'prove a blessing'. 'The dear Queen likes to surprise,' was Olivia's comment in her letter to Venetia. 'Contrary,' was Venetia's terse translation.

Given the date of the birth, there was no doubt that the newcomer would be named Albert, after his great-grandfather; he was given in addition the names Frederick (after the Emperor Frederick) Arthur (after his great-uncle the Duke of Connaught) and George (after his father). The Queen had been delighted at the birth of his brother David, and had pointed out more than once that it was the first time in history there had been three direct heirs and the sovereign all alive at the same time. The birth of Prince Albert was a reassurance on the 'heir and a spare' principle; though the *Morning Advertiser* congratulated the princeling with the pious hope that 'he may never be called upon, as his Father was, to step into the place on the steps of the

Throne vacated under such sorrowful circumstances by an elder Brother'.

Christmas approached. For several years Venetia and Hazelmere had been spending it with the cousins down at Wolvercote, but this year the plan was to stay at home and to entertain the four little Compton children in the nursery along with their own four. Henrietta was still unwell after her miscarriage, and Venetia hoped by taking the children away to give her a period of peace and quiet – as well as amusement for them in having their cousins to play with. She invited Lizzie as well, but Lizzie said she preferred to stay and look after her mother.

However, two days before Christmas an urgent telegram came from Ravendene, saying that Harry was ill and asking – almost ordering – Venetia to come. She showed it to Hazelmere.

'It doesn't sound good,' he agreed.

'He looked very ill back in August,' Venetia said, and found, foolishly, that she needed to sit down. However little they had had to do with each other in recent years, however cool relations had sometimes been between them, he was still her brother, and to think of him dying was horrible, like a hole being torn in the fabric of her life. Marcus, her other brother, had died in Khartoum, suddenly and violently, and there had been nothing for her to do but mourn. But this time she had been given notice, and while the common cant was that it was a blessing to 'have time to say goodbye' she half wished Nancy had not thought to send for her until it was too late. It was too hard to have time to anticipate her pain as well as to feel it.

But the death of a duke was always a matter of protocol and gravity, and she had her duty to do. She sent a hasty note off to the Comptons, for it seemed unlikely that she would be back in time to honour her engagement with them, and she and Hazelmere set off for the station. The train was a bad one, stopping everywhere. The weather was cold and damp, the countryside dull green and brown, and the light of the short day was dreary. Hazelmere had provided them with reading-matter from the book stall in the station, but

Venetia felt too apprehensive and restless to read. She tried not to think, looking out of the window at the endlessly passing farmlands and the sun, swollen and red behind the cloud bank, rolling down like a great ball in a bowling alley towards the bare trees of the horizon.

A carriage was waiting for them at Ravendene station. She recognised the driver – a relic from her father's day. 'How are you, Corby?'

He was evidently pleased to be remembered. 'Very well, my lady, thank you.' The offside horse turned its head to look at her and she went automatically to caress it. A nice pair of matched bays. Harry had always had good taste in horses. 'It's a sad day this, my lady,' Corby went on, watching her. 'His Grace such a young man, and hardly married no time at all.'

'Yes, it's a dreadful thing.'

What he meant was *without an heir*, but it would have been indelicate and impertinent for him to say so. The horse nibbled at her glove, and she stroked its ear and leant towards its comforting warm smell. She had not thought about that aspect until now. Harry had had plenty of time to get an heir, but Nancy was still childless, and she wondered – she wished she didn't, but she wondered – whether the marriage had even been consummated.

Hazelmere made a small sound of impatience, and she turned obediently and went to climb up into the carriage. He settled beside her and was about to make a comment, but seeing her set profile he desisted, and they did the short journey in silence.

It was her mother who came down to meet her in the entrance hall as the butler took their coats; her mother at seventy-three marvellously strong and well – smooth-cheeked, white-haired, still straight, but growing a little stout now.

Venetia kissed her, put her arms round her, and felt comforted. Her mother evidently felt the same, for she said, 'Dearest Venetia. Somehow nothing's ever quite so bad when you're here. John, dear, thank you for coming.'

Hazelmere kissed his mother-in-law, reflecting that she

was the only person, since his own mother had died when he was twelve, who had ever called him by his given name.

'How are you both?' the dowager asked.

'We're well, Mama, but how are you? Is it all falling on your shoulders again?'

'Poor Nancy is quite overcome, and no wonder. What a dreadful thing for her, poor lamb, and with her mother and father in America, too far away to support her. She's in her room resting just now. Come up to the red drawing-room and have some tea. You must be perished. You're the first: Olivia and Charlie will be here later, and Batchworth and Anne hope to arrive tomorrow.'

Those words told Venetia all she needed to know. She stopped at the foot of the stairs, where she had been shepherded by her mother. 'It's bad, then?'

The dowager duchess seemed suddenly to grow pinched. The brightness left her face. It was like seeing a plant touched by frost. 'He's dying,' she said. 'The doctor thinks it will only be a matter of hours – days at most.'

Her son, her only son now, was dying. She remembered the moment of his birth, the wonder of him, the joy of a son after two girls who, however much she loved them, could not inherit. And then, not just one son, but two! The twins, Harry and Marcus, laid in her arms by a weeping maid, little, perfect things! She remembered that moment so clearly, and there seemed to have been almost no time between then and now. But Marcus was dead and buried, and now here was Harry dying, dying at forty-two.

'Oh, Mama,' Venetia said, and all her love and pity was in those two words.

'We are not meant to outlive our children,' Charlotte said bleakly. 'Sometimes I think it would have been better if I'd died in the Crimea.'

'Not for me,' Venetia said starkly. 'Not for Papa, or any of us.'

The dowager seemed to draw on something inside her, straightened up and shouldered the burden once more. 'Of course not,' she said gracefully, smiling. 'Silly and selfish of me. Come upstairs and have some tea, and then we'll see if Harry's awake. There's a trained nurse with him, and the doctor calls in every two hours or so, so he's being well looked after.'

As they warmed themselves at the fire and sipped tea, Venetia asked, 'What is it, Mama? Is there no hope?'

'Oh, it's a mixture of things, the doctor says. But you know what his life has been like these past years, better than me. You can't go on abusing your body in that way without paying the price. You can talk to the doctor when he gets here – you'll understand the detail better than me. But he says there's nothing to be done, and he's a good man.'

It seemed unreal to be sipping tea and eating shortcake beside the fire while her brother lay dying somewhere nearby. It was the first time she had been here since her father died; but nothing had changed. Nothing had changed since her childhood, in fact: the furnishings and decorations were those of her great-grandfather, from whom her father had inherited the dukedom. Papa had been too – what? respectful, perhaps, to change anything; Harry too indifferent. He had entertained here with his mistress, the actress Alicia Booth; later with Gussie as his hostess. (Gussie dead too – it was too hard!) And Nancy did not seem to have left any mark on the place – she had been little here, living mostly in Southport House in Pall Mall. So it was to the worn red plush wallpaper, shiny horsehair and crimson velvet of her childhood that Venetia had returned for what must be the last time.

Dr Hillier arrived, was introduced to her, and asked her deferentially if she would like to come with him to examine the patient. Male doctors did not generally show such respect to female ones, and she wondered, absurdly, whether he thought her high rank somehow improved her abilities.

'Yes, go, darling,' Charlotte said. 'I'm sure Dr Hillier would value your opinion.'

Harry was in the principal bedroom, which had once been her father's. She was surprised he had not preferred something more modern and convenient. The bed was even larger than the State Bed in the King's Bedroom, which hadn't been used since George IV bestowed the honour of a visit on Ravendene. It was an ancient thing of oak like a great dark ship, its high tester and curtains of faded crimson-spotted cream like furled sails, gleaming strangely in the twilight. The rest of the furniture was George II and III, huge dark mahogany pieces that yet failed to fill the vast spaces of the great room with its twenty-foot-high ceiling. Dark oil paintings of hugely wigged ancestors and favourite horses stared down from the red-silk-covered walls patterned with fleur-de-lis. There was no gas-light at Ravendene, and the heaped fire and many candles seemed to make no impact on the dusk gathered in the corners and across the ceiling, as if it were waiting to take him away. *Death of a Duke*, she thought involuntarily. It was like one of those huge gloomy paintings of a generation ago.

The nurse was modern enough, nun-like in her immaculate white and her serenity, but reporting efficiently in the language of medicine. Hillier offered Venetia first place with a gesture of his hand, and she stepped up to the bed and looked down at her brother. He seemed shrunken and gaunt, his face waxy and pinched, like an exaggeration of his appearance in August. His eyes were open but he showed no sign of seeing her: they were fixed on nothing as he struggled to breathe. His heartbeat was rapid, faint and irregular, his temperature elevated. She stepped back and let Hillier take his turn, and he returned to her at the foot of the bed to say, 'No change since this morning. The respiratory decline has been gradual but continuous. I do not think he will last the night.'

Venetia agreed with him, but found suddenly that she could not speak. She bowed her head in assent, feeling as though she were pronouncing the death sentence on her brother. She went alone back to the bedside, but he stared on unseeingly into the middle air and did not seem to know she was there.

When she returned to the drawing-room Nancy was there, remarkably self-controlled: Venetia had expected collapse or hysteria.

'You've seen him? What do you think?' Nancy asked, looking up with horrible hope in her eyes.

Charlotte was looking at her too, and Hazelmere. There was no escaping now: she had to say it. 'I agree with Dr Hillier. I'm sorry, Nancy, but there's no hope.'

Nancy's eyes filled with tears, and her throat worked for a moment or two before she could speak. 'What – what is it? What's killing him?'

'His heart is failing, dear,' Venetia said gently. 'The involuntary muscles that make it beat, and those that allow him to breathe, have been weakened to the point where they can't go on working any more.'

'Does he – is he – does it hurt?'

'No. There's no pain.'

Nancy obviously wanted to ask more, but couldn't, so she nodded and turned away. Charlotte held out a hand to her, and she went and sat beside her on the sofa.

A little while later Olivia and Charlie arrived. Olivia flew to Venetia's arms, her cheek cold and her hair smelling of the outdoor air, just a little foggy. The sisters hugged each other, long and hard and silently. *Now there's only the two of us left*, was the thought of each, though neither spoke it aloud.

They all waited, mostly in silence. There was nothing to do and nothing to say. Sometimes one of them would try to make conversation, but voices seemed too loud, and no-one could concentrate enough to keep a subject going. The fire burned down and a footman came in to make it up again; the large French clock on the chimneypiece, flanked by vast bronzes of Hercules wrestling with lions, ticked lightly and rapidly, while the long-case monster in the corner tocked low and slowly, seeming almost to hold its breath between each heavy beat and the next. Charlotte was wondering whether she should nudge Nancy into doing something about dinner – it would at least help to pass the time – when the door opened and a maid came in.

She curtseyed, her eyes fled about the room, and she said, 'Excuse me, Your Grace, but His Grace is awake and is asking to see her ladyship – Lady Venetia, that is, Your Grace.'

'Just me?' Venetia asked.

'Yes, my lady.'

Aware of all the eyes in the room on her, Venetia obeyed the summons. In the great bedchamber she found that Hillier had returned without announcing himself and had removed his coat as one prepared to stay. He made a movement to resume it as she entered but she waved a negation. 'Not on my account.'

'He's awake and asking for you,' Hillier said. He met her eyes. 'I don't think it will be long now. He's sinking fast.'

'You had better send for the others, then,' Venetia said. She approached the bed. The eyes were still staring just as before, but now as she came into his range they moved and fixed on her. His breathing was noticeably worse. She took up his hand and felt for his pulse, and that was weaker too.

'Harry,' she said. 'It's me, it's Venetia. You wanted to see me?'

He stared at her, struggling to breathe – his mind struggling too, she thought.

'You had something you wanted to say to me, or ask me? Take your time, I'm listening.'

His hand tightened on hers for a moment. His lips moved. It was a huge effort for him to speak, and the words came as individual gasps, thrown out on the small exhalation between dragged-in breaths. 'Wanted. To say. Sorry.'

Tears sprang to her eyes – stupid, weak tears. Sorry for what? Sorry to whom? To her personally, for having cut her off from the family and from her inheritance? Sorry to everyone in general for the pain his unsatisfactory life had given them all? To Nancy for having married her? To God for having wasted his talents? He had left it too late to particularise: he had not the strength or the breath left to explain. But he was Harry, her brother, and she had loved him, as one does, through it all. She squeezed his hand. 'It's all right,' she said; and then, in case it had not been for her, 'I'll tell them. It's all right, Harry.'

Still he stared, and the struggle behind his face was not just for breath. He needed something more. 'Be at peace,' she said. 'All is well.'

His hand relaxed then, and he sighed, as if in relief; but the sigh went on and on, and there was no indrawn breath to follow it. The struggle left the face, and it seemed to smooth out; the insistence left the eyes. He seemed to go from her like someone sinking down into dark water, visible for an instant as a shape, like an after-image, and then gone. She laid his hand down on the counterpane and leant over to roll his eyelids shut, holding them a moment until they stayed. Grief was a sharp pain in her chest, and she had to straighten and stand for a moment with her back to the room, until she had enough control to turn and signal to Hillier that he had a duty to perform.

There were things to do, and Charlotte and Venetia did them, with Norton's help. It seemed to fall naturally to their lot, and unspoken between them was the awareness that it was good to be busy at a moment like that. For the others, there was nothing but the languor of bereavement and a cliff of forbidden topics hemming them in. Charlotte had been through it all once before, when her husband had died. It brought it back to her, and she lived again through that desolation of loss.

Alone with her mother in Harry's business-room, looking through the chaos of his desk, Venetia asked, 'Who does the title go to now?'

Charlotte answered at once as though she had been waiting for the question. 'I've been trying to think. Your father was an only child, of course. His father had two brothers, Alfred and George. George never married. Alfred married Lavinia Fauncett – she was the aunt of the Mrs Fauncett you met when you lived with Emma and went to all those women's rights meetings, you remember?'

'Yes, of course.'

'Alfred died long ago, and though he had three children they were all girls. Your grandfather also had a sister, Mary, who married the heir of the Earl of Preston, and they had sons, but the title can't pass through the female line, so that's no good. That means we have to go back to your great-grandfather, the first duke. He had a brother, and I'm pretty sure that line hasn't failed. I seem to remember old Dabs saying something about it when Marcus died, because of course at that point he became the heir presumptive – the unknown did, I mean. Naturally we always assumed – or hoped, anyway – that Harry would marry and have a son.' She stopped abruptly and pressed her lips together.

'Poor Nancy,' Venetia said. 'I can't help wondering—'

'Don't,' Charlotte said, quite sharply. 'It does no good. Nancy's his widow, and that's that. I suppose,' she said, with huge regret, 'that I shall have to give up the dower house to her. I've lived there so long I've started to look on it as my own. I did hope I might see my time out there.'

'You can always come and live with us,' Venetia said. 'The children would love it, and though the house isn't large, we can always make room. A squeeze doesn't matter when it's people you love.'

Charlotte was amused. 'To think of hearing you saying something like that! You were always the most ducal of my children! But there's no need for you to squeeze any more, at any rate. Your inheritance will be substantial, and I see no reason to make you wait until I die before you can enjoy some of the income of it.'

'What?' Venetia said, startled.

'It was different when Harry was going to come in for it,' Charlotte explained. 'I couldn't very well give you what would be his one day. But now it is to come to you, you might as well enjoy it soon as late.'

'Mama-duchess, I don't understand you,' Venetia said patiently. 'What inheritance? You mean your own money?'

'I mean the Chelmsford money,' Charlotte said. 'You know that I was the Countess of Chelmsford in my own right before I married your father. The estates fell together as long as there was a male heir. But the Chelmsford title can pass to a female as well as a male, so now poor Harry's gone without an heir, they diverge again. You're my eldest surviving child, and the direct heir. When I die you will be Countess of Chelmsford, and the entailed estate will come to you.'

Venetia was almost too surprised to speak. 'Well, there's a thing!' she managed to say at last.

* * *

Old Mr Dabs, the family solicitor, had passed on some years ago, and it was the son of his partner, Mr Rigsby, who attended to discuss the legal and testamentary consequences of the duke's passing. He confirmed to Venetia what her mother had told her.

'The ducal titles and estate go to Mr Frederick Fleetwood who is the . . .' He paused and counted down the generations on the family tree amongst his papers. 'The great-great-grandson of *your* great-grandfather. It is most fortunate that your great-grandfather's brother William has a clear line of descent from eldest son to eldest son, so there can be no doubt about it. The connection is remote enough as it is and it would have been inconvenient, to say the least, if there had been any further complications.'

'Indeed,' said Venetia.

'The estate he inherits will be a little depleted, I'm afraid, your ladyship. His late Grace has not been, I'm sorry to have to say, a very careful caretaker.'

'But he did at least marry money.'

'Indeed, your ladyship, but Her Grace's – I should say, Her *young* Grace's – father was a man of some business sense, if I may put it like that, and he made provision for the present melancholy situation. The marriage settlement provided that in the event that His Grace was to die without issue, a large proportion of Her Grace's dowry would revert to her.'

Venetia almost laughed. Culpepper was a canny old fellow after all. Culpepper money was not to be thrown away without good reason. If there were to be no little dukes with Culpepper blood, all bets were off.

'So the new fellow will not have everything?'

'Not quite, your ladyship.'

'Do you know him?'

'Mr Frederick Fleetwood? I have had correspondence with him, your ladyship. On the sad occasion of Lord Marcus's death it was necessary for me to investigate the possibility, at least—' He seemed to find this line embarrassing and abandoned it. 'He is not a gentleman of large means, but he has respectable employment in the civil service, and is married with, I believe – er – yes, five children.'

'Any of them boys?'

Rigsby seemed unsure whether she was being jocular or not. 'Three, I believe, your ladyship.'

'Well, thank heaven for that, at least,' said Venetia. She thought for a moment. 'It will be a very great surprise for him. Or at least, a very great change. From civil servant to prince of the realm in one leap.'

Rigsby permitted himself a twinkle of the eye. 'He and his family live in what I believe is called a *villa*, your ladyship, in Sydenham, which is a suburb to the south of London.'

'Good Lord,' said Venetia. And suddenly she felt sad. A clerk from Sydenham would be coming to take over her father's house and estate, the place where she had grown up, the park she had ridden over so often that she knew every tree and hedge. It was the end of something very great, a huge piece of her life, and indeed of history – Papa had been a great statesman as well as a duke. His successor might prove to be an excellent man, of course – but still, it was the end of an era.

'And you will now inherit the Chelmsford estate from Her Grace your mother, your ladyship.'

'Will it be difficult to unravel from the Southport estate?'

'A little, your ladyship. But we may hope and pray that I shall have many years in which to do so, if I may be permitted to say so, your ladyship.'

'You may,' said Venetia.

It was a sad Christmas. Venetia and Hazelmere went home for Christmas Day to be with the children. Olivia and Charlie had leave from the Queen to stay for as long as they needed it, so Venetia felt able to go. Then Venetia went back to Ravendene; Hazelmere stayed at home and was to travel down again for the funeral.

The new duke came the day before the funeral to inspect his kingdom. Venetia thought him a nice enough fellow: in his late forties, tall and rather thin with a little of a clerkly stoop, gold *pince-nez* and a round bald patch in his curly greying-dark hair like a monk's tonsure. His coat and black tie seemed new, but his trousers and waistcoat, though of good cloth and cut, were evidently well worn, and his boots, though well polished, had been economised on in the purchase. A decent, hard-working family man, Venetia thought, of the sort she met every day professionally. He seemed utterly bewildered at finding himself where he was: he must never in his inoffensive life have expected that immeasurably distant dukedom to come to him. The first time one of the servants addressed him as 'Your Grace' he started, and then stared with his mouth a little open, unable for the life of him to respond. Venetia thought that one thing more would make him burst into tears.

He was not helped, poor man, by the interview with Mr Rigsby who, faintly resenting that the ducal domain had come to this, lectured him for over an hour about the huge responsibility an estate and title like this entailed. He was shy with Olivia and Charlie, no doubt because he had been told they were part of the royal household, and Nancy was too sunk in her own grief and anxiety to welcome him. Venetia noticed that even her mother, usually the most affable of people, was being somewhat grand with him, perhaps unable to help comparing him with her loved late husband. But it was a feature of the English system of nobility, and its greatest strength, that the younger sons of peers are commoners, and have to make their own way in the world, and so situations like this were bound to happen from time to time. And besides, it was Harry's fault, not the new duke's.

So she went out of her way to be kind to him, and to give him someone to talk to. There must be many things he wanted to ask, and no-one to appeal to. In the afternoon of his arrival she invited him to tea in her private sitting-room, and when he put his head tentatively round the door in response to her 'Come in!' she smiled warmly and said, 'Come and sit down. I thought you would prefer to have tea quietly with me rather than formally with everyone else. This must all be rather a shock to you.'

He sat down with pathetic gratitude. 'It is, it is indeed, my lady. I think I can safely say it was the last thing in the world I expected. The very last.'

She smiled gently. 'I can understand that very well. But you mustn't call me "my lady" now. You are "Your Grace" and far above me in rank.' He blushed and began to apologise and she said quickly, 'No, please don't. I did not mean to embarrass you. It is a little difficult, isn't it? Normally one knows just what to call the duke – it is Uncle John or Papa or one's little brother. Do you think it would be stretching the point too far if we were to call each other "cousin". That would do away with many difficulties. May I call you Cousin Frederick?'

'Oh, yes, please do, my lady.'

'Cousin Venetia.'

'Cousin Venetia,' he said, and for the first time a little of the tension seemed to slip from his face and his shoulders. She poured him tea and moved the bread-and-butter closer, and he took a piece without seeming to know what it was. 'Yes,' he said, 'I have been fairly rocked to my foundation by this business. I knew from things my father said that Great-grandpa had been a titled man, but it wasn't the sort of title that passed down so I took no notice, and really, it all seemed so long ago and far away it was like . . .' He paused, lost for a simile.

'Like King Alfred and the cakes?'

He laughed, and in that instant looked younger, handsomer, and more like a duke. 'Yes, just like that. Schoolboy history.'

He looked at the bread-and-butter he was holding, recognised it, and ate.

'It will be a great change for your wife, too,' Venetia suggested.

'Poor Maria! She didn't believe me when I first told her. She thought it was a joke or a tease. Even when I showed her the letter, she thought it had been got up by some of the fellows at the office as a prank. There's a fellow there called Cheeseman who is always up to something or other. Oh! I beg your pardon, my – Cousin Venetia. I did not mean to make light of the situation. Your sad bereavement—'

'Don't upset yourself, Cousin Frederick. At the worst of times one can find things to smile about.'

He looked at her shyly. 'I believe – that is, someone said – that you are a lady doctor. Is that true? I beg your pardon if it is another tease . . .'

'No, it's quite true. I have a practice in Town.'

'Then that accounts, perhaps, for your being more – more approachable than – than I expected.'

He had navigated past two mines in that sentence, and she rewarded him with more bread-and-butter. 'This is exceptionally good bread-and-butter,' he said, perhaps for something safe to say.

'You will be able to have as much of it as you like now,' she smiled.

That seemed to be the cue for him to be frank. 'It has been a struggle sometimes, I don't mind confessing, just to make ends meet. I have a good position and there is always hope of promotion, but with five children there never seems quite enough money. I don't know how it is, but one of them always seems to be ailing something, and doctors' fees are so shocking—' He stopped again. 'That is . . .'

'Yes, I know. It's true! But we have to live too. I have four children myself.'

He smiled with relief that she was not offended. 'Children are expensive, from start to finish. Will I be rich now? I didn't fully understand everything that lawyer fellow was telling me.'

'I don't suppose for a minute that he meant you to. Rigsby is a good lawyer but the firm has been taking care of the estate since my great-grandfather's day and I suspect there's a little resentment of a newcomer. It will pass, but you mustn't let him intimidate you. You are the boss now!'

'I'll try to remember that.'

'As to your question – well, most of the Culpepper money will go back to the Culpeppers, and my brother Harry was not a good custodian. Besides that, there seems to be a general falling-off of stocks, and farming is in a bad way, so the rents are poor. Then there will be the funeral expenses and debts to pay, and of course the wretched death duties. They will all take their toll. But in round terms, and from the perspective that you and I share as working people – yes, you will be rich. Rich enough, I suspect, for anything you and your wife are likely to want. As long as your children don't have their heads turned and take to spending your fortune for you . . .'

'My children,' he said. 'Yes. Freddie, my eldest, is now Lord Turnhouse, so Mr Rigsby told me. It's hard to believe. And my little Mary – my pet – is Lady Mary Fleetwood. It's quite a turn-around. It will change all their lives.' It seemed a daunting prospect, and he frowned in thought. Venetia nodded sympathetically.

Then something occurred to him, and he brightened. 'But I'll be able to send the boys to good schools now. That must be a good thing. And Mary will have the chance to marry really well.'

'You see,' Venetia said, 'there is good in every situation. Have some of this shortcake. You'll find it's exceptionally good, too.'

CHAPTER TWENTY

Venetia and Hazelmere went home directly after the funeral. They had the children, and Venetia had her patients, to attend to; and though she liked the new duke she did not want to see the rest of his family, whom she imagined – perhaps unfairly – straining at the leash to come and see what they had got. Most of all she did not want to see them unworthily installed in what had been her parents' place, and in her family home.

As they drove away from the door, Hazelmere slipped his hand under the rug and took hold of hers in silent sympathy. Venetia looked out of the carriage window at the dear familiar park, and was glad it was not possible to see the house. She did not suppose that she would ever see house or park again.

So she was not at Ravendene when the letter arrived for Charlotte, a very properly expressed letter of condolence from the American man who was employed in Mr Culpepper's shipping office, whose name was Morland. 'From researches I have made I understand that you and my grandfather, Benedict Morland, were connected in a business as well as a family way, so I hope you will not feel it is too presumptuous of me to offer my very sincerest condolences for your most sorrowful loss.'

In the middle of January, 1896, Charlotte came to London and stayed with Venetia and Hazelmere while she looked for a house.

'There's no need for me to squeeze in with you, much though I appreciate your offer,' she said to Venetia. 'I've been living rent-free at the dower house for years now, so I have quite enough to take a little house of my own for as long as I'm likely to need it. I'm used to being by myself, and Norton does everything for me. Just a small place will do – somewhere nearby, so that we can see each other often.'

'I know better than to try and persuade you against your will,' Venetia said. 'But remember the offer is still open if you change your mind.'

'And my offer is the same, if you want to move to a larger place.'

'Thank you, but I don't think so. Not at the moment. I like this house, and it's convenient. The only reason for wanting a larger place was to make room for you, if you remember.'

'Very well, then, each shall keep her own. I shall send for the agent tomorrow to find me somewhere neat and not too far away.'

'Is there such a hurry? Surely Cousin Frederick doesn't mean to throw you out by your heels?'

'Darling, such violent language! No, not at all. He's as meek and compliant as a mouse; but you see Nancy wants to live there, and there isn't room for two households.'

'Nancy wants to live in the dower house?'

'She's taken a fancy to it, it seems.'

'But that's not fair! She's hardly ever been at Ravendene. It's your home!'

'*Was* my home. You know how these things are arranged, Venetia.'

'The King is dead, long live the King.'

'Just so. There's no sense railing against it, darling.'

Venetia thought of her brother Marcus, and how uncomplainingly he had accepted that as the second-born son – even by such a short time as separated the birth of twins – he should have nothing but his wits to live on. He had left Ravendene without a murmur, though it must have been dear to him too.

'It's just that things seem to have fallen apart so suddenly,' Venetia said, with a sigh. 'And Nancy was never like one of us.'

'That was Harry's fault,' Charlotte said. 'Poor girl, she must have been very lonely. But she will marry again. Her father will see to that.'

'I don't doubt it. Having got her dowry back he can stake it on another horse. What will he buy for her this time? A marquess?'

'Perhaps she'll marry for love,' Charlotte said soothingly, and reminded by the Culpepper connection, said, 'By the way, I had such an interesting letter of condolence. I have it in my reticule – over there, darling.'

Venetia fetched the bag and Charlotte gave her the letter to read. 'Oh, yes, I remember Mr Culpepper mentioned this man to me some years ago. He asked me if it was likely he was related to Henrietta, since he said his people came from Yorkshire. I told him I thought there was no likelihood, and that was that. I never heard any more about it. He really is related, then?'

'So it seems. If Benedict was his grandfather, he must be a son of Mary Morland, who married her cousin in Carolina.'

'But Culpepper said he was a Yankee – from Boston, I think he said, not the South.'

'Oh, well, I dare say the family moved. Things must have been difficult in the South after the civil war. I know Benedict thought it strange that he never heard any more from Mary. He assumed she was dead, because otherwise he was sure she would have found a way to get word to him.'

'Of course she would have. The obvious answer is that she *was* dead – she and all her family – and that this man is an impostor. He's hoping to make something for himself from the connection. Now, isn't that much more likely?'

'What a cynic you are! Yes, I suppose so – except that he has never tried to play on the connection before, and his letter is very proper, and does not ask for anything. I've half a mind to see him, just to find out what the story is.'

Venetia laughed. 'There you are, he's playing you like a fish and you're half landed already.'

'Oh, Venetia! There's no talking to you on this subject, I can see.'

'None at all. I never knew Cousin Benedict, so I've no curiosity. But just on probability, I think there can be nothing in it. The man's a faker.' A thought occurred to her. 'Oh, but Mama, if he should get hold of Henrietta! Benedict was her father, Mary her sister – it would be dreadful for him to raise false hopes in her that the family had survived. I do think you ought not to encourage him in any way. Poor Henrietta's not in any state to be able to withstand a plausible rogue.'

'Very well, I shall leave well alone. But I think you are worrying for nothing. If he were going to prey on Henrietta he would have done it long ago, surely? What was to stop him? And he might be the real thing, after all.'

'He hasn't preyed on her because she isn't rich enough to tempt him.'

'Well, then, she should be safe enough, shouldn't she?'

The newspapers were full of South Africa: Mr Chamberlain's first year in office was giving him plenty to do. The problems arose mainly from the discovery in 1886 of a huge goldfield on the Witwatersrand in the Transvaal. Transvaal, under its president, Kruger, had been granted independence in 1884 subject to British suzerainty and control of foreign policy. But the Boers wanted nothing less than full independence for their state; and their dream was complete domination of South Africa.

The gold find had caused thousands of prospectors to flock to the Vaal, most of them British, and over the years Johannesburg had become a great city. But the government of Transvaal treated these 'Uitlanders' harshly, denying them the vote or any civil rights, and taxing them harder than their Boer neighbours, both by direct taxes on the mine profits and indirectly by enormous duties on imported machinery and other mining requirements.

Such was the richness of the field, however, that even though a large part of what they got was confiscated by Kruger's government, the Uitlanders still felt it was worth getting.

'There's Kruger's justification,' Hazelmere said to Venetia. 'He says, "You needn't have come, and since you have come, you must put up with whatever conditions we impose."'

'A very complete answer,' Venetia said. 'However, he needn't have admitted them in the first place. Surely having done so, he ought to treat them fairly?'

Kruger's policy so filled the coffers that from being the poorest state in South Africa Transvaal soon became the richest. The most worrying thing was that Kruger spent much of the money on buying armaments, and was flirting with other European powers with a view to gaining their support in taking over the whole of South Africa. Given the ancestry of the Boers, it was not surprising that they looked to Germany first, nor that the growing anti-English feeling in Germany prompted the Kaiser to respond warmly.

'The Kaiser and Kruger,' Venetia mused. 'What an ominous sound that has.'

Kruger was one man bestriding South Africa like a Colossus; the other, appropriately, was Cecil Rhodes, managing director of the Chartered Company and Prime Minister of the Cape. While Chamberlain was worrying about Boer ambitions and the persecution of the Uitlanders, he was also being plagued with demands from Rhodes concerning Bechuanaland. Bechuanaland lay between the Cape and Rhodesia, the territory owned by the Chartered Company which was just being opened up. The southern half of Bechuanaland was British, governed from the Cape, the northern half only a protectorate, still ruled by its native chiefs. The railway from Cape Town ran only as far as Mafeking, on the border between the two halves, and Rhodes wanted the Chartered Company to take control of the Protectorate so that the railway could be continued all the way up to Rhodesia.

Three Bechuana chiefs travelled to England to protest that they did not want their country to be placed under Chartered Company rule. Chamberlain heeded their pleas and conceded only a strip of land to Rhodes, just enough for the railway, along the border with Transvaal which lay to the east.

Kruger meanwhile, resenting the Cape's dominance of trade, especially of imports, which he wanted to come in through a Portuguese port and by rail to Pretoria in northern Transvaal, began disrupting overland routes to the Cape, blocking the railway and the river crossings; until in November 1895 Chamberlain was forced to send an ultimatum, to which Kruger yielded.

'There is going to be trouble,' Hazelmere said at that time. 'Chamberlain fully expects that there will be an outbreak in Johannesburg. The Uitlanders sent a petition with thirty-five thousand signatures to Kruger, but he refuses to right their wrongs.'

'What do you mean, an outbreak?'

'An uprising. A rebellion. Arms and bloodshed. Salisbury's prepared to send out an envoy to mediate if – or when – it happens, but I wonder if that will do any good. The Boers are stubborn and ambitious. It's the dickens of a mess.'

This had been the situation when, on the 29th of December 1895, Chamberlain received a report that Rhodes meant to take Uitlander matters into his own hands, and mount a raid on Johannesburg with as many armed police as the Chartered Company could command. Chamberlain at once sent a strongly worded cable to Sir Hercules Robinson, the High Commissioner, forbidding the raid; but it was too late. Dr Jameson, the Chartered Company's administrator, had left Pitsani, on the border of Transvaal, on the evening of the 29th with 350 mounted police, 120 Bechuana police, eight machine-guns and three pieces of artillery.

The whole government was appalled. 'To launch an attack against a state with which we are at peace is indefensible,' Hazelmere said. 'No matter what the provocation – and I believe Rhodes's brother is one of the Uitlanders – it cannot be justified.'

'I can hardly believe it of Rhodes. What does he think he's doing?' Venetia said. 'It's not his business to declare war.'

'It's pure filibuster,' Hazelmere said. 'Chamberlain must repudiate it.'

The raid – Jameson's Raid as it became known in the press – was a hopeless miscalculation even in military terms, and on the 2nd of January the raiders were stopped at Doornkop by Boer machine-gun fire and surrendered on the promise that their lives would be spared. Chamberlain, meanwhile, denounced them in Parliament and sent a telegram direct to Kruger repudiating them in the strongest terms.

From that point matters quickly worsened. The following day the Kaiser sent a telegram to Kruger congratulating him on having put down the armed attack against his state 'without appealing for the help of friendly Powers'; and lest there should be any doubt that this meant Germany felt it had the right to interfere, contrary to the settlement of 1884, and would do if it deemed it necessary, the Kaiser ordered the embarkation of troops from German East Africa. They were to join up with a naval detachment from three German naval cruisers which were already lying off Lourenço Marques, the whole force to go on by rail to Pretoria.

It was an act of war. The newspapers were full of indignation and horror. 'The Nation will never forget this telegram,' thundered the *Morning Post*, while the First Royal Dragoons, of which the Kaiser was honorary colonel, was so incensed that it cut his portrait to pieces and burned it. The general public was shocked. Most people outside the circle of Court and government, used to seeing France as the enemy, had assumed that Germany under an emperor who was the Queen's grandson could never be hostile. Now the full extent of Germany's antagonism to Britain was laid bare.

'The Kaiser must be mad,' Venetia said. 'Quite mad.' She remembered his behaviour at Cowes – ungoverned, needlessly provocative and thoroughly ill-mannered, given that he was a guest of the country – and considered that if he could behave like that in private, there was no reason to doubt he could behave the same way in public matters.

The government met and took swift, decisive action, manning and despatching a squadron of armed ships strong enough to crush anything afloat. The Portuguese, in whose territory Lourenço Marques was, refused the German force permission to land, and the German government backed down and made suitably apologetic noises.

'Though I don't believe for a moment they really are sorry,' Venetia said. 'It was only because they realised they could not win the "scrap".'

'I'm sure you're right,' Hazelmere said, 'but my fear is that they'll use the despatch of our squadron as an excuse to build up their own navy at an even faster rate. It won't have made them love us any more, and relations between our two countries were not of the best anyway.'

'Well, it can't be helped,' Venetia said. 'We have to do what's right. Chamberlain repudiated the raiders, and Germany had no right to interfere.'

In Transvaal, the leaders of the raid were put on trial and four, including Rhodes's brother, were condemned to death, the rest to imprisonment and huge fines. Only with great difficulty did Chamberlain manage to have the death sentences commuted, and the ringleaders handed over to British custody so that they could be brought back to England to stand trial. Cecil Rhodes resigned as Prime Minister of the Cape, but great damage had been done. Before the raid Rhodes had enjoyed the support of the Dutch community in Cape Colony and in Orange Free State: now he had lost the goodwill of both. And in Transvaal the Uitlanders, who made up half of the state's white male population, still had no rights, no justice, and no recourse.

Towards the end of January 1896 Venetia received an invitation to Tommy Weston's wedding. He was to marry Beatrice Abradale in St Margaret's on the 2nd of February.

'A cold sort of time for a wedding,' she commented. 'What on earth am I to do about it?'

Hazelmere raised an eyebrow. 'Do you want to go?'

'I think in the circumstances it's a great impertinence to ask us. No, impertinence isn't the right word. It shows a lack of tact and sensitivity which I find staggering.'

'I take it that means no?'

'I don't in the least want to go – do you? But I can't help

thinking of the children. They don't know the truth about their mother, and if we are to keep it from them . . .'

'Quite so.'

'How will they feel if everyone avoids their father and his new wife? It amounts to punishing them for his sins.'

'It's a dilemma,' Hazelmere admitted.

A visit from Fanny Weston clarified matters a little. 'It's a horrid time of year for a wedding,' she told Venetia, 'but the thing is Papa wants it done before the Season starts, because he wants to bring me out this year and it means my new mama can chaperone me.' She said *new mama* with a certain awkwardness, though with less than Venetia would have anticipated.

Fanny would be nineteen in March, and it would have been more natural for her to have been brought out the previous year, but that would have entailed asking someone to sponsor her, and to the eyes of the public Venetia would have been the natural choice. Evidently Tommy had feared she would refuse, so he had not asked. Now it came to her that perhaps his reasons for remarrying were largely for the sake of the children, and that she ought not to judge him so harshly. Then she thought of Emma's poor swollen dead face – a picture she had managed of recent months to banish from her memory – and her feelings hardened again.

'Ada and I are going to be bridesmaids,' Fanny went on, happily unaware of the ferment in her ladyship's mind. 'Ada's so excited, because of course she won't come out until next year, so this will be her only chance to dress up and be seen for a whole year more! Our dresses are so pretty: white gauze over pale pink satin, and wreaths of myrtle and white heather on our heads. Tavy and Edie are wild with envy. You should hear naughty Edie badger Papa to be a bridesmaid too! But Papa says he loathes the idea of small children being paraded behind a bride at a wedding, like monkeys dressed up. Edie doesn't know whether to be more mad at being called a monkey or a small child!'

So the thing was decided in Venetia's head without further agonies. She could not spoil it for Fanny: sitting opposite her chattering, all eagerness, she looked heartbreakingly like

459

her mother, with her sweet face and soft, curly brown hair. Venetia could never like Tommy again, could never forgive him, but for the sake of Emma's children she must have friendly relations with the Weston family, and welcome the unknown Miss Abradale as their new mother. Young as she was, Venetia reflected, at least she was unlikely to prove the cruel step-mother of legend when and if she started to produce a family of her own.

February brought news of another wedding. It was not on such a grand scale as the Weston–Abradale wedding, so there was not a full report in the papers, only a paragraph in the 'recent marriages' column. There was every chance that Lizzie might miss it, but somehow the name jumped out of the page at her as she leafed idly through one morning after Jerome had gone to the City.

The wedding took place in St Stephen's Church, Ealing, Middlesex on February 8th of Edith Alice Barclay, eldest daughter of George Cameron Venner of Mount Pleasant, Ealing, and Dryden, eldest son of Ernest Paget of The Lodge, Primrose Hill. Mr Venner and Mr Paget are partners of the well-respected Paget and Venner Merchant Bank. The bride was dressed in an exquisite gown of white zephyr and ivory silk crêpe, with a long veil depending from a coronet of pearls. The embroidered train was carried by two of the six bridesmaids who followed her, beautifully dressed in primrose yellow spotted muslin over white silk taffeta. After the ceremony a hundred guests enjoyed an elegant luncheon at the Castle Hotel, before the happy couple left for their honeymoon in Italy.

It was not much, but the words conjured up a picture as clear as if she were looking at a series of photographs: the church, the congregation, the proud parents, the new hats, the carriages, the little crowd of onlookers outside always ready to brave any weather to see a bride arrive. Then the organ struck up some triumphal tune, and she sailed down the aisle like a ship coming into port, her sails white and gleaming, the lesser vessels of the bridesmaids bobbing in her wake. (Six bridesmaids – was Polly one of them?) In Lizzie's imagination it was she who took the leading role, floating in white zephyr and ivory silk crêpe on blissful feet towards the figure of Dodie, waiting at the altar. He turned and smiled at her. She saw his sweet, loving smile, his adoring look. *Oh, Dodie! Why couldn't you have fought for me*? Her eyes filled with tears. The answer, of course, was that though he had loved her, he hadn't loved her *enough*. So here she was in her twenty-fourth year and now surely beyond hope. No-one would ever want her now. *On the shelf* – that dismal phrase. She was doomed to be an old maid, to live without love all her days.

Her mother came into the room, and she hastily folded the paper and thrust it away, but tears made her clumsy and attracted the attention she had meant to avoid.

'What is it, darling? Lizzie, are you crying?' Henrietta crossed the room and sat beside her daughter anxiously; saw the crumpled newspaper on the floor and guessed the rest. 'Is it something about Dodie?'

Lizzie nodded. She managed to say, 'He's married. Oh, Mother!' And then the tears broke through. Henrietta held her while she sobbed, and after the first tumult had eased, Lizzie felt how comfortable it was to have a dear mama to lean on, someone who knew all her concerns and cared about them all, large and small. She was not so *absolutely* unlucky or forlorn. She sat up, blew her nose, accepted Henrietta's handkerchief with which to wipe her eyes, and at length was able to say, 'Over now. Sorry. Foolish of me. I won't do that again.'

'Darling, you're entitled to cry,' Henrietta said. 'It's the hardest thing in the world to be parted from the man you love.'

'It was just reading about the wedding in the paper and thinking about what might have been. But I shouldn't have indulged myself. It was weak and wrong of me.'

'You're so hard on yourself, Lizzie,' Henrietta said.

Lizzie noticed then how worn and anxious her mother

461

looked, and was ashamed all over again. 'Not hard enough. I should have been thinking about you. My troubles are nothing compared with yours. Are you still feeling very bad?'

'No, darling, not so very. A little sad and a little tired, still, but that will pass. It's Papa I'm really anxious about.'

'Yes,' said Lizzie, thrusting her own situation to the back of her mind and thinking about him. 'He does seem to have been – well, different lately. Cross and moody and not like himself at all. He never laughs or smiles like he used to, and hardly even talks. Picks at his dinner, too,' she remembered – and Papa had always enjoyed his meals.

'He's worried about something – very worried – and he won't tell me what it is. I know it's something to do with his business. Lizzie, I'm afraid he may be in trouble.'

'Trouble?'

'It's what I was worried about in the beginning. You hear so many stories of people failing on the Exchange. But when I said that to him at the beginning he said it didn't happen any more, and that as long as you knew what you were doing it was quite all right.'

'You think Papa is failing?'

'I don't know. I'm so very afraid he may be.'

'But what does it mean? I mean, what would the results be?' Henrietta did not want to say the words, but her silence worried Lizzie as much. 'Mama, will he be—?'

'Bankrupt.' Henrietta said it at last.

'Surely, surely it can't be that bad?' Lizzie said. She found she and her mother were holding hands tightly, like two people hiding in the dark, and hearing the footsteps outside. Henrietta didn't answer, and Lizzie took a deep breath and said, 'You must ask him. Today, as soon as he comes home. Whatever it is, it's better to know. And it may be something else, something much less—'

They looked at each other, reading the same dread and foreknowledge in each other's eyes.

'You're right,' Henrietta said at last. 'I will ask him. I expect it's nothing serious, really.'

Whistling in the dark, Lizzie thought; and then, with hard humour, *At least it's taken your mind off Dodie*. A real, solid, practical disaster was an effective antidote to a broken heart.

Jerome came home in what had become his usual manner lately: his face set, his mouth grim, his eyes distant. He barely greeted Henrietta, asked when dinner would be ready without seeming to want to know the answer, and went straight to his study. Henrietta exchanged a look with Lizzie, gathered her courage together and followed him.

He was sitting at his desk, staring at nothing when she came in, but looked up irritably and snapped, 'What is it? Am I not allowed a moment to myself at the end of a long day?'

She ignored the question. 'You've been worried for a long time. Something's wrong, isn't it? You must tell me.'

'Oh, *must* I?' he said, glaring at her.

She stood firm. 'Yes, I think you must,' she said steadily. 'I am your wife. What affects you affects me.'

He stared a moment longer, and then his tense anger crumpled and his shoulders slumped. He looked so tired and afraid it frightened her, and she wished for a foolish moment that she had not provoked this, that she could have gone on living in ignorance a while longer. She shook the thought away and went round the desk to him, to lay a tentative hand on his shoulder. 'Is it very bad?' she asked.

He nodded slowly. 'Yes. As bad as can be.' He placed his hand over hers and chafed it drearily. 'I'm sorry, I should have spoken to you before. I suppose I hoped against hope that I could escape, and then I need never have worried you.'

'I've been worried for months. Don't you think I saw that you had something on your mind?'

'Of course. Stupid of me.' He pulled away from her and stood up restlessly, walking to the window, though it was dark outside and there was nothing to see. 'It's the worst news, Henrietta. I have failed. The business is under the hatches. We're done for.'

She felt a cold dread in the pit of her stomach. 'Tell me,' she said.

'It started with the South American railway shares. They'd been doing so well, and then they collapsed.'

'Yes, I read about that in the paper. Was it very bad?'

'The stock was my first big success on the Exchange and I suppose I was foolishly attached to it. I had too great an exposure there, and I held on too long. I lost a small fortune. So I had to make it up somehow.'

Her mouth was dry. 'You didn't—' She couldn't conclude the sentence.

He turned and saw the question in her face, and his mouth turned down bitterly. 'No, I didn't do anything illegal. Did you think that of me?'

'No, I didn't. Of course not. But—'

'The way to make large sums of money quickly is on the more volatile shares. But you have to know exactly when to buy and sell. Timing is everything. Mine was not quite as perfect as I thought. I lost as much as I gained. And like a gambler, the more I lost the more I had to go on gambling.'

'Oh, Jerome!'

'Easily in but not easily out, as the lobster said in the lobster pot,' he said, with a grimace. 'I'm ashamed to have been caught in such a hackneyed way. And now I have found out that Harwood has been doing things behind my back. There's a mine in South Africa – a false claim about a find there – I'm afraid he may know more than he has told me about it. At all events, large sums have been lost and if it is proved that the false claim was fraudulent—' He stopped and passed a weary hand over his eyes.

'How bad is it?' she asked.

'It's only a matter of time. When settlement day comes, it will emerge that I cannot meet my obligations. I will be declared on the Exchange, and that will be that. I'll be ruined. And the next stage is bankruptcy.'

There, he had said the word at last. She stared, her mouth too dry to speak. She remembered suddenly his words that evening when they had come back from Hatfield. 'They can take my money and my reputation and this house and everything in it,' he had said. She understood their import now. He had not been speaking figuratively, but surveying a future possibility she had known nothing about.

Jerome went on, speaking more easily now that the dam was broken, 'Harwood did not come in to the office today. I don't know where he is. I suspect he has been doing other things I don't know about. I spent the day trying to find out what. If he has been dishonest, he may have run abroad. I sent a message round to his place but there was no reply. I think he may have cut and run.'

'How – how big is the amount?'

'I haven't computed it yet, but it is huge. I have no way of finding a tenth of it. I shall certainly be declared bankrupt.'

She saw that he was trembling, and the fear of the future was vanquished by her present need to comfort him. She went to him, and he put his arms round her. 'They'll take everything,' he said. She held him tighter. 'Everything we have.'

'We'll get by somehow,' she said, as women do at such moments. 'We have each other.'

'Oh, my darling, you don't understand! It's not just a question of giving up luxuries, retrenching. They'll strip the house. Every stick. The remainder of the lease will have to be sold. We'll be thrown out on the street.' He made a sound that might have been a laugh under different circumstances. 'I was talking about sending the boys to Eton – now I'm wondering how I shall even be able to feed them.'

'It can't be as bad as that,' she cried.

'It's worse,' he said, with a sort of relish now – punishing himself. 'The motto of the Stock Exchange is *Uberrime Fidei*. It runs on trust, and a failure to settle is the worst crime there is. They cannot treat it lightly. There will be denunciation, not only on the Exchange but in the newspapers. An honest business may go bankrupt through ill-luck without shame, but I will be disgraced. That's what I've brought you to.' He pushed her away, turned from her, walked across the room. 'It's all I've ever brought you. I made you marry me against your conscience, and you've suffered ever since. It was my action, my arrogance that led to your being cut by the likes of the Suttons, and now I've brought this on you. It would have been better if you'd never met me.'

Separated by the width of the room, she saw the utter despair in his face, and found there was a worse fear yet than that of financial ruin. She had heard and read of it often enough: of a man ruined and facing bankruptcy taking his own life.

'No,' she said. 'You mustn't say that. Jerome, please, look at me! Promise me – promise me you won't leave me all alone!'

He did not understand her. 'What? Leave you?'

She stood rigid, like a soldier under discipline. 'Please,' she said again. 'You won't – you won't – *hurt yourself*?'

Enlightenment came at last like a tumbling wall. He stared, seeing her properly, seeing through his own concerns. 'No! Darling, no! You can't think I would do that. What, and leave you to face it alone? What kind of wretch would I have to be to do that? Oh, my love, even though I've brought you nothing but sorrow, you are the only bright thing in my world – you and the children.'

'It's not true,' she said. 'You've brought me all the happiness in my life. I don't care about anything, as long as we are together.'

He held out his arms and she went to him. 'Together, then,' he said, kissing the crown of her head. 'We'll face it together.' But he still didn't think she had any real understanding of the trouble they were in. Well, perhaps that was best. Let her live in ignorance as long as possible.

Safe in the circle of his arms, Henrietta thought of how she had faced the prospect of poverty once before, and could again. She didn't think he had any real understanding of how little ruin and disgrace mattered to her. They would survive somehow, as long as they were together. Let him only not despair. All their previous peccadilloes were as nothing against that. Despair was the worst sin of all.

There was a strange period of numbness that followed, when nothing seemed entirely real to Henrietta. She told Lizzie what had happened, and saw at once that Lizzie grasped it in a way she had not. Lizzie was sharp, clever, read the newspapers, and had talked on a far more masculine level both with Jerome and with Dodie. She understood money and what the stock market was, where they were a mystery to Henrietta. It was Lizzie who asked what it had not occurred to Henrietta to ask: 'What about your money, Mama? Will they take that too?'

Henrietta didn't know. She put the question to Jerome the next time he came home. It took him a while to come back from his anxious, churning thoughts to understand what she was asking, and then he said, 'No. No, they can't touch that. Thank God – or rather the Married Women's Property Act. Your sixteen hundred pounds is safe.'

'Then we shan't be completely penniless!'

He shook his head, almost smiling. 'Dear love! Eighty pounds a year for the seven of us to live on?'

She knew it was absurd, impossible; but from that moment she could not quite despair. The difference between utter pennilessness and eighty pounds a year seemed to her absolute. She had known when her first husband's will was proved that she could not keep herself and Lizzie on eleven and six a week, and it was even more certain that she could not keep herself, a husband, Lizzie and the four little ones on thirty shillings. But a ridiculous, unjustifiable seed of hope had been planted in her heart and did not die.

But when the blow came, it was dreadful indeed. Settlement day arrived, the cat was out of the bag, and Jerome and his partner were declared on the Stock Exchange. The next day the bare fact of the failure was announced in the newspapers. Harwood, who was unmarried and had no dependants, had indeed gone abroad, so there was no-one to take the attention from Jerome. First estimates of the failure were in the order of fifty thousand pounds, a sum so large it put Henrietta's twelve hundred properly into context for her.

After that it was a matter of waiting. Jerome could no longer trade, and his bank account was frozen. His club required his resignation. An enquiry was put in train concerning the dealings over the gold mine and his and

Harwood's part in them. His creditors began to call in their debts; at home tradesmen's bills were presented, and gradually, as the news circulated, credit was cut off. People looked at Henrietta in the High Street, neighbours crossed the road rather than talk to her, and Emma reported, indignantly, that in the Park, nannies who had been friendly now chose another bench and would not let their children play with hers.

It was like a gradual shrinking of their world, a withering as of plants in a drought. They drew together, avoided contact with the outside world, simplified their lives. Henrietta turned off the servants, using the money she had in hand, left out of housekeeping, to pay them up to date. She did not tell Jerome, suspecting that he would chide her for parting so soon with what they had so little of; but she could not treat them badly. Servants, having no power, were often turned off with no pay for one excuse or another when it suited their employers, but Henrietta had been brought up at Morland Place where consideration for one's servants was considered the mark of a gentlewoman and a Christian duty.

Edie, who had been with them for such a long time, and Fanny Dark, who had grown very fond of them, both cried when they left. Emma, however, refused to go. 'You can't take care of the children all on your own, now can you? To say nothing of the cooking,' she reasoned. 'Master won't drink your coffee, ma'am, not if it was ever so.'

'But I shan't be able to pay you,' Henrietta protested. 'Don't you understand that we are in trouble?'

'Lord, ma'am, you're like my own family now,' Emma said stoutly, 'and family don't up and leave when trouble comes a-knocking.'

Henrietta tried to protest, but Emma wouldn't be budged, and underneath she was very glad. Emma was so calm and practical, and such a comfort, understanding very well, from her childhood, how things had to be managed when there were a lot of mouths and little money. Between them she and Lizzie and Emma could get through the work and care for the children, but she knew it was Emma who did the lion's share, and it was she who managed most of the cooking. Henrietta swore that she would find a way to pay her back one day – one day when things were normal again. She had to believe that things *would* be normal again. How did one live otherwise?

The directors of the Stock Exchange met to discuss the case, and, given that Harwood had fled abroad, and from what they knew of Jerome, they concluded that any actual wrong-doing, if any were discovered, would be the part of the former and not the latter. A date was set for a meeting of the creditors. When that was held, Lizzie explained to her mother, they would probably resolve to take the case to court, to have Papa declared bankrupt so that they could at least recover some of their money. That was the point at which everything would have to be sold. Until then, they would carry on as they did now, living on Henrietta's thirty shillings and whatever else Jerome could borrow informally from friends – friends who did not mind if they never got it back. Henrietta did not ask how they would manage *after* bankruptcy. She was too afraid that Lizzie might know the answer.

She wrote to Venetia, explaining everything, not wanting her to hear about it from the papers or from gossip.

> The name of Compton will be dragged through the mud, and though you do not share the name, I will not call on you again, for fear of involving you. Thank God Amy and Macdonald are abroad. Patsy wrote with her sympathy, but Vivian Laine has too much to lose if his reputation is touched to allow her to call on us. It is sad but I do understand perfectly, and that's what I want to say to you. Your friendship has been the most important thing in my life after my husband and children, and this awful calamity will not change my affection for you, nor my belief in yours for me. You must protect your family and your career at all costs.

The letter brought Venetia hurrying to her side. Henrietta was shocked. 'You must not!'

'Nonsense! Do you think I care for reputation?'

'Dear cousin, your patients – the paying ones – will care. You know that. You can't risk your livelihood.' She saw that Venetia accepted that point. Amongst the nobility, such things might perhaps be shrugged aside, but Venetia's patients were mostly members of that respectable middle class, like the Pagets and the Suttons, who cared very much about propriety and appearance and avoiding scandal.

'Well,' Venetia said, 'I don't have any patients in this area, so I shall be safe in coming to visit you here, even if you can't come to me. But how are you managing?'

'Oh, very well. I have a little money of my own,' Henrietta said, but her lips trembled.

'Tell me the truth,' Venetia urged.

Henrietta gave in. 'It's like an awful nightmare, except that I can't wake up. The tradesmen won't give us credit now, so I have to buy everything with cash, but I have so little of it. We seem to eat soup, mostly. Emma makes it. It's nourishing, I suppose, but it's hard to explain to the children why it's the same every meal. And Jerome hardly eats anything at all. He's so tired at the end of the day, he hasn't the heart to eat, and soup is not what will tempt him. I feel as if I'm failing him. Surely someone cleverer than me would manage things better? Oh, Venetia, I don't even know how to get by from day to day: I daren't think about the future.'

Venetia fumbled for her purse, and emptied it into Henrietta's lap. 'Take it. It isn't much, but it may get you through a day or two. At least buy some mutton for them.'

Henrietta should have refused it, but could not. 'Thank you,' she said. 'Bless you. I can't tell you what it means to me – not just the money, but your friendship.'

'We will always be friends.'

'Yes, we will. But you mustn't come here again. You say you haven't any patients here, but someone will see you, and talk. There is always someone who recognises you, and they are always the ones who love to gossip. I learnt that before, over that other business. I don't want to be the cause of damaging you.' Venetia tried to protest but she hurried on, 'No, really, I mean it. We'll still write to each other, and one day, when all this is over—'

'Yes, of course. It will be over one day. Even scandal does not last for ever. Don't forget our children are destined to be great friends!'

'You're so good to me.'

'That is what family is for,' Venetia said.

Family! Emma had said it, and now Venetia had said it, and it made Henrietta think. Family! She could not appeal to Regina, for Perry had never forgiven her for marrying Jerome, and though she and Regina corresponded, she would never be invited over their threshold again. But Teddy – ah, that was different, wasn't it? She and Teddy had been the closest of the family when they were children, and he had accepted her marriage without demur. It was because of him that she had sixteen hundred pounds of her own and not six hundred. It was to her he had written about taking his little bastard nephew into his household, and again when he had married the child's nurse. She had wondered a little at that, as anyone might, but had written her warmest congratulations to him. Love, she had reflected, could come in many guises, and Teddy, a gentleman of independent wealth, was in a position to marry where he loved without asking anyone's permission. The girl was much younger than him, an orphan of no family and no fortune – a servant girl, to be blunt – and no doubt there would be tutting from many quarters. But Henrietta had reasoned that he was hurting nobody; and he had spoken of love. So she had responded with all the warmth she could summon to her pen.

To Teddy she would appeal now. It was not only proper, since he was the head of her family, but it was also right. As she would have helped him if their cases were reversed, he would help her. And he was a man: he could tell her what to do. But, she decided, she would not tell Jerome what she was doing until she got a reply. He might just forbid her to write. Men could be so sensitive, and he might think it touched his pride.

* * *

The directors deemed Jerome innocent of actual wrong-doing, which was a great weight off his mind, and Henrietta's. He was still disgraced, but there was no taint of criminality to bear.

Spring came, the chestnut buds in the park fattened, the garden was full of squabbling birds and the grass of the small lawn grew bright green and shaggy, now that there was no gardener to cut it. The London Season started, and Miss Fanny Weston was presented at a Drawing-Room and proved one of the most popular and pretty of the débutantes. In Athens an international athletics meeting was held, called the Olympic Games after the ancient Greek contests once held in the wooded vale of Olympia; though few nations took part, it was intended to hold them every four years in the cause of international amity, and it was hoped that eventually every country on earth would send competitors. In Matabeleland there was a native uprising and white settlers were murdered; Cecil Rhodes went almost alone and unprotected to the Matapos and persuaded the chiefs to surrender. In London the government set up a committee with Lord Rothschild as chairman to investigate possible schemes for providing old-age pensions for the aged poor. And in Cambridge the idea of degrees for women was again put to the vote in the university and defeated by a massive majority.

These events, both domestic and strange, passed the Comptons by: their world had shrunk to a narrow focus of impending misery. The creditors appointed a trustee from amongst their numbers to represent them, and took their case to court. It came on in May. All Jerome's finances were gone into, his records scrutinised, his failure confirmed, and his bankruptcy was declared. There was another article in *The Times*, which seemed to Henrietta's flinching eyes to be printed in darker type than everything else so that it stood out from the page, as if it were being shouted from the house tops. His failure was much greater than first suspected, owing largely to the activities of the missing Harwood. More than a hundred and thirty-five thousand pounds was owing, a sum almost beyond imagination – certainly beyond discharging.

Strangely, now that the court case was over and the worst was known, a weight seemed to lift from Jerome. He seemed suddenly to be able to bear it much better – able, even, to joke a little.

'Well, my love,' he said, his voice lighter than it had been for over a year, 'we are done for. We have your sixteen hundred pounds to live on, and next week they will throw us out of this house and sell all our furniture and belongings. I am not allowed to have a business again, and if I get a job, they will distrain a large proportion of my wages to pay my creditors. How will it end, I wonder. I hope not in the workhouse – they separate husbands and wives there. Can we sustain life in a single room in the Devil's Acre, like those poor wretches Venetia talks about? Perhaps we could sell the children. What do you think we would get for them?'

It was then that she told him about her appeal to Teddy, and what Teddy had replied.

'Morland Place is empty,' she said. 'The fire left part of it damaged, but the rest is inhabitable, and Teddy says we can live there for as long as we want. He will pay for any large repairs that need doing to make it sound. There is still some furniture there – heavy old stuff that no-one thought it worth while to sell, but it's something. And there's the kitchen garden and the home farm – the land and outbuildings – still attached to it, as well as the park, and Teddy says if we like to farm it, we can.'

'As his tenants?'

'Well, in a way. We wouldn't be paying him rent, of course. But you see, he doesn't like to see the land go uncultivated.'

'No good landowner would.'

'I suppose we'd be more like caretakers than tenants. But we could grow and raise nearly all the food we need, and there's firewood, and with my little bit of money, we could get by.'

She looked at him anxiously. Would his pride rebel? One corner of his mouth turned up and she had the uncomfortable feeling that he could read her every thought, including the one about concealing from him the other thing Teddy had said, that he would give her money if she needed it, enough to set themselves up and to be comfortable.

'My love, you don't need to try so hard,' was what Jerome eventually said. 'We shall be homeless next week, and if it is nothing else, Morland Place will be a roof over our heads. How can I refuse your brother's kind offer? We must go somewhere, and where else can we find a house large enough for three adults and four children at no cost?'

'You don't mind, then,' Henrietta said.

'Mind?'

'That I asked him. You aren't angry with me?'

He laughed, and it was almost his normal laugh. Almost. 'If I can't provide for you, how can I blame you for asking someone else?'

It was not quite the right answer, but it was near enough to break down Henrietta's caution.

'I'm so glad. I didn't want to hurt your feelings in any way.'

'No, love, you haven't hurt my feelings,' Jerome said, with a strange expression.

'I've loved living in London,' she went on, ever more cheerfully, 'but the way things are now I think it will be best for all of us to go right away. At Morland Place we will be out of the way of prying eyes; no-one there need know anything about all this. And think of all that space for the boys to run about, and the fresh air, and good country food! We can live on next to nothing there; and if we should like to try our hand at farming, I know Teddy would help us. You used to say that you would like to have a place one day. I know this wouldn't be your own, but – well, we'd be safe, and I think we could be happy.'

In so far as he'd had a chance to think at all in the last five minutes, he had been thinking of Morland Place as a temporary refuge, while he licked his wounds and worked out what on earth he could do next. Now, catching hold of her hands, he looked down quizzically at the faint pink in her cheeks and the brightness of her eyes, and realised something else was going on here.

'You're really happy about this, aren't you? You're really looking forward to it?'

She looked at him uncertainly. 'Not happy about the situation. Of course I wish none of this had ever happened. But as a solution to our present problems . . .'

He drew her against him so that she should not see the pain in his eyes. 'Tell the truth and shame the Devil,' he said lightly. 'You're as happy as a lark at the thought of going home, aren't you?'

Henrietta didn't answer, afraid of saying the wrong thing; but, her face resting against his chest, she closed her eyes and imagined Morland Place. Yes, he was right, it was the thought of going home that pleased her. *Home*, the most haunting word in the English language: everyone carried the feeling and the need it represented in his heart. But it was more than that to her, though she didn't expect him to understand. How could anyone not born to it know what Morland Place meant to a Morland?

CHAPTER TWENTY-ONE

Henrietta received a letter by hand from Charlotte, Dowager Duchess of Southport, enclosing fifty pounds.

I implore you not to be too proud to accept the enclosed, which is offered as one mother to another to help with the immediate expenses of removal of your family to Morland Place. You and I have not met, but I knew your father very well and honoured him. I have only met your brother Edward once – in August 1872 when he applied to my cousin Fanny, who was living with me, to buy the other half interest in the mills in Manchester. He struck me then as a warm-hearted and right-thinking person, as his present actions towards you demonstrate. Would you be so kind when you see him as to pass on to him my heartiest regards?

I believe Morland Place is a wonderful old house, and as your childhood home it must be very dear to you. As you may perhaps know, I have a house nearby – Shawes – which however I have not visited for years. Perhaps it may suit me to see it again in the not too distant future, in which case you and I may meet at last in Yorkshire as we never did in London. If I do travel north, I shall try to persuade Venetia to come with me and – with your permission – see the house in which my grandmother was born.

Quite apart from the welcome fifty pounds, it was a wonderful and comforting letter to Henrietta, with its entire lack of censure, its warmth and kindness, the reminder of the family connection, and the hint that not only might she and Venetia meet again, but that they might even be neighbours. It was something to bolster her against the bleakness of being stripped of all their possessions and made homeless.

Jerome was determined that since they had somewhere to go, she should be removed from the scene before the last act was played out, and she was certainly not eager to see their home dismantled. So she was to go to Yorkshire with the children ahead of him, while he remained to see the sale go through and finalise the last details of his ruin. Teddy was agreeable to having them at Makepeace House for a few days until Jerome could join them, but Henrietta felt they ought to start as they meant to go on. Quite apart from the disturbance it would make in Teddy's life, she felt it would upset the children more to taste the comforts of luxury again for a few days rather than settling in to Morland Place from the beginning.

So she asked Teddy only to meet them at the station and escort them, and to arrange for their luggage – such as it was – to be transported from there to the house. Teddy replied with a hearty telegram, 'I'll be there!' and so it was settled.

Emma, whose wages had been the first thing Henrietta paid out of the fifty pounds, was a little unnerved at the thought of going to Yorkshire. 'That's such a long way, ma'am. They say that's like a foreign country up there, and wild and savage too. Is that right that the men wear skirts, and it snows all year round?'

Henrietta laughed – and enjoyed the feeling that she could laugh again. Going home was making her feel quite light-hearted. 'You're thinking of Scotland. Yorkshire's not like that. It's pretty much like the countryside round London, really, except that the people talk with a different accent.'

'I'll never understand a word anyone says,' Emma mourned. 'That was hard enough with Londoners, and trying to make the shopkeepers know what I wanted.'

Henrietta grew serious. 'Emma, dear, you don't have to come. I would be unhappy about taking you so far away from your family unless you were really sure. You needn't be afraid to say if you would sooner leave us, though I'd be very sorry to see you go.'

Emma's eyebrows shot up. 'Go? Leave you? Lord, ma'am, how could you think it? I can't leave my children after all this time. And how'd you get on without me in a foreign place, with wild animals and funny food and such?'

'Very badly indeed,' Henrietta said. 'Come with us, then. I should have hated to have to face it without you.'

So early on a bright June day they set out for the station, the luggage having been picked up for an even earlier train.

'I shall be no more than a week behind you,' Jerome said. 'Perhaps less. I've no desire to linger here. I wish you didn't have to manage this journey alone, but—'

'Alone?' Henrietta said.

His lips quirked. 'You know what I mean.'

'Teddy will be there to meet us at the other end. There's nothing to worry about.' She didn't like being parted from him, even for a few days. It made her afraid that something would happen, a cold superstition that they would never see each other again. She crushed the feeling down, resenting its intrusion into her new happiness.

Jerome shook hands with Jackie and Robbie and bade them sternly to be good and help their mother, kissed Frank and Jessie and ruffled their hair, hugged Lizzie briefly, and then helped them all into their carriage. Henrietta gave him both her hands, and they exchanged a long look. Then she said briskly, 'You don't need to wait until the train pulls out. You must have a thousand things to do.'

And he read her thoughts, touched her cheek with one finger and said, 'Begone, superstition! I shall see you in a few days – and you'll have so much to do in the mean time, you won't even notice my absence.'

But he didn't wait for the train to pull out; and she forced herself not to lean out of the window and watch his retreating figure for as long as she could see it.

The train pulled in under the glorious curved canopy of York station on time, and ten years and six months after

Henrietta had last left it on the London train. The boys were racing about the compartment like mice in a box, so Henrietta wasn't able to get to the window to see if Teddy was there waiting. She and Lizzie and Emma collected their bags as the train sighed and jolted to a halt, and grabbed various limbs as they whisked past them.

'Boys, stand still! Be quiet! Now when we get off, you must stay close by and not wander away. Frank, keep tight hold of Lizzie's hand. Emma, if I take Jessie, can you manage to hand the bags out?'

Crowds were pouring off the train, porters were scurrying up with trolleys, there was a racket and bustle as great as anything in a London terminus, but as Henrietta stepped down onto the platform, the first thing she saw was Teddy, standing calmly like a rock in a stream a little way off. He was just the same dear old Teddy, a little slimmer than when she had last seen him, but still dressed as smartly, his curly brown hair, so like her own, untouched with grey as he lifted his tall hat in greeting.

The children grew quiet, and the little group of refugees stood close together, suddenly uncertain in this strange place. Henrietta felt absurdly shy for a moment, and saw that Teddy did too. He slipped his fingers into his fob, pulled out his watch and consulted it – needlessly, since the enormous station clock was there above him – and said, 'Just under one minute early. Excellent time-keeping. It's a good train, this one. Non-stop from Peterborough, isn't it?'

Henrietta's shyness passed, and she smiled warmly. 'Dear Teddy, I'm so very glad to see you!'

He smiled too, replaced his watch and held out his arms to her. They embraced; and then he said, 'Don't tell me this is little Lizzie? This lovely young woman? I don't expect you remember me, do you?'

'Of course I do, Uncle,' Lizzie said, and kissed him.

'I don't remember you,' Robbie said boldly, and Jack, with more understanding of the gravity of the situation, jabbed him hard with an elbow to silence him.

'Boys, behave,' Henrietta said hastily. 'This is your uncle

479

Edward. Say how-do-you-do politely. This is Jack, this is Robbie, and there's little Frank, and Jessie.'

Teddy shook hands with the boys, saying, 'How d'ye do, how d'ye do, but it's Uncle Teddy, my dears, to you. None of this Edward business – too late in life for that. And is this really my niece?' He bent over Jessie. 'I thought perhaps it was an angel come down to visit us. Will you kiss your uncle, my poppet?'

Henrietta was astonished at his ease with the children, given how little he had always cared for them, and reflected that marriage and, perhaps more significantly, taking care of George's bastard, had changed him. On the tail of this thought she asked, 'Are we to meet Charlotte and the boy today?'

'Yes, yes, they are at Morland Place now, waiting to meet you. Since you would not come and stay with us, they insisted on it. Too many to be at the station, you understand – never would have got into the carriage. This sensible young woman is your nurse, is she?'

'Much more than that. Emma is one of the family now.'

'How d'ye do, Emma? Is this all the luggage? Yes, your boxes have gone on ahead – saw them collected myself this morning. Porter! Yes, just this. I've a four-wheeler waiting outside. Come along then, everyone. Your long journey is almost over.'

In the growler, under cover of the children's eager chatter, Teddy leant across and patted Henrietta's hand. 'Chin up, little sister. Things might have been a great deal worse.'

'My chin is up,' Henrietta assured him. 'You've been so very kind to us, I should be an ungrateful wretch if it weren't.'

'Oh, none of that! It's nothing at all – and, you know, there's a benefit to me in it too. Not that that's why I did it, but I think this may turn out well for both of us.'

'I hope so.'

'And June's a good time to be beginning – not farming, of course, I don't mean that, but here's the good weather, and you'll have the whole summer to settle in and see what needs doing. Coming here in the dead of winter would have been a very different business.'

'You're right, of course.'

'So look on the bright side. You might think of it as a holiday, you know. There's no need to be deciding anything for several months yet, and I dare say you could do with a rest.'

Henrietta agreed gratefully, and Teddy sat back in silence so that she could look out of the carriage window at the familiar scene. When they left the main road and turned onto the track, she felt such a pang of familiarity and longing it brought tears to her eyes. She had roamed and ridden over every inch of this land. She was familiar with every bush and tree, path and rill; now her children would have the chance to love it too.

The track widened, white with summer dust, curving gently to accommodate the features of the land, as some ancient walker had once meandered, laying down the path for ever. There was the great oak tree, hundreds of years old, out of which Georgie had fallen when he was ten; it had lost a massive lower limb since she saw it last, but it was green and vigorous still. The hedges were thick and overgrown, needed cutting or they would thin at the bottom, she thought. The hawthorn flower was nearly over, but the wild roses were coming into bloom, pink faces peeping up from the tangle of honeysuckle and bear bind. Would Jessie make herself coronets as she and Regina had used to? The boys would discover where the best nuts were and gather them for her, as Teddy had, cracking them between two stones. They would pick blackberries, too, at peril to their fingers. They would learn how to suck rosehips without choking on the seeds, and how to get a sip of honey from a honeysuckle flower; they would learn about the tender young lime leaves children called bread-and-butter when she was a girl, that were good to eat.

Now there was a smudge of buildings in the distance, which grew rapidly until she could distinguish the new stable-block George had built – empty and sadly dilapidated now – and then the group of old barns and coach-house, and then at last Morland Place itself. Its shape was imprinted on her mind so long ago that if everything else were wiped

from it that would surely remain: the outer walls, drawbridge, barbican, the line of the moat, a hint of chimneys
behind, all sketched against the sky.

They slowed and turned over the drawbridge and pulled
through into the yard. Henrietta drew a breath. Yes, there
was devastation where the fire had destroyed the new wing,
a heap of rubble and charred wood between the outer wall
and the blackened brick of the old house. There was the
doorway, which had been knocked between the two, boarded
up, and the window above boarded too, presumably where
the glass had broken in the heat, and the roof rather clum-
sily repaired. The yard was full of last year's dead leaves and
dead grass, fresh weeds were sprouting from between the
cobbles, and the gutter of what was left of the stable block
was hanging off, with a fine large patch of emerald moss
across the ground and up the wall to show how long it had
been like that.

But her eye could eliminate all that, as it could eliminate
the changes George and Alfreda had made to the kitchen
side and stables. The face of the old house was the same,
the warm red brick and the tall chimneys, the windows
reflecting the bright June sunlight, the great door seeming
somehow welcoming even though it was shut, with the stone
panel above it on which, indistinguishable from this distance,
was carved the Morland hare, leaping blithely over the sprig
of heather, and the words *Deo Gratias*. Thank God – yes,
thank God! She had come home, and home was still home,
and welcomed her.

As if he had heard her thought, Teddy leant across and
said, with satisfaction, 'There'll be a Morland at Morland
Place again. It never felt right to me all these years without
one.'

She needed to hold on to that thought, and revive it from
time to time, as the desolation struck her again and again
in a host of tiny details. The emptiness, the shabbiness, the
neglect were hard to bear. It was like losing her mother all
over again, that sense that the comfort had gone out of life.
In her childhood Morland Place had been a small kingdom

in itself, home not just to the Morlands but to a host of servants, all living and working to a comfortable routine, mutually dependent but self-sufficient from the world outside. From the fishponds and orchards, through the laundry-room and the brewhouse, to the library and chapel, everything one might need for a civilised life was provided by the house and the estate. It was so empty and silent now, she felt even the ghosts had departed.

Teddy's wife (how strange that sounded!) was waiting for them in the great hall, holding the boy by the hand. Charlotte seemed to Henrietta a nice young person, quietly spoken and remarkably pretty. Teddy introduced her with obvious pride, and though her manner was gentle, Henrietta sensed a firmness underneath it that surprised her a little. This was no ordinary servant-girl raised above her station. Charlotte had intelligence and self-respect, and though she was grateful she was not overwhelmed, and conducted herself with a natural authority that said there was nothing to wonder at in her marriage to one of York's leading gentlemen. Henrietta was intrigued by the relationship between Charlotte and her brother. In public he was gallantly devoted and she was respectfully fond, but what they might be to each other privately eluded her; why precisely Teddy had asked Charley to marry him and why she had accepted.

Even more startling to her feelings was the sight of the boy, Edward Bone, son of Alice the housemaid and her brother George. If there had been the slightest doubt in her mind that George was the father it must have been dissipated by the ten-year-old's face, for he was startlingly like. He was a little shy and uncertain – and perhaps being back at Morland Place roused unwelcome memories – and he held Charley's hand tightly and greeted Henrietta unsmilingly, glancing up at Charley as if for reassurance. He was ten, going on eleven, almost a year older than Jack. While the adults talked, the boys eyed each other cautiously, looking for those intangible signals that tell whether friendship, indifference or enmity is ahead.

But first there was something more important on hand.
'You must all be terribly hungry,' Charley said. 'I suggest

we eat first, before we look over the house – don't you think so?' She appealed politely to Henrietta, and Henrietta appreciated the gesture.

'I think that would be an excellent idea,' she said. And then, doubtfully, thinking of the empty kitchens, '*Is* there something to eat?'

Charley smiled. 'We brought a picnic luncheon, enough for everyone.'

'Lunch!' Teddy exclaimed, rubbing his hands. 'Shall we have it outside? It's such a fine day, it seems a shame to be indoors. Now, then, which of you strong lads is going to help carry things out?'

They had their picnic in the sunshine on the Long Walk, on the bank of the moat and out of sight of the damaged part of the house. Charley and Teddy had brought rugs to sit on as well as a luncheon basket of kingly proportions, out of which came cold ham, cold chicken, watercress, buttered rolls, pasties, anchovy scones, cheese straws, sausage rolls, curd cakes, fairy cakes, buttered buns, biscuits, apples, apricots and cherries, together with wine, lemonade and ginger beer to drink. Henrietta thought her children's eyes would fall out of their heads at this cornucopian feast, after weeks of soup varied only by rice pudding. Their carefully taught manners might have gone by the board had not astonishment curbed them.

When everyone had eaten enough for the time being, the children, having decided that they were going to be friends, asked permission to go and play. Teddy exhorted Edward to show the newcomers around the gardens but not to go too far, and Emma sternly commanded Jack to take care of Jessie and not to let her fall in the water. Charley and Lizzie were striking up a tentative but interested conversation, and Emma was simply enjoying sitting in the sun, so Teddy invited Henrietta to come for a walk with him around the moat.

'I'll have to get that section of the roof repaired properly,' he said, as they strolled. 'I'll get the men to start that next week. Best to do it while the weather's fine and the evenings are long. And I'll have them brick up the doorway to the ruined wing properly while they're at it. Alfreda's new bedrooms and sitting rooms were damaged, more by smoke than fire, but you wouldn't want to use 'em as they are. If I were you I'd just shut them off and lock the doors for now – there's more than enough room for you without them. Otherwise the house is all right. Ah, here's the place where the moat was blocked, you see? Part of the bank came down. I had it cleared out, but that wants a bit of work, too. The poor swans didn't know what to think . . .

'I had the chimneys swept, so that's all right. And the kitchen range ought to be in working order, which will save you having to light the big kitchen fire. There's plenty of coal in the cellar, and of course there's firewood all over the place. You can get those boys of yours to look for it – best way for them to find their way around . . .

'Beds, now: we found the Butts Bed stored in sections in the attic.'

'Yes,' said Henrietta, 'I remember when Alfreda had it removed. She wanted to throw it away but the carpenter wouldn't allow it – said it was an heirloom.'

'So it is. Anyway, I've had my man put it up in the east bedroom. Thought you and Compton would like to use that. Not sure the mattress is up to much. We may have to see about that, but it will do for the present. The nursery is still furnished, so there are beds for your little ones and the nurse, and Eleanor's Bed and that big armoire are still in the blue bedroom so I thought that would do for Lizzie. Charley's had our maids over to make them all up with fresh sheets and sweep the floors a bit. So at least you can go to bed when you like.'

'Teddy, you're so kind.'

'Nonsense. Least we could do. Now, you said you had your own pots and pans?'

'Yes, they let us keep those, and one set of china and the everyday silver.'

'Good-oh. I didn't think you'd feel like cooking this evening, though, so Charley's put a cold supper in one of the pantries, and the whatnot for breakfast tomorrow; and there's a table and chairs the Craikeses used – only kitchen stuff, but it'll do for now. As to furniture, there are all sorts of odds and ends around the house and in the attic – nothing very pretty, of course, but there's probably enough to be going on with. I haven't had any of that moved, because I didn't know how you'd want to arrange things, but I can send a man over to help you when you decide where it's all to go.'

'I'm sure we'll manage without taking your man away from his work.'

He stopped and turned to her. 'Believe me, I'm glad to do anything I can for you. I've missed you, dear old Hen, and I'm more pleased than I can say that you're back – though I'm sorry it happened this way, of course.'

'You're my dear kind old Teddy,' she said, 'just the same as you always were. Do you remember when you came back from Oxford after Papa died, and you gave me a necklace? Silver filigree daisies. It was the first grown-up present I'd ever had. I have it still, you know.'

He smiled slowly. 'Didn't the duns take it, then?'

'They said it wasn't worth anything. But I'm glad they left it, because it's worth a lot to me.'

He turned again, taking her hand and tucking it through his arm as they resumed their stroll. 'The thing is,' he said, 'you needn't feel too horrid grateful, because you'll be doing me a favour just being here. Houses need someone to live in them, and paid caretakers can't be trusted the way I can trust you.'

'Don't you really want to live here? I know you didn't while you were a bachelor, but now you have a wife, and you may have children some time—'

'I have the boy.'

'Oh! Yes, of course.'

'Well, at any rate, I'm happy where I am. I don't want to live here, but it hurt me to see the old Place neglected. So this is a fine outcome for all.'

'And if we farm it for you—'

'Yes, well, no need to talk about that now,' Teddy interrupted. 'When Compton comes we can have a fine old jaw about it and see what's what. But you'll need plenty of time to settle in and get the house the way you want it first, so you needn't worry about farming just yet, not until next year at the soonest. In the mean time there are fish in the fish ponds, plenty of fruit and vegetables in the kitchen garden, and I'll see you get other stuff, milk and meat and so on. And,' he added before she could thank him again, 'I'm teaching Edward to shoot, so if you like your eldest boy could come out with us, and see if he can get you something for the pot now and then. Only pigeons at the moment, of course, but later on . . .'

'Pigeons make nice eating,' Henrietta said. 'And Jack will love you for ever if you take him shooting! I can see you are going to make a perfectly magical uncle. I can't get over how good you are with the children all of a sudden. When Lizzie was born I could hardly get you to look at her.'

'Oh, I was young and foolish then. Edward's opened my eyes to a whole new world. He's a splendid little fellow, you know, and when you think what an unfortunate beginning he had, it's wonderful how he's shaping up.'

'You're fond of him.' Henrietta said.

'Of course I am. He's my nephew – why shouldn't I be?'

Henrietta didn't pursue the subject. She had suddenly thought that if Teddy was as fond of the boy as he seemed, he might want to adopt him; and then in ten or eleven years' time, he might want to give Morland Place to him, which would mean the Comptons would have to go. Well, well, she must not be ungrateful. Teddy was generosity itself, and by the time Edward was grown up, her own boys would be too, and if necessary she and Jerome and the girls would find somewhere else to live. It would be hard to leave Morland Place again; but she would not think about that now.

Instead she said, reverting a sentence or two, 'If you teach Jack to shoot, I can show him how to snare rabbits. Old Ellerby, the keeper of Acomb Wood – do you remember him? – he showed me when I was a girl. I'll teach Edward too, if you like. Don't you think they'll find that impressive in a mere female?'

'There's nothing mere about you,' Teddy said. 'Never was. I'll bet you know how to fish, too.'

'Not with rod and line, but I can tickle a trout with the best of them. It takes patience, and a woman's touch.'

'Woman's touch be damned! When I was a lad I took the biggest fish in the world out of the bottom fish pond – do you remember? Must have been four or five pounds . . .'

'Of course I remember. You got such a beating for it!'

'Lord, yes! Father handed me over to old Wheldrake, the tutor. Could he whack, the old tyrant!'

'You needn't sound as if you admired him for it.'

'Oh, boys need a licking now and then to keep 'em in order. Never did me any harm. I say, do you remember the time Georgie and I brought that wasps' nest home?'

Reminiscing happily, they strolled on round the moat, under the curious eyes of the swans.

It was like a glorious holiday. Though there was plenty of hard work for the women, it was work with hope to it, and the satisfaction of creating order. It made them cheerful, so that they chatted and sang about it all day long as they fashioned a new home out of emptiness.

The children simply ran wild, excited as dogs. They thundered up and down stairs and in and out of empty rooms, chasing each other round and round the house, thrilled at having two staircases so that they never had to retrace their steps. They explored every room and cupboard of the great old house from attic to cellar. Then, outside, they ran madly, shrieking with sheer pleasure, over endless grass that knew no touch of perambulator wheels, through gardens innocent of bath-chaired colonels and uniformed nannies. They revelled in unfettered movement, almost drunk with the sheer space all around them, theirs to explore, unpeopled, and with no activity forbidden.

It wasn't long before Robbie slipped into the moat, Jack fell out of a tree, Frank got stung by a bee, and Jessie got tangled up with some blackberry runners, scratched her cheek and left quite a chunk of her hair behind in the process of getting free. Lizzie worried about the injuries, but Henrietta only laughed and said it was good to see them looking like proper country children. Emma said if they hurt theirselves once they'd learn not to do it again, but the rule seemed to take a long time applying itself. On the next day Robbie slipped while running full-tilt down the great staircase and rolled down the whole flight with a sound like a chimney brought down by a storm; Jack cut himself on a hoof-paring knife that he found, involuntarily, in a heap of straw in the stables; and Frank found a forgotten jar of pickled onions in a distant pantry and ate them all, not only making himself extremely sick but managing to get the pungent vinegar all over his clothes and even in his hair. They seemed, however, to be held in a magic capsule that prevented them from hurting themselves seriously. And in between endangering life and limb, they partook of the most amazing picnic meals, never in the same place twice, and never the sort of mutton-hash-and-rice-pudding meals that a well-brought-up child comes to expect. It was no wonder they were as happy as larks, or that Jack said to his mother – breathlessly, throwing his arms round her briefly as he passed her during some chasing game – 'I *love* Morland Place! Can we stay here for ever?'

When Jerome arrived, tired and drawn and depressed a week later, he found the beginnings of a home set up, and, had he known it, an amazing amount done. The kitchen had been swept, the floor scrubbed, the walls newly white-washed, and the range blackleaded; the pots and pans and china had been unpacked and put away, and with the table and chairs set up it had become the new centre of family life.

For their sitting-room Henrietta had chosen the dining-room, which had a good fireplace and was the closest public room to the kitchen. Later when they wanted a dining-room they could set it up in the dining-parlour – the smaller of the two rooms Alfreda had made out of the great dining saloon. The drawing-room and sitting-room on the south side of the house were too badly smoke-damaged to be usable without a great deal of work.

'But they'd be much nicer, looking over the moat and the gardens, and getting all the sun,' Henrietta said. The dining-rooms only looked onto the inner courtyard and were rather dark. 'It must be our long-term goal to get them cleaned up so we can use them.'

She and Emma and Lizzie had taken up the dining-room carpet and beaten it, cleaned the wallpaper with damp bread, dusted and polished everything, and assembled a motley assortment of furniture in there from all over the house. Jerome followed her obediently as she showed him what they had achieved, but he seemed unable to be impressed with it, and his comments were few. He ate his dinner at the kitchen table that evening with a look of bewilderment, and did not even take pleasure from the bottle of wine Teddy had sent over especially for him. Henrietta was hurt and disappointed, but reasoned to herself that he was tired, and that he had little to rejoice about. Morland Place was not *his* home.

But he slept soundly that night, despite the inadequacies of the ancient mattress, lulled, perhaps, by the silence and velvety dark outside, and the sweet air coming in at the window – so different from London. He slept so heavily he did not move all night, and once or twice Henrietta touched him nervously to make sure he was still alive; and in the morning he woke refreshed, his mood lighter, and ready to appreciate the good luck which had followed the bad.

The next week the workmen arrived to start the repairs, and Teddy arranged for Henrietta and Jerome to borrow horses so that they could ride out, partly to get away from the builders, but mostly so that she could show him all over the estate. It was wonderful to Henrietta to be on a horse again after so many years, and though she knew she'd be stiff the next day, she could not resist urging her mount into a canter at every available opportunity.

'I had no idea how much I'd missed it,' she said breathlessly, as they pulled up at the end of a track. She patted her mount's neck, and thought, wistfully, that she had better enjoy it while she could, for riding was unlikely to play much part in her life for the foreseeable future.

It was lovely to see old favourite places again, and to show them to Jerome, who had always, as long as she had known him, spoken of an interest in the place of her birth. In telling him the little stories she had in connection with this place and that, she lived again the happy times of her childhood, when she had roamed these woods and fields unfettered and unworried about the future.

They stopped on the top of Cromwell's Plump in the middle of the day to eat some sandwiches Emma had hastily assembled for them after breakfast. Sitting on the grass, holding the reins and patiently pushing the horses' noses out of their lunch, they talked about the situation.

'I know I am in no position to exercise pride,' he said, 'but I don't like the idea of living on your brother's charity for ever.'

'It isn't wholly charity,' Henrietta said. 'Teddy says that when my father died, Reggie and I were supposed to have been provided with dowries out of the estate, but he didn't specify the amounts and left it to Georgie to arrange it. And of course Georgie never did, either because he forgot or because Alfreda wouldn't let him part with the money.'

'I don't see how that's relevant.'

'But it is, you see. Even though Georgie squandered most of his fortune, Teddy inherited what was left, and the part of the estate that Papa left to Teddy has thrived and multiplied. So I ought to have a share of that.'

'Darling, even if you had been given a dowry, you wouldn't still have it now. It would have gone to Fortescue when he married you. And when he died, it would have gone with the rest to create a monument to him in his old college. Come to think of it,' he added soberly, 'you seem to have had to do with thriftless men all your life: your father, your brother, and both your husbands.'

'It wasn't your fault,' she protested, but he silenced her with a look. 'At all events,' she went on, 'don't talk any more about pride and obligation.'

'No, you're right. I mustn't. It's a luxury I can't afford. But what is to become of us?'

'Teddy wants to talk to us both together about it. But I think his idea is that we start off with just a few chickens and ducks and a house cow or two, and work up gradually. And instead of being rent tenants, we'll go back to an older system, and pay him in tithe.'

'How much is a tenth of nothing at all?'

'Oh, it will soon build up. And simply taking care of the land will improve its value, so he loses nothing.'

'I doubt whether farming at that sort of level can pay nowadays. You know – or you ought to – how bad things are in agriculture these days.'

'Mmm, yes, but that's the old-fashioned sort of farming. What one has to do nowadays is to specialise.'

'Specialise?'

'This is for the future, of course. But here we are, sitting under the walls of a great city full of people, who all have to eat. Fruit and vegetables and milk and eggs: that's what will pay.'

'Market gardening?'

'Yes, and we have the market right there under our noses.'

He laughed suddenly. 'You sounded like a farmer's daughter just then.'

'Well, so I am – in a way. Anyway, if you're willing to try, Teddy will start us off, and I think in a few years the scheme will be doing so well we'll be able to pay Teddy back and give him rent in money instead of kind; be proper tenants, and put it on a legal footing. In time,' she added eagerly, 'we may make enough to discharge your debts.'

She wished she had not said it, seeing the light in his face dim a little. 'That it should come to that – that my wife should have to rescue me by her own labour.'

She would not be put off. 'You quite mistake the matter,' she said cheerfully. 'You will be labouring ten times harder than me, I assure you. Milking the cows, tilling the fields – did you think you were going to sit in the counting-house counting out your money while I did it all?'

He put a hand to the back of her neck and drew her to him to kiss her in a sort of homage. 'I am humbled by your courage. And I promise you I shall throw away gloom from this moment on and buckle to with a good will. Doesn't the proverb say, "God loves those who do their duty with a glad word and cheerful heart"?'

They sat in silence for a while, looking out over the country, with nothing to disturb them but the horses' grazing, the juicy crunching, and the steady little tugs on the reins. The warm June sun fell on them like a blessing, the sky was achingly blue, darker than chicory, almost cornflower-blue; in the distance an ing put down to hay was a blond corner on a green handkerchief field; and further off yet, sheep grazed, scattered like petals, too far away to hear their voices or their bells.

'It's beautiful country,' Jerome said at last. 'We'll be happy here. And we *will* make a success of it – I swear it to you. One day I shall discharge my bankruptcy, and then the first thing I shall do is to buy you a – a diamond necklace. There!'

'Darling! What would I do with diamonds? Make it a horse.'

'Much better idea. A horse it shall be.'

'I've had another idea: it's a plan for the more distant future, of course, because the stock would cost money to set up, but I think we might breed horses again. Not race-horses, like poor foolish Georgie, but draught horses. Think of all the places they're needed – railways, breweries, collieries, omnibus and tram companies. We have wonderful grazing here – why not?' She took a quick little breath in, looking around at the land beneath them. 'Oh, wouldn't it be wonderful to have horses at Morland Place again? Think of it!'

'I'm thinking,' he said obediently; but he was looking at her face and thinking how beautiful she was, and how lucky – how enormously, undeservedly lucky – he was.

In February of 1897 there was a ferment of excitement amongst the supporters of women's suffrage. Suddenly, and at short notice, they were promised a day in Parliament to bring the Women's Suffrage Bill. Anne Farraline came to tell Venetia and could hardly keep still for agitation, walking up and down the room as the words poured from her.

'At the last minute we thought Arthur Balfour would go back on it and take it away from us, though Frances was confident – or said she was – that he wouldn't, because of having had to do so before. But Chamberlain has been chipping away at him – I do dislike that man! – and right up until tonight there was still the chance that it might be cancelled.'

'But it's sure now?'

'Oh, yes! Mrs Courteney sent me a note to say Leonard says it is definitely to come on. I do hope the House will be full. Wyndham and Begg have been rushing about talking to people all day, reminding them of their promises. Oh, Venetia, I can't believe we are actually going to get our time! Salisbury's an honourable man, I'll say that for him. And to think Mrs Fawcett is missing it all! She's holidaying in Athens, you know – how mad she will be when she hears! You will come, won't you?'

'My dear, I can't – I have work to do.'

'Work? Whatever it is, it can't be as important as this! You must be there. Surely, surely you can't think of missing it?'

'Well – I could put off some of my less urgent cases, perhaps, and be there for part of the debate.'

'Yes, do, do!'

'But don't raise your hopes too high,' Venetia begged. 'You know you have some very staunch opponents in the House, some of whom have great influence – Herbert Asquith, for instance. And a great many more who say they support you will go the other way in Division.'

'But this time it will be different,' Anne said, her eyes bright. 'I just feel it in my bones.'

'Well, bless your bones! I hope you're right.'

Venetia rearranged her day as best she could, and was present in the gallery for the last part of the debate. Her hopes were still not high, for though the House was full, there was no atmosphere of excitement on the benches; indeed, the majority of Members seemed hardly interested in the proceedings at all, and one or two, slumped low with their chins on their chests, appeared to be asleep. Her one comfort was that though the general standard of debate struck her as poor, the opponents of the Bill spoke by far the worst: the greatest amusement to be had was from Mrs Hallett, sitting beside Lady Frances Balfour, whose snorts of derision and disgust were quite audible in the Chamber, and who had to be restrained at times from shouting at the enemy below.

Venetia's hopes had not been high, so when the results of the Division were announced, her surprise was almost equal to her delight: the Bill was passed by a respectable majority. The women were overjoyed, almost beyond speech. It was twenty-seven years since the House had accepted the female franchise as a principle: twenty-seven years of unremitting work by women like Millicent Fawcett to get them to this point.

Anne was jubilant. 'I knew it! I told you, didn't I, that I could feel it in my bones?'

'You did. I am so very glad for you.'

'For me? For all of us! Leonard Courteney really believes we shall do it this time. He thinks we'll get it through. Everything looks set fair. The Division lists show a few shocking rats – people you wouldn't have thought it of. But quite a few new friends, too, which is encouraging. Wyndham and Begg have done wonders! And Chamberlain didn't speak against us, which I count as quite something. But now we have the committee stage, and there's a lot of hard work ahead of us, keeping everyone up to the mark, and trying to win over public support. You will help, won't you, dear Venetia? Let me wheedle you.'

'I will do what I can, but you know I am too busy to write letters and speak at meetings.'

'I know, darling, I don't expect that of you. But you do have influence, and you'll speak to friends, won't you? What about Campbell-Bannerman? I know you like him. Can you enlist him? And get Hazelmere to use his influence, too. He could be worth quite a few votes to us when it goes to the Lords.'

Venetia promised to do what she could, though she had less faith in her influence than Anne did. There were formidable forces still ranged against them, however. The newspapers were almost incoherent with rage over the Bill's passing its Second Reading. Scorn was poured on the Movement. *The Times* said in its leader that the vote was wanted only by a handful of ladies of masculine ambitions.

'The experience of every man is that the overwhelming majority of women are perfectly content to wield influence in feminine ways and have no desire to be mixed up in the dirty business of politics.'

Even the *Daily Chronicle* warned the Liberal Party not to pursue the women's issue while so many men were still outside the franchise. It also said that the vote had first been proposed in order to right various women's grievances, but as so many of them had been addressed since then, there was no need now to proceed with enfranchisement.

As the weeks passed, it seemed that many Liberal MPs agreed with this view. At any rate, Anne, driven to frustration, told her cousin that they seemed to feel that having voted for the Bill and shown their support for the principle, they had done all they needed. 'Without actually saying so, they let one understand that it would be pleasanter for everyone if we dropped the Bill now and saved them the awkwardness of actually having to do anything about it.'

But when the end came, it was done without putting the MPs to the trouble of proving or denying their support. The Third Reading came on in May, and the women's Bill was next in the Order Paper after the Verminous Persons Bill. Henry Labouchère, that implacable enemy, stood up to talk about verminous persons, and waxed witty on the subject for three hours, to the great and noisy appreciation of the House, until all the available time was spent and the women's Bill had to be dropped as 'talked out'.

So the great hope was ended, and the disappointment of the Movement was equalled by the anger and despair that their opponents had resorted to such a 'dirty trick'. Now the whole process had to be begun again, and who knew when another day would be granted? Not for another twenty-seven years, perhaps.

Only two good things resulted from the episode. First, public opinion was moved to feel that the women had not had fair play, and several newspapers carried articles saying that while they did not approve of women's suffrage, they disapproved far more of MPs using such mean tactics to avoid discussing the subject seriously.

The second good thing was that the divided and scattered elements of the women's movement were persuaded that there was a great need to pull together. As a result, all the small local franchise societies and the two large London ones decided to amalgamate into one National Union, with Mrs Fawcett unanimously elected as president. Now as they began the weary task all over again from the beginning, they did at least speak with one voice, and were the stronger for it.

CHAPTER TWENTY-TWO

In September 1896 the Queen had remarked, and noted in her diary, the day on which she had reigned longer than any other English sovereign in history; and in June 1897 she would have reigned for sixty years – her Diamond Jubilee. There must, of course, be a great celebration.

Hazelmere, who had been at Windsor with the Prince of Wales during a visit by the Prime Minister to discuss the matter, said to Venetia, 'It's such a delight to see Salisbury and the Queen together – the liking and the trust between them is very soothing.'

'Well, of course, she's known him all his life. He was a page at her coronation. And he is a very likeable person: no pride about him or self-consequence.'

'That's just it,' Hazelmere said. 'They both have such a plain, matter-of-fact attitude towards their respective positions. Here they are governing between them not only Britain but an empire of a hundred million people, yet for all the fuss they make about it, you'd think they were the squire and the vicar discussing the parish. To them it's just a duty, a job they have to get on with – nothing to be puffed about.'

Mr Chamberlain, the Colonial Secretary, wanted the jubilee to be a celebration of empire, and that suited the Queen very well. She was passionate about the empire herself; and besides, she did not want to have to invite the Kaiser, which would be inevitable if other kings and emperors were to be present. So the decree went out: no crowned heads. Instead the prime ministers of the self-governing dominions would be the guests of honour.

Chamberlain dreamt of a multicoloured pageant, of representatives and uniformed soldiers from India, Australia, South Africa, Hong Kong, Borneo and Cyprus, all marching through the capital to show how people of many races could join together as one peaceful family under the benign shelter of the Crown.

As the actual anniversary fell on a Sunday, it was decided to hold the celebration on Tuesday June the 22nd. The Queen was to drive in an open landau from Buckingham Palace to St Paul's Cathedral where a service of thanksgiving would be held.

'The dear Queen is very concerned about the length of the service,' Olivia said one day, when she and Venetia were having tea with their mother. 'She's told the Archbishop that she won't stay if it goes on longer than twenty minutes.'

Charlotte laughed. 'That sounds like her!'

'But how will she manage the steps?' Venetia asked. 'Isn't she very lame now?'

'She means to stay in her carriage, and have the service take place outside. The Duchess of Mecklenburg-Strelitz said it was a shocking idea to be thanking God out in the street, but the Queen said quite sharply that the duchess ought to remember Who else used to preach in the open air.'

'I heard,' Venetia said, 'that there's to be a cinematograph picture to be taken of the service.'

'Yes,' Olivia said. 'The Queen was so impressed with the one that was done at Balmoral last year, when the Tsar and his family were visiting, that she thinks it would be a good idea to take one whenever there's an important State occasion.'

'Did you see it?' Venetia asked. 'I can't imagine what it must look like.'

'Well, it's just a lot of photographs joined together on a reel,' Olivia said, 'so that when you wind them along the people seem to move.'

'Like a magic lantern?'

'Yes, a little. We were all out on the terrace so as to get the best light, and we were told to walk up and down, and the children jumped and ran about, while the man turned the handle. Then when the pictures were shown, there we all were, you know, moving about just like life – only all in grey, of course,' she added, in the cause of honesty. 'And rather fuzzy and blurred. And a little jerky, too. But still, it was remarkable.'

'What happens after the service?' Charlotte asked, returning to the jubilee.

'The Queen wants to be driven round some of the poor streets of the East End, so that the people there have a chance to see her.'

'Talking of streets,' Venetia said, 'I suppose London will be crowded again, and getting about will be impossible on the day. Remember the golden jubilee?'

'It's likely to be even more crowded this time,' Charlotte said. 'There are so many things planned, aren't there, Livy?'

'Oh, yes. There's the schoolchildren's address in Hyde Park, and the garden party at Buckingham Palace—'

'Yes. We've had invitations to that.'

'And there's another, separate garden party for Members of Parliament only, and then the military review in Windsor Great Park.' Olivia smiled suddenly. 'Do you know, the Queen is learning a speech in Hindustani so that she can address her Sikh soldiers in their own language? Isn't that like her? It's frightfully difficult, because she can hardly read now so she's having to learn it by heart, but she won't give up until she's mastered it. Don't you think that's touching?'

'Is she looking forward to it all?' Charlotte asked. 'It must be quite a strain for someone of her age.'

'She sees it as a duty, I think,' Olivia said. 'But she is looking forward to the family dinner on the Monday night. The dear Empress Dowager is coming from Germany for that. The Queen even plans to leave off her blacks for the occasion. She has a very splendid dress planned, all over gold embroidery, from some cloth made in India.'

'I suppose you will be wanted that evening,' Venetia said. 'You know that the new duke is planning his own jubilee dinner the same night at Southport House, and has asked us to go?'

'Yes, he sent an invitation to me and Charlie, but we had to refuse,' Olivia said. 'Shall you go?'

'I was rather hoping to get out of it,' Venetia said. 'I expect it will be both dull and embarrassing.'

'Oh, darling, do accept,' Charlotte said. 'I shall pretty much have to go, and the poor man does need our support. It will be too bad if we all snub him. And you know,' she added temptingly, 'you'll get the best view of the procession the next day from the roof of Southport House, and he's bound to ask you if you go to his dinner.'

'No, Mama-duchess, not that!' Venetia laughed. 'I'll go to his dinner, if you insist, but nothing more. Besides, Lord Rothschild has invited us to bring the children to see the procession from his house in Piccadilly, and that's much more convenient for us.'

'Oh, very well, I'll accept half a victory,' Charlotte said. 'It occurs to me that the view from Chelmsford House would be just as good, if it weren't let out. When you inherit it, along with the title, Venetia, you might decide to take it back and live in it.'

'It's a little large for my way of life. I'm just a busy lady doctor, you know.'

'Hmm, perhaps. But think of little Violet's come-out: the ballroom is one of the loveliest in London. Wouldn't you like to hold her ball there, in your own house, when the time comes?'

'As Violet is only six years old, I think that's a decision I can safely defer,' Venetia said.

Charlotte shook her head wisely. 'Time passes more quickly than you can imagine, my darling. It seems like only yesterday that I was planning *your* ball.'

When Olivia left to take the train back to Windsor, Venetia stayed with her mother for a while, and they talked of the children and other agreeable topics. Then Charlotte said, 'By the way, darling, talking of houses and property . . .'

'Were we?' Venetia said, amused.

'On the Humpty-Dumpty principle, of going back to the last conversation but one,' Charlotte said, 'I have been thinking a lot about another property of mine, which I haven't seen in quite a while, and I thought that, after the jubilee celebrations are all over, it might amuse you to take a little trip with me and have a look at it.'

'And where is that?'

'My house in Yorkshire, Shawes. I had it repaired many years ago, and stayed there for a few months, but I haven't seen it since, though I've had an agent keep an eye on it, in case I should ever want to use it again. And as it will be yours when I die . . .'

'I wish you would stop talking about when you die,' Venetia said crossly.

'Very well, then, I will. But Shawes is a lovely house, one of the best examples of Vanbrugh's work, and of course it's only a walk across the fields from Morland Place.'

'I thought you'd never been to Morland Place?'

'I haven't. At the time I visited Shawes, for reasons I won't go into I never left the grounds. But I've always wanted to see Morland Place, and it occurred to me that perhaps you might like to, as well. It would be a pleasant holiday for the children – lots of fresh air and space to run about. And, of course, you'd see Henrietta again. What do you think?'

'It sounds a wonderful idea,' Venetia said. 'I couldn't take time off until August, but it's always an object to get the children out of London for a month or so then. I had thought we might go down to Wolvercote again, but this would be even better. Do you really think we could?'

'Of course – what's to stop us? And August would be perfectly suitable. It will take time to make sure the house is fit for an invasion, and to get everything ready. And August in York means race-week, which will be something to entice dear John to come with us.'

'He usually shoots grouse in August. Are there grouse in Yorkshire?'

'Of course, up on the moors.'

'Then I think I can answer for him. I'm sure he has a curiosity to see the old place.'

'I wonder,' Charlotte mused. 'You know, I hadn't thought about the grouse, but it would make a perfect excuse to do my old house up and have a party there every year for the races and the shooting. I haven't had many gay times since your father died, and I do love a sporting party. The country is lovely there for riding, too. If I establish a precedent, then when I – that is,' she checked herself at Venetia's look, 'you might like to keep it going in your turn. Much nicer to have one's own house for holidays than hiring one, or going to stay with people.'

'It sounds to me as though you just want an excuse to spend money,' Venetia said.

'Why, so I do,' Charlotte said peacefully. 'And I do *love* to do up a house. Doesn't every woman?'

At Morland Place the jubilee was a thing of interest though not great moment. York would have its celebrations, a service in the minster, flags and bunting in the street, a fancy-dress ball, a civic dinner and a great many private ones. Teddy was planning to entertain and had devised a rather pleasant scheme, of hiring a steamer to sail down the river and back, with a grand luncheon on board for family and a few friends. 'It will be something that the children can enjoy too,' he explained, 'which, if I give a dinner like everybody else, will be out of the question. It would be too bad to leave the children out of it.'

As well as Henrietta and Jerome, he had asked Perry and Regina to come with all their brood. After long thought and some negotiation, Perry had agreed that he could meet his errant brother- and sister-in-law without suffering too much corruption, as long as it was on neutral ground. Jerome was inclined to snub them for the long insult to his wife, but Henrietta begged him not to.

'It would be unkind to spoil Teddy's party. He's so happy about it, and pleased with himself for thinking of it. And a mended bridge is better than no bridge at all. I miss Regina, and I haven't seen the children in eleven years.'

So it was agreed; and Henrietta allowed Teddy to slip a little extra money to her so that Lizzie at least could have a new dress for the occasion.

'I'm inviting all the nice young men I can find who aren't otherwise engaged, so we want her to look well,' he said.

'Bless you, Ted,' Henrietta said. He was so kind and thoughtful towards her and her family, and had a firm desire to see Lizzie well married. Henrietta's only doubt was whether she could persuade Lizzie to accept a new dress when no-one else would be having one. She would have to put some thought into how to manage that.

Life at Morland Place was establishing a routine, though it had taken longer than Henrietta, in her coming-home euphoria, had anticipated. There had been adjustments to make for everyone, and they missed the modern conveniences they had grown used to in London. Oddly, though, Emma, on whom the heaviest burdens fell, bore them the most lightly. 'It's just like hoom,' she would aver stoutly. 'Only grander.'

It was not just the lack of shops, public transport and entertainments nearby, or the darkness and isolation outside at night which made any sort of going out a thing to be planned well ahead, or even the distances in a large house across which things had to be carried – coals, food, water. Life was more difficult at a very basic level. There was no piped water, which meant hours of work at the pump every day, and forced them to learn more economical habits. No piped water meant no wash-down water-closets, which Lizzie now found rather disconcerting, having forgotten the smell of privvies, and what it meant to have to empty slops. No piped water also meant baths were a great deal of hard work, and all of them were glad that some previous moderniser had installed the big range in the kitchen, which had a large boiler attached to it, otherwise it would have been a matter of boiling kettles.

They could not send laundry out, so it all had to be done at home in the laundry-room, which had a huge copper with its own furnace. There was no gas at Morland Place, and Henrietta had forgotten just how much hard work was involved in filling and cleaning lamps, and how poor the light from a candle was, especially in a big room.

But the beauty of the fine old house compensated them for the extra labour, and little by little they were bringing it back to life. Jerome had started, with the help of Gatson,

Teddy's carpenter and handy-man, to rescue the drawing-room and sitting-room, stripping out the smoke-damaged paper, repainting the ceiling, cleaning the carpets and so on. One evening he said to Henrietta, 'I've been thinking that while we're about it, it might be just as well to restore it to the way it was before your sister-in-law altered it. What do you think? Do you remember what it was like?'

'Oh, yes. It was lovely. It had the most beautiful old linen-fold panelling – but Alfreda hated it, thought it was dark and gloomy.'

'Gatson thinks the panelling is probably still there. It would be a great deal more in character with the house than floral wallpaper. Shall we try?'

'Oh, yes, do,' Henrietta said – glad, as much as anything, that he had discovered an interest in the house.

That was Jerome's project; Emma and Lizzie meanwhile were doing the great hall, gradually cleaning all the marble and waxing all the wood; and one day Jerome and Gatson lowered the great chandelier in the hall and the women spent several evenings taking it to pieces and cleaning all the individual drops.

One of Henrietta's first self-imposed extra tasks had been to reclaim the chapel. She had crept in there on the first evening when everyone else was on their way to bed, and by the wavering light of the candle it had looked astonishingly, wonderfully unchanged. The altar was bare, and the sanctuary lamp was out, but the ancient statue of the Lady was still on her altar in the lady-chapel, and Henrietta had gone straight towards her, as towards a friend. It was wonderful that she had survived. Without realising it, Henrietta was smiling. The gilding of the Lady's face and hands caught the candle-light, which chased across her age-worn features so that, for a moment, it looked as though she were smiling too.

'It's me,' Henrietta had whispered foolishly, her heart full. 'I've come home.'

So in the spare moments between all her other tasks, Henrietta had swept and washed the floor, dusted and polished all the woodwork, cleaned the marble and brass of the memorials; and when it was all bright again, she had relit the sanctuary lamp, and made sure there were always flowers for the Lady on her altar. One day, she thought, we may have a chaplain again; but until then, there was the small cheerful tribute of her daily prayers to stir the still air. Soon Emma found her way there, and found the lady-chapel a place where she could comfortably say her own prayers; and Lizzie took to visiting it at odd moments, when she needed to be quiet and think. Gradually the chapel came back to life, and to Henrietta, Morland Place felt right again: it was like a beating heart, something you never noticed until you listened for it, but were aware of on a deep, unspoken level.

Life was harder than it had been in London, and there was always too much work and not enough hours in the day, but the work felt purposeful and good, food tasted better, sleep satisfied more. Henrietta watched Jerome slowly recover, his shoulders straighten, the spring come back into his step. On the day he came into the kitchen whistling, with a pair of rabbits he and Jack had shot, she knew that not only was she home at last, but he was too. Whatever the future held, to be here at Morland Place with her dear husband and her family was all she asked.

As well as the work of the house, there was the land to tend. Though they were not yet doing much farming, the plans were shaping up. Teddy had bought two in-calf heifers in the autumn, both of which had had heifer calves in the early spring, so the nucleus of the future dairy herd now existed. Once the heifers calved, there would be milk to spare for sale, and Henrietta meant to find someone to teach her how to make cheese, too. All of them had learnt how to milk, though Lizzie was the best at it, and was generally the one to take care of the cows.

They also now had two dozen chickens and half a dozen ducks in the fowl-yard, which grazed in the orchard during the daytime. The children were responsible for collecting the eggs, feeding, and shutting them in at night. In the autumn everyone had turned to for the fruit harvest, and the unusually large crop of cider-apples had prompted Jerome and Jack to have a look at the cider press and with the help of Gatson to get it working again. The resultant brew was rather successful, and they were able to sell most of it to the Hare and Heather, providing, after paying Teddy his tithe, the first cash Jerome had earned since his bank-ruptcy. That had cheered him up enormously, and given him more confidence in their future. Now he was keen to try pigs, and having spent many evenings reading everything he could lay hands on about their feeding and ailments, he was waiting for a good opportunity to open the subject with Teddy. Henrietta could have told him that his reticence was unnecessary – Teddy would have bought any stock he liked just for the asking – but she understood that Jerome had to find his own way at his own pace.

He and Lizzie between them had taken care of the kitchen garden, with help from Davey Walton; and though it was only expected to supply the house this year, they were learning how the thing was done so that, perhaps next year, they would be able to put more area under cultivation and start doing it properly.

Though it was hard work for everyone, they were all looking healthier and happier. The children loved the life, though Henrietta was beginning to worry that they were becoming as wild as rabbits and ought to have some schooling. Emma seemed perfectly happy, though she was glad when Teddy had quietly provided a daily charwoman to help with the cleaning and laundry; and Henrietta was learning to cook properly, finding a pleasure in preparing meals from their own produce. The freshness and flavour of everything was noticeable, and made up for losing the convenience of Kensington High Street. That life seemed very far away now.

What they were doing, she was aware, was a sort of apprenticeship, and when they had served it and were confi-dent, Teddy would stock the place and take on help and they would farm properly, for profit. It was his kindness and tact to allow time for them to settle in, and for Jerome's mental wounds to heal. Henrietta was sure it would pay well enough to support them all. Her only worry was for Lizzie, that shut away here at Morland Place and seeing no-one, she would never have a chance to wipe out the memory of Dodie Paget, to meet the right man and marry. She did not want her sweet, clever daughter to dwindle into an unpaid dairymaid, and she was grateful to Teddy for taking the problem into consideration.

She wondered whether the forthcoming reunion with Perry and Regina would help. They entertained a great deal, and their eldest children were of an age to be useful to Lizzie. Perhaps, she thought, she could persuade them, even if they could not forgive her, to invite Lizzie to stay: she, after all, had done nothing to offend anyone and was the child of a perfectly proper union. Henrietta thought of balls at the Red House, parties and picnics, and all the other kinds of fun the young Parkes would come in for, and pictured Lizzie having her share in them. Pretty soon her imagination produced a handsome and wealthy young man who fell madly in love with Lizzie, and added a satisfying concluding scene in church complete with flowers, veils, and the younger Parkes as bridesmaids. Well, why not? She resolved to do everything in her power to promote the possibility.

While she was still dreaming about this, a further happiness was promised in the form of Charlotte's proposed visit in August, bringing Venetia, Hazelmere and their children. Venetia wrote of her mother's plan to make it a regular thing, and the idea of seeing her dear friend and cousin again on a yearly basis almost took second place to the thought of house parties at Shawes. They would provide wonderful opportunities for Lizzie to meet suitable young men. Now the faceless bridegroom of Bishop Winthorpe gave way to a minor member of the aristocracy with generous acres and a ministerial career.

Henrietta's sense of humour interrupted at that point and she laughed at herself for being a horrible matchmaking mama and an impractical, day-dreaming fool besides. And in any case, she thought, what she wanted for Lizzie was a happy marriage, not a grand one.

But all these delights were still to come when a letter arrived at Morland Place, addressed to her, which caused her much mental disturbance, some pleasurable and some not. It was from a man who signed himself Ashley Morland, a name which sounded somehow familiar even before she read the letter, though she could not think who he might be.

Mrs Compton, Dear Madam [it began formally],
   First of all I must beg your indulgence for writing to you when we are not at all acquainted. I have had the honour to meet the Dowager Duchess of Southport, who has spoken to me of you, and I hope you will take that as sufficient introduction for this letter, whose purpose you will discover if you will be so good as to read on.

Henrietta was perfectly willing to read on, only hoped that the gentleman's scrupulousness would not force him into any longer circumlocutions. Fortunately, having got to the matter of his letter, he became more direct.

I believe, madam, that I am your nephew. My mother was Mary Morland, who was born at Morland Place and went to America in 1854 to marry Fenwick Morland of Twelvetrees Plantation, who was my father. My mother's father was Benedict Morland, whom I believe I did meet at one time in America, though I could be mistaken about this as I was only about five years old at the time and the memory is vague.

Henrietta stopped at that moment as a sudden painful memory of her father came to her. Yes, her father had gone to America when she was a little girl, and stayed away what had seemed like years to her then. She remembered her mother's sadness when he was away and the excitement of his homecoming. Sister Mary she didn't remember at all – an older half-sister, who had married and gone away when Henrietta was still an infant in arms,

509

though she remembered seeing a miniature of her, very beautiful and golden-haired, which her father had always treasured.

But, she thought with a frown, Mary and all her family had perished in the Civil War. What could this person be about? Ashley Morland? Yes, the name was right. She remembered now that Mary had had three sons, and two of them had been called Preston and Ashley after the great rivers in Charleston. She couldn't remember the name of the third son.

She read on.

My father was killed in action during the war, at Gettysburg, and at the end of the war my mother married again, to her cousin Martial Flint who had served with great honour right up to the Surrender. There were two sons of the marriage, my half-brothers Nathan and Daniel, whom I love very dearly. They perhaps helped to console my mother for the loss of my younger brother Corton, who died of typhoid in the last year of the war.

Corton? Yes, that sounded right. She thought that was the name she had heard her father mention.

Not to weary you with too long a tale [the letter went on], things were very bad in the South after the war, with great persecution of Southerners, high taxes and confiscations, making it all but impossible to make a living. Food was scarce and sickness and disease were rife. After enduring great poverty and hardship my poor mother succumbed, also to typhoid, in 1869.

So she did die! That was why there had been no word – though why they did not write to Papa about her death Henrietta didn't know. But perhaps if they were in very dire straits, they could not afford to, or did not think of it. When you were struggling to survive, writing letters became a luxury.

My step-father had many friends in the North from before the war, and, despairing of life in the South, took us four boys and went to Boston, where friends secured him employment in a shipping firm. There we lived ever after, and my three brothers live there still. I, however, was taken with the desire to travel, and came seven years ago to England, which I liked so much I have now made it my home.

My reason for writing to you is that I have always had a strong desire to see Morland Place, where my mother was born. Learning from Her Grace the Duchess that you, my aunt, were now living there, I hoped that perhaps you would indulge my wish and allow me to call on you. I propose to take a vacation from my employment at the end of May and to travel to York, which I believe is a beautiful city well worth visiting. If during my stay there I might come and see Morland Place, and meet my maternal relative, I will be the happiest man alive.

Henrietta sat in stillness a long while when she had finished the letter. Could it be true? A nephew – Mary's son – alive and in England, contrary to everything she had believed all her life. Oh, if it were true, how terrible that poor Papa had died not knowing it! Losing Mary had broken his heart, after which he had been unable to bear Mama's death. Had he only known Mary's sons had survived, he might not have despaired. She felt a surge of anger at the unknown Martial Flint that he had not found the means, or the will, to write in all those years. If he could not write from the South, why had he not written later, when he was settled in the North? She supposed that with Mary dead he had felt no attachment or connection to England. He did not care enough even to write and tell his father-in-law that his grandsons were still alive.

She stood up and walked to the window, feeling disturbed. Her first instinct was to tear up the letter, her second to write an angry refusal; but as she grew calmer she told herself that it was not this man's fault. He had grown up in a different place and a different culture, and England to him had always been a remote thing, perhaps a fairy tale, not in any way his concern. Now he was here, he liked England, and his thoughts had turned to his own history. That was laudable enough, wasn't it? If he wanted to see Morland Place, why shouldn't he? It was a noble old house, well worth looking at: in Henrietta's childhood it had been open to the public for a shilling. And she had a great curiosity to see the child of the sister she had never known.

She showed the letter first to Jerome and Lizzie.

'Really your sister?' Lizzie said. 'And you don't have any memory of her?'

'None at all.'

'The letter sounds all right,' Jerome said. 'He expresses himself well, and I can't see what he could have to gain by making it up.'

'You don't think he's an impostor?' Henrietta asked.

'If he were, he'd have been sure to find out by now that we have no money, and we'd have never heard from him. No, if he's in the shipping business, he might well have a fortune of his own. An importer, not an impostor. What a difference a consonant can make!'

'Do ask him to come,' Lizzie urged. 'Think how sad, if he tries to meet his only family over here and they snub him.'

'If he was so lonely,' Jerome said, 'why did he wait seven years to write?'

'I expect he was busy.'

Jerome laughed, and ruffled her hair. 'What an absurd girl you are. Well, I don't mind if the fellow comes here. Write and tell him he may,' he said to Henrietta. 'But you had best tell your brother, hadn't you?'

'Yes, of course. I wonder if Teddy knows any more about it than I do?'

But Teddy didn't, though he did have a very faint memory of Mary. 'Beautiful and laughing, and she sang like an angel. I was only about four when she went away, though Georgie used to talk about her sometimes. And I remember Mother saying once that if Mary hadn't gone away, she might have kept Georgie in hand, because he adored her when he was little. She was tremendously clever, too. I got the idea that Mother thought her wasted on the American fellow, though he was nice enough.'

'So you don't mind if this Ashley Morland comes to visit?'

'Not at all, if you don't. I shall be interested to meet him. He may have some tales to tell. Perhaps Charley and I will have him round to dinner. Pity nearly all the family portraits have been sold – he'd have liked to see his ancestors, perhaps.'

The early part of May had been cool and damp, but towards the end the winds changed and brought proper summer weather to the Vale of York. It would have been very pleasant weather for sitting in the shade of a tree all day and reading a book, or going for a long ride through the woods. The children found it perfectly congenial for roaming the fields all day, paddling in brooks, and trying to emulate their mother's fishing prowess in the river; but for Lizzie there was hot work to be done in the walled garden and the greenhouses.

She didn't mind being a 'farmer's daughter'. It was a very different life from the idleness of pleasure she had enjoyed before their fall from grace, but she found it much more satisfying. To grow and tend things made her feel she was achieving something; and she loved Morland Place, and liked to feel that she was improving it in her small way. But she was lonely, there was no doubt. She was too busy all day long to think about it much, and in the evenings there were the children to play with, mending to do, Papa to play cards or chess with, Mama to talk to.

But in the silence of night and the spaces of her large bed, it came to her. She missed the closeness she had shared with Dodie. Her love for him had faded, and she hardly repined at all now, sure – almost sure – that they would not have been happy in the long run. But she had no friend, and she was sure all of Uncle Teddy's well-meaning attempts to marry her off would not result in her finding one. She saw the closeness between her mother and Papa, and it made her ache. She wanted that for herself; but she was nearly twenty-five, and her time was past. Dodie had stolen her youth, and she could not have it back.

Still, there were pleasures to be had, and she fixed her mind on them, determined to be cheerful. The jubilee celebrations would be fun, with Uncle Teddy's river-trip, and the ball in York to which Mama and Papa were determined to take her. And lest things fall flat afterwards, there was the visit of Lady Venetia to look forward to in August. Mama said there would be a visit to the races at least, and that there would be bound to be parties of some sort at Shawes.

And before all that, tomorrow indeed, the unexpected cousin from America would be calling. Mama was planning a better-than-ordinary dinner, in case he meant to stay for it, and had discussed with her whether they should do something about a bedroom for him as well.

'He might want to stay. It would be dreadful to have to turn him away for want of a bedroom.'

'Bedrooms are not the problem,' Lizzie had said. 'We have all too many bedrooms. What we haven't got is beds.'

'We could take one of the beds out of the nursery and put it in one of the bachelor's rooms, and Robbie and Frank could share.'

'It would look like a nursery bed, though,' Lizzie had pointed out. 'Black iron frame, narrow and hard.'

Her mother laughed. 'You obviously don't know anything about bachelor's rooms, my love! They were always Spartan, and the beds always looked like nursery beds! I'm sure if we scurry round we can find enough bits and pieces for one room. I've seen a ewer and basin up in one of the servants' rooms in the attic, and you can spare the little table from your bedroom for one night, and the mahogany chair, can't you?'

'Yes, of course – and the middle bachelor's room has a cupboard built into the wall, so if we put him in there, there'll be no need to worry about a wardrobe.'

'He could have our bedside rug, and the two brass candlesticks out of the servants' hall.'

So it had been decided, and now the room was all ready.

Lizzie had taken pity on the putative occupant by moving in a painting of a horse from the red room to make it seem less bare, and planned tomorrow morning to pick some flowers and put them in a vase on the table for a welcoming touch.

This afternoon was hotter even than the morning had been, and at lunch Henrietta noticed her daughter was rather pale.

'You really mustn't work in the walled garden again in this heat,' she said. 'You're looking quite fagged. Put on your shadiest hat and go for a walk this afternoon.' And knowing that Lizzie would feel guilty about taking a walk purely for pleasure, she added, 'You might take a basket and see if you can get any wild strawberries. The first ones ought to be out now – you know the places along the hedges and round the pastures. If you don't pick them the foxes and hedge-hogs will have them, so you might as well.'

Lizzie was willing enough to be persuaded, and knowing the wild strawberries were just a subterfuge, she put a book into the basket with the intention of finding a shady place to sit and read. She set off across the drawbridge and out into the hot sunshine. Her companion was delighted to be going out, and rushed ahead, whirling in mad excitement. He was a young brindled wolfhound, of the sort that had been bred at Morland Place for generations, and he had been a birthday present to her last September from Uncle Teddy. When the squirming puppy had been put into her arms she had wanted, absurdly, to cry, for it seemed just like dear Uncle Teddy to realise that she was lonely and longed for something of her own to love. She had never had a pet before. Her real papa would not have cared for animals about the house, and it had not seemed the thing to do in London. Mama had delved into her memory and come up with the recollection that Morland dogs were always Kithra, or Kai if they were bitches, so Lizzie had called the brindled pup Kithra with a happy sense of restoring one more piece of its stolen history to Morland Place.

Whether her mother had expected it or not, there were quite a lot of strawberries, gleaming in the shadow of the hedge banks like tiny crimson jewels. Lizzie worked her way out along one side of the lane and back along the other, filling the basket with the tiny, scented fruit. Kithra pursued ends of his own, plunging headlong into bushes and intriguing holes in the hope of rabbits, his hind-quarters wagging enthusiastically, coming back to Lizzie every few minutes to make sure she was still there and still smelt the same.

She had almost reached the drawbridge again when she heard the sound of a horse's hoofs. Kithra ran up and jabbed his muzzle into her hand in warning – his kind never barked – and she straightened up and turned to look.

A bay road horse was approaching. Kithra ran to it, circled, looking up at the rider, then bounded back to Lizzie, and stood, nose up and searching, tail already swinging in willingness to make a new friend. The rider was a man neatly dressed, but wearing a wide-brimmed hat – practical in this weather but not at all fashionable, or what a gentleman would ordinarily wear. It looked rather peculiar, and made Lizzie smile, not in ridicule but with an odd pleasure that someone should mind so little how he looked that he would choose comfort over style.

He reined in the horse a few paces away, touched his hat and called, 'Hello, there.'

'Hello,' she said. 'Have you lost your way?'

'Why should you think so?'

'Well, this track does go to Acomb, but by a very round-about route, and there's nothing else along here.'

'What about that very splendid castle?'

'It's not a castle, it's a fortified manor house,' Lizzie told him kindly.

'It's Morland Place,' he informed her. 'I've never been here before, but I'd know it anywhere. It speaks to something atavistic in me.' He loosed his feet from the stirrups and jumped down, pulling the reins over the horse's head. Kithra ran up to sniff his boots, and smiled, his whip-like tail revolving so hard it imparted an ecstatic wiggle to his entire back end. 'Hello, pup,' the man said. 'You're a nice feller! What's his name?'

'Kithra.'

'Kithra? That name sounds familiar. Did my mother say she once had a dog called Kithra?'

'You're the American cousin,' Lizzie realised, wondering how it had taken her so long. 'But you're not supposed to come until tomorrow. Did you forget the date?' It was not a remark of polished politeness, but she felt unaccountably jumpy and put off her stroke by this man's sudden appearance.

He didn't seem to mind her bluntness. 'No, I didn't forget. I just thought I'd like to sneak up on it and catch a glimpse of it before it knew I was here, so to speak. I hope you don't mind?'

'Why should I mind?' she said, and added, '*Heureux qui comme Ulysse a fait un beau voyage.*'

'How kind of you to put it like that.'

He stopped right in front of her, only a pace away, and pulled off his hat. His hair was thick and fair, brushed straight back from a fine, broad forehead. His face was firm with authority, lightened by humour and intelligence. It seemed familiar to her. She thought that he bore a faint resemblance to Dodie. But no, this was a grown man, and Dodie had been only a boy. It must be that Dodie had borne a faint resemblance to *him*. Perhaps, she thought confusedly, this was what she had seen or recognised in Dodie – that he had looked a little like this man whom she would one day meet, and had always known.

There was one notable difference from Dodie: these eyes were the most brilliant, imperishable blue. They looked straight into hers now, and he smiled, and Lizzie felt something like a soundless explosion in her mind, like being struck painlessly by lightning through her head and down into the middle of her body. What was it? She felt she knew him already, in some deep, indefinable way. Her mouth was dry, and though she knew she ought not to stare, she couldn't take her eyes from him. She just wanted to look at his face, his eyes, the way his firm lips lay against each other, faintly smiling.

His expression changed minutely. 'You wouldn't by any

517

chance be a Miss Compton, would you? The young lady of the house?'

She nodded like someone in a dream. The horse sighed, shifted its feet, and then put out an enquiring nose to Lizzie. Automatically she gave it her fingers, and it mumbled them a moment hopefully, then turned its head away. Kithra sat down with puppylike suddenness in the dust and scratched hugely behind his ear with a hind foot.

'Then,' the man said, as if it gave him great pleasure, 'we're cousins. I am so glad to meet you. Won't you shake hands?'

He extended his hand, and she went to shake it, found the basket in the way, put it down, and held out her own – nervously, as if he might be charged with electricity. But his hand was warm and dry, large and firm, a thing of safety and comfort.

'I am Ashley Morland,' he said. Having taken her hand, he did not let it go; and she really, really did not want him to.

'I'm Elizabeth Compton,' she managed to say.

He was staring at her now, much as she was staring at him, with a sort of half-puzzled, half-recognising look.

'Tell me, Cousin Elizabeth,' he said, in a rather strange voice, 'do you know the meaning of the expression *coup de foudre*?'

DYNASTY 1: THE FOUNDING

CYNTHIA HARROD-EAGLES

Set in the years 1434 to 1486, the first glorious volume
of the Dynasty series is an enthralling historical novel
with Wars of the Roses as its background. Power and
prestige are the burning ambitions of domineering, dour
Edward Morland, rich sheep-farmer and landowner, as he
sets out to arrange a marriage that will secure his
empire s future. And Robert, his son, more poet than
soldier, idolises his proud young bride, Eleanor, ward of
the influential Beaufort family.

Used to gentility and grace, Eleanor is outraged at having
to marry the son of a Yorkshire sheep-farmer, but she
must obey despite her consuming secret passion for
Richard, Duke of York. Time creates a bond, both
passionate and tender, between the apparently ill-
matched husband and wife; for Eleanor s warmth and her
love for life are as great as her rigid sense of justice. This
remarkable woman is at the centre of a pageant which
blazes with colour and life.

Robert and Eleanor s marriage is the founding of the
Morland Dynasty. Life holds for them prosperity and
success   all too often mingled with tragedy as they are
embroiled in the civil strife which has divided families
and sets neighbour against neighbour.

DYNASTY 23: THE CAUSE

CYNTHIA HARROD-EAGLES

In 1874, the wedding of Lady Venetia Fleetwood is the talk of London. Invitations are eagerly prized, not least by Venetia s cousin George Morland and his socialite wife Alfreda, preparing to journey down from Morland Place in Yorkshire for the most glamorous event of the Season.

But on the eve of the wedding a bombshell hits Southport House. Venetia s fiancØ discovers that she means to continue in her attempt to qualify as a doctor. Horrified, he forbids it absolutely. Venetia, half afraid of her own determination, calls the wedding off, and from being the talk of the Season, it becomes the scandal of the year.

For George and Alfreda the disappointment is acute. Alfreda consoles herself with elaborate building plans for Morland Place and ever more lavish entertainments. Both refuse to believe that extravagance is driving George ever closer to bankruptcy, to losing the one thing he values above all else   his land . . .